"Wolf has created a richly detailed, complex fantasy universe populated by intriguing characters who will continually surprise readers throughout the briskly paced tale. Gray is a particularly well-developed protagonist, and [the novel] refreshingly allows the villainous characters to change... A strong, confident fantasy novel [and] an impressive, page-turning adventure for fans of the series."

— Kirkus Review

Citadel of Fire

To Becci who believed; and to all my fans and friends who saw fire when it was only an ember.

FARHAVEN
Frizzian Coast
Ester
Kalvas Ocean
The Dragons Tooth
Mountains of Soot
Kalvas Ocean
The Abyss

VASTER
Tacrian
LANDER
Cloudfell Town
Cloudfell Lake
Aster Plains
Helians Desert
Drymaus Forest
Helvas Forest
ELVAS

FARHAVEN

The Abyss

Burai Mountains

Death's Gates

The White Plains

DE'GRAEL

Sobeku Plains

The Green Valley

Moonshire

The Silvas River

Burmen's Bank

Lakewood

THE LOS

DAERVAL

e´Dol

ity

Kimdel

Merkal Desert

The Gold Road

EASTERN KINGDOMS

The Crags

Tower

The Wastelands

Maiden´s Mane

OMS

Other novels by Matthew Wolf

THE RONIN SAGA
The Knife's Edge
Citadel of Fire

Contents

The Tale of the Ronin

Long ago, the world was in chaos. Twelve kingdoms fought for wealth and power, creating an age of darkness. Kings were killed by their trusted subjects in the dead of night, and citizens were thieved from their homes by those sworn to protect them. Soon, men turned on brothers, fathers against sons, and nature against man, for the greed of the twelve kingdoms consumed all…

The world turned dark, as rain ceaselessly soaked the lands, and crops withered, until death and misery replaced hope.

Then one day, a robed figure changed the fate of history.

Tales differ, some offering that he came across the ocean, others said he descended from the clouds in motes of shimmering light, while fewer still believe he simply was a man born of a different land. But all agree *the nine* were at his side. The Ronin. Warriors who wielded different powers of wind, water, fire, sun, moon, leaf, metal, flesh, and stone.

The robed figure came with a contract. The war would end and the lands would know peace, but in exchange, he demanded The Three Rules, creating laws for the land and establishing the Great Kingdoms.

However, if any ruler grew greedy again, the nine Ronin would unite, and with the might of their elemental powers they would siege the unruly kingdom. No army could stand before the Ronin as they cleaved a path to the throne, cut off the head of the greedy ruler, and ordained a new monarch, one that would ensure true peace or be replaced once more.

For a thousand years, peace was known. The lands rejoiced as crops bloomed, and the people breathed sweet air without the stench of blood. They felt sunlight upon their skin and laughed freely. All was well… but nothing can stay good forever. One day, a blade of light was stolen, and the Ronin were blamed as the war returned. The people named this dark time the Lieon, meaning "everlasting fight." And the once-heroes became the villains of mankind.

Rumors spread of the Ronin's betrayal... tales that Kail, their leader, had turned mad, wandering the land and killing all until he disappeared into the forest, while the rest of the Ronin joined the side of darkness. In the end, evil was thwarted but not conquered, sinking back into the lands, seething and waiting to return.

Time wore on and the lands began to grow again from the rubbles. Tales floated upon the winds as bards and minstrels spun accounts of the war and the evil sworn to return… An evil known as the Ronin.

The Three Rules

One

Only nine of the twelve kingdoms will be chosen and deemed "The Great Kingdoms", those who bear the eternal elements as their sigil: wind, sun, leaf, fire, moon, water, stone, flesh, and metal.

Two

The warriors known as the Ronin, with nine magical swords, will be bound to the kingdoms—each matched to their elemental power in turn. Baro will be the ambassador for the metal kingdom, Seth for fire, Hiron for water, Aundevoriä for stone, Aurelious for flesh, Dared for moon, Maris for leaf, Omni for sun, and lastly, their leader, Kail for wind. They will be the peacemakers of the land, the arbitrators of justice.

Three

A prophecy will be forever engraved upon the walls of each Great Kingdom, words to spell the future of the world.

The land of Farhaven is full of Great Kingdoms, but only the city of fire sits at its heart—a hub of magic, might, and power, where the spark ignites the sky for all to see and wonder…

— Evistos the Songseer, Bard to the Patriarch

Farhaven broke the day the Ronin fell.
Not from fire or brimstone, but from lack of unity.
Without cause or master, we roved like wolves.
What once was beautiful now turned to waste.
The burnt trees, the fractured cities,
The fissured land, and broken homes—
All will be rebuilt, and we will find a home,
Until even the seed of fear is washed and worn
Like a river rock set in an old inn's hearth.

But what is truly thieved is our memory:
We must remember. We must not let truth fall to ruin.
Our birthright, our place in this world is tied to the elements,
And the elements to them.
We are bound to them and them to us—
They are the home we have lost.
They are the rightful guardians of the land.
This truth will redeem the world.

— Renald Trinaden, The First Leader of the Devari, taken from his lost journal entries 16 years after the war ended, during the Exiled Time

Golden Lies

Prologue

Before the Patriarch, all of Farhaven lay.

Standing high in the great keep, he could see the world beneath him, stretching out endlessly—waiting to be opened like a book beneath his hands. With his level of the spark, all of it was just beyond his fingertips.

To the east, past the turquoise waters of Cloudfell Lake and a town cast in perpetual low-lying fog, lay the now desolate Great Kingdom of Stone—destroyed during the great war of the *Lieon*. To the west, he saw the shadowy Narim Foothills, the Great Kingdom of Moon. Beside it lay its unlikely neighbor, the Great Kingdom of Flesh, a land of man and beast toiling beneath the harsh sun and its religion of the Mortal Being. And lastly, to the south, many miles away, past the vineyards of Sevia and lands with roving brigands, sat the deserts of the Great Kingdom of Fire.

But now the Patriarch sat in the Great Kingdom of Sun known as Vaster.

The breathtaking green landscape stretched below him. Upon the rolling hills far below the grand keep and in between the bleak cliffs of stone, the land was painted verdant with hardy bushes and evergreens strong enough to withstand the bite of the harsh winter and a brilliant sun, which now filled the air with the presence of their faint aroma.

Farhaven was a land of magic, of possibilities.

A *dying land*, the Patriarch knew.

A man cleared his throat, and the Patriarch turned to see a liveried servant. He was a stooped, gray-haired man with a face like a prune. He was old enough to look as if he'd survived the Lieon. But with no real spark, the Patriarch knew the old man's age was infantile compared to his own. This high in the fortress of Vaster, he was obviously a high servant of Lord Nolan. Faint beads of sweat formed upon the man's temple as he opened his mouth to speak, but no words came out.

The Patriarch raised a brow in question. "Yes?"

The man bowed to his waist, his gaze falling to the polished floor. "The great Steward of Vaster, Lord Nolan, will see you now, your eminence," the servant said, croaking out the words.

The Patriarch dipped his head, and the servant led the way.

Together they maneuvered through halls with richly woven gold rugs, passing large, elegant rooms filled with priceless vases and other pointless material extravagances. On the walls, mosaic windows let in colored light, showing the varying kingdoms' symbols and their corresponding colors: leaf, stone, water, sun, moon, flesh, metal, and fire. All nine save for wind, of course, the banished element. As always, the familiar copper flame symbol of the Great Kingdom of Fire was a comforting sight for his weary gaze, reminding him what he was fighting for.

In between the glass mosaics were ancient tapestries depicting battles from a millennium ago. The Lieon, the war that had nearly destroyed the world. Though over a thousand years ago, he remembered it still, like a dream within a dream.

Nearby, guards in silver and gold armor stood like figurines at the mouth to every hall and room, each bearing the Sun Kingdom's mark on their resplendent plate mail.

At last, with the servant leading the way, they reached a grand double door of hammered gold. In its center was a huge insignia of the sun. Each door was the weight of twenty men and the worth of a city. The Patriarch sighed inwardly. *Such needless things we mortals do to prove ourselves.*

The old servant stopped before the doors, looking nervous again.

"Shall I introduce you, my lord?" he asked.

The Patriarch touched the man's arm, gently. "No need," he said and wove a thread of flesh, intricate but subtle, and the tension in the old man's body seemed to visibly evaporate, and he breathed a sigh. "Be at ease, old friend." With that, the Patriarch drew upon his spark again, issuing a thread of metal. But before the magic could work, the huge doors glided open as if weightless. *Hinges fused with magic—artifacts from the Lieon,* the Patriarch knew.

Inside, a man in brilliant plate and white silks stood staring out the window. Upon his entrance, the man turned swiftly. Nolan, Lord of the Sun Kingdom, was tall and broad shouldered, which made him nearly equal to the Patriarch's imposing height. He had a youthful face, which now wore a deep look of concern. His hair was still brown and full, but parts were graying with age and the stress of his station no doubt.

Despite being a lord in title, Lord Nolan was only the steward of Vaster—the Kingdom of Sun had not had a king since the great war of the Lieon had disposed its last ruler. However, he wore several pieces of armor made for a king over his white robes—robes less brilliant than the Patriarch's of course. Upon his shoulders sat golden epaulets crafted to look like eagles in flight. His wrists were clasped with gilded bracers depicting a bursting sun, and a golden belt cinched his waist. But for all his grandeur and surroundings, the difference between the two men was as clear as the distinction between dawn and dusk. Still, Nolan was a proud and allegedly virtuous man, a man full of *light*—a trait all inhabitants of the Sun Kingdom were said to possess. But standing before the Patriarch, the most powerful wielder of the spark in all time, Nolan was just a man.

"Forgive me, my liege," Lord Nolan said sincerely, bowing almost as deeply as the old man had done. "As soon as I discovered it was you, I told my servants to bring you without hesitation. I assure you, your delay was *completely* unintended, though still inexcusable. It's just… You *must* understand, no guest so prominent has ever arrived without an entourage in tow." The sun lord scratched his graying temples and chuckled. "Honestly, I've had minor governors of my provinces arrive with a small fleet of guards, servants, and practically their *whole* house in tow, and you… a ruler of a great kingdom arrive alone, *and* unarmed."

"Unnecessary heraldry," he replied calmly. "And as you know, I do not need an army."

"No, *the Patriarch is an army unto himself*, or so the stories say," the man said, hiding a shiver and giving a sly smile. "Luckily, I am too young to remember a time when the world was not at peace."

The Patriarch glanced around at the furnishings. He stood upon a floor of snowy marble. A sun was embedded in its center. The ceiling was tall, constructed of hundreds of glass facets, letting the sun stream in and fill the chamber with golden luminescence. None of it mattered to him. He was searching for something else.

He felt a presence lingering in the air.

A *woman*.

All other threads of the woman's presence were masked. *She's powerful.* Not nearly as much as him, but she'd had time to cover her tracks. *My unintended delay*, he reasoned, hiding a bemused smile. *No matter.* The petty perfidy of nobles and the squabbling of kingdoms were of no import to him.

What mattered was the world, and it was dying.

"Bring in the rest of the nobles," the Patriarch declared, looking out the window. "I have ordered all of the Great Kingdoms here, if that is acceptable…" He spoke with the authority of his rank to make even the proud sun lord hesitate.

"*All* of the great kingdoms?" Lord Nolan gawked.

"My presence—" the Patriarch began, turning back. "I am here for a reason, Nolan. As we stand, the world is on the precipice of a new age, one balancing between light and darkness."

"You speak of the rumors…"

"We would be blind to ignore the truth. Whispers spread of a darkness rising within the Deep Mines, the black caverns beneath Yronia."

Nolan shook his head. "Yronia, the Great Kingdom of Metal, was destroyed in the great war. It is dead," he said in a flat tone. "Walls bashed in by the enemy. Nothing lives in those dark halls anymore.”

“Nothing but death,” the Patriarch answered.

Nolan’s brows furrowed. “What do you mean?”

“Upon hearing the rumors of Yronia’s wakening, I sent some of my best Reavers to investigate alongside several dozen Devari two weeks ago. They have not returned, and they never will,” he said plainly.

Nolan’s eyed widened. “You cannot mean…” His hand fluttered to his side, fingering his belt inlaid with scrolls of gold, as if seeking his sword that was not there.

A *missing sword. Ironic*, he thought, *for a man of sun*. “Whatever there is in those halls, it’s nothing of light. The darkness has spread beyond Yronia. Nodes are appearing in great numbers, trying to hold the deserts north of the Gates together, but magical beings are dying,” he said. “Something is awakening…”

“You mean the ancient evil, don’t you? But they…” Nolan hesitated, “*those nine*, they were destroyed in the *Lieon*, during the war—”

“—No,” he interrupted smoothly, “that evil has been banished and put to rest, for now at least. This darkness is something else entirely.”

“Something else?” Lord Nolan questioned.

“It is a prophecy of death,” he answered. “An insidious disease that masquerades itself as strength, but it is not. Even as we speak, it seeps into every home and every Great Kingdom under the guise of truth and light, eating away at us from the inside out.” The Patriarch lifted a hand and a tiny flame of fire formed, swelling into a molten orb. It floated in the air, suspended, burning proudly when its surface changed. Black veins forked across the fiery orb’s surface like a spreading poison. “It is not an army, not yet at least, but a mantra that corrupts, led by a singular purpose: to turn the world to shadow.” He waved his hand and the orb was consumed in roiling darkness.

Nolan swallowed and asked slowly, “How long do we have?”

“Not long,” he replied. “It grows quickly… and it will not be contained by anything, not the well-guarded borders of the elves, the might of my Reavers, or even the high walls of Vaster. If we do not stand together, by the time we turn to face it, it will already be too late.”

“Then what do you propose?”

His hand made a fist and the black orb burst into flames, leaving only a strange smell in the air like fetid water and rotting flesh. "If we wish to save Farhaven, the time to act is now."

At his words, a knock sounded.

Puzzled, Nolan's silver brows drew together, but he called out without turning. "*Enter!*"

A woman servant entered, closing the door behind her as if she was being chased. Sweat poured down her face, dampening her livery. She caught her breath, trying to gather herself before the two powerful men.

"My lord," she said. "The kingdoms… they are here."

"How many?"

"*All of them.*"

The sun lord's jaw clenched.

The Patriarch turned grandly and reached out. With a flick of his finger, the huge double gold doors flung open, slamming against the walls and shaking the sun-lit chambers.

A stream of monarchs entered with airs that could knock a lesser man over from a dozen paces away. Clad in rich silks, ceremonial armor, and thick pauldrons, they jostled for rank and position. It was a tributary of gold and silver, all polished to gleam. His gaze passed over a few of the most notable men and women, listing off their names and titles.

King Darmin of Covai, the Great Kingdom of Flesh, had a soft face and ripe belly, his plump fingers laden with glittering rings—yet his eyes were deceivingly sharp. Dryan of Eldas, the new ruler of the Great Kingdom of Leaf, wore his lavish pale green armor, his Elvin features absent of all emotion as always. King Owen Garian of Median, the rebuilt Great Kingdom of Water, High Elder Fari of Menalas, and Havas of Ester, and so forth. Though none were more powerful than the sovereigns of the Great Kingdoms each were kings, queens, or ambassadors of their own right, hailing from all over Farhaven. Together, they comprised the rulers of the world.

They cast sly looks to one another, and behind their gazes, the Patriarch saw plots of political maneuvering brewing, for each held feuds as old as the kingdoms themselves, steeped in blood. But today, they had promised to set their quarreling aside, if only for discussion.

"So, this is it?" said King Owen Garian, sovereign of the Great

Kingdom of Water, a mountain of a man with a long, blue-tinted beard as if he'd been born of the sea.

"It seems so," said another, Havas, ruler of Ester, who seemed nothing more than a stooped old man, save for his cane that was made entirely of rare white gems from Ester and Menalas' joint renowned mines. "The meeting to decide our fates."

Lord Nolan rushed forward, addressing them all in grand tones.

Calmly, the Patriarch turned and looked out the gleaming windows back onto the land—they sat high above it all, looking down protectively upon the denizens of the world. And he knew the full circle quirk of fate. It was much like the meeting within Morrow that decided the future of the lands those thousands of years ago. His lips curved slightly, glad for it.

Last time, the council had failed, and the world had been plunged into darkness. Of course, they had stopped the evil of the Kage and their dark army, barely, upon Death's Gate, only for the evil to return and *ultimately* be banished by a young man with a powerful sword. But the true evil wasn't gone. The abyssal darkness of the Lieon still lingered and now it was returning. The council had failed, but this time would be different.

This time the darkness would not be so easily quelled.

Hands clasped behind his back, the fading sun illuminated his face as he inhaled deeply, relishing that scent that was not a scent. Here, in the gleaming mirrored columns that shone with the fading sun—aside from the perfumed guests—there was no smell.

Absence, he thought curiously.

The room had grown quiet. A stillness settled that he felt to his ancient bones. Turning back, he saw the monarchs' faces, hard or soft, impatient or serene, all proud, and all anticipating.

As the founder of this meeting, all were waiting for his word.

The Patriarch threaded bits of light and flesh into his voice so his words soared. "As the rulers of the lands, we are upholders of all that Farhaven stands for, but the peace and serenity we have treasured and even taken for granted these last many years is about to change. Evil is rising. A darkness takes its form, sinuous and pervasive, but still cloaked in shadows..."

He raised his hands and orbs of fire appeared in the air, and the hundreds of mirrors burst with light, banishing any trace of darkness in the golden room. "Now is the time of vigilance, for watchful eyes to turn to your own fair borders and beyond. Now is the time for unity. Scattered and broken from the Lieon, we are a family who has lost its brothers and sisters… Seria of Water, Narim of Moon, Lander of Stone, and Yronia of Metal… Their losses have made us as reclusive as a widow, sheltering ourselves behind our high walls, but we must see ourselves whole once more—for, broken, we will fall. That is why I have gathered you upon this day… a day that marks the tides of change and the eve of a new age," he intoned grandly.

Each ruler hung on his every word.

And the Patriarch smiled, gamely. "It is time."

Facing Death

Zane couldn't cool the fire in his veins. Nor did he want to. They had stolen everything from him, and he would take it back, piece by piece. The thought resounded in his head like a tolling bell, and he gripped the gold coin purse tighter as he tore through the desert back alleys, ignoring looks and pushing those who got in his way. He turned a corner and ran face to face with noise, color, and the crush of bodies.

A procession.

Perfect, the young thief thought. Sheathing his blade, Zane slipped into the folds of the crowds. Sweat and dust filled his nose. The heat of bodies was stifling, but he continued, moving past eager looking men, women, and children. They ignored him, oblivious to the danger he was in. They were all too busy watching the lavish affair in the main thoroughfare beyond. The people of Farbs loved such spectacles. Reavers, Devari, and their ilk, while greatly feared, were also respected like royalty. *Royalty who could incinerate your body to ash for looking at them the wrong way.*

All knew it was forbidden to enter a procession in progress.

Only once had he seen a man take a step into the streets, and a Devari, emotionless, had cut him down faster than a cutpurse reaching for a coin. Zane had seen death, but this was different. Had it been out of rage or even greed, he'd have understood at least—for both emotions he'd seen in men for as long as he could remember. That moment however... It was the coldest thing he'd ever seen, as if the Devari were cutting a dead branch. A man no more flesh and blood than a hunk of stubborn wood born for kindling. The procession had ambled on as if nothing had happened, the dirt street soaking up the man's blood like a thirsty patron.

All in all, Zane didn't care for the spectacle one bit. He caught glimpses of camels, horses, and bare-chested, muscled men carrying a lecarta among other impressive sights—none of it mattered. He cut a path through the crowd, spotting an alley just as the masses began to stir. Looking back, he saw movement behind him.

Grom was pushing a fat merchant out of the way while Salamander stalked behind him. Zane saw his eyes. An unquenchable fury roiled in that dark gaze. Immediately, Zane ducked, but he knew it was too late—Salamander had seen him. *Blood and dust, how is the man not dead?* He cursed. *He can thread,* he reminded himself—a fact that meant his death if the foul man caught up with him again. Zane thrust himself through the sweaty mess of bodies. Staying in
10 a half-crouch, as fast as he could, he scurried, hoping not to stir the crowds and give away his position.

For a brief moment, Zane rose to gather his bearings, and saw movement from the opposite direction. *More of Darkeye's men,* he knew. He felt it in his gut. They were like arrows flying from all directions, and he was the haystack. Behind him, he saw the bustling procession. Red cloth ribbons waved in the dry air. A band of musicians played flutes, drums, zirods, shambles, and tarzas, ushering the display forward.

He took a heavy breath, eyeing the rumbling ground beneath him. A calm came over him, clashing with his always-thundering heart. *They will capture and kill me,* he realized.

If it were just him, he'd risk it. But he had to think about Hannah. They'd come for her too. They'd been pilfering from Darkeye's Clan for months. *They will want blood, and they won't stop with me.* But he was cornered with no way out. Worse yet, if he moved into the thoroughfare, he would be cut down. The crowds crashed around him, and he could see Salamander's snide, wrathful face bobbing over the heads, nearing with the others at his back.

Something rough grabbed his arm. He turned to see Snaggle, another one of Darkeye's lackeys. The man's foul tooth stuck out over his bottom lip. He wore ragged strips of cloth. They hung loose on his bony frame while a tight cap hugged his skull, wisps of hair sticking out from underneath. Zane held the man's eyes and slyly reached for his blade.

"Ah-ah, I wouldn't," Snaggle said, showing off his awful grin as he flashed a glimpse of his long, rusty dagger—curved like his tooth—from within the pockets of his clothes. The man was hideous, but he wasn't slow. He'd cut Zane to ribbons before his hand would touch his blade, and then he'd leave him bleeding out on the dry desert street. "Where's the money you stole, you little rat?"

Zane's fist clenched tighter around the coin purse. "It goes to the people. To those who need it. The real lost souls of this city."

"Fool," Snaggle said with a disgusted sneer. "Don't you know? You fight or you die. It's that simple. What you're doing, protecting and suckling those sad men and women, is wrong. It goes against the code of the street. They don't deserve life." He scoffed. "You of all people should know that, little rat. It's the code of the thief."

Zane ignored the man, glancing back. Salamander was drawing closer. Zane felt the noose closing around his neck. His heart was now thundering. There was nothing he could do. It was all over. Die here, or be taken back and let Hannah suffer Salamander's awful wrath. There was no other option now, and with his back pressed to the procession, there was nowhere to run. He felt true despair rise in the pit of his stomach, overwhelming the roar of the crowds.

Unless... He glanced at the long train.

Suddenly, he had an idea. He visibly slumped, letting go of the rage that always boiled inside him. His head lowered.

"Ah, we've finally broken you! I didn't think it was possible... It seems in the end, you were nothing but a scared rat that needed to be flushed. Salamander will be glad to see the smug fire wiped..."

Zane stopped listening as Snaggle's grip loosened in victory. He smiled as Salamander pushed through the last of the crowds. Zane looked up. He felt fire and pride rush inside him. Snaggle choked on whatever words he was saying upon seeing his eyes. Zane pulled his arm from the man's now-loosened grip and leapt into the street.

To his death.

* * *

Zane jumped before the caravan.

A collective rush of gasps, like a gust of wind, sounded from the crowds as the giant procession came to a screeching halt. Zane could only hear the pounding of his heart in his ears, but beneath that, he sensed the silence.

The musicians had halted their playing, the dancers no longer danced, and the crowds watched in frozen horror.

He stood like a statue—head high and hand far from his blade.

Before him was the largest, most opulent lecarta he'd ever seen. In shape it was little more than a box on poles, but its sides were inlaid with thick gold while silver curled from its four corners like thorns. Anything that wasn't covered in gold was draped in dark red cloth, the foreboding color of the Citadel. The cloth was a thick, rich weave, which made his own clothes feel like rags hanging from his frame.

Carrying the lecarta were nine shirtless, heavily muscled men who wore baggy red pants—their dark skin was oiled and glistened in the light of the burning midday sun. Zane was no slouch, but each man's arm was the size of his thigh. But that was not his fear…

Closer still, were two men wearing nondescript clothes of brown and tan to blend in with their surroundings. Unlike normal guards, they needed no armor. Upon their backs were cloaks depicting two crossed swords.

The cloak of a Devari.

The two men held strange postures, heads down with knees heavily bent, and shoulders turned. *Fighting stances*, his street-wise mind told him—the one that had kept him alive. It always warned him before imminent death. The Devari eyed his dagger. Without hesitation, he reached to throw it away. As his hand touched the handle, he felt steel before his throat. He looked up into the coldest eyes he'd ever seen—frozen blue orbs.

"One fool move upon another," the man whispered.

Somehow the Devari had crossed the span of twenty paces faster than he could blink. Zane closed his eyes, realizing what a hair-brained move that had been. He remained still, aside from slowly retracting his hand. "I was only trying to toss it…"

"A foolish move before a Devari. Your hand would never touch the blade."

He swallowed. It caused the blade to bite deeper, slightly cutting his throat. He spoke softly but urgently, "I mean no harm."

The Devari's hard angled face seemed to judge him. That long nose, slanted eyes, and sharp jaw tilted, as if seeing into him. Zane felt a strange chill, and the hair on his arms stood on end. *Threading?* he wondered. *But how?* Devari didn't have the spark, not like Reavers and Arbiters at least—those who could manifest the innate spark in all life and then *thread* to extract elements from the world, anything from fire to flesh, and wield them as powerful weapons. To some it was simply called magic. But he had heard of something called the ki, a power of the Devari to sense another's emotions.

The chill left Zane, like icy fingers gripping his heart only to pull away. It was unnerving, but he didn't resist.

The Devari spoke at last. "You speak truth. I sense your fear. Curious… One would never know looking at the fire in those strange eyes of yours." He sheathed his blade, backing away.

Zane remembered the crowds. They all held their breath, watching as if they had just witnessed a miracle.

"Go now before I change my mind," the Devari said.

Nodding his silent thanks, Zane moved when there was a commotion. He didn't waste time second-guessing his dumb luck. Suddenly, he felt his limbs stiffen, a frigid chill entering his bones, his blood cooling. He stumbled and fell, his face hitting the dry desert ground. He sucked in dust, trying to rise, but it hurt to move. Every muscle felt aflame, as if being prodded with a thousand needles.

Still, he cocked his head, peering over his shoulder, and he saw a fearsome sight.

Six women and six men on horseback approached. They wore scarlet robes. The robes of a Reaver. At their head was a man dressed in black trousers and a vest so deep a blue it appeared black as well, and over that, he wore an oiled, dark coat that draped over the sides of his huge stallion.

The leader came to a halt just before the lecarta. He was stooped and his eyes glinted from within his hood like black gems, but his face was hard to see. "What is going on here?" Silence. "Someone speak before I lose my temper..." For the first time in ages, aside from Darkeye's men, Zane felt an instant hatred. Everything about that oiled tone was filled with righteous self-importance.

The Devari spoke. "He meant no harm, Sithel."

Sithel snorted. "I will be the judge of that, Devari."

Who was this man who led Reavers and commanded Devari?

"Rise," Sithel ordered. A Reaver at his side with three stripes on his cuffs lifted a hand. Like a puppet, Zane was lifted into the air to stand upon his feet. Yet his limbs were not his own—he felt as if a steel thread ran through his body, holding him in place. It was terrifying, and he hated not having control. *Let me go*... his body raged, but he bit his tongue, knowing one wrong word could mean his death.

"What's your name, criminal?" Sithel asked.

He held the man's terrifying gaze. "Zane—" he hesitated "—and I am no criminal."

"Then why do you interrupt my procession, Zane?" Sithel asked, moving closer, his horse looming above Zane. Zane could smell sweat and a rank darkness emanating from the man. "It is, by law of Farbs, illegal to interfere with Citadel affairs. Does this not look like Citadel affairs?"

Zane's body began to shake, suffocating beneath his bonds.

"Are you both blind and deaf? Speak!" Sithel barked.

The fire within Zane raged. *Release me,* it begged. Meanwhile, Zane tried to find words through his rising fear and frustration, forcing them out. "It was not my intention. I... was forced to..." He tried to move, but his bonds held him tighter than the noose around a murderer's neck. He choked, feeling as if his whole body was slowly dying. He could not be caged, and every fiber of his being railed against it. He needed to move or he would explode.

"Intention or not, you are here. Speak straight, for I am losing patience..."

"First, let me go," he sputtered. "I swear, I will not run or fight."

"Is it that unbearable?" Sithel sneered. "Sad. You seemed stronger than that."

His eyes bulged and his body shuddered as his eyes rolled to the back of his head, losing consciousness. "Release ... me..."

Distantly, he saw Sithel flick his hand in annoyance. The bonds fell and Zane sagged, falling to the earth, vomiting as if a darkness was purged from his body.

Sithel spoke, "Your next words will be your death or salvation. Choose them wisely."

Still breathing ragged breaths, Zane realized he was in a corner. If he admitted stealing, even if it was from Darkeye, he would be jailed or even killed. In Farbs, stealing was a crime often met with death. He breathed in the dry dust, staring at the tan ground before him, desperately trying to buy himself time.

"Answer!" Sithel bellowed, spittle flying from his mouth. "Enough stalling!"

In the corner of his vision, between the heads of the crowd, he saw a glimpse of Salamander. The thief smiled—a sinister grin. He knew Zane was stuck. A lie was as good as death, and so was the truth. *I should have fought and fell to Snaggle and the others.* At least, there he would have had a chance. *A slim chance, but at least a chance.* Against twelve Reavers, two Devari, and this man? There was no hope.

He gritted his teeth but suppressed his fear and rage and rose, standing tall. He took a deep breath and summoned his voice, "I—"

"—Let him go," the Devari interrupted. It was the same one who spoke earlier, with the fearsome features—long nose and sharp jaw. "This is not our way."

Sithel looked confused and curious but, before he could respond, the Reaver at his side with three stripes whispered in Sithel's ear. Zane thought he heard the word *orphan*. He didn't know what the stripes meant exactly, but he figured it denoted rank. The others all had two or less. A light entered Sithel's eyes, and his steed danced beneath him, feeding off its rider's excitement. "It is decided. The boy will come back to the Citadel for questioning. It is the Patriarch's will. Now take him."

The bare-chested servants moved forward.

Zane felt his heart drop. *Death.* That was what questioning meant. It was a mounting rumor that had only taken hold in the last few months that boys and young men were taken to the Citadel for "questioning" and never returned. Always, it was orphans, those without family.

The Devari stepped forward, countering the muscled servants. "I've read his mind and his intentions. The ki tells me he is no threat."

Sithel raised a single brow. "What are you trying to say?"

"That I will not let you take him."

"This is the Patriarch's will, Devari. Question it again and risk everything."

The two Devari pressed together, looking like cornered lions, and their hands went to their blades. "This is not the Patriarch's will. This is Arbiter Fera's will," he said.

16 Sithel quaked with anger. "You dare to speak Citadel politics in front of these heathens?"

"I do what I must. You will not take this boy or any other boy back to her."

"*Stand down,*" Sithel hissed. It was whispered, but it couldn't have been harsher if he had bellowed it.

Both Devari unsheathed their blades.

The crowds gasped.

The quiet Devari leapt.

Sithel's dark eyes flashed dangerously as he nodded. The man fell to a pile of ash. The first Devari, Zane's defender, cried out and lunged for Sithel. The Reaver at Sithel's side waved a hand, smirking. The Devari suddenly gasped as flames sprung from his clothes. He tore his tunic and shirt from his burning body with one hand, still running. With his other hand, he tossed a dagger. It flew, lodging itself in the three-stripe Reaver's throat. The man gurgled blood and fell from his horse, dead. Abruptly, a roaring ball of fire seared the air to collide with the charging warrior. The Devari cried out as the fire consumed, eating away at the screams. Zane watched, unable to look away, feeling sick. At last, Sithel waved his hand. The fire vanquished. In its place was a body blackened like burnt meat, his smoldering clothes clung to his charred flesh. Zane gagged as the awful smell hit him.

Silence, like the pall of death, hung in the air. It had all happened so quickly. Zane slowly backed away, knowing that if there was a time to run and honor the Devari's sacrifice, it was now or never.

Sithel sniffed the air like a rat as his head swiveled, turning to Zane. "Where do you think you're going?"

The Reaver at his side snapped his fingers and nerves pinched in the back of Zane's legs, wincing in pain as he collapsed to the ground. He knew they were controlling them by threading the element of flesh. He snarled in rebellion, but there was nothing he could do.

"Really now," Sithel said, pulling back his hood to expose his features to the light of day, and Zane balked. With black eyes, sunken cheeks, and sallow skin, the man looked as if he'd been born in a dark pit, more creature of night than human. His long ebony hair sucked in the light and seemed to move about his face like writhing snakes. By contrast, it made his pale skin appear almost translucent. He picked his filed teeth with a long, black fingernail and spoke again. "We've made far more of a spectacle out of this than necessary. Now I'll ask only once. Come with us quietly, won't you?"

Zane seethed, his blood rising again. "You mean do I care to die quietly?" He was no longer afraid. Instead, seeing the Devari die had filled him with a mounting rage.

Sithel shrugged. "Choose what words you will."

He made a gesture, and men moved forward to grab Zane. His fear spiked.

"I..." Zane thought of the most outrageous lie he could. "I'm not an orphan."

Raising his hairless brow, Sithel laughed. "Is that so?" He sounded amused and doubtful, yet the large, approaching men hesitated, if only for a moment. "Well, where is your precious family then?"

"My family..."

"*Lad!*" A voice called, sounding over his thudding heart, coming from the crowds. All turned to the sound, including Sithel and the other Reavers. The throng parted, revealing an old man with gray hair, a beak nose, drooping cheeks like soggy bread, and a hunched back. He leaned heavily on what looked like the gnarled root of a Sansa tree made into a staff. "Boy, light and flesh, there you are! I should have known if I let you wander off on your own, you'd have the whole Citadel crashing down on your head!"

"Who are you, old man?" Sithel questioned.

The old man hobbled to Zane's side, seemingly oblivious to the danger. The crowds seemed equally perplexed. "Who am I? Isn't it obvious? I'm his father!"

Zane's mouth parted.

Sithel looked to him, and he swiftly wiped the look from his face and nodded as confidently as he could. "This … is your son?" Sithel asked, looking suspicious but not entirely disbelieving.

"Are you hard of hearing, young man?" the old man questioned and chuckled to himself, eyeing Zane. "Well, I suppose the resemblance isn't easy to see. He's got his mother's looks mostly, and her knack for finding trouble. But that nose, sure as sugar, is mine!" Zane eyed the man's large nose and realized it was much like his own bold nose—in fact, it looked almost identical, albeit bigger. Old men's noses always did seem to grow with age. *Coincidence*, he told himself… And yet… *Could the old man really be my father?* Zane shook his head. No, it couldn't be. But the man was saving his hide. Zane realized he'd better fall in line and quick.

"Sorry, da'. I know you told me to get a new bridle for Jess, but this procession was in the way, and the only way through was … well, straight through."

The old man, his back turned to the others, flashed Zane a wink of approval. Then he turned back to let Sithel see his disappointment as he wagged an admonishing finger. "See? How many times have I told you? You have a good head on you, if only you'd actually use it. Now, apologize to this man quickly, and we'll be on our way."

"I'm afraid not," Sithel sighed. "This is Citadel business now, old man, and your boy is caught up in it. He is coming with us."

The old man rubbed his chin. Again, he wondered who the old man was… *Didn't he know whom he was talking?* "Oh, really? Taking my own boy from me in front of all these people? Is that truly the will of the Patriarch? Is that what the mighty Citadel has come to now? Noble Reavers stealing boys from the street and killing their own Devari?"

"Silence!" a Reaver with two stripes shouted with a snarl. Zane saw the old man's words sink beneath their skin, and he hid a grin. *He plays a dangerous game.* It reminded him of Terus, a street game where one lived or died by the flip of a dagger. "You stand before Reavers, men and women who can peel the skin from your bones. Show some respect!" The ground rumbled, and the lecarta's red drapes wavered.

In that moment, Zane saw something behind the drapes—a brilliant flash of blue. It was so bright and mesmerizing that he took a step towards it, wanting to touch the miniature, azure sun. A chill flashed through him. He took another step, passing the old man pretending to be his father. His blood felt on fire and yet frozen all at the same time. Zane reached out just as the drapes settled but, at once, the image was gone. Shaking his head, he wondered: *What was that?*

"Mighty powerful words…" the old man said softly, and a dangerous note entered his voice. "Powerful and foolish, seeing as the word Reaver means 'protector of the people', but I suppose you've forgotten that…"

The Reaver who spoke bristled, then raised a hand as if to thread.

"Enough!" Sithel spat. "You forget your place, Calid."

Why did the man stop? But as Zane looked around, he saw all the crowds wore vigilant looks and realized it was clear Sithel and his minion were treading too far. Taking a boy from his own father before a crowd of witnesses was something that Zane suspected even the Patriarch would hear of. The Citadel, while growing darker, still heeded to the voice of the citizens.

Calid's mouth worked soundlessly. At last, the two-stripe Reaver lowered his head. "Apologies, my lord."

Sithel turned his horse and spoke over his shoulder. "Take your son and go, but, if we meet again, know my mercy has its limits."

With that, he rode off, back to the head of the procession.

The old man ushered Zane towards the crowd. But Zane stopped for a moment. He eyed the ash pile that was once a Devari then the broken, burnt body of the blue-eyed Devari. Several muscled men grabbed him, putting him on their shoulders and carrying him away. *Is he dead?* Zane wondered. The man had saved him, sacrificing himself. *Why? I hadn't asked it…* He hated owing anyone anything, and now his life was indebted to a man who was likely dead. The old man tugged Zane's arm, and he let himself be taken. Whispers sifted through the crowds, following them. Men and women, merchants, beggars, mothers, fathers, all stared at him as if he were a leper and a Reaver combined—looks of fear and respect.

Behind them, music filled the air as musicians took up their instruments, and the procession carried on as if it had never been stopped.

He followed the old man through the thicket of people like he was pressing through a field of wheat. The old man hobbled, using his gnarled staff to gently push the crowds out of their way. Most parted for them easily though, trying to glimpse the one who had been at the center of it all. As they moved, Zane couldn't help thinking about Hannah, about that strange man, about the guilt of the Devari and his death, but strangely, most of all about that blue orb.

At last, they broke through the last stand of people as if parting the clouds. Zane breathed a sigh of relief. He hadn't realized how much he hated being around so many people.

He took in his surroundings.

The alley was bright but empty. They were in a nicer part of town, one closer to the Citadel. He could see those tall, black towers above the adobe walls that crowded them from either side.

He turned to his savior.

The old man appeared taller and less hunched. Zane shook his head. Was he seeing things? Suddenly, the air rippled like heat waves and he gawked. The old man faded as if just a mirage, and in his place was a tall, regal looking man with broad shoulders. He was still wizened in years, but his face was smoother, almost handsome. The drooping white brows became thick and dark. His eyes—those eyes… No longer were they dull and glazed with the film of age, but penetrating and brimming with great wisdom and mystery. This was no mere man, Zane knew. Authority and power resonated from him the way the sun radiated heat. He wanted to avert his gaze, but there was something kind and settling about the man's face.

"That was closer than I intended. Far too close." His voice too had changed, deeper and full of control—but still it bore the fearless undertone. "I had not thought this day would come so soon…"

Zane narrowed his gaze. "Who or *what* are you?"

The man smiled, giving a grandfatherly look. "You do not look like I was expecting. You're taller, and blonde ... but you have his eyes." Zane shook his head. *Is the man mad? Is that the danger I sensed?* But he was curious too. The mysterious man spoke again, "We were lucky this time. In the future, you must avoid that man you just met and the one called Darkeye. Both are dangerous, more so than you could possibly imagine."

Despite himself, Zane chuckled. "Is that so? I'm not sure if you know this, but I didn't exactly intend on running into that man, and everyone knows to avoid Darkeye. I'm a fan of danger as much as any man, which is not at all." As he said the words, they sounded like a lie. *Stealing from Darkeye? Is that how I avoid danger?*

"It will not be easy. You will be pulled towards Darkeye like a string drawn by a loom."

The younger man put a hand to his head. "How do you know this? And who are you?"

"Someone you can trust," his savior answered.

"No offense," Zane remarked, "but I only trust two people in this world, and you aren't one of them."

"Beware that sentiment," the man said. "For a heart does not open easily once it is closed." The man's eyes flashed in pain and anger, but then the image was gone, as if never there.

Whatever this man is, Zane realized, *above all, he is dangerous.* He shifted his stance, reassuring himself with the dagger at his hip and said, "Listen, thank you for saving me. I owe you, and you should know that I always repay my debts. But... Whatever it is you're offering, I don't want any part of it."

The man sighed, looking distant, lost in memory. "I remember a look much like that from a young man very close to your age. It is sad when such mantles of power and duty are placed upon those so young." *What is he talking about?* "For now, Zane, I simply come with words of caution and a gift. Take this, and *don't* lose it." He pressed something cold and metallic into Zane's palm—a silver figurine of a squat man, a sword resting across his lap. Zane held it, puzzled. "One last thing: when the time comes, you can trust the man who speaks with the winds."

Speaks with the winds...? The man talked in riddles. But before he could say anything, the mysterious old man turned and walked away. Beyond the alley, the flow of traffic returned to the city—the procession long passed. Zane called to him. "*Wait!* I don't even know who you are! At the least, tell me your name…"

The man paused and looked over his shoulder. Backlit by the sun, Zane saw the wisp of a smile. "Ezrah," he replied.

Dark Things

Silver bugs bobbed in the night air like dancing lanterns. Their potent glow seemed like orbs of frost, and Gray dared not disturb them but flowed between them.

Dragon Finds the Roost.

Morrowil spun above Gray's head then plunged, diving for an unseen foe's heart. It was almost unnecessarily extravagant, and he would never do it in battle for the time it took, but it was powerful. Gray didn't stop. With his eyes flashing open and closed, he moved through the forms—forms which he didn't know until he began moving. They came to him like a dream, forming pictures in his mind. *Beetle Skims the Water.* He made short sprinting bursts, legs and arms straining with a series of fast thrusts.

Too open! he told himself.

Fluidly, he backpedaled into *Crane Fans its Wings*—like wind, Morrowil cut, parrying his imagined enemies in a figure-eight motion. Sweat beaded on Gray's brow, concentration intensifying. *I must go faster*, his mind pressed. But his muscles burned. *The mind is stronger than the body*—a quote that wasn't his. Devari. He shut the thoughts out and lost himself to the forms. *Crane Fans its Wings* met *Darting Snake*, which flowed awkwardly into *Thief's Reprisal.* Every move was aggressive, hard, and unrelenting.

Find balance! his fighting side instructed.

He ignored it. He ducked, evading a pretend blade that would've taken his head and rolled smoothly across the ground. Mid roll, he grabbed a fistful of dirt. As he came to his feet, he flung the dirt in the imaginary opponent's eyes and cut down. Morrowil sparked upon the bits of granite sand. *It would never work against a Devari.* Again, it was his own voice, his own doubt. Without slowing, he whipped the blade around his body, cutting down a charge, then dove, rolled and with a cry—

Too open! Kirin yelled.

That voice… His concentration shattered like a brittle sword. Morrowil slipped from his sweaty grip. He opened his eyes. The sword lay upon the ground, pulsing a brilliant silver as always, beating back the night's gloom.

"Kirin?" he voiced aloud.

Silence, save for his heavy breathing and the subtle hum of the bugs.

"I know you're there…" he said, fearful and curious.

There was a rustle of movement behind him. "Gray?" a voice said.

Gray turned.

Ayva's blue shawl was wrapped around her slender frame, staving off the cool night air. She was back to pleated riding skirts and brown boots. Despite the darkness, and not for the first time, he noticed her subtle curves. He looked back to her eyes, glad of the darkness as his cheeks heated. She wore a look of innocent confusion.

"What's going on?" Ayva asked.

Suddenly, as if upon seeing her, life and reality seemed to settle around him again. Gray panted, taking ragged lungfuls of strangely sweet air, for Farhaven's magic permeated all things, and he felt it with every breath. They were in the desert, and had been for the past week. Though the map Karil had given them didn't show distances, they'd estimated the journey would take a full moon's cycle to reach Farbs. But Gray found it hard to trust the simple piece of paper, for the desert seemed endless, broken only by odd patches of forest, meadow, or stream. Once, they'd even seen a waterfall. How did such a thing occur in this arid landscape? Farhaven was strange and extraordinaire indeed, and he had a feeling they'd only brushed the surface.

He shook his head and smiled, rubbing a hand through his disheveled hair and feeling sweat run down his arm. It reminded him that he needed to bathe and cut his hair—it nearly touched his shoulders now. "Just a little training," he said, "nothing to worry about. What are you doing up? It's still my watch, isn't it?"

"It is," she said, "but I can't sleep..." She eyed the nearby darkness, then asked hesitantly, "A second ago, were you just talking to yourself?"

"Probably..." he admitted with a wince, feigning embarrassment to hide what he truly felt: pure and utter confusion. Kirin was supposed to be dead and gone... Killed when he thrust the sword into the stone. He was only Gray now, but it sounded too much like he was convincing himself. "It's weird, I know, but I've done it for as long as I can remember." He hated twisting the truth, but dealing with the idea of Kirin was something he didn't know how to broach with her. *Are you there?* he thought again, probing his mind.

Ayva seemed to relax. "I talk to myself when I'm bored too, breaks the tedium of a long watch," she admitted, her judging gaze turning away at last. Gray hid a shiver. Sometimes he felt as if they were waiting to see something inside of him.

They are looking to see Kail, Kirin whispered, amused.

You're back...

Ayva smiled and raised an amused brow. "What are you talking about? I never left, Gray."

"What?" he asked instinctually.

She neared and touched his bare arm. "Darius and I are with you. You know that."

Gray grimaced, he hadn't realized he'd said it aloud, and she took it... He must have sounded vulnerable. "I know," he said confidently. "I couldn't do this without you two, nor would I want to." He meant it but changed the topic. "Yet how much longer do you think we'll have to travel this cursed desert?"

"I'm not sure," she answered. "Judging by the map, we're probably a few days away from a town called Tormen that butts against a large river—which, by the way, looks huge. If the map is any indication, we could fit a hundred Sils within this Umai River." As always, her voice became entranced, and Gray imagined being here, in Farhaven, was like a dream come true for her. He wondered, *is that why she doesn't sleep?* As if Ayva was already dreaming, and to sleep was to wake from this adventure. She continued, "Then beyond the river, it becomes real desert all the way until we reach Farbs."

"*Real* desert," he repeated with a snort, "Great."

She chuckled, sitting down on a nearby rock. "You know, you're beginning to sound a little like Darius. I think he's rubbing off on you."

"Oh, really? I'm not sure if that's a good thing."

"Not at all," she said with a smile.

"Well, that's just dicing terrific!"

This time, Ayva laughed deeply. It was truly pleasant—sweet, pure and feminine—and it banished all the darkness from his mind. He was glad he could make her laugh. Darius always seemed the one for that. "Can I ask you something?" she said suddenly.

"You just did," he said.

She gave him a level stare.

Well, perhaps his humor wasn't *as* good as he thought. Cursing the sudden awkwardness, he sat next to her, staring off into the darkness, seeing glimmers of what lay upon the horizon. He almost thought he could see a stand of trees. The bugs danced in the air, their silver glow setting a serene ambiance to the moment. Behind him, over his shoulder, he saw the faint outline of Darius' sleeping roll, and he thought he could hear the rogue's raucous saw-like snores. "Go ahead," he told her.

"Well… First, what's worrying you? You seem annoyed by this desert, more so than any of us."

"It's going to sound silly, but I don't like the quiet."

"I think I know what you mean…"

He shook his head. "It's more than the silence." *I feel it in the air,* he thought, but instead said, "Nothing has happened since we started our journey."

"Isn't that a good thing?"

"I don't know," he said. "But I fear something is out there."

They both grew silent, staring into the distance, into the night. "And it's just what, watching?" she asked.

"Or waiting…" he said ominously.

Ayva shivered as a nearby glowing beetle floated closer. She reached out her hand, and it landed on her finger. Through the intense shine, Gray could make out furry feelers, large pincers, and a blue shell. *Frost bugs*, Ayva had called them. It and its brothers gave off a strange buzz, but rather than being annoying or incessant, the varying buzzes created a kind of harmony—a quiet song even.

Ayva spoke. "The stories say there are infinite types of creatures within Farhaven. They say the elves attempted to name them all long ago, but it was just as easy to name all the stars in the sky—there's simply too many. These beetles glow when feeding, and they sustain themselves off the very air and magic of Farhaven—that glowing dust you see sometimes. But normally they dwell in caves and have no glow. I read once that their light is a defensive mechanism, but if you touch their feelers in just the right place…" She touched it gently, and sure enough, the insect's glow vanished like a flame winking out. Ayva smiled, but then a grave look crossed her face. "Just as surely as there are creatures who are innocent like this one and feed only off the magic in the air, it only stands to reason that there are a thousand creatures out there who feed off more than just magic and are much more dangerous." Again, she touched its feeler, and its glow returned. The frost bug flew away into the black abyss.

Gray whistled through his teeth. "How many books *did* you read?"

She smiled. "Too many and not enough. But none of them ever prepared me for the real thing."

"What else?" he asked, sensing that wasn't her main question.

"What are you training for?"

He shrugged. "That's obvious enough, isn't it?" Ayva looked away, staring into the darkness. And he could tell she was avoiding something. Gently, he grabbed her chin and pulled her gaze to match his. "Tell me. We're friends. You can tell me anything."

"I…. I don't know what's going to happen when we reach Farbs," she said. "Karil told us that we won't be able to get into the Citadel, this place you're from. I'm not as afraid of the dangers from outside as I am from within. I heard you talking to yourself. I'm worried about what will happen to you when we get there. Maybe your old self will return. Maybe you'll realize that it was bad, or perhaps it will even overtake you." Ayva gripped his arm, eyes narrowing. "Or worse yet, I fear you left that place for a reason. What if they are waiting for you to return, only to kill you as soon as you enter?"

He sensed her fear, her vulnerability, and he even felt his own. Something rose inside of him. A long moment passed. He felt his heart beating harder and harder. Looking down, he felt Ayva's fingers graze his hand, and he gripped back. He gazed up, staring deep into her blue eyes. The silver glow from his sword illuminated her features, small nose, freckles, and soft, pink lips.

At last, Gray cleared his throat, finding his less-than-steady voice. "I guess, in the end, we'll just have to watch out for each other."

"Agreed," she said, holding his eyes.

The moment lingered, and Gray felt his heart wanting to pounce from his chest.

"Well," Ayva replied, suddenly rising, and, despite the deep night, he thought he saw her cheeks color and her voice sounded breathy, but he might have been imagining it. For when she spoke again, it was clear and confident. "I suppose if I have the next shift, and since Darius took *both* my shifts last night, I should get some sleep or the fool will never let me hear the end of it."

Gray nodded, standing as well, though a part of him missed the warmth of her.

They faced each other.

Again, his heart pounded against his ribcage.

"Goodnight," she said with a smile, moving away.

Grabbing his sword from the ground, he watched her retreat back into the darkness. His fingers tightened, feeling its glassy smooth handle. Gray realized he was grinning like a little boy who'd just won … *something*. As always, it was difficult to connect his youth to things when he didn't have memories. He wiped the silly look from his face and eyed Morrowil. The sword's glow beat back the shroud of night, but it did nothing for the sensation of eyes watching him from the shadows.

The blade gave him strength and confidence lately, but he would not let it control him again. He would have to be careful, but he had found a balance with the sword of power. The more he poured himself into the blade, the more power and abilities it seemed to grant. But there was a trick—the sword's powers mimicked its owner. A wicked man would find corruption, and an honest man, the power of light. So to tip the scale in his favor, Gray had to trust himself. He had to believe in his actions wholeheartedly to keep the sword in equilibrium.

He wondered if that was Kail's downfall during the great war of the Lieon. All was turning to darkness and death, he imagined. Kail, the leader of the Ronin, surely would have needed the blade and its power. The man would have demanded more and more from it, and the blade would have given it. Yet, as loved ones fought and died, and the world crumbled beneath him, Gray could only imagine that each request must have been mired in Kail's own dark fear. *The blade only echoes its owner*, he thought again. With fear growing like a cavity within the legend, shadows of those he loved feasted upon his soul, and the blade upon them in return. Ultimately, it was not the blade that had borne a terrible darkness, but Kail himself. Though he had made it right in the end, giving up Morrowil and helping destroy the Kage, the truth was clear: the greatest Ronin and most powerful warrior of all time was done in by his own fear, his own doubt.

No, Gray would not fall victim to that. For once, he trusted himself and his path.

He smiled and grabbed his sheath with its silver and gold-worked vines—the elaborate scabbard Mura had found at the Gates and given him. The thought of the hermit sent a pang through his heart. Already, he missed the man and wished he were there. Mura would know what to do. But the hermit was with Karil, and that was where his duty lay. As for Gray, his duty lay here. He would see the hermit again, he vowed, but for now, they had their own paths.

Setting aside such thoughts, he reached for his shirt when—

What are you training for? Kirin asked from within the darkness of his mind.

I thought you were gone…

Why? his former self asked.

I had two paths to choose at the Gates, Gray replied. *One was to remember everything and destroy the world, the other to forget it all and sacrifice myself. I chose the second. You should be no more.*

But I am you. And you are me. 'One never truly loses one's self, Gray, even if they forget their name or their way.'

Those words… *Whose words are those?*

Silence, then the voice spoke distantly. *What are you training for?*

For them, and for me… Because it's all I can do.

Do you truly believe you can take them? Devari? Reavers?

I don't want to fight anyone.

But I didn't ask that. Not want. If you have to, if you're forced to, would you be able to take them?

No one can force me to do anything.

Sometimes taking a life is necessary… The way he said it—as if he was implying something greater.

Is she right? Are you evil? Gray asked.

Are you? A vision flashed in Gray's mind. A face. Vera. His sister—and he *had* killed her. He may not have dealt the final blow, but he had killed her. No, she had chosen death, and, in truth, she had died long ago.

Semantics. You pinned her to the stone, and let Kail behead her.

Gray shook his head, casting away the thoughts. He felt his gaze grow hot, tears brimming in the corner of his eyes. "Leave me be," he said hollowly, feeling a gnawing emptiness in his gut, reminding him of Kail and the legend's descent into madness. No, he thought adamantly, then aloud, "I'm not Kail. I made the right choice."

You did, but there's a power inside you. You just might be able to face them all… But you must not run from the truth.

Gray reached back and felt the nexus, swirling at the edge of his thoughts, waiting patiently. But when he gripped it, it was not pure and blinding like it had been at the Gates. Still, over the past few weeks, it had slowly grown. With each night of training, he felt it build, as if throwing logs onto the fire.

I will be powerful, but I will keep my conscience, and I will be rid of you, he thought decidedly. The words were like an axe head, felling his doubts.

Kirin seemed to balk, but only whispered, Soon then…

When? he asked impatiently.

Farbs. There you will find me. There we will meet again.

And one of us will win this body, Gray stated, but he felt it sounded more like a question—a terrifying question. Who would win? Would he be absorbed by Kirin? Just become a voice trapped in the back of Kirin's mind? Or would he fade completely?

Gray watched the shadows. Something was out there. He waited fearfully for his former self to respond, to confirm his fears, but nothing came. Gray looked down and realized he was holding the broken pieces of his pendant—the stone necklace, and a piece of his past—when a vision filled his mind.

A *black keep.... Dark stone walls... A man running in fear as bookcases crashed down around him...*

Just as quickly as it came, the vision dissipated, leaving Gray wondering who the man was, if it was past or present, and why it had come when he was holding the pendant. But instead, all he was left with was Kirin's mocking voice, a fading echo in the back of his mind.

Soon... Soon we will meet again.

The Nodes

Light and shadows flickered across Ayva's vision.

Those sharp gray-green eyes taking her in, seeing into her... She felt her hand reaching out, her heart quickening. Her palms turned damp. She leaned forward and—

Ayva's eyes snapped open. She put a hand to her brow, shielding her gaze from the morning sun. She was still in her bedroll and, in the peripheries of her vision, she saw Darius packing up his things and brushing down his spirited cormac. The majestic beast pranced with energy despite days of hard travel.

Her thoughts returned to her dream. *Gray.*

Absently, she grazed her lips with her fingers. Shaking her head, she put the confusing bundle of thoughts and questions to the back of her head and rose. Yawning, she took in their camp. The ground beneath her feet was soft sand. From it, tubers and the occasional plant sprouted. Nearby, a strange purple and green succulent bristled with finger-length spines, multihued like a rainbow bed of nails. That was tame for Farhaven.

She'd seen tall plants, short ones, plants that looked like rocks or even animals. One plant, she remembered, had floated, with no base! She had wanted to examine it closer, having not heard of it in any of the stories, but Gray and Darius had advised against it. They didn't know what they were dealing with, and she knew they were right.

She remembered Karil's words. *You venture in a new land that is beautiful and dangerous. Be careful.* Well, she didn't remember the words *exactly*. But it was something like that. Of course, Karil would have said it with perfect eloquence and poise. Light and flesh, she already missed Mura and the others. How had that happened?

Ayva rose and began stuffing her bedroll into her pack, ruminating on her friends.

Taking back the Kingdom of Eldas—one of the Great Kingdoms—won't be an easy task. That much was clear even to Ayva, but if anyone could do it, it would be Karil and the others. Part of her was jealous. *What I wouldn't give to see the City Within the Trees*—another name for Eldas, a city with a thousand lights, their buildings suspended in the colossal great trees. It was home to the elves. It was also the kingdom of Leaf. Each Great Kingdom held dominion over one of the nine elements: leaf, water, fire, stone, moon, sun, flesh, metal, and of course, wind. The notorious element of wind made her think of Kail and Gray—one a mad, powerful legend, and the other her close friend. And yet, somehow, they were the same person.

She wondered if Kail still lived. Gray said they were dead, that he had watched Maris, the Ronin of leaf, die before his eyes, but there was something in the way he had said it… As if he believed there was something missing, like a book without an ending. Surely, the Ronin weren't dead. She couldn't imagine such epic beings vanquished so easily. Truthfully, she'd never felt particularly close to them, aside from Maris, but their loss made her feel oddly hollow even now, as if a great light had gone out in the world with their passing. *No*, she thought with a smile, absently stuffing in a pair of breeches she'd rolled up and used as a pillow, *the Ronin are not dead.*

Her thoughts went back to Gray. That moment… Despite the storm of uncertainty that welled inside her, and all the confusion of what they faced ahead, she had felt so secure in that one moment.

She caught Darius looking at her curiously over his shoulder.

Her cheeks flushed and she looked away, pretending to busy herself with shaking out her bedroll. *Dice!* she thought, stealing the rogue's curse, *I'm a little girl again… Wasn't it just yesterday I was hanging from a dragon's talons?* She must have looked like a boy pining over his first sword, or a patron falling for the wiles of Willow's enchanting voice and harp.

Thoughts of her father's inn almost drew her back to a dark place, but she veered away, thinking back to the Ronin and the final battle at Death's Gate. *Wasn't it less than a year ago that I didn't even think Farhaven existed, let alone the Ronin?* No. That was never true. Ayva had always believed in something more, and only when Gray showed up did those dreams become a reality.

Gray…

She shook her head, coming full circle. *I miss Mura, Karil, and even that stone-faced Rydel, but I wouldn't choose to be anywhere else in the world, or with anyone else for that matter.*

"Dice, who took my pipe?"

She looked over and saw the rogue mumbling and cursing, peering into his bag. "No one took your pipe, Darius. Maybe you just misplaced it."

"Someone took it. I'm not pointing fingers, but it was right here, plain as day, and now it's gone…"

"Don't you have three others?" she asked.

Darius paused his frantic rummaging and looked up. "Well, sure, but that one was my favorite. I'd worn it in just right. A good pipe is like a good pair of boots, and—*bah,* you wouldn't understand."

Ayva shook her head, amused. *Perhaps I spoke too soon.* She looked down. Her hand gripped a silver scabbard, which she had hidden beneath her makeshift pillow. She admired the beautiful, intricate weapon. As long as her forearm, the lacy scabbard had scrawled silver patterns too complex to decipher. It dazzled as if encrusted with diamonds. She unsheathed the blade. Its steel shone like a full moon on a dark night, even in the morning sun. A gift, like the cormacs, from the Elvin queen.

Tucking the blade into her belt, she rose and approached the rogue. Looking around, Gray was nowhere to be seen. His pack and bedroll had already been seen to. "Where's Gray?"

Darius shrugged. "He said he'd ride ahead and scout—something about being restless." He looked up, pulling tight the last strap on his cormac. "Between you and me, he was acting a little strange. More so than normal."

"Oh, really?"

Darius lifted a brow. "What's got you smiling? You look like someone just asked you to the Harvest Festival."

Ayva hadn't realized she was smiling. She resumed a smooth face. "Nothing, I just think you two are funny."

"Why's that?" He grabbed her bag and moved to her cormac, strapping down the pack.

"Well, lately, he's acting more like you, and you, more like him," she said with a casual shrug. As she said the words, she realized that added another confusing layer to what had happened last night.

Darius had already rubbed the animals down. Their silken coats, now free of dust, glistened in the desert sun. Her steed was chewing on the strange cud Karil had given them, the animal's long, graceful neck dipping like a willow tree's branch, silent as always. "Wait, what's that supposed to mean? How so?" he asked.

"I wouldn't worry about it."

"Well, I wasn't before, but *now* I am. Gray's fine and all, but he's always so … dutiful."

"Looks like you just answered your own question. Who's strapping down the animals? Who's making sure all the night watches get covered?" She shrugged again. "I'm just saying."

Hand frozen on the cormac's strap, Darius' mouth worked but no words came out. "I…" he stumbled, and then cursed, tugging the already fully tightened strap and grumbling to himself. She heard some interspersed words as she finished cleaning up the camp. "*Dicing … Gray … cormacs … women.*"

"Let's get a move on," she said. "I don't like the idea of Gray traveling alone, even if it's to scout ahead."

Darius grumbled, but made no objection as they mounted their steeds and started forward, leaving their camp behind. Before they left, they always made sure to brush down their camp with a large frond to ensure no one could tell anyone had been there. As for their footprints, they'd figured occasional winds would cover their tracks. She wasn't sure what they had to be afraid of, but there seemed to be no sense in taking any chances. She couldn't imagine Farhaven having bandits or thieves, but at the very least, it put her mind at ease.

As they rode, she took in the landscape. The desert was dappled with bright green bushes that moved, swishing without so much as a hint of a breeze. She looked to the rogue who wore a pensive face as he stared at the desert ahead. "Darius?"

He looked over at her, swaying in his saddle. "Yes?"

"What are you thinking?"

His eyes scrunched, looking thoughtful. "I don't like the silence of the past few days."

"Gray said as much. He thinks there is something watching us," she revealed.

"I hate to admit it, but I think he's right," Darius said with a shiver. His hand idly reached for the dagger in the folds of his new clothes. She was so accustomed to the rogue's secondhand rags that the fitted dark coat, polished boots, and deep black pants he now wore seemed odd. He wore an earth-green cloak of Elvin fabric and design, a long pointed hood with vines embroidered on its edge, which Karil had also gifted them. And while he often complained about the color—"the very worst of colors" as Darius put it, "no color that resembles vomit should be respected"—he still seemed to wear the cloak with pride. More than once she had seen him admiring the meticulous Elvin needlework—the flowing vines and silver-stitched leaves so graceful and vibrant that they almost appeared alive.

Now, as he scratched his patchy stubble with his eyes fixed ahead, she realized she had grown comfortable around Darius—almost more so than Gray. There was less mystery around the rogue, but still she knew he had his secrets, as did she. For instance, why else was he here? The rogue seemed pulled by something more. Maybe they both were, she admitted. But who had Darius left behind in Lakewood? Sometimes she wanted to ask, but she saw the pain in his eyes when she brought up Lakewood. For both of them, it was still too raw a wound to discuss.

"This land…" he continued, "it's strange. I've never felt so at peace and yet so on edge all at the same dicing time. It's like an inn full of music and cards that I'm sure to win, but beneath the table everyone is brandishing their daggers."

She nodded in agreement. "We'll just be careful."

He agreed, and they continued until Ayva saw something on the horizon. A stand of bright green glimmered. It looked like a forest.

"Do you see that?"

He nodded. "It's real." Sometimes there had been false images. Mirages, she had read.

"Do you think Gray is in there?" she asked.

"I'm not sure, but don't stray too far from me." With that, he spurred his cormac—*Mirkal,* he had begun to call it. When she questioned earlier why or what it meant, he had shrugged, saying it simply "felt right".

She nodded and veered her cormac closer. It listened with the slightest of commands. In fact, she didn't even remember pulling her reins—it was almost as if the beast had *felt* her intention and reacted.

They neared quickly.

That was good. Sometimes things could seem a mile away and take days to reach, and other times a place may seem impossibly far and take mere minutes. The desert was strange that way. She wondered if such was the case with all of Farhaven.

They stopped at the edge of the stand of trees. Inside, light illuminated the glade, streaming down like pillars of brilliant gold. The trees were thick, as if she had ventured into the heart of an ancient forest. Otherwise, there was no Gray, nor sign of life.

Darius grumbled to himself, "Fool! What is he doing? Getting himself lost without us?"

"Right? I thought that was your job," she said then patted her cormac—she would have to come up with a name for the beautiful animal, but nothing yet had felt right. "Well, no use waiting out here," she said before the rogue could retort, and she spurred the creature forward.

"Argh, wait up!" Darius cried, racing to catch up.

They entered, and cool air met them. Ayva took a deep breath and felt a heavier magic in the air. She saw more motes of gold floating before her eyes. *This place... it is truly magical...* As they wove through the majestic trees, she saw signs of life. Flowers dappled the bright, moss-covered ground—red, blue, green, white, purple, and a hundred other colors Ayva didn't even know existed. Nearby, butterflies the size of her head flitted from branch to flower. Their wings were silver and gold. She found her breath taken by the beauty of it all. Even Darius whistled through his teeth at the sight. They wove through a last batch of willow-like trees, and Ayva gasped at the sight before her. At her side, Darius cursed.

Beyond them was a large clearing. In the center, there was a body of water, large enough to be bigger than a pond but smaller than a lake, and around it, life flourished. There were mushrooms the size of stools with speckled tops, and ferns that dipped their branches into the cool water. The ground was grass in most places, and in others, moss that was green, blue, and even blood red. Huge, shelled creatures moved slowly amid the cerulean water, several of them awkwardly scooting upon the grassy ground, like reptilian children learning to walk. At the other end of the lake, Ayva saw a flock of green-feathered birds standing on two long legs, bathing. They looked up at their entrance but then paid the humans no mind. Above the water, dozens of butterflies danced among the hanging specks of gold.

"Dicing dice," Darius cursed. "What is this place?"

Ayva shook her head, at a loss for words. Quickly, she dismounted and approached the water. Darius joined her. The warm sun blanketed her, and she felt alive, as if feeding off its vitality. Smaller butterflies flitted around her, and she heard an enchanting hum in the air like music. She reached down to touch one of the shelled reptiles and felt a hand upon her shoulder. She nearly leapt out of her skin. Turning, she saw Gray's familiar face wearing an impish smile.

"Gray!" Immediately she rose and hugged him. At first he didn't respond, but then he returned the gesture, and she felt his strong arms. She pushed away. "You nearly scared me half to death! What did you think you were doing, leaving us like that then jumping out of nowhere? Where have you been?"

Standing there, Gray looked different. *Powerful,* she thought. Tall and broad-shouldered, he wore his usual threadbare gray cloak with its crossed swords, but now he wore new clothes, another gift of Karil's—dark pants and a shirt with a fitted gray vest, cinched by a leather belt with a white-metal buckle. Upon his arms were leather bracers with silver accents. Stubble from the days of travel now began to grow evenly along his cheeks, and dark brown hair dangled about his shoulders. He held her gaze, just like the night before, making her swallow. "To be honest," Gray said, "I saw you both a bit ago, but I wanted to see your reaction to this place. It's amazing, isn't it?"

Ayva was silent, raptured in the moment. The sun grew toasty upon her cheek, and she held up a hand, watching as the butterflies danced around it like a pole in the center green of the Harvest Festival, wanting nothing more than to let the moment continue forever.

"Amazing, indeed," Darius breathed, "but *what* is it?"

"It's a sanctuary," Gray said.

Drawn back by her curiosity, Ayva questioned, "From what? And how do you know that?" He seemed to know more and more of late, but where was he getting his answers? Did he have some book he'd not shared?

"I'm not sure," he answered. "But whatever the reason, it explains why we haven't seen much of the inhabitants of Farhaven until now."

"And as for how you knew?" Darius asked.

"I'm a Devari."

Ayva raised a curious brow. "And that means?"

"I thought you had heard Karil or Maris explain it," he said, but she shook her head. "Well, Devari live in Farbs. I guess they, and I, have this power called the ki. I'm not very good with it yet, but it allows me to sense other beings, humans or animals, to feel how they feel."

"Like empathy?" she asked.

"That and more. I literally *am* those creatures for a time, inhabiting their bodies with my mind."

"That sounds ... terrifying," Darius said with a shiver.

He shook his head. "It's not really. In fact, it's amazing to truly connect and understand another creature. I can feel these animals. They are afraid, but here they feel safe... Like a beast in a self-made cage. A cage they feel is closing in around them."

Darius snorted, "Thank you, but no thank you. I prefer staying in my own skin."

Ayva smacked his arm. "That sounds amazing," she said. "A true gift." To understand another living being fully was a thing she tried to do but knew no one could truly accomplish until one could feel what others felt.

At that moment, a bloody cry split the air. Ayva jumped, grabbing Gray's arm. Darius leapt as well, reaching for his blade in his black-green coat, twisting and turning as the cry continued, echoing through the woods. Across the lake, creatures bolted into the dense foliage while birds took to the air and the shelled beasts skittered into the water's depths.

"What in the light was that?" Darius asked.

They looked at one another, and Ayva knew that each was thinking the same thing.

It sounded like the cry of a child.

Ayva realized her fingers still gripped Gray's arm. She let go. He offered her a smile of reassurance, but she knew him well enough by now to see uncertainty behind his piercing gray-green eyes. He looked ahead sternly. "We need to investigate."

"Oh, of course, go on ahead! Meanwhile, I'll just make sure this lake doesn't go anywhere." Darius hunkered down, sitting cross-legged.

"*We,* Darius," Gray said. "We cannot afford to move alone." He looked to Ayva.

She took a deep breath and nodded. "Together."

Darius grumbled, but as always, she tuned him out and moved to her cormac.

They mounted and moved into the woods together. They passed tall trees, their roots sprouting from the ground. Between the folds of their bark, she saw flowing silver, moving as if alive. *Silveroots,* she knew—a rare type of Farhaven tree whose sap was pure silver. The cry sounded again, louder this time. *So close,* she thought. Suddenly Darius' cormac—*Mirkal*—took off into a full gallop as if sprinting after the sound.

"Darius!" Gray said, reaching for the reins, but he was too slow.

"*Help!*" The rogue cried out in surprise, but then he was gone.

Ayva spurred her cormac hard, and Gray did the same. They raced through thick trees, ducking beneath low-hanging branches until they heard another sharp scream. Darius. They parted the last stand of trees. Ayva pulled hard on her reins to slow the animal's gallop, but before she could, the cormac stopped dead still, nearly catapulting her over its head. When she settled, she took in the scene.

Darius hung upside down in the air, suspended from a bough high above by a thick rope that was wrapped around his ankle. Before him was a woman with fiery red hair spilling over her shoulders. Horror and anger warped Darius' face, and Ayva realized the woman held a dagger to his throat.

"You fool!" the woman seethed. "You let her get away!"

"Let who get away?" Darius stuttered, bewildered. "What are you talking about?"

Her dagger pressed closer.

Gray quickly dismounted, striding toward the woman. Ayva saw he held Morrowil—its tip aimed at the woman's nape, ready to cut. "If your blade moves another hair, you will find your head and body no longer joined. Now, let him go," he ordered. Ayva shivered. For all the world Gray pretended to not be Kail, sometimes … he sounded… *No*, she thought, refusing to think of the mad legend as Gray.

The woman, hearing the threat in Gray's voice, slowly backed away from Darius.

Quickly, Ayva threw her leg over the saddle and fell to Darius' side. She eyed the ropes on his ankle. Ayva had seen some knots in her time, but nothing like this. It would make Ole' Rubis, Lakewood's weaver, flounder in red-faced confusion.

"Get me out of this cursed thing—all the blood is rushing to my head." Darius pulled himself up to untie his bonds.

"I wouldn't…" the woman whispered.

Darius paused. "Why?"

Ayva ignored her and moved to help him.

"If you untie him, you will die."

"Is that a threat, stranger?" Gray asked stepping forward and pressing Morrowil to the woman's slender throat.

Ayva took her in finally. Though a dark, dust-cloak hid her frame, it did nothing to detract from her looks. Fiery red hair framed a heart-shaped face. It fell in waves like a waterfall across her shoulders. Her eyes were light brown, soft on anyone else, but on her, they were russet daggers. She eyed all three of them like curious playthings. The woman was gorgeous, in a rough-hewn, hard way. If anything, it only made her all the more attractive, like a flower that bit back.

"My name is Faye. And it is the simple truth. The rope is oiled with a poison, and anyone who touches it will die." She said the words so plainly, as if speculating whether there would be rain or sunshine.

"Then we can just cut it with a sword…" Gray looked to Ayva. She nodded, unsheathing her dagger. It blazed white, sucking in the clearing's light.

"Well, that's not a bad idea on its own," Faye mused, "but still he will die."

Ayva hesitated, hand wavering.

"Spit it out," Gray ordered. "Why?"

The woman nodded to three different points, "In the bushes there, there and there, are fine poisonous darts aimed directly at your friend here. If anyone dares so much as breathe upon that rope, they will fire, triggered by a pulley system. It's a fairly simple trap, but an effective one."

Ayva ground her teeth. "Enough. You created it, so you know how to disarm it. Tell us."

Faye raised a single brow, eyeing Morrowil's point. "May I?"

"Throw your blade on the ground first," he ordered.

"Well, unless you want me to cut rope with my teeth?"

"Fine. But one wrong move…"

"Right, right, and I'm dead. I got that." Gray lowered Morrowil. Faye moved fluidly, cutting something within each of the bushes a dozen paces away that circled the clearing. "There, that should do it," she said and stuffed her long, curved dagger into a sheath behind her back. She looked too well practiced at that, Ayva thought. All three stood, frozen. "Well, go ahead, and cut him down."

Ayva moved to cut the rope, but it was too high to reach, especially with her dagger. If she could jump and… She reached into her mind, leapt and… Something fizzled, and the rope snapped. Darius fell with a grunt, hitting the soft forest floor.

Suddenly, Ayva saw Faye dash, blade withdrawn.

Everyone moved at once. Gray raised a hand. Darius cried out, reaching for his blade. Ayva moved to jump before him, raising her dagger, but they were all too slow.

The woman was *quick*. She sliced but then missed, only cutting the air, then froze, as if purposively. She knelt, putting her dagger upon the ground and raised her hands meekly, though it looked like steel pretending to be soft.

Darius lay on his back, hands shielding his face. "Dice! What just happened?"

Gray's hands slowly fell to his side. He moved before Darius and picked up the two halves of something.

A wooden dart.

Faye smiled. "Seems I forgot one. My mistake."

Gray growled and dropped the halves to the ground. "I don't know whether to thank you for saving his life or end you right here for nearly taking it," he said.

She shrugged. "I merely righted a wrong—take it as you will."

Ayva offered her hand to Darius, helping him up.

"Thanks," he said sincerely. He *was* changing, she realized. He rose, brushing his pants and cloak free of dirt and dried bits of leaves.

Faye moved to rise and she grunted, a look of confusion crossing her face. Ayva saw that thick roots were twined around her leg, holding her in place. She would never have reached Darius, she realized. "What is this?" Faye asked. "Which of you did this?"

Ayva felt a shiver and looked to Gray. "You can…"

Gray shook his head. "It wasn't me." He looked to Darius.

All three eyed the rogue. Darius' face was deathly pale. "I…"

"Enough!" Faye snapped, growling and drawing their attention back. She was bound in vines fully now, her arms and wrists trapped at her sides. "Release me this instant!"

Gray moved forward, but Darius rose. "Wait," he said. His eyes narrowed as if concentrating. On the roots? Or perhaps on something in his own head… He raised his hand and slowly, the roots unfurled, slinking off of Faye's foot and disappearing back into the ground.

Ayva's throat went dry, taking a step back. "How did you…?"

Darius shook his head, looking confused. He looked to his hands as if they were not his own. "I don't know… I just felt it. Sitting there, waiting."

"It must have come to your defense, rising out of need when you thought she was going to attack you," Gray said. "Just like mine…"

"No," Darius shook his head, a sudden fire and fearful edge in his voice. "It's nothing like yours."

Gray was silent.

Faye snorted. "An Untamed. That's all you are."

"What's an Untamed?" Darius asked, voice shaky.

"An untrained Reaver," she stated, rising to her feet calmly. Ayva saw she had lost her dark grey dust-cloak somewhere in the chaos. Now her full-figure was revealed, and it nearly made Ayva blush.

She wore fitted red and black cloth mostly but at the arms, light chain mail glimmered. On her shoulders were thick leather pads. Yet the cloth and armor did nothing to hide an ample bosom and alluring hips. A heavy-belt cinched her thin waist, accentuating it.

A long, curved blade sat on one hip and a small crossbow sat on the other. Ayva saw a throwing dagger in one boot and a few smaller ones attached to the inside of her arms.

Ayva had never seen so many weapons in one place. Well, maybe once or twice, but always by a fool sauntering into The Golden Horn—her father's inn—acting as if more weapons somehow meant he was more dangerous, when the truth was the opposite. No one could wield that many weapons at the same time and hope to be effective. Ayva had no doubt Faye could handle every one of those weapons and more.

Darius stepped towards Faye, anger in his eyes. "You say the word like you just ate a bad lemon. What's an Untamed and why do you despise them?"

Faye hesitated. Suddenly, she leapt with dagger in hand, attacking Gray. Taken aback, Gray raised Morrowil in the nick of time, parrying, but Faye didn't slow. With her other hand, she unsheathed her long sword cutting and slicing in a whirling blur.

What is going on? Ayva thought frantically. "Stop it!" she shouted.

Gray barely had time to parry one before the next attack came. Ayva saw, however, he was starting to gain control as he rolled backwards and assumed a stance. "What are you doing?" he yelled at the woman angrily.

Faye only smirked. She attacked again, moving faster. Steel rang as Gray blocked the first two strikes, but they were distractions. A kick came through, smashing him in the chest. He flew back, but somehow, instead of toppling over, he righted himself. *Wind*, Ayva knew.

The vile woman faltered in confusion, but it didn't slow her much. She leapt with a cry. Gray growled, flowing from form to form with brutal efficiency, but his attacks grew angry and wild. They were powerful, but even Ayva could see he was leaving himself wide open with each attack. He roared with a downward strike. Faye sidestepped it, just by a hair, but it could have been slow motion with all the ease and effortlessness she portrayed. The blade sliced past her face, missing. Faye cut with her dagger, slicing his wrist. Gray slowed, but didn't stop. Yet Faye was still moving too. She hit his wrist hard with the flat of her long blade, and Morrowil fell from Gray's weakened grip.

It had all happened so quickly that Ayva could barely comprehend it.

At her side, Darius moved.

Faye twisted, and the blade fell upon the rogue's throat, nearly cutting it. "Ah, I wouldn't, Untamed. I would like to keep you alive. It is the greater of the two rewards."

Gray lunged for his blade. In one smooth movement Faye sheathed her dagger and unhooked her crossbow, holding it at Gray's temple. He froze, gripping his wounded wrist.

"Now, before anyone decides to do something foolish and die, including you, *girl*," she said, eyeing Ayva with a cool sneer, "I would highly advise against it. I truly don't think all three of you could take me, but I know sure as sugar that I can take at least two of you before I go. And that's a promise."

Ayva cursed. She felt so worthless. Her palm sweated as she held her dagger, knowing if she moved the woman would kill all three of them. At her feet, her eyes caught something. The rope she had cut. It was blackened, as if burned, not cut.

Gray spoke, drawing her attention. "Why are you doing this?"

"Well, besides you being a very pleasant surprise? Mind telling me where you learned to move like a Devari? *Like* being the operative word, of course. Did you watch one by chance or…" She pursed her lips, eyeing him like an inferior puzzle. "No, perhaps you aided one somehow, and he taught you a few moves? Or could you be a failed Devari?"

Gray was silent, his eyes a bottled storm. Ayva had seen that look before—she hoped he wouldn't do anything stupid or rash.

Faye snorted indifferently. "Well, I do hope you'll tell me, but either way, the real reason is that an Untamed will fetch a heavy gold purse from the Citadel's coffers. Of course, I could kill him and drag his corpse back, but a dead Untamed isn't much use to the Citadel. Granted, they'd prefer that over him wandering about and causing mayhem." She paused and looked down at the sword at her feet. Morrowil. She slowly knelt, keeping her crossbow and sword outstretched. "Now this… I have never seen anything like it. Truly a blademaster's sword. Whom did you steal it from?" She looked up. "Move a muscle and I will kill you both before you can say, 'I'm a dead fool'." With that, she sheathed her crossbow and reached for

Morrowil.

She touched the blade and gasped, crying out in pain and falling to her knees. She dropped both weapons and clutched her stomach, vomiting violently. At last, she looked up through bleary-eyes. Still, she breathed thinly as if she'd been punched hard in the gut. "You… *How?* Such pain… How do you bear it?"

Silently, Gray reached out. The blade lifted into the air as if on its own, falling into his hand. "I am its true wielder. It doesn't pain me."

Faye looked confused and bewildered. "You… You're no Reaver. That was wind…" If she looked fearful before, now she looked terrified as if she looked upon a monster, and yet... Ayva couldn't read the woman's features. Something about her looked almost excited.

Around them, the forest began to rumble as if waking from its slumber. The ground rattled beneath her feet as if an army marched beneath them. The music of the forest, calls of animals, and all else went silent in its wake.

The woods shimmered. "What's going on?" Ayva asked, fearfully.

"This sanctuary is no longer safe…" Faye said slowly, rising.

The rumbling grew louder. Ayva's whole body shuddered, terror rising inside her as reality seemed to rip in two.

"Dice!" Darius cried. "This is the end!"

Gray roared over the rumble. "No longer safe? What do you mean?"

Faye shouted as the world began to disappear. "*They* are coming."

The Underbelly

Zane twirled his rusty dagger. Its dulled point spun in a well-worn rut in the stone. *His* rut. It was the only place in the world where he felt safe to sit and think, where he didn't feel a blade creeping closer to his back. His finger touched the dagger's base, stopping it each time before it fell. He sat upon a stone ledge, watching the river flow in the corner of his eye.

He was in the sewers of Farbs, often called the Underbelly. Tan, earthen brick surrounded him, hanging above his head. The stone was cut at sharp angles as if sheered by magic. Meanwhile, the gurgle of water was ever-present, echoing faintly off the cavernous walls.

While it was relatively clean, it was still the Underbelly. Moss and mildew clung to the corners of the stone and near the water's bank. A few paces away, his dark cot lay, his few belongings tucked in the corner. Hannah's bed was not far from his, though she had made it more of a home. A green awning covered hers, and stacked boxes she'd gathered made a sort of makeshift fort. Bits of jewelry lay on a nearby box, and a thick nail held a few of her different cloaks.

Zane looked down. In his other hand was the strange statue—the squat, silver man with a sword resting across his lap. It was cold and smooth, save for the sharp point of the sword. As his thumb rubbed the figurine, his thoughts churned and guilt burned his insides, thinking about the Devari and the old man. *What am I waiting for?* "I must be going crazy," he whispered, spinning the dagger harder.

"I wouldn't argue with that," a voice answered.

Zane looked up, clutching his dagger, as Hannah entered from the arched entry beyond, the only entrance in the cavernous room aside from the watery canal. "Sister…" She was a few years younger than him and pretty, with hazel eyes and flaxen hair. She had a round face, but when she smiled, it was perfectly shaped. He had worked hard to protect such beauty and innocence in this foul place.

Hannah's gaze fell to his shoulder, gasping. "What in the seven hells did you do to yourself?"

"I was attacked," he said simply with anger in his voice, but not towards her.

Cursing, Hannah dropped the bundle in her arms, rushing to his side.

"Those fools tried to sneak up behind me in an alley after I stole their gold, but they're clumsy as a six-legged cerabul." She *tsked* through her teeth, chiding him, her eyes full of concern and fire as she examined his wound. His insides twisted at the sight, her big, worried eyes sending him a pang of guilt, and he muttered, "It's not as bad as it looks. Besides, I took a couple of those dark pills Father gave me in case of a moment like this. They've dulled the pain quite a bit."

"Dulled your senses too," she said and touched his arm, wincing. He followed her eyes. He'd taken his vest off, and now a tear in his shirt from Grom's hammer exposed bloodied skin and a dent in his flesh. It's true, the drugs fuzzed his mind a little, but the pain was mostly drowned by his burning anger. "It doesn't hurt at all?"

He shook his head. "Only a little," he lied.

Hannah sighed, grabbing a shirt from her nearby bed, ripping it into strips, and wiping the blood free. "How could you not get this healed?"

"I was waiting for you."

"Well, I suppose that was smart. But I'm not sure if I can heal this, Z. I've only healed scrapes and bruises with the spark. This is..." she swallowed. "I'll have to set the bone back in place. Using flesh is more difficult than most other elements. I could set it wrong and you'd be in pain for the rest of your life, or I might just grow you another arm."

Zane spun his dagger. "Sounds useful."

"I'm serious, Z."

He stopped his spinning dagger. "I trust you."

"Of course you do," she sighed again. "You always trust me."

"Have you ever given me reason not to?"

She grumbled something beneath her breath but moved closer to his side, sitting upon the stone ledge, and she closed her eyes, concentrating. Her cold hands touched his shoulder. Zane's skin prickled. The hairs on his arm rose as her threads sunk beneath his flesh. "The bone is fractured," she griped. "An Untamed should not be doing this. This is a Reaver's work."

"A Reaver would never help me," he replied in a burning whisper. But as his other hand rubbed the statue, he remembered that man. Ezrah. He should have asked him to heal his shoulder. The man seemed powerful. Surely he was a Reaver of some rank. But at the time, more pressing things had commanded his attention.

"This is going to hurt," Hannah declared.

Zane grunted in understanding.

Suddenly, he gasped as his heavy muscles twisted, being pulled aside. Despite the drugs and all the pain tolerance he'd developed over the years, it truly hurt. His dagger fell from his grip as pain lanced through his limbs. He cried out. The sound echoed off the cavernous walls, mixing with the babble of water. His eyes sprouted tears and blackness threatened, but he held on to consciousness. Muscles made way as bone shifted back into place, and then cracks were filled. At last, the muscle was laid back on top, and flesh was knit. He felt every bit of it, searing and sharp.

At last, Hannah stepped away, sweat upon her tan brow. She gave a rattled breath. "There, I think it is done." She squinted at him, looking impressed. "I'm not sure why I'm surprised, but were it anyone else, they'd have passed out or worse from the pain of a healing of that severity."

Or worse? Zane wondered, but didn't want to ask. He rubbed his shoulder, feeling smooth flesh where broken skin had just been. "You've got it backwards. Anyone can take a beating, but you and your magic… That is truly special, Tovai." The name meant 'beloved' in sand tongue, a term of affection between brothers and sisters. Realizing how he sounded and seeing the surprise on Hannah's face, he cleared his throat gruffly. "Thanks," he added at last, a little more under his breath.

Hannah merely smiled. "Of course."

Zane returned to spinning his dagger, thoughts spinning as well. *Ezrah … that Devari … burning magic from the air … the Citadel … a blue orb … that wretched man, Sithel … and even the shadowy enigma, Darkeye…* Each flashed in his mind's eye, one after the other.

"What is that?" Hannah asked, shattering his thoughts. He looked up to see she had pointed to the statue. "And where'd you get it?"

Zane's thumb froze on the silvery surface. He eyed the squat little man with the sword that rested across his lap. A memory flashed before his eyes as if he was seeing again the strange old man shedding a hundred years of age from his face in a mere second.

"Well?" she asked.

He debated lying, but he would never lie to Hannah. Anyone but her. Reluctantly, he told her about Ezrah and Sithel and Darkeye. He recounted the events of the procession, softening the accounts of violence.

50 Nearby, a wide stream ten paces wide flowed slowly as she listened.

"What are you going to do?" she asked when he finished at last.

He rose, shaking his head as he watched the churning waters. His fist clenched around his dagger's handle. "I'm not sure. I don't know what to do for once. I can't save the Devari because I don't know where he is. That is, if he even is alive. And the same is true for the old man." He felt weird calling the man *old*. Sure, he was older than Zane, but he appeared too wise to be simply called old. *Father* was old—this man was ancient. Father, of course, wasn't Zane's actual father, though he was as close as anything Zane had ever had to a dad. *Father* was a protector of the weak. He looked over all of them, Hannah and the other Lost Ones—if Darkeye was the scourge of the Underbelly, Father was the savior.

"And this man, Ezrah, he gave you that?" she asked, nodding at the statue. Zane nodded. "Can I see it?" He reluctantly handed it over, and she fondled it carefully as if it would break. "It's beautiful, but strange."

"Can you sense anything in it? Any magic?"

Her brows furrowed. "I'm not sure," she said. Her eyes narrowed, and her round face pinched attentively. At last, she sighed, shaking her head in frustration and disappointment. But beneath that, she looked exhausted. "I'm sorry, I wish I could help."

"You shouldn't expend any more energy. Remember what Father told us. As an Untamed, you don't know your limits. Without proper training, it would be easy for you to go beyond them. You could die." An Untamed was a wielder of the spark who was not trained by the Citadel. Untamed were looked down upon, feared by most people as a danger to themselves and others. Zane knew that wasn't true. Not entirely at least, but he did fear for her. Since they were little, Hannah had been sought by the Citadel. More than once, he had pushed her to become a Reaver for her safety, but she refused each time. He understood her hesitance. He felt his blood rise even thinking the word Reaver.

"Thanks for that reminder."

He shrugged. "It's the truth."

"It's always the truth with you. And I'm fine. It's just a little headache," she said while standing, and staggered. Zane was there in a flash, grabbing her and lowering her to her bedroll beneath her awning.

"This is why I'm the one who lies for us. You're a horrible liar."

Hannah didn't resist as he laid her down in her bed, pulling her blankets up. A small sweat had formed across her forehead. *Spark fever,* he knew, cursing his foolishness. He had taken too much from her with the healing. She didn't know her limits. He wet one of the cloth strips from the waterway, and knelt at her side, cooling her brow.

"You've used too much of the power. You're having a spark fever. It will go away soon, but you need to rest, all right?"

Eyes closed, Hannah nodded weakly.

Zane rose. He felt fingers clench around his hand, stopping him. "Where are you going?" she whispered, eyelids fluttering open.

The old man's silence and the debt for the Devari had turned Zane into a cauldron of anger and confusion. And he was tired of stewing in his own wrath. He had to do something.

Gently, he peeled her fingers free. Grabbing a dark pill from his pack, he sat back at her side, patting her warm skin. He wished he had some Silveroot, but remembered that it would do nothing for a malady of the spark. Silveroot healed the body, and the spark was the mind. "I'm not going anywhere," he answered. "I'll be right here. Now take this." Hannah grabbed the dark pill and swallowed it.

She gave a sigh of relief then asked, "Brother?"

"Yes?"

"I'm glad you're all right," she whispered and then was asleep.

Zane laid back, resting at her side, thoughts turning back to the Devari and Ezrah. He held the statue that now stood tall—the little man looking almost proud. The statue's closed eyes looked calm, mocking Zane's broiling thoughts. He looked to Hannah, watching as she muttered in a fever dream.

She was the symbol of all that he had lost, and all that this cursed city had taken from him. But she was also the symbol of all that was still good, and all that was worth fighting for. He rose, moving to the water's edge. His hand tightened as he watched the water churn and flow, the statue pressing into his flesh. Unfurling his fist, he saw the small sword had punctured his skin and blood was beginning to well. He looked up.

"Where are you?" he whispered.

But only the quiet babble of water answered him.

Sanctuary

Zane made his way through a series of sandstone tunnels, moving with purpose. In his hand he gripped the statue, knowing if anyone would have answers for it, it would be Father.

The Underbelly was a complicated labyrinth of tunnels and running water. On his right, he passed a wide ramp that led to the surface. Two sentries flanked the ramp—an old man and a middle-aged woman. Eyeing the knobbed clubs in their hands, which they leaned on like walking sticks, he held back a sigh. What good would those do if Darkeye and his men ever came? They would be just as suited to wielding a dead fish for all they were worth. They gave him nods as he passed.

"Shade," the woman said in greeting.

He merely nodded in return, heading deeper into the Underbelly.

Hopefully they would never have need of those sentries. The Underbelly was massive, and they were deep and difficult to find. He passed more tunnels and empty chambers, the stone cut with odd, angular edges like leftover puzzle pieces. The gurgle of water permeated the air, echoing off the walls and befuddling the senses.

At last, he reached a huge cavern.

The Sanctuary, others called it, or the home of the Lost Ones.

Ahead, several sentries stood beside tall torches on stands set into the stone floor. They watched him warily until his figure resolved itself in the light. Their faces relaxed.

Zane almost passed them but hesitated. "What's with the looks?"

A big man named Tiberius spoke. "Sorry. Just rumors, Shade."

He lifted a brow, waiting.

Tiberius glanced to the man next to him nervously. Both men were taller and wider than Zane, but they looked like youths scolded by their mother. "Well, it's silly, but Lucky said he saw something in Shadow's Corner..."

"Something?"

"He said he saw a man cloaked in black. He said it was Darkeye." The big man gripped his iron-studded club tighter, eyeing the shadows.

Zane growled. "You're going to believe a ten-year-old's lies, Tiberius? You should know better than to spread such things. You're as bad as a fishmonger's wife." Tiberius looked embarrassed. "Who's he telling?"

"Everyone," said the big man. "Father's trying to quell the whispers, but it's put a darkness in everyone's step."

"I'll have a talk with him."

"Thanks," Tiberius said, looking relieved.

Zane grunted and moved on.

The Sanctuary was little more than a gathering of low-lying tarps and bodies in a massive cavern of tan stone. It was dark now, but during the day, light from conduits to the surface illuminated the whole cavern. For now, it was simply a meadow of fires. Zane breathed in deeply, smelling stale air and food, and his stomach rumbled. He maneuvered through the bonfires, eyeing the quiet forms of sleeping men and women. Despite the time of night, many were awake.

Moving through the crowds, some reached out to him, whispering thanks for the recent shipment of food and coin he'd delivered—filched from Darkeye's warehouses. Yet most of the faces that looked at him were newcomers. With the Patriarch opening up Farbs to outsiders, the Lost Ones' flock had nearly tripled in size. Zane felt the pouch at his side, again courtesy of Darkeye's Clan. *It won't last us the week*, he knew, *and we'll be starving again.*

Pushing dark thoughts aside, he made his way to where he knew Father would be.

The Healer's Terrace was a rise of stone that overlooked the rest of the cavern. Zane's eyes glanced over the injured as he passed them. There were men and women swaddled in bandages, and others sipping water and broth, being nursed back to health from malnutrition.

He saw Father immediately. He was whispering to an injured older woman, touching her on the shoulder warmly. As if sensing Zane's presence, the man turned.

Father was tall, but he stooped as if he were perpetually ducking beneath a low-hanging doorway despite the vast ceiling above them. Zane knew it was the weight of leading the Lost Ones that weighed the man down. His face was heavily lined, showing his age. His hair was white with streaks of gray, and thick brows like white moss dropped over his hooded gaze. He wore simple white robes with bronze trim, the bottom hem dirtied a dark brown from the Sanctuary's floor. Those dark, soulful eyes found Zane's, filled with compassion.

"My boy," Father said, embracing him.

"Father," he replied, stepping back and bowing his head.

"Where is Hannah?"

"Resting," he said. "She isn't well. She has spark fever."

Father shook his head with a sigh. "I've told that girl to be careful. What happened this time?"

Zane motioned to a nearby box. "Perhaps you should sit."

Father lifted a bushy white brow but complied. "Tell me everything." And Zane did. It was the second time he'd told the story, and it came easily. Again, he glossed over some of the rougher bits of violence, and this time he avoided the Devari's sacrifice entirely. He didn't want to think about that, for it only made his blood boil.

Father nodded all the while, and when Zane finished, he breathed a heavy sigh. "I see. I wonder who this man is…"

Zane shrugged. "The man didn't wear the scarlet robes of a Reaver, or any stripes of rank. There's no way of knowing."

"No, this man does not strike me as a Reaver. You said he talked back to the man named Sithel, but then hid his nature and identity? And yet he has the spark… Did he have a name?"

"Ezrah, he called himself."

Father's eyes widened. "Are you certain?"

Zane nodded. "I am. Why? Who is he?"

"You, my boy, just encountered an Arbiter."

Zane felt a chill run down his spine, and he swallowed, at a loss for words. Arbiters were legends. Men and women who had lived thousands of years due to the strength of their spark—some stories said they were not even human. "How do you know?"

"That name… It is a very old name, but as a child I heard my mother speak of the promotion of a man to the rank of Arbiter when she was just a little girl. A promotion to Arbiter is news spread throughout all of Farbs, and a great ceremony is held. This man, she described him much like you did. She said his name was Ezrah. Arbiter Fera is better known throughout Farbs, and of course, the Patriarch is an Arbiter as well. Three Arbiters, each with varying power."

"How powerful is Ezrah?" Zane asked.

"Only the Patriarch is more powerful," Father declared.

Zane suppressed another shiver. He had met a man—if he was just a man—who had talked to the Patriarch. A man stronger in the spark than nearly any who had ever lived. And he had questioned, even *challenged* the man. Well, Zane would not back down to anyone, even if he were an Arbiter. Still, as he rubbed his hands together, they were damp with sweat.

"I would be careful, my boy, and heed his words with great care. Do not steal from Darkeye, at least not for a while, and avoid this man called Sithel at all costs."

Zane eyed the injured nearby, taking in their frail frames or sad, gaunt faces. The occasional moan of pain rose above the quiet of night and the hiss of nearby torches. Feeling anger to his bones, Zane fingered the statue's sharp point within his pocket. At last, he shook his head. "I cannot abide by that, Father. We need more food. Before the newcomers, we barely had enough food to feed the Lost Ones. Now? Without new supplies, the Lost Ones will be starving before the end of the month."

"It is not as bad as you say," Father replied.

"No, it's worse," Zane countered. "I've heard the tales, Father… Bloodshed on the Aster Plains, roving bandits near the vineyards of Sevia, and strange red-sailed ships raiding the Frizzian Coast. They even say the Algasi are traveling north, being seen as far as Vaster, pilfering as they move." Zane laid a hand upon Father's arm. "I know the consequences too well. I *choose* to risk myself."

"You risk your life for us so that others may live. Though it has been a burden upon my soul for too long, it has been necessary, but this time it is too dangerous, Zane. I forbid it."

Anger and compassion swirled together in Zane's head in a confusing mix. "You cannot stop me," he said finally.

"I can and I will," Father replied. "If you care for me, you will not do it."

"Or what?"

Father's brows drew together, and his benevolent face turned dark. "I will exile you. For your own good, but I will do it."

Zane looked away feeling hurt, his jaw clenching reflexively.

"Come. Let us talk of such things no more. You came to me for more than just this. What else bothers you?"

With a sour taste in his mouth, Zane let the matter drop, for now. He pulled out the statue. "Do you know how to make this work?"

"Where did you get that?" Father asked, looking amazed.

"The Arbiter."

"Did he say anything else?"

That look in Father's eye… "Have you seen it before?" he asked.

"No, I've only heard of such things. This is clearly an item of the Citadel, an object of magic made by the Reavers." Father looked up, and spoke, "When did it change?"

"How did you know it changed?"

"My great grandfather was a famous blacksmith. Mother would tell me stories. Tales about how he worked for the Citadel when it was a place of peace. With the aid of Reavers, he created objects of power like this one. This however… I feel it is much older, likely made during the Lieon when the transporters were created."

"What does it do exactly?" Zane asked.

"If I am correct, one can communicate over long distances with it."

"How?"

Father shook his head. "I'm not sure. But I know that the statue reflects the mood of the owner. The Reavers of old would implant their personalities into the objects, creating a sort of miniature version of themselves. That is why I doubt this one was given to you in this position."

"What do you mean?" Zane asked.

"You see how the figurine is holding its sword?" Father asked, gesturing to the statue. The little man had his sword raised, and his knee's bent, as if he were walled in by imaginary foes.

"He looks in trouble, almost afraid."

"Your friend is in danger," Father affirmed.

"From whom?" he asked.

"I do not know, but I dread the thought, and would not want to find out myself. For any man who causes an Arbiter to fear must truly be death itself."

Zane nodded, swallowing nervously. *Father is right… Who in the seven hells of remwar could cause an Arbiter to be afraid?* Even the way Ezrah had handled a dozen Reavers and the oily Sithel was effortless and without a shred of fear.

Suddenly, Zane remembered the purse at his side, which he'd stolen from Darkeye. It had nearly gotten him killed, drained Hannah, and caused all this madness. Casually, he handed it to Father. "Here, before I forget."

"Thank you, boy. We will put it to good use."

Again, he pressed. "It will not last us long, Father. It is not

enough."

Father merely smiled, his sage eyes crinkling. "We will make do, my boy. We always do."

How could he be so calm, so sure? Didn't he see what Zane saw? With a sigh, Zane moved to rise. "I need to get back to Hannah."

"Here, take this," Father said, handing him a small pouch from his belt, "It's herbwort. It should reduce the fever's bite a bit. And tell her to see me when she is feeling better, all right?"

Agreeing, Zane embraced the man one last time then left. Gripping the statue tightly, fear sunk beneath his skin as he made his way down the Healer's Terrace and back into the heart of Sanctuary, Father's words ringing in his head: *Any man who causes an Arbiter to fear must truly be death itself…*

Burning the Nexus

As quickly as it had come, it ended. Gray looked around. Dry desert and soft sand surrounded them. Above, billowing clouds perched in a bright blue sky. The forest was just gone. As if it had been a dream… *How is that possible?* he wondered.

He saw a horse in the near distance. Faye's, he figured. Besides their three nervous and confused cormacs, the land was barren for miles on end. "What just happened?" he whispered, looking to Faye who gazed into the distance. Even though the rumbling had stopped, she looked even more afraid. Gray realized it wasn't over.

Darius breathed a sigh, unaware, but Ayva felt it too. She gripped her small, but brilliant dagger, turning in all directions.

Then, a small black dot appeared on the horizon. Gray watched. Slowly, it grew. Then faster, becoming a thin black mass stretching across like a blanket of darkness—as if night was a tangible thing. And it was coming.

Nearby, Darius choked. "That can't be real…" the rogue whispered. "Can it?"

Gray grabbed Faye's arm. "Can we outrun it?"

She shrugged off his hand. "Not unless you're faster than the wind."

The words made Gray hesitate, but at last he shook his head.

"What is it? And how do we defeat it?"

"They are an evil from an ancient time..." Faye answered without turning. "They feed off of the magic of this land. But unlike other creatures, they feed and never stop. They cannot be satiated. They seek safe havens like that Node that was here, hoping to devour it and all its magical inhabitants."

"Are you saying we can't defeat it?" he asked.

"No. A flux of Darkwalkers cannot be stopped."

"Well if we can't outrun it, and we can't defeat it, what in the blasted seven hells do we do?" Darius shouted.

Fayed smiled darkly. "Die with honor."

Darius swallowed. Ayva closed her eyes, uttering a prayer. The darkness was getting closer. Faye gripped her sword and dagger tighter, watching the dark host grow with each passing second.

"No, this can't be it..." Gray voiced. Think, Gray! He yelled, forcing his mind to work. What would Kail do?

The ground shuddered with their approach, his teeth chattering.

Abandon us, Kirin voiced calmly.

And it hit him. Fear and uncertainty pounded in his veins as he decided. "I have an idea..." he said loudly. "Everyone gather close."

Darius' eyes widened. "Dice, are you thinking what I think you're thinking? And why didn't I think of that earlier?"

"What are you running on about?" Faye asked sharply.

"I will attempt to move us," he proclaimed.

Ayva touched his arm fearfully. "All of us? Is it possible?"

"How on earth..." mumbled Faye curiously.

Beyond, the dark swarm was beginning to resolve itself—Gray saw individual black beasts and he thought he could see wings and claws. "Quick!" he shouted, motioning the others to his side. Ayva grabbed his arm. Darius grabbed the reins of the three scared cormacs—Gray was glad they were Elvin steeds, for horses would have run long ago. The rogue's fingers dug into Gray's shoulder.

Gray delved into his mind, finding the nexus. It pulsed, a beacon of light and wind. But it was not nearly as strong as he'd hoped. He tried not to think about his rising dread and how the ground heaved. He pulled upon his power, remembering the threads Kail had woven upon the Gate in order to *shift*. It was not easy, like trying to dredge up the memories of a dream long forgotten, but, slowly, it came. One thread wove on top of another, until the complex tapestry formed a whole. He opened his eyes and terror filled him.

Wind swirled around him, rising higher and higher.

But beyond, the dark mass was nearly upon them. Distance was tough to tell, closer and farther were often arbitrary in this land, but he estimated less than sixty breaths away.

Faye eyed him, and he read her eyes. Fear and mistrust, and a burning curiosity… Clearly she feared him and the power of wind, and he knew she feared little. He extended the ki, and touched Faye's body with it. He ran into a wall as dense as steel. Emotions. They flooded him—strength, certainty, uncertainty, chaos, hate, anger, fear and, finally, sorrow. So many emotions, he thought. His eyes snapped open, and he made his decision. Gray reached out his hand, white eddies flowing over his arm.

"Gray? No! What are you doing?" Darius shouted. "She's evil!"

Faye looked at him, confused. Her pretty face held an innocence he had not seen before. *An innocence like Vera's?* Kirin asked. He silenced Kirin. "Why?" she asked.

"Call it mercy, or call it empathy."

"Are you a fool? I just tried to kill you and steal your friend for ransom."

His hand extended further, wind curling around it.

She backed away, closer to the dark horde. "No, I don't trust you."

"You have no choice," he said calmly, voice cutting through the din.

The darkness was getting closer.

"Leave her, Gray," Darius yelled. "Let's go, they are getting closer!"

Ayva grabbed his arm, eyes burning. "She's *not* worth it, Gray."

The ground rumbled louder and louder. The black line was a tidal wave, rushing towards them.

He looked to Ayva. "Did I not already tell you about empathy?"

"And would she have done the same for you?" Ayva asked, voice trembling from the sound of the rising rumble that rolled like thunder.

"Tell me the truth or abandon me now!" Faye yelled. "Why?"

Using threads of wind, Gray's voice cut through the noise like a dagger. "The truth is simple. I have questions and you have answers.

That's all. I will call a peace for now if you promise to answer them. Your reward is your life."

She gritted her teeth. "Peace then." She made the word sound like a foul curse.

He gripped her leather-clad forearm, pulling her close. Faye whistled and her horse galloped to them. "Hold on tight," he yelled. Plugging their steed's ears and shielding their eyes with wind to keep them calm, he pulled upon the nexus and his power. The dark tide neared. So close. *More power,* a voice yelled. He felt it rip at him, pulling at his bones and deeper, sucking the life from his very core, and he poured everything he had into the threads. Still, it was not enough. *It's not going to work.* Fear and panic flashed inside him, and sweat popped from his pores.

"We're not doing anything, Gray! Nothing's happening!"

The darkness was nearly upon them. He made out terrifying, inhuman faces, dark wings, and thousands of fast moving long-legged limbs, as the evil crawled, galloped, and dashed across the plains like abominations.

The power flowed through him like a torrent, taking his breath. He couldn't breathe. He ignored the suffocating feeling in his lungs as they were wrung of air like a wet rag. Still, more. More was required. There were too many to move, he knew. *You can have more. No, you must have more,* Kirin voiced, *but you must lose control.* Maris' voice echoed distantly: *Pulling more than you can handle will drive you insane or burn you to a crisp.* He ignored that too and let the power fill him completely. It obeyed, and then took control, seeping and filling every nook in his body until he could contain it no longer. *No more,* he pleaded, agony wracking his body, but still it came… It burst from him as if splitting the seams of his soul. He fell to his knees. Words and screams sounded distant and muted. Please… he begged, in a daze, limbs weak and numb. But Kirin was louder, stronger. *More!*

Too much.

He opened his eyes.

Through the gauzy haze of white, he saw black creatures reaching through the torrent of wind. Something clawed at his arm, screeching, and he cried out in pain. Then, everything vanished, winking out of existence.

Still, the power grew.

The threads bolstered themselves like white steel cords, growing and going far beyond his limits. He saw fire in his mind. It burned at the nexus, and he felt his mind ripping in two. Dread filled him. The power, his very core, was being eaten alive. In a rush, he let it all go. The wind died, as if he were being burnt alive and leapt into a body of water. Distantly, he felt something soft between his fingers. His eyes opened and closed, slowly.

He saw green blades, and then it was all gone…

* * *

Gray's world formed slowly. Nearby, a man lay on a marble floor. His white robes were ripped to shreds, pulled to his waist to expose a horrid sight. The man's face was hidden in shadows, but what he could see was an abomination.

His tan skin laid flayed open, and where it wasn't, it was crisp and blackened from searing fire… Diseased vines crawled over his body, thorns puncturing and oozing blood, pressing deeper with each passing second…

The man cried out in agony—one long endless cry.

Gray wanted to run, to flee this awful nightmare. But he couldn't. Instead he pressed closer, hoping to save the man, and just as he almost resolved the face…

His eyes snapped open, breathing hard—seeing a green canopy overhead.

Alive, he thought.

But his thoughts were filled with only the dream. Who in the seven hells was that man? And why did Gray feel such a strange and powerful urge to know? As if he was being guided, *pressed* to remember. But it was just a dream, Gray told himself. Wasn't it?

He pushed the dream aside, and noticed for the first time that he lay on a bed of grass and curling vines, vines just like the ones that had wrapped around Faye's limbs, trapping her after Darius had…

"*Darius…*" he whispered, remembering the rogue and his power.

"Yes?" Darius shot up. Gray hadn't seen him lounging against a gnarled tree. He seemed to blend into the forest as if one with it.

"Where am I? What happened?" he questioned, feeling groggy. His head throbbed as if bludgeoned by a cudgel. Repeatedly. He looked around, taking in his surroundings.

They sat in a flat, grassy dell, hemmed by towering trees. A faint trickle of water announced a stream, and he saw it flowed down a nearby slope feeding into a small, translucent pond where birds and more butterflies flitted. Even from here, he saw brightly colored fish swimming beneath the surface. Beside the pond sat a huge batch of dark green mushrooms, at which several deer-like creatures nibbled.

"Faye says we're in another smaller Node, a forest just a week from Farbs," Darius explained. "We've jumped ahead considerably. You nearly got us to our destination with that little stunt of yours."

"My little stunt..." Gray repeated, and sudden fear gripped his body. *The nexus...* He reached into his mind. The swirling ball of air was there, sitting extraordinarily quiet. For a moment, something felt different about it, but it passed. It was still there, and that was all that mattered. He breathed a heavy sigh of relief, slumping back down upon his strange bed of vines. When had he grown so attached to his power? He held onto it, not wanting to let it go. "It nearly cost us everything," he said, trying to sit up, and groaned. He hurt everywhere. *Is this the repercussion for drawing upon my power like that?* It must be, for he knew he'd threaded too much. He was only glad it wasn't worse. At his side, he saw Morrowil. He grabbed the blade, holding it to his chest, drawing comfort from its presence.

"Ah, but it worked! My ma' used to say that sometimes a foolish man is great, and a great man is a fool, but one can never tell which is which if both have success."

"What's that mean exactly? I'm too tired for sayings."

Darius scratched his head of unruly brown hair. He'd combed it once, Gray thought he remembered, at Karil's camp, but it was growing more and more unkempt in the past few weeks. "Not sure, but you're a foolishly great man in my book."

Gray smiled. "Thanks, Darius." He eyed his arm and saw a thin bandage. "What's this?"

"Faye's doing," Darius remarked. "When you got us here, one of those things got through. Before I could turn around, she'd killed it and it disappeared in a bout of flame. After that, she insisted on your rest and set us up in this glade." He shook his head, "Dice, I hate to admit it, but somehow she's gone from villain to friend." Though the rogue didn't sound entirely convinced himself.

"She promised peace, for now," Gray said, feeling suddenly weary. *So much power.* It was Kirin's voice, not his. It sounded dangerously similar to Vera, and he silenced Kirin, shutting him out of his thoughts forcefully.

"What do you remember?" Darius asked.

"The last thing I saw was wind and … a black limb, and then it was all gone."

"Yes, that wicked thing…" The rogue shivered and looked to a nearby tree, pointing to a cloth-wrapped bundle.

Gray whispered, "Is … that it?"

"It is. Faye wanted to keep it. Said no one had ever separated a limb from its body. Usually the things just burn like tinder to a flame if killed, or so she says," Darius admitted.

Suddenly, he remembered those vines that had held Faye. That power. "Darius… Back in the other Node, when Faye tried to kill you and you grabbed her, how did you do that?"

"I'm not sure…" Darius answered, squirming in his black vest. "For a flickering moment, I just saw this thing floating in my mind, and I told it what to do."

"…What sort of image do you see?" he asked cautiously.

He saw a haunted look in the rogue's eyes. "I see a leaf."

Gray felt his heart stop for a moment. Life, curiosity, and excitement pounded in his veins. "A leaf?"

Darius shivered, looking away. "Perhaps I should leave you to get some rest." he said and rose. "You've been out for a bit, but I'm sure you're tired and you don't need me jabbering in your ear about leaves and vines and—"

"—Darius," he said, interrupting the rogue.

Darius paused. He looked at Gray curiously. Gray opened his mouth, and then hesitated. Using the ki, he delved into Darius. He felt guilty, like he was invading the rogue's personal space, but he needed to know. What he felt surprised him, taking his breath. He felt strength and confidence, but beneath that—*terror.* It wasn't just fear, but unadulterated dread and doubt, like a pool of boiling water beneath a thin layer of ice just waiting to crack. How was the rogue not shaking visibly? That, at the very least, took strength of will. Pulling away, he returned to his own body. *Why is he so afraid?* Gray wondered, and then he realized… Darius was terrified of what was inside of him. *Wasn't that how I was?* The unknown. He's scared of what he is and might be. *How can I possibly tell him?* No, maybe now wasn't the time…

"I…"

"What is it, Gray?" Darius asked with a pale face, but his voice still remarkably strong.

He shook his head, "Nothing. Don't go is all. I don't need any more rest, and well… I could use your company."

The rogue smiled. He didn't need to use the ki to sense some of the fear and tension flee from Darius as he sighed, settling back down. And Gray understood. Already feeling confused and strange because of his new power, he didn't want to be alone as well. Gray noticed that Darius was whittling something. "A new pipe?"

"My last one was stolen," he declared.

Gray looked around. "Where's Ayva?"

"Your girl went looking for more wood, at my request," a calm, collected voice said.

Gray groaned, sitting up to see Faye approach. She no longer wore her dust cloak, he noticed. It was warm here—though a steady breeze rolled off of the nearby pond, cooling him.

Red hair like spun fire shook around her face as the woman laughed. It was feminine, but strong. "Funny girl, that one. She wouldn't leave your side—not until I ordered her to, and she made me promise to burn this cursed arm, as well. Guess they both are like that," she said, eyeing Darius. "What did you do to earn such loyalty?"

"Dice," the rogue said. "We're called *friends.* Don't you have any?"

"Not really, no," she said matter-of-factly.

Darius cleared his throat. "Well then…"

Gray drew their attention with a word. "Faye. About those questions."

"Already, eh? You're a man of business, I see." She shrugged. "It's no matter to me. I hold my word, and I promised peace, at least until I answered your burning questions. After that, however, I promise nothing. If I so desire, I can kill you and steal your friend to claim his Untamed bounty. Deal?"

He nodded. "Fair enough."

Darius snorted. "So much for friends."

"You have too little faith in me, Darius," said Gray.

The rogue guffawed, gesturing with his half-finished pipe. "Do I now? It doesn't take a blademaster to see you're exhausted, having spent every bit of your power and more. Besides, I already saw what happened to you when you *had* energy and fought her. It wasn't pretty."

"I'd have to agree with your friend's assessment. It's not too late to back out," she said. "I'll keep my word, either way."

"It's more a matter of my faith in you, Faye."

"Equally foolish," she replied.

"I've seen your heart," he answered. "It's not all bad."

"But it's not all good. How can you trust a speck of light amidst the darkness?"

He laughed, but it hurt his ribs. *Did I break something?* Gray wondered. No, but every bone and muscle hurt. Breathing alone was agony. "Don't you see? The very fact that you're arguing with me proves that you have at least some good in you."

"Or I'm just argumentative and don't like to be wrong. Besides, 'some good' means 'a lot bad'," she said, flipping her dagger in the air casually and catching it by the blade repeatedly. *Terus?* A memory whispered, showing a brief glimpse of clay streets and a dark game. He shook it off as Faye shrugged at last. "I'm done talking you out of it. It's your choice either way. I care not. Questions are an easy price to pay for my life."

"Then the bargain is struck," he said.

"What bargain?"

Gray twisted and saw Ayva. He winced, knowing she would give him an earful or more if she knew what had just happened. Already, he saw the fire and anger that passed between the two women though they stood thirty paces apart.

"Oh, nothing. Gray just bargained our lives for a few measly questions," Darius said, and then leaned back upon his elbows, a grin spreading.

Gray growled at Darius. *Great. Throw logs onto the fire then back away.*

Ayva whispered, "You… *what?*"

"You two are making too big a deal out of it, honestly. The deal was already set. We have a truce."

"For now," Faye said with emphasis, and then flipped her dagger and stuck it into a nearby Silveroot.

Ayva smoothed her riding skirts, tucking her dagger away in her leather belt, and then sat on a nearby log. "You're a fool, Gray. But at least you're a living fool. I don't know how you moved us all out of that predicament, but it was truly something…"

Gray was listening, but only barely. He watched as Faye dug her dagger deeper until it found the tree's vein. Suddenly sap poured out, flowing over her dagger, and then dripping into her cupped hands. When it was full, she neared him, and spoke in a gruff tone, "Sit up and drink this."

He looked at her skeptically. "That… can't be good for me."

She raised a brow. "Oh, do you know more about Farhaven than I do? How long have you lived here exactly?" She smiled thinly when his words failed him. "That's what I thought. I'm guessing you somehow crossed the Gates and, up until now, have only managed to survive by sheer dumb luck and the faintest bit of knowledge."

"Don't drink it," Ayva said. "If that's a silveroot tree, then that's silver."

Faye sighed. "It's not silver. Well, not exactly. It's a type of silver essence and—look, just drink it or don't."

He held Faye's gaze, searching the truth in her eyes. There was no hint of deception. He debated asking her again and threading the spell of truth he'd done on the Gates—though the memory of how he'd done it was hazy—but everything told him she was telling the truth. At last, he nodded. She casually put her fingers to his lips, and he drank. She was cautious not to let a drop spill, and he gulped the cool liquid down. Over her shoulder, he saw Ayva flash him a curious glance, and he nearly let the sap spill. It was surprisingly sweet with a tart note, if a tad viscous. "That's not half bad," he said at last. As he said the words, he felt a strange vitality flow over him. His ribs that only a second before stung in agony with every small breath now only smarted. He took a huge lungful of air and felt almost no pain. "That's … that's a miracle."

"No, it's magic," Faye said.

"It's trickery is what it is—that's a Silver—"

"Look, girl. I can put up with that fool walking into my trap and ruining my carefully laid plans, and even your friend presuming to understand my true intentions when he doesn't, but I will not stand idly by as you attempt to lecture me on the natures of this world when you know nothing." She ripped her dagger from the tree and rammed it back into its sheath.

Ayva's lips drew into a tight line. "Nothing?"

"Nothing," Faye repeated flatly.

"Try me," Ayva said, standing straight, lifting her chin and looking down her freckled nose.

Faye snorted. "Fine. Have you all been getting a good night's rest?"

"Not really," Gray admitted.

"More or less," Ayva said evasively.

"Not a wink. Like my bed is full of burs," Darius chimed.

Ayva shot him a venomous look.

"And do you know why?" she asked.

"Because we are strained and stressed, traveling from sunup to sundown, that's why," Ayva answered. "It's a wonder we sleep at all."

"You're a foolish girl indeed. And wrong. It's because Farhaven is full of magic. We live longer and have fewer diseases. In the same way, we require less sleep. Your bodies have no idea how to adjust to it. You will acclimate hopefully with time. However, initially, most people sleep less and less, their bodies getting restless because they are overly sensitive. Others sleep more. So much so that they become addicted to the sleep and its satisfying effects. You can die by sleep in Farhaven."

The notion was mind-boggling. He realized they had experienced the exact pattern that she had just described, and part of him wanted to stay awake forever.

"And *that* is one of the simplest symptoms in this land. If you thought you knew Farhaven, please realize that you *don't*. They are just the foolish and likely misguided fancies of a little girl who reads too much and knows too little. Now move aside and let your friend ask his questions so he can be done with me, and I can be done with you," Faye said sternly, pressing past Ayva, knocking her shoulder roughly. Ayva looked as if she'd been slapped, and hard. He couldn't see her face, but her entire body practically quivered.

Gray swallowed, and he felt Darius' tension beside him.

Ayva hesitated, but turned around. Her face was surprisingly smooth. She spoke, addressing him as if the woman at his side did not exist. “Gray, this woman seeks something… I promise you it is not to leave. She will be a thorn in our sides as long as she stays. So please ask your questions quickly so we can be rid of her.”

With that, she turned and walked away.

“Ayva!” he called, but she didn’t slow. He thought he saw her body shaking as she disappeared behind a tree.

Cursing, Darius rose and followed her.

“Did you really have to do that?” Gray asked.

Faye rolled her eyes heavily. “Was I wrong?”

“No, but you didn’t have to beat her down for her lack of knowledge.”

“That girl needed a dose of reality. You all do. I might have been a tad rough around the edges, but the truth is the truth. If she kept sauntering on with her eyes closed, she was destined to run straight off a cliff.”

He saw wisdom in almost everything Faye said, yet it was veiled in a kind of half-truth that ignored the feelings involved in the situation. “Ayva was right. You’re obviously shrewd, at least about this world, and so far, you’ve been true to your word, but you have no idea what empathy is.”

“And I have no need for it.”

“I believe that will cost you one day.”

She flicked a hand. “You presume too much and talk too much. Now ask your questions.”

Gray rose higher from his seated posture but grunted in pain. *I guess Silveroot isn’t a cure-all.* “What were you doing in the woods when we ran into you?” he asked.

“Hunting,” she replied, thinly.

“But what were you hunting?”

“Ah, a much better question. I was hunting a rare creature that resides only in Nodes. That darkness you saved us from, those creatures are called Darkwalkers. They require the spark to kill, a lot of it—”

He interrupted her, “But Darius said you killed one.”

“Or,” she continued, “Someone who knows exactly where to hit it. All creatures have a weak spot, even Darkwalkers. A quick cut or two to the area near where their heart should be sends them up in flames."

"That doesn't sound so hard."

"One touch from a Darkwalker is death. They don't even need to be strong or brutally savage, though they are. They hold a plague that feeds off the spark inside of us all."

"But what if we don't have the spark?"

She sniffed. "All beings have the spark. The only difference between someone like me and a Reaver is one can more easily manifest the spark, and some are simply stronger than others."

Absently, Gray scratched his arm realizing it was healing *already*. As he listened to the nearby gurgling brook, he remembered something and looked at his bandaged arm. "That thing… it touched me, so how am I not dead?"

Faye rocked back. "I… have no idea," she admitted, eyeing him like a puzzle. "You should have been dead long ago." *Perhaps it's because I have the flow and not the spark*, he wondered, but he wouldn't voice his secrets unless he had to. Still, it was something to remember. Despite sitting, he felt suddenly dizzy and put a hand to a nearby root for balance. "Famished?" Faye asked.

"Now that you mention it…"

Pulling out a strange fruit from her bag, Faye threw it to him. "Eat."

Hesitantly, he bit into the strange purple flesh, teeth jarring from the crunch. At least it was tasty, and he *was* starving. Gray shook his head, realizing he'd gotten sidetracked. "You said you were hunting a rare creature. Why, and what was it?"

"It's called a Phox."

"Then what was that child's voice?" he asked skeptically.

"It was the beast I am hunting. They can disguise themselves with sounds and even distort their image. They are truly cunning beasts," she said and sniffed. "I nearly had it too, before your fool friend let it get away. Phoxes are cleverer than you or I, not to mention faster and stronger." She paused as if thinking, putting a finger to her soft lips. "Yes… That makes sense. Perhaps it sensed your presence and pulled you toward me with that little trick, altering its voice so it could get away."

Gray had trouble hiding a smirk. "Sounds like you're outmatched."

Faye didn't rise to his provocation. She shrugged, chainmail rustling lightly. "Alone, they are dangerous—very—but not without weaknesses. Phoxes are meant to hunt in packs. Against a pack, I would have no chance. Death would be certain. This, however, is the very last *wild* one of its kind, so there is nothing to fear."

"Why would you want to hunt the last of its kind?" he said, suddenly angry.

"I said it is the last wild one. There are some who keep Phoxes as prizes, but they are uncontrollable."

"And this one?"

"If I'm right, their pack leader. Their Matriarch… a female," she said and snorted, "Which of course, just happens to be the smarter and faster of the two genders, *as usual*."

"What's so special about Phoxes anyway?" he asked around a mouthful of fruit.

"Phoxes have one great ability above all others. A Darkwalker's touch has no affect on them, and they can sense their presence. They are the natural predator of those abominations, and they are nearly all but extinct."

"You plan to breed them," he said in realization.

Her full, red lips twisted in an amused smile. "Enough questions."

He could tell he had pushed too far into that subject. "No, at least tell me what a Node is. What is this place?"

"Farhaven is in danger. The magical creatures of this land aren't safe. Haven't you wondered why you haven't seen much in the way of life on your way here? Something dark is brewing, taking over the lands."

"The Darkwalkers?"

"They are just a sign of it—a mere byproduct but not the root of evil. Nodes are sanctuaries for the good creatures of this land, intended to keep them safe." She looked around and picked up a patch of glowing green moss. She ran her thumb across its bumpy surface and where her finger grazed it turned scarlet as if sensing the danger in Faye's words. "That is why this place changes daily. When we wake tomorrow, it will be gone. And it's never the same twice. It responds to good magic, that way creatures of light can find it, but beasts like the Darkwalkers cannot. That is why the last wild Phox flees from Node to Node."

Gray neglected to retort that the Darkwalkers had found the sanctuary, but the rest of it did seem to add up. "That makes sense," he said, realizing that's the sensation he'd felt: *fleeting safety*. He continued to twiddle the blade of grass then looked up with a breath, "That's all I wanted to know, aside from one last question." With his other hand, he idly touched Morrowil's hilt that sat in his lap for reassurance, keeping positive thoughts in his mind's eye.

Faye waited uncertainly. "Why do I have a feeling all those questions were just leading up to this one?"

"Join us," Gray said.

She laughed loudly. Louder than he'd expected, and birds flew from the nearby trees, finding other shelter. "You can't be serious."

"I am."

"The others hate me," she replied, brows scrunching as if he were mad. "Why do you want me around? And it's not just for safety—you're too blindingly stubborn just for that reason."

"You're right," he admitted quietly. "I wasn't entirely truthful."

"Then tell me now. The whole truth, and I might just do it."

"I…" He stared into her light brown eyes, framed by red curls. She was beautiful. No, how could he possibly think that? As he held her gaze, his heart thumped loudly.

She bit her lower lip in curiosity, waiting for his reply. "Well?"

He shook his head, focusing. "You asked me earlier how can you trust a speck of light amidst the darkness? The answer is simple. I was that speck of light in the darkness. Only the faintest ray of light led me from true darkness. It's was *them*. They believed in me even when I didn't believe in myself."

"I see…" she said. "So it is deeper, as I expected. And you believe I can do the same?"

"It depends."

"On?"

"On what you desire," he replied, and he saw her intelligent eyes narrow. "You see, they gave me hope, but that was only the rope. I had to choose to grab it and crawl out of that dark pit."

Faye looked away, as if thinking. He wanted to read her with the ki, but refrained. Absently, she pushed a stray a lock of scarlet hair, placing it back behind her ear with one hand, as she dug her dagger's tip into a nearby tree's root. At last, she looked up, meeting his gaze.

She drew near. He felt her warm, sweet breath. A wisp of her hair touched his face. Gray didn't flinch. Her red lips twisted and she spoke. "You have my word. I will help you, Gray, but you will listen to me as an equal and not as a servant. This is payment for you saving my life, and then we are even. Also, after I get you to Farbs, I want one of your cormacs. You'll have no need of it there."

"What do you plan to do with it?"

She sniffed indignantly. "Eat it, of course. Cormacs are quite the delicacy."

Gray stifled a gag.

"I plan to ride it, you fool. I'm not greedy or hair-brained enough to sell a cormac."

"Is that all?"

"One last condition," she said, running a finger along the smooth steel of her blade. "I wish to teach you *si'tu'ah.* It is the sand tongue. In your language it means 'The Way of the Sword'."

"Why?" he asked.

"I enjoy a challenge," she said. "And a sparring partner is a rare thing for me. Back in Farbs, no one will play with me, and I miss the practice." Something in the way she said the word "play" gave Gray pause to wonder how many of her "playmates" were still alive.

He saw her hidden motive, of course. *I want to discover what you are,* her eyes spoke. *Devari? Reaver? No, what are you?* He imagined her thinking. It was clever. Teaching him in order to learn something he would otherwise not disclose. "Deal," he replied.

"Excellent." Faye flipped her dagger, caught it by the handle then dragged its fine edge smoothly across her palm. Blood spilled forth. She wiped the flat of the blade clean across her sleeve, and then handed it to him. "Sorry, I trust my honor, but not yours. A blood pact, however, is binding."

"How binding?"

"Farhaven will hold you to it," she said simply, mysteriously.

Without pause, Gray grabbed the blade and cut his palm, sucking in a hard breath, water forming in his eyes. How had she not even flinched? He subdued the pain and gripped her hand firmly.

"It is done," she said, still a breath away.

"What's going on here?"

Gray straightened. "Ayva," he stuttered. "We…"

Her pretty blue eyes narrowed, taking them in. Hurt. Like a dagger to one's heart. The ki read it in the air, so heavy. At last she shook her head with a fallen look, turned, and left.

"Well then," Faye laughed and slapped his shoulder, making him groan in pain. "I'll take my leave on that note. That's a perfect introduction to us as traveling partners."

"Where are you going?"

"You need rest, unless you were planning on limping to Farbs?"

He shook his head. "I'm fine. We need to move."

Immediately, she was pressing him down, a dangerous look in her eyes. "No. You are seriously injured. You may not feel it, but you need rest or you may die. I've seen Reavers with a hundred times your experience fall victim to over-threading or spark fever. They are fine one moment and dead the next. The spark inside you is drained. Moving will drain it further, and it may vanish completely. One cannot live without the spark." She stood, turned to walk away, and hesitated, speaking over her shoulder, "Sleep well, *friend*, for there is no better rest than within a Node."

With that, she was gone, her slender form moving into the trees.

Kirin laughed inwardly. *Didn't you learn your lesson with Vera?*

He ignored the voice.

You must face harsh truths if you wish to succeed. The Citadel has broken men stronger than you or I.

It broke you, didn't it? Gray asked harshly.

Us, Kirin replied. *You're speaking to yourself.*

Gray had a sudden image of the rainy night he had arrived at Mura's house—remembering nothing, as if woken from a dark dream—breathless and bone-weary, glimpsing the smoke curling above the trees from the cozy fire-lit hut. Then he remembered the blade in his hand. Morrowil, covered in blood. "Maybe we are one," he voiced aloud, "but I am not a murderer, and before I accept you, you have to tell me… What happened? What is it you did to make us forget?"

Kirin wailed in pain, then dwindled into obscurity.

One way or another, Gray decided with a breath, *I will be rid of you.* He looked around his silent camp. *I need to apologize to Ayva. But what can I say?* He put it aside reluctantly and let the sensations of the Node fill him. He needed strength. He needed his flow repaired. Of course, he hadn't told her that the power inside him was the flow and not the spark. He didn't know much about either but had read in *Tales of The Ronin* about them both. The analogy used between the two was always 'the nine lakes'. The flow was the nine lakes themselves where all magic, including the spark, drew from—*a lake of wind, water, fire, stone, flesh, metal, leaf, moon, and sun.*

Some lakes were bigger, and thus it was said some elements more powerful than others, and while the hierarchy was often debated, it was always well-known that wind was the strongest, for it was a lake imbibed by one man alone. The spark was the lake's residue… the fog, sleet, foam, or ice that clung to its surface, more varied in form but always and inevitably weaker for it was never the true source. Yet the spark could mix and match: a threader of the spark like a Reaver could blend water with fire in the same way sleet or ice mixed with the water's mist. The flow, on the other hand, could never pull from anything but its original source. In that way, while inferior in raw power, a threader of the spark could do creative blends of magic that a threader of the flow never could…

Beyond the tale of the nine lakes, however, Gray knew little to nothing about his power, apart from what the Ronin Maris had taught him.

Gray returned to his body.

It trembled with fatigue like a leaf in the wind, weak from overuse of his power. A random seed of fear hit him thinking about his power…

Reassuring himself, he grabbed the nexus and saw something. The ball of wind flickered for a second. Part of it was missing. A small but gaping hole, like a burned patch of crops. "No…" he whispered. He tried to gather his power, but it didn't come—as if there was a missing link between him and the nexus.

"It's gone," he said in horror.

Sensai Roots

The girl opened her pack and grabbed something. Faye noticed and her muscles tensed. Swiftly, she reached over the girl's shoulder, grabbed the curled root and threw it into the nearby lake, then walked away without saying anything.

Ayva gawked like a noble with a lighter coin purse. "Why did you do that? Those were Sensai Roots!"

"Sensai Roots gone bad."

The girl hesitated. Good, at least she had that much sense.

Faye shook her head, sitting down heavily and busying herself with oiling and sharpening her dagger. The scrape of stone against steel filled the glade, but she felt a pair of eyes on her.

Beyond their grassy camp, night had settled around the Node. Here, in this place, even darkness was filled with light and magic. Blue frost bugs hovered above the white pond, which now glittered, lit by the full moon. Beneath the water, silver and orange fish darted—big ones. The air held bits of magic in it too, little blue and white specks. They fell upon the nearby moss, and the moss glowed as if warmed by the touch of the spark.

The Node filled Faye with a restful sensation as usual, and the moment was peaceful and serene.

She hated it.

Nearby, a fire crackled, sparks of red and black spitting into the air. It was cooler in this Node, but the fire was not for warmth. A black, sinewy arm burned in its center. Darkwalkers would burn given time. She covered her mouth from the strange stench, like rotting corpses mixed with something sour.

The girl continued to eye her like a slighted serving girl. At last Faye sighed and spoke without looking up. "Things don't spoil the same in Farhaven. Some things stay good for months or longer, others only moments. But spoiling doesn't equate to sickness like in the weak lands of Daerval. Did you see the black tops of those roots?"

Ayva nodded, slowly.

"That means death."

"But it was so subtle… How?"

Faye felt her jaw tighten. She stabbed her dagger into a mossy patch. "Because! You are a swaddled babe in a new world and, as such, you are completely out of your element. This is a world of subtleties." Again, the simple words were like a blow to the girl's gut.

But this time she took an even breath and extracted another leather pouch. She upended it onto the mossy ground. "And these? Bulba Flowers?" They were purple and brown flowers, alternating, their petals finger-thick.

Faye smiled. "Try one."

Ayva eyed her like a deadly Uni Asp. "Are they…"

"Poisonous? Not at all."

The girl's eyes never left her. She grabbed one, put it to her lips, and bit. Immediately, she gagged, spitting the parts onto the forest floor of the Node. "*Ugh!* I've never tasted anything so horrid! It's like rancid meat… How can that be? You poisoned me!" She scrambled for the nearby water skin, gargling and spitting in disgust.

"No. They just taste awful. One has to be on the verge of death to eat a Bulba Flower. They are fairly nutritious however."

Ayva scrubbed her tongue with her fingers, eyes still watering.

"Stop embellishing," Faye said, but she knew the girl wasn't overreacting. It was that foul.

"Why do they taste that bad?" Ayva asked.

"Their bitter, foul taste is a defense mechanism against predators like you."

"You could have warned me," she said.

Faye rose angrily. "I'm growing tired of your ignorance. For my sake, and for your own, just don't touch anything anymore, ever. I promised Gray I would get you all to Farbs in one piece, and at the rate you're going, I won't succeed." Ayva held her gaze, blue eyes burning with hatred. At last, she lowered her head. *Good*, Faye thought, feeling a tad pleased with herself. The girl had a surprising backbone. One she didn't deserve if she couldn't take the truth.

Gray approached.

With a strong jaw, nose, and piercing green eyes, he was handsome, she admitted to herself again. Despite the slow aging of Farhaven, she guessed he was her age, or a year or two younger, but he appeared more youthful. She liked that. Not to mention, she had seen the way he looked at her. Not like most men, but still—beauty was beauty. Fortunately for him, she had no *real* interest in such things. To her, it was like admiring a painting, or, better yet, the craftsmanship of a fine sword. Yet… She hesitated. There was a darkness in his eyes that he tried to hide.

He took in the tension of the glade, but ignored it and spoke, "You two ready to leave? Ayva?"

Ayva rose. "You're well enough to ride already?"

"Gray," Faye said. He turned to her. Yes, there was a hollowness to his gaze, but he had the practice of a Devari, hiding all emotions, just like her father had taught her.

Darius, the fool, came leading the three cormacs, the longhaired steeds with dazzling white coats.

"You all worry too much. I'm well enough," he answered at last, but he sucked in a tight breath, touching his ribs.

Faye snorted. "Foolish man."

Ayva looked at her in agreement, but then shook her head, as if uncomfortable with that.

"We've a long way to go, and no time to waste," Gray said.

The four stood in a strange, awkward silence.

"Well? Are you going to tell them?" Faye said.

"Tell us what?" Ayva asked.

"Faye is coming with us," Gray announced.

Ayva's jaw dropped. She strode forward to Gray, her body quaking in anger and exchanged a string of heated words. Faye watched impassively. At last, Ayva ignored her, looking to Darius. "And you're all right with this? The woman who tried to take your head back to the Citadel on a platter riding along with us?"

Darius shrugged, abashed. "I tried to talk him out of it at first, like you, but really, Ayva, he has a point. The woman has already told me seven different ways I nearly died on our journey up until now. We know nothing of Farhaven, and we're still a week away from Farbs. Listen, I don't like her any more than you do," he looked to Faye, "No offense, but I don't."

Faye shrugged.

Darius continued, "I hate to say it, but we need her." The fool, aside from the girl, was the farthest from warming to her. He was street-wise, she sensed. Faye smiled calmly, amused by the whole interaction.

"She's coming," Gray said firmly. "We need her."

Ayva's eyes burned with a quiet fury.

Something flashed between those two—a mere flicker, but Faye knew people, or at least knew how to watch for signs. Something between them was breaking, or had just broken.

Darius rubbed the back of his head nervously. "C'mon, Ayva. It makes sense and you know it."

"You're pathetic," she snapped. "Both of you, and when she turns on us, you'll see. Oh sure, she plays a decent game at acting the savior, but she is dark to the core." With that, she grabbed her smaller cormac, leapt into its saddle, and started off.

Faye made her face smooth, saying nothing.

"I really hope we made the right decision," Darius grumbled, taking to his steed.

Faye held Gray's eyes. He glowered at her, dark and brooding. *Handsome indeed*, she thought. She knew he was judging her, trying to see into her. She felt something prick upon her skin, hairs rising. *Ki?* She eyed him, curious. *Perhaps there's more to this Devari stunt than I figured.* Casually, she rebuffed his attempt, erecting a shield of emotions just as her master—and father—had taught her, a useful trick she'd learned growing up within Farbs, surrounded by Reavers and Devari.

Frustration seeped into Gray's features. He sheathed his curious blade in its kingly scabbard of gold and silver and mounted the cormac, riding up to her side.

"Don't disappoint me or I will kill you myself."
Her smile deepened, slightly. "Yes, master."

Si'tu'ah, The Way of the Sword

Faye found herself riding beside Ayva and watching the woods. Butterflies, dragonflies, and songbirds moved about them, fluttering from tree to tree. The soft, lilting song of the Node plied her, but she ignored it, thoughts turning to Farbs and her mission.

She would get the beast, and she would return with it in hand. Then he would listen to her, and give her what she wanted. Iris was waiting for her, she told herself. *At the next Node I will find the leader of the phoxes and take her back, unharmed. 'A hunter never loses its prey'*—echoed her old master's voice.

"Teach me."

Faye twisted, looking shocked. Her surprise put a smile on the girl's face. "Teach you?"

"Did I stutter?" Ayva asked. Faye growled. "That is, unless you think you are a poor teacher and know less than you think you do."

"I am a poor teacher. Teach yourself."

"Ah, but you just said I will die if I attempt such a thing."

Faye had trouble not biting her own tongue. *Fool*, she thought, speaking to herself, maneuvering through a last stand of Silveroots. Her horse, Yarish—in the sand tongue it meant *long strider*—stepped lightly down the grassy hill. She said nothing.

"Let's start simple, shall we? I ask questions, you answer them.

That's all."

"I shall think on it." Faye rode in contemplative silence.

As they left the safety of the Node and entered the Reliahs Desert, a fear slipped beneath her skin. Tan dunes sat in the far distance. Nearby, it was simply sand and grass. She warily eyed the east and west, looking for signs of the Darkwalkers. Nothing. But she knew there were other dangers out here besides Darkwalkers. The Reliahs Desert was infamously perilous. Bandits and predators abounded, not to mention the sudden shifts in the land called tremors. The temperature alone could change faster than a pickpocket's hand. In one lungful you could inhale stifling heat, and in the next exhale a frosty breath.

She thought about Ayva's proposal. Reluctantly, she admitted she was right… Faye couldn't let her die. She never broke a promise. Especially not a blood pact—Farhaven would extract the price from her. And slapping the girl's wrist every time she turned around was not only impractical, but also tiring. Not to mention that teaching allowed Faye a chance to show at least a glimmer of the knowledge she'd acquired under *his* tutelage.

"Surely, the ever-wise Faye wouldn't want to break a promise and endanger—"

"—Fine," she said, cutting her off. *Backbone indeed*, she thought. "You will be my apprentice. But if we do this, we do it the right way. The Farhaven way," she said and felt a toothy grin crease her face. "You will call me *Sunha*, and I will call you *Diaon*. One means 'the learned', and the other means 'knows nothing'. I assume you know which is which." Ayva bit her lip. It was a habit Faye had noticed when the girl was truly frustrated. "This is a common tradition in Farhaven from master to apprentice. See? Your first lesson. But know this: I will not be easy on you."

"I understand," Ayva said.

"No, you do not," Faye said. "When I was a Diaon, I would rarely answer wrongly. But when and if I did, *my* master would whip me, beating me fiercely until once-healed scabs oozed, or until I coughed blood from my mouth. 'To know the pain inside is to know true failure,' he would say." She unbound her armguard and pulled back her sleeve to expose a thick white scar that ran wrist to elbow. "He preferred to keep the wounds temporary. I was of more use…

unblemished. But this one was his reminder."

Ayva looked horrified, but she kept it hidden well.

Faye's vision flashed back to her past.

He stood over her, but her vision swam, dark spots floating before her eyes. The room spun. I'm losing too much blood, she knew. No, he was wiser than her. He would know her limits. Dimly, she heard his words. He was asking her something.

Respond!

"Where is pain, Diaon?"

"Everywhere, Sunha," she whispered, sputtering blood.

Wrong. She felt it before the words left her mouth. It had sounded like the right answer… Why? Why was she such a fool? His hand lifted, obscuring the sunlight behind him from the single high barred window. The room was a small square with only weapons of death, a bucket of cold water, a small cot, and books. Her room.

His hand lowered, falling to his side. She hid a sigh of relief, for that would surely get her beaten. He answered in a dark voice, like crackling thunder, "At one time, I might have agreed, but I have evolved beyond such notions. Pain is a tool, and it is only in your mind, Diaon. Make the mind strong, the will unbreakable, and your knowledge deep, and you will not suffer the only true pain—the pain of defeat."

The vision shattered.

She found herself in her saddle, riding quietly, listening to the soft clop of her horse's hooves. Patches of green grass and dry desert stretched ahead. Behind them, she felt Gray and Darius' presence. They were laughing. *Friends,* she thought, remembering the fool rogue's words. The girl's gaze was hot on her, but she ignored it and spoke. "I will not be so hard, but I will not be soft either."

Ayva said, "You may think me weak, but I can handle more than you think."

Faye eyed the girl sidelong. She had a pretty face. Light freckles speckled her cheeks, and fine, short-cropped, brown hair swayed slightly as she maneuvered her cormac—elegant steeds of the elves. *How?* she wondered. The elves would never give away a cormac. Then she shook her head. It made no difference to her. She saw strength in Ayva. The girl's light blue eyes were not hardened like hers, but they held a surprising note of perseverance. Knowing a person's limits was a talent of Faye's. She had to know, so she could break them.

"We have one week until we reach Farbs," she announced. "I have promised to train Gray in *si'tu'ah*, or the Way of the Sword. That comes first. With my remaining time, I will teach you the wisdom of this world." She allowed herself a smile. "It's hard to say which is more vital to not dying. Together, you will be a formidable couple."

Though she meant the words without sexual implication, the girl's face grew a red as dark as Sevian wine. *Oh really? Interesting*, she thought. Faye herself despised sex, but all knowledge was useful—simply a tool like coin to be saved, and then used when the moment was right.

"Let's begin now," Ayva said.

Faye lifted a brow, imploringly.

"...Sunha," Ayva added, reluctantly.

She sighed. "Ask."

Ayva nodded. "What other dangers are there in these lands?"

Faye's eyes nearly rolled at that question. So many answers... "I will answer this, Diaon, but from now on be more specific. Use the knowledge of the books you read, and I will dispel fact from fiction."

"Yes, Sunha," she said, almost servile.

Yes, she will learn, slowly, but she will learn, Faye thought, and began listing the multitude of dangers in the Reliahs Desert, answering questions from how a Tumai plant could heal one's burns, to the history of dragons—dating back to their blood feud with the race of elves—to which Great Kingdoms had been lost or destroyed during the Lieon. All knew that wind, water, stone, moon, and metal had fallen during the great war, though now water was rebuilt upon the sea, moon was still standing but run by thieves, and stone was said to exist secluded somewhere in the east. The questions veered this way and that in topic, but mostly focused on the many perils of the land.

After traveling awhile, Faye was exhausted. Blood and dust, did the girl's questions never end? She had gotten better about narrowing her questions, allowing Faye to answer in the simple, concise manner of a Sunha. Moreover, she was surprised by the girl's previous knowledge. Only a little surprised, but still surprised. Granted, it was riddled with inaccuracies like weevils in two-month-old bread.

What was more amusing was that the falsities were often less grand than the actual truth of Farhaven. She would have stopped long ago, but the girl's ravenous hunger for knowledge, and the way she soaked it in like a Suntha Sponge, was fascinating. Her light blue eyes grew with every word. She seemed to retain all the information as well—a harsh grilling had ensured that. *The girl was born on the wrong side of the Gates, surely.*

Ayva opened her mouth.

"Enough," Faye said at last. "That shall do for now, Diaon."

Ayva looked disappointed, but luckily for her she nodded. "Yes, Sunha..." and then, "Thank you."

Faye hid her surprise, eyeing the girl as she swayed in the cormac's saddle. Ayva wore her typical pleated gray riding skirts. Her answer was docile, but nothing about her features looked soft. In only a few days, the girl had grown harder and wiser. Faye would have to be careful of her, but she found herself nodding in approval. Then, immediately, Faye grimaced inwardly. *She's still just a foolish girl,* she thought forcefully.

An oasis sat ahead. It was little more than a pool of water and several trees—a mockery of even the smallest Node, she thought. The two young men had already dismounted. Gray knelt beside Darius at the water's edge, chatting.

She approached.

"Do you think it's still watching us?" Darius was asking.

Gray shrugged. "I'm not sure... I haven't felt it since Faye arrived. Perhaps..."

Darius cleared his throat loudly, indicating her approach. *Watching us?* The thought made her think of her prey. She couldn't forget that was her main goal, but for now, she had other snakes to skin. Gray quieted. Calmly, he washed his face with the warm water and looked up.

"Your turn," Faye told him, nodding to the magnificent sword at his side. She wished she could touch it but remembered the horrifying agony it had given her last time. She didn't make the same mistake twice, especially not one as painful as that.

"You look exhausted," he said, eyeing her. "We can wait if..."

She chuckled, but it held no mirth. "Underestimating your opponent is a bad place to start when learning *si'tu'ah, apprentice.*"

Faye emphasized the last word and looked to Gray's sword again that rested in the sand. "Pick that up." There was a clear threat in her voice. Darius rocked back, and she knew Ayva must have been sending her daggers.

"Or?" Gray questioned.

"You still do not trust me, do you? What do you expect me to say? That I will cut you down where you kneel?" She laughed and this time she was amused. "No, Gray, I don't need to threaten you with violence. Farbs and the Citadel will do that for me. I am no easy foe, but I am nothing compared to a hundred Devari, and a keep full of deadly Reavers, and to top it off, several Arbiters—more legend and myth than actual living beings. If you wish to live, you must learn. If not, then die. It makes no difference to me."

With that, she walked away without waiting.

Gray's eyes narrowed, and then he grabbed Morrowil and rose. "So be it."

* * *

Flipping back her scarlet hair, Faye circled Gray, appraising him. He stood silently, waiting. "You are too aggressive. Too wild. You need control. Devari are masters of their bodies and their environments, in perfect harmony with everything, including their enemies. Like a horse, you chomp at the bit, but you must accept it. Without having balance, you will die."

The words sounded familiar. Control. He thought he had control. His grip tightened on the blade in his hand, feeling its smooth hilt. Control over Morrowil perhaps, but what she suggested was different. Now he needed control over his own body. And yet… He reached, feeling for the nexus, and felt his gut lurch. It sat, waiting, but just like last time, a part was missing as if a sickness was eating away at the swirling ball of air. He lifted his hand, summoning it. He waited to see eddies of wind swirl around his palm but there was nothing. It was like reaching for a handhold and falling upon his face. His power was there, he knew, but he just couldn't touch it. How do I bridge that gap? He tried to imagine filling the gap in the nexus, as if patching a hole in a leaking boat, but nothing happened. Frustrated, he turned his attention back to Faye.

"You're right," he said simply.

Nearby, Darius lounged back on his elbows and Ayva sat cross-legged, watching. Somehow he was afraid to have them watch—why was that? He'd faced the Kage, Saeroks, Vergs and dragons with them at his side… Why was fighting Faye making his palms sweat?

"Of course I am," she snorted from behind him, still circling. "You attack wildly, attempting to make up for the gaps in your training."

"Then help me fill in those gaps," he voiced, hoping it sounded like less of an order and more of a plea. Abruptly, he felt a slight break of wind from behind him and he twisted, lifting Morrowil in the nick of time as her blade crashed down upon him. Metal rung.

Faye squinted. "How do you sense my movement? Can you hear me?"

Gray shook his head. "It's the wind."

"I thought your power was gone?"

He felt his skin prick. "How did you…" Ayva and Darius watched, but she had said it so that only he had heard.

The pressure of her blade spiked and she leapt back, skidding along the sand. Her head rose. "This is your first lesson. You must sense the emotions of others, when fighting or merely talking, and then read what they are hiding and what they are intentionally exposing. Then, take both and use it against them. That is *si'tu'ah*. Your blade and mind must be one."

"You are a fearsome opponent."

Faye laughed. "Flattery will get you nowhere," she replied and attacked.

Gray raised his sword, but the slice to his head was a feint. She took her blade across sideways towards his torso, spinning. Morrowil flashed, parrying. But her foot extended as she spun, hitting his feet, and he stumbled, falling onto his rear. Dust puffed into the air, and when it cleared, her sword sat before his eyes, wavering, ready to strike.

"I learned that from another, a tribe of warriors," she explained. "*That* is *si'tu'ah* as well. Take what your opponents teach you and use it against them. Everything in fighting is a lesson, but you must have ears that listen, eyes that see, and a mind that adapts," she said, tapping her temple. Her curved blade still hung before his eyes, its steel point reflecting the bright sun into his eyes.

Gray cleared his throat, eyeing the blade.

Faye grumbled and grudgingly dropped it, extending a gloved hand.

As she did, he grabbed it, put a foot underneath him for weight, and swept his other foot in a smooth arc. Faye, however, saw it coming and pulled away, but he gripped her hand tighter, tugging her in. As he swiped her legs from beneath her, she fell hard onto her rear. "Am I learning?" he asked, rising.

Faye looked up at him from upon the ground, and he thought she was hiding a smile, but he couldn't tell. Suddenly, she rolled, grabbed a fistful of sand, and threw it at him, clouding the air. Gray coughed, and something flickered in his mind. A small gust cleared the sand from the air. In its place, was Faye, both blades raised. Something popped into Gray's mind. It felt ancient, yet new. *Monk pushes the Darkness*—gripping Morrowil in one hand, he parried her sword to the side. But her dagger darted towards his throat. He slipped it, slightly, and used his forearm to smack her other arm aside. The weight of his strike made Faye stumble forward. Without slowing, he brought his hand up to his ear and chopped towards Faye's throat. He stopped, pulling the blow in the last second. Her eyes were wide, staring into his.

He tried to hide a toothy smile of his own.

"You *are* learning," she said. "I've never seen that form. Where did you…?"

"Another life," he replied.

"Impressive," she said, but she didn't look impressed with her red ringlets curling around her smug face. She sounded as impressed as if the sun had decided to rise in the morning. "But you must not always rely on your forms."

Gray nodded. "I've heard as much before, but it's hard." Mura had told him that… Thoughts of the hermit made his heart clench, but he stuffed them down. Knowing Mura was safer with Karil than with him was a comfort, a small one, but a comfort nonetheless.

"Then whoever told you was wise. Forms are but a tool. They will work sometimes, but other times you must simply give into instinct. Besides, all things have flaws…" she said and gestured with her eyes downwards. Something tapped his thigh. Between his legs, he saw Faye's blade.

He swallowed. "But I still won. My attack is more deadly," he insisted.

"Interesting opinion," she remarked, "I doubt all men would see it the same. But who was quicker?" she asked and Gray realized he hadn't seen her blade at all. "Ask yourself, if I was, would yours even hit? And is it a risk you'd be willing to take again?"

Gray growled, pressing back. He leapt at her, flowing from form to form, faster and faster, more and more aggressive. *Vixen's Revenge.* He blocked upwards, and then struck down. She parried easily.

Faye held his parry and barked, "You are stronger than this. Show me!"

She thrust his sword away and chopped from both sides. *The Breeze Flows East.* He ducked, rolling to the side. When he looked up, she was there. *So fast!* He dipped his head again, but her dagger clipped his ear. He snarled, shoving down the pain, and launched into a series of attacks, blade crashing down upon her, using all his strength. Steel met steel, ringing into the open desert, but she seemed unaffected. He continued to hammer down, and she flowed backward, blade meeting his at every angle.

She leapt back and aimed her sword at him. "Your weakness is

not in your muscles, Gray," she stated. "This is your next lesson: you were limited by Daerval, but you are limited no longer. You must give in to your powers and to the magic of Farhaven. We are all made of the elements around us. Give into those elements. Let them give you strength."

Gray hesitated but didn't argue. He took a deep breath, letting the magic in the air flow into him, giving him life and power. His limbs felt lighter than before, his steps almost buoyant. Exhilarated by the sensation, he charged again. This time his blows *were* different. They became heavier, stronger. Faye grunted as he hammered down. Elation and triumph filled him. Through the blur of weapons, he saw her wisp of a smile and *felt* her satisfaction. And then…

Faye twisted, redirecting Morrowil. She cut to his neck and thrust to his belly. Gray couldn't block both and he moved to leap back, when her foot smashed down upon his. Her blades raced and she froze, a breath away.

She had won.

Gray's world returned. He dropped to one knee—exhausted. How long had they been fighting? He realized he was sweating profusely. It soaked his clothes and matted his long hair to his face, and he tasted salt upon his lips. Faye, on the other hand, wasn't even breathing hard. How could that be? She was just too strong.

Calmly, she nodded and sheathed both weapons. "Enough training for today," she announced. "You've learned much."

Frustration rose inside Gray as he eyed her back. "No," he cursed quietly and she stopped without turning. Nearby, Ayva and Darius watched. They had witnessed the whole thing he knew, and he felt weak, all over again, weak like he had been when he didn't understand his power and the darkness inside of him. Weak like when he'd been chased and nearly killed without knowing why, when his home and life with Mura had simply been shattered in an instant, leaving him alone and frightened. He tried to silence his insecurities, but his teeth ground in rising frustration. He hadn't realized how much his confidence relied on him being the one who was strong and in control. What was he now? "I've learned only that you're too fast. If a Devari has half the skill you have, I won't have a chance. Sure I got you once, but how often can I rely on remembering ancient moves?"

Faye twisted. Her light brown eyes glinted dangerously. "You think I am fast? I am nothing. I am stronger than you certainly, and many others, and perhaps I can even take an average Devari, but there are plenty of others much faster and stronger than I."

"What is a Devari anyway?" Darius asked, sitting by the pond and playing with a handful of sand.

"Warriors who wield the ki," Faye answered.

"Well that's helpful," Darius said sarcastically, "but mind explaining it to someone who isn't from this land?"

"What's the ki?" Ayva asked politely, making Gray raise a brow.

"It is empathy at a whole new level. The ki is the ability to understand someone's feelings so deeply that the line between two bodies blurs." Darius made a yakking sound but Faye ignored him. "The ki was said to once exist in all humans but was lost over the ages. No one knows how or why, but it is speculated that we broke from it when we made kingdoms and sought division over unity, greed over love." She scoffed. "Not that I believe that load of horsedung, but the fact remains that only Devari wield the ki now. And some of them can wield it stronger than others."

"Some?" Gray asked.

She looked north, as if seeing the Citadel in the distance. Gray had a flashing image of a black keep. It was Kirin's memory. "I've heard of one in particular. Before I left Farbs there were whispers of a new Devari."

"The Devari have leaders?" he asked. "I thought they were simply guardians of the Citadel and protectors of Reavers."

"It is rare," she admitted, "Devari are brothers. There are no real ranks among them, save for their leader. The last one died years ago. I remember it clear as day."

Something inside Gray stung and Kirin wailed. Then, just as suddenly, the voice turned silent as if disappearing into a dark abyss. *What was that about?* he wondered.

Faye continued, "But there hasn't been a Devari strong enough to take the position. Until this man."

Gray hesitated. "Strong enough? Is there some sort of test?"

"You could say that. It's a trial of strength, willpower, and skill that breaks many a man who attempts it," she said. "To become their leader you must be able to defeat twenty Devari in battle." *Twenty?* Gray gawked and Faye continued, "Devari have been around for thousands of years, since the very Citadel was founded, but it is a feat only few have ever achieved."

"You mean this man…"

"He would make me look like a fumbling child," she replied.

Gray shivered. Were there others who could rival the Ronin? How could he possibly defeat someone like that? No, there was no one stronger than Kail, or so the stories said. But Gray knew he was no Kail. Not yet, at least. The man had lived a thousand lives of men… He had a long way to go. Thinking of Kail made him think of that look the legend had worn before Gray had transported into the center of Death's Gate, when he had accepted his ultimate fate: to slay the Ronin. He still remembered the legend's face, a look in his eyes as if he held a secret. As if his death wasn't truly the end. Gray glanced over his shoulder at Ayva and Darius.

"Be satisfied with your progress today," Faye said firmly, drawing him back to the moment. "You may not be a Devari yet, but you learn quickly. Before we are done, I will make you into one, or, if I can, something better…"

Gray nodded, excited and a little afraid. *Something better?* He wondered. Faye walked past Ayva and Darius. She said something quietly to Ayva, and Gray thought he heard a word on the breeze. *Diaon? What could that mean?*

A Duel for Honor

They moved through the bright day, making progress. So far, it was a peaceful day, promising a respite from the chaos of the past few days. Faye felt alone with only the dogged sun above burning like a golden flame, and her web of troubled thoughts.

Well, if not for that stubborn girl…

Again, she answered Ayva's questions until her throat grew dry from talking or until Ayva failed to answer a question correctly. Silence was her punishment for now, and for the girl, it was clearly the greatest of punishments as she sat sullenly in her saddle. They moved past a bumpy patch of sand when, suddenly, there was a cry. Faye twisted, looking behind.

She tensed.

Gray knelt on the ground, spear points a hair from his head as a full circle of tan-clothed men stood around him, yelling angrily. Sand still sluiced, falling from their slender frames. The fool rogue lay unmoving in the sand. His cormac made a bemoaned sound somewhere between a neigh and whimper, nuzzling its rider, while Gray's Elvin beast watched the exchange placidly. A man taller than the rest stood closest. At his side, two tan-clothed men held small bows aimed directly at her. Their skin was caramel in color, and they had dark eyes and black curly hair.

"Algasi," she cursed.

"What is going on?" Ayva whispered fearfully. "Where in the seven hells did they come from?"

Faye cursed her own foolishness, seeing the disturbed pocket of sand nearby. They had been lying in wait until they had left the Node. Algasi warriors were legendary, and their patience was equally renowned. *"Has siwth sun reggal sith tu vi ren nus,"* she said smoothly.

The tall man with broad shoulders eyed her uncertainly. All she could see were his white-gray eyes as his face was hidden behind a white cloth mask. He was the only big one of the tribe. Algasi were small, slender people, but they moved like sand serpents. She knew she could not reach her daggers or sword before they cut Gray down, if not all four of them. At last, he spoke, "Regar." She had asked to be released for they were only "simple travelers". *No* was his answer. She doubted he believed her.

"Tell him we mean no harm," Gray said. Immediately, the spears pressed tighter to his throat, stopping him from speaking. He swallowed, raising his hands higher in submission.

"I tried that," Faye answered flatly. There was only one move now. Ever so slowly, she drew back her dust-cloak. The leader of the Algasi watched. Still moving as if through quicksand, she pulled off her crossbow and threw it down. Then her daggers. Then her sword.

"What are you doing?" Ayva whispered in a fierce undertone.

She replied through her teeth, keeping her eyes forward. "Put down your little dagger, and perhaps they will let us go."

"And if they don't let us go?"

"Then they will capture us as prisoners and use us as target practice for their younger ones in training." The girl hesitated, reading her eyes and seeing she was not joking.

Ayva growled. "Does everything in this cursed land have to try to kill us? I refuse. We cannot be prisoners!"

"You have no choice."

"That's the difference between you and I," Ayva said in a low but heated voice. "We always have a choice." At the words, she *felt* the girl's heat. *Such anger, but how is that possible?* Faye wondered. No, she must be imagining things—heat exhaustion surely. Ayva dismounted her cormac and approached their leader slowly with her hands raised.

Gray tensed nearby but couldn't move.

"What are you doing?" Faye shouted. "Stop!" Ayva ignored her. Still, she kept her dagger hidden, but the Algasi were no fools. "Girl, move no further. They will slit you from ear to ear! Let me talk to them, I—"

She felt sudden warmth burning her throat. The dryness of the desert? Her throat went numb, words falling short. At the same time, the Algasi leader held up his hand, stopping Ayva's advance. "Do as I say, Faye. Translate this."

The burning abated and she spoke. "My name is Ayva. We mean no harm. Simply give us back our friends, and we will be on our way. Take what you will from us, but know that we have little but our lives."

Faye translated.

The man didn't smile, but a twitch creased his lips for a moment. "Dalic un savas. U suroth sel es, Ayva." With a knuckle, he tapped his forehead and then his broad chest. It was an Algasi greeting, a rare privilege. Algasi found power in names and did not give them out freely, much like elves. He continued. "Du sa vi aruni al Algasi. Sun suh to morla. Murs u tal in ni sutin. Se suh tu swahala."

Faye translated. *"Dalic is my name. I see your light, Ayva. But that is not the way of the Algasi. We must take something of worth. These are our lands and you have trespassed. There must be a price."*

"Then take me," Ayva said.

Faye looked at the girl calmly.

"Faye, do not translate that!" Gray said then choked as a spear jabbed him.

"Don't worry, Gray," the girl said, and then looked at Faye, a fierce intelligence in her blue eyes. "I don't plan on going, but it's clear they value strength. Say it, and see his response."

Faye sighed but translated. The man listened, his white-gray eyes hard. At last he spoke and she echoed his words. *"Full of fire and light indeed, as if Algasi blood flows through you. But what you say makes no sense. What stops us from taking all of you?"* Faye snorted. "I told you. They know they have the upper hand. This is what I was trying to avoid."

Ayva watched the ground and then twisted, as if suddenly remembering. “Challenge him to an Honor Duel.”

Faye laughed. The sound made Dalic’s eyes narrow, and the other Algasi shifted uneasily on their feet, gripping their spears. She knew they were a breath away from spilling their blood upon the sand. She lowered her voice. “Are you mad? They will kill you before you can blink. Then they will kill all of us.”

“Me?” Ayva lifted a thin brow. Faye hesitated, catching on. “You see, if I recall from what I read *and* what you told me, Algasi are the ones who will choose their opponent, and they *always* choose the strongest. If I’m correct, that means they’ll choose you.”

Again Faye laughed, but she kept it under her breath. Cursing herself for teaching that fool girl, Faye couldn’t help but be impressed. *At least I taught her well.* “What makes you think I’ll agree to that?”

“You don’t have to, but it’s our only option unless you have a better idea…?” Faye tried to think of one but admitted inwardly that she didn’t. Ayva continued, “An Honor Duel grants the victor freedom and one request.”

“What makes you think I can win?”

Ayva shrugged. “I didn’t say you could.”

Nearby, she saw Gray watching tensely, obviously craving to speak, but surrounded by the fearsome sand people, he was forced into silence while the fool rogue remained unconscious.

“You plan to kill me off so quickly?” Faye asked.

“No, but if you are as strong as you claim you are, well, then perhaps you have a chance.” Ayva nodded to a nearby Algasi, a man like the others with black curly hair, brown skin, and a hooked nose. Oddly enough, the warrior had only one arm. A clever smile crossed Ayva’s face. “Besides, just because they choose the strongest of us, doesn’t mean you have to choose the strongest of them, correct? So surely you can beat a one-armed man.”

The girl was trying to goad her. A juvenile attempt. She scoffed inwardly as it wasn’t working. Faye realized she was grinding her teeth. Well, maybe it was working a *little*. But the girl still had no idea what she was asking.

Algasi were weapons, born and bred. They trained from sunup to sundown, beneath the burning desert sun, to be stronger and faster than an average man and to endure immeasurable pain. She counted eight Algasi when she noticed several had a black-band upon their wooden spears—the mark of an elite warrior, *Mundasi*. She shivered in memory. Faye had seen a Mundasi fight two Devari and nearly win. In the end, by reading the Algasi's moves, only one Devari had died, and the other had barely lived. A normal Algasi was only slightly less threatening.

"If I win," Faye voiced, sounding more confident than she felt, "who's to say I won't just choose my own freedom and leave you all in the dust?"

Again, the girl looked impassive. It was growing infuriating. "If you let us die, you will be breaking your bond and your word. But the truth is there is no assurance. It is your call. *If* you win."

Faye dismounted and strode forward. Dalic and the other warriors had watched the whole conversation quietly. Somehow she felt as if he had understood every word. Very slowly, she reached for her long, curved dagger and then her sword. The Algasi watched her, raising their own weapons, but before they could move she crossed the blades over her heart, dipping her head.

The formal challenge to an Honor Duel.

Dalic spoke. "Whom do you choose?"

"You speak the common tongue?" she asked in surprise.

"It is common for Hutäs, or *clan leaders* in your tongue, to learn," he said confidently, if haltingly.

She snorted. *Algasi*. "Whom do you choose?" he repeated.

Ayva nodded to the one-armed man. Everything in Faye agreed. Her survival instincts were strong. Her street-sense had even picked up on the slight limp in another man, noticing their weaknesses and debating which was the least of a threat, like searching for the runt in a litter, though every runt here was deadly. Every fiber of her being and of her tireless tutelage pointed to the one-armed warrior.

She motioned to Dalic. "You," she said.

Ayva drew near, speaking in a harsh whisper for only her ears. "What are you doing? That man... He is clearly the most dangerous of them all."

"I know," she said softly.

"Then what are you doing? Have you lost your mind?"

Perhaps, Faye thought, but remained silent. Though she could not see the man's face, she felt him smile beneath that white-cloth shroud. Dalic bowed his head, slightly. He accepted.

A dozen paces away, Gray risked death to croak, "Faye… *No…*"

She ignored him, stepping forward.

Dalic moved back, preparing. The man rolled his lithe shoulders, moving from side to side, warming up in the sun's light. At last, he pulled down his white shroud. He grinned—showing a hard, angular face full of excitement. He was handsome, but raw like an uncut stone. Then his gaze focused, like the sun's light through a thick looking glass, ready for battle. An Algasi handed him his spear, and Faye saw that it held *two* black bands. She had never heard of such a thing.

This man was not her equal in the slightest.

Today, after years of avoiding it, she would die.

Unintended Consequences

Darius' skull throbbed.

Dust filled his nostrils. Suddenly, he heard the ring of steel upon steel and the scuffle of feet. Someone was fighting. There was a cry—muted and feminine. *What the…?* He moved to sit up, but froze. A strange instinct warned him against it. Slowly, barely, he cracked open his eyelids. Light flooded his vision.

He saw a boot in the corner of his gaze, and the glimpse of a spear hovering before his face. *Captive.* He cursed inwardly. *Where are you, Gray and Ayva?* Surely they must be held captive too, but Darius couldn't risk moving or his captors would notice. He took in the scene beyond.

Nearby, upon the dry desert, Faye faced a mountain of a man. He was not wide—not unless a blade could be considered wide—save for his broad shoulders, which would have brushed a door's frame. Hunched, he looked like a large cat ready to pounce. In one hand he held a spear with a thick, steel head and two black bands upon the wooden haft. Dust colored fabric like his own previous rags draped the man's huge frame. Casually, he rose to his full, impressive height and spoke a strange, jumbled mess of words. Darius wondered if the knock to his head was making his hearing fuzzy.

Faye was breathing hard, looking ragged and on the verge of

defeat. Through the haze of his lashes, he saw blood. It dripped, staining the desert ground at her feet. The man, on the other hand, wasn't breathing hard at all. All exhaustion seemed to flee as Faye cried out, launching at the man. She was a whirlwind of steel and anger, fluid like water, but then unpredictable like a pike amid the reeds. How had Gray stood up to such a woman? Her sword and dagger flashed, cutting and swiping, and between the gaps of each attack, she launched kicks, elbows and even knees. But that man.... Darius couldn't believe it. He moved as if sloughing through water. Nothing she threw hit, as if he were smoke. No, he realized, he was just quick. Too quick. Worse, his rock-like face never changed. It was as if he were merely dancing, as if he were reading her moves before they happened. Dice! Darius had never seen anything like it. And he realized, suddenly, that the man was not attacking. Not once even. He simply backpedaled along the desert as Faye cried out in a rage of fury, exhausting herself.

Screaming at the top of her lungs, Faye cut at his neck wildly. Suddenly, the man stopped dodging. He halted, and Darius *felt* Faye's surprise. *His opening*, Darius knew and choked. He had just been waiting, calmly biding his time. The man slipped an attack
that would have taken his head by a hairsbreadth and stabbed. The spear lunged for her head, impossibly fast. She ducked. But the man was still moving. He thrust again and again, three, four, five times and more, faster than Darius' eye could follow. Faye dipped, dodged, and weaved, evading one after another, her breath coming harder and harder. She was keeping pace! *Dice, she can do it!* He thought, watching in amazement. Suddenly, the man twisted. His long leg sliced, raising a fan of dirt. Faye, her eyes focused on the jabbing spear, didn't see it coming. He swept her feet, and she hit the dirt like a sack of bricks, air pressed from her lungs. Darius swallowed, blinking. When he opened his eyes, the man stood over her. The spear's head hovered above Faye's heart, inches away. Still, the man wasn't breathing hard, and looked as if he hadn't broken a sweat.

Faye lowered her eyes, defeated. Her hand touched something at her side, but he knew it was a death sentence. The man's muscles tensed.

Darius reached inside. The Leaf floated in his mind, lines golden and glowing. Fearfully, he gripped it. Immediately, he was opened to his surroundings even with his eyes closed. There were few trees out here, but he felt dead roots deep beneath the earth as if this place had once been full of life. Unsure of what he was doing, he reached for them. *So far*… But still he pulled, anger and pressure building in his mind.

He opened his eyes.

The man's spear descended.

He cried out, feeling root and earth breaking beneath him. *Almost there!* A boot stomped hard onto his back, pushing him to the ground. Suddenly, the pressure was gone as cries erupted. Darius felt the air break. Without wasting a second thought, he rolled to one side. A spear's tip dug a chunk of earth out where he had just been. He looked up. A one-armed man with brown skin and black hair even wilder than his own stood over him, attacking, spear flying again towards his face. But Darius was ready. He kicked, hitting the man square in the chest with both feet. The man took the blow, flying back. Rolling to his feet, Darius saw the chaos before him.

Ayva was running, sprinting for safety. Nearby, Gray knelt, surrounded by four different spears. Yet the men watched fearfully as turmoil exploded around them. Roots burst from the ground, hundreds of them. They grabbed some men, holding them in the air and lashing at others.

Closer still, Faye knelt, frozen. The tall man before her growled, but a thick, gnarled root held his spear, halting the killing blow. Confused, but only for a second, the man dropped his spear and looked around, watching the disorder. Sweat knit across Darius' brow as he propelled the chaos, pushing the roots to grab and flay. Suddenly, the power was too much to hold and his concentration broke and the roots collapsed, lifeless once more. Darius sagged, exhausted.

The tall man bellowed, drawing all eyes. Darius saw that he gripped Faye's throat, holding her above the ground. "No more tricks! You've broken the duel and have lost all honor. Now you all must die." He nodded to the four men surrounding Gray. "Kill them all."

Ayva shouted, "No!"

"Ayva, save Faye!" Darius ordered.

He saw her expression twist, but she nodded.

The four men around Gray raised their spears.

Darius concentrated. With the last bit of his failing power, he focused on a huge, ancient root deep beneath the sand. Slowly, it rumbled. Its presence and his became one. Darius' eyes snapped open and he thrust his hand up, driving the root like a spike through the earth and into the center of Gray and his captors. Earth sprayed like water into the air, buying Gray a split second. He dove, rolling and reaching for his sword. But one of the warriors, unperturbed by the exploding ground, was quicker.

"Faye, shield your eyes! Now!" It was Ayva's voice.

A light burst in the corner of his vision, blindingly bright. Darius was forced to shelter his gaze as well. When he opened his eyes, he saw the leader. The man groaned, stumbling and clutching his eyes as if temporarily blinded.

Faye rose, standing over the man who reached for Morrowil, "Go ahead." The man grabbed Gray's blade then screamed, falling to his knees. Faye nodded, as if satisfied, then kicked Morrowil towards Gray. Another warrior leapt at Gray from behind with a black-banded spear.

"Gray!" Darius cried out.

But Gray was too slow. He twisted and the spear flashed. Suddenly, Faye pushed him, taking his place as the black-banded spear found its mark, piercing her shoulder. She cried out but then kicked the man in the groin with all her might. The warrior merely flinched. It was all the time Darius needed. He lifted his hand, directing the ancient tuber. His body quaked, every muscle straining as he lifted the colossal root. It rose into the air and then fell, landing upon the warrior and pinning him to the ground.

Looking around, Darius saw the leader. Face dark as death, the Algasi leader snatched his two-banded spear and stalked forward. *Well, I guess his vision is back*, Darius realized. Glancing around, he swallowed. The other warriors had dealt with the remaining roots and now made a slow death-stalk towards Darius, weapons in hand.

Ayva, Gray and Faye fell in at his side, backing up slowly.

"Well, that *seemed* to be going well."

"You fool, you shouldn't have interrupted our duel. Now you've gotten us all killed."

Darius shook his head, dumbfounded. "Are you serious? I saved you! You were about to die!"

"Better me than all of us," she replied with a shrug.

"It doesn't matter," Gray stated, interrupting. "Got anything left in that bag of tricks of yours, Darius?"

Darius shook his head, eyeing their approaching death. "I wish." It was true; his whole body felt as if he'd just run from the Lost Woods to Death's Gate and back. He was drained. And even if he did have the energy, he had conjured those roots out of need. He had no idea what he'd just done. "Can you get us away, Gray? You know, use your power again?"

"I..." Gray faltered. He closed his eyes as if searching, and then shook his head, looking afraid and defeated. "Not this time."

Ayva nervously gripped her dagger in her hand. "Then what do we do?"

The men stalked closer still, their dark faces with hard eyes ready for the kill, like hawks corralling a field mouse into a corner for the final blow.

Faye spoke. "We can't fight this. It's time to run." She put two fingers into her mouth and whistled. Her horse suddenly whinnied, galloping towards them from the east. The cormacs, intuitive beasts, turned and followed Faye's mare. The warriors twisted, but it was too late as the steeds galloped through their ranks. The leader pivoted, whole body twisting as he stabbed, his spear piercing its target. Faye's horse cried out, falling, but the cormacs burst through. Faye shouted, but there was no time.

Leaping up on his mount, Darius grabbed a distraught Faye and pulled her up behind him. She winced, grabbing her wounded shoulder. Then, kicking his heels into Mirkal's flanks, Darius charged, bursting away from the sand-colored warriors and into the desert beyond.

* * *

The sun was a ripe blood red, hanging just above the horizon in the west when they at last stopped to make camp at a large Node just before the rolling, endless dunes.

Gray wanted to put as much distance as possible between him and the Algasi. Faye had said that many of them could run for miles on end without tiring. That had put him and the others on edge.

Nearing the Node, he slowed.

This sanctuary was not like the others, more dirt and sand, and less greenery. The majority of trees were smooth poles with huge green fronds. They drooped as if drowsy, glad for dusk and a respite from the relentless sun. Gray could understand that sentiment. At the center was another large pond, but it looked shallow. He doubted at its deepest it would reach his waist. There were no animals, save for the buzz of some nearby beetles. Yet bits of gold—magic, he knew—hung in the air above the water, which reflected the full moon above.

He dismounted and patted his cormac, thanking the beast for working so hard. Even the cormacs, seemingly tireless beasts, had begun to slack. Their fine-coats had worked up a slight lather. *Let the Algasi chase us here*, he thought, then rescinded his words immediately. *Spirits send they don't.* He knew they couldn't face those warriors again. Not without an army at their back.

Faye swung smoothly from Darius' mount and strode to the nearby pool.

"Faye," Gray said. She said nothing, washing her hands at the water. "I'm sorry."

"'*Just as the bright sun sets and darkness falls, so too must all things fade with the sands of time*,'" she whispered, and he realized she was quoting something.

A silence settled over the four, Ayva and Darius looking to him.

"Yarish was a good steed, but it's fine," she said, her back turned. "As long as you keep your promise." Her voice was calm and indifferent. But as she knelt at the water's edge, dipping her hands in and washing the dirt of travel from her tan face, he sensed her hurt. Not the ki, but *si'tu'ah*. It was evident.

"What does that mean?" Ayva asked, "What promise?"

Gray shook his head. "Nothing."

Darius made a loud, exaggerated cough. "Sorry to interrupt, but does anyone want to tell me what in the seven hells of remwar happened back there? What were those things exactly?" He leapt from his cormac and tied it to a nearby tree.

"Algasi," Ayva said. "Sand warriors. Stories say they are a nomadic tribe that roams the lands near the Rehlias Desert. According to many tales, they were once citizens of the great kingdom of Vaster. After the war, it was said they banished themselves for the guilt was too great."

"What guilt?" Gray asked.

"The guilt that they started the war. It was Omni's sword that was stolen. The sun blade was never recovered and many believe it was the catalyst for the Lieon. The Algasi felt the blame for the countless victims of the great war."

"That must be when Omni and the Ronin took the blame for the war," Gray said in realization.

Ayva bobbed her head. "Precisely, for they were the only ones who could hold the blade."

Gray shook his head, amazed. "How do you know all this?"

She smiled, looking pleased. "I was always fascinated by the Algasi, and Faye filled me in on the rest.

Faye said nothing.

Gray looked at her, pondering. The woman had tried to sacrifice herself for them… Hadn't she? Or was that just another ploy? Gray had figured Faye was the type to always have an out. She was a survivor. Then what was that back there? Had she truly attempted to give her life for them?

"No offense," Darius said, raising his hands, "but I didn't ask for a history lesson, Ayva. I just want to know what happened. The last thing I remember was riding along, laughing, and then, whack! Lights out! Where in the world did they come from?"

Ayva grumbled. "Just because you say no offense, doesn't mean it's not offensive, Darius. Idiot."

Darius, taking off his cormac's saddle and brushing the creature down, merely shrugged. He seemed to pay a lot of attention and care to the beast. But Gray could understand, for they weren't like normal creatures. Sometimes, he almost felt as if they understood him when he talked.

"They were hiding in the sand," Gray explained.

"*In* the sand?" the rogue exclaimed, "That figures. This whole land is a dicing deathtrap. But how is it that I'm always the one who gets knocked out? Remember Lakewood? Same dicing thing!"

Gray hid a smirk. It was true. "But this time was different. What you did, Darius—" he shook his head, remembering the army of roots that, like a hundred fingers of earth, had sprouted from the land "—it was truly magnificent. You saved us."

Darius looked embarrassed. He scrubbed a hand across his

mouth. "I did a little, sure, but it wasn't me that saved us. It was her." He nodded to Faye.

Suddenly, Faye rose, let out a small groan and staggered, falling.

Gray darted, grabbing her as she collapsed. She was limp in his arms. He cursed, furious at himself—how could he have forgotten? She had pushed him out of the way and taken the spear that was meant to take his life. He lifted a hand. It was drenched in blood. Without thinking, he pulled back her layered leather and mail armor. He saw the wound. It was on her shoulder, but cloth covered it. He set her to the ground and pulled her shirt down, exposing her shoulder and her chest.

"What are you doing?" Ayva exclaimed, aghast.

He spoke heatedly. "I need to clean and bind her wound, and quick. Her clothing is in the way. If I don't, she will surely die." He looked up. Ayva's face was pained, conflicted. "We can't let her die, Ayva. She sacrificed herself for us. This is partly your fault, and mine as well. It's all our fault."

Ayva looked ready to retort when Faye coughed. "Water..." she moaned.

Surprisingly, Darius was at her side, a skin of water in his hand, putting it to her dry lips.

Cursing, Ayva grabbed her dagger and leapt upon her cormac's back. "I'll look for some Silveroot then. Don't let her die before I get back," she said, as if an order, and then dug her heels into the animal's flanks, heading deeper into the Node.

"Can we trust her?" Darius asked. Again Faye moaned, head lolling to one side. *She's unconscious*, Kirin whispered to him. *She's lost too much blood...*

Don't tell me that. Help me or stay quiet.

"Gray?" Darius asked.

He looked up. He must have said it out loud again. Ripping bits of red and gray cloth from Faye's clothes, Gray dipped them in the nearby water and quickly cleared away the wound. Much of it had crusted, clogged with dirt and sand. He brushed it aside as carefully as possible, but as he did more blood spouted like a fountain.

At his side, Darius gagged, averting his gaze.

Something isn't right about this... Kirin voiced. *She should be worse. Not even a Devari would stay upright with a wound like that.*

She's lost a lot of blood, but less than she should have.

What do you mean? Speak quickly!

I think something is still stuck in her, slowing the flow of blood. A piece of the spear perhaps…

And?

It may be the only thing that has saved her thus far, but if it gets into her bloodstream…

What? he pressed.

She'll die.

Tell me what to do, he ordered.

Kirin hesitated.

Now, Gray insisted, growling inwardly. He didn't know what he could do if Kirin refused. There was no threat he could give to the voice, aside from trying to shut it out or banishing it once and for all when he got to Farbs. But at last, his old self spoke.

You will owe me.

Gray nodded without hesitation, accepting that bargain. As he did, a shiver traced his spine. Somehow it felt more binding than the blood pact with Faye. And then Kirin began to instruct him in a calm, authoritative tone, and he set about cleaning, sanitizing, finding a tool to extract the shard of spear… Distantly, he heard himself order Darius to make a fire. He was amazed at how much his Devari side knew. He almost felt as if he could touch that pool of knowledge, as if he didn't need Kirin. He tried to pull it out himself, to break down that barrier, but it was like trying to grip the reins of another's horse. Too far to reach. For now, he knew, the key to that door was held by Kirin.

It still may not be enough, Kirin voiced, as Gray worked feverishly.

It has to be…

"Gray," Darius interrupted, "can we trust Ayva to find the Silveroot?"

"Go with her," Gray said absently, if only to have him out of his way. He needed to concentrate. He looked to Faye's shoulder. With a deep breath and mentally preparing himself, he lifted a makeshift pair of pincers—really just two metal sticks that Mistress Hitomi had given them back at the Shining City, which he'd kept as a memento until now.

Heat them first, Kirin ordered.

Gray didn't question the voice. It knew more than he did. He stuck the metal sticks into the fire, fingers growing hot.

Darius rose. "You sure you know what you're doing?" he asked nervously, still keeping his gaze away from Faye's exposed chest.

"I don't, but Kirin does."

"Kirin?" Darius asked.

Gray shook his head. "I'll be fine. Go help Ayva. Silveroot might be the only thing that can help her now."

Darius bobbed his shaggy head, leapt swiftly upon his cormac, and took off into the Node, leaving Gray with a silent Faye. Watching the glowing orange metal cool, he looked to the wound. *Are you with me?* he asked inwardly and Kirin concurred. The wound swelled with blood, and Gray began, rooting for the spear's sliver using Kirin's voice as a guide. It was chilly out, but sweat broke out on his face in concentration. He continued and felt the land darken around him, the orange fire illuminating his work. Kirin had intended the fire for two purposes, he realized. His heart pounded in his chest as he lifted flaps of flesh, searching, all the while struggling to keep his hands from shaking.

Too much blood, Kirin said with a note of fear. *I've never seen this much...* Gray had never heard emotion in Kirin's voice. Usually, it was just forward and confident. It terrified him to hear that fear.

Will she live?

But Kirin had no answer.

SECRETS

"Ayva?" Darius called, but there was no answer.

This Node wasn't large, so where the dice could she have run off to?

Darius maneuvered his cormac around several large trees with smooth bark and large fronds upon their crest, looking like a jester's green hat only missing its bells—*dola* trees, Ayva had informed him. Truthfully, the cormac didn't need much guiding. Wherever he looked, the beast went, almost sensing it before he did. He patted Mirkal fondly.

"Good boy," he said. "Good cormac."

Suddenly, Darius choked as something lodged in his throat. He went into a fit of coughs, hammering his chest, and at last a tiny golden bug jettisoned out of his mouth. It flew and landed on a dola tree. He watched, dumfounded as the golden beetle melded with the bark, disappearing entirely.

What the…? Darius shivered. He ignored it, pretending it hadn't happened. He seemed to be doing that a lot lately. Too much. He looked at his palm. *My power… Summoning those roots felt like moving a mountain with my bare hands.* But he had done it. He dipped into his mind, and there the Leaf floated serenely. Waiting.

"Go away," he whispered, shutting his mind. As the Leaf winked away, he felt a strange sense of loss, as if he were shunning a part of himself, or cutting a finger from his hand.

No, he thought adamantly as he scoured the trees for some trace of Ayva. *Aside from the cormacs, this land can keep its blasted magic.* Give him a bit of gambling, a pretty barmaid, and perhaps a little bit of adventure. Scratch that, no more adventure. Back in Lakewood, he had pined for the thrill of sword battles and honor duels. *What a fool I was,* he thought. Now he realized adventure was just another word for deathtrap.

His cormac found its way, stepping past rust-colored bushes and a last stand of dola trees. A haunting song hung in the air. It was almost inaudible, but he could hear it. Again, he shivered… It was as if the Node was alive and singing.

Suddenly, in a strange, white-sanded clearing, he saw it.

A large Silveroot tree. There were no other trees around it. It was the largest tree he had ever seen. It lifted its bushy branches towards the dark desert sky, as if pleading to escape this cursed land as well.

"*Ayva!*" he called again. No answer. Darius gruffly threw one leg over Mirkal and landed upon the ground. "Wait here," he told the beast firmly. Any other animal and he would have felt silly, but as he looked into those large, unnerving white and green eyes they seemed to comprehend. *Did it just nod?* He shook his head, turning back to the tree.

He scanned the tree line nervously, but the desert was quiet, save for that song… He realized it was louder. He felt it humming through him, chilling him and sending shivers through his body. *What is this?* he thought, fearful and excited. Darius felt tears spring from his eyes, and he gruffly wiped them away. He looked back to the huge Silveroot. It sat calmly, as if waiting. *Just like the Leaf,* he thought.

Unsure of what he was doing, he took a step forward. The hum continued to grow, resonating through his limbs. He felt alive. The Leaf pulsed in the back of his mind, urging him to grab it. Darius ignored it, pushing it away, but not far. Another step. The hum grew louder, coursing through him, and his heart pounded. He realized, suddenly, that all this time that hum had been *pulling* him here.

Reaching the tree, Darius' grimace faltered. He let out a soft breath, taking in the tree. The trunk was wider than a dozen men with arms linked, and it sprouted from the crystalline sand. Inside the folds of its bark, huge veins of silver flowed, glowing brilliantly. He craned his neck up to see the tree's branches spread over him like a giant protector. "Dice… It's beautiful."

Unsure of what he was doing, he reached out and touched it. A jolt of something flashed through him. Not of pain, but of understanding. Empathy. He *felt* the tree, its ancient wisdom, and its deep roots. He felt balance. Then something pulsed. *Life.* It throbbed like a beating heart, just as clear and true as his own. He nearly staggered back, wanting to run for Mirkal and leave this bizarre place, but something kept him rooted there with his hand to the craggy bark.

Suddenly, a voice spoke.

Not in words or pictures, but in *feeling.* It was something else entirely. An understanding.

Darius rose, not knowing when he had begun kneeling. He circled the tree, keeping his hand to its surface. Then he saw it. There was a slight bulge in the tree's trunk and a flash of green.

Still with no idea what he was doing, he opened his mind to the floating Leaf. It came, as if bursting through a floodgate. With his power in hand, Darius peeled back strips of bark, gently and one at a time, to unveil a glimmering green sword. Vines and roots twisted around the brilliant blade as if the tree had grown around the sword. *Or perhaps the sword had been born from it,* he thought. He reached out and the vines fell, releasing it. Grabbing the golden hilt, he lifted it to the light of the moon. Deeper in the tree, he saw its sheath, equally resplendent.

"Dice…" he whispered. It must have been made for a king, he thought, for it was magnificent. From the broad head, it slimmed down then flared out slightly again at the sword's hilt. The hand guard was a radiant bronze that fanned outward like two golden fronds. In the center of the hilt was a green diamond. A leaf was imprinted in its center. He twisted the blade in his hand, the moon glimmering off its surface. It appeared to be made of thick, bright-green glass, which smoldered, casting his skin in a faint flush of emerald. As a whole, the blade looked akin to a long leaf, but slender and unimaginably deadly. He had never seen anything like this. He hesitated. *Morrowil.* Then Darius shook his head. *No, it's nothing like Morrowil.* It felt right in his hands—light, yet sturdy, as he chopped at the air, imagining foes before him. The blade whistled and cut the air smoothly when a voice sounded and he spun.

"Darius, is that you?"

Ayva? Dice! Darius threw the blade into the nearby rust-colored bushes, wincing. *Wait … did I just?* His thief instincts had kicked in, and throwing the goods seemed the most logical answer. Reason settled in and he debated retrieving the sword from the bushes, but something made him hesitate. He looked back just in time to see Ayva appear from behind the huge Silveroot.

"You found it!" she exclaimed, and then heaved a heavy sigh. "Why didn't you say anything? I heard footsteps but was afraid…"

"I … uh…"

"Wait, why are you here?" Ayva's brows furrowed, her pretty face squinting unattractively. "Did Gray send you? Did that fool really think I wouldn't look for the Silveroot?"

Darius' mind still reeled, unsure of what in the seven hells of rem-war he had just stumbled upon. Somehow he felt as if he had nearly been caught with his hand filching one of Sophi's freshly baked apple pies. And he realized he didn't want Ayva to know because he knew where those questions would lead… A magical sword much like Morrowil waiting for him, calling to *him*? He'd tell her, surely, but on his own damned time for once. "Well," he coughed into his hand, "it's not exactly a secret, Ayva. You don't like her very much. In fact, I'd go so far as to say that you downright loathe her."

Ayva's short-cropped hair swayed as she shook her head. Darius wondered for a moment when and why she had done that. He always liked girls with more hair. Not that he viewed Ayva like that. She was more like a sister than anything, a self-righteous, often overbearing, but warm-hearted sister.

Ayva answered, "I can't deny that the woman is infuriating. She thinks she knows everything and *then* some, but have you both gone completely mad? I wouldn't go so far as to kill her!" She barely gulped down the word *kill*, face blanching at the notion.

"No?" he asked absently. His gaze flickered to the bushes. *I hope I didn't break it.*

"Of course not!" she said, "Besides, I know as well as either of you that she saved us."

Well, if he'd broken it, then at the least it would still fetch *some* gold surely, he thought. Inwardly, he cringed. No, a sword like that couldn't be pawned, no matter how much money it was worth. "Sure, sure," he said nodding, half-listening. "You may not kill her, but would you truly want to save her? There's a difference."

Ayva hesitated then spoke. "This is a silly conversation, Darius. Let's just get the Silveroot and get this over with." She moved to her cormac, and came back bearing a waterskin. She emptied out the water, and then withdrew her shiny dagger. She plunged the blade into the tree. Darius cried out, and recoiled simultaneously. Sharp pain bloomed near his heart and his fingers groped at his chest. Ayva peered over her shoulder. "What's wrong with you now?"

He shook his head. "Nothing, I'm fine." But he knew what had happened. He had felt the tree's pain, sharp and real as if it were his own pain—as if the dagger had pierced *his* flesh! Ayva still looked at him uncertainly as the viscous, silver sap flowed over her dagger and into the empty leather flask.

"Why do you hate her so much?" Darius asked curiously, trying to change the subject. Still, he winced. *For such a big tree, this hurts a lot,* he thought, eyeing the towering Silveroot. He felt as if the monarch tree was watching him like a wise old man.

Ayva's jaw muscles clenched, and she spoke, "Because she is tearing us apart. Don't you see it?"

The pain abated and Darius raised a brow. "What are you talking about? We're still together." And he laughed darkly. "Of course, we've nearly died six different times in the past few days alone, but I almost think that's drawing us closer together if anything."

Ayva sniffed, looking away. Anger burned in her eyes. "You don't get it, Darius. This task proves it. Gray didn't even trust me to save a life! Before this all started, the way he looked at me…" She faltered, and Darius thought her cheeks took a spot of crimson, but it was gone just as quickly. "He looked at me fondly, as he does you. Now? I've been made out to be some sort of criminal, a villain even, and worse yet, she's the one who nearly tried to take your life! And don't tell me she's changed. I know people, Darius. I've seen them all my life walking into my father's inn," she said, voice gaining momentum like a boulder rolling down a hill. "Some would parade, wearing fine silks, and others plain wool, but, beneath their clothes, I saw their true nature. The simple man with a heart of gold, or the nobleman who'd rob and spill your blood just to watch your reaction… Faye is the second. She might be helpful, but she's just a creature of curiosity and chaos." Darius thought how much that curiosity part sounded like Ayva, but he kept his mouth shut. He knew when a woman was speaking her mind that it was best to let her do so.

The waterskin filled, she corked the top and rose. She grabbed his arm fervently, staring up into his eyes. She spoke passionately, "Darius, you have to trust me. Faye is not good. She will betray us. I can see it… You have to help me convince Gray that she cannot stay."

"She might not even survive the night, Ayva," he said and nodded to the Silveroot.

"Oh, I know her type. She'll survive. The ones rotten to the core don't fall so easily."

Darius swallowed, looking into her gaze. Her words were a slice of truth that he knew all too well, and, despite himself, he realized he was nodding. At last, he shook his head, exasperated. "Let's discuss this with Gray, all right? It'll all work out, I promise. But for now, we better go save her or all this is just pointless yammering." Darius thought of the sword just lying in the bushes like just another weed. *I can't grab it now, not without Ayva knowing.* He wanted another moment to himself to take in the rare find. It seemed a shame, but he would have to come back for it later. Darius looked to Mirkal. The creature approached knowingly, and he leapt onto his sloped back.

Ayva's lips pressed thin, and then she breathed a deep sigh and mounted her steed. "Then let's go, but think about this before you make your decision: If I am wrong, we lose a traveling companion, but if I'm right… You saw what she did to Gray and how she fought against Dalic. Let's hope I'm not right," she said with a shiver and dug her heels into the cormac's flanks.

Together, they raced back. As they left the moonlit clearing, Darius looked over his shoulder frequently, where the lone Silveroot and the majestic sword remained.

* * *

Gray felt Ayva and Darius before he saw them. They appeared out of the darkness, riding toward him. Despite the dim light, he saw the sternness in their faces, but he noticed Ayva held something in her hand. Swiftly, she dismounted and fell to his side.

"Is she…?"

"She's alive. For now," Gray answered.

Ayva looked down and stiffened, catching sight of his hands in the light of the flickering fire. They were covered in blood almost up to his elbows. He hadn't washed them yet, as he'd just finished. Gray extended his hand for her waterskin and she ignored it, moving around him to kneel at Faye's side. "I'll do it," she said firmly.

Darius cast him a strange, almost worried look, before dismounting.

Not knowing what to make of it, Gray knelt beside Ayva, watching as Faye's breathing came thinly. With a leftover waterskin, he washed the blood from his arms. Seeing it now, removed from the moment, anxiety filled him. It was hard to believe that so much blood was even in a person.

You did the best you could, Kirin whispered. It was kind, but it held no hope.

"Help me lift her up," Ayva instructed.

Darius fell to his knees, helping Gray lift Faye, setting blankets and bedrolls beneath her. With a swift and practiced hand, Ayva uncorked the flask, opened Faye's mouth, and poured the thick, silver liquid into it. Rolling in and out of consciousness, Faye gagged. She shivered, shaking her head and spitting out what little had gone down.

Ayva grabbed her chin firmly. "Drink," she pressed. "Drink, Sunha. Please…" Suddenly, miraculously, Faye's mouth opened, if only slightly, and Ayva poured. The liquid flowed, and Faye drank until the last drop. Gray and Darius exchanged curious looks.

"Sunha?" Gray asked.

"Something between me and her. A bargain, much like your blood pact. I call her Sunha, and she calls me Diaon."

"What does it mean?" Darius asked.

"Diaon means 'one who knows nothing'," Ayva answered softly, rising and putting the waterskin back in her cormac's pack.

"That's not very flattering," Darius mumbled, wisely beneath his breath.

Gray's eyes tightened, watching Ayva's back. He saw it took strength for Ayva to aid Faye, but now he saw its depth. The woman had taken everything from Ayva. Her knowledge was her passion and her confidence, and the woman had crushed it at every turn—pointing out every flaw and inaccuracy in Ayva's words about Farhaven. He cringed inwardly. *What a fool I am*, he realized. A part of him had hated Faye for superseding his role as the one with strength, for taking his confidence, but he saw now that Faye had taken so much more from Ayva.

Gray moved toward the water and began to wash the blood that was starting to dry on his hands. "What was the bargain?" he asked, but he had a feeling he already knew.

"To learn," Ayva said simply, still busying herself with the pack upon her cormac, keeping her back to him.

"Ayva," Gray said and rose. He touched her shoulder and she turned. Tears filled her blue eyes, and he felt his throat clench.

"Did you really think I would let her die?" she asked.

He shook his head. But part of him had wondered.

"I'm not evil," she said firmly.

"I know that, Ayva. I just..." He looked away then back at her. "I'm sorry. I should have trusted you."

"And why didn't you?" she questioned, tears now gone.

"Because you've changed," he said, speaking the words before thinking. A silence hung in the air as she looked at him, trying to gauge his tone. He wasn't sure how he meant it... It wasn't bad, was it? But that innocence. As he looked at her, he saw it fading like frost before the sun.

"I haven't changed," she said. "You have." But even as she said the words, she stood straighter and spoke clearer. Still, she touched his shoulder compassionately, letting him know she had not meant the words callously. The way she did that reminded him of someone.

Gray searched for words. "We need her, Ayva. Don't you see?"

"No, Gray. You need her."

He hesitated, for once his words falling short.

"I see it in your eyes. I know you, Gray, and I know why you think you need Faye."

"What do you mean?"

"Her darkness. You think it's like yours. You think if you can save yourself then you can save her just as easily. But you can't. Your heart, though once shrouded in shadows, is pure and full of light. It was only a veil of darkness. I've seen Faye's heart, and it is not pure." She shivered. "I don't know what happened to her, some evil training, but she is tainted and loyal to no one! She will betray us when she gets the chance."

"I can't believe that..." Gray said, shaking his head, and looking to Darius who sat back, watching the exchange with hard eyes. "You both saved me when I didn't believe in myself. You gave me hope. Faye needs that as well."

"No, she doesn't!" Ayva shouted. "Why do you persist in trying to change things that you cannot change?"

Gray swallowed, unable to answer. "It doesn't matter." Every word she said cut through him like a knife carving to his very core. He couldn't deny it. But it wasn't the whole truth.

"That's not it ... is it?" she asked, as if reading his mind. Ayva pressed closer. He nearly backed away. Something in the way she moved—fluid, strong, and purposeful. Her hand lingered on his arm as she looked deep into his eyes. "You still think you have a darkness inside you, don't you?"

"I don't know what I have inside me," he answered. "I am still Kail's progeny, Ayva, no matter what you say."

Nearby, he saw Darius shuffle uncomfortably. *Does he still fear me for that?*

Ayva smiled, touching his chest as she looked up at him. How could he ever think she was merely soft? Surely she was soft, but those eyes—they held a coldness too. Her father's death, her mother's... *How much has she sacrificed to be at my side?* She spoke, "Your darkness is gone, Gray. You're no longer bound by Morrowil's evil. Saving her does nothing for you. And..." she hesitated, "I think you believe Faye's redemption is also a way to absolve yourself of Vera's death."

"I..." he faltered. "I can't abandon her, especially not when she's injured. It doesn't feel right. Besides, she's promised peace."

"And that assuages your fears? Blood and flesh, Gray, the ones we need to fear *always* say that."

Gray hesitated, looking at the unconscious Faye. She looked peaceful.

Ayva spoke firmly. "Look at me, Gray."

He did, and he realized whose eyes they were. *Omni's*. It sent a shiver through him.

"You realize that *you* made the decision to have her with us. Come to think of it, you've made just about every decision since we've arrived in Farhaven." She pointed to all three of them. "But we're a team, Gray. We're all in this together. Sure we follow you because we believe in you, but when you make decisions like that, you put our lives in danger as well. And then you don't even consult us? It's just plain wrong."

She was right. He had made a decision without them, putting himself above them, and it wasn't right. He had to fix that, even if it meant doing something else that went against what he believed. "You're right."

Ayva's hand fell from his arm in shock. "I am?"

Again he nodded. "I should have asked you first. We'll put it to a vote," he said. "If Darius decides she should go, then that is what we'll do. Otherwise, she stays."

Darius leapt to his feet, raising his hands before him defensively, and shaking his head. "Oh no, you two aren't going to blame this on me."

"What do you mean?" Ayva asked.

"I don't like not being in the know on something, but this is different... No matter what I decide, I'm wronging one of you. No, sorry, I don't want any part of this. Keep Faye, lose Faye, I don't care, but don't make me decide or I'll just dicing choose to kick both of you out, and then we'll see—"

"—Darius," Gray said, interrupting the rogue's rant. "You have to choose. No one will blame you either way."

"You say that now," Darius grumbled.

"Please," Ayva said.

The rogue looked between the two, judging their hard eyes. At last, he sighed. "Fine, but this isn't fair." He eyed Faye who lay on the ground, unconscious. Darius scrubbed his chin, cursing to himself. Ayva's body tensed. "We go on without her," he said at last into the silence. Ayva breathed a heavy sigh of relief and embraced the rogue.

Gray felt a dark, emptiness inside him as soon as the words left Darius' mouth.

Darius pulled away. "But!"

"But what..." Ayva asked, obviously trying to contain her enthusiasm.

"We stay with her until she is no longer at death's door, leave her supplies enough that we are sure she is safe and, lastly, never ever put me in this position again."

Ayva nodded. "Deal."

Gray moved away. He felt a hand on his shoulder and turned to see Ayva.

"Gray..." she said, searching his eyes. "I'm sorry... But this *is* for the best."

He kept his face emotionless and gave a nod. He couldn't help but feel as if he had lost something. It wasn't just his stubbornness, was it? No, Faye somehow had become more than just an outsider, and she had done nothing wrong. Not yet at least. Leaving her like this... It felt wrong. "If you say so."

"Gray, don't be like that," Ayva said. "She is splintering us. I'm simply removing that splinter."

"Well, you convinced me," Darius said, lounging back down on his bedroll. "As long as we find a way to keep our hides intact and make it to Farbs without Faye. She seemed to know every danger these lands hold, and I hope I'm wrong but I've a gut feeling that desert ahead has a few surprises for us."

Ayva kept her hand on Gray's arm. "That's the thing, Darius, I've prepared for this. I've learned more in the past day or so than in all my time in Daerval. I know what lies ahead, at least enough to get us to Farbs. I promise."

Darius bolted up suddenly and moved to his cormac. "I'll be back. I forgot my... waterskin... back at that old stump." With that, he left.

What is he up to? Gray wondered. He knelt beside Faye, putting a hand to her tan skin. It was scorching hot. Grabbing a wet cloth, he patted her forehead. Nearby, he saw a flat piece of bark. On it, a sliver of steel lay covered in blood.

With a sigh, Gray rose, and Ayva touched his arm.

"Gray," she whispered.

He looked down into her eyes, gaze distant. "Yes?"

"Please, don't..." she said, pained. "I've seen that look of yours before. I don't like it."

Gray smiled. "You were right, Ayva. You don't have to worry." With that, he grabbed Morrowil. "I'll take first shift." And he left her there, looking to get away from that gaze and away from Faye. He needed time to think, to be alone.

You're always alone, Kirin whispered.

Gray felt a cold fury rise. The voice had helped him this night. He admitted there was no way he could have done what he had for Faye without Kirin's aid, but now it mocked him. He silenced it, closing his mind. Gray felt something break, like a door shattering and then laughter.

Kirin's.

You can't get rid of me that easily. The closer we get to Farbs, the stronger I become. Besides, you owe me. Don't forget that.

"I haven't forgotten," he said calmly, finding a rock to sit on and setting Morrowil on his lap, watching the darkness that no longer watched him. Nevertheless, he wished he had his power. Without it, he did not feel *whole*. It wasn't right that he had grown so accustomed to it, even reliant on it, and so quickly. *At least I have Morrowil*, he thought, feeling the smooth, white handle. He had a flashing memory of Death's Gate again. He recalled how the hilt had shattered as he had thrust the blade into the altar and stopped the Kage and the rising darkness, simultaneously. He eyed the snow-white handle that seemed to swirl as if made of slow-moving wind. Despite its silken feel, its grip was firm, almost tacky as if his hand and the hilt were one. While the original hilt had shattered, the elves had crafted a new one. Now it felt even more right than before. *What is broken can be remade*, he thought. *Reborn.*

He sensed a frustration inside him. Kirin was waiting for an answer.

Stars flickered above like frost bugs caught in a spider's black webbing. He replied, "I will repay my debt, and then I will cast you from me once and for all."

Kirin was silent, and then his voice came again, loud and near, as if a hot whisper in his very ear. *Ah, but soon you will meet me. Perhaps you will realize I am not something to fear, but to embrace.*

"We will see," Gray said and began his watch.

The Citadel

Cresting the giant dune, Gray pulled his cormac to a halt.

He couldn't believe his eyes.

Beyond the low, rolling mounds lay a vast city that sprawled for miles. He felt his mouth part in awe. Even from this distance, he could tell those walls were huge, perhaps even taller than the Shining City. Before the outer wall was a sea of green, blue, and red dots—tents and haphazard buildings, a ramshackle smaller city. *Smaller*, Gray scoffed. A dozen Lakewoods could fit within it with room to spare.

The kingdom took his breath away. "Farbs," he whispered.

Aside from colorful tents, the Kingdom of Fire blended with the endless desert. It reminded him of a flesh-colored awning, save for one building. A black structure rose above all others. The keep of the Citadel was like a patch of darkness the bright, desert sun had forgotten to banish.

He looked to Ayva at his side. Her eyes watered, taking it all in.

Darius whistled through his teeth. On his back he bore his strange new find. *A green sword?* Gray wondered. It seemed too coincidental. Not to mention, it reminded him of another man's sword. Maris' blade, called Masamune, had looked similar, if less ornate. The rogue had said few words about the blade otherwise, but had glared them each down as if expecting Gray to pry the leaf-shaped blade from his hands. It was almost too much to take in. All he knew for certain was that blade belonged to Darius, just as Morrowil belonged to him. Eyeing Farbs, Darius spoke in wonderment, "Look at that… I never imagined…"

"I had," Ayva said, shaking her head slowly. "I dreamed nearly every day, trying to picture, to *see* the Great Kingdoms in my mind—Eldas, Vaster, Seria, Narim, Lander, Covai, Yronia, and of course Morrow and Farbs. And now it's real," she whispered. "Finally."

Darius snorted, resuming his look of indifference, but he kept glancing at Farbs in fear and awe. "Now that we've seen it, we can go home, right?"

"This is just the beginning, Darius," Gray said, and prodded his cormac forward.

"Why do I feel like when you say that it's just another way of saying, 'Hey Darius, more daggers will be pressed to your neck'? Speaking of which, why is it always *my* neck? Maybe next time you can risk your neck and—"

Ayva let out a sudden, joyful cry, racing past them, galloping dangerously fast down the steep dune and raising billowing clouds of dust and sand. Any other animal would have broken its neck *and* hers, but the cormac took the decline easily.

Gray smiled, and Darius laughed at his side.

"Seems ditching Faye was a good idea after all," Darius said.

Swaying in his saddle, Gray swallowed. He eyed his hand upon the reins, seeing the mostly healed cut from Faye's dagger, and a memory took him.

Gray heard a rustle. His heart shot into his throat, and he twisted to see Faye's eyes crack open. She took in her surroundings. It was the same oasis, but they had set up camp a little more, with a lean-to tent to shelter their supplies, a bigger glowing fire, and a makeshift picket for their cormacs. Nearby, pots and pans hung from a nearby dola tree.

She sat up, squinting. "Gray…?"

He smiled. "Welcome back."

Faye groaned, falling back. She pushed back her scarlet hair, gazing up at the stars, wide-eyed. "I'm alive," she said, sounding … disappointed? No, that must have been his imagination.

"Barely," he answered.

"Where ... are the others?"

"Ayva is collecting food, and Darius is looking for more kindling."

"And you? You're just sitting here looking miserable while waiting to see if I die or not?"

"Something like that," he answered. It wasn't too far from the truth. He had grown more distant lately, watching Faye and waiting to see a change. He hadn't realized how attached to her he had become. Now, seeing her awake, he felt it was the first time he could smile in days.

Faye groaned. "Will you stop grinning like a fool? It's giving me a headache."

He stopped grinning, but laughed. "It's a pleasure to see you too."

"Something is chafing like cured leather undergarments," she grumbled and pushed back her blanket to see his handiwork, eyeing the now bandaged shoulder. It was bloody. You'll have to change it soon, Kirin whispered. "Where did you learn to do this?"

"Impressed?"

"Not really," she said. "I could have done better while unconscious, but..." She hesitated. "I suppose it's not that bad. Thank you." Her hard eyes softened, if only for a moment.

Gray looked away, feeling his heart race. He chastised himself. It reminded him too much of Vera's effect, though Faye didn't seem to be doing it intentionally. At last, he shrugged. "It wasn't my doing, really. But I'm just glad you're not dead."

"That's the sweetest thing anyone has ever said to me," she said.

He almost laughed, but it died in his throat. She wasn't kidding, was she?

"I'm joking, Gray. Mostly."

He cleared his throat, nodding.

Faye sighed and moved to rise.

Gray was quicker though. He pushed her shoulder down, gently but firm. "You're not going anywhere. You need to rest, Faye, just as I did. Unless you plan on limping to Farbs?"

"Familiar words," she said with a smirk, and then sighed again. "Watching over me like this, I've a sinking feeling this is going to go to your head."

He hid a smile. "Probably."

"I'll be well tomorrow. Then I'll make you pay for it in training."

"Training?"

Faye sniffed. "Don't think I've forgotten your lessons just because I was about to die. Si'tu'ah awaits, apprentice. And you are getting better, but you are still not a Devari. And don't forget, even with my help, you will always have to avoid some, like the Leader of the Devari, or you will not survive a day in the Kingdom of Fire."

Gray choked, and averted his gaze. "I won't forget." He rose. "You should rest now, we'll talk tomorrow." Without another word, he moved into the darkness and away.

Something touched his arm, the vision broke, and he found himself staring into Ayva's compassionate blue eyes. He realized she had pulled back, letting Darius ride on ahead. "You look troubled," she said, emotions churning behind her eyes. *What is she thinking?* he wondered.

Without thinking, Gray delved into her thoughts using his ki, and nearly gasped. *Such light…* But beneath that gleaming beacon, he felt worry and a strange desire. It was a yearning to mend, as if she gazed upon a broken pot. *Mend what though?*

You, you fool, Kirin answered.

Gray squinted, hesitating. He wanted to mend what was between them too, but he wondered how much Ayva thought their fissure was *his* error, as if *he* were the broken one and not their joint failing. He felt suddenly slighted by Ayva's gaze.

A fool's distinction, Kirin said. Gray was growing tired of the voice calling him a fool.

"I'm not a broken pot," he said calmly.

He retreated from her mind. Though ki was not an intrusion exactly, more like a higher understanding of another's feelings, he still felt guilty, as if he had pilfered her thoughts.

"I'll be fine," he replied at last. Despite the darkness and guilt he felt, somehow he did believe those words. This path, it felt more right with each passing day. Now seeing Farbs, his task solidified. A new purpose filled him, one that he'd been waiting for… waiting since the day he had to flee Farbs and Farhaven and cross Death's Gate into Daerval.

That was the day his life had started.

After traveling for a while, the sun sank below the sand's horizon, and they slowed on a small plateau that looked out over the city. Gray halted. "We're still hours away. We'll camp here tonight, outside the Gates," he announced. He looked at the two of them, remembering the promise he'd made. *We're a team.* "If that's all right?" he added.

Ayva smiled. "Much better. We'll teach you yet."

Darius was already dismounting. "Fine by me." After their makeshift camp was set up, Darius plopped down nearby, humming a simple tune to himself as he began to whittle:

"Oh, simple path,
You hold no sway—

Oh, darkness too,
You'll find no hold.

Oh, cloud and mist,
I push on through.

But sweet face, you vixen you,
You hold my gaze, and true heart too!"

Gray saw the wood was finally starting to resemble a pipe. Though he was bone-tired, Gray eyed Farbs, hesitating with his hand upon his pack. Something told him the night wasn't over.

"Gray…"

He turned.

Gently, Ayva took his wrist, pulling back his sleeve to reveal the sinuous black tattoo. "Have you thought about how we're going to get around that? Karil said that Farbs doesn't allow outsiders, and we won't be able to enter the Citadel without your mark…"

He shook his head. "I have a few ideas, but nothing certain."

"Faye might have known," Darius suggested, not looking up from his pipe.

Ayva opened her mouth, but Gray spoke first. "That path is behind us. She can no longer hold our hand. This is our task, and we must look forward. I think I know how to get us inside Farbs. Once we're inside the walls, we'll gather information as best we can and figure out the Citadel and how to get inside." He kept his face smooth and voice strong, but inwardly he wavered.

In a new world and a new city, how many mistakes could they make? For all he knew, a single question to the wrong person could mean death. But they had made their decision. They would find a way, with or without Faye.

Darius and Ayva nodded firmly, looking buoyed by his words.

"One question," Darius said, looking up. "What exactly *is* our plan? You know, generally speaking."

"To discover the old me," Gray answered, lying.

"That's enough for me," Darius said with a shrug.

Ayva's eyes didn't let him go though. She whispered so the rogue couldn't hear. "What's your real reason? Last time I checked, you were done with your old self." Occupied with his pipe, Darius didn't seem to notice.

"I'm done with my old self but, unfortunately, it's not done with me. I have to figure out what happened all those years ago."

"And?" she asked.

"And… I'm going to look for the prophecy that named me in The Knife's Edge."

"Why?"

"I have a feeling it's not done with me either," he answered darkly. "Something in what Vera said…"

Ayva smiled in the darkness. "Whatever your mission, we're by your side."

He touched her arm warmly and smiled, thanking her. For the first time, he felt a spark return between them as she smiled back. They set up watches, deciding against a fire to avoid being seen by any unwanted eyes from the city, and settled down for sleep.

Gray took first watch. Again, he needed time to think. He stared at the city, watching as it darkened, and then, like a sun illuminated, the whole thing came to life, glowing like a thousand yellow frost bugs. His breath was taken by it, amazed as he was to be here and seeing it at long last.

Ayva sat up in her bed with a sigh. "It's beautiful."

Darius merely cursed, rolling over in his sack and facing away.

"I'm not sure I can even sleep," Ayva whispered, lying in her bed. "I'm too nervous and excited."

Gray heard snoring. Darius was already asleep, he realized, the rogue's snores carrying over the sands. *How is he so loud?* Half-jokingly, he hoped the fool's saw-like snores didn't alert any guards from Farbs.

"You should find rest where you can," he advised, gripping Morrowil tightly, watching the golden city. It was like a lantern in the night. It looked so welcoming from there, but he knew the truth. "We will need it, all of us. Tomorrow we begin the next step of our journey." Gray looked over his shoulder and realized Ayva was asleep as well, whispering soft words as she slumbered.

Despite his serene surroundings, Gray was glad to take first watch, as sleep seemed far away, and he felt overwhelmed by it all. He breathed in the scents of the warm, dry air, listening to the faint song of insects, but mostly he liked the quiet. He savored it, knowing it was the last moment of silence for a long while. Inevitably, however, his gaze fell to the city in nervous excitement. "I can't believe it…" he whispered to himself. *I'm actually here.* His home, his birthplace, sat before him like a treasure chest waiting to be opened. His answers.

And tomorrow, you will see me… Kirin said. Emotion had returned to his voice. He sounded eager, calm, and confident, like a grizzled warrior preparing at dawn's light for the coming battle.

And Gray whispered in reply, "I'm ready."

The Voidstone

Ezrah sat hunched over the ancient tome.

He cursed softly. What *was* he looking for?

Soft light flickered from his lantern as it sat nearby on the polished table. The table was worn and smoothed by touch from centuries of use. The flame in the glass lantern was real, though it was fueled by his power. He'd made sure it was soft and white—a perfect hue for reading. Otherwise, aside from several orange flames in brackets upon the walls, the library was shrouded in darkness.

He was in the most restricted library of the Citadel, high in the dark keep, a place of power and knowledge. Only Arbiters and their servants were allowed here. It was the most secure place in the entire castle.

He turned the page. It crinkled, crisp and brown from age—perhaps the oldest book in the entire Citadel. That made it one of the most ancient tomes in all of existence. Still, it held nothing. He gave a thin sigh and pushed it aside.

He looked up.

Outside, the city shone golden.

Farbs.

It was a dangerous and beautiful city. He loved the Great Kingdom of Fire, but dark events now conspired in the heart of his home.

He sought to put an end to it. He would not let the world be consumed by shadow. It seemed hard to believe, seeing the lights and beauty outside that large, paned window. A city full of life. Beyond the walls, in the city itself, people amassed in celebration. He could almost hear the sounds of laughter and cheers as a round of fireworks exploded in the night, illuminating the sky a bright red.

The Festival of the Moon.

It was the reason there were no guards watching the far door, and no red-liveried servants to dust the nearby shelves. It was utterly quiet. The shadows nearby reminded Ezrah of his duty. Drawing a deep breath, he grabbed another book from his large stack. *Tu Redghao a' Yronia* read its spine with faded gold lettering, or, in the common tongue: *The Reliquaries of Yronia*. It was about the Great Hold, the treasury of the Kingdom of Metal, home to the Ronin once-named Baro. Yronia was no more, sadly. It was one of the few Great Kingdoms out of the nine that had been destroyed in the great war of the Lieon. Backed against the Summits of Soot was a cloudy mountain range, resembling and named after the white soot that used to burn from the once-famous Great Forge of Yronia. It still existed, but the city had been abandoned since the war. He had seen it, long ago. The kingdom now was little more than a ruined mass of steel, its great walls twisted and melted while wind blew hollowly through its cavernous insides.

The tome in Ezrah's hands was old, but not nearly as old as the others. He almost set it aside, but hesitated. He had heard faint rumors of dark things stirring in the Kingdom of Yronia. Perhaps…

He peeled back its heavy cover and read. Time passed, and he grew engrossed in the pages with their ancient objects of magic: A long and plain rod of silver that could divine the truth in words when both bearers touched it; an intricate statue of a woman holding a baby that could make *something* grow faster—what it grew exactly Ezrah couldn't decipher; a cone-shaped object made of purple metal that could alter one's voice—or simply amplify or nullify all sound in a room. Nearly all were objects of great magic, and all were lost to the sands of time. Each had been created long ago when Reavers were at their most powerful. Ezrah felt his blood stir. He wished he'd been alive to question those ancient Reavers and their vast knowledge. Of course, one man *had* been alive since the Lieon. The Patriarch, ruler of the Citadel, still lived.

Ezrah turned the page.

A flush of blue light emanated from the pages where a brilliant illustration of an azure orb was drawn. Faint lines of dark blue and white were etched into its surface like cracks. Ezrah realized his heart was thundering as he read, fingers following the lines of text.

'*At last, after dark months of endless trial and error, it is done. It is an object not of creation, but of utter destruction. As anticipated, the stone consumes, eating like a ravenous beast. We had intended it to be a weapon against the dark Ronin—the ones we now call Kage—to drain them. But even the wisest among us did not foresee the fatal flaw. All life contains the spark.*

Upon its creation, it fed upon those nearest, killing them all. The greater the power, the greater the devastation. Realizing our fault only too late, we attempted to destroy it. To date, all efforts have been futile. Now, after nearly a hundred deaths of our brothers and sisters at the hands of this instrument of death, The Order has ruled unanimously: we will lock it away in the deepest, darkest vault we know. This journal is the only testament of its existence. Of those that still live, all have been sworn to secrecy. We now bury it never to be opened again, beneath steel and stone, locked away with powerful magic within the Great Hold. May none ever have to gaze upon its deathly glow again, and may light send this object to the depths of hell.'

Beneath the entry, in huge, dark, bold text, were the words:

THE VOIDSTONE MUST NEVER BE USED.

He hesitated, fingers pausing. Ezrah looked up from the page, feeling sweat bead upon his brow. What had they done? He thought. What was the voidstone? He knew sacrifices had been made during the Lieon, great sacrifices, and he'd heard of objects of war created to battle the overwhelming forces of evil, but this? It had sounded like they had created an object to end all life. *Desperation makes a smart man become a fool*, he quoted the Patriarch, knowing it all too well himself. He looked at the nearby shadows and flickering flames upon the walls.

It was too quiet.

Ezrah's jaw tightened. He lifted the white flame out of its glass container. It floated forward, and he let it bloom, growing and illuminating the ancient library. The shadows receded, showing seemingly endless rows of shelves, stacked with books upon books. The walls were lined all the way to the high ceilings. The musty scent of worn pages hung in the air, but, otherwise, there was nothing.

No, Ezrah thought. *Something doesn't feel right.*

He twisted, looking to the only door in the room, a huge arched entrance made of Silveroot. It was reinforced with a heavy metal bar and a ward of magic. Silence. He closed his eyes and sifted his senses, feeling the stone beneath his feet. He slid the sensation outward and beneath the door. He felt the pressure of feet on stone. Someone was there, and they were coming. Immediately, his power flooded through him, filling him with life as it always did. Yet something staggered in his mind as he reached to touch the spark. Pulling upon his experience, he held on.

As he did, his mind railed. *How is it possible?* He'd set up countless wards along the hall. *Not to mention, I should have felt another wielder of the spark and…* In the corner of his vision, the page glowed blue.

The door burst, splinters flying.

Something flew through the air. A dagger. The steel froze right before his throat, and he quickly twisted threads of steel to send it flying back. Ezrah heard a dying grunt, but he didn't hesitate. He began threading other elements. Fire mixed with stone flew from his hand forming globes of angry, molten stone, racing towards the now vacant door that exploded upon impact. He felt heat on his face as his robes were singed, but he didn't flinch. The fire receded and shadows stepped through the doorway. Ezrah faltered, but only for a split-second. With threads of Leaf he hefted huge bookshelves into the air, then hurled them like arrows. As they hit the shadows, he ignited them in a roar of flames. More figures appeared in a black mist. He felt the stone beneath.

Still, nearly a dozen.

You cannot fight this, his mind yelled.

With that thought, Ezrah ran. Without looking behind him, he threaded the stone in the ceiling and brought it down on his assailants, but more still came. He weaved between tall bookracks, extracting threads of water from the air behind him and setting them aflame, creating a steam that made it hard to see with the naked eye. He heard the cries and shouts of his attackers, and he stopped momentarily to touch the ground beneath him and sense their numbers when, suddenly, his power stuttered, falling short. In nearly five hundred years of life, he'd never felt anything like it. *What am I fighting?* And despite all his power and strength, he felt weak. He pushed it aside. Vaulting past rows and rows of books, he headed deeper into the ancient library.

With his heart pounding, he pulled for his power again as he ran. Luckily, it came. He removed brackets of metal from nearby bookshelves and, with a quick plying of threads, he fashioned them into spikes and laid them upon the ground.

I've only to wait until Devari or other Reavers are alerted.

Passing small windows, he saw more fireworks explode in the sky and he remembered. The grassy grounds of the Citadel were empty. No guards, Devari, or Reavers would be roaming these high quarters, and those who had remained would not hear a thing over the explosion of fireworks and festivities.

He was alone.

Ezrah reached a sudden wall. He looked around. Only shadows. *Have my traps worked?* His breathing was too loud, and he used a trick he'd learned as a Neophyte, twisting threads of flesh and expanding his throat to soften his heavy breathing.

He put a hand to the stone wall. A corridor lay beyond. He would need more of the spark, and he pulled upon the silken pool in his mind. It was placid normally, but now it was tumultuous as a tidal wave that threatened to crash. As he had done a thousand times, he summoned a roar of power. It flushed through his limbs. Pressing a hand to the wall, he dissolved stone. Suddenly, a chunk of the wall before him disappeared, as if the doorway had been there all along. He stepped through to the lit corridor. Then he looked back and filled in the hole. The wall was seamless once more. He let out a breath of relief, glad to be out of that dark room when…

Ezrah gasped. Something came over him. His pool of power rattled, growing hotter, burning and searing his mind. He fell to one knee and looked up just as a hunched figure rounded the corner at the far end of the hall, his mottled red and white robes whisking. His staggered gait halted and, despite the distance, he *felt* a smile crease the crooked man's features when a dozen shadowy figures materialized at his side wearing strange black armor that was molded to their skin. Ezrah's heart darkened. *Nameless*—Reavers who were twisted to the dark in the great war. Gritting his teeth, he rose. It felt as if a mountain of stone sat upon his shoulders, weighing him down.

A soft clap resounded through the lit hall.

"Well done," the man said with a greasy smile as he walked forward. That's when Ezrah saw it. From the folds of his sullied white robes, the man extracted a palm-sized orb of feverish blue, holding it aloft. It pulsated, filling the hall with azure light. Even from this distance, Ezrah saw silver and dark blue cracks along its surface. It seemed to crackle with power, as if *feeding*.

The voidstone.

As the man approached, Ezrah drew upon his power. All the while, he kept his face smooth, feigning defeat. The spark wavered, but it came. He closed his eyes. *Give me everything*, he requested. Drawing a long breath, he dredged deep, pulling his power into him. It came in a rush and filled him, but he asked for more. It seeped into every pore, flowed into every crevice, permeating him with translucent light. He felt as though, if he opened his eyes, he would see himself glowing. He asked for more. He reached into his very soul, soaking in every last drop. At last he opened his eyes, and prepared threads the size of mountains that would level everything in their path—that would bring the massive Citadel to the ground. For he knew that object of power could not be taken, and must not be used.

Life itself hung in the balance.

The man was almost to him, unaware of what brewed inside him. Ezrah kept his face calm despite the torrent of power that thundered through him, waiting until he was nearly a dozen feet away. And then, he struck. Accepting his death, Ezrah let his power explode. He gasped as it charged out in a surge of light and darkness. His body filled with agony, and the spark in his mind burned like a conflagration. Then, there was darkness.

At last, he *felt* something. *Strange.* He should feel nothing. All he saw was darkness, but through it Ezrah felt... Pain. It was sharp and excruciating, like daggers pressed into his flesh. He opened his eyes despite the stabbing pain and saw the bloodstained hem of robes dusting along the stone. He was still alive; the Citadel was still here. Ezrah tried to speak. "I..." his voice was hoarse, barely audible.

A hand grabbed his hair, pulling him up, and he looked into soulless brown eyes. The Nameless at his side didn't even seem as empty as this man. "That was … impressive," the man said.

The man's black hair dangled about his pale face. His expression—nose wrinkled and eyes sharp like beads of dark glass—reminded Ezrah of a rat. Along with his hunched posture, Ezrah half-expected a tail to squirm from behind the man. He nodded slightly, and two of the Nameless standing beside him disappeared into mist and reappeared again behind him, dragging him to his feet. At the man's hip, his hand rested casually on the wire-wrapped handle of a long sword. His boots were oiled and black as night, as were his leather pants. Worst of all were his robes, making Ezrah's body coil in rage and disgust. They might have been white at one time, but now reminded him of a butcher's apron soaked in blood—some of those dark red splotches still appeared wet as if recent and not given time to dry. The man surveyed Ezrah with those empty eyes. "I am Sithel," he announced, a false smile adorning his thin lips. He cocked his head to one side. "You haven't noticed yet, have you?"

Then it hit him. Ezrah reached for the spark but… "My power…"

"It's still there, but it's fleeing," Sithel stated. "Perhaps you can catch it."

Sithel was right. The spark was receding, racing away. *A trap?* His mind shouted. *It doesn't matter. Without the spark…* The thought was too terrifying, and he shot after it. Ezrah reached out mentally, but the spark raced away. He pushed harder, deeper, digging into the dark recesses of his mind. He almost had it, almost felt it, life and warmth flickered, but it slipped, brushing past his fingers. Deeper he pressed, into the bottomless pit of his mind, but it was too fast. In the moment before it collapsed, he sent out a message, jumbled, but strong. He shot it towards a knot in his mind, a portion of himself that he had been unable to reach until recently.

At last, dwindling to a tiny dot, his power was gone. Despair hit Ezrah like a building collapsing upon him. *I am an Arbiter,* he thought forcefully. *I will not fall here.* But without the spark what was he really? He tried to maintain his calm, but it shattered.

"Is it gone?" Sithel asked.

Ezrah merely stared at him, pure hatred and despair battling inside of him.

Sithel shrugged. "I suppose that's confirmation enough. You should be glad you're not dead. One as powerful as you should have died instantly being this close to the voidstone." He hefted the terrible, dark blue orb. It sucked at the light of the room. He felt it eating away at him, as if devouring his life force. "A pity too. I was told that if you died it would be *unfortunate,* but only that. Now that you live? Well, now I must keep you alive—if you behave."

Ezrah remained silent, his despair still welling, and beneath that … pain, excruciating and sharp. His body pleaded for him to end it all, but to that too, he remained stubbornly silent and unyielding. "I see that look in your eyes, Arbiter," Sithel continued. "It's the same look they all get. None seem to care much about life without the spark. The stronger the spark, the greater they wish for death. Yet I'm surprised by you…" his gaze narrowed, as if trying to comprehend. "You would think, with your level of strength, you would be practically begging me for death."

"You… first…" Ezrah managed. *Oh gods, why does it hurt so much? Isn't the spark gone?*

Sithel laughed, slightly. "Amusing. Well, perhaps you are stronger than the others in more than just the spark."

"What do you want?" Ezrah breathed. He was a limp weight in the Nameless' grip, and he barely felt their knife-like fingers clawing into his arms.

"It's not so much what I want, but what my master wants… No, what he *will* have. I will attempt to break you, but you are just one piece of the puzzle, a small means to a much greater end," Sithel spoke, rolling the voidstone from hand to hand. "With this finally in our grasp, we will be able to take even the most powerful and bring them to their knees, cowering. But again, even that is just one small thread in the fabric that *he* weaves."

"What does he seek?" Ezrah pressed.

"Dominion."

"Why?" he croaked.

Sithel snorted. "Does it matter? All that matters is that he *will* have it."

Ezrah knew this had been coming. He'd read it in the prophecies, seen it from every angle, felt the darkness rising over the centuries. Even before he helped Kirin, now Gray, flee the Citadel and run to

Daerval, he knew this was coming. But to see the pieces unfolding before him? It was too soon.

"We know you've been plotting against him, seeking to rectify the darkness he spreads, but you are merely a weed. The Kage—"

"—The Kage are dead," Ezrah snapped. "A failed plot of your master."

Sithel's eyes glinted darkly. "Ah, but the Kage were just the beginning, Arbiter. A mere torch that announced *his* hand. A hand that will set the world aflame. And just as the voidstone drains the spark from any but the one who holds it, he will drain the world until there is nothing left. Without the Ronin, there is no one to stand against him now."

Ezrah's eyes flashed, betraying him. He looked away, but it was too late.

Sithel laughed, throwing his head back. It filled the brightly lit hallway. "You are a fool. Again you think to hide what we already know. All along he's seen your plans, allowing you to continue, but only recently you moved too boldly."

Recently… Ezrah's mind clicked, recalling the boy.

Sithel gave another thin-lipped smile. "When you made your move in the marketplace, he decided it was time. We will find the boy soon, one way or another. It is already in motion. Your plan to reunite the reborn Ronin is futile. It will fail, just as surely as you have failed."

Ezrah felt the last dredges of his life being sapped. He suddenly saw it—an essence in the air, flowing from him into the sapphire orb. *His life*. "The prophecy…" he choked past his pain. *"It will… see you undone. There is… always a way."*

Again Sithel cackled. "You mean the Knife's Edge? Not this time, old man. My master did not anticipate that boy before or your tenacity. But this time, it is all accounted for now. This time, the prophecy is irrefutable."

Pain consumed him, becoming too much. *"The world… will know…"*

"The other Great Kingdoms?" Sithel asked calmly. "They will be just as powerless."

"*I…*" His vision began to fade.

"The best part is that no one will know you are gone. You keep to yourself in places no one can go," Sithel explained with a laugh. "You are the second most powerful wielder of the spark in all the world, and no one will even miss you."

And there, Sithel was wrong. Even as all turned to black, and agony seared his mind and body, Ezrah had one last thought, one last flickering hope. With the last bit of his power, before he had lost the spark completely, he had sent a message. Now that he was close, the presence, like a small knot in his mind, had returned, despite the pendant being broken…

Gray was there.

Save me, Ezrah had sent.

* * *

Gray was standing amid a small stone room. The wall was heavily curved, and based on the smaller neatly joined stonework… *I'm high in a tower*, Kirin whispered, familiar with keeps and battlements.

Nearby was a small wood board with glass figurines. A *game*, he realized. It looked like someone was still playing. But where were they? Against the far wall was a large table of strange white wood, polished to a glow. Aside from the walls filled with books, and a soft rug beneath his boots, the room was empty. Outside, rain fell lightly.

"Where am I?" But Kirin was silent now.

The room was very familiar, yet when he tried to remember, nothing came. He moved to touch a figurine on the board. A squat orange piece that looked like a flame. His hand reached out and—

Gray!

His mind flashed, something sparking in his head like a firework. Not pain, but urgency. He twisted, but saw nothing, only tomes and a wooden door. *Maybe it came from outside?* he wondered, moving to the door, but with his first step, the world flickered. With his next, the stone around him crumbled, falling away.

Air and noise, time and space distorted as he fell into a void of black. Gray felt his mind ripping. He shouted, but nothing sounded. *This is a dream*, he thought forcefully, forcing himself to wake but, still, darkness buried all sight. He felt as if he were moving, wind coursing around him with the speed of flight. As if he was being dragged *somewhere*.

At last, it settled, and Gray saw light.

He focused, as if peering through a tempest of wind.

Figures stood in a white hall.

All but one wore pitch-black armor. Shadows breathed from their lithe frames, and Gray's blood froze. In their clawed grips, a man hung half-dead. Straggled silver hair fell about his face. Those features... They were familiar, yet not.

Hunched over him, was a seedy-looking man in a black coat. Gray watched as the man limped forward, and his pale, sickly complexion, cast in ominous blue, twisted in satisfaction. He spoke, thin lips curled in a cruel smile. Gray tried to listen, but noises jumbled together as if he listened through a tunnel of wind. In the man's hand, a bright blue light pulsated.

The nearly dead man looked up, eyes staring into his soul.

"Save me," the man whispered, but his lips didn't move.

Gray felt terror in the sending.

Flash.

Gray was standing in a chamber. It was the same one from his vision in the desert, but this time it was clearer. The room was circular and windowless. Four men and four women stood in a circle around... something... Gray needed to get closer to see. He moved, walking without walking. He saw the body. The tortured man. Gray's skin crawled. It was the same man. He was stripped down, brown and white robes pulled to his waist. Red marks flayed his body as if from a whip, and his silver hair fell across his face. Beneath him, a star was inlaid on the marble floor in black and red glass with eight points. On each point was a symbol, and on each symbol one of the robed men or women stood. Even through the blurry, tempest-filled vision, he saw their looks of concentration. Horror filled him.

The old man's eyes were closed, his screams now silenced.

Was he ... dead?

Gray... The word came, faint and fractured and anguished. Gray clutched his heart. How? How could he bear such agony? *Who* was this man? *Remember...* The man breathed, and something sparked in his mind.

Memories.

Pain flooded through Gray. He fell to his knees, in front of the man who was being tortured, but in his mind Gray was remembering the past. He opened his eyes, seeing through a haze of tears, and he had one single, burning thought. At the same time, wind began to fissure around him, crackling. The circular room and scarlet-robed men and women distorted like wet paint running, and then finally it shattered.

The vision burst. Gray jolted upright. His breathing was ragged, and he held his heart, still feeling pain and sorrow spiraling through him as reality settled back around him.

The desert was quiet.

Sweat ran down his temples, mingling with his hair. The night was still cold, but Gray threw back his covers. Nearby, Ayva and Darius were still sleeping, though the rogue's snores rumbled like rocks down a hillside. Gray touched the ground as if to reaffirm it, forcing his thoughts back to the moment and away from the nightmare. But he knew it was more than just a nightmare. Just as he knew who that man was.

"Ezrah…" he whispered.

Save me… The words lingered in the air, like a faint echo.

And Gray answered, "I'm coming for you."

A Citizen of Farbs

Darius woke and wordlessly began packing up the camp. There wasn't much to do and, soon enough, he was brushing down Mirkal and preparing to head out. The others were still asleep. He'd have to wake them up soon. He looked over his shoulder and saw Ayva stir. She looked so peaceful just lying there—her mouth parted slightly, hair draped across her delicate features. *Why am I thinking like that?* Well, she was beautiful, just … not his type.

He looked to Gray. He slept like a stone, as if dead. Even his brows were bunched, as if he were *always* deep in thought. *Even while sleeping?* A man has to let go *sometimes.* There was a rustle, and, when he spun, Ayva stood before him. When had she awoken? He looked down, and realized she was still in her shift. Blood rushed to Darius' head. That thin white cloth didn't hide much. He could see her outline clearly, slender body with curves and all. He gulped. "Ayva…" he breathed. She put a finger to his lips and pressed closer. Her finger was warm, or was it cold? He couldn't tell.

He looked over her shoulder. Gray was still asleep.

"He doesn't have to know," she whispered, brazenly, though a bashful spot of red colored her cheeks.

All words fled Darius' mind. What was wrong with him? A beautiful girl was standing before him. Nothing was wrong with that, was it?

“Stop thinking so much,” she said.

What *was* wrong with him? That was *his* line. He growled in reply. “I’m not. It’s just, this is … unexpected.”

“Isn’t that your style?” she asked.

He smiled wryly. “Maybe a little. But…”

She drew near, silencing him, pulling her body against his.

Warm.

Reaching out, he gripped her waist, accepting her.

A sharp pain pierced his side, then Ayva, Gray, and all else faded abruptly. Darius’ eyes snapped open. Light blinded him, and he grunted. He looked up and saw Gray’s face smiling down on him. “Good morning.”

Darius groaned. A *dream?* “Why’d you kick me?”

“That was me,” a soft voice said. Looking into the light of the sun, Ayva’s face slowly resolved itself as she blocked out the burning orb. Her lips curved in amusement. “Did I break you from a pleasant dream?”

“I…” he faltered.

“You were grinning. It must have been good,” Gray said.

“It *was* pleasant.” *More or less,* he added inwardly, feeling confused and still trying to slow his racing heart.

Gray laughed and moved away.

“Wake up, Darius. You have to see what Gray has done,” Ayva said excitedly. She was wearing a strange get up. Lately she wore a split riding skirt, but now she had on fitted tan pants and a soft white shirt. Over it was a golden jacket with a few obscure symbols upon its hem. It seemed familiar.

“What’s with the getup?” he asked.

“I’m a citizen of Farbs, just like you’re about to be,” she answered, twirling in display, “Like it?”

“It… suits you,” he admitted.

She beamed and asked, “What was your dream?”

“My dream?” he repeated, looking around. The camp had been packed up and even Mirkal waited, prancing his hooves, excited to move. A lie ran through his head. *A serving girl had just given me a big portion of mutton and…* He stopped his mind. “It was nothing.”

“No?”

Gray tossed him something and Darius caught it. "What's all this?"

"Your clothes," Gray answered.

Darius held up a shirt that was a green so bright it hurt his eyes. "Where did you get this?"

"I couldn't sleep," Gray answered.

"So you decided to become a seamstress?" he questioned.

Ayva was practically bouncing on her toes, pawing at her newfound clothes. "If so, then it's safe to say he's one talented spinster. They're perfect..." A dreamy light entered her eyes, that faraway look she got sometimes, which Darius was growing oddly fond of as she whispered, more to herself, "It's just like I always imagined."

She *did* look great in it, and… *No.* Darius shook his head. Something wasn't right. "You stole these, didn't you?" he asked Gray sharply.

Gray nodded. "For once, you're right."

Darius scrubbed his chin, looking to Ayva. "And you're all right with this?"

Ayva blushed. "Well, I'm not exactly *happy* about it. But what's done is done, and it was necessary."

He grimaced. *Necessary*… Darius hesitated. Though Gray looked eager and almost impatient, there were dark circles around his eyes. "What has gotten into you? You look exhausted. And this was risky. What if you had gotten caught? You've become an increasing fool lately and…" he silenced himself, realizing there was heat in his voice. Why was he angry? He was thinking too much. This act was exactly something he would have done at one time not long ago. He turned away.

He felt a hand upon his arm and saw Gray's smile. "You're right, Darius. It was foolish and reckless, and I should have consulted you two first. Of course, I fear we will have to do more of these acts if we are to succeed in Farbs, but this was necessary."

"What happened?" Darius questioned, seeing through his words.

Ayva raised a brow. "What do you mean? Gray has simply found a way in."

He shook his head. "No, Darius is right. Something has happened, and I have to tell you about it. Both of you. Please sit," he said, motioning to the ground.

"I'm fine standing," Darius said.

Ayva raised a brow at him but quietly sat. "What happened?"

Gray took an even breath and spoke, "Last night, I had a dream. But it was more than just a dream. It was a vision," he said and pulled from his pocket what appeared to be dust as if ground from stone. "This was a shattered pendant I'd carried until yesterday. When I awoke, it was simply dust. Before it was turned to dust, it held magic, and through it I received a message."

"What kind of message?" Ayva asked.

"A man spoke to me. As he spoke, my past spoke as well."

Unexpectedly, Ayva tensed. *Fear? What is she afraid of?* Darius wondered. "You remember your past?" Ayva asked with trepidation.

Gray shook his head. "No, not yet. But I remember this man."

"Who is he?" Darius questioned.

"His name is Ezrah. He's my grandfather."

"Your grandfather?" Ayva repeated, "That's… I can't believe it! I'm so happy for you, Gray!"

Gray smiled, but then a dark look came over his features like a shadow. "I wish that were all... Ezrah is being held captive. I saw an image of a room and eight wielders of the spark torturing him for information as we speak."

Horrified, Ayva put a hand over her mouth.

Silence settled and Darius strode forward and gripped his arm. "I'm sorry for questioning you. I should have known you would only take such risks out of dire need."

"You were right to question," Gray said. "I would have done the same. But I know now what I have to do."

"And I'm with you."

"Right," Ayva agreed, "But what's our plan? How do we get him back?"

"That's the thing… I figured out our entry into Farbs after stealing these from a clothesline at the border of the outer city last night, but I still don't know where Ezrah is located."

"What did the room look like?" Darius asked. Gray described it in detail and he nodded. "That's enough information for me. Let's get a move on." Quickly, he changed into the green clothes. *Why does it have to be green?* he thought with a grimace. *Why not black or even a drab white?* He hated green. Well, his cloak was different, but at least that was fine, dark green wool and not this silly bright stuff. Darius moved to his cormac, grabbing his sword.

Ayva raised a hand. "Just wait a moment, Darius!"

"What?" he asked, leaping upon Mirkal.

"What are you thinking?" Gray asked hesitantly.

Upon his steed, Darius smirked. "Get us inside the gates, Gray, and I will find out where your grandfather is held. I can't promise we'll get to him in time, but if this city looks anything like I anticipate, it'll be full of thieves' dens and shady inns—a ripe fruit for the picking when it comes to information," he said, spinning upon Mirkal, feeding off the beast's excited energy, or perhaps it was feeding off of him. "Well, are you ready?"

Both Ayva and Gray looked dumbfounded.

"Trust me," he said, holding Gray's gaze.

Gray nodded at last, taking to his mount.

Ayva grumbled something and then threw up her hands. "Well, no use arguing," she said and leapt upon her cormac smoothly. "Lead the way, fearless leader," she said sarcastically.

Darius made an overly elegant bow and looked ahead.

To Farbs.

* * *

After several hours of riding, they neared the city. Though Farbs had looked huge and near, Darius had realized it was deceptive. It was further away than he'd imagined, and, as a result, far larger.

They approached, entering the outer city and, despite the warm air, a chill entered Darius, as if diving into a frozen lake. Behind him, Ayva and Gray rode, watching their surroundings. *What has gotten into me? he thought, I'm parading around like some sort of fool hero. That's supposed to be Gray's job.*

As soon as they passed the first few blue and green tents he realized their mistake. Men and women stared at them, eyeing their Elvin steeds as if gazing upon royalty.

"They aren't used to the cormacs," Gray whispered. "Perhaps we can stable the animals once we get inside the gates."

Darius gave a subtle nod. "Good idea. The less eyes on us, the better." They were surrounded by life, hundreds of eyes making him itch in his clothes. A hawker shouted to them as they passed, selling shriveled roots on a long table. A group of men talked in a circle beneath the shade of a large, orange awning. In the next square, a statue poured water from its six mouths, and crowds gathered to fill buckets and urns to the brim. One woman, oddly enough, passed them while balancing a pitcher upon her head. People came and went, dressed in colorful clothes. Soon, Darius realized his silly green clothes were in fact the norm. Twice he saw a man with green robes even brighter than his. Women wore light vests like Ayva's, but none quite so flashy and of such fine material. Well, if anyone could pretend to be a noble, it was her. Even Gray's white vest with dark leather lacing and gray pants were common too, just less so than Darius' attire. *Good, let me be the most normal one for once,* he thought.

Abruptly, a cluster of men with shaven heads walked before him as if blind. He pulled hard on his reins to avoid trampling them and almost cursed when Ayva touched his arm. "Sons of the Flesh," she explained, sidling her beast closer. "They are from the city of Covai, the Great Kingdom of Flesh. Best not to upset them."

Darius realized they all had the same brown and white robes that were dirty from travel. In their hands, they held coarse ropes

that they wound and unwound around their fists as they muttered to themselves in a deep hum, walking through the crowds.

"What are they mumbling about? And what's with the ropes?" he asked, watching as the crowds avoided them like the moldy onion in a once-tasty soup.

"It is a chant, a prayer to their god, and the ropes inflict pain," she said.

"Why?" Gray asked.

"I'm not sure of all the reasons, but Faye said it is a gesture of piety. They believe life is pain and that one must embrace it. It helps remind them of their mortality. Oh, and they say it reminds them to resist the temptations of the flesh." Darius scoffed at that. *Life is meant to be embraced, reveled in even, not resisted.* Ayva continued, "In every city, they roam, converting those who wish to join their path, simply called *The Way*. They are the largest spiritual sect in all of Covai, and perhaps all of Farhaven."

"Are they dangerous?" Gray asked softly.

"Faye said only to avoid them. They are nothing to fear if you stay out of their way, but those who interfere find themselves in a whole heap of trouble."

They pressed forward with Darius leading the way. All the while, he wished they could avoid the looks their steeds brought them, but at least the people of Farbs were more or less accustomed to such oddities. By their looks, cormacs were obviously rare, but not unheard of. Still, he pulled his green cloak around him and sunk deeper into his cowl.

Ayva and Gray pulled closer as a dozen or so guards neared upon tall steeds. They wore chainmail and plate, and Darius squinted from the reflecting sun. In their hands were long halberds or colorful pikes. *Colored weapons*? Darius scoffed and then remembered the green sword upon his back. *Well*, that's *different*, he thought. The guards barely cast them a second glance as they rode by, their armor clanking as they headed into the desert.

Eventually the three of them approached the tall, tan-colored gates. The flow of people increased like tributaries joining a larger river. They found themselves in a main thoroughfare that was wide enough for ten carts to move side by side. On the edges, fewer tents and more buildings had been constructed, seeming more and more like a real city.

He felt strangely invigorated as they rode, as if he *hadn't* slept upon the hard ground. No, he felt alive. It was magic he realized and shivered. It was like that sometimes. Though he'd never tell the others, a part of him was excited. He wanted to help Gray, and he couldn't wait to see what would unfold once they entered Farbs.

The giant gates sat ahead, wide open. The crowds swelled, moving towards them, and Darius felt as if he were caught in a wind tunnel, being pulled in.

Most of the people traveled on foot, looking dirtied and worn—there were so many of them. *What has happened?* Darius wondered. It almost reminded him of Lakewood's survivors. He sighed upon remembering that, glad to know the villagers were safe at long last.

"What's going on?" Ayva asked. "These people... They look displaced. As if we just missed a war."

Gray looked equally confused.

Darius touched the shoulder of a man who walked at Mirkal's side. The man looked up, startled. "Greetings. The name is Darius. Where are you all coming from?" he asked bluntly. Well, he was one for subtlety *sometimes*.

The man's round eyes looked at him nervously, as if confused why he was talking to him. Darius took in the man's tattered blue clothes. They were wide around the collar, cuff, and sleeves. It was a fashion stranger than even his own green garments. Yet he noticed embroidery and a heavy gold stone around the man's neck. And of course, the way his nose stuck in the air like he'd just wafted some bad cheese. *Nobility?* he wondered.

"I'm Jurad. I hail from Sevia," he answered. "Why do you ask?"

"I've been meaning to get a new shirt, and I just admired the cut of yours. Is it..."

"The finest cut of Sevia silk, from the Duvai provinces, of course," Jurad huffed, and then smiled. "You've a fine eye for cloth."

"Why thank you. I pride myself on it," Darius lied. "I've always said, 'even the lightest piece of Sevia silk is worth the fattest piece of gold'." The words sounded sour and false on his tongue, but he spoke smoothly. He felt Ayva and Gray, the heat of their gaze on his back.

Jurad bobbed his head, looking pleased. "That heartens my soul." Then his sun-tanned nose wrinkled in disgust. "Too many young men nowadays can't tell a fine piece of brocade from a swatch of beggar's woolens! Of course, I don't have to tell you that Sevia silk is the finest silk in all of Farhaven, and Duvai is..." The man hesitated. "Wait a moment. Farbian garb, but light skin, and Elvin mounts... I've never seen humans quite like you. You three... are you... are you from Eldas?"

Did he just call me an elf? Darius thought, not sure whether to laugh or be offended. He cleared his throat, but Gray spoke instead, "No. We come from the south."

"South?" Jurad questioned, suddenly wary. "There's nothing south. Not since the Lieon and those cursed nine destroyed nearly all the lands. All that remains is a few patches of green amid an endless desert. That and the once Great Kingdom of Yronia—that heaping mass of steel is little more than scraps where only shadows skulk and rumors stir. Beyond that is Death's Gates, and none but the elves venture beyond, into that false land, without magic."

Darius' heart beat faster, caught in their lie. Not that it mattered if the man discovered them, he supposed, but it was an old habit—that racing pulse. Seconds felt like hours as the man's eyes gauged them, and Ayva spoke. "He means we've made a hard journey to the south. We're from Cloudfell Town."

Jurad mopped at his sweat with a kerchief and turned his scrutiny north, through the crowds. "You have the look of Cloud folk, hard-bitten people but somehow soft too. Sadly, they've no eye for good cloth."

"Right," Gray agreed, joining at last. "We've made a hard journey here from Cloudfell and just purchased new clothes. You look a bit travel worn yourself. How fairs Sevia?"

"You haven't heard?" the man asked as the mass of bodies lurched forward.

The gates grew in size as they neared. It nearly took Darius' breath away, looking up to the dizzying heights of those tan battlements. Spikes crested them, and guards moved about, watching the endless procession push through.

"Heard what?" Ayva asked him, moving closer.

"Sevia is… Well, it's a mess. I'm not sure how you avoided it to be honest. The trade routes are nearly all shut off from here to the Frizzian coast. Bandits rove the countryside in droves, assaulting anything that moves and seeking coin and blood. Sure we had them before—Sevia isn't as safe as other places. I mean it's no Vaster, where there are laws just for stepping on a patch of grass. But now? It's worse than ever! There've been more deaths in the past month than in years combined."

Nearby, an older woman with a round, black bun on her head chimed in suddenly, having overheard. "It's not just Sevia. My name is Semi. We live near the foothills of Narim, near the coast. A week ago, we'd gone to town to fetch some supplies, and when we came back…" She spoke with a shiver, and a man at her side—her husband, Darius figured—put an arm around her slender shoulders as he held her close, issuing soft words of comfort. She stood straighter, continuing. "Our home, our crops, all of it was burning. Everything gone, decades taken from us in a fiery flash."

"Not even a fight," the man at her side said. "If and when I find them, I'll bleed them dry."

"Who could do that?" Ayva asked softly.

"I know who," Semi answered. "We never saw the ones who'd

done it, but weeks before that we'd heard tales of strange men. Red-sailed ships, they said, assaulting the Frizzian coast, and rumors say they be in the habit of taking prisoners." Her voice lowered conspiratorially. "As if the villains are amassing, planning a city of thieves or the like."

Jurad grunted. "I've heard as much. Fearful rumors. And I thought Farbs was bad," he added under his breath, eyeing the nearby people. Some had taken interest in their conversation, but most looked too huddled in their own tattered clothes and thoughts to contribute, gazes fixed ahead.

"But Farbs doesn't allow outsiders. What are you planning to do?" Gray asked.

"Well I figured you all knew," Jurad stated, looking confused. "The Patriarch has opened the gates of Farbs, lifting the ban. That's why all these people are fleeing like there were a fox in a rehn's coop. However, I'm not planning to stay long. I'm from the noble house of Carah, and we've come to petition for men to help make the trade routes safe again. Sevia is vital to the prosperity of all the lands. Farbs needs us. Now I only hope the Patriarch's compassion is as

notorious as they say."

"We hope only to make enough coin using Targa's skills as a blacksmith to go back home and rebuild," Semi said. "They say Farbs is full of coin, if one knows where to look."

Darius wished them the best of luck, and with the others at his side, they pressed forward, weaving through the walking masses.

"I can't believe there's this much sorrow and chaos," Ayva said.

"Remember what Faye said about the Nodes?" Darius said. "Something about Farhaven and magic being attacked. That's why the Nodes were appearing, acting as safe havens. Now Farbs is a sanctuary."

"What if the Nodes were just the beginning?" Ayva whispered.

"I hope not, but it wouldn't surprise me. Bandits, raiders, and bloodshed?" he shivered. "Dice, the world seems to be going crazy outside these walls."

Gray made a grunt of agreement. "Farhaven is under attack."

"But by whom? The Darkwalkers aren't the root of it, are they?" Darius asked.

Two guards were helping a fallen man to his feet nearby. They grew silent for a moment until the guards passed.

"We'll find out soon," Gray said. He sounded afraid yet hopeful.

"Right, first Ezrah, then the darkness that is conquering the world," Darius announced. He expected a laugh or perhaps a rise out of the two, but instead, they merely nodded. Nodding? Darius guffawed silently. *What have you gotten yourself into, Darius?*

They reached the gates. Dozens of guards with red-cloth shrouds watched the crowds enter, helping order traffic as best they could. A few nearby guards eyed their cormacs, but luckily none said a word. As they moved beneath the tall sandstone archway, Darius couldn't help but feel like he was willingly entering into the jaws of some enormous sand beast. He passed through and a chill sunk beneath his skin. He shivered and looked to Ayva and Gray.

"Did you feel that?"

Both nodded.

"Magic," Ayva said, awe-struck.

"It was testing us," Gray said. Darius waited for him to say more, but Gray froze, looking up to the sky.

"Gray? What is it?"

A screech pierced the air. Darius jumped, nearly vaulting from his cormac. In a searing flash, memories came of dragons and death upon the golden walkway. He twisted in his seat and was hit with a rush of air. He cursed, ducking.

When he looked back up, he saw the image of a beast, flying through the air with huge white wings. It twisted nimbly, disappearing around a corner. *Is there a man riding it?* He shook his head, wondering if he was dreaming again. He must be dreaming, for what in the seven hells kind of person would ride a flying beast? A *madman*, Darius concluded. He leaned over, nudging Ayva. "What in the world was that?"

"Gryphons," Gray explained with a light in his eyes. Before Darius could ask more, they pressed past the gates and into the streets of Farbs proper, and Darius found himself slack-jawed again.

The large circle before them was nothing remarkable—well, nothing remarkable for Farhaven that was—but in its center was a bedazzling sight. Darius stared at an enormous sphere. It was twice as tall as any building he'd ever seen in Lakewood. And even *more* oddly, it hovered a foot above the ground, suspended by nothing but air. Its surface was glassy and translucent. He dismounted and found his feet moving on their own. In a daze, he reached the sphere and his fingers grazed the surface.

Water.

A huge dome of water, like a bubble that hadn't been popped. He pulled his hand back. The water reformed, seamless once more. "How is it not falling?" he whispered.

"It must be a spell," Ayva replied, eyes wide.

"It is," said Gray. Darius watched Gray glide his hand through the water in amazement. "Every Arbiter is known for their grand creations—this is one of his." His last word was said fondly, with emphasis and a quirk to his lips.

"Whose?" Darius posed.

"Ezrah's," Gray answered.

"Really?" Ayva asked, breathless. "Your *grandfather* made this?"

"How do you know that?" Darius questioned, dubious.

"My past," he retorted, smiling and inhaling a deep breath of the warm desert air as he gestured grandly. "These streets, the gryphons, the magic at the entrance... All of it is coming back to me." Even Ayva looked rejoiced, and Darius' felt their enthusiasm spreading to him. It was infectious. He shook his head, wiping the grin from his face and looking back to the sphere. Beneath the floating globe, a fountain of water spouted, constantly feeding it. All around, people gathered, citizens and newcomers alike. They dipped in their hands to wash their dirtied faces or fill their buckets, flasks, and even barrels.

"Well, if your grandfather created it, it must be safe," Darius said, cupping his hands and drinking.

Ayva followed suit and made a sound of delight. "It's delicious!"

Thirsty and his throat raw, Darius drank deeply. Energy and life flushed through him. The water was crisp and slightly sweet. It was the tastiest water he'd ever had, and he didn't even know water *could* be tasty.

As he drank, he took in the square.

Beneath him were paved white stones flecked with red, but beyond that, he saw dirt streets. All around them, buildings sprung into the air, taller than anything in the Shining City. They were mostly clay but reinforced with wood. Between them sat dark alleys. Darius felt his dagger in the folds of his clothes and shifted his shoulders, reassuring himself with his new blade. As beautiful as this city was, those alleys were a testament that it was also destined to be equally as dangerous.

After rinsing the dirt from his face and hands and refilling the waterskins, Darius mounted. He gazed over the many heads, feeling reinvigorated from the strange water. "No use waiting here," he announced.

Gray was at his side immediately, looking more alive than Darius had ever seen him before. Ayva brushed the last bit of dirt from her gold vest and mounted. ' "What's the plan?"

"Simple," Darius answered. "Let's find ourselves a dirty hovel. If I remember correctly, Gray, you still owe me that beer from the Shining City."

Gray laughed, scratching his head. "Is that so? Why don't I remember that?"

"Mind like a steel trap," Darius said, tapping his temple.

Ayva snorted. "Exactly. Nothing going in or out."

Darius grumbled, hiding a smile, "Bah, just follow my lead." He prodded Mirkal forward just as Gray spoke.

"Wrong way," he announced.

Looking back, Gray was grinning like a man with a rigged set of dice, and Darius sighed. "I'm not sure if your returning memory is going to be annoying or a relief," he replied.

"Both, probably," Gray answered.

With that, they sifted through the dusty streets, and Darius took in the sights.

Inns and taverns littered the main thoroughfare. Their swinging signs held strange names like The Flute and Tarsk, Reaver's Rest, Blind Marksman, Silveroot's Sap, Caverns of Mendari, and a few he couldn't even pronounce. He whisked down a narrow alley and found darker buildings. People still moved about, but fewer now, and they wore hooded expressions despite their bright attires. Darius heard the scurry of rats in some of the darker alleys between the buildings. He was getting closer.

Gray was silent, merely eyeing the shadows as they rode. Their white, silken haired cormacs seemed out of place in the murky alleys. "I'm afraid I won't be of much help here. It seems my memory is a bit fogged when it comes to the darker warrens of Farbs."

"Is there one you're looking for in particular?" Ayva asked him.

Darius replied, "A good inn is neither too nice, nor too dingy. Information lingers somewhere in the middle." He nodded to a sign that read, The Blue Boar. It had a painted image of what he guessed was supposed to be a boar. Noise and laughter emanated from behind the closed door. He heard a splintering crash and the breaking of bottles from an erupting fight. "Well then…" Darius hiked up his belt and glanced to the others. "Let's start here."

A Ronin's Luck

Gray was growing frustrated. Six inns and two taverns later, they *still* had nothing. He wished he could help Darius more, but he was useless. This place was completely unfamiliar. Besides, he admitted, he wasn't used to digging for information. He didn't seem to have the skills for this sort of thing. He took it as a good sign, hoping it meant his previous self wasn't of the nefarious ilk, but still... It didn't explain Kirin's maniacal laughter and the feeling of death clinging like residue upon his hands... Gray shook the thoughts free like a dog shaking off water.

More to the point, they were no closer to finding his grandfather.

Darius had done his best, but no one wanted to talk. As soon as the Citadel was mentioned, all grew predictably silent. True to Darius' word, they were now in a dark hovel called The Drowned Rat. They had quickly realized that the deeper and darker they went into Farbs, the more they would find, but still no one was willing to talk.

He sat at a bar with Ayva at his side and pretended to drink his frothing ale. Gray sniffed it again. It smelled sour like milk gone bad. He didn't know much about ale, but he presumed sour wasn't a good thing.

On a rickety stage, a woman plucked at a strange, seven-stringed instrument and sang. It was an odd up and down melody, though enchanting, and he listened half-heartedly.

"The rusty trail of time,
It passes on and on,
Till we forget what's come an' gone:

Of battles fought
Of love lost and won,
Of heroes gained and villains made,

But bards, they do remember—
In moonlit taverns they spin their tales,
A history that winds, left and right it goes,

But always back it comes, to tell of fabled foes:
Those legends, myths, and enchanted men
Who fight for what was right,

But all were lost to darkness,
And Kingdoms retreated to lofty walls
To stow away their hatred.

And the rusty trail of time
Continues on and on—
Till we forget what's come an' gone..."

Her voice drifted on, and despite the intriguing subject matter—he knew what *legends* the song was referring to and which name it was pointedly avoiding—Gray's attention turned. Even with the time of day, the tables were packed. Men, big and small, sat huddled over their drinks, wearing dingy clothes and even dirtier faces. They cast wary glances. A few of their eyes lingered, but not on *him*. Ayva ignored it mostly, but Gray felt anger brewing at those looks. Casually, he touched Morrowil, reassuring himself.

"How's he doing?" Ayva asked.

Gray glanced over his shoulder to see Darius chatting with a man twice his size, both in width and height. The man leaned forward, his chair straining as he listened to the rogue talk. Gray reached into his mind, drawing upon the nexus. It wavered and sputtered—that black cavity was still there, as if someone had taken a bite out of it. Tentatively, Gray extracted a thread, praying it wouldn't shatter. The thread came, but slowly, and he twisted it into a familiar spell and reached out. He cupped the air before their mouths and pulled it toward himself.

Words floated, sifting into his ear.

"Well, I can tell you one thing for certain. I'd wager all my coin that a procession like that is hiding something. And trust me, I know a thing or two about hiding."

"Is that so…" the large man said dubiously. "How do you figure?"

"Obvious, ain't it? It's the oldest trick in the book! Make a flashy show to keep the dull-eyed crowds smiling, all to conceal the rabbit under the hat. The buried treasure. But I just wonder where they would try to hole up something like that," Darius said.

Gray knew what he was talking about. Among other unusual rumors, they'd heard of a strange procession, more grand than anything the citizens had ever seen before. It had everyone in a buzz, questioning: What was it about? Were they hiding something? Who was the man with the black coat? Gray didn't care about any of that. He continued to listen, knowing the rogue was leading the conversation towards information.

"Better to not wonder," the big man hissed, suddenly nervous. "I don't want to know what Reavers be hiding."

"No?" Darius asked. "I suppose that's smart, avoiding danger and all. But I can't help but think … something they'd take all that effort to hide must be worth its weight in gold. Dice, a man could buy Eldas itself and still have more than a few coins to rub together." Darius rubbed his chin as if pondering. "I only wonder where something like that would be held…"

At last, the man looked thoughtful. "You're clever, friend. Too clever for these parts. Now cut to the chase. I'll help you if I can. What do you want?"

Darius took a sip of his beer and his mouth twisted from the sour taste. I wasn't wrong, *Gray thought.* *"The Citadel," the rogue said softly.*

The man's face darkened. "Better face a Devari in a duel than answer questions about the Citadel," the man said. "Sorry friend, you'll have no help from me, or from anyone else if they've got half a brain."

Darius grumbled and rose. "Thanks, friend."

"Bit of advice, if I might," the man said, gripping Darius' arm. The rogue gestured for him to speak, but Gray knew that look. It was the same one he had before Darius had pinned a snake in the desert in the blink of an eye. "Word on the street is that the Citadel is not right of late. Something is happening. Dark events, I tell you. Whispers of Reavers turning to the dark, and the Citadel is…"

"Is what?"

"War is coming," the man breathed. Raising a ponderous brow, the big man let the words linger, then pushed his girth away from the table and stalked to the tavern's door, letting in a flurry of cold wind, before it swung close with a thud.

"Gray?" Ayva asked, touching his arm. "You have that look again…"

Gray shook his head, returning.

Darius neared as he downed the rest of his ale, and then slammed the flagon on the bar. "Another please," he said, gesturing to the lanky tavern owner.

"I don't know how you can manage to drink any of this swill," Ayva said, brushing imaginary dirt upon the bar. "It's a shame this place is even allowed to exist. Really, it's a disgrace on the name of inns and taverns everywhere. My father would never allow such a thing in The Golden Horn."

Darius merely shivered. "Honestly, after news like I just heard, I'm willing to drink anything."

"What'd he say? Does he know where Gray's grandfather is being kept?"

"No," Gray answered.

Darius choked mid-gulp, spitting out his new drink. "*Gah!* Will you cut it with the eavesdropping, Gray? Dice, it's uncomfortable as is. Not to mention, your leering is going to make these fools suspicious. And as for what he said, it was the same as before, only worse. The Citadel seems to be stirring. People are afraid."

Gray cleared his throat.

"Is that all?" Ayva asked.

"He mentioned war," Darius admitted.

Ayva swallowed. "Could it be true?"

Gray was silent. *War*... Part of him thought Farhaven would be different, that a land of magic would have evolved beyond such things. But he knew it was a silly notion. There would always be war where greed and power flourished.

"I'm not sure," the rogue said, "I'm as likely to trust a newt as I am anyone in this gutter. Now come on, we're getting a few too many looks, and this place has served its purpose. Let's find another." Darius was right. The leering men were now openly staring, and several of them rose to finger daggers at their waists and flash hungry grins—revealing missing or rotting teeth. Gray moved for his sword when he felt a hand on his wrist. He turned to see Darius. "It's not worth it," said the rogue with a furrowed brow. "Your grandfather, remember Gray? Not Ayva's honor."

Gray released his breath, pulling his hand away. "You're right. No use dying over fools." Were the words Kirin's or his? It was becoming difficult to tell.

"Precisely!" Darius said. "Or better yet, how about just no dying?" Ayva looked at them curious, but was too far to hear. Darius threw an arm around Gray's shoulders, then flung a few coins he'd gambled for on the bar. With his other arm, he grabbed Ayva jovially. But as they left, Gray put himself between the men and Ayva, hand resting heavily on Morrowil's hilt.

Outside, light blinded Gray and he shielded his eyes.

It was still midday, but after the dimly lit tavern, it felt like they'd just stepped out onto the surface of the sun. Upon Darius' advice, they'd found a stable for their cormacs at a nicer part of town a while back, paid for it with Darius' gambling winnings, and had resorted to walking. Whatever helped them blend in, he thought, as a pair of men cast them sidelong glances.

They entered a dark red building with white letters that spelled The Bloody Axe. Again, they found nothing. There were fearful whispers, but the woman's mouth shut as soon as the word "Citadel" passed Darius' mouth.

The Swine's Tale.

Nothing.

The Beggar's Hand.

Again, nothing save for the threat of a dagger in Darius' back.

As they left a rickety building with barred windows and a sign that read The Giant's Gizzard, Gray grabbed Darius' arm, pulling them to a halt. Frustration boiled inside of him. It was now nearly night time. *Hours wasted and we've gotten nowhere,* he thought. His other hand was a fist in his pocket, clutching the dust from the former pendant. He watched as a few men and women wearing black and red rag-like clothing moved around them.

"What is it?" Darius asked, looking worn and equally frustrated, and more than a little drunk.

"You've done better than Ayva or I could ever do, but this isn't working," Gray whispered fiercely.

"No, you're right," the rogue agreed.

"Time is wearing thin, and thus far we've only found out that he's being kept in the Citadel. We've still no blasted idea *where* he is inside the keep, or even *how* to get in… Let's face it, this is turning into a lost cause." He felt a thread of despair weave its way into his voice.

"What do we do?" Ayva asked.

Darius gripped Gray's forearm. "We can't give up yet," he said. "We have to keep trying."

He held the rogue's gaze and felt some of the mantle of darkness slough from his mind. He heaved a sigh of relief. The look of perseverance and confidence on Darius' visage gave him hope. Gray remembered Morrowil as well. He could not give into despair or the sword would feed upon it—*I will never be Kail.* "All right," he said. "Though there has to be a better way. At this point, we are more likely to get stabbed than to get information."

"I've got one last idea," Darius said. "The darker the establishment, the more they seem to be willing to reveal about the Citadel. But we've been far too tame."

"What are you proposing?" Ayva asked hesitantly.

Darius didn't smile, but his eyes took on a wild look and he answered, "I'm saying it's time we find the most foul, most ruthless inn in all of Farhaven and hope someone has the guts to speak."

"I don't like the sound of this. That just sounds like an easier, faster way to get stabbed," Ayva replied.

"No, he's right," Gray said. "It's a long shot, but it's our best bet. One last chance, but if we're doing this, let's not go halfway. It'll have to be the darkest, deepest hole we can find."

Darius gripped his arm with a mischievous grin. "Deal."

"This is a fool's plan," Ayva said fearfully.

"Well, then it's perfect," Darius answered and started forward.

* * *

They wove deeper and deeper, night settling in around them. They passed buildings that only seemed to stand because they leaned against one another for support, most of their windows boarded or shattered like a brawler's broken teeth. Darius' eyes flashed, watching every shadow in every nook. He saw Gray was doing the same, but he didn't know where to look, not like Darius. His fist was white-knuckled around Morrowil's hilt.

The man's white-knight routine is going to get us killed! And yet... He felt a goofy smile crease his face. He admired, no, he liked that about Gray! That sense of honor and morality was reassuring in a world gone mad. And the world *was* mad. But not to Gray. To Gray the world was black and white, *good* and *bad*—a comforting thought to the truth of an uncaring world full of gray-matter.

Gray-mattered. He giggled at his own inner pun, feeling light-headed and drunk once more. Trying to sound sober, Darius touched Gray's hand, pulling it away once more. "Careful. A threat of a fire could burn the whole house down." He wasn't sure what that meant exactly. He was drunk, but it sounded reasonable. A spark could cause an inferno? Maybe that was the phrase. Regardless, Gray understood and removed his hand, but he still watched the shadows.

He was right too. Threats were everywhere, but not where they expected. Gray's eyes passed over a bald man with a toothless grin—but Darius saw the man's stumble lead him purposively towards Ayva.

Faster than an adder, Darius slipped his dagger free and pressed it to the man's side. Their gazes met in a flash and Darius shook his head. The man sneered, but his hand slunk back into his smelly, threadbare coat—a hand that clearly gripped a shank or some other crude weapon—before stumbling on.

"What was that about?" Ayva questioned. "You just ran straight into that man, Darius. How drunk *are* you?"

Gray merely squinted.

"A little," Darius lied. The world was beginning to spin. He felt the ground lurch beneath him, and he gripped Gray's arm for balance. "I probably shouldn't have tried to outdrink that man at The

Giant's Gizzard. Or—" he burped "—perhaps it was spiked." The thought sent a cold flush across his skin, and he hoped he was wrong.

"We can call this off," Gray said.

Darius shook his head. "No."

A group of men approached.

Ayva nervously walked closer to Darius. She assumed the air of indifference—a necessary mask he assumed she'd learned from working in her dad's inn. Still, the men were making a straight line towards them. As if he'd feigned his drunkenness, Darius lunged. He snatched Gray's collar suddenly and shoved him against the nearest wall. In the corner of his vision, he saw the men pause.

Gray cursed. "What in the—"

With an overly extravagant flourish, Darius whipped out his dagger. His fingers felt fat, nearly dropping the blade. Sweat flashed across his skin in panic, but he held on, spun the dagger in the air then put it to Gray's throat. "Enough!" he shouted, loud enough for all to hear.

"Darius!" Ayva shouted.

"You're leading me nowhere! Give me all the coin you promised and now, or I'll do it!" His grip loosened just enough, and Gray's eyes widened in sudden recognition. Darius belched, and it made his throat and mouth taste like bile. He suppressed a grimace, hoping Gray didn't smell what he'd issued.

Gray recoiled, as if in fear, but more likely in disgust. "Please, I promise!" he shouted, voice quaking. "Whatever you want, I'll give you."

Darius snorted. "I knew you would. 'Course the band won't be happy with just your coin. They wanted your life too. Lucky for you I'm the merciful sort. But you try *anything* foolish or hero-like, and the street will drink your blood. Quickly now, or I'll tell the others! They'll be coming soon, and they're thirsty for violence." He sneered and Gray feigned horror. He was shaking! Dice, he was *good*.

"I..."

He felt a tap on his shoulder and he spun, but his boot caught on something and he tripped, falling upon his rear. Through his blurred vision, he saw Ayva with an amused smile.

"I was just going to say, they're gone."

The alley they were in was now completely empty. It was without a doubt the darkest spot they'd been in so far. The only life he saw was a scurrying rat, and even it seemed to be running away. Even the occasional mangy dog or feral cat they'd seen before were nowhere to be seen. The buildings around them crowded close, blotting out the sky above as if casting a perpetual moonless night. The dirt beneath Darius felt wet and grimy. A stale smell hung in the air, like moldy water mixed with something rotten.

Darius groaned, rubbing his butt. "Who's gone?"

"Uh, those vile looking men? They left as soon as you mentioned others coming. How drunk *are* you?"

He waved it off. "That hurt more than I expected. What did I land on?" He looked down and saw a long, white bone, as if from someone's leg. "I hope that's not human." A hand shot before his face and he recoiled. When he opened his eyes, he saw Gray wearing a silly grin.

"That was the smartest thing I've ever seen you do," Gray said.

"I got the idea from this guy I know. Did it seem familiar?"

"Very," said Gray. "In Lakewood, when your gambling nearly got you in over your head."

"I still insist it was not my fault," he grumbled. "But yes, you saved my skin back then, and now I saved yours. So we're even, deal?"

Gray laughed. "Deal."

Darius didn't mention that Gray had probably saved him a dozen times after that, but if he didn't remember, then he didn't need to be reminded.

"Funny, that was our first meeting, all three of us," Ayva said.

Darius took Gray's hand and shot up, wavering on his feet. "Well—" he belched, covering his mouth and eyeing their pitiless surroundings "—let's hope this isn't an ending to that beginning. If it is though, it'll be a beautiful ending!"

"You're scary when you're drunk," Ayva said.

"That's the idea," he answered.

"That's not—"

Darius stopped suddenly.

"What is it?" Ayva asked, reaching for her white dagger.

Darius looked ahead, nodding.

At the end of the dirty, dank street was a huge building, bigger than all the others. It had open windows. Smoke emanated from them like from tiny mouths, and shadows indicated there were people inside. But his eyes were rooted to the swinging sign that was shaped like a leaf. He swayed, eyes narrowing. "It couldn't be…"

In green lettering it read: Maris' Luck.

"Is that…? That can't be the same one," Ayva said.

"It is," Darius replied.

"But Faye said"—she lowered her voice despite the vacant alley—"even to say the word *Ronin* is a crime punishable by death."

"This place is dangerous, Darius," Gray said.

"Right," Darius said. "Then this is the one?" He reached out, touching a building for balance. It felt slimy. He retracted his hand as if he had touched fire, wiping it on his crude green clothes.

"Maybe we should go to one a little less ominous," Ayva suggested, stepping back. The inn seemed to *breathe* darkness. "The Dragon's Tooth was just back there, or perhaps…"

Darius shook his head. "This is the one." With that, he stepped forward, heading towards the solid oak door. Above it, the leaf-shaped sign rattled as if from a breeze, despite the windless alley. He heard voices and the sound of eerie music beyond. The sword on his back felt hot. Quickly, he scooped a handful of grime and dirt from the ground, wiping it on his face and clothes, and gestured the others to do the same. Both did so without pause, Ayva grimacing as she did.

With a breath of confidence, Darius grabbed the door, pulled it open, and ushered the others inside.

Filthy Liars

As Zane walked briskly, his fear was replaced by anger, blood simmering as he moved among the Lost Ones. He saw many helping those around them even before they helped themselves. They looked up at him, and despite their torture and torment, despite all the hardship they'd endured until now—a city casting them to its dark depths—many still had hope in their eyes. They were strong. Their minds and wills had been battered, but they pressed onward.

Salamander was a fool to think these people weak, Zane thought, but they did need his help. He would not let them die. No matter what Father said, even if it cost him his exile, he would not let a single Lost One—man, woman, or child—starve. Not if he could do something about it.

Suddenly, he saw a familiar group in the distance, huddled around a fire that sat at the bank's edge. They were backed against a huge pillar whose broad base was lit by the fires. In the day, however, the pillar was even more impressive—a monument rising up towards the vaulted ceiling high above, as if supporting all of Farbs with its girth.

"Zane!" a reedy youth called, standing. "Have you eaten?"

The others batted at him, yanking on his leg and trying to silence him. But the youth ignored them, flagging Zane over eagerly.

Grudgingly, Zane veered towards them.

Steam rose from a nearby kettle that hung over the low burning fire. In the dim light from the flickering flames, he took in the three youths. Rygar was short but stout, like a stump. As the most senior, his too-small brown rags bore the Lost Ones' emblem.

The other two were new. As such, they still had their thief names. Dasher was quiet as a breeze, wrapping his arms around himself and looking nervous at Zane's approach. He seemed as if he was trying to disappear in his own clothes. Lastly, Lucky, the one who'd summoned him, was tall but scrappy. Blond hair much like Zane's topped his head, but it was oily and he'd styled it to stick up at odd angles.

Dasher ladled a bowl for him.

Lucky snatched it, handing it to Zane. "Here you go, Shade," he said, dipping his head.

Shade, he repeated inwardly, finally addressing the name.

In the desert, shade was protection, a respite from the tireless sun and even a symbol of life and generosity. It was a name many of the Lost Ones had begun to call him. It had happened faster than he

had expected, and now nearly everyone was calling him that. Bringing food and coin to the Lost Ones had gained him the title, he assumed, but Father said it was more.

Zane sniffed the bowl. Rat soup, he determined, eyeing the murky green liquid and its thin shreds of meat. In truth, it was little more than broth, but at least it was something. He settled down, his back to the huge column as the others watched him.

"Sorry, Z. We tried silencing Lucky. He didn't mean to wake anyone up. He's still learning the rules," Rygar, the oldest of the bunch, explained. While Rygar was barely more than a boy, he had been a Lost One nearly as long as Zane. Still, Rygar was starting to gain a little stubble on his cheeks, and his kind nature was slowly gaining backbone, perhaps due to his deepening voice—a confusing baritone like a man twice his size.

"It's all right," he replied simply.

"I don't get it. Why do we have to be silent?" Lucky asked.

"Silence is our best friend as a Lost One," Zane said. "Hiding has kept us alive."

"But aren't we hidden down here?" Dasher asked nervously.

"These walls are thick as buildings, but the caverns echo and carry noise like a Reaver's voice," he explained. Zane had seen a Reaver wielding the spark speak in a voice that had boomed over a thousand heads.

The three nodded, looking nervous in Zane's presence. He sat back, lounging and sipping the hot broth in silence. "Don't mind me. What were you all talking about?"

"Dasher here was just telling us about the rumors," Rygar said, matter-of-factly.

Dasher flushed red. "No, I wasn't!"

"Sure you were, something about outsiders?" Lucky pressed.

Dasher sighed. "All I heard was that there were some outsiders asking all sorts of questions in the Shadow's Corner."

"So?" Lucky asked.

"So," Dasher voiced, "They said they'd been to a dozen inns already, asking after the same things again and again."

"What kind of things?" Rygar pressed.

Dasher eyed Zane then shrunk further into his clothes. "Stuff about the Citadel."

"They're looking for trouble then. Asking about the Citadel leads to no good," said Rygar, stirring the soup and shaking his head. He lifted a spoonful to taste. "Was that all, Dash?"

"Yeah, what'd they look like?" Lucky added.

Dasher shrugged. "All I heard is that it was two boys and a girl. And they rode in on cormacs."

Rygar choked, spraying soup.

"*Cormacs?*" Lucky sputtered. "You can't be serious, can you? Elvin steeds! Were they elves then?"

Dasher shrugged again. "Don't ask me. No one said. And I've never seen an elf so how would I know?"

"Cormacs…" Rygar breathed. "I bet selling one of them could fetch enough food for all the Lost Ones for at least a week or more!"

Lucky rocked back then scoffed. "Well, it's not *that* impressive."

"Oh, ya? What's more impressive than cormacs?" Rygar asked in his oddly deep rumble.

"*I* heard something to make a Devari quake in his boots!" said Lucky.

"Go on," said Zane, hand stilling upon the statue in his pocket.

Lucky swallowed, looking suddenly squeamish. "Well, I don't know if it was true, but I heard that a man in black with a huge dark cloak was seen about The Shadow's Corner. They say he moved like a nightmare. Salamander and a few others were following him like a bunch of faithful hounds."

"Who was he?" Dasher whispered.

Rygar was spooning the soup absently, spilling it upon the dusty stone.

Lucky licked his lips, leaning forward, and then whispered, "*Darkeye*."

Silence held the three.

Zane spoke suddenly, drawing their eyes. "Where'd you hear this?"

The boy looked as if he'd just been caught in a trap. Lucky was a notorious liar. Not bad at heart, just still a young thief to his core. He could see it in the boy's eyes. *Old habits are hard to kill*, Zane admitted to himself. "If you think I'm lying, I'm not!" Lucky protested quickly, raising his hands defensively, then crossed his heart with a finger. "String me up by my toes and call me an elf, but *I'm not lying*."

"Where?" Zane asked. "The truth."

Lucky rubbed his skinny arms uncomfortably. "Fine, I'll tell ya, but don't be angry, all right, Shade? At least, don't tell Father. I don't like it when he's mad." Zane gnawed on a particularly chewy piece of rat, holding Lucky's gaze. Lucky threw up his hands. "Stop looking at me like that! I'm sorry! I … I was casing, skimming for easy pickings by the gates from all them new outsiders arriving from fancy places. *That's* when I did see that dark-looking man." He shivered. "See? I told you, it wasn't no lie."

"You know that's not our way," Zane said softly.

He gripped Zane's arm with one hand, holding his gaze with teary eyes. Zane felt a tug on his coat, but when he looked down he realized he was imagining things. "I… I know it was wrong," Lucky pleaded, drawing his attention back. "Please don't exile me. I won't do it again, I swear!"

Zane brought out his dagger, brushing it along his cheek in thought, hearing the scrape of stubble. It was a habit of his. With his other hand, he reached into his purse. Fishing from the pouch, he grabbed a heavy silver piece and tossed it to Lucky before rising.

"What's this for?" the boy asked, confused.

"I always reward valuable information with coin. You needn't steal any longer, Lucky. I'll let you go this time, but if you do it again, I'll toss you out of here myself," he said. Lucky smiled and pawed the silver coin with delight. "One last thing—split it."

Rygar and Dasher's eyes widened.

"A whole silver?" Rygar boomed excitedly, voice cracking and his cheeks coloring.

It was his last silver, but Zane knew they would use it well. Both were good lads: Dasher, soft and spritely, and Rygar generous and as gentle as a leaf on the wind, a boy more likely to spend it on others and not himself.

"Wait a second," Lucky squawked, "but I had the—"

"—Lost Ones aren't about greed, Lucky," he interrupted sharply. "You'll find that out soon enough. And if you spend it without sharing, I'll know." He tossed the bowl into Lucky's hands and stalked back into the night. Moving through the campfires like a shadow, he saw a figure in a dark gray coat standing at the edge of the Lost Ones' camp, near the sentries.

Two faces he didn't recognize guarded the Sanctuary's border, watching the night nervously. The face of the dark coated man resolved itself, and Zane breathed a sigh of relief. When had he been holding that?

"Zane." Trev beckoned, ushering him towards the light of a standing torch.

Zane approached. With scraggly brown hair and bright green eyes that were widely set, much like jewels placed in mismatched sockets, there stood Trev, second in command of the Lost Ones behind Father. He was lithe and light-skinned, and many of the younger female Lost Ones seemed to find him attractive. He was several years older than Zane. Trev looked strangely nervous, watching the shadows as if creatures lurked within.

"What is it? What's wrong?" he asked.

Trev leaned in closer. "I heard you talking with Father recently."

"You were eavesdropping?"

The lean man shook his head, looking affronted. "No! Well, technically yes, but unintentionally. I only caught snippets. I heard your argument with Father, how he wants to exile you."

"Then you misheard. It's not like that," he countered.

"No," Trev said, placing a hand on his arm. "I did not mean to make it sound that way. I know Father, and you are like his son. I'm sure Father is only doing it because he cares for you."

Zane pushed Trev's hand away, kindly but firmly. "He is, but he is wrong this time."

"Exactly. We need you, Zane. Without you and your thieving, we would starve."

"Enough flattery," Zane snapped. "What do you want? Get to your point." He glanced at the shadows as if moving to leave when Trev spoke up, voice gaining urgency.

"This morning I overheard something… something dire that could change the fate of the Lost Ones *for good*. No more thieving, no more starving. An end to the suffering and misery. Naturally, once I heard that, I remembered your little spat with father and realized this *could be* the solution to all our problems."

The hair prickled on the back of Zane's neck. It sounded too good to be true, but his curiosity, his burning desire to save the Lost Ones was like an unquenchable fire in his gut. "Go on," he bid him at last.

Trev lowered his voice so the nearby sentries couldn't hear. "A shipment for Darkeye is being delivered to the Eastern Gate. From there, they will drop the cargo off in a warehouse nearby."

"And the source?"

"Very reliable."

Zane ran his tongue across his teeth, feeling the sharp edges as he thought. "What's in them?" he asked finally.

"I'm not sure. All I know is it's valuable. Very valuable. It will be a hard blow to Darkeye." The words were a soft spot for him, every blow to Darkeye was a good one.

"The muscle?"

"Nearly a dozen, all disguised as Farbian guards."

Zane raised a brow. It wasn't unheard of. Darkeye often employed Farbian guards or had his men pose as them. "I can't take a dozen men, especially not if they're Farbian guards, and I won't kill a man who isn't of Darkeye's brood."

"That's the thing. A dozen men to escort, but there will only be two guards at the warehouse, and both are Darkeye Clan to the bone."

"Why two?"

"That's the kicker," Trev said, looking anxious. "It's a Citadel warehouse."

Zane nearly laughed, but the look on Trev's face was deadpan. "That is a twist indeed. But it makes sense—I would never expect two guards and a Citadel warehouse to hold Darkeye's goods."

"Exactly," Trev agreed. "And if I'm right, just one of those crates is worth its weight in gold."

"I wish you knew what was in them," Zane said.

"Me too. But it doesn't matter. Take it and we'll find out later."

Everything about the job sounded perfect, aside from the Citadel's warehouse. While it was safer than one of Darkeye's, it was risky for other reasons. But it made sense and was immensely clever. Hiding Darkeye's goods within the Citadel's holdings was something Zane would never expect. It sounded just like Darkeye. But how had the man pulled such strings? Was Darkeye employed by the Citadel, or did he finally have a foot in the door of that dark keep? It seemed impossible. The two forces had seemed like oil and water. But either way, it was dangerous news. "Intriguing but, unfortunately, I only receive my orders from Father. He tells me about the shipments and knows the routes better than anyone."

"But he won't be helping you anymore, will he?" Trev stepped forward, looking anxious. Perhaps that look of his, that fear, was actually sympathy for those in need. He didn't know Trev well but, without the man, Father would have had trouble keeping the Sanctuary functioning as it did.

Zane gave an uneasy sigh. He hated disobeying Father, but this was necessary.

"It's your call," Trev said at last, "I won't force you."

"First, you couldn't force me, not if you had a dozen of you. And second, I don't deal with liars."

Trev reeled. "What?"

"I know when a man is lying better than anyone. After all, a master can recognize an apprentice when he sees one. And you aren't telling the truth, at least not the whole of it. Tell me what you're hiding, or I walk."

Trev stood straighter, eyes hardening. His timid fearfulness fled.

"The whole truth? Well the truth is I don't like you. I never have. Father confides in you, but I don't see why. I've seen the way you move and the way you eye everything like a threat, as if curiously wondering whether you can kill it or it can kill you. In the end, you are just a weapon without a sheath. "

Zane made no move, he stood quietly. Trev sounded truthful. "Then why even talk to me? Why approach me now?"

"I didn't say you weren't necessary. A weapon has its purpose."

"Then you wish to use me? To wield me?"

"You help us, you help the Lost Ones. Prove yourself this time, and I will consider trusting you."

"Interesting, asking me for help with one hand, and striking me with insults and accusations with the other." Anger simmered just below the surface. Trev was an ass, but at least he was an honest ass. "Give me one reason I should help."

"Because it's not for me, it's for them," Trev said, motioning to the fires of the Lost Ones in a fierce whisper. "And if it was me, and I had your skills? I wouldn't think twice."

Zane held Trev's bright-eyed gaze. "You're nothing like me." The nearby torch flickered, and the cloying scent of burning fat hung in the air. It mixed with the acrid smoke, which lingered between them like an ill omen.

Unable to hold his gaze, Trev looked away. "Well?" he pressed nervously, sweat from the hot torch dappling his brow.

"I'll do it," he said at last, "but not for you."

The lissome man let out a sigh of relief, looking over the Lost Ones as if he had just stopped a flood from taking them away. The man gave him directions and Zane pivoted without acknowledgement, his cloak whipping behind him.

"Wait!" Trev called and Zane hesitated. "If you want, I can show you."

He glanced over his shoulder. In the dancing light, the man looked concerned. Though he did not care for Trev, perhaps the man was only trying to do what was best. Just as Zane was. "That won't be necessary. But you could do me one last favor." He pulled out the latest herbwort Father had given him. He laid it in Trev's hand and gave directions to their hideout. "Give this to Hannah. Tell her I will see her soon."

Trev nodded. "Certain you don't want me to come?"

"I'll be fine. Like you said, it's what I do best."

With a grave smile, Trev replied, "I'm sorry for doubting you. You're a good man, Shade."

"No, you were right about me all along," Zane admitted, turning away, then added in a fiery rasp, "but I will make them fear this weapon." With that, he moved away into the shadows once more, hand on his blade, readying himself for a night of blood.

A Red Night

As Zane left Sanctuary, heading to the surface, he saw glimpses of moonlight on the walls. The light came from airshafts leading upwards. Dawn was only a few hours away, he figured.

At the fork between the ramp to the surface and the path that led to his hideout, he wavered. *Hannah.* His fist tightened. He looked back to the wide ramp. *She will have to wait.* Two new guards stood at attention, young men Zane didn't recognize. They gave awkward salutes, but he paid them no mind, quickly moving on.

He wanted to hurry and return before Hannah awoke. He didn't want her to worry about him, not when she was barely beginning to recover from the spark fever.

As he climbed, the gurgling of water faded and the air changed, becoming hotter and less stale with every step. At last, he took another turn and was at the mouth of the Underbelly—it was one of many. Hundreds of these existed around the city. Most were simply drainage outlets. Of course, there was a main entrance to the sewers, but this wasn't it.

Ahead he glimpsed a dark alley.

Zane skulked forward, clinging to the shadows. Aside from the soft clop of hooves and the rattle of a nearby cart, the streets were quiet, almost vacant. Shreds of light from the moon shone on the tops of nearby buildings.

Pushing his hood forward, Zane stuck to the darker alleys, moving like a phantom. Soon enough, he reached the building. It was just as Trev described it, plain and dark. He slowed when he spotted two Farbian guards wearing conical helmets and thick chainmail. Upon their leather chest pieces was the red flame of Farbs, symbol of the Great Kingdom of Fire.

Directly behind them was a small side door bearing the Star of Magha, the insignia of the Citadel.

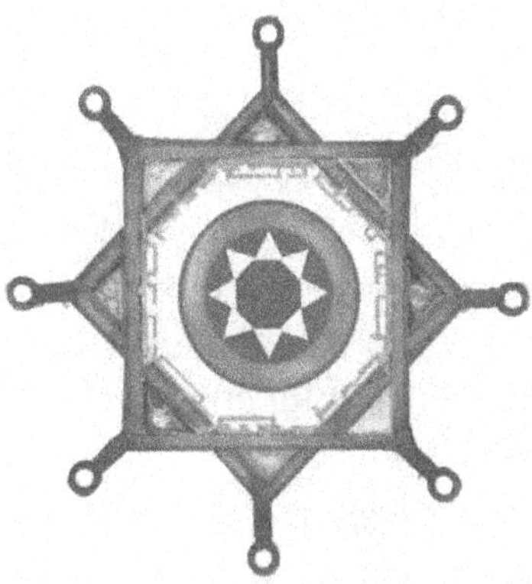

The guards watched the silent night, oblivious to Zane who stood in the shadows. Ignoring them, he moved around the building, looking for another way in. He paused, seeing a high window. If he could reach it… it was perfect, but there was nothing near it. There were no boxes to prop himself up on, and as he touched the sheer wall, he felt that it was almost slick like metal with no good handholds. He eyed the nearby adobe building, calculating its distance and the height of the roofs. It was his best chance.

Scaling the earthen building was easy, with its series of wood poles, gaping windows, and rutted handholds. He glanced to the street beyond, hoping no one saw the dark-cloaked figure clinging to the tan building. Zane scooted into the vestige of shade as he climbed to the summit. Crouching low upon the rooftop, he looked back down. *Thirty paces*—a fall might not kill him, but it would surely break bones. Before him, maybe ten paces away, the Citadel's warehouse was a black box. He had misjudged. The roof was taller. That was going to be difficult, but not impossible.

Sure enough, in the dirt streets below, a cart appeared, surrounded by twelve Farbian guards. It rattled its way to the warehouse's main door, but just before it passed out of view, Zane caught sight of a man at their head wearing two crossed swords on his cloak.

A Devari.

What was a Devari doing here? Had Trev simply not known or was it something else? Either way, Zane couldn't handle a Devari. Immediately, he looked for a way down, to abandon the whole thing. Just then, hooves sounded on dirt as all twelve guards rode back the way they came, including the Devari. When the last cart passed out of sight, Zane fixed his gaze upon the warehouse's ledge. Upon his third breath he bolted, legs and arms pumping. His foot pressed against the lip of the building and he flew, air whistling in his ears, until he slammed against the black wall. His hand gripped the stone's ledge, but then slid on the smooth surface. Scrambling nervously, he felt a sudden crevice and he dug his nails in, holding on and stopping his descent. With an angry breath, he looked down.

The window was just below him.

Suddenly, his swinging legs felt purchase. There must have been a score in the smooth, stone wall, allotting him a foothold. He tested it. It was firm. He used it, and then he felt another. His anger wavered, curiosity replacing it. The three lucky finds got him to the window's ledge, just barely.

Only Zane didn't believe in luck.

Silently, he slipped through the open window and into the warehouse. The window led onto a wood platform that overlooked the huge building's insides. He was in the rafters he realized, a landing not much more than a series of crisscrossed wood planks hanging above the storeroom below. Zane took in the sight like a blademaster assessing the quality of a sword. The room was empty of life, only boxes and barrels stacked haphazardly, looking like a gutted carcass with only the inedible bits left behind. And then he saw it... In the center sat a chest, bigger than all the rest. It gleamed strangely. *Too open*, he thought, grimacing. He didn't trust it, but he'd have to get closer to find out. He found a coil of rope. He gripped it, moving to fasten it to something when—

It was already tied down. He examined the knot. *Sturdy*. Something about the type of knot unnerved him too. He peered down to where the rope would land, but saw only darkness. Impassively, he noticed his hand holding the rope. It was shaking slightly. *Three oddities are enough*, his streetwise voice told him. *Leave this place*.

Paranoia, he thought gruffly, shoving it down. It was easy to have it in a job like this, and the bigger the job, the greater the mistrust. Still, he ignored the rope, went around to the far end of the rafters, found another cord and made his way down. As he landed, he saw the box in full.

Dull, hoary light from an unseen source lit the lower warehouse.

The shipment sat ahead. Now he saw it in full—not a box but a plain white Silveroot chest with rusted metal rivets. The Silveroot glowed faintly. Others might have been discouraged by the plainness, but Zane knew differently. What was often most valuable was rarely gilded in gold, for only a fool would hide their jewels with more jewels. No, the way it sat all by itself *was* special. He had a gut feeling that whatever was inside was no mere meal ticket. It was much more... perhaps even a new life for the Lost Ones—all of them. His heart hammered in his chest, harder than it ever had. At last, he could save them.

He stalked forward when his arm suddenly trembled. *Fear?* Zane was in his element, why was he afraid? Another step and his blood grew cold and hot simultaneously. Something wasn't right, like a sour smell hanging in the air. But time was running out. Ignoring it, he pushed forward. He took another step, his foot entering the light, and sweat beaded upon his brow.

Against all instincts, he took another step when he heard voices.

He had to close his eyes and concentrate just to make out the hushed tones.

"That little snitch was supposed to have him here hours ago."

"I don't trust one of those weaklings," said another. *"Turning in one of their own, no less."* He laughed softly. *"Imagine the look on Shade's face once he sees the truth of it."*

"Well, I just 'ope the raid on that rat's den is going better than this."

The first chimed in again. *"That is only half the pain he'll feel, watching his beloved wretches die before his eyes!"*

A third hissed. *"Shut your mouth. I think I heard somethin'."*

Zane's hot blood chilled to ice. Horror sunk beneath his flesh in realization… He backed away, mind reeling in anger, confusion, and fear. He tripped over a lump. His hand touched something wet, and soft. Raising his palms to his eyes, he saw blood, and then took in the body of a guard. Gritting his teeth, Zane staggered to his feet, ignoring his terror.

As he moved, retracing his steps as fast as he possibly could, shoving down his fear and foolishness, he had one single thought, one burning realization—this wasn't just a trap for him.

Sanctuary was under attack, and Hannah was in danger.

Wrath filled him, and he only prayed he wasn't too late.

* * *

Zane reached the last rung of the Underbelly. Beyond the next bend was the fork between his hideout and Sanctuary. His tired legs didn't slow, and he kept on running. A sinking feeling in his gut hit him as he rounded the corner.

Two bodies lay at the base of the wide ramp, unmoving. As he neared, he saw it was the lifeless corpses of those same two young men. Their faces were twisted in horror, as if they had looked upon a nightmare…

Words flashed through his mind.

Any man that causes an Arbiter to fear must truly be death itself.

Zane pushed down the words, grabbing a long cudgel from the youth's body and moving on, anger flowing through his veins. As he ran, his thoughts churned. He felt fear and terror for Hannah, and for the Lost Ones. But coating it all was ire for Trev and his treachery. The fury tugged at him, threatening to suck him in, but he wouldn't let it. Nor would he let it subside. Instead he channeled it, using it to fuel his tired limbs and sharpen his panicked mind. His anger was a blade, and he unsheathed that weapon in full. Trev was right in the end—now he would see the truth of it.

Sprinting hard, he reached their hideout quickly. At the corner he pressed against the wall, withdrawing a small mirror from the folds of his clothes. Angling it, he peered around the bend. A man stood to the right of the arched entryway, rusty sword in hand. He was big—much bigger than Zane. Upon the shoulder of his soiled, dark rags, Zane spotted Darkeye's crest. The thug watched the shadows uneasily. Zane's fist loosened, letting his hand slide down to the heavy cudgel. With his other hand, he put away the mirror and snatched a nearby pebble, lobbing it into the slow moving stream. It plopped. The thug spun, looking away, and Zane charged, racing like a shadow across the distance. Just before the man twisted, Zane cried out in fury. His muscles flexed and the cudgel snapped with the power of his fury, breaking upon the man's back. The man buckled, falling like a heavy sack. Indifferently, Zane dropped the weapon and walked through the entry, anger and fear roiling off him in waves.

Immediately, he took in his surroundings. Empty.

The boxes were shattered, and Hannah's little enclave was in pieces, awning and bed overturned. A struggle, he assessed with a clenched jaw. His own bed was a mess as well—his few rare belongings scattered or missing. Nearby, he saw a note tacked to the wall. Hannah's favorite necklace hung from it. He ripped it off the wall and read.

Come to The Lair of the Beast or the girl dies.

-Darkeye

Darkeye. Could it really be? Ezrah's words echoed in his head once again: "You will be pulled towards Darkeye like a string drawn by a loom." *Come to The Lair of the Beast.*

The Lair was Darkeye's hideout. It was essentially a deathtrap, regardless of Ezrah's prophetic warning. It was a place all thieves avoided like a plague. To enter was death. He crumbled the note, eyeing Hannah's heart-shaped necklace as memories flashed through him…

He found Hannah by the river. He heard soft sobs. As he moved to her side and sat, she stifled her tears. Still, her gaze was distant. They sat in silence, and he tried to issue comfort by his presence alone.

"Why did she have to die, brother?" she whispered at last.

Zane tried to find his words. He was never very good at these things, but the silence weighed on him. She looked to him, waiting. "Sometimes…" he began, "sometimes things just happen, Hannah, and no matter how hard we try, we can't change it."

"But she was just a little girl…" Her voice shook with emotion.

Zane felt his anger nearly succumb to sorrow, but he held onto it. It gave him strength. "There was nothing you could do. Perhaps… Perhaps it was her time."

"I refuse to believe that," she said, fist shaking as she watched the river. Her delicate features twisted in pain. "It was this city's fault. These people!"

"No," he answered. "It was Darkeye's. He starves the people and makes them think only of greed."

"I suppose, but how could no one see her starving in the corner? How could no one help?" Her voice broke, and she shook her head. "Is this all life is? Just meaningless death and destruction? Those that live and those that die, simple pieces on a board? And those that live… Are we truly the lucky ones?"

Zane felt the fire inside him churn as he thought. Life was simple—that was the way he lived. Living or dying, fighting or running. It was how he thought, but he knew it was not who he was. Long ago, he'd purposefully made the choice to think this way. With too many hard choices, keeping everything simple, when he knew it wasn't really the case, was the only way. It allowed him to make choices quickly and be strong when others would falter. If he thought in shades of gray, he doubted he would still be alive now, or at least he would be a hollow creature—filled with the misery of all he had seen. But Hannah was different.

He spoke in a whisper. "Do you see the river?"

Hannah looked up, curious, and wiped her tears. "Yes, why?"

"It moves forward. If it sees a rock, it splits, moving around it. It may dry up one day, or flow over another, but it continues. Death does

happen, but life continues, Hannah. The river continues and so must we. And as for that little girl? I'm not so certain death has the final say, for where does the river go when it passes around the bend?" he asked quietly.

Hannah sniffled. "You know, you're kinda good at this."

Slowly, he grabbed her fist and unfurled it, placing the heart-shaped necklace in her palm then folding her fingers around it. "She wanted you to have it. It was hers. Cherish it, and cherish life, sister—there is still much left to see around the bend."

Zane returned to the moment, hearing the river babble, just as it had done then.

He tossed the note but pocketed the necklace, focusing his rage. He examined the struggle. He saw blood on her blanket. Fear rose, but he fed it to his torrid anger. "She is alive," he whispered fiercely, reminding himself of the note. They would not kill their leverage. *Not yet at least,* he prayed.

"For now," a voice answered.

Zane twisted.

Salamander stood in the arched entry, a smile on his pockmarked face. Long, midnight black hair hung in strands around his features. His grin spread. "Are you ready to die, rat?" In his hands, a ball of fire swirled, growing and eating at the air. Without a second thought, the fire hurled towards his head.

Zane dove just in time. It roared over him. Heat touched his skin as it crashed and burned Hannah's makeshift shelter. Two more came, right on its heel. He dove behind a pillar and it exploded, shaking the cavern. The next ricocheted off the wall. He raised his arms, sheltering himself as flames exploded near his face. Breathing hard, Zane felt his fire rising.

He heard Salamander cackle, sounding near the entrance. "Come and face me, rat! No more hiding! If you beg me, I might even tell you where Hannah is being held." Three more balls of fire exploded against the column. The cavern shuddered repeatedly. Zane looked up through the flames. A crack had formed in the ceiling. Two more balls of fire rocked the room, and the crack grew, the room threatening to collapse.

"Enough!" Zane bellowed.

The onslaught of fire stopped.

He stepped out from behind the column. Casually, he picked at a burning ember on his coat and flicked it aside. He looked up to Salamander, anger reaching a peak. He felt as if he could make the man explode with his eyes alone. For a moment, the man flinched beneath his fiery stare.

"Give her back to me," he ordered. "If you do, I might spare your life."

Salamander laughed almost awkwardly, taken aback by his comment. "You're bold, I'll give you that. But you will die here."

"Why did you attack me at the warehouse?"

Salamander grinned wickedly. "We had to get you away. It's a shame those fools didn't kill you there, but I doubted you would fall for that trap entirely. But they did their job, I suppose—keeping you away and all that. You see, every time we got close enough to wipe you out, you somehow sensed us and moved the Lost Ones to a new dirty hovel where you could peck at us like a disease, like a *little* conniving rat gnawing at scraps." Salamander took a deep breath, easing out the anger in his voice, even smiling. "So, I thought to myself, how on earth do you stomp out a rat's nest? And do you know the answer, little rat, *hmm*?"

Zane said nothing, his fury rising.

"It's quite simple really. You lead the rat to food. And when the vermin's gone, you squash his nest and burn it all. Every. Last. Rat." In Zane's core, something burned. But Salamander continued, voice slick as oil, "But there's one fatal flaw. How do we get that little rat to smell the cheese and take the bait? Well, that was even simpler." Salamander's gaunt face twisted, eyes glittering. "We needed to get a rat of our own…"

Zane put the pieces together and he felt the hairs on his neck rise. "Trev," he breathed in fury.

"Darkeye minion to the bone that one," said Salamander with a grin.

"Trev will find a traitor's death at the end of my dagger, just like you."

"Sadly not," Salamander said darkly. "It is fitting that in the end I should be the one to bring back your corpse and claim the reward on your head." The man's hand lifted, and a molten ball of fire formed from thin air, growing like a blister. Zane retreated, feigning fear, circling the man, and moving back slowly. Salamander continued stalking forward.

Zane's heart thumped, watching that fire. "Why me? What does Darkeye want?"

"He didn't say, and I didn't care to ask. Your head on a pike is enough for me." Another step.

"Why would he take Hannah? Just to lure me?"

"Oh, surely you know. The girl is an Untamed." Zane continued to back up. Salamander gave an oily sneer and added, "She will make a fine addition to our stock."

Zane spoke confidently, simply. "I will kill you. You will live for now, but one day I will wipe that look from your face, and watch as you die, afraid and confused."

"Silence!" Salamander bellowed, spittle flying. "You abandoned those you love, and now you will die!" The ball hovered, emanating heat, making sweat run down his ruddy features. He cried, throwing the fire. Zane dashed. He had positioned himself close to the bank of the river. It was paces away. The fire roared, gaining on him as he dove.

The fire streaked by him, igniting his clothes. At the same time, he pierced the water. The fire raged above him, a muted roar. It lit the river, and sent torrents of water into the air, rocking him like a boat in a storm. But he pushed forward, and the water carried him quickly downstream. Still, he swam harder. At last, after what felt like an hour later, he came up, gulping for air. Quickly, he stilled his breath, waiting to hear the splash of another, to see if Salamander had followed, but there was no sign. The man couldn't swim, he figured—most of Farbs couldn't. What need was there in a land full of sand? He almost wanted to breathe a sigh of success, but Salamander's words sunk beneath his flesh, filling him with dread and more anger.

Hannah, a part of Darkeye's clan. The thought was somehow more terrifying than her death.

He pushed it aside, continuing on.

After a while, he debated leaving the river and returning to the tunnels, but the stream was taking him where he wanted to go. And through the murky water, he spotted torchlights bobbing in the dark tunnels. The forms of men were big and wide, moving in organized packs much larger than anything like the Lost Ones.

Darkeye's brutes, he knew.

And so he stuck to the river, letting the warm waters take him deeper. He kept his head low, breathing through his nose as he skimmed the water's surface. Occasionally, a lantern or torch passed too close and he dipped beneath the water, holding his breath and swimming until the currents carried him onward.

Zane hated being submerged in water. *Give me dry, desert heat over damp, humid weather any day.* Besides, being surrounded on all sides felt all too similar to being trapped and suffocating. He couldn't stand to be restrained. But for now, he was glad for its shelter.

At last, he reached Sanctuary. He saw more fires, and the grand cavern ahead. Suddenly, he heard cries and moans, cutting through the air. He stiffened.

He was too late…

Voices rose above the gurgle of water.

"Should we hide?" the man asked. "Salamander tol' us Zane maht be comin' to save his lil' los' rats any moment now."

"And? What's yer stinkin' point?"

The big man shifted uncomfortably and answered, "He's no slouch, Vurpil, nah' like these vermin."

Vurpil laughed. "Oh yeah? What's he gonna do? Take us both?"

"But them rumors—'aven't you 'eard? They say he's made of shado' and fia'."

"That don't make no sense," said the smaller one brazenly. "Which one is it, shadows or fire?"

Zane grabbed the bank's ledge and walked out before them. "Both."

The brutes froze, eyeing the dripping man before them as if they were dreaming.

He felt his anger form, hardening him, forging him. His blood was a torrent of fire. He reached for his dagger behind his back and… He stiffened. *It's gone.* It must have fallen out when he dove into the river. Both men saw that look in the flickering torchlight. They grinned and attacked at once.

Vurpil, the smaller of the two, swiped with a spiked bludgeon, aiming at Zane's head with a wild cry. Zane ducked beneath the man's strike, rushing forward. Using his momentum and his funneled anger, he punched the smaller brute in the stomach. Hard. Vurpil doubled over as the air was knocked from his lungs and his cry was squelched. The man tried to rise, but Zane's fists crashed into his hunched back, sending him to the ground. The other, bigger thug was charging with his sword upraised. Zane slipped the strike as it came down, narrowly missing his back, and then he kicked the bigger man in the chest with all his ferocity. The man flew through the air, splintering the nearby torches, and landing with a grunt. Zane approached. The big man moaned, rubbing his chest—likely several of his ribs were broken. He coughed, and sputtered, "Oi' knew you were some kina' blasted demon…"

Zane bent and grabbed the torch from the ground as the man continued to groan and blather.

"But Darkeye ain't human either. Not even mortal." He cackled and sputtered more blood. "You… Even you don't stand a chance. Him an' Salamander'll wipe you and yer pathetic kin off the face of this damned earth…" Zane rose, approaching. The man's eyes grew wide and wild. *"DO YOU 'EAR ME?!"*

Zane didn't break stride as he kicked the man in the face, knocking him out and moving on. He entered the camp and desolation hit him.

Fires like before lit the cavern, but these were not cooking fires. Tents, bedrolls, and all else burned as far he could see. The dead littered the ground—both Darkeye's men and Lost Ones. Mostly Lost Ones.

He found himself moving, eyes filmed, as he took in corpses he had just seen living and breathing. Now they looked into another world. Zane had seen death, but this was different. He saw a little boy. His torch tumbled from his grip as he dropped to his knees.

Rygar…

The boy's blond hair was tousled, his too-small clothes torn to tatters. In the boy's crumpled fist something glinted. Gently unpeeling Rygar's frozen fingers, Zane saw the fat silver coin he had given the boy. Nearby, he recognized another little body—Dasher. Fire and sickness boiled inside of Zane, and sadness threatened to overwhelm. He closed Rygar's wide, lifeless eyes with one hand. With his other hand, he closed the boy's fist around the coin. Whispering a prayer, he grabbed his torch and moved on. Smoke saturated the air, stinging his eyes and burning his nose. Beneath it all, he smelled the metallic stench of blood. He quickened his pace, making his way up the Healer's Terrace where he found what he had been dreading... He shied his gaze, sucking in a thin breath. Slowly, he looked back, taking in the fallen man's white robes with their dirty-brown hem.

Father was dead.

Zane opened his mouth to bellow his anger, but in the last moment swallowed it. Instead, he breathed a tumultuous breath, avoiding the vacant stare of the man who was the closest thing he'd ever had to a father. Arm trembling, he uttered another soft prayer and closed Father's eyes. Quietly, Zane rose, moving to the water. A mantle of fury, deeper than he'd ever known, came over him as he dropped the torch with a hiss and submerged himself in shadows. Breathing in the darkness, Zane turned, eyes latching onto a destination far beyond. He knew what he had to do, where he had to go—to a corner of Farbs where the deepest shadows and all dark news resided.

He moved. Water still dripped from his clothes as he strode, feeling a strange power rumbling inside him. He moved up a smaller

tunnel, having to crouch as he pushed forward. A part of his rage wanted, no *demanded*, that he take the main tunnels out. The path they expected of him. It beckoned him, begging him to lose himself, to kill without abandon. But his anger was his to control, and he would not let it consume him. He would not risk himself and die, only to let Hannah be lost to the hands of Darkeye and his men. He would see her to safety, no matter what, and vengeance would be served.

But there was only one place to find his answers, only one place that would know how to storm The Lair of the Beast and live. It was still a fool's task, but he would not fail.

Maris' Luck waited.

Then Darkeye would meet his torrid wrath.

A Bet of Blood

Gray sat in the corner of Maris' Luck.

Thoughts of the man returned like a dream.

They were close, huddled over a flickering fire as the white storm assailed them.

Kail was the cause of that storm. More than that, now he knew why Kail had sent the storm—to ward off Vera and protect them as they reached the Shining City. But that wasn't known back then, and the memory consumed him once more.

He watched Maris. The man sat quietly, and Gray took in his characteristic white hair spiked up like a flame, his timeless, moss green eyes and sharp features. Most intriguing to Gray, Maris had a perpetual quirk to his thin lips, as if always in on some dark joke that all the world was blind to knowing... Huddled against the cold, the Ronin cradled a steaming mug between his frayed, fingerless gloves and shivered. Even so, he found it odd that the man could be cold, could feel things like others. The stories had made it all a big, confusing pile of truth and fiction in his head. A Ronin. He was immortal, was he not? Maris caught him looking and, nervously, Gray turned. "You make a man unnerved with a look like that," the Ronin murmured, his breath misting in the cold air.

"Like what?" he asked.

"Like I'm not really alive. Like I'm something from the stories."

The words were too close to the truth. He searched for words but found none, and at last grew silent. Gray poured his gaze into his dark brew as he waited for the awkwardness to dissolve like thawing ice. It wasn't that he didn't have questions. If anything, he had too many, but where to begin? He wanted to ask if the man was immortal, but he couldn't bring himself to do it, so he asked his next burning curiosity. "The others," he whispered, "do you miss them?" Maris had left the other Ronin to aid Gray in his path—a path where survival seemed less likely day-by-day, where there was little doubt that the Ronin were gone forever.

But Maris' answer cut beneath the wind. "I shall see them again… one day."

The way he said those words… So certain.

The wind picked up, Kail's litany, as if in answer, and Gray looked back into his dark brew.

He returned to the moment.

That time… so long ago. Gray felt like a different person from the confused, insecure boy, but how long had it really been? Months at most. Now here he sat in Maris' Luck, an inn named after the legend. He felt an odd vacancy, missing the man, and yet…

He found himself gazing at Darius, and was reminded of Maris' smile. Yet where Maris' smile held little warmth, as if hardened over the centuries like weathered stone, Darius' held mirth. *The Ronin of leaf's words echoed in his head: "I shall see them again … one day."*

Suddenly, Ayva spoke, drawing him back to the world and the dark inn.

"I don't like these looks," she said as the men eyed her. "They are worse than the others." She was at his side, again feigning drinking. Despite the fact that he sat between her and the rest of the packed inn, lecherous men *still* leered at her. He hated it, wanting to touch Morrowil, but he remembered Darius' words back in the alley. *A single flame could cause a fire…* or something like that. Either way, better not to antagonize these men and cause more trouble. Besides, many of them looked like they could fight—again it was Kirin's knowledge, but he agreed with it, eyeing their surly looks and dark blades. He wondered if he would even win that fight, especially with his power not working. That thought grated on him, but he tried not to think about it as his eyes surveyed their surroundings.

Maris' Luck was clearly a place where only the darkest thieves congregated, though there was a strange energy in the air. Much of the inn was cast in a fog of pipe-spoke. Beneath that, half-broken tables and chairs crowded the inn. Sordid men filled them, scratching their scruff, exchanging dark whispers. Collectively, it created a drone of noise.

Gray watched as a short little server with a red apron wobbled up to a table, plunking down two dented cups of ale. The dwarfed man had avoided their table entirely. It wasn't a good sign. *There are no women here,* he realized. Suddenly, Gray felt eyes on him, hot and burning. His neck tingled, and Kirin wanted to touch Morrowil. He looked around, searching for that specific gaze. A cloaked man sat at the black ash bar. Behind it was the innkeeper. He was a wiry old man with a face like a corpse and eyes that looked to have seen more death than a grave keeper. His hand scrubbed at the same dirty spot with an even dirtier rag. His other hand was missing—a smooth stump in its place. All the while the innkeeper watched them with a dark scowl. Was that the gaze he felt?

At least Darius seemed to blend in. He'd pulled his collar high around his neck and wore a sour look. He didn't seem to be faking it. Still, compared to the rest of the inn, he was a pup in a wolf's den.

Suddenly, there was a cry and a man crashed to the floor, shattering a chair.

A dagger protruded from his back and dark red blood pooled.

Gray froze in disbelief.

"Is he…?" Ayva breathed.

Darius ribbed him with an elbow and whispered hard. "*Look away, both of you. Just act normal!*"

"Normal?" Gray retorted, anger rising. "Are you still drunk? A man was murdered before our eyes!"

Darius let out an even breath. "Look, I don't like it any more than you do, but this was the plan, remember? Ezrah is waiting. If anyone knows how to enter the Citadel and get him back, we'll find him in this foul pit."

"Then we do nothing?" Ayva questioned.

"Not if you want to live," Darius hissed in reply. "Do you think you can take all these men? If so, then I'm not the one who's drunk. If we get into a fight, we won't do Gray's grandfather any good."

The other men were already settling back into their chairs, laughing and playing cards as if nothing had happened. The dead man just laid there, the puddle of blood growing.

Ayva sank back into her chair. "It still doesn't feel right."

"Then mind telling us your plan?" Gray said, trying to be calm.

"It's coming right now," the rogue announced.

"What's that supposed to mean?" Ayva asked.

"You lot lost?" A rasping voice asked.

Gray looked over his shoulder to see a man, smaller than he anticipated, but no less threatening. He was a hand or two shorter than himself and slender as a blade. His sleeves were rolled back, exposing lean, muscled arms covered with bright-white scars. He wore simple rags, aside from a fitted black vest with silver trim that Gray figured looked respectable at one time but now was fraying at the seams. *Something he must have stolen*, Gray assumed. On his vest's upper right corner was a badge—a bloodshot eye on a field of black. At his hip dangled a dozen different shaped daggers—curved, straight, and jagged. The man's face was lean, as if someone had boiled the fat from it for food, leaving only skin and bones. His sunken jaw muscles worked as he chewed on a long wooden toothpick, and a single hollow eye gauged them like scraps of meat. The other was covered by a red eye patch.

Darius took a long, leisurely sip of his ale. "Lost? Hardly. This is the best ale in town. How could we pass it up?"

"You must be the clown," the man snarled, one eye squinting. Darius tipped his head as if in thanks. "I've a jest for you then. What're you gonna do when I take that pretty thing at your side and have some fun with her?"

Three more men rose from a nearby table and joined the foul man's side, looking ready to do the deed right there. Each wore a similar badge, if less ornate. "She is pretty, Adorry. Both my eyes aren't as keen as your one, but you weren't lying after all!" said a fat man rubbing his mouth with two fingers—the other three of his fingers were missing.

"Lay off, Bones—she's mine first," said a smaller man, sidling forward.

Gray felt his hackles rise. Ayva's leg touched his. It was shaking. He grabbed her hand. Luckily, her face was smooth, almost indifferent—he didn't know how she did that. Gray touched Morrowil, but it would be useless in this cramped space. He saw the scene unfold in his mind, imagined kicking the table onto the three men and cutting into the leader first... But what then? They would be swarmed like bits of food beneath a host of ants.

Darius, however, ignored them all.

Adorry raised his hand, stopping the smaller thief before he reached Ayva. "Speak," he said, leaning forward. Darius said nothing. Adorry slammed his hands down on the table, spilling Ayva and Gray's ales across the splintered wood. "I'm talking to you," he hissed.

Still, the rogue remained silent, sipping his drink coolly.

"Seems he ain't afraid of you like we are, Adorry," said Bones snidely.

"He should be," said the third, a tall man.

Adorry's one eye squinted cruelly, and quicker than light, he bashed Darius' drink from his hand, knocking it against the nearby wall. "I'm not afraid to kill a man who doesn't talk. Takes some of the joy out of it, but it's all the same in the end."

Gray was about to open his mouth when Darius made a move. Slowly, the rogue drew out his dagger and gestured to the one-eyed man's belt filled with knives. "That's a lot of fancy metal. Can you use those or are they just for show?"

As he spoke, the other men burst into laughter. The fat man, with the incongruous name of Bones, dribbled spit, and the shorter, squat one cackled, slapping his leg. The tall lanky man's mouth fanned wide in a wicked grin, showing jagged teeth and one long, curved tooth. Adorry, however, was expressionless. It was somehow even more terrifying. "More or less," the one-eyed man rasped, breathing his rank breath upon them.

Darius spun the dagger in his hand casually, as if pondering. "And are you a betting man?"

"For the right price? Always," Adorry answered, as if amused.

Kirin was still shouting danger, just as he had done since the moment they entered this place, or, for that matter, the moment they entered Shadow's Corner—but now Kirin was truly afraid. He felt as if the one-eyed man was hiding something.

Darius raised his arm, pointing. All turned. Twenty paces away, a post held up the roof. On it was a round slab of a tree trunk hung by a thick nail. It had painted rings—green, blue, yellow, and then finally red for the dead center. The wood looked scarred by a thousand knives. "I challenge you to a game of daggers."

"What's the wager?" asked the fat man, licking his lips.

"Let's say a man wanted to get into the Citadel, unscathed, would you know such a thing?"

Daggers and swords loosened in their sheaths all around them.

"The Citadel?" Adorry scoffed. "You truly are a fool."

"Do you or not?" Darius pressed.

"I know a way," the man said indifferently.

"Then that's my wager. Information. If I win, you tell me how to enter the Citadel and leave … *alive*."

Adorry smirked again. "Valuable information in the right hands, but why would you three weaklings want to enter the Citadel?"

"That's not part of the deal."

The one-eyed man laughed coldly. "And what's in it for me?"

"This," Darius said, dropping a pouch onto the table. It clanked. It was all their money—the silver Karil had given them back at Death's Gate, and what little Darius has scrounged from gambling. Beneath the table, Gray elbowed the rogue. If Darius gambled and lost all their money… Then he realized—their life was on the line. It really didn't matter what Darius was gambling.

"Ah, that's a fat purse!" squawked the stout thief, reaching forward.

Darius pulled it back quickly.

Adorry fingered a blade at his waist as if thinking, then sneered. "No deal."

"Why not?" Ayva asked.

"Because I'm just going to take that from your cold corpses anyway. You have nothing to offer me I can't already take—and *will*," the man said, then his hollow eye panned to Ayva suggestively. Tension mounted, and Gray's palms began to sweat, gripping Morrowil until it hurt. He reached for the nexus but again it flickered, sputtering and dying like a flame with too little wick. "Kill them," Adorry commanded abruptly, and metal rung as his men unsheathed their swords, stalking forward with the lust for blood in their eyes.

Gray pleaded, searching for his power, watching the men approach. *Listen to me!* He bellowed in his mind. But there was no answer.

"*Wait!*" Darius shouted, rising. The men didn't slow. Gray gripped the bottom of the table, preparing himself. "If you kill us now, you'll never get the true bounty!" the rogue yelled. The men hesitated. Behind them, Gray saw a good portion of the nearby patrons were watching curiously.

"What true bounty?" Bones asked with greed in his eyes.

"Cormacs," Darius answered quickly.

"Elvin steeds?" the short one whispered. "Adorry, those be worth a fortune! Two hundred, no three hundred Farbian gold coins at least!"

"He's lying," the tall man said, moving forward and raising his blade.

Adorry lifted a finger. "Wait." The tall man stopped reluctantly. "Let them live for a moment, Snaggle. You have one last chance, boy. Explain quickly."

"We have cormacs," Darius said. "Three of them. But if you kill us now, you'll never know where we stashed them. If you win, however, we'll tell you. You'll get the cormacs *and* the coin. If we win, the information."

"And your lives I suppose?"

"Naturally," Darius said with a shrug.

"Congratulations," replied the one-eyed man. "You have yourself a deal."

What in the seven hells of remwar had gotten into the rogue? He was gambling their lives with this man like trading a bushel of wheat for a jug of milk! But somehow Gray couldn't *really* be mad. Fearful, surely, but not angry. Somehow, he felt that was the best deal they were going to get from this man. Now, light just send that Darius wins.

The commotion resolved, the rest of the inn gradually went back to their previous rabblerousing. The clank of cheap coin and the grate of laughter and dark talk returned to its normal hum.

"Shall we?" Adorry stalked towards the dartboard.

Darius scratched his head, turning back to them.

"Why do I feel like we just bargained with the devil?" Ayva breathed.

"I only have one question," Gray said, eyeing Darius. "Can you win this?"

"We'll see," Darius replied. "That man seems … talented."

"It's because he's no mere thief," Ayva explained, rubbing her brow in frustration. "This is my fault. I should have told you earlier, but Faye told me all thieves have thief names in Farbs, like your friends Snaggle and Bones."

"What's a thief name?"

"They're names orphan boys and girls seek to earn—often crude nicknames given by their peers related to their physical appearance, meant to belittle." Ayva's fist tightened in anger. "It's a barbaric practice associated with the loss of innocence… But to many, it's a badge of honor—for within the world of thieves, you either have a thief name, or you die."

"And Adorry?" Gray asked.

"A rare handful of men and women don't have thief names, like Adorry."

"Why him?"

"The men who don't are named by a man they call *Darkeye*."

"Darkeye?" Darius questioned.

"Leader of the Darkeye Clan. He and his men run most of Farbs—the darker side of it at least. Faye said he's almost never been seen. He's a man of myth and legends. But she said we would have to avoid his clan at all cost."

Gray didn't like the sound of that. He hoped this man was just a myth, but around him, myth and legends always turned out to be real too often. "Then why is this man named by him?" he asked, returning to the point.

"It's a mark of prestige—a name that means something in the sand tongue, like *warrior*, or *cruel one*. Most importantly," she said with a heavy gulp, "it means he's one of Darkeye's officers. Foul as he is, Adorry is clearly a man to be feared."

"Darius?"

Darius was staring at Adorry as he spread his dozen varied daggers down on a nearby table, laying them meticulously, as if preparing himself for torture. Gray eyed the rogue. Darius seemed different, not far away at all now, but focused. From the top of his sword's sheath, a faint green light pulsed, as if feeding off the rogue. At his name, Darius looked back calmly.

"We don't have to do this," Gray said softly, eyeing a nearby back-door. "If we run now, we might get away and—"

"—No, it's too late," Darius said and then smiled. "Besides, without this man, your grandfather is as good as dead. We have to do this."

"But can you?"

"We'll find out, won't we?" he said, grinning. Then he rose and strode forward.

Ayva muttered, "This was a bad idea."

"We have to trust him," Gray said. "Darius knows what he is doing."

Light help us if he doesn't, he thought, and followed.

* * *

A ring of men now surrounded them. Dark chatter still hung in the air, but the nearest chairs had been pushed back and a crowd had begun to watch.

Adorry pulled back his sleeves. "As the one who was challenged, I have the right to decide who goes first," he decreed. "Unless you disagree?"

Darius gave a mock nod of servility. "By all means."

Adorry smirked. "You first."

"That's quite generous of you."

"Not really. I'd prefer to let you have a sliver of hope before I take it away is all," Adorry said. It was not a boast. The man sounded as if he were simply stating a fact.

Yet the fat thief, Bones, chortled. Adorry's other two lackeys merely watched. Both of them still had the same bloodlust in their eyes, fingering their cruel blades. *You have to win, Darius,* Gray entreated, but then wondered what would happen if the rogue did win. Would those men attack anyway? *At least not before we get our information,* he prayed, placing a hand upon Morrowil. *Let them stay their hand at least until we find out how to breach the Citadel.*

Adorry moved aside for Darius, pointing to a red line. Gray tried to imagine the line was paint and not blood as Darius moved forward with a breath. He stood twenty paces from the target. The slab was no bigger than two hands side-by-side. It was a hard shot as it was.

Darius lifted his arrowhead blade, eyes focused on the target.

Yellow, blue, green, and finally, red. Four rings.

Silence hung. Gray felt as if he could cut the tension in the air with a knife. *C'mon, Darius.* With a breath, the rogue released the dagger. It whistled through the air, plunking into the hard wood.

Red.

Darius' blade sat dead center. Commotion in the inn went to a standstill. All eyes fell to Darius, who, to any stranger, wore a deadpan expression. But Gray saw the smirk.

"Blood and flesh!" Foulfoot, the short thief, screeched. "First try!"

"*Luck*," Bones muttered.

Whispers and grumbling spread among the other seated thieves.

"Did you know he was that good?" Ayva whispered in Gray's ear.

"I had a feeling," he admitted, and in truth it was just a feeling. He was hopeful but afraid, though he had hidden it. Fear was no use here, not when men like this fed off of it. "Do you remember the snake in the desert? The one he nailed from a dozen paces away in the dead of night?"

"I'd nearly forgotten," she whispered, and then she bit her bottom lip excitedly. "I think Adorry might be the one in trouble."

Gray flashed a smile, but, inwardly, he wasn't certain. Something told him they shouldn't be so confident, not yet at least. And when he looked to the thief himself, it confirmed his fears. Adorry's face could have made stone look expressive. The only distinguishing mark was a slight twinge to his thin lips.

"Impressive," Adorry declared. But he didn't sound impressed at all.

"Beginner's luck," Darius replied humbly and moved aside.

Adorry stepped forward. "We shall see." From the table, the man extracted a long blade with jagged edges like teeth. His one eye squinted. A deadly calm entered his face. He gave an even breath, and with a practiced flick, the dagger flew. Wood *thunked*.

Red.

Dead center, even closer than Darius'.

Ayva released a thin breath.

Nearby, gasps escaped from the other ruffians. Gray looked to the tall thief, Snaggle. The man's grin spread, revealing a jutting tooth. Both knew this was far from over.

Adorry turned to Darius. "Not luck," he said, stepping back.

Darius swallowed, retrieving his dagger from the board. Another man pulled Adorry's out. Stepping back to the red line, Darius gave a breath and threw, the dagger hitting home. *Blue.* Gray's throat tightened. Blue was the third ring. Two away from red. Not good, he thought. A round of laughter rose from those nearby. Adorry pushed him aside, stepped forward, and threw.

Thunk.

Red again.

Adorry snorted. "Perhaps it was just luck."

Gray touched Morrowil just as something caught his eye. A man in the far corner. He was hooded, smoking from a pipe and cast in shadows. *Danger.* It was Kirin. Reaching out with the ki, he tried to feel for the man, but as he touched him, his second sense recoiled in pain. It wasn't a wall of stone like Faye's had been, but a burning bulwark that seared to the touch. He couldn't tell, but he knew the man's expression changed within that hood.

He retreated, racing back into his own body.

Ayva gripped his arm. "Are you all right? What just happened?"

He realized he was scowling. Shaking it off, he dipped his head to the far wall. "You see that man?" he asked. Ayva followed his gaze to the dark corner, giving a nod. "He's been watching us the whole time."

"Who is he?" she asked.

"I'm not sure, can you tell anything about him? Anything Faye might have said?"

Ayva shook her head. "No. But as a daughter of an innkeeper I can tell you he is dangerous. He's not drinking, and all the nearest chairs and tables to him are empty. He might even be more dangerous than this Adorry fellow."

"Dicing great," Gray whispered, stealing the rogue's curse, looking back to the board as another gasp escaped the nearby crowds.

Darius' blade sat in center of the red ring.

Adorry's sat in the yellow. The fourth ring, farthest from the center.

The thief's face was a mask of confusion and anger. "That … that can't be…"

"What happened, Adorry?"

"Something from the floorboards up and tripped me!" he shouted.

Ayva gave Gray a look, and he hid any expression, but inwardly elation lanced through him. Did Darius just…? Darius, however, looked the most confused and innocent of them all. Gray knew that was usually a mastered expression from the rogue, but this time it seemed truly genuine.

Nearby, men looked to the thief-leader as if he were mad. Adorry, seeing this, quieted. He flashed Darius a smooth grin. It contorted his gaunt face oddly, like thin dough stretched over too big a pie tin, as if he couldn't spare the flesh to smile. "Seems you lead. But as the challenger, I go first now. Step back," he snapped, pushing Darius aside.

"As you wish," Darius said, hiding a sneer behind a smile. Gray could see Darius' anger, though luckily, he kept it in check.

Adorry grabbed the cruelest looking blade he had from the table—a spiked, curved dagger that looked like a large, bent needle with thorns. The thief-leader gave three even breaths, then his eye snapped wide. Gray's heart pounded. Such confidence. The man threw. The blade twirled end over end. It hit.

Again, red—but the very center.

"What does that mean?" Ayva asked. "Did he win?"

Gray shook his head. "No, but almost. Darius just has to hit red as well and he'll win. Anything less and he loses."

"Exactly," Bones said, "But he has to hit more center than Adorry's last hit."

"Who says?" Ayva replied. "They're even!"

"Besides, there is no more center than that," Gray said, scoffing.

"Well, I'm sure he'll find a way," Adorry announced.

Darius' said nothing. Instead, he strode forward, all eyes on him as he yanked his dagger free from his last throw, and strode back. Gray had never seen him like this. The rogue's dark eyes narrowed on the board. At his side, Darius' finger flitted. Gray knew that gesture—it was the same one Maris used to do. The full name of the inn hit Gray like a sack of bricks. *Maris' Luck*, he realized. *Dice, I hope that's true.* Was it simply fate they had entered here?

He felt Ayva sidle closer as Darius raised his blade.

Adorry suddenly spoke, "We've been playing wrong this whole time. You've been cheating."

"What do you mean?" Darius protested, shaking with restrained ire. "I haven't stepped over the line once!"

Adorry shrugged. "Perhaps. But the odds are unfair. I have one eye, and you have two. Thus, you've been cheating."

"How is that his fault?" Ayva said, bristling.

Chairs slid back and Gray's muscles tensed. He saw it all panning out before him: bloodshed and death—falling to these vile men in this dark place without ever saving Ezrah. Just as the tension reached a peak, Darius raised a hand. Men froze. Gray saw the rogue's jaw muscles spasm, clenched furiously, but all he did was give a mock bow. "Fair's fair," he declared and put a hand over his eye.

All around, men roared with laughter.

Adorry and the tall man, Snaggle, merely sneered.

Gray knew Darius had barely held his own with Adorry with *both* his eyes. With just one and no sense of depth? The rogue was doomed. Gray tried to hide his rising fear, but he knew that, unless a miracle occurred, Darius would lose. The others knew it too. Snaggle and Foulfoot moved forward, just slightly, preparing themselves. At the bar, Gray saw movement. A slender cloaked figure was watching, pipe smoke curling from a deep hood. *A third danger? How many murderous men does this hellish pit breed?* he thought with rising anger, but he registered the threat and turned back to Darius as the rogue let out a heavy breath, raising his dagger with one hand, and covering his left eye with the other.

Subtly, Gray lifted Morrowil from its ornate sheath, clearing it so it wouldn't stick when drawn. As he did, he realized this whole thing had been a fool venture from the very start. But it was too late. Now he simply had to be ready. With that thought, he prepared himself for Darius to lose.

He prepared himself for blood.

An Unexpected Guest

Darius gripped the dagger in his fingers. It felt slick. The metal pinched between his thumb and forefinger. He felt another trickle of sweat run down his temple. He wiped it with his shoulder and focused on the target.

It wasn't easy. The wood slab seemed to waver like a drunkard, zooming in and out. *Stop thinking that way!* He shouted inwardly, and gave an even breath. Again, his fingers flitted at his side nervously. In the corner of his vision, he saw Adorry. The fool watched him smugly. Gray and Ayva weren't far—their eyes were even worse. *Hope and fear.* He pushed it all aside, remembering the lessons his pa had taught him so long ago.

Find the center, he thought, repeating his father's words.

The world pulsed.

Breathe.

It pulsed again, and he was lost in a memory.

"Breathe, boy!"

Darius was in a dark room. In the nearby forge, a bed of glowing red coals smoldered. It was the only light. The room smelled of metal, sulfur, oils, and sweat. His eyes watered from the stifling hot air. Why couldn't they do this outside? he had asked. His father's retort was simple: Because the world isn't always fair. One day when you grow up, you'll see that.

The world wasn't fair, sure, he thought, eyeing the target before him. But it wasn't all bad either… But he'd kept his mouth shut of course. Arguing with his father wasn't worth it. Even if he wasn't beaten for his "sharp tongue," the man might stop teaching him. It wasn't his dad's fault really—Darius just didn't see the same darkness as him. Perhaps he was simply less wise than his father.

In the end, he would never ruin it by talking back. His father was so focused on his duties as a blacksmith that to be taught daggers by him was a blessing Darius wouldn't toss away.

His dad yelled again, something about breathing, but Darius was focused.

The metal can sat square in his vision. His eyes narrowed, holding the blade tighter. He reared his arm up like his father had told him—nice and slow and always even—and then loosed. The dagger flew, skimming the tin can. It clattered against the wall into an assortment of hanging tools—tongs, hammers, and chisels—and then fell into a water trough.

He looked to his father, feeling his failure to his bones.

"Did you breathe?" the man asked softly, fury in his eyes.

And Darius let out the breath he was holding, shaking his head.

Darius returned back to the moment.

Breathe!

And he released a pent up breath. His arm trembled, and the weight of eyes hit him from all around, but his father's words hammered through him. *Breathe and ignore it all.* And like a blade being dunked into the quench tub to be tempered, the weight of the eyes and the heat of the moment evaporated. There was only him and the wood slab before him. That was all. With a last breath, he unleashed the dagger.

It soared, spinning end over end.

But it wasn't going to hit. The blade's trajectory carried it close, but with his covered eye, he had misjudged the center by a hair and that was enough to lose it all.

Darius had lost. Again fear and disappointment spiraled to his core as if he felt his father's judging gaze upon him once again. At the same time, something pulsed. Pushing his childhood guilt and even his current dread aside, he saw something … something brilliant in the corner of his mind. He pushed further, trying to feel it, to *see* it. He pushed through a last barrier, like breaking through a last stand of trees and there it was.

The Leaf.

He gripped it. Abruptly, he felt a connection to the building around him—every piece of wood, every splintered chair or rough-hewn table. But it was distant and faint, like trying to cling to a wisp of smoke. He looked up.

The dagger was still flying.

Time seemed to have slowed to a snail's pace, but it was still moving. The dagger was about to miss. Darius reached out, lifting a hand, but it moved too slowly. His mind was what moved—his mind was faster. He touched the slab of wood. It listened, if barely, like a limb that was not his own. He begged it, pressing it to move. But it was rooted by the thick nail. No, he thought in dread as the dagger made its last rotation. Please! he pleaded. The dagger flew. Darius pulled. The wood trembled, his mind shook and then—

There was a loud *thunk*. His heart beat like a steel drum in his chest, and sweat poured down his face. He twisted, looking around, and saw surprise on the rough faces of those nearby. Darius eyed his shot and breathed out—the only sound in the otherwise silent room.

The wood slab had split down the center. One half was on the ground—Adorry's dagger was no longer inside the wood but had clattered uselessly to the side. The other half of the slab still hung. Darius dagger was in the dead center. It had pierced the wood all the way to the hilt, consuming the entire red circle.

"Is that center enough?" he asked.

Adorry's jaw hung.

Another thief exclaimed, "The young fool has won!"

A sudden, gruff round of cheers went up from the nearest thugs, mugs clinking and tables rattling. Darius realized they didn't seem to care who had won, just that someone had lost. Of course, those affiliated with Adorry weren't cheering, they wore dark looks. The rest of the inn turned at the sound of cheering as well, casting peeved looks, distracted from their dark talk, but quickly returned to their business.

Ayva embraced Gray in triumph, and he squeezed back until he noticed various glances. They both cleared their throats, and he set her on the ground and turned back to the scene.

Darius looked to Adorry himself. "So… That information."

The man's hollow face twitched in fury. "You cheated," he seethed. "No one else saw that? The blade was clearly off path and then something shifted the board!"

He shook his head, amused. "No, *you* cheated, and the whole way might I add, and I still won fair and square." In a way, it was true—it was *his* power he'd used.

"You broke it in half! How does that mean you won over me?"

"Sounds like a win to me!" a thief at a nearby table exclaimed.

Another man, missing his teeth, chimed in, "Aye, but go easy on Adorry, fellas. It's his first loss. He's allowed to whine like a little girl." Uproarious laughter and cheers sounded at that, louder than before, accompanied by more clinking of pints. A dagger whistled through the air, hitting the toothless man in the throat. The thief gurgled and fell over, lifeless.

Darius eyed Adorry who held two more daggers in his hand.

"The bet?" Darius asked, swallowing.

Adorry snorted. "The bet is off! You broke your end of it, and no one cheats Adorry Droverson. I don't know how you did it, but you must be an Untamed or something else vile like that. You'll be a fine catch for Darkeye when we take you back to The Lair of the Beast as a prize. He'll decide what to do with you then. As for your friends, we have no use of them. You lot should never have wandered in here. It's a crying shame about the cormacs, but I'll have to assume you were lying about those too." He gestured to Snaggle, Foulfoot, and Bones. "Grab the liar; I'll handle the other two." Adorry's hands flashed, flinging two daggers towards Ayva and Gray.

Both moved, but they were too slow.

Darius delved inward, grasping the Leaf. It waited. He gripped something and flung it. A table hurtled through the air, catching both daggers, and then crashed against a pillar.

An awkward silence filled the air, all four men taken aback.

Darius shouted, "If any of you move, I'll strike you all dead with my power!" *Lying again?* But fear and anger flowed through him. He almost felt it was true. The men hesitated, clearly fearful—but it only lasted so long.

Adorry's sneer widened. "*Enough!* I'll end your filthy lying if no one else will!" His hands and arms flew, flashing faster than Darius' eye could follow, and a dozen daggers flew through the air, hurtling towards him like raining steel. Darius reached for his power, but as he gripped the Leaf, it slipped through his inexperienced fingers like water. *No!* he bellowed.

At the same time, the door to the inn burst, a silhouetted figure stood lit by the murky inn's light. Sudden fire flew forth. The fiery bolt roared across the space between Adorry and Darius and crashed against the far wall, sending out sparks. Twisted hunks of glowing hot metal clattered to the inn's floor.

All turned to the sudden stranger who was still moving, striding forward. He crossed the distance and came to a sudden halt.

He wore dark rags and a heavy wool cloak. Strangely, Darius saw his clothes dripped with water. He threw back his soggy hood to expose a hard, rugged face with dark scruff and ratted blond hair. He was muscled and broad, though not tall. He was, perhaps, a hand shorter than himself, but the way he held himself was like a man twice his height. But worst of all were those eyes…

The stranger's gaze flowed over them all like a tempest, surveying quickly as if looking for something. Those fiery, copper-colored eyes looked at Darius, and he felt his blood heat from their sheer rage. But then they passed over him. *Who in the seven hells is this man?* He looked no older than Gray or him, but that pain and anger… It was enough to rival a hundred men. Finally, the man's eyes caught on something.

The bloodshot badge Adorry wore held his gaze.

"You…" the stranger seethed.

The bubble of silence and confusion shattered. Adorry gripped a dagger and lunged at the man, but the stranger snatched Adorry's arm and brought his knee hard against the man's elbow. There was a loud crack of bone. Adorry cried out in agony. Swiftly, the stranger grabbed the man's throat and raised him into the air. No one had time to move, not even Snaggle, and the other thieves still gripped their swords as if bewildered about whom to attack first.

The stranger spoke in a low burning voice, commanding all attention, "You're going to help me now, or I will break every last bone in your body. And if any of you try to come after this man, this is what will happen: I will kill him first, and then I will kill you."

Adorry quivered, grasping his shattered arm in pain and choking as the stranger held him aloft. "What… What do you want?"

"The Lair of the Beast. You will take me there."

The thief-leader's hollow eyes fanned wide, but they were nothing compared to the fury of the stranger. Darius was almost surprised Adorry hadn't ignited in flames yet from that gaze.

Darius saw his friends. Gray gripped Morrowil, and Ayva at his side held a curious orange glow in one hand and her translucent-white dagger in the other. As for the rest of the inn, most had risen, clutching weapons, while some huddled in the shadows.

"Never," Adorry jeered and then roared, *"KILL HIM! KILL THEM ALL!"*

And the inn exploded in chaos.

The door crashed open, and men in dark rags wearing the same badges with a bloodshot eye upon their shoulders poured into the inn. At the same time, Snaggle sliced at Darius, who leapt back, but the man was quick. He rolled beneath another lunging strike and came up near his dagger. He yanked it from the red center, and threw it at Snaggle. The man parried the blade with ease, charging forward. Suddenly, the man gasped and keeled forward. Darius saw a dagger sprouting from Snaggle's back. Darius looked around but had no idea where it had come from.

All around him, a battle raged as steel clanged and wood exploded. In the center, he saw the stranger holding Adorry aloft as he fended off a clutch of thieves—though most looked afraid to confront the stranger and his burning ire. Darius felt something hot on his back. *His sword.* He reached for the blade just as fire roared, racing through the air. It was coming straight at him. He ducked, barely missing it, and it seared through a wood pillar like hot iron through parchment. The inn groaned as if about to collapse, floorboards shaking beneath his feet and then settling. Darius pivoted as a figure barreled into him, sending him tumbling back and crashing into the bar. His head smacked hard wood, and there was an explosion of pain. His senses blurred, his vision clouding. Something heavy rammed into his gut. He gasped, wind knocked from his lungs. Rage mounting, Darius pulled at his sword. Its ring filled the air.

Abruptly, the body upon him went limp. His vision cleared as he saw the man, Foulfoot, fall dead with another dagger to the back.

Dazed, Darius looked up.

"Faye..." he whispered.

Faye sat on a nearby barstool, looking down on him. Calmly, she pulled back her hood, and ringlets of red hair spilled out, framing her tan face. Her dark, round eyes, however, watched him mysteriously. All in all, she looked bored.

"What in the seven hells of remwar are you doing here?"

"Saving you, it seems. Twice now," she replied.

"*I*—" he began angrily.

Faye cleared her throat. "Behind you," she said coolly with a nod.

Just then, a thief barreled towards Darius with a long sword in hand. The big man swung the huge blade. Darius parried, barely in time. But instead of metal clashing, his sword sliced the thief's blade in two, as if melting the steel. The man faltered in surprise, eyeing his stump of a sword. Darius, equally shocked, shook his head and smashed the hilt of his blade into the man's skull, knocking him out. At the same time, something fell upon his foot. Two more daggers and two more thieves, he realized.

"Three, and four," Faye said, counting her tally upon her hand. "You really are beginning to owe me. Also, I noticed you don't kill. It's admirable, but foolish. These are murderers and cutthroats, Darius. They would not be so valiant in the same position." As she spoke, he noticed her eyes linger on his green blade.

Darius growled. He didn't have time to argue morality with her. He twisted, looking for Gray and Ayva through the din. He spotted them on the other side of the inn pitted in battle against a group of thieves, one of which was Bones. Gray was working curious forms, parrying and attacking with Morrowil, mostly keeping them at a distance, but they were closing in. Darius realized it was only a matter of time before that noose cinched.

"Mind debating this later and helping me now?" he asked.

"This isn't my fight," she answered, turning back to her drink. In her other hand she puffed on a familiar-looking pipe. And he realized it was *his* pipe! It was the one he had lost. *How in the...*

From across the inn, he heard Ayva cry out.

"Faye!" Darius shouted furiously. "They are going to die!"

She sniffed and leaned back as a dagger soared through the air, barely skimming by and crashing into the wall behind the bar, shattering bottles. "As I seem to remember, you three abandoned me. This seems a fitting retribution."

Darius snarled in anger, turning. She was useless. He charged forward, looking to cut a path through the men, but there were too many. As he kicked one down, three more replaced him. It was a losing fight. Between the mesh of two men's swords against his green blade, he saw Gray was tiring and Ayva was surrounded. Only four men remained, but it was just too many.

Gray took a cut to his hand and Morrowil fell. The men swarmed around him.

Through the tangle of men and swords, something caught Darius' eye. A presence, strong and powerful. The Leaf in his mind pulsed. A man. He sat in a far stall, the only one not participating in the fighting. Darius sidestepped a dagger's thrust that would have taken his arm, watching as the man rose and moved through the storm of battle, avoiding swords somehow as if made of smoke. He stopped in the center of the battle.

Calmly, the man unsheathed his sword. The ring of steel and a roar of fire echoed off the walls. Eyes fell to him and his fiery sword, and ruffians dropped their weapons with a look of terror.

"What in the..." Darius whispered.

Suddenly, the two men before him threw their blades as if the fools were gripping snakes. Confused, Darius rubbed his head, eyeing the now defenseless thieves. He was tempted to attack, but reluctantly, he straightened and stepped back. Still, he sure as dicing hell wasn't going to drop his sword! In a matter of seconds, all fighting in the inn had ceased. Silence reigned. The copper-eyed man even looked surprised, but he still held his sword. His other fist gripped Adorry's hair.

Holding his burning sword, the man spun in a full circle, eyeing all in the room. His hood was still up, so Darius couldn't see his features, but he took in that blade. It was a curious looking sword. Thin flames coated its surface, hissing. Fearsome surely, but Darius didn't see what was so intimidating about it when—

As the man rotated, he spotted his cloak. Two large crossed swords. It was just like Gray's cloak, if less dirty and threadbare. A Devari. The Devari spoke in a low, dark grate. "If you value your skin, run."

None moved.

"Leave or find the might of the Citadel crashing down upon your heads." Each dark thief stiffened at his words, but still none moved.

"*Now!*" the Devari bellowed at last, and they sprang into action, bolting for the door, many ignoring their weapons as they fled into the night. The last one left was Adorry—he still cowered in the stranger's grip. "Him too," the Devari said, raising his blade to the stranger's throat.

The stranger's hand gripped his blade tighter. "I need this man."

The Devari's burning sword hovered closer. "I won't ask again."

The stranger looked conflicted. He lifted his sword, but at last he angrily shoved Adorry to the ground. The thief-leader, cradling his broken arm, rose with a satisfied grin.

"Run," the Devari breathed.

Adorry spat at their feet and skittered away. As he reached the door he spoke. "Count your breaths, Shade, for they will be your last. Darkeye has great plans for you. You won't live to see the morrow!" he said with a cackle and slammed the door.

Shade? Who was he talking to? Darius wondered. *The stranger?*

With the last thief gone, a strange silence settled over the inn.

A Battle of Wind and Fire

Darius rushed to Gray's side, helping him to his feet. Ayva stood as well. They were both beaten up—Ayva had a bruise upon her cheek, and cuts and scrapes marred Gray's arm as if he'd just been tossed down a rocky hillside, but all in all, it was nothing serious. *How did we survive that?*

Faye, Darius remembered, turning. She still sat at the bar, sipping her drink and puffing smoke from his pipe as if nothing had happened. She had turned around now and was sizing up the room.

Both the Devari and the stranger had engaged in some sort of epic angry staring contest, and both seemed to be winning *and* losing. Darius looked towards the backdoor, wanting more than anything to not be involved in that. Quietly, he tugged on Gray's arm. "Let's get out of here before…"

"No one else leaves," the Devari declared.

"I wasn't planning on going anywhere," Faye replied coolly. "But I am curious as to why a Devari is in this cursed place. The Citadel's presence, sadly, does not extend to Shadow's Corner. You are a far away from your home. Perhaps even more so than those three," she said, nodding in their direction. "And they at least are fools who don't know any better."

Darius wanted to be angry, but a part of him agreed with her.

They were over their heads. Far over their heads, and he was the one who had got them into it. *Great, now I'm playing the dicing hero.* Darius saw Gray. He looked as if in a trance, gazing at the Devari.

"You let them all get away…" the copper-eyed young man seethed. "I needed that fool, Adorry, and you released him without even a care."

"He was not yours to keep," the Devari said.

"Nor yours to send away!"

"I see your pain, but your anger is blinding you. Or do you really think that man would have aided you? He would have led you to The Lair of the Beast and then fed you to the beast itself. If you think otherwise, then you are a fool."

The stranger still shook with anger, but he seemed to see reason. At last he gave a thin, hard sigh. "It was my only chance…"

"Your only chance for what?" Gray asked suddenly.

All turned to him.

The stranger eyed him curiously, his copper eyes narrowing. "To save a life."

"Whose life?" Ayva asked gently.

"What's it to you?" he replied, without turning.

"Please, perhaps we can help," Ayva insisted.

Raising a dubious brow, Darius tugged on her sleeve, but she didn't flinch. *Ayva! What are you thinking?* he growled inwardly. *Isn't one impossible mission enough?*

The stranger looked to Ayva, and some of his fire seemed to visibly dissipate, but his voice was still cold. "My sister's." Darius dropped his hand and swallowed. The others looked uncertain as well. *That explains his anger.*

"We can still save your sister, Zane," the Devari answered.

"How… How do you know my name?"

Slowly, the Devari pulled back his hood. Darius winced, repressing the urge to look away. Sharp blue eyes were the only true feature on the Devari's face. The rest of it was hideously scarred. It shone in the inn's pitiful light, bone-white. Some parts were smooth and taut, looking almost unharmed, while others were twisted and overlapping like tight strands of rope.

Zane gasped. "You…"

"Victasys," he said, nodding his scarred head in introduction.

The fiery young man looked rattled by the Devari before him. "How did you survive?"

"It's a long story," Victasys replied.

"I'd be willing to hear it," Faye called casually from the bar, puffing smoke.

Darius' head swiveled in confusion. "Wait, you two know each other?"

"He saved my life," Zane stated.

"At nearly the cost of my own," the Devari replied.

"I..." Zane hesitated, the fury in his eyes faltering. He held the man's gaze with difficulty. "I'm sorry for whatever you had to endure, but I never asked for it."

Victasys' eyes hardened. "I didn't do it for you."

"Then why?"

"I saved your life because Sithel was wrong. You just happened to be in the center of it," the man answered matter-of-factly. "And I did not say it to garner sympathy or to guilt you. But if I had to choose again, I would do the same. That it nearly cost me my life was simply the truth."

"And they just let you go after all of that?" Zane asked.

"No, I'm no longer a part of the Citadel, nor truly a Devari."

Faye laughed, amused. "Then that was a grand bluff indeed, '*might of the Citadel!*' I never knew Devari had a sense of humor."

"We don't."

Darius almost laughed, but his mirth perished at the look in the man's eyes. His scarred face hadn't shifted. His laughter died in his throat. No one in the room moved. He looked around, confused, as Victasys eyed Faye like a viper. She merely sat upon her stool, legs crossed, puffing quietly. "You still have yet to answer me," she pressed. "Why did you enter Maris' Luck, Devari? Do you have a death wish?"

He snorted. "No one would kill a Devari."

"They might try."

"Not if they value their lives."

She sniffed. "Ah, but many don't."

Zane stepped forward, gripping the Devari's arm, interrupting the two. "Enough bickering. Victasys, you said you know a way to save Hannah ... to save my sister. Please, what is it?"

The Devari sheathed his blade, the fire winking out as he slammed it home. "The Lair of the Beast is a breeding ground for evil. It is the home of Darkeye's Clan. That you attempt to venture there is tantamount to suicide."

"Then you're of no use and I go alone." Zane moved to the door.

Victasys moved, seizing Zane's shoulder, stopping him. "I did not say I would not go. But walking into the The Lair of the Beast without a plan *will* be certain death. I've already been brought back from the brink once—I do not wish it again."

"How *did* you survive?" Zane asked.

Victasys' eyes seemed to glaze in memory. "I owe my life to one man, a wielder of the spark the likes I've never seen before. He saved me when I was but a breath from the grave. His name was Ezrah."

Gray choked, stepping forward. "Ezrah? Are you sure?"

"Why do you ask? And who are you?" the Devari questioned gruffly.

"My name is Gray, and please," he insisted.

"I'm certain," Victasys said. "I would never forget a man like that."

"Isn't that…?" Ayva whispered, casting a subtle look to Darius.

Darius nodded mutely. *Gray's grandfather*, he thought in astonishment.

"Where is he?" Gray asked, having crossed the distance between the two.

"How do you know him?"

"He is my grandfather."

Victasys looked astounded, though it was difficult to tell on his face.

"He's your grandfather?" Zane repeated.

Gray nodded.

"He saved me too," the blond-haired man confessed, "I got myself into a bit of trouble after stealing gold from Darkeye's men. To avoid them, I jumped into a procession of Devari and Reavers. Looking back, it was a fool's move, but my hide was saved when a man came forward claiming to be my father. It was your grandfather. He makes a strong impression." The heat in his voice went from anger to admiration.

Gray smiled. "I don't know him well, but I've a feeling that sounds about right."

"I'm going to make a guess," Faye said. "That this man, this Ezrah, is how a Devari ended up in this abysmal place."

"A good guess," Victasys said.

"It was less of a guess I suppose and more of an elimination of possibilities," Faye replied. "I've never seen a Devari down here, nor had those men, which by the way was likely the only reason your little stunt worked."

Victasys smiled for the first time, taut skin twisting. "The power of confusion is never to be underestimated." Darius grunted agreeably to himself, knowing that all too well from his gambling misadventures.

Gray touched the Devari's arm, turning him. "Please, what did Ezrah say to you?"

"Very little. We met in secret. He healed me, and then helped me escape before Sithel returned to finish what he'd started. I was under constant watch from Jian, so it wasn't easy, but Ezrah knew exactly where to go. With the use of a hidden transporter, I escaped." *Transporter? Jian? Sithel? What is he talking about?* Darius wondered. The man continued, "Once we got out of the Citadel, he gave me strict orders to visit an inn called Maris' Luck and stop what he named 'a battle of wind and fire'. He didn't know when, only that something *would* happen. I sensed that he was entrusting me with the lives of those he cared about. I sensed his compassion, and that is why I am here, answering your questions..." Victasys scratched his jaw and growled, "Of course, the next time you can tell your grandfather a timeline would be nice. For days I've been coming here, dealing with these foul folk."

"Wind and fire..." Gray repeated, "Those words sound like prophecy."

"You mean to say that your grandfather knew this battle was going to happen all along?" Darius whistled through his teeth. "Why do I have the feeling that every bit of this was set up? Like a card game, and Ezrah knows all the hands..."

Gray's eyes grew cold. "You'd be right, Darius, save for the fact that he is in chains and being tortured."

Darius cleared his throat.

Nearby, the others tensed.

"How do you know this?" Zane asked fervently.

"I've seen it," Gray answered, his gaze distant. "I saw him held captive by a group of Reavers within the Citadel."

"Then someone is one step ahead of Ezrah, pulling the strings," Ayva declared, moving to stand at Gray's side.

"Perhaps it's Sithel," Zane said, looking to Victasys.

"Who is this Sithel character anyway?" Darius questioned, flipping over a nearby chair that wasn't broken and sitting on it backwards. He sheathed his sword and stuffed his dagger away, resting his arms on the chair's back.

"I'm not sure where he came from," Victasys said. "He just showed up recently and started commanding others. Reavers listen to him, and so do many Devari. I couldn't sense the spark on him, but he seems powerful."

Zane made a disgruntled sound.

"What is it?" Gray asked.

"Are you sure you saw what you saw?" Zane replied. "That your grandfather is in danger?

"I only wish I was wrong. Why do you doubt it?"

"You don't know?"

"Know what?" he asked curiously.

"Ezrah, your grandfather, he is an Arbiter," Zane said.

Darius was just confused, watching the others' reactions of confusion and awe. Victasys seemed thoughtful, nodding, while Ayva's eyes split wide as if she'd been bitten by a snake.

Faye was more adamant than all. She strode forward. "Who told you this?" she asked.

"A friend," Zane said, emotion wracking his voice. "He's dead. But before he died, he told me Ezrah was an Arbiter. He was old. His mother as a girl had watched the man's promotion to the rank of Arbiter. How did you not know this?" he asked, looking to the Devari.

"Aside the fact that I'm new in town, the identity of Arbiter is generally kept a mystery. All know that the Patriarch is the most powerful and highest ranking, and only recently, with the kidnapping of young boys, has Arbiter Fera revealed herself. But the identity of the rank two Arbiter has always been a mystery. But when he saved me I should have known. There was an aura about him... I've never seen such power. That he is taken..." Even the Devari looked fearful, and *that* scared Darius more than the rest.

"Mind filling us in on what an Arbiter actually is for those who aren't from Farbs?" Darius voiced.

Ayva answered. "Arbiters are the most powerful wielders of the spark. The Citadel is split up into ranks of those who wield magic. Neophytes, then Reavers, and finally Arbiters—there are only three Arbiters in existence." He thanked Ayva, glad *someone* was filling in the blanks.

"This is ominous news…" Victasys whispered.

Darius looked to Faye. She seemed oddly silent now, watching the others.

"Why isn't the whole Citadel in an uproar if the second most powerful wielder of the spark is missing?" Gray asked.

"Precisely because only a rare handful even know of his identity, let alone know where he is or how to reach him," Victasys explained. "It is a means of protection for the most powerful against those who would attempt to seize their place."

"What do you mean?" Gray asked.

The Devari waved the matter off. "We do not have time to give you three a whole lesson on the Citadel and its division of hierarchies. Suffice it to say that power is everything within the black walls."

Ayva spoke, "You mean to say that, if one were to gain more power in the spark than even the Patriarch, then he or she would become an Arbiter of the highest rank?"

"She catches on quick," Victasys said in admiration.

"Of course," Faye replied. "Ayva is—or *was*—my pupil. My *Diaon*." The way she said it, sounded like Victasys' compliment was meant for *Faye* rather than Ayva. Ayva's jaw grit, and she stared daggers at the woman, but she said nothing.

Gray spoke. "That makes sense why the Citadel isn't in an upheaval at least, but still, who could take down the second most powerful man in all of Farhaven?"

Darius had pulled out his dagger and was spinning it in his palm as he listened. But at Gray's words, the dagger wavered, nearly falling. Even Darius didn't know what all this Reaver-Arbiter-Devari business meant in full. Sure he was quick to gather whom to fear, and wisely so, but the second most powerful man in all of Farhaven? He shivered.

"This news means more than you know," Victasys proclaimed,

his scarred hand tightening around his sword's pommel. "I've been hearing dark rumors of the Citadel breaking, of Reavers turning to the dark. This Sithel and the Reavers whom he keeps as pets are the beginning. I fear that the Citadel, my home, is on the verge of war."

"With whom?" Darius asked.

"Itself," Victasys said.

"Then how can no one see it, this rising darkness?" Gray asked.

"Others see it," he admitted. "Many of my order are worried. But it's been building slowly for years. Reavers growing darker, learning more forbidden arts, Devari ignoring the codes, and more—the whole keep, despite its dark façade, was once a shining bastion of peace, Reavers meant peace; now Devari are dreaded, and Reavers are demons. The Citadel has become a den of iniquity."

There was a silence as it sunk in. Darius scratched at the hairs on his arm that stood on end. "It's true…" Zane said. "I've seen the darkness spreading."

"It's just like what we heard in every inn and tavern," Gray said, hand tightening on Morrowil. "The world is darkening."

"The Patriarch must be warned," Victasys announced abruptly.

"And who would tell him? A banished Devari? A thief? *Me?*" Darius questioned, gripping his dagger tighter. "Not to mention, if this Patriarch is as grand as you all make him sound, I very much doubt a single one of us could even get close enough to touch his highness' bathwater."

"Interesting way of putting it," Faye remarked, nose wrinkling. "But I'm in agreement with the rogue for once. Ezrah must be saved first. Only he can undo the darkness of the Citadel, and from the inside out. At the very least, he may be able to warn the Patriarch."

"Then what must we do?" Ayva asked.

"We have to save him," Gray said.

Zane rumbled, shaking his head as if breaking a spell. "No, your grandfather can wait." He looked to Victasys. "How do I get into The Lair of the Beast, Devari?"

Victasys grimaced. "Sadly, I do not know a way in, but I will help you if I can. But the truth is they will likely kill us as soon as we enter their borders. A Devari can still hold sway within the Shadow's Corner, but the Citadel holds no sway in The Lair of the Beast. Not unless we bear the bloodshot eye."

Gray spoke, "Wait, you can steal those badges, can't you?"

"That's easy," Zane said, smiling at last.

"A start," Victasys admitted.

"I can gather them. I know where to look without drumming up any questions about missing members of their order. Any other good ideas?" Zane asked.

"Perhaps we can gain entrance as newcomers seeking to join Darkeye's clan," Gray posed. "With a thief name and a decent background…"

Zane looked hopeful and Victasys rubbed his chin, nodding.

Darius scratched his head. It sounded feasible, but could it really be that easy?

"It won't work," Faye said. "It's a start—but that's all it is. Breaching The Lair of the Beast is no simple feat. Darkeye is many things, but he is not a fool."

"How would you know? It could work," Ayva insisted.

"It won't. First off, there are passcodes, secret tunnels, and a hundred other traps that none but an initiated clan member would know. And even if you get past those, to get to where you want to go—the heart of the Lair—you would need officer clearance, and no silly badge will work for that. You'll need Darkeye's Mark. Besides, those men aren't brainless pawns like the rest. You saw Adorry Droverson. They're smart and deadly, and he's the runt of the litter. They'll see through your ruse before you can bat an eye and kill you before you draw a drop of blood.

"And *even* then, if by some cursed miracle you get through all that, you've forgotten the best part! *If* your sister is held within the prison, you'll have to confront Darkeye himself, for that is the heart of his home."

Victasys gave a breath, looking troubled. "She speaks the truth."

"Of course I do. I'm not a nitwit like all of you," Faye said with a final huff.

"I can take Darkeye," Zane announced.

Faye laughed, but Zane flashed her a fiery look, and she merely rolled her eyes.

"From what I've seen, I sense you are a skilled fighter, Zane, but if you think you can take Darkeye alone, you are a fool," the Devari said bitingly. "I've brothers more skilled than I who have fallen to

Darkeye's blade." Victasys' fist clenched at his side. "Whispers say that he wears three patches of the crossed-swords from fallen Devari upon his own cloak, sewn together like badges of pride. He is vile to the core, and he is not to be taken lightly."

"Besides," Gray added, "The way that Adorry spoke, it sounded like they are waiting for you, Zane, as if they are expecting you will come for her. You're the worst one to go out of all of us."

Darius expected Zane to lash back, but something swirled in his eyes. "Your grandfather said as much," the fiery man said.

"What do you mean?" Gray asked.

"When he came to me, he warned me of facing Darkeye or Sithel. He said it was in the prophecy that, if I did, it would spell my death. But I will not stand by idly," Zane countered fiercely. "I would rather die."

"And die you will if you enter Darkeye's home," Darius said.

"Then what would you have me do? Lay down like a tamed hound as they torture my sister?"

Tamed? Darius thought, eyeing the fiery Zane. *What is the man's definition of tamed?*

"Join me and save my grandfather," Gray proposed suddenly. Zane raised a skeptical brow, but Gray continued, "It's your only real option. If you confront Darkeye, you'll die. But you and I, with Victasys' skill and knowledge of the Citadel, can rescue Ezrah from the Citadel's clutches." He shook his head as if seeing a sudden nightmare. "I've seen him … in a dream. They are torturing him endlessly. I *feel* his pain." Gray looked up suddenly, eyes burning. "I fear he will not last much longer. With your help…"

The inn's door crashed open and a foul-looking ruffian stood in the entry. The ruffian froze. Quickly, he took in the now empty room with its broken chairs and shattered tables, the strewn pieces of glass, the dozens of abandoned swords, daggers, and clubs upon the ground, the bodies and, finally, the six conversing individuals. His gaze panned from Faye, to the fiery Zane, and then at last glanced to Victasys, eyeing the man's cloak and fearsome face. Each time, his eyes grew wider. Slowly, he backpedaled and closed the door. Darius heard his footsteps racing away.

"Think he's going to alert someone?" Darius asked.

Faye spoke, "Doesn't matter. This place is no longer safe. If Ezrah knew to send the Devari here, then it's safe to assume that whoever captured him could know of it as well. Not to mention, no one stays long in Shadow's Corner and lives." Faye plucked daggers from nearby corpses, sheathing them in her leather belt as she moved towards the door, opening it. Outside, despite the dark alley, dawning light peered down. "Well, are you coming?" she called impatiently.

Gray sheathed Morrowil, Victasys and Zane following suit.

Ayva shook her head, baffled. "Are you all crazy?"

Darius shrugged, giving his best look of innocence. "C'mon, Ayva. We can't stay here any longer, and I don't particularly want to," he said, looking around at the chaos. Nearby, the big man Darius had hit upon the head groaned, trying to rise. When Darius looked back, the others were already out the door. Grabbing Ayva's arm and ignoring her protests, Darius rose. He tossed a few coppers upon the bar's counter, nodding to the old innkeeper who trembled, looking confused and afraid behind the bar. "Thanks," he called.

As he moved to the door, the big brute saw Darius. The man snatched his broken sword and growled, rising. He swung. Darius barely sidestepped. He brought up his dagger and hit the man square in the head with his pommel, knocking him back out. Ayva looked at him, impressed and shocked. "Still want to stay?" he asked.

She growled in reply.

Darius grinned, and with Ayva at his side, he left Maris' Luck, moving into the waiting dawn, following Faye and the others.

A Joint Decision

Faye had led them to a small room that felt far more cramped after the large inn. *But at least with far less dead bodies*, Gray admitted darkly. It was quite a ways from the Shadow's Corner in a surprisingly nice district of Farbs, with clean streets, and tall, grand buildings. Citizens of this district wore silks or other finery, and a good bit of jewelry too. As they'd approached, he'd glimpsed the dark spires of a keep rising over the buildings.

The Citadel.

They were close, he knew, and Gray felt its pull, even now, through the thick walls around them. He could still hear Ezrah's bloody cries like a faint echo in his mind. Somehow, even in waking, the dream seemed to persist. His jaw clenched. Time was running out.

Taking in the room, he didn't know what to expect—it was Faye after all.

The walls were clay and thick, likely to obscure prying ears. The only window was small, covered with iron bars, and set on a back wall. On the left side of the room was a cluttered table, and beyond that a small bed. On the opposite wall was a row of hooks holding an arsenal of weapons: wooden clubs—some with metal studs or thick nails—flanged maces, swords of all shapes and sizes, even a few pole-arms on a rack, and finally, several chains, each attached to a heavy iron ball with wicked, curved spikes like metal thorns. A *Senduku*, Kirin said, *a type of Farbian flail.* Gray nodded then shook his head, shutting the voice out. Kirin had been silent since leaving Shadow's Corner, and he rather preferred it that way for now.

All in all, Faye's place was more like a quaint prison combined with a cozy armory than an actual home.

Darius grabbed something round, smooth, and white from the table. Gray realized it was a skull. The rogue's hand froze in realization, and he let the skull clatter to the floor. Ayva stood near the weapon-rack by the door. Her hand fingered a pair of iron manacles with a thick chain.

Faye quickly stalked to the window, glancing out.

"This is where you live?" Gray whispered.

Nearby, Darius brushed dust off a chair and plopped down, kicking his heels up onto the slender table that held stacks of books, writing paper, and other strange instruments.

Faye casually knocked his feet off. "I once called it home, but no longer."

Gray realized the truth of her words. Dust hung over everything—a thin coat that testified to her absence. Then he realized the oddity he'd felt: books lay open, blankets on the nearby bed were still tousled, and even food, or what had *once* been food, sat on a plate, molded and emitting a foul stink.

He neared the plate. "Seems you left in a hurry."

Dead flies dappled the crusted platter.

Faye looked to him calmly. "A clever deduction."

"Running from something?" Ayva questioned. She still stood near the door, as if expecting to run at any moment. She clutched her arm, looking about the place with dubious eyes. Gray shivered as she and Faye exchanged looks that could boil water.

Faye merely smiled. "Please, sit," she said to Victasys and Zane, motioning to two chairs beside the door, pointedly ignoring Ayva.

Victasys took a seat.

"I'd rather stand," Zane said.

Ayva took his seat with a smile.

Faye shrugged.

"Ugh, that stinks," Darius said, holding his nose. "Mind throwing that out?"

Faye grabbed the moldy plate and dumped it on the ground. "Better?"

Darius grumbled.

"Is there a point to this place?" the fiery man asked abruptly. "Why are we here?"

Silently, Faye grabbed a sword off the wall and tossed it to Zane. He caught it in one hand, casually. Faye smirked. "I thought this a fitting place to prepare for what's to come. Besides, no one knows of it. As of this moment, it's the safest place in all of Farhaven."

Zane admired the blade, as did Gray. It was long and curved, and the steel shone brightly, lit by streamers from the window. It was no Morrowil, Gray thought, but it was still finer than any weapon he'd ever seen otherwise, well, aside from Darius' blade now, and perhaps the Devari's odd sword. "A fine weapon," Zane admitted. "But I don't need it, and coming here was a waste of time. I've no time for this." He moved to the door.

Gray stepped forward. "You can't save her by yourself, Zane," he said, holding the man's copper gaze. It was hard—like staring into the sun.

"I do owe your grandfather a debt I promised to repay... But Hannah... Who will go to save my sister? I *will* not abandon her," he fumed, but then hesitated. "But if what you said before is true, none of us can enter The Lair of the Beast."

Silence reigned. A fly buzzed and Darius swatted at it.

"I'll go," Faye proclaimed.

"Why would you help?" Ayva asked in disbelief.

"Because I can," she said sharply, "*and* because I owe Gray my life. If he wishes for Zane to aid him, then I must do this."

Gray remembered those dark fearsome beasts. *Darkwalkers*. The memory of their escape came back to him, and he could almost hear the rush of wind, just as he had when they had barely escaped. The broken nexus pulsed in his mind, as if mocking him, and he pushed it aside.

That incident seemed like ages ago now, but he knew it couldn't have been more than a week past. Still, he felt like a different person compared to the Gray that had first entered Farhaven.

"You saved my life as well," Gray admitted. "All our lives."

Faye pulled up a chair, sat on it, and leaned back, propping her foot up on the table. Darius grimaced as if jealous. "If you call nearly dying to that cursed Algasi saving your life, then you have an interesting perspective. No, I failed and you saved me, even if you abandoned me after. Still, I always repay a debt."

"As do I," Zane said, eyeing the Devari.

"There is no debt to repay," the man said, his tone almost scolding. "Like I said, I did not do it for you."

Ayva stood up in frustration. "Why is no one addressing the main issue here? How exactly *are* you supposed to help, Faye? Unless you bear Darkeye's Mark, you'll die inside that dark pit just the same as any one of us."

Faye dropped her foot from the table and sat up straight, pulling her shirt down and exposing her upper shoulder.

Gray tensed.

A white scar shone in the shape of an eye—Darkeye's Mark. The eye was more ornate and a sword pierced its center, molded from scar tissue. It was striking in contrast to Faye's tan skin, though obviously it had faded with time. How had he not seen that before? Then he realized it was on the other shoulder not the one where she had been wounded by the Algasi's spear.

Zane growled, lifting his sword to Faye's throat. "That's the mark of a Darkeye officer… How did you come by that?"

Faye looked unperturbed by the blade, eyeing it as if it were a child's stick. "Are you going to kill me with my own sword after I offered to save your sister?"

But Zane's fury didn't falter. His eyes were burning cauldrons.

Guiltily, Gray reached out, using the ki. As his senses touched Zane's body, he nearly collapsed. He sucked in a sharp breath. *Sorrow.* The pain of it took his breath away, swirling inside him so heavy his knees threatened to buckle. It was an agony that made his eyes well with tears. He felt death everywhere and saw the bodies of those he cared for at his feet, while blood stained his hands. But washing over all of that was pure anger. He wanted to cry out until his lungs exploded, or to attack, shattering anything nearby and breaking it to a thousand pieces. It was too much to handle. He fled Zane's body, returning to his own, and breathed heavily.

Ayva was watching him curiously, but he avoided her gaze and looked at Zane. The copper-eyed man stood straight, every part of him trembling with restrained fury. He saw him differently now, feeling if not knowing Zane's anger. What had he lost? He was so different from Gray, and yet that anger was somehow so familiar… Gray shook his head, wishing to understand him more, but he feared entering Zane's body again. *How can the man bear it, let alone keep his face so stoic?*

Zane spoke in a grave tone, "Darkeye has killed my friends and family, rooted us out like rats at every turn, and now he's destroyed my only home and all those I love. And you, you stand for every dark deed he's ever done."

"If you want to kill me, then do it. Light knows I deserve it," Faye said calmly.

"This isn't right," Ayva voiced. "Don't do it, Zane. Spirits know I don't care for her much either, but this isn't right."

Zane ignored her. His face was a mask of fury. Gray feared what he'd do if he tried to interrupt. "Answer me," Zane said. "As his minion, the blood of innocents stains your hands… How many have you killed?"

"Hundreds," Faye said hollowly.

Zane growled, charging forward, pressing the sword tighter to Faye's throat.

"Drop the sword, boy," Victasys said. He was standing now, blazing sword unsheathed. Darius had jumped up from his seat, but Gray merely held his hand over Morrowil, hoping he wouldn't have to use it. He felt something in Ayva, a tension, as she held on to the edge of the table.

"Give me one good reason I shouldn't cut you down right here," Zane said, and Gray knew the threat was not idle. Not after what he'd felt.

"*Hannah.*" Faye's single word cut through the air like a dagger. The sword at her throat wavered but didn't drop. "If you want me to save your sister, I can do it. They trust me," she explained. "As for my past, it is simply that. My past. It was a dark part of my life that I've tried harder than you can imagine to put behind me and atone for. I know I will have to answer for it one day, but if you want me to save Hannah, then I would recommend putting down that sword."

At last, Zane dropped the sword. Victasys sheathed his blade as well, flames snuffing. Faye leaned back in her seat again, undisturbed by the fact that she had come so close to her death.

Ayva released a pent up breath.

Darius cursed and sat back down. "Well, at least that's behind us. Now if we don't have one person trying to slit another person's throat for more than ten seconds, I think we'll call that a victory."

"Wait, why did you leave?" Ayva questioned. "Don't tell me that you grew a conscience."

Faye replied, "I grew a reason to live."

Gray felt the words in the air. They felt truthful.

"And what's that?" Ayva questioned dubiously.

Faye's eyes darkened ominously. "I don't have to tell you," she answered, heat finally entering her voice.

"You do if you want us to believe you," Ayva retorted.

"She's right," Gray said. "What reason do we have to believe that you're not still one of them?"

She laughed. "Beside the fact that I've saved all your lives a dozen times over and just killed a good portion of Darkeye's recruits in that inn alone? Not a single reason. Sadly, one cannot ever leave Darkeye's clan. Once you join, you are in it for life. That is why I fled, and why you found me in the desert. While I'll never serve Darkeye again, I can never truly be free of him."

"It's true," Zane said.

"How do you know?" the rogue asked, cleaning his nails with his dagger, rooting out the grime and dirt of the Shadow's Corner as he leaned his chair against the wall. The action reminded Gray of Maris.

"I ... was a part of them once," said Zane. "No more than a single day I served Darkeye, until I realized the horror of what I was doing. I left, but I have been hunted ever since, for that and other reasons."

"If you left them, Faye, won't they wonder why you are back now? Won't it seem curious?" Gray asked.

Faye merely smiled. "Perhaps, for those who remember, but Darkeye's clan is made mostly of a constant inflow of new recruits who are simple dimwits or cowards who will tremble before an officer. Besides, out of the officers, only a few will know me."

"Why is that?" Ayva asked.

"There are not many who outranked me, aside from Darkeye himself."

"*Dice!*" Darius cursed, as his dagger froze mid-pick. "I *really* don't like this..."

"Exactly!" Ayva added. "For all we know you could be Darkeye!"

Faye sighed. "That's beyond foolish. If I were Darkeye, I would have killed you all a long time ago."

"Great, *that's* comforting," Darius grumbled.

She continued, "I would simply have swarmed Maris' Luck with my men and been done with this nonsense. Besides, if I was Darkeye, I wouldn't have nearly died to an Algasi, even a two-stripe one."

"I hate to admit it, but everything she says has the ring of truth," Zane said.

"Then how will you get past the officers who know you?" Gray asked.

Faye stood up from her seat. She flipped a small dagger from her sleeve, and it flit amid her fingers. She walked closer to him, hips and narrow waist swaying seductively with each step. It reminded him too much of Vera. "As you know, I can be very convincing," she replied. "A lie or two, and I will be back into their dark folds."

"No, I don't like it!" Ayva said. "How can we possibly trust her?"

Faye twisted and a dagger flew through the air, hitting the wall paces from Ayva's head. Ayva stiffened, and a glow blossomed in her hand. The ring of swords filled the small room, Morrowil in Gray's fist, ready. Darius had risen in his seat, gripping his green blade. Faye merely sneered. "How dare you... Trust *me?* Out of anyone in this room, I'm the only one who has reason to mistrust. Tell me, who got you to this point? Exactly how long would you have survived without me? I aided you at every step, and what did I get? You deserted me, leaving me half dead. Then I return to Farbs only to save your worthless hides yet again. I even offer to help you when no one else can. And what do you do? You treat me like dirt. All of you," she said, glaring at each, until her gaze rested on Gray. He grew hot under her accusatory stare but refused to look away. "Whose idea was it, Gray? Was it yours?" Faye whispered.

He held her gaze stubbornly. "It was a joint decision."

Faye laughed and then looked to Ayva. "So it was yours then."

"*All* of us decided," Ayva agreed, emphasizing the words.

"And you?" she asked looking to Darius. "You were glad to leave a nearly dead woman in the middle of the desert?"

"Don't look at me like that," Darius said. "We both know you can handle yourself beaten and bruised better than most men can on a good day."

"Compliments. Strange to leave me out to die, and then shower me with praise."

"It was the truth. That's all," Darius said stubbornly.

"I see you four have a past," Victasys interrupted. "But if you haven't noticed, there are more important things at hand than such childish bickering. We need to work together or we will fail separately."

"What he said," Zane added, stepping forward. "So if you don't mind, either help me or shut up. I'd appreciate it—because, as I see it, this woman is our only chance."

Gray touched Ayva's shoulder. "Zane's right. What other option do we have?"

Zane grabbed a sheath from the wall, then rammed the blade home, and stood tall. "It's my sister—I say she goes."

Faye gave a nod. "I appreciate your trust."

"Unfortunately, I don't trust you," Zane admitted. Gray still saw Zane shaking. "But it seems you're our only option. If you betray us, I will find you, and I will kill you."

Faye laughed. "That's one way to treat someone who is risking her life for you."

Zane's ire wavered. "Please… Save her. I will be in your debt."

Lightly, Faye dipped her head. "I will do my best."

"Then who will go to save Ezrah with me?" Gray said.

"You cannot enter the Citadel without the mark of a Devari," Victasys replied.

Gray pulled back his sleeve. "I bear the mark."

Victasys eyes narrowed.

He swallowed. "Do you know me? That is, who I once was? I might have gone by the name Kirin."

All but Ayva and Darius seemed shocked by his question.

"Kirin?" Faye questioned coolly from her seat, looking intensely interested.

"Who you *were*? What kind of man are you?" Zane asked.

A *lost man*, Kirin said, laughing in the back of his mind. But Gray ignored them both, eyeing the Devari. Victasys uttered at last, "I do not know you, or the name Kirin. But you're not a Devari, so how do you bear the mark?"

"Another life," he said simply.

"Well," Zane voiced. "If I cannot go to save Hannah, for it is certain death, then it seems I'll join you, Gray, to save your grandfather and repay at least one of my debts." He glanced to Victasys, and Gray saw the copper-eyed man was hoping to repay more than just Ezrah's debt. "My sword is yours."

Victasys sighed. "Were you not listening? You must have the mark."

Zane pulled back his sleeve, exposing a sinuous black mark. "I do not know where I got it, but I've had it as long as I can remember."

"Mysteries upon mysteries," the Devari breathed.

"Indeed," Faye said.

Gray turned to Victasys. "Well? You said my grandfather saved your life, this is your chance to repay that favor."

"You two may bear the mark, but you have neither the memories nor the skills of our kind. I will be surprised if we make it past the entry. Beyond that, I am not even a Devari myself any longer. I was banished and disgraced."

"You still move like one, and that's enough for me," Zane said.

"How many know of your banishment?" Gray asked.

"Few, I suspect," Victasys admitted. "But Zane does not even possess the cloak."

Faye moved, opening a door to a tall chest. She grabbed something and tossed it through the air. Zane snatched it, and Gray glimpsed twin crossed swords.

"How did you get that?" Victasys questioned threateningly.

"Relax, Devari. It was a gift," Faye said genuinely. Zane swiftly shed his tattered shroud, replacing it with the Devari's mantle. "It suits you nicely," she observed.

"Now, what was that you said?" Zane asked, standing smugly at Gray's side.

The Devari growled. "You two don't know the first thing about being a Devari."

Zane smiled thinly. "I'm a quick study."

And Gray sheathed Morrowil with a nod. "Time is running out. It seems a short lecture will have to suffice." At the same time, Zane moved to the wall of weapons. He sheathed a dozen daggers up his sleeves and in his leather belt.

"So be it," Victasys said with a heavy breath. "Then it is decided. Zane, Gray, and I will save Ezrah, while Faye and you two will go to save Zane's sister."

"How the… How did I get wrapped up in this?" Darius replied.

Faye snorted. "I don't need them. They'll just get in my way."

"We're coming," Ayva insisted.

"And how exactly are you supposed to get past the guards without the mark?" she asked.

Ayva's eyes were like blue daggers, as if waiting for her moment to strike. She held up the metal manacles, chain rattling. "You said Hannah will be in the prisons, did you not?"

Darius made a strangled sound. "Dice, I don't like where this is going…"

Faye laughed. "You would willingly shackle yourselves? Put yourself in *my* hands? Why?"

"If it saves a life, gladly," Ayva said.

"Do we really need *two* prisoners?" Darius asked. "Isn't one enough?"

"Besides," Ayva said, ignoring the rogue, "I don't believe you'll be able to trick those guards, not without a cover that is believable. And what's more believable than this? Also, if it comes down to a fight, you won't be able to handle Darkeye alone."

"If it comes down to a fight, we'll all be dead," Faye replied.

"Then trust that it won't," Ayva said.

"Fine," Faye conceded with a twist of her lips. "*Together.*" She made the word sound like a curse.

"Uh… Do I get a say in any of this?" Darius voiced.

"Do you really want to leave two women alone and defenseless, Darius?" Gray asked, smiling.

"These two? Defenseless?" he scoffed. "As much as a badger in a corner is defenseless."

Ayva lifted a brow and Faye smirked.

Darius grumbled, "If you're trying to guilt me with those looks, it won't work. You all go play the fool heroes, but I'm staying right here!" he said, flopping down upon the rumpled bed and crossing his arms.

"Did I mention that I put scorpions in my bed incase intruders ever returned?" Faye mentioned.

Darius yelped, leaping to his feet and brushing down his body furiously.

Faye picked up a scorpion from the ground letting it scuttle across her finger.

The rogue growled, looking to Gray. "Defenseless? *Really?*"

Gray shrugged, hiding a grin. Victasys' expression was humorless, but Zane looked amused.

"*Alright*, fine," Darius griped, "But if we're going to do this, let's get it over with. No use waiting around."

Faye cleared her throat and followed as Darius threw open the door.

"You best leave your sword here, rogue," she said.

Darius grumbled. "My sword goes where I go." Snatching a sheet from the bed, Darius shook it, and a few loose scorpions fell to the dirty ground. Deftly, he wrapped the sheathed sword, strapping it low upon his back to hide the handle. All done, he placed his hands upon his hips, looking satisfied with himself. "Better?"

Faye lifted a brow with a sigh but didn't object, and Darius headed for the door without waiting for an answer. Gray followed, squinting from the sun as they walked out into the light of day.

* * *

Gray waited with the others, exchanging plans while Faye was inside. She had to change clothes, she had said. Just then, the door swung open and she stepped out. Gray swallowed just to keep his jaw from dropping.

Faye now wore a wholly different outfit. A large pauldron sat on one shoulder with layered plates, each of which came to a sharp point. The dark metal looked like dragon's scales. The top plate's spike rose high enough to shield her cheek. More dark-plated metal covered her chest, flaring at the collar. Deep brown leather adorned the rest of her, molded to her body like a second skin, accented with dark silver lines. Heavy metal vambraces were cuffed onto her slender arms. She wore a black cloak as well, its pointed hood pulled far forward, hiding her scarlet hair. Her eyes were now darkened, a smoky black shadow encircling them, making them appear like light brown lanterns staring out from the shadows of her hood. Lastly, weapons decked her body, maces, swords, daggers, and more.

All in all, the effect was truly menacing.

The woman looked ready for a war all by herself.

Faye moved into the desert street, hips swaying—the tight leather and plate armor accentuating her alluring curves. Gray hid the desire to turn away when her gaze passed over him, flashing a seductive smile. She joined the other two.

"What are you preparing for?" Ayva asked.

"For anything," Faye replied.

Ayva's lips made a tight line, but she said no more.

Gray eyed Ayva and Darius standing beside Faye in the dirt street. He felt suddenly strange splitting from them. They'd spent so much time together that to part now felt somehow wrenching.

"We'll see you soon," Ayva said firmly.

"Soon," he agreed.

"And after you've rescued Hannah, we'll meet back here," Victasys stated.

"So be it," Faye agreed. "As you know, even if we don't run into any obstacles it'll take us a full day to make it into The Lair of the Beast. I know how you worry, but don't lose any sleep over me," she said with a wink.

"I'll try not to," Victasys replied.

As always, Gray couldn't tell if the man was joking or not. His face was a bluff rock. He shrugged it off, eyeing Darius. *Stay safe,* he urged his friend inwardly. Darius looked to Gray and nodded. *You too.* Then the rogue shook his head, looking confused at what just happened. *Did I just…?* Gray questioned, as a memory flashed through him of the Ronin talking to one another without talking.

But before he could question the strange knot in the back of his mind where Darius' voice had rang, the three said their goodbyes and Faye dragged them off towards The Lair of the Beast.

"You ready?" Zane asked, looking to Gray.

"Ready as I'll ever be," he said.

Gray felt peculiar. Less than an hour ago both these men were complete strangers. Now they were going to risk their lives together. *Fate,* he thought with a sour feeling. Would he ever have any control over his life? And yet the rest of him felt at peace, as if Zane and the

Devari's presence were familiar and *right*, even.

"Stay close and follow me then," Victasys said, leading them into the increasingly crowded desert streets. The Citadel loomed, waiting in the distance. Gray eyed the dark spires jutting high above the buildings like black gloved fingers on a huge hand.

Home, Kirin voiced.

Lucky

Where is it? Lucky thought in rising terror.

He held back a whimper, feeling for his small dagger. With his hands bound behind his back, it wasn't easy. He felt nothing. The rough rope chaffed at his small wrists. *It's gone,* he realized. They took his blade.

He took a deep breath, trying to not let panic take over. He knew how easily such a thing could happen. When he was alone, in the dark, waiting for big men to grab him and kill him for stealing their coin or food, the panic was always heavy. He breathed in and out, slowly, just as he would back then. But still his heart was loud, pounding, slapping against his ribcage. It didn't help that he heard the others' fearful breaths.

He glanced right and left and saw boys his age, some younger, some older in a long row. Most were softly sniveling while tugging on their bindings. Some were openly crying. Lucky felt a flash of pride—he wasn't crying. Not yet at least.

Lucky tried to calm himself by taking in his surroundings.

He was in a darkened courtyard. Grass cushioned his knees. Above his head, through a mesh of Silveroot branches, he made out a sliver of a moon. A *thief's moon*. It was a pickpocket's best friend. Normally, he felt comforted by the dark, but now the darkness felt different. Lucky was scared.

He felt something sharp in his pocket. He shifted upon his knees, but he almost fell to his face. He forgot his feet were bound too. *What is it?* he wondered, feeling the small, sharp object digging into his side.

The statue.

The one he'd stolen from Shade.

He looked up, eyeing the men who watched them— dark brutes with muscles that gleamed in the faint moonlight.

"What do they want of us?" a boy whispered to his left.

"I don't know, but I'm scared," said another, tears streaming down his dirty face.

"Where are we?" asked a third with a quivering voice.

"The Citadel," Lucky answered in a low breath.

"How are we going to get out?" asked a little girl, Vitsu, with a woven cap tugged to the brim of her eyes. Vitsu had been a Lost One he'd seen a lot. Shade favored her. She was nice, always helping others. Lucky grimaced in memory, feeling jealous still. But why was she here? Strange when all the others were boys.

 Just then, at the glowing entry to the courtyard, a figure appeared. Lucky stiffened. Help, he thought, gaining a flicker of hope. Maybe it was a Reaver or a Devari. He'd avoided both like a disease in the streets of Farbs, but surely they would see a bunch of boys and save them from these men.

"Lucky?" Vitsu voiced, louder.

"Hush," Lucky said, "someone's coming."

The figure walked down the keep's steps, heading toward them.

As he approached, Lucky felt his fear spike.

The man strode forward, bearing a strange blue orb in his hand. It crackled, lighting the darkened courtyard a scary blue. With each step, grass died, burning and turning to ash.

As he neared, Lucky's heart darkened. Something prickled along his skin. It hurt, like a flame drawing closer and closer. With the man's next step, the other orphans began to whimper and cry. Lucky stuffed down his terror, breathing evenly.

The man came to a stop.

He towered over them. With a long black coat and dark boots, the man blended with the night, save for his face. His hair was dark, too, and greasy, appearing like wriggling snakes smeared in oil. Lucky cringed eyeing his pale skin that sucked in the moon's light. The man stood, judging them, muscled thugs at his side. Suddenly, looking at the man, Lucky saw an image of blood.

He clenched his eyes against the recent memory.

Sanctuary … under attack…

Blood and cries of Lost Ones. Men, women and children. Fire and chaos.

Lucky returned to the dark courtyard, trembling.

The blood still stained his hands. He tried to hold back the tears. He'd seen Father die. Father had been kind to him. Lucky never fit in with the Lost Ones, not really at least, but Father had given him food, water, shelter, and clothing. Father had trusted him when almost no one else did. He'd thought Lucky could change, stop thieving and become better. He was wrong, but Lucky *had* tried. That was more than anyone else had done. Lucky felt his throat tighten, anger rising inside of him. No, Father didn't deserve it.

"Master Sithel," the biggest of the brutes said in a voice like gravel.

Sithel's gaze scanned over the whimpering boys. "Where did you gather this wretched lot?"

"It seems someone attacked the Sanctuary. We found these boys wandering, lost."

"And do any have families?" Sithel questioned.

"No, all orphans, master."

"Excellent," Sithel breathed.

"Please don't kill us," a little boy cried.

Sithel loomed over the little boy with a cruel smile. "I have no intention of killing you, little one. Not unless the prophecy demands it." Lucky shivered. This man was death.

"Then what do you want of us?" Vitsu asked in her small voice.

"To discover a truth, child."

"What truth?" another little boy asked.

"You shall see," Sithel said and raised the blue sphere. It pulsed an eerie light. It was beautiful. But above all, Lucky knew—it was evil. Pain shot through his limbs like a hundred needles. He tried to breathe but it was difficult. It was as if someone had just walloped him in the stomach, hard.

Others at his side cried out in pain too.

"Please stop!" several cried.

Holding the orb out, Sithel approached the first boy in the line. The boy cried out loudly. *Please someone hear!* With tears in his eyes, Lucky watched in horror as a strange face appeared in the air like a spirit. His dread rose. It glowed orange, like a mask of the boy. The boy's cry pitched as the face was sucked out of him and into the evil, blue orb. The orb drank it in like a sponge, as if craving more. The orange essence flowed into the orb until the boy's skin grew ashen. At last, Sithel pulled away.

"Not him," he declared.

The other orphans were now all sobbing.

"What was that?" one whimpered.

"The spark," Lucky breathed. He had seen a Reaver die. The man had keeled over like any other, and then a strange orange essence had fled from his body, rising into the air. It was the spark.

Sithel approached the next boy.

"Please … no," he cried.

But Sithel merely smiled as the blue orb ate, and the boy's spark fled, racing into the evil sphere. "So sorry, child…" he said, but his eyes held no remorse.

"Let me go, please," said the little boy, his voice hoarse.

Sithel pulled away, if only for a moment, and the boy gasped a breath. "You will each seek forgiveness, but know that I cannot give it to you. For you see, we are all cogs fulfilling our roles, mine more grand than yours. But the truth remains that the prophecy is more important than us all. In the end, feel grateful that you play such an important role." With that, he pushed the terrible orb forward, draining the orange essence and the boy fell forward, lifeless.

One by one, he moved down the line, the blue orb hovering before him. And each time, a boy cried and then crumpled. At last he reached Vitsu. The blue orb sucked at her. Her cry peaked, louder than all the others. More and more.

"*Stop!*" Lucky cried. *Please*, he thought, *no more.*

But still, the orb pulled, taking more. Vitsu's skin grew ashen, her cheeks sunken, and her eyes hollow. Her cry suddenly ended, and she fell over, as if dead.

Lucky's heart thumped, his breathing hard and fast. *Is she…*

Sithel shook his head, as if annoyed. He knelt down and threw off

Vitsu's tight cap. "This one isn't even a boy. How many times have I told you no girls?"

"I… It was a mistake," a brute mumbled nervously. "The girl's cap, I didn't see— "

Something flashed. Steel rang. Lucky saw something hit the ground with a sickening thud. A *head.* Lucky's body quaked. The brute's body stood for a second, and then toppled over, headless.

"No excuses," Sithel hissed. "Get him out of my sight, and take the girl back to the streets." Another brute tottered forward fearfully. He grabbed the thug's body, grunting as he hauled the corpse away. Sithel twisted to Lucky. His dark eyes gleamed despite the moonless night. His blue orb floated amid the darkness, crackling, but he sheathed it, throwing a black cloth over it.

Lucky was visibly shaking. He couldn't stop himself.

"How old are you?" he asked.

Lucky gulped, but the lump in his throat felt stuck, like swallowing dry bread with too little water. He tried speaking but it came out in squeak.

"Try again," he said calmly.

"Ten," he breathed.

"I see," Sithel said, smiling. But his eyes didn't smile.

"What did you do to Vitsu?" Lucky asked, a tremor in his voice. But he felt anger too.

Sithel sighed. "Sadly, some cannot handle the voidstone. Life is the spark. But her spark was too small. It drained it right out of her until there was nothing left. She may still live, but I doubt she will be the same. You cared for the girl?"

Lucky hesitated, but shook his head. "She was just a Lost One, like me, but why are you doing this? Vitsu…" he sniveled, holding back tears. "She didn't do anything wrong."

"Right and wrong are of no consequence, little one," Sithel answered. "They are meaningless words, worn out by an era of weaklings. If you are strong, you live. If you are weak, you die."

Lucky had heard those words before… Darkeye's men said them, and even more of late, spoken like a growing plague. Lucky hated the words now and the man before him. "You're evil," he breathed.

Sithel's grin grew, showing black, pointy teeth. "You mistake me. I am not evil. I am but the hand of the greater good. A tool for a grander purpose, just as you are." His breath smelled like the innards of something long dead. Lucky's heart pounded. He tugged at his bonds hard. This man… The light of madness shone in his eyes. Lucky wished he could stop trembling, stop his streaming tears, but fear held his body. "Now, let us see if the voidstone can find the truth within you. Let us only hope you are stronger than your friend."

Sithel withdrew the black cloth, and the blue orb pulsed. Lucky's throat clenched. He tried to look away but couldn't. The orb drew his gaze and he was lost in its swirling colors.

"Do you sense it?" Sithel asked, his black eyes glowing.

Lucky felt something being *pulled* from him. His skin prickled. *What is this?* he thought in terror. *Look away!* But he couldn't. It felt as if his very soul was being wrung like a wet rag, squeezed from his body. An orange light appeared in the air before him.

My spark.

The blue orb ate his spark like a hungry beast. "Please," he sobbed as tremors ran across his arms. Sithel continued to watch him, like a curious bug. Lucky tried to speak, to beg him to stop, but nothing came out as the world began to blur, fading as all dimmed.

Distantly, voices sounded, talking. So far away…

"What is the plan now?"

"We kill this boy and the others. They are no more use to us." It was Sithel's voice.

"But what about the Arbiter?" a man said, fearfully.

Distantly, Sithel laughed. *"I do not listen to her whims, you sniveling scum."*

"And what about that old man? He's still not breaking."

"Yes, he's surprisingly resilient, even for one of his rank. Go now, and tell the Reavers I have need of them. I've a plan to break him once and for all."

Lucky felt himself slipping like a fall with no hold. His eyes fluttered. He was so tired. *Sleep.* But something inside him shouted. *No! Stay awake!* The sphere glowed darker and brighter at the same time. Pulling at him. The deep sleep drew him in, and he couldn't resist it any longer. Somewhere, Lucky felt fear to his bones. *Is this it?* Lucky thought in dread.

"What is this?" a woman's voice questioned darkly.

Lucky gasped. The blackness receded. He felt as if a dark, suffocating blanket had been thrown over him, and now it was suddenly gone. When his vision cleared, he saw the slender outline of a woman.

Nearby, Sithel's head scraped the ground. "Arbiter Fera," he whispered. Lucky heard sharp fear in Sithel's voice. *Who is this woman?* He swallowed, looking up as life returned to his limbs. Arbiter Fera stood with confidence. With her back to the thief's moon, her frame was black as night. The faint light illuminated a shine of raven hair. It flowed to her slender shoulders. And Lucky knew deep down that this woman was strong—very strong. The air before him trembled with power, and he felt his small body tremble as well.

"Rise, my pet," she said as if talking to a faithful hound.

Sithel stood, looking shaken.

"Explain yourself," she instructed softly.

"Arbiter?"

"This boy. He is not the one. Then why is he on the verge of death?"

Lucky saw the other brutes sprawled on the ground in submission.

"I… I had to make sure," Sithel said quickly.

She snorted, softly. She made it seem pretty. "If they have spark, it is proof enough. I told you before—the boy we seek is different. He carries the *flow*."

The … flow? Lucky thought, trying to think, his head still ringing in pain. He'd heard of such a thing in stories. Stories about the Ronin. Is that what she was talking about? But the Ronin were dead and gone in the war long ago…

"I will do better next time," Sithel replied meekly.

"That, or you will die. Simple choices, Sithel," she said calmly, standing in the darkness. "Now, let's see if you did better with the rest of your orders. Where did you find these boys?"

"Upon the streets, Arbiter."

"And do they all match my descriptions?"

"Every word. They are what you requested."

"Hand me the prophecy," she demanded. Sithel withdrew a paper from his sleeve, handing it to her, and she read quickly in the dark moonlight, then handed it back. "These are all too young. You were wrong."

"How?" Sithel breathed, sounding afraid.

"The prophecy says the boy will be at least in his eighteenth year."

Sithel shook his head, looking afraid for the first time. Lucky felt a shred of hope. *Kill him*, he begged. "Surely, there must be a mistake. I followed your orders faithfully, mistress. I swear it."

"This time, it is not your fault. The prophecy has faded from our minds yet again. We must not forget to read it or we will continue to forget the truth. Now take them and go, but do not fail me again."

"Yes, mistress," Sithel breathed.

Lucky looked to the deadly woman and tugged desperately at his bindings. He felt the bristly rope bite into his flesh while his eyes looked for an escape, letting the blood run down his fingers. She approached slowly. Arbiter Fera knelt before him. She had a pretty face with smooth, pale skin that matched the white moon. Her full red lips twisted, but it reminded him of the cold hard floor of the cave in which he slept.

Lucky flinched. "Please ... don't kill me..." Hot tears streamed down his face, and he realized he was crying openly now.

She extended her hand and he cried out, closing his eyes.

When nothing came, he opened one eye. He watched as she calmly reached in his pocket, pulling out the statue. She admired it, fingering the little man's sword. "Where did you come by this, my child?"

"A friend gave it to me..." he lied.

"A curious friend. What's his name?"

"*Shade*."

"And where is this Shade now?"

Lucky hesitated. There was a hunger in her eyes. "Why? What do you want with him?"

The woman smiled deeper. Arbiter Fera *was* pretty, and she looked at him calmly, almost kindly. But Lucky shivered. Those eyes were distant—he could have been just a scrap of meat to this woman. "You wish to protect this friend of yours? Such a valiant little thief." A strange light flashed in the woman's hand that held the statue. *Magic*, he knew. But then it was gone. She tucked the statue back into his pocket. "Keep it." Suddenly, Lucky felt his tight bindings snap. His arms fell to his side. He looked around, ready to run. But he'd seen her magic. She would just blow him to pieces with her power.

"Are you going to kill me now?" he asked, terror in his voice.

Arbiter Fera cupped his wet cheek softly, almost tender if it weren't for the fire in her eyes as she pressed something into his palm, cold and hard. He looked down. A gold Farbian coin. The single coin was more than Lucky could ever earn in all his life, more dream than reality. With it, he could feed the Lost Ones for a month with *real* food—roasted chicken, fresh loaves, and more—not those moldy scraps they were used to... But as he looked back up at Fera's face he wanted to drop the coin and run, for he knew that compassion was just a mask. Beneath it, he felt her eyes peering, looking hungrily into the depths of his soul for *something*… "No, little one. Tonight, it seems you are lucky. But in exchange for my coin, you will deliver a message… Tell your friend Shade something for me, will you? Tell him to see me—it's very—" she leaned in closer, voice breathy "—*very* important." She hit something suddenly. A stone in the ground. A strange purple sphere appeared in the air. "Now go."

"What… What is that?" he whispered.

"Your freedom, little one. Take it quick."

Lucky didn't question. He staggered to his feet, gripping the precious coin in his sweaty fist, and stumbled into the purple sphere.

Marching Towards Death

Ayva strode down the desert street, watching Faye. The woman walked ahead of her and Darius, dark cloak wavering with deadly purpose.

She looked like she had when Ayva had first met her, only a hundred times more fearsome. Ayva eyed those weapons again, nearly gawking. Maces dangled from a leather belt. A one-handed crossbow sat at one hip, while her long sword hung at the other. Throwing-daggers were strapped against her arms, and she saw more peeking from her heavy metal vambraces. A short blade was tucked into each of her knee-high boots. Again she knew those weapons were not just for show, though Ayva couldn't help thinking Faye looked like a pincushion of bristling steel and plate armor.

"Where are we headed?" Darius asked. "This place is … *nice*."

They moved through dry desert streets in the early dawn. A few men and women moved about, each dressed in rich, colorful silks. The buildings were tall—blocking the early morning sun and casting a cool shade on the wide roads. The streets were clean, not a beggar, hungry animal, or even a scrap of trash in sight. Mostly she saw tall inns or wide, squat buildings looking like palaces for nobility. Gardens were frequent, brightening their tan surroundings with water and greenery. The lushness seemed out of place in such a dry environment. Though it was beautiful, it rubbed her wrong. *Why do men build such things when others go hungry?*

Darius occasionally shot her worried glances, but Ayva made sure her face showed confidence. Mostly the rogue shrugged his shoulders, as if feeling for the blade to reaffirm its presence. She could understand the feeling, especially where they were headed. The cold steel of her small dagger, tucked in her boot and pant leg, gave her equal comfort.

Their surroundings continued to get even grander, almost absurd. Men and women walked amid the buildings and now paved streets, each moving with a full entourage of servants. Ayva passed more courtyards, gold-roofed buildings, huge water fountains, and lacy bridges. A cushioned seat with four poles whisked by Ayva, carrying a woman draped in silks. Four muscled men held it aloft. For a split moment, she admired their tan bodies, but then the thought went sour. She realized they were just more pieces of decadence like the silver and gold gilding on the seat's exterior, or the jewelry in the woman's hair.

Ayva caught sight of a large reflection pool where children tossed fat coins towards large, brightly colored fish. She wanted to snatch the coins from their stubby fingers and give it to those she had seen in the drab, ramshackle part of Farbs, those with the hollow faces or stooped backs. *Those who truly need it,* she thought.

But that was not why they were there.

Zane's sister first, she thought, *then this backwards city second.*

"This isn't the way to Shadow's Corner," Ayva called to Faye's back. The woman ignored her. Gritting her teeth she strode up to walk beside Faye. "I thought we were headed to Darkeye. Where are you taking us?"

Faye didn't spare her a look, but her red lips twisted. "Who said The Lair of the Beast is in Shadow's Corner?"

"It's not?" Darius said, scratching his head of unruly brown hair.

"Where then?" Ayva asked, undaunted.

Faye replied, "True darkness doesn't just hide in the seedy pits. It is everywhere. It parades itself in fine silks, or sits at tables filled with food while others go hungry… It lurks even in a child's eyes." Faye said without a hint of amusement. "But most beguiling is that false glimmer on a king's crown, that smudge of blood on a priest's perfectly white robes. Look closer, dear Diaon, and you'll find that true darkness is everywhere."

Ayva shivered. The woman had a chilling way with words sometimes... And a pretty awful outlook on the world. A noble woman with voluminous robes of blue and red silk passed her. Her brows were thin and painted on, and golden hoops hung in her ears. Powders and paints made her skin appear flawlessly smooth. Ayva had never seen anyone look so rich and dignified, and yet she was like a painted doll, eyes vacant and lacking substance. This whole place was missing something, like a shell—fine and beautiful on the outside, but hollow within. "You still didn't answer my question," she said. "Where is The Lair of the Beast?"

At her words Faye came to a sudden stop.

They stood before several huge buildings. Each building had seamless, tan walls that were four-stories high. Silver rod-iron balconies and crawling green vines adorned their outer walls. Between the gaps of each building were bright courtyards filled with lush trees in full bloom. Ayva heard the babble of running water. Arched bridges of fanciful silverwork connected each building at every story. More trailing foliage hung from them, creating a waterfall of emerald green that obscured the courtyards beyond.

A shining silver sign read, "The Noble Beast."

Ayva's heart dropped. "Is ... this it?"

"The greatest darkness is that which can survive and even thrive in the brightest light," Faye said mysteriously, and pushed open the grand double doors, entering. Ayva steeled herself and followed, Darius mumbling a string of curses behind her.

As she entered, she was shocked again. The inn was *not* an inn. Sure, it had several tables—only several—and a long bar where a gangly-looking man stood wearing a grimace. There were even casks piled high on the far side of the room, gathering dust. Otherwise, the room was barren, empty of people and furniture, as if it had been gutted and carved of its innards like a pumpkin for the Harvest Festival. There were none of the normal signs of an inn, no stains or floorboards worn by feet—nothing. It was a strange feeling for Ayva. An inn to her was a place of comfort and familiarity, but this was just a sad, eerie copy.

Darius shivered. "Dice, this place makes me more jumpy than

that dark pit with Adorry and his cronies," he muttered.

"It's a front," Ayva breathed in realization. In fact, the only worn part of the inn was a path from the door to the bar, and the floorboards creaked as they walked, as if there was a huge cellar beneath. "What's beneath us?" she asked.

"The beast's chambers," Faye said with a predatory grin.

Ayva suppressed her fear, unwilling to give Faye the satisfaction.

They approached the innkeeper, another worn looking man with petulant eyes. *Are all innkeepers in this land such dour folk?* she wondered, proudly thinking of her father, who seemed to be growing larger than life in her head day by day. "What can I get for you? Perhaps a room? Or a plate of food? Our roast duck is the finest in all Farhaven," the innkeeper slurred, polishing a mug Ayva knew had never been used. The way he said it sounded like a line he'd said a thousand times.

"No duck," Faye said. *"The bloodshot eye sees all."*

"Strength is life, weakness death," the innkeeper droned in reply.

Faye inclined her head. "Wise words."

The man sneered and pulled at a handle that was shaped like a bottle. Miraculously, the bottle-filled wall slid back as if on metal-rollers, unveiling a vaulted tunnel. Faye barely waited for it to open all the way, striding forward. Ayva followed closely. As she passed, the man gave her a lecherous grin. She tapped into her mind, reaching out, and the man yelped as if a fire had just been placed beneath his rear. She let the tiny burst of light fade, hiding a satisfied smile. Grumbling, the man shut the door behind the three with a thud.

Ayva breathed out, unaware she'd been holding her breath.

"Sure it's smart to use your power here?" Darius asked.

She raised a brow. How had he known?

"Your power?" Faye questioned, torches lighting her beautiful face.

Ayva sighed. "It's nothing, just lead on."

With a shrug, the woman motioned to the manacles in Ayva's bag. "Best put those to good use now." Ayva did as she said, shackling her hands together. The manacles were seamless metal with only a tiny hole for a key, which she held in her pocket. She'd made certain the act of reaching for the key and unlocking her bindings wouldn't be too difficult. She *was* in Faye's hands, but Ayva wasn't *wholly* mad.

Darius bound his wrists as well, cursing the whole while.

"Mind telling us what we're in for?" the rogue questioned.

"I wouldn't know where to begin. Just stay close to my side and look servile."

With that they marched forward, towed behind Faye like two docile and fearful prisoners. They moved through the tunnels, heading deeper. Suddenly, she saw a bright light ahead, along with the sound of voices and footsteps.

Faye slowed and jabbed Ayva with an elbow. "Wipe that look from your face, girl, or you're going to get us all killed."

"*What* look?"

"That petulant fire in your eyes—the one that says you want me dead," Faye answered. "No prisoner I've ever held continues to wear that look. Not in my presence."

At her side, Ayva's fist tightened, her fire and anger rising. What had this woman done in her past life? How much blood had she shed? Just how many men and women had cowered in fear of her? She said she wanted to move beyond it, but there was no way to trust that. *Of course she would say that,* Ayva thought. *And yet... Don't all people deserve a second chance?*

Reluctantly, Ayva made her face as meek as possible just as they turned the bend and saw a group of sword-bearing guards arguing. Each bore the bloodshot eye upon their sleeves.

At their appearance, the guards turned.

Faye approached, head high and back straight—a queen amid her servants.

"Name yourself," said the biggest guard, brandishing his blade.

"Faye Tumai' Sliverus," Faye intoned. Her voice—it had suddenly shifted. It was darker and full of importance. Ayva shivered.

The other men seemed shocked by her words too, stiffening. All dropped their hands from their blades, and several fell to one knee reverently.

"I've heard that name," said a wiry Darkeye thug nervously.

"An officer," breathed another.

Somehow Ayva knew that Faye was no simple officer.

The big man swaggered forward. He was two-hands taller than Faye, but still she managed to look as if she was looking down her nose at *him*. He grunted, unimpressed, stepping forward threateningly. "An officer? And what is an officer doing without any of her followers?" He took another step, closer still.

"Take another step, I dare you," Faye breathed.

The man laughed, and his booted foot lifted. Suddenly, his eyes split wide. Ayva hadn't seen the dagger. She was certain no one had, especially the big brute. But Faye was cleaning her blade between her two fingers, flicking the blood onto the man's body.

"Any other objections?" Faye asked softly.

The rest of the smaller men fell to their knees. "Proceed, Officer Sliverus."

And they did, moving deeper into the tunnels, which were now wide enough for two carts to pass side-by-side. The tunnel broke, opening up to a sudden chamber that took Ayva's breath away. High above, she saw the dirt roof of the cavern. It fell hundreds of paces, to a wide basin beneath. A broad ramp spiraled down, hugging the sides of the cavern to the basin below. The whole thing was shaped like an inverted cone. All along the spiraling ramp were tunnels from which hundreds of men came and went. Down in the basin, Ayva spotted a swarm of structures like a small city.

Darius' mouth worked at her side, soundlessly. "What in the dice…" he finally breathed.

Faye shot him a look as two big men passed, carting prisoners of their own. The Darkeye thugs cast Ayva and Darius wary glances, just as Faye snapped. "*Move, you sacks of meat!*" Ayva gasped as something sharp jabbed her lower back, pain blossoming.

Luckily, the men continued on, laughing.

Ayva let loose a breath, subduing an acrid look meant for Faye, knowing the woman had drawn blood with her sword. But Faye's eyes were simply cold, brown embers as she guided them along the path, spiraling deeper and deeper. Darkeye's thugs passed them in a steady stream. Most prodded prisoners of their own, treating emaciated men and women like human refuse. Ayva was surprised to see so many Darkeye thugs were women, but she knew the path of evil was equally appealing to all.

As they spiraled deeper, she glanced into the dark tunnels using the corner of her vision. She noticed some led to bright paths while others were dimmer. On some paths, men wore clothes that practically fell from their bodies, carrying shoddy goods and half-broken boxes. The deeper they went, though, the fancier the loot and the thugs.

Eyes fell to them, as if wanting to question or perhaps even just to snatch the prisoners. The brutes looked like hungry beasts wanting scraps, but a mere glance from Faye sent them running. She had thought previously that Faye was always comfortable with any setting, but this was different. This was truly Faye in her element.

Men muttered things to Faye, eyeing her clothes as they passed, or the ornate bloodshot eye upon her breast. Their words reached Ayva's ears as she kept her head bent.

"Purge the weak, and find your strength."

"Kill the weak, protect the strong."

"Weakness, death—strength, life."

And most frequently, *"The bloodshot eye sees all."*

To some, Faye merely nodded, the rest, however, she ignored. Only to a few truly deadly looking men did she murmur something in reply, but no more than a word.

They reached the bottom of the pit and Ayva had no trouble maintaining a look of fear, though she had difficulty not reaching for her hidden dagger.

The Lair of the Beast.

It was a small city, if a city could be purely evil. The floor of the basin was filled with men, women, and beasts. Sounds and sights flooded them—grunts, shouts, cries, the clashing of steel from nearby smithies, the hiss of steam, and a hundred other sounds and smells assaulted Ayva. But even worse were the sights.

Cages littered the ground.

As they walked, Ayva had to suppress her anger, seeing sad faces behind those rusted iron bars. Animals were caged as well—dogs, boars, goats, horses, and even stranger creatures.

They passed a cluster of huge cages, twice as tall as any man, and Darius gasped. Ayva eyed beasts with huge white wings, bodies of brown animals, giant talons, and faces like a regal birds. *Gryphons*, she knew. The gryphons moved about in their cages restlessly, flapping their wings, causing gusts of wind, or screeching loudly. The worst were the ones that didn't move. Ayva eyed an older gryphon with brown, molting feathers. It eyed her with huge, intelligent blue eyes, and Ayva's heart hurt. She had trouble not rushing to the cages and shattering the locks, but instead, she made a vow.

I will save you, she promised.

"We're nearly there," Faye whispered softly as men, women and children shuffled by, all shackled in a long chain. Ayva's fist tightened at her side, rage welling. Distantly, she nodded. *Let us save Hannah and be out of this foul place, at least until we can return with an army in tow.*

They passed another set of cages stacked high, and in each were creatures that made Ayva's heart clench. They were pale white beasts, almost human looking, save for distinct differences. Huge, bright silver eyes watched the three—too keenly and too predatory-like. Silver hair spiked from their shoulders like furry pauldrons. They were neither muscled, nor lean. Long, silver claws retracted from their human hands, in and out rhythmically. And many growled, showing long, shiny fangs, slavering with hunger. But most strange of all, they all bore short horns, translucent in color, many of them warped or thorny, others simply straight. They bashed them against the heavy cages, rattling the ground and sending small shivers through Ayva.

"Phoxes," Faye explained in a low whisper. "All males, however, the females have huge, ornate horns… If there are any still alive."

"What are they doing here? What does Darkeye want with them?" Ayva whispered, eyes to the ground—it was hard, though, to keep her gaze from returning to the curious creatures.

"Phoxes are powerful creatures. Not to mention they are the only things untouched by a Darkwalker's killing touch. However, they are feral, and utterly uncontrollable."

"Then why does Darkeye want them?"

"Darkeye seeks the last females," Faye replied. "Tales say that among the females there is a Matriarch. And some say that the Matriarch will even bond with a human if she deems you worthy. If one can do that, then the males will obey that man or woman to the death. Of course, most who see a phox in the wild, let alone the Matriarch, simply die a quick death."

Ayva swallowed. "And what then?"

"Darkeye cannot contend with the might of the Citadel … but with an army of phoxes at his command?"

Ayva shivered, looking away. She didn't want to think of a man like Darkeye with an army of foul thieves *let alone* magical creatures.

It was a fearful notion. They entered a large burrow at the bottom of the pit. "Beware the next bend. These next men will be Darkeye's Officers."

They rounded the corner.

The tunnel was wider and darker, even though torches burned on the walls. It was as if the darkness was too strong, repelling the light of the fires.

Ahead, a horde of men waited before a set of tall pikes that were planted in the ground and aimed at them. A few bigger, better-dressed men sat at a wide table, playing cards or conversing in low voices. The rest wielded crude weapons and stood at attention.

Suddenly, Ayva recognized one of the men. He was smaller and sat at the table, complaining loudly. He cradled one arm in a sling while his other was lacerated with a host of bright white scars. At his hip was an assortment of serrated daggers, like broken teeth from a cruel beast. His one eye shifted as they approached, squinting, then widening in recognition. The man's boney face twisted in a slow, wicked grin.

Adorry Droverson.

250 The man rose from the table, sauntering forward. "Well, well, what a pleasant reunion! So you've captured these two, finally. I knew it would be only a matter of time until one of the clan brought them in. Where exactly did you find them?"

Faye, however, ignored him, approaching the biggest officer. "We come under Darkeye's orders. He wants these two without delay."

"The mark," the big officer ordered gruffly.

Faye pulled down her upper-sleeve—a flap had been built in to show her branded skin, shaped in the image of an ornate Bloodshot Eye. The man grinned with a nod and began to exchange words with Faye that Ayva couldn't quite make out.

Adorry moved to Darius, sniffing the rogue like a mangy hound, face grimacing. "I smell your fear…" True enough, the rogue stared straight ahead, but terror etched his features. *Is he still feigning?* Ayva wondered. If he was, it was truly believable. "Did you really think you'd get away with it?" Adorry asked snidely.

Darius' fear flickered, a smirk flashing across his face, but then it was gone.

Adorry looked confused, as if questioning what he had seen. He looked around. No one else seemed to have noticed Darius' reaction. With a snarl, Adorry backhanded Darius across the face with his good hand. Blood sprayed the dirt. "I'll be glad to see you hang for trying to make me look the fool. Darkeye will enjoy breaking you," Adorry said then looked to Faye. "Beware of this one, he is a foul Untamed."

Ayva realized Adorry must not have seen Faye reveal herself at Maris' Luck. The man was not only buying the ruse, but also somehow *reinforcing* their ploy.

Faye pulled her sleeve back up. "His power is meek," she said, "Only a weakling would fear it."

Adorry snorted, not rising to the taunt. Ayva saw fear in the man's eyes as his gaze glanced to Faye. In fact, each officer eyed Faye's menacing form of dark plate, fitted leather, and spray of weapons with trepidation. It made Ayva want to shiver—who was the true monster, the one they followed or the ones they were trying to avoid?

Faye grabbed Ayva and Darius' chain and yanked them forward, but as she did, Adorry slid before her like a serpent, blocking her path. "Why have you no men? You've just a few little rats following on your tail like pups looking for their mother's teat. Speaking of which," he said, leering at her chest.

Faye ignored the man's gaze. "Let us pass."

The two other officers and their horde of men stood aside.

"Move aside, Adorry. It is Darkeye's will," said the biggest of the three officers, a man with an unruly scar that split his face. "Besides, this one should not be messed with, even you should realize that."

But Adorry didn't budge. "Oh I'll let her go soon enough, Gundar. But before I do, I think I'll take one as a prize and payment for my broken arm. Anyway, I'm sure Darkeye won't mind having just one prisoner to toy with," he said with a laugh then gestured to several men. They lurched forward, grabbing Ayva's arms before she could react.

Instinctually, she fought. She wanted to cry out, to tell them to get off as their greasy fingers pawed at her and their rank, sour breaths suffocated her, but Faye had been clear. Her prisoners did not react that way. Ayva clamped her eyes, feeling their hands but forcing down her fear. She would not give away their ruse and be the one to doom Zane's sister. She would rather die.

"Now, you may go," Adorry announced. The men's hands continued to grope her more and more, and terror rose over Ayva's barrier of calm as dreadful thoughts surfaced, a scream rising in her throat.

"Let go of her," Faye whispered. It was a voice so cold it made Ayva open her eyes despite the vulgar men around her.

Faye hadn't moved.

"I think not," Adorry replied haughtily.

Faye's hand glided slightly closer to her mace.

Several large men stepped before her, blocking her path to Adorry who merely grinned. Faye's hand crept another sliver closer. The men gripping Ayva reached for their blades—their fingers tightening on her nervously. The tension mounted. Then, as if it was a cord, it snapped. The two brutes near Ayva dove at Faye's back. Small roots sprouted, breaking earth. They grabbed the men's feet, and the brutes' faces smashed into the ground. The other men blocking Adorry with their bodies leapt at Faye with a cry. Faye's hands flickered. Two daggers found their mark, one lodging itself in the first man's throat, the next dagger in another man's chest. Both fell, looking confused. Two more men replaced them, moving faster and

stronger. Daggers bounced off their leather armor, as if metal plate was beneath it. They sneered, slashing for Faye's head. Casually, almost bored, Faye ducked. She withdrew two maces, caving in the first man's head, then, breaking the second man's knee. The man reached for his knee, opening his mouth to cry, but a sword suddenly flashed from Faye's sheath, cutting the man's scream short.

Both crumpled, silent.

Four men dead, and two injured in a matter of seconds.

Adorry watched it all in both fear and confusion. His one eye narrowed on Faye, face quivering with rage. Suddenly, his one good arm moved with lightning speed and daggers flew through the air. One hit Faye, clattering off her armor, but then Ayva realized it was just a distraction. Four bits of steel hurtled towards Ayva's face. She wanted to flinch, but instead she dove into her mind, pulling out of desperation. Something flickered—a bright white sun—and she summoned strange threads into the air. Bright light flashed. Metal sizzled, dropping from the air. *One, two, three.* All but the last dagger fell harmlessly to the ground… The last dagger flew, nearly reaching her. Ayva's power wavered. *No!* She screamed inwardly, grasping at the sun as its light sputtered, dying. *Work!* She commanded, reaching and pulling hard. But the white sun vanished like a snuffed flame.

The dagger flew.

Ayva closed her eyes, waiting for it to hit.

Silence.

Suddenly, she realized her breathing was all she heard. She cracked open her lids and saw a piece of steel floating between her eyes. Faye's armored hand held the dagger tightly. Her brown eyes now glowered like burning slits. *She caught the blade*, Ayva realized. Blood dripped from Faye's glove and she threw the dagger aside. Voice robbed from her throat, Ayva nodded her thanks. Faye grudgingly returned the gesture.

Turning back, Ayva saw that Adorry lay dead—several fletched arrows sprouting from his chest, and Faye's crossbow still held in her other hand. The other officers were silent. They had watched the whole thing without moving. Their men numbered easily three-dozen, and they wore mixed expressions of fear, confusion, and hatred. Ayva thanked their luck. If the rest of the officers had joined the tousle, none of them would be alive.

Faye straightened, turning back with the air of a monarch having just executed an unruly subject. She looked around, as if daring any of them to object. Then, she snatched Ayva's and Darius' chains and shoved them forward.

Slowly, the officers moved aside, and their men parted like a dark sea. With Faye in the lead, Ayva and Darius made their way deeper into the tunnels.

"How in the seven hells did we just survive that?" Darius whispered.

"Luck," Faye said darkly. "Adorry both legitimized our ruse and nearly foiled us."

But Ayva knew it was not luck. As she eyed Faye, she had a flash of guilt. Perhaps the woman was good.

"I'm just glad that fool is dead at least," Darius muttered.

"Never be glad for death," Faye said. "For Adorry's death might be our doom or salvation. One can never tell the future."

"He was an arrogant, lecherous fool," Darius countered. "He deserved it."

"I've done worse than that man. Do I deserve death?" Faye asked, and Darius' mouth shut, disgruntled. "And if I did and was dealt it, what would have been your future without my help? No, better not to judge the dead, and better not to talk anymore. Voices can be heard from far away, and some are even more skilled than I am at hiding in the shadows."

Ayva eyed the nearby shadows with renewed fear, peeking around every corner as if it were moments from revealing a new attacker. With that, they wound their way deeper and deeper into the belly of the beast.

A Path to Salvation

Dust filled Gray's mouth as he followed Victasys. The sun blazed high in the sky, beating down on their backs as they strode with deadly purpose. They drew closer to the Citadel, the black spires rising.

Ezrah.

Gray set his jaw.

Every second they delayed, the man was that much closer to death. He pushed faster. The streets grew more crowded, but the manner of people changed. The common folk of Farbs thinned, the bright dress changing to dark red and black.

Victasys' long legs took him quickly through the throngs. He hid his scarred face deep within his hood, but Gray saw that hood shift, taking in everything. He wondered if Devari could use the ki to sense danger. It made sense. A threat was just a result of emotions, wasn't it? If the man sensed a thief's blood rising, or the anger of a slighted patron, then perhaps Victasys could even sense the attack *before* it came. The thought set off a realization in Gray. That's how he had avoided injury, walking through Maris' Luck as if made of smoke.

But something bugged Gray much deeper than Victasys' special powers. And he spoke suddenly, his curiosity burning a hole in his gut. "Do you really not know me?"

Victasys didn't miss a step. "I do not."

Gray shook his head. "But if I lived here, how is that possible?"

The man responded without turning, "All Devari live within the Citadel, save for a rare few. Some of them reside in one of the other nine Great Kingdoms, serving as emissaries of the Patriarch and the Citadel. Until a year ago, I lived within the Great Kingdom of Sun as a councilor to the steward of Vaster, Lord Nolan. When I heard of threats of war close to our borders, and unrest in the heart of my home, I requested to be sent back to Farbs. As a result, much of my life has been spent beyond the walls of the Citadel." Gray narrowed his eyes. If Victasys was disappointed with being separated from his home for so many years, the man hid it well. He almost wondered if the Devari actually had emotions.

Zane was still staring ahead, but Gray knew he was listening too. Both men were more attentive than rabbits listening for a hawk.

Motri…

It was the name of his hawk. Well, a hawk, as it wasn't really his. But Motri had saved his life by alerting the elves to come to their aid at Death's Gate—of course only after he had inserted the blade into the stone and stopped the Kage, taking a dark blade in the gut in return. Without the hawk and the high elf healer, however, Gray doubted he would still be there. He wondered where Motri was, hoping the strange, intelligent bird was still alive.

Returning to the moment, Gray gave them details about the room where Ezrah was being held as they moved. Victasys spoke, "That most closely matches the Vaults, a dangerous place."

"Are you certain?" he questioned.

"The Star of Magha is the eight pointed star you described. It's the Citadel's emblem. It stands for the eight elements of the land—Water, Stone, Metal, Flesh, Sun, Moon, Leaf, and, of course, Fire. It is the power all Reavers and Neophytes can wield to greater or lesser degrees."

"What about Wind?" he asked.

Zane and Victasys looked at him uncertainly. "Wind is the banished element," the Devari said, eyes narrowing. "No one in the world can wield Wind, and it is forbidden to speak of it, just as it is forbidden to speak of the nine forbidden ones."

Gray noticed Victasys' voice wasn't afraid or resentful, but cautious. He decided to risk his luck and test the man. "You mean the Ronin," he said. "And you don't believe the stories, do you?"

Victasys snorted. "Long ago I discovered the truth. The Ronin were not evil."

Were not… Gray thought. *Is he right? Are they gone for good?*

"What does any of this have to do with the Star of Magha?" Zane questioned gruffly. "How does this help save Gray's grandfather?"

"The Star of Magha is as old as the Citadel itself. It is inlaid into the ancient stone of the keep in only three places, each of particular significance. One is placed in the Oval Hall, a place where Neophytes are tested and rise to the rank of Reaver … if they pass the grueling Seven Trials."

"The other two?"

"Another is located in the Patriarch's grand chambers. The last star is said to be within the Vaults."

"Then where are the vaults?"

"Below the Citadel."

"Where exactly?"

"I do not know," Victasys admitted.

"Then what?" Zane asked, interrupting. "We just saunter up and ask someone where they are torturing the second most powerful man in Farhaven?"

"I doubt that will work," Victasys replied matter-of-factly.

Gray laughed, but it died in his throat.

The two men weren't joking. In fact, Victasys looked to be considering Zane's question seriously. *What have I gotten myself into?* They were mad. He hoped at least Ayva and Darius were faring better with Faye. The woman was fearsome, but at least she wasn't crazy. Then again, after hearing about her past and knowing at least some of who she had been, could he ever look at her the same? Gray shook his head—now was not the time for such thoughts.

Victasys looked over his shoulder. The sun lit his hood. His scarred face shone a glistening white as he took in Morrowil. "By the way, that sword you hold, I've never seen its like. Where did you get it?"

"Its owner no longer needed it," he replied honestly, if perhaps too quickly.

It was an evasion, but the words were true. Kail no longer needed it, for the Ronin were no more. *Weren't they?* he wondered again. The book in Gray's bag written in another language and the scrap of Kail's cloak made him hesitate.

Luckily, Victasys looked convinced. "Still, you hold a blade of kings in your hand like a simple training sword. Even if you two aren't Devari, I will at least teach you to hold your swords like one."

Zane opened his mouth to object, but Victasys spoke in a low, commanding tone, guiding them firmly through everything from postures, to hand positions, and a hundred other things, some minute, others drastic. Gray's mind boggled at the amount of information. The man was a fount of knowledge.

Who could have known a fist touching the blade's hand guard—or *sobri*—was a hidden way to unsheathe one's sword? With a simple squeeze a swordsman could loosen his blade from the scabbard for a smoother draw. But if a skilled swordsman saw the move, it meant "draw or die." How in the seven hells of remwar could one even detect such a subtle thing? Or that a thumb upon the guard meant an outward threat, but was less dangerous because it could just be a

swordsman's warning. Overwhelmed, Gray avoided touching Morrowil as a whole, afraid of the implications. But he listened raptly, soaking in every morsel of information like rain upon the dry desert.

As Victasys finished instructing the two on how to speak like a Devari, a file of Farbian soldiers clanked past Gray in shiny plate, a woman in scarlet robes at their head. She had two black bands upon her cuff. She moved confidently, emanating power. Something inside him jolted, Kirin shifting restlessly. Gray waited, but his former self grew silent once more.

"A Reaver," Zane said at his side. "You've never seen one before?"

"I can't remember," he admitted.

"Your past life?" the fiery man asked.

He nodded.

"A strange thing to lose your memories," Zane replied. "I can't imagine forgetting all I've ever known. I've often wished selfishly I could forget my past, my dark deeds. To forget sounds like a blessing."

Gray watched two men arguing over a piece of a fruit, and replied, "Do you think so? Would you willingly forget about Hannah?"

Zane looked thoughtful. "No, you're right, I suppose."

"Light always comes with a price of darkness," Gray uttered. *Those words*… were they his own? Kirin muttered inside his mind, just a distant laugh. Gray gave an even breath. "No, it is more a curse, and one that I intend to undo," he said, speaking to both Zane and Kirin.

Zane chuckled. "You speak in riddles. You truly are like your grandfather."

Gray laughed, warmed by that thought. "If only I knew him."

"Be glad at least you discovered him," the man said. "Some could only wish to be so lucky."

It was true. He had family, at last. Gray had never cared for such things. Granted, in the dark of night, he would sometimes wonder who his parents were, and imagine their faces, but he never missed them. He supposed it was hard to miss what you never had. But now he knew he had a grandfather. Gray had *seen* him. He was real. And he wasn't willing to lose him now.

Gray stared ahead, his eyes hardening upon the huge, black stone keep in the distance that brushed the wispy clouds above. *I'm coming*, he thought again, clutching the pendant's dust in his pocket.

"We will save him," Zane said suddenly.

Gray felt strangely comforted by Zane and his presence. Those hooded eyes, a bright copper, though unusual, didn't unnerve him. Even as they pressed through the streets, he saw others shy from Zane's stare. But Gray saw the fire of truth and the passion of strength in his gaze. *Who is this man?* he wondered not for the first time, feeling an inexplicable connection towards Zane.

"It's unsettling not remembering anything of your old life," Gray admitted as they moved past a group of colorful stands. "I don't really mind it most of the time because I still have memories. Memories with Ayva, and Darius, and others." He remembered Mura too and his insides twisted, missing the man and his gruff smile. Even Karil, he missed dearly. Gray continued. "I am still *me*. I don't seek who I once was anymore, but it's still odd. I mean, you know more about my own grandfather than *I* do."

Zane shrugged. "I suppose. But I know nothing of my parents. They died when Hannah and I were only infants. The only person I ever cared for aside from her was a man I called Father."

"What was he like?" Gray asked.

The man's wrathful face broke into a sad smile. "A kind man. And from the little I could tell, much like your grandfather. But he was just a man. Your grandfather is an Arbiter."

What exactly is an Arbiter? Gray thought.

Victasys appeared at his side, gliding in like a shadow. "Arbiters are legends."

Gray hesitated.

"The ki senses many things," the Devari said, eyeing him shrewdly. "The more attuned one is, the more they can sense your feelings. Zane mentioned Arbiters, and your curiosity spiked.

"Arbiters are no mere mortals. A Reaver alone is something to be feared. They are powerful and you must avoid them. You can watch for the stripes at their cuffs to determine their strength," Victasys whispered. He nodded to a one-stripe Reaver who passed with a gaggle of gray-robed children. "A Reaver of two stripes is vastly stronger than a one stripe. Remember that."

"And Arbiters?" Gray questioned.

Victasys mulled the question over, a silence settling until Gray thought he wouldn't answer. At last the Devari spoke with a storytelling air, "I've seen a three-stripe Reaver issue a stream of fire wider than a river to level a hillside with one sweep of his hand. But a three-stripe Reaver does not hold a candle to the weakest of Arbiters. Arbiters are gods of the spark. It is likely your grandfather has lived for a thousand years."

Gray shivered. "How is that possible?"

"The spark is life, and life is the spark. The greater the spark, the greater the life force. I do not say this lightly or to scare you. You simply must know what you are getting into. If someone has your grandfather, then we can only assume they are equally powerful. Therefore, we would be more than wise to prevent a confrontation, for nothing short of an army of Reavers will be able to stop an Arbiter or its like." He eyed them each seriously. "Understood?"

Both agreed, unable to do anything else beneath that gaze.

"Good. Now your last lesson," Victasys said. "I will teach you to block the ki. Other Devari will attempt to sense you with it. If you do not have a barrier up, they will discover you are imposters, for all Devari can shield their emotions."

"And if they do discover us?"

"The crime for intruding is death."

"Great," Gray said.

Zane's heated expression didn't waver.

Quickly, Victasys explained how to seal emotions away in a compartment within their mind. But as he instructed and Gray obeyed, he felt another strange presence. It reminded him of when he had talked to Darius. He reached to touch it. But before he could try to define the sensation, they took a corner, breaching a set of tall adobe buildings and entering a huge clearing.

Straight ahead sat a huge black keep.

The Citadel.

It sat like a block of hewn obsidian, draining the light from its surroundings despite the bright, dawning sun high above. Awestruck, Gray took it all in: hundreds of tall parapets, sharp crenulations with roving guards in shining plates, and a sea of battlements. The whole thing could have held a hundred Lakewoods within its walls.

"We're here," Victasys announced. "Just remember what I taught you."

Zane grinned. "This is looking more like a deathtrap with every step."

"Don't sound so excited," Gray griped.

"Just expectant," Zane replied and ribbed him with an elbow. "Besides, I'm curious what you can do with that sword of yours."

Mad indeed, Gray thought as they approached the giant black gates. But he simply held his breath, and Victasys led the way. A steady stream of Farbian guards poured out of the giant open gates. Inside, he glimpsed green courtyards and a wide staircase. A small file of young boys and girls walked at his side, led by a young girl in drab gray robes—all entering the Citadel as well. They looked terrified. *Neophytes,* a part of him remembered something.

He clenched Vera's hand tighter, gazing up at the impossibly tall, black walls.

"Are you afraid?" she asked.

He shook his head. "This is what we wanted, remember? Soon we'll be Neophytes and we'll never go hungry." He could almost feel the gray robes on his body already, replacing his tattered rags, and he practically trembled in excitement. And fear too, he admitted.

She nodded, her tiny face trying to look confident. "You're right.

Just don't leave me, all right?" Vera said nervously.

"I promise," Kirin replied.

I promise...

The vision shattered.

Vera...

Gray realized he had crossed the distance of the courtyard, a span of time suddenly gone, and they were standing on the other side of the gate. To his right sat a gatehouse with iron spikes upon its roof. Directly in front of him were two Devari. They blocked his path. One of them was tall with black hair. He was even younger than Gray. An older Devari was standing a breath away, hand on his sword. His hair was plaited into a single silver braid. A *komai tail*, a voice whispered. Kirin. Crow's feet at the older man's eyes tightened.

Gray sensed the tenseness in the air. The man was waiting, he realized. *The Devari must have asked a question. What was it?* he thought frantically.

Victasys strode forward, but the older Devari raised a hand, holding him back. "I didn't ask you, brother. I asked this one."

"Come again," Gray said. "I was distracted."

The Devari's face didn't waver. "Do I know you?"

"I'm back," he replied. He shook his head. *What did I just say?* Fear flashed through him.

Kirin, he cursed inwardly at the voice.

"Back?" said the younger Devari.

"From our mission," Zane filled in smoothly.

"I know your face, but it's changed..." the older Devari said, squinting, "Who *are* you?" The threat in the man's voice was undeniable.

Victasys remained silent, watching Gray. It was on his shoulders, and he remembered the man's commanding words: '*Match strength with strength, for no Devari values weakness*.' "A brother in arms," he replied, voice hard. He touched his sword, putting his thumb to the sword's guard—its *sobri*. A threat.

Though hidden in his hood, Gray felt the scarred Devari's approval.

The gray-haired Devari hesitated visibly.

The younger Devari behind him spoke, "Relax, Sunji. There's no need for this."

"Listen to your friend," Zane breathed in fury, falling in at Gray's side.

"Enough of this. You've avoided my question for the last time. Lower your ki, now," Sunji demanded, putting his fist around his hilt. *Draw or die*, Gray knew. He had to lower his ki now, but he knew if he did the man would shatter everything they had planned. The crime for intruding was death. They would never save Ezrah. It would be all over.

You better get me out of this, or I will... Gray threatened his former self.

You will what? Kirin challenged.

Sunji's sword scraped, slightly.

"Brother—" Gray said, reaching out with a hand. "Stop this. Please. Feel free to test me." He felt Victasys tense at his side, knowing the depth of what he just offered. *What are we doing?* Gray questioned. It was Kirin's choice. Not his. *They are going to discover us! If you get us killed...*

Then it'll be hard to seek vengeance on me, won't it? Kirin retorted calmly.

Gray growled and felt Sunji reach out with his ki. Gray's barrier dropped—the small compartment in his mind opening as he allowed the gray-haired Devari inside his conscience.

Sunji's face contorted. Gray shook, feeling his hand sweat upon Morrowil's hilt. Two Devari they could take, but how many would jump upon them once the battle started? It was hopeless. Zane's blade cleared another inch in its scabbard. Victasys moved closer, readying himself.

At last, the aging Devari slammed his sword back into his sheath. "Forgive me, Dundai. I have not seen you before. How was the Black Marsh? Are the Algasi still advancing north?"

Gray replied absently, dazed. "They are making their way to Vaster still, but we held them back as much as we could." Again, the words weren't his but Kirin's.

Sunji nodded. "It's not like the Algasi at all. They do not care for the affairs of this world, or so we've always been told. Something must be happening. Are they hurting the unarmed at all? Those in the countryside?"

Gray took a guess. "No."

"As I thought," Sunji replied. "Their prize is greater. But what do they seek?"

"I wish I knew," Gray said honestly.

Sunji sighed deeply, blue eyes looking away, as if seeing the world crumbling beyond the black walls. "The world stands upon the brink of destruction. We must seek to stop it as best we can—I only wish the Devari had both the answer and the strength to stop it."

"If you seek unity and peace, then what are you doing questioning a brother at the tip of your sword?" Zane said furiously.

Gray waited for the man to snap back, but he simply nodded, sorrowful.

"The tide of darkness has changed me," Sunji answered sullenly. "But still, it is no excuse. We must stand together as brothers. Forgive me for questioning you so, brother." He said, looking to Gray sincerely.

"You're forgiven," Gray replied, as if grudging.

The man held out his tan, leathery arm laced with scars. And Gray remembered Victasys' counsel. *The Devari greeting.* He clasped Sunji's arm heartily, showing his strength. Victasys, still menacingly silent, stepped forward and motioned the two men aside with his presence. And together, they moved away, joining others entering the Citadel, taking the wide steps swiftly.

"What in the blood and dust was that?" Zane whispered. "I've lied in my time, but you? That was like a completely different man! And a believable one too."

Gray kept his teeth from gnashing.

A thank you would be appropriate, Kirin voiced.

As soon as they reached the Citadel's grand entry, breaching the last of the massive steps, Victasys grabbed Zane and Gray. He pulled them aside, behind a sea of colossal black pillars, each the girth of ten men with their arms linked. High above, a domed ceiling of gold, silver, and glittering blue gems sheltered them. Most importantly, it was out of the flow of traffic and away from ears and eyes, aside from the occasional glance. "First, pull your hood up. Second, explain yourself," Victasys said darkly.

The scarred Devari's silence had been unnerving, and Gray was almost glad to hear him speak at last. *Almost.* The man was a thunderhead. "What is there to explain?" Gray said, looking over his shoulder as a young gray-robed flock noticed the three Devari huddled by the pillars, staring at them with fear and respect. A guard ushered them on, deeper into the wide hall.

"What you did..." Victasys said, looking flabbergasted. "That was impossible."

He swallowed. "What did I do?"

"You changed your ki. *Willfully.*"

"And?"

"You don't get it," Victasys growled. "You didn't just alter your emotions, you somehow implanted entirely different ones."

Zane shook his head. "Sorry, still not following you. Your brief sketch on how to be a Devari didn't really explain this. How is that strange exactly?"

"How to explain it to you two fools..." Victasys grumbled, "To put it simply, it would be like trying to remember something that someone *else* has forgotten. It's not possible. It is a thing of myth."

Zane let out a breath, and then scratched his head. "That does sound confusing."

"I'm not sure what you're so upset about," Gray said. "I got us out of there, didn't I?"

Victasys made another disgruntled sound. "Alas, now I wish I'd asked more about your past, for I fear it will get us into more trouble yet." He turned to Zane. "And you? Any large, dark secrets to unveil?"

Zane grunted. "No. And I agree. Based on that little encounter, I fear Gray's past is not done with us so soon. But it's all the more reason to find Ezrah, and quickly. I don't want to waste any more time here. Hannah is waiting for me." He left unstated that Faye and the others had to succeed first for that to happen. But Zane's fire wasn't something Gray wanted to question. Not without expecting to get burned.

Victasys exhaled thinly. "So be it. Follow me."

With that, they left the columns and moved back into the flow of the crowds. The hallway was wide enough for four carts to move through side by side. It opened up abruptly into a huge chamber, and Gray's next step faltered.

Even Zane, at his side, fell short with a curse.

The hall was breathtaking.

Fiery opals were set into the floor, smoldering like small flames just beneath the marble's surface. On the far walls, white crystals glittered. The walls themselves were fashioned in a bizarre but symmetrical pattern of shapes. Each of them glowed, refracting light. Gray realized the faceted walls were meant to extract the natural light from outside and reflect it all over the great hall. The result was an ever-present bloom of soft white light, bathing his skin. It made all those in the hall appear divine, like spirits sent from above. Gray peered up and held back another gasp.

Simulated clouds swirled, skimming across a dome of bright blue. The clouds flowed as if alive, forming shapes and strange patterns. It mimicked a real sky, if the real sky was a thousand different shades of blue, and clouds were made from the dust of glimmering stars. It was truly remarkable, and Gray wondered if he could ever look at the sky without feeling it somehow paled in comparison. Granted it was not as opulent as the entry hall, it was far more stunning in his eye.

With the gems, clouds, angular walls, and crystals, the vast chamber appeared cut and polished from a glorious mine, and then shaped by a master craftsman's hand. *Wayfarers' Hall*, Kirin said. He sounded unimpressed. As if there could be places grander than this. Gray snorted. He didn't believe it.

In the center of the vast floor was a statue of a man. It towered ten men high, looming like a giant among giants. The man was clothed in elaborately carved robes that fell about his form gracefully. His face, wizened but not old, held wisdom, power, and truth. In one hand, the man held a scepter, in the other, a huge *real* flame burned brightly, cradled in the figure's upturned palm. Who was this man?

A second figure knelt at the robed statue's side. And Gray knew instantly who it was.

Seth.

The Ronin was carved immaculately. It was as if the legend had returned to life, grown a hundred feet in size and girth, then been frozen in stone forever, immortalized. Seth's hard, angry face was just as Gray remembered it. It stared outward, as if seeing beyond the grand chamber, past the hall, to something no one else could see. In the man's hands, of course, was the Ronin's famed blade, carved to scale. One swing of that stone blade, Gray imagined, could have smashed Mura's hut, leaving nothing in its place but splinters the size of toothpicks.

Yet most stunning were the sounds and colors.

On the far walls, hundreds of purple spheres opened and closed making a droning *vwoom*.

Over and over again it sounded. Soft individually, but together it created a humming chorus like a host of men in prayer, like those they had passed at the entrance to Farbs. Gray watched, stunned and fearful as men and women walked casually into the spheres, and then disappeared, each *vwoom* resonating through his limbs.

Transporters, Kirin said.

Suddenly, the teeming of voices and even the droning of Transporters was dulled as a ripple appeared in the crowd coming toward Gray, Zane, and Victasys.

The ripple spread, approaching.

Hundreds parted like fearful insects scattering, and at the center of the now hollow corridor was a woman. From far away, Gray took her in. She had raven hair that flowed to her shoulders. With her head bent, he couldn't make out her features aside from a heart shaped face and pale skin. Her robes were a pure white, but they were laced with gold filigree, and her cuffs and skirt that brushed the marble floor were trimmed in black. She bore no stripes of rank. In her hand she held a thick tome, her gaze absorbed in its pages. Abruptly, more men and women stepped nervously aside, revealing a horror that made Gray's hairs stand on end.

A gangly beast crawled by her side, using a dozen, long, multi-jointed legs and arms. Those limbs moved too fast. They appeared neither bone nor flesh, like black knives ringing on the marble floor. From it, darkness emanated, shadows eating at the light. Yet there were white parts to the creature too: translucent horns, silver eyes, long fangs, and splotches of white hair. Gray didn't know what to make of it, but he knew distinctly what its darker side was.

Darkwalker.

With the horror trailing at her side like a misshapen pet, the woman strode down the path created for her. She seemed oblivious to the others around her—or perhaps uncaring. Power hit Gray like a wave, crashing against him and stealing his breath. His knees quavered. The sensation was different than anything he'd ever felt. He was torn between grasping his neck and clutching his heart, feeling a heady mix of terror and awe. This woman was death and life all wrapped up in one, and he knew instantly.

An Arbiter.

And they stood straight in her path. Gray glanced around, realizing the truth of that statement. *None* stood near them. Not a single soul. He didn't see Victasys. But the rest of the crowds had parted and now watched him and Zane in fear.

Gray's mind raced. Where could they go? There was nowhere *to* go. If they ran back, the woman would only see that oddity and notice them even more, and if they jumped into the crowds? No, the crowds watched them like an anomaly. They would stick out like a fly swimming in fresh milk. Gray's heart thumped faster, hands sweating as the woman's steps glided closer.

Something droned nearby.

It distracted Gray, but he couldn't move. He was rooted, his gaze fixed and limbs frozen. Somehow the woman was still not looking at them, but she was drawing nearer. The creature at her side still moved, a mass of flashing white and black limbs, scrambling along the marble. Gray felt as if each step of the Arbiter rattled the floor, shaking him, and spiking his dread.

Vwoom.

It hummed and pulled him from his fear.

Gray felt something well up inside him. The Transporter. At the same time, a white sphere appeared in his mind. He grabbed at it, and the mantle of fear and the awe-inspiring power that rooted him diminished.

A hand gripped his shoulder. "Come now!" Victasys breathed, pulling them as another Transporter opened a dozen paces away.

Gray looked away for a split second and saw the Arbiter was almost to them.

When he looked back, the purple sphere was nowhere to be seen. The Transporter was gone. *No!* He thought, dread rising, sweat flashing across his arms. In the corner of his vision, the Arbiter was nearly upon them. Victasys smacked the wall. To Gray's surprise, a block of stone slid into the wall and a purple sphere appeared from thin air. The Devari shoved him and Zane in then dove headfirst after them, just as Gray saw the Arbiter's gaze pan up.

The purple light coated him, taking his vision. He felt stuck in solid stone. Light and time distorted as he floated in nothing. Then, as quickly as it came, it was gone. He hit something hard. His hands gripped a stone floor. Dazed, he looked around. Gray saw they were now in a strange wide hallway with a series of windows on one wall. *Where ... are we?*

Victasys pulled Gray to his feet.

"Who was that woman?" Zane asked, brushing himself off.

"Arbiter Fera," the Devari answered. "She is one to be feared and avoided like death."

"I sensed that," Zane grunted. "But what was that thing at her side?"

Gray shivered, remembering that horrible looking beast.

Victasys answered, "It's an abomination. Arbiter Fera has been experimenting, breeding the magical creatures of this world. She considers herself an inventor of sorts, and all the Citadel fears her creations, especially that beast."

"It seemed like she was looking for something," Gray said, hoping to change the topic.

"You used your ki, didn't you?" Victasys said. "It's true. According to rumors, she is searching for orphan boys." He dipped his head towards Zane. "It is part of why I saved his life."

"And why Ezrah saved me as well. He pretended to be my father," Zane explained.

Gray looked around. Outside the windows, he saw more green courtyards with soldiers and several Devari. Haystacks riddled with arrows and wooden dummies hugged the long wall. *A training grounds*, Kirin said. *One of many.* "Where are we?"

Victasys looked up and down the empty hall. "I don't know."

"*What?*" Zane asked. "*How?*"

"Like I said, I was trained here, but I've never lived long in the Citadel."

"Then where are the Vaults at least?" Gray questioned.

"They are below us," Victasys said, "but I do not know the way."

Gray's grip tightened on Morrowil. "Then what do we do?"

"We've only one option. We search," Victasys replied.

"Aimlessly wandering? This place is far too large," Gray said.

“Agreed—we’ve no time for that,” Zane growled.

Gray opened his mouth when a sudden image appeared. He tried to speak but images flashed in his mind, almost painfully. *Hallways… Rooms… Turns…* Everything sparked as he was seared with memories. His eyes snapped wide with a sharp breath. He realized the other two were looking at him. Ignoring their looks, he started forward. “The Vaults are this way. Follow me,” he ordered. And he didn’t have to look behind, or use his ki to feel their looks of incredulity and uncertainty.

Victasys silently joined him, matching his strides.

Zane fell in at his side as well. “And I thought we were the mad ones.”

Gray wanted to laugh but he merely nodded. “Me too. And if my previous self is correct, the path ahead is a treacherous one. In the end, perhaps we’re all mad. I just hope we’re not too late…”

Don’t die, Ezrah, he prayed. *We’re coming for you.*

A Rising War

The tide of war was rising. Karil felt it in her bones.

Outside the tent's window, the camps churned with commotion, an array of sounds and sights—the clang of swords on swords, the twang of bows, and ring of blacksmiths' hammers.

They were in the green fields of Belegrun, just outside the Forest of Aenor. It was several days' ride from Eldas, the location chosen purposively, like a mother keeping watch on its child—*if* the child was a Great Kingdom, taken and being held hostage by an evil known as Dryan.

She took a deep breath, looking back.

Four elves stood at attention. Each of them was a high-ranking member of the Lando, elf warriors—the small, brilliant pieces of her father's crown shining upon their elfin chainmail. Their pointed ears stuck out through their long, silken hair. She felt a special affection for the Lando, and an undeniable debt, for they had saved her life, whisking her out of Eldas when her father was assassinated. They had believed in her when few had.

Looking at them, she still felt strange being a half-elf in charge of an Elvin army, but she did not allow herself to question it for long. Questioning led to uncertainty and uncertainty led to failure. And she could not fail. Not when the lives of her people were at stake.

"What would you have us do?" asked Tunmai, the highest-ranking of the Lando.

"Send out more messengers," Karil commanded at last. "All the Great Kingdoms must know. Eldas will not be taken without a fight."

"The same message?" the elf asked.

"No," she answered. "This time tell them Eldas is under siege. Mention nothing of Dryan or his rebels."

"And if they still do not respond as you hope?" Rydel asked from behind her.

"Then we press on," she pronounced with the true strength of a queen—her father would have been proud. "We will siege Eldas with or without their aid and free our people, taking back what is rightfully ours."

"At your command, my queen," Tunmai said.

The other elves clasped fists to their hearts, moving out of the enormous command tent.

The tent was tall, with a peaked canvas roof. A dozen tables were scattered about, holding maps, markers, scrolls, and other signs of an impending war, and her bed sat at the far side, still made. Sisala had made it two days ago. Karil had not slept since. She was beginning to feel fatigued to her bones, but there was too much to be done and seen to. She would sleep soon, she promised her tired limbs as she rubbed her brow, but not yet.

Beside her throne sat a cup of tea that had gone cold and a stack of letters, most of which she'd already read. It was a dismal litany of bad news: raids on the Frizzian Coast by strange red-sailed mercenaries, upheaval in Menelas and Ester—rumors that the two mining cities were at one another's throats over the discovery of a strange new metal, not to mention that bandits were moving in droves around Sevia, attacking merchant caravans upon the Aster Plains, and the Algasi were moving north, towards Vaster.

That last bit was troublesome enough on its own—for few knew the history of the Algasi and the city of Vaster, Great Kingdom of Sun. Few but the elves. It was almost enough to set her stomach churning as if she'd eaten a bad *dumai* root. But she hadn't. In fact, she'd barely eaten anything at all. If Sisala found out—and somehow she always seemed to—the short, stern-faced elf would chide her with a firm tongue. At that thought, she expected the straight-backed servant to barge into the tent and force one of her noxious remedies down Karil's throat, as if thinking of her would be enough to summon her, like the children's stories of her youth.

At her side, Rydel made a sound, displeased.

"What is it?" she asked.

"I don't like the way you dealt with those emissaries from Covai earlier."

Covai was one of the Great Kingdoms. They had been pinning much on their allegiance with all the Great Kingdoms to win the war. But none of the responses had been what she'd hoped for so far.

She touched the armrest, feeling the smoothness of the rare purple heartwood beneath her palms. Her whole throne was made of it. Surprisingly the Lando had been able to bring it here, all the way from the Relnas Forest, the only place where heartwood resided. Well, *aside* from the forbidden forest of Drymaus—home to the magical Dryads, beings made of wood, leaf, and moss, as well as the dragons—but not since the Lieon had any dared to cross those treacherous borders.

The heartwood reminded Karil of her childhood, of her father, of Eldas and the spire. Of her home. She replied softly, "Sometimes *liking* is a luxury a queen cannot afford. Long ago, I learned to act out of necessity."

"I am aware of necessity," Rydel replied. "They wanted to give their aid. We could use them."

"Did they?" she asked. "More accurately, it seems they wanted to know if I was worth supporting. They never promised to send recruits to aid our war, nor did they even question Dryan's rule as legitimate or false."

Rydel's jaw tightened, but he remained quiet.

She hated it as much as he did. Yet Karil was queen now, she could not afford to deny such truths. With her father, King Gias, dead, and then her mother's proclamation of the final prophecy that took her life—the very prophecy that foretold the Ronin's return—Karil was in charge. Of course, she wished more than anything that her father was still alive to rule with his wisdom and his strong hand, or her mother to guide her with her loving, quiet serenity, but it was not so.

Rydel moved, his grand hando cloak, denoting his high rank,

flapped as he strode to the large window in the otherwise empty tent. He looked out as the camp moved with purpose.

"You are restless, my friend," she said. Summoning roots from the nearby tree, Karil brought the cup made of Seria porcelain to her lips, sipping on minty water. It had long gone cold, but it helped to soothe her stomach. Some elves would be displeased using nature for such a mundane task, but for Karil, embracing her spark, her ka, and using the element of leaf was a treasured act. Moreover, touching the leaf made her feel connected to the glorious forests she had left. And she needed that bond now.

"Is it so obvious?" he said quietly without turning.

"It is," she answered with a sad smile. "I've rarely seen you like this. It seems lately I am even more elf than you."

He gave a hard breath, turning back. His clothes were black, but he'd taken to wearing upon his shoulders the dark green spaulders of the Lando in homage. His wide shoulders tapered to a narrow waist that held two swords—each of which were like second appendages to the blademaster elf. Dark hair fell from his chiseled face and bright blue eyes held a quiet intensity. His Elvin ears were longer than most, and his eyes more angled. Even standing still, he seemed to be moving subtly, always ready to strike. Even the formidable Tunmai and all other Lando feared Rydel like a black susa snake. He was in the highest rank of all Elvin warriors, the last of a dying race that had guarded royalty. Karil knew of no one more powerful and more passionate. He was her mentor, her guardian, and a beloved friend. But his mood of late troubled her even more than the reports.

"Speak your mind, dear friend," she told him.

Looking out the window at the teeming makeshift city, he answered softly, "Whatever I say, you already know."

"Speak it anyway."

He looked back, his eyes orbs of fury. So strange to see so much emotion in an elf. "This is not a war that can be won, Karil. Not as we stand now. We have barely one legion of elves. Dryan has ten legions, and he is gathering more. Elves are joining him by the hour, flocking from the eastern woods of Relnas, and even the fringes of the Drymaus Forest. They see his rule as inevitable."

"Numbers are not everything," Karil answered.

"It is not just numbers, my queen," Rydel replied sternly. "And this truth you must see yourself. Aside from a rare few, most of our so-called warriors are no more than half-trained younglings—this is the first time many have wielded a blade, and we expect them to be our frontlines against Dryan's armies? Against the *Terma*?"

The Terma's allegiance with Dryan troubled her greatly. Terma were elite Elvin warriors—only one rank below Rydel, but there were hundreds of them under Dryan's black fist. Somehow the dark elf had swayed her father's once-loyal warriors, and now he commanded them like personal servants.

I will find out how, she vowed. *And soon…*

"You say they are untrained? Then train them," she replied, undaunted. "My father always said, 'Do not look to the fault in your weapon, but use its strength. If you pinpoint its only flaws, then that is all you will see.'"

"I remember that well," Rydel said. She knew Rydel had been like a son to the great elf.

Thoughts of her father made her throat clench, but she swallowed. Her voice gained strength. "You are our greatest weapon, my dear friend. Teach them to fight." She left unsaid that she was doing the same with him, by focusing on his strength. Rydel was *her* weapon.

He nodded. "I will do my best."

Rydel's tensed shoulders eased, but his strikingly handsome face, even for an elf, did not seem to relax too much. Karil rose, touching his arm. "Is that all that worries you?"

"You know the rest as well. The Great Kingdoms. They will not fight for us."

Outside, Karil watched a stream of elves and men. One man pushed a heavy cartful of armor and weapons, sweating under the load, and two more joined him, helping press the cart forward. She smiled to herself, finding it a fitting metaphor. "That is not wholly true, my friend. Out of the nine Kingdoms, two of which were lost to the great war, we have heard back from only a small handful. Covai is a blow, and one I wish we did not have to suffer. But they, aside from Menalas, are the farthest from us. They believe this war will not affect them."

"Then they are fools," Rydel said calmly.

She shook her head. "I wish it were so simple. I believe Dryan has used his powers of deception. The world does not know a Great

Kingdom has fallen, that Eldas is overrun. Covai simply see it as an exchange of power. In this, we underestimated Dryan and his connections."

"What are you saying?" Rydel asked.

She had not voiced this, not to Rydel, not to her high-elf councilors, nor her trusted healer, Jirah Dawnbringer, not to anyone. But Rydel was not just anyone. Karil gave another heavy sigh. "I believe Dryan is not working alone. I fear a greater power and evil is at work, one moving Dryan like a puppet upon a grand board of *yudai*."

"Who?" he asked.

"I know not yet, but I will find out. But more importantly, we are not without our own plans. We are not as alone as you think we are, my friend." He raised a dark eyebrow, but she merely smiled. "You shall see soon enough. Now come, let us quell your earlier fears." Karil strode forward, convincing herself she was not tired.

"Where are you going?" he asked as she reached the tent's flap.

"You said it would be better to let me see with my own eyes the chink in the armor of our forces," she said, hiding a smile. "So? Show me." Instead of giving the elf a chance to deny or argue, she pulled back the tent's flap and entered the sunlit day, into a host of sights and smells.

Letting the sounds of training swarm around her, Karil moved forward. Rydel was suddenly at her side, appearing like a phantom. He said nothing, and together they moved through the camps.

Elves in masses dropped to one knee as she passed, armor clinking as they settled to the grass-trampled ground. She gave them nods in return. She knew it was not a thing all elves did for their king or queen, but they did it for her. At first, she'd feared this post, dreaded it even. Not until the boy had plunged the blade into the stone, and she had crossed back across Death's Gate had she decided to take up the mantle of queen in full. Of course, she had the training that was required. But what was she compared to her father, the great King Gias? Still, that fear lingered in the back of her mind, but she shoved it and her half-elf inadequacies down. These were her people. The looks they gave her as she passed spoke of only one thing.

Trust.

And she would not betray that trust—not if it ran her to the bone, and not if it cost her life. Not for anything.

They passed into the training ground, which was little more than a large field with hundreds of rings of men sparring in a furious clash of metal and wood. The most advanced of them held metal blades, but the freshest recruits were required to learn first with the wooden swords, halberds, dulled pikes, and staves. But just because they were wooden, did not mean they couldn't do harm. Karil could still remember her countless bruises and bloody knuckles from Rydel's training sword.

More men bowed to them, refraining from falling to one knee while in the midst of training. Wooden fences surrounded the field, trailing into the distance.

Karil passed a huge set of weapon racks filled to the brim: nusais, single-edge bolos, halberds, pikes, swords—broadswords, claymores, even massive zwinzals—quarterstaffs, full-staffs, katars, bows, crossbows, *senduku*, and more, each she had trained with at one time or another in her royal instruction. But could she remember her training she wondered, eyeing the assortment. Her favorite was the nusai, a sword with an oblong head, and a horned cross guard used to catch and break other swords.

Sadly, most of their weapons were in shoddy shape. All metal
now came from the joint mines of Menelas and Ester, and, with their civil unrest, their borders had been shut down tighter than a Landarian seal. Karil had attempted to force her way in, for they needed metal like a drowning man needed air. But her messengers had been sent away with the threat of violence. Her only other option was the Mountains of Soot and the infamous Deep Mines—those ancient, abandoned caves of metal beneath Yronia, the once Great Kingdom of Metal. She had debated sending men there. She was sure the Deep Mines were still full of ore—the stories said the mines were endless caverns of iron, copper, and tin. From there, her blacksmiths could smelt it down with ease, but Karil had delayed the order. She'd heard foul rumors of a strange darkness brewing in the giant forlorn halls of Yronia. She feared what those rumors meant.

Karil turned her thoughts away, focusing on the men and women around her, elves and humans alike. They sparred, creating a cacophony of thwacks and ringing steel. To her right, a female elf moved like a serpent, evading the blows of five male humans.

"So tell me again, how is our army deficient?"

Rydel sighed. "Five untrained humans against an average female elf. It is nothing to brag over. A hundred of those humans or twenty of those elves could not take a single Terma. You can see—every one of these men or women are untrained, outside of battle and within. If they don't fold from the Terma, Dryan's legions will finish us off. We cannot siege Eldas like this."

"Then what would you have me do?" she asked, not really expecting an answer.

A hand gripped her arm, stopping and turning her. "Find another way," he said, holding her gaze. "I believe in you. *We* all do. There must be another way, my queen."

She smiled, softly. "There is no other way." Nearby, a group of men watched two men spar. "Besides," she said, "the true strength of an army is not always so easy to see. Sometimes, it is what is beneath the surface that shines."

"Karil, you cannot honestly believe that this rabble can stand against Dryan…"

She moved towards the group of sparring men. "I choose to believe that, given the chance, men and women, human or elf will rise

to the occasion, that there is a hidden strength in all." With that, she approached the circle.

"What are you doing, Karil?" Rydel asked as he followed.

Karil's lips twisted. "It's time to test the might of our armies."

Rydel growled, saying something, but she didn't listen. As she approached, several men recognized her and immediately dropped to one knee. Others continued fighting for a few more strikes and then stopped, their wooden swords falling as they rushed to their knees.

"My queen," uttered a big elf—the instructor leading the group of humans.

"Your name?" Karil asked.

"Unmia," he said dutifully.

"This group. They are untrained, yes?"

"Yes, my queen. These are the newest group of warriors."

Perfect, she thought. And she could recognize many of these men and women—boys barely old enough to shave more than once every few weeks, if that, and girls looking just beyond the stage of playing with dolls. Admittedly, as a princess, Karil had never had that phase, but she'd heard of it. "Great," she said, loud enough for all to hear.

"Then I will spar with one of them." She pointed to a boy roughly the age of Gray, and he reminded her of the young man as well—with intelligent green eyes, and a tousle of brown hair. He held his sword with confidence, despite the fear in his eyes. "I choose you," she declared.

The young boy swallowed, but strode forward to the center of the circle.

"This is not a good idea," Rydel said at her side, not sharply, just calmly. He'd regained his Elvin restraint.

"Why not?"

"Because a queen does not do battle with her own men."

She extended her hand to another girl her size. Face fearful, the girl understood, handing her weapon over to her queen. Karil realized it was a wooden nusai, with an oblong head. *What luck!* "What was it you said once?" she asked Rydel with a smirk. "I am not like any normal queen?"

He growled and glowered at the green-eyed boy. "If you hurt the queen, you will pay for it, boy."

If the boy looked afraid before, now he looked petrified.

Karil sighed. "If the boy holds back, how is that an indication of his limits, of his capacity? Besides, don't you have faith in me, *master?*" She emphasized the word. The big elf Unmia looked completely aghast. Even some of the other boys and girls looked awestruck. Word of Rydel's prowess had already wormed its way into nearly every ear.

Rydel hid a grimace. "No offense intended, my queen, but it's been a while since you've had my teachings, let alone held a sword. Your other duties have been more pressing, as they are now."

She ignored him, and strode to the center, meeting her opponent. Her fine cloth robes brushed the grassy ground, restraining her movements. Another hindrance she'd have to be wary of… The boy swallowed again, but his grip tightened. *Good, he has strength of heart.* "Don't listen to him," she commanded, noticing the boy cast Rydel nervous looks. "Simply do your best to land a blow."

"My queen?" he asked shakily.

"Your name."

"Logan," he replied.

"Well, Logan, consider it an order. I, *Karil yl' Silvar*, hereby order you to hit me," she said in a hard voice, raising her nusai blade. With that, the boy nodded, and she attacked.

The light blazed as she charged, hammering down from above. Logan was quick however, raising his blade just in time. She connected, swords thwacking. His blade sagged, and Logan grunted. He was obviously stronger and taller, but he didn't expect her ferocity. Agilely, she flicked her blade, adding power from nothing. Logan was blown back. He grunted, looking up, readying his blade. But she was on top of him, instantly. Her knee hit his gut—*hard*—and he fell to both knees, gasping.

Are you all right? she asked inwardly. But she would not voice it, nor would she go easy on him. Karil needed to prove to Rydel that even the weakest of them were strong, and even more importantly, prove it to *them.* Instead, she spoke. "Get up. The enemy will not stop when you are on your knees. When the time comes, they will finish you where you lay without mercy."

"But you are not my enemy," the young man said—sounding more a boy than she'd hoped. Was this how Gray had sounded when she had met him? But now he was no longer just a boy, his adventures had forged his strength. She had to do the same with these young ones—whether she liked it or not—if she wanted them to live.

"If you train with ease in practice and expect mercy or a simple fight when the time comes, then you are a fool or a dead man, or most likely both."

Luckily, a fire sparked in the young man's face. Logan's features twisted in anger, and he lifted his wooden sword, ready to lash out.

"*Calm, boy!*" the elf captain barked, "Remember serenity over rage, for a calm mind conquers all!"

Karil remembered these words well. Ironically, they had been hammered into her as well. She found that peace now. Similarly and surprisingly, Logan's mask of rage contorted, his features smoothing with a breath—and he attacked.

His moves were not the angry swipes of a young man now, but the tactical strikes of a swordsman. He struck at her left flank. Her nusai flickered, blocking. He hit her right. Again, she swung the nusai, flicking his sword away with a force called *jang,* not magic, but simply the skill of an advanced swordsman—a pop sounded as Logan's sword was repelled forcefully. But unlike a novice, he *used* the extra force. The blade's momentum swung to strike her head again. And she realized he was testing her.

She smiled, impressed, as a thin sweat broke out on her face.

In the corner of her vision, Karil realized the crowds were gathering to watch. Sweat stung her eyes as she worked the forms, but still she glimpsed men and women join the swelling group who watched their queen battle amidst them. She heard cheers distantly, but she did not waste time thinking on it.

Logan roared, pressing harder, and she continued to block, parry, and redirect, flowing back smoothly.

"Careful, boy—she's baiting you!" The elf captain called.

Rydel growled. "Whose side are you on?"

Karil listened between the sounds of strikes. It was difficult—with the speed and fury of the young man's strikes, her attention could not be spared as much as she had anticipated. Again, she saw the crowds swelling, hundreds watching.

"Apologies, Hidden," the captain said, referencing Rydel's rank with deference. "That's my queen, but not now. For now, he's my student, and she's yours. You may do as you like, but I will see mine well-trained."

Heart, Karil thought happily. But the captain was right. As Logan rained a fury of blows, looking for an opening, Karil found her moment. Subtly, almost delicately, as if sidestepping his blade in slow motion, she spun, blade flashing. It landed near his neck.

But he was not there.

She tensed, feeling the wind part at her back. His blade. She dove, narrowly dodging the blade's tip. She rose, lifting her blade, expecting a strike from above but it was a thrust. Narrowly, she dipped her head to one side. Logan's sword knifed past her neck, skimming flesh. Karil growled. She knocked his blade away with her nusai, adding *jang*—an added power given to the blade when a last moment flick or twist was applied. But the blade didn't shift... Logan somehow had added his own *jang*, and his sword rested near the nape of her neck, held back barely by her own blade.

"Almost," she breathed through gritted teeth.

A tense moment hung, the crowds watched expectantly.

"Her feet!" the captain called suddenly.

Karil's leg swung, sweeping Logan from his feet. He fell hard.

She leapt upon him but he kicked frantically. She raised her blade, resting her palm against the flat of the blade to take the blow. It sent her back several feet. Logan leapt up. He charged with a cry, and his sword arced, fast and full of calculated fury. Her nusai caught it smoothly. She twisted her blade hard, snapping his wooden sword in her hooked crossguard. The wood shattered, half of his blade falling. But before Karil could rejoice in victory she felt wood touch her neck. Slowly, she twisted, eyeing a *second* blade—a short wood dagger—that Logan had hidden behind his back.

The young man panted, looking both confused and elated. He eyed his dagger as if almost unsure what he had done. His brown hair fell into his eyes, and he looked around, bewildered.

He had won.

Whispers of excitement sifted like a breeze through the amassed throng. Karil rose to her feet. Logan's dagger dropped. He watched her with dread, as if preparing for his execution. Instead, Karil smiled widely. She grabbed his arm, and held it up.

Cheers burst, ringing through the crowds and echoing out over the vast field. She felt pride in the pit of her stomach as she held his sweaty wrist that was limp with fatigue.

He had won, besting her, and in so doing, she had won.

They could fight. Now all saw their strength. It was undeniable.

"Thank you," the boy said, rattled.

Karil merely smiled, bowing to him and turning, moving through the crowds. Men and women bowed low to her, as if seeing what she had done and thanking her. It was odd, surely, to see their queen fight alongside them, but that was where she belonged.

As she moved back to the command tent, Rydel joined her side.

She looked at him out of the corner of her eye, lips quirking. "Well?"

Rydel looked to her unflinchingly. "Yes?"

"Can I say I told you so, or will your elf pride not allow it?"

"I can admit when I was wrong," he said.

She laughed. "Then now would be the time."

The stony elf gave a nod. "As always, you are impressive, my queen, and the boy had more fight than I was anticipating. Perhaps there is more than meets the eye to this rabble. And I do not belittle them because I wish it, I simply fear the odds."

"The odds have been stacked against us before," Karil said, grabbing a kerchief from her pocket and dabbing sweat from her brow.

"That was different," Rydel replied.

"How so?"

"The prophecy of The Knife's Edge was a long shot, but it was not our battle. This is our fight, and I do not see a path of salvation, razor thin or not. This time, Karil, the odds are even worse."

She growled, finally growing frustrated with him. "But how do you not see? This was the weakest of our group. If he can fight, then so can our army. Trust them, Rydel. Heart will be our key to victory."

"And if heart does not kill a Terma? If heart is not enough to cut down thousands?" She knew his words did not come from a place of anger or derision towards her. He was simply a general seeing the layout of the battlefield with cold calculations. But that was not a battle—not all of it at least. Wars had been won and lost on strength of heart and mind alone.

"If the enemy thinks us soft and few, we will use that against them. We will hide easier, sift among their faceless masses effortlessly, and whittle them down one by one until *they* are few. If they think us poor and famished, we will use that, taking from nature, becoming the forest itself so they cannot find us with all the armies of Farhaven combined. And we *will* fight, my friend, with sticks and mud if we have to."

"And when we fall?" he asked.

"Then we will rise again," Karil replied turning to him and this time gripping *his* arm. Firmly. "Until there are none left," she vowed. "I promise to break him, Rydel. Dryan will meet his end beneath my sword. Now do not argue with me again on this matter. Simply see it done."

As if simply needing to hear *her* conviction, the elf gave a deep bow. "As you command."

Just as he turned to leave, a messenger approached. Garbed in the green-black armor of the Lando, she saw a familiar face. Karil's heart lifted. She held her breath in anticipation as he approached. This is what she had been waiting for. "My queen!" Temian called, approaching swiftly, weaving through the combatants. He was breathing hard, though his features were masked in characteristic Elvin impassivity.

Blond hair fell halfway down his back. The full elf appeared almost typical of the Elvin race. While Temian was not particularly high-ranking amid the Lando, he was perhaps her most loyal warrior. He had been there since the first day, and had even taken an interest in Gray before the young man had left the camp. She could talk to him of Gray, Ayva, and Darius, and he seemed equally intrigued. He believed, as she did, that those three were destined for much more.

He neared, coming to a halt.

"Temian, what news?"

"We have him, my queen."

"Have who?" Rydel asked calmly.

"Where is he?" Karil said to Temian. Her heart pounded in excitement.

"In your command tent as you ordered, my queen," Temian said swiftly. "But he is not alone. He is surrounded by fifty of the Lando, our very best."

"Who?" Rydel asked again.

"A Terma," Karil replied.

"You captured a Terma?" Rydel said, disbelieving.

"I told you I had other plans in motion, dear friend. I dared not involve you. It was risky, and I had a feeling you would advise against it," she said and looked to Temian, putting voice to her true fear, "Did we lose any?"

"Two Lando."

Karil's heart clenched. "How?"

"They fell to the Terma before we had him in bindings," Temian said sadly, looking down. "Despite sneaking up on him, the traitorous wretches are still as dangerous as a susa snake in the brush—*Terma*." He said the word with such disdain. All her elves felt the same. She was sure if he were human he would have spat in disgust.

Karil let out a heavy breath. "They were brave warriors. We will honor their memory and give them the funeral rites of nobility." It was a rare thing, but not unheard of, save for heroes of war. Suffice it to say, it hadn't been done for hundreds of years.

Temian hesitated. "A true honor, my queen. Sadly, we could not retrieve their bodies. But it is not necessary, for all know the truth. It is spreading quickly. Their sacrifice was not in vain, their deaths are already seen as legendary, their lives remembered well."

With difficulty, she summoned a smile. She was heartened by the elf's words, but it was not enough. She knew hundreds more would die, but these were the first casualties of the war. They could not ignore their sacrifices or see them as simply figures on a board, or they would be no better than Dryan. "Still," she insisted, "we will see the pyre rights fulfilled. Gather anything you can in place of their bodies—tokens they held, their blades, anything treasured their families do not wish to keep, and prepare their souls to meet with the Eternal Spirit.

"We must let others see the price of victory, and what is at risk if we lose. And let them know that each life is valued dearly."

Temian gave an unexpected, deep bow. "I will see it done. You are truly a blessing sent to us by the spirits themselves. Your father would be proud, just as we are."

Karil warmed under the praise, but simply smiled. "Thank you, Temian. Now, see it done and meet me in my quarters afterwards, there's much still to be done." The elf bowed again, whisking away.

"How did you do it?" Rydel asked.

In the light of the morning sun, the cloaked elf was still a shadow, his grand Lando cloak shrouding his muscular frame and brushing the ground. But Rydel's long dark hair was resplendent, his bright eyes filled with pride. "I shall tell you all," Karil answered. "For now, come with me. The training of the others can wait. If it's all the same to you, I'd prefer to have you there when I question this Terma."

"You think I would be anywhere else?"

Again, Karil's heart warmed and together they moved through the camps towards her tent, to discover the truth behind the Terma.

* * *

Karil's tiredness fled as they approached her tent. Emblazoned upon the tent's side was a glorious black leaf with gold embellishment. It was huge, two or three people in height at least. Two smaller ones were stitched upon the tent's flap. It was the symbol of the Great Kingdom of Leaf, of Eldas.

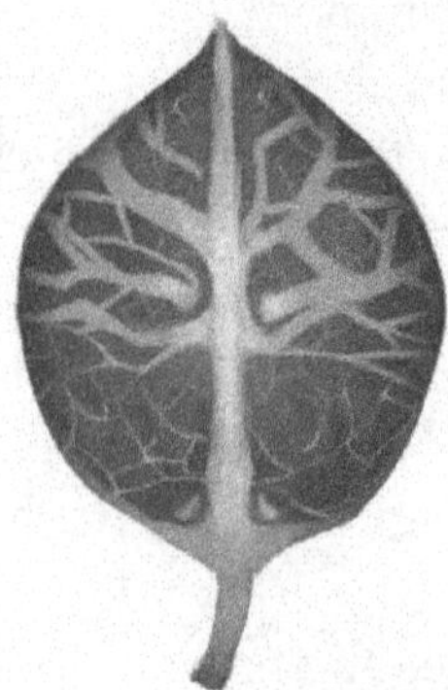

Rydel touched her arm as they reached the entry. She understood, and let him go first. Two elves pulled back the tent's flap, and Rydel moved with deadly intent inside the shaded tent.

She followed.

Inside was dark. After the bright sun, Karil felt blinded. As her eyes adjusted, she saw it was crowded. Dozens of elves bearing the armor of the Lando made the giant command tent seem small. Upon their breasts nearly all bore a piece of her father's crown, a badge of rank and honor. Their swords were unsheathed and ready. They made a giant spiraling ring of armor, guarding a lone figure.

In the center, on his knees, was an elf with his head bowed, light illuminating his dark blond hair that touched and coiled upon the floor. He wore a simple green tunic and white pants, both torn to shreds. Karil saw the armor of a Terma stripped in a nearby pile—dark plates of black with faint gold vines. It made her shiver in memory. Most strikingly, a dozen sword tips rested against the captive elf's neck.

The elf looked up upon her entrance. Karil froze. His expression. It was … full of sorrow. It confused her. She expected angry or stoic, but not this. Otherwise, he seemed utterly uncaring of the sharp blades upon his flesh. That didn't surprise her. She did not think a hundred elves were overkill to guard a Terma either, even if they were her best warriors.

Rydel strode forward.

The forlorn eyes caught her guardian's and the Terma stiffened, looking afraid, if such an elf could look fearful. "*Hidden…*" the elf breathed, and then remarkably pressed his head to the ground. "Brother! We thought you had all died. My name is Hadrian. Are you the last of your kind?"

Rydel looked baffled, obviously taken aback by the Terma's voice, as if Hadrian were talking to an old friend, or a brother-in-arms.

"Are you certain you got the right one?" Karil asked a nearby elf captain, Lannor, the highest-ranking in the room aside from her and Rydel.

"Certain, my lady," Lannor said sternly. "His armor is proof. If that were not enough, before we captured him, Sunvai and Leahwin fell to his blade. He moved like a Terma."

So those were their names... she thought, storing them aside. Sunvai and Leahwin.

Hadrian spoke suddenly, "I... What do you mean? I killed two of your men?"

Karil shivered. "You ... do not know?"

"It's a ploy," Rydel said, pulling her aside. "My instincts tell me there is something he is hiding."

"And what kind of ploy would it be?" she asked in a whisper. "He knows we will not set him free."

"Dryan is crafty. The Terma is simply a pawn covering for his master."

"No, brother," the Terma said. His hearing was remarkably good, even for an elf. "It was not me. Whoever did this, it was not me. I swear it."

Karil spoke clearly. "You killed two of my men, traitor. If you believe your lies will save you, then you are sadly mistaken. Tell the truth or I will set Rydel upon you and pry it from you the hard way."

Hadrian shook his head. "I swear on the Eternal Sp—"

Steel rung. Karil hadn't seen Rydel cross the span, but his sword rested on the elf's neck. But Hadrian didn't look afraid, instead, his eyes looked pained. "*Silence!* Do not muddy the Eternal Spirit with your foul lies. Speak truth now or I will cut you down where you kneel," Rydel seethed. "And know I am not so easily deceived." The Terma's eyes searched Rydel's.

At last, Hadrian gazed to Lannor. "How? How did I do it?"

"With ease," said Lannor darkly. "You had no mercy."

Hadrian shook his head. "That does not sound like me."

"Yet you smiled upon their deaths. I saw it myself."

"I saw it too," another elf said. "He grinned as he cut them down, as if reveling in killing his own kind, taking some kind of sick delight in it."

Hadrian shook his head softly. "No… It cannot be…"

"He's a monster," Lannor said.

"Then, if what they say is true, perhaps I deserve death," Hadrian voiced forlornly.

"And you will get it," Karil declared, striding forward. The ring of elves surrounding Hadrian tensed, pressing swords tighter like a collar of steel barbs. Again, she knew it was not an unnecessary precaution, but she needed to see if he was evil, and she could only see that with bait. She motioned their swords back. She held his gaze. It was an unnerving green hue, but she made her silver gaze equally fearsome. This man *had* killed, *had* taken the lives of her men, and she knew it had been easy for him, possibly even enjoyable.

At last, Hadrian's head fell. "Kill me, then, and be done with it."

She unsheathed her dagger, put it to his chin and lifted his head. "Not yet. Not before you tell me everything. What do you remember of your capture?"

Hadrian looked away, as if trying to remember. "I remember … woods… I was on the border of the Relnas Forest, on a mission. It seemed an odd order, to scout in the Yurili Pass, for it is not secured by our forces, but I followed the order anyway."

"Go on," Karil pressed.

"I…" Hadrian's eyes squeezed. "I had just moved into the valley when there was movement in the brush on my right. It seemed suspicious. And so I trailed around it, moving to a higher vantage spot… That was when the true trap was sprung. I saw it just before it happened."

"Continue," Karil said, feeling her anger rise, dagger pressing tighter.

Hadrian's faced twisted, pained, but not by her dagger. "I remember green armor… Two elves in the bushes. I wanted to warn them to put down their weapons. I tried. I remember. I opened my mouth and…"

"*And?*" she questioned.

There was a long, heavy silence as sweat broke out on Hadrian's skin. The elf grunted in pain and exertion.

"Tell me!" she commanded. "What happened next?"

He looked up, eyes bloodshot, shaking his head only slightly. "I can't…"

Her anger was growing, but she was getting nowhere. She felt a hand on her shoulder, and Rydel pulled her even farther aside, speaking low enough to ensure he couldn't hear. "I do not trust him."

"I fear it is not so simple," she replied. "His words seem too true. There is something missing here, but I cannot put my finger on it. Either way, I do not believe we have seen the full Hadrian. We will have to question him further, but I don't believe he's going to tell us anything now. Luckily, he's not going anywhere."

"I don't like it," Rydel said. "He should not stay here, and you should not have brought him here."

Karil looked to the elf captain, Lannor, gesturing him over. "Lannor, did you do as I said in full? Was he blindfolded?"

"All the way, my queen. He knows not where he is."

"Good, then blindfold him again and take his hearing this time—I don't care if you have to stuff wax in his ears or deafen him, but do not let him have any sense of where he is going."

"Where shall I take him, my queen?" Lannor asked.

"I've had Temian prepare a tent that will suffice. It is on the eastern border of the camp. Take him there. Keep him bound and blindfolded, and set a guard of at least ten on him at all times."

Lannor, dutiful to the core, simply clapped a fist to his heart and went to see it done.

Rydel's teeth ground. "It is not enough."

"We've enough bindings to shackle a stagfal," she said. Stagfals were huge beasts, the size of a small dragon, moose-like in appearance, but bigger all around and with skin thick enough to deflect the keenest spear. "It will have to do, my friend."

"And why do we not simply execute him? You said it best—he killed two of ours. He will not avoid justice."

"I believe there's much Hadrian has yet to tell us…" she said, meaning more than her words implied. "He is a mystery I seek to crack. Besides, his knowledge of Dryan's forces alone—their movements, positions, and numbers—is vital if we seek to find a chink in *their* armor. You know as well as I, this elf is our first edge in this war, our best weapon yet. I cannot—no, I *will* not—throw it away. He is too important."

"Even if he is lying?"

"He is not lying..."

"Believe me, this will not be the end of this elf," Rydel said oddly. "There is something more to him."

"What are you saying?"

He looked towards the elf as he was pulled to his feet, bound, blindfolded, and deafened with waxed cloths stuffed in his ears. Hadrian complied without so much as a twitch of a muscle. It was good he did. Rydel replied at last. "What he said ... *my kind* ... he seemed to know too much. He seemed worried that I was alive, or surprised to see it so."

"Perhaps the other Hidden are being hunted by Dryan," she posed.

"Perhaps," Rydel said mysteriously.

Karil cleared her throat, watching as Hadrian was hauled to his feet. "I don't believe I've ever asked you, but how many Hidden are there left?" She felt odd asking. She should know, but it was not a topic Rydel ever seemed to want to talk about, like a family he had lost and could not bring himself to rekindle the harsh memories.

"Just two that I know of, but the way he spoke ... it seemed too familiar. As if when he asked, *your* kind, I felt he wanted to say something else..."

Karil hesitated when Hadrian, with his guard of fifty Lando, was marched forward.

Hadrian suddenly stopped before her. Despite the swarm of guard around him, Karil felt a flash of fear as his blindfolded eyes turned towards her. She *felt* his eyes, burning. *How? My scent?* she wondered. A thin smile passed across his face, but it was gone just as quickly, leaving her to question whether it *had* been there.

"Sunvai and Leahwin was it?" the Terma asked in a dark voice. "I will remember their names."

Anger boiled inside her. She stepped forward, and pressed steel against Hadrian. His fair skin peeled, blood dripping from her blade. Calmly, she pulled out one piece of waxed cloth from his ear and hissed, "You do not have the right to remember their names"—finally feeling her human side—"*nor* the need, for you will not live to see the light of day ever again."

Again, the hidden smile—but this time, she knew she had seen it.

"Peace upon you, my queen," Hadrian said. "May you discover the truth soon."

She stuffed the waxed cloth back and gruffly motioned to his guards. Several elves jabbed him in the back, drawing blood. Calmly, leisurely, Hadrian looked forward and continued out the tent. With his head high and gait measured, he appeared as if a king escorted by *his* guards.

Lannor stopped at her side.

Unfurling her sweaty fist, Karil instructed, "Double the guard and, upon their lives, impress upon them vigilance at all times—tell them I will check on them myself to be sure." Lannor bowed low, and moved out, following the captive and the host of Lando.

Rydel suddenly gripped a nearby officer's arm. "Have any who are able to lift a sword, those not attending the prisoner, meet me in the center field."

The officer's thin lips quirked in a smile he could not hide. "Yes, Hidden." He moved, but then paused, looking almost anxious for an elf. "And .... might I say, the Lando rejoice to have you as their teacher at last."

"They will not be rejoicing long," Rydel said with a subtle grin. "Nor will you be so happy when I run you through your paces long into the night and you're bruised and battered from head to toe. But you will be ready, for I will see you fit to fight even the Terma." Karil shivered in memory, yet oddly longing for those days. The lessons had been hard, but the pain had been simpler, if still sharp. The elf looked fearful as well. Yet oddly, he looked even *more* excited as he clasped a fist to his heart and ran off to see it done.

"I will go now," Rydel announced turning back to her. "I must see to making our forces strong."

Karil felt her heart warm again. "Thank you, my friend."

"That's one thing you never have to do," Rydel replied, sliding his sword smoothly in its sheath at one side, opposite its twin brother, and grabbing the tent's flap. "But you are welcome regardless, my queen. I will do my best."

"I know you will."

Rydel paused, holding the tent's flap, revealing again the bustle of war. Something crossed Rydel's stern features—a dark, brooding look but then it was gone. "Be careful," he said simply, at last. With that, he slipped into the light of day. But before he did, she heard one last strange word, murmured in thought.

A word she had heard Hadrian use.

Brother…

Dreams and Deeds

Meira worked the threads flawlessly and brutally.

She was a natural.

Sweat beaded upon her brow, forehead wrinkling in concentration. But the sweat was not from exhaustion. She worked harder, knowing it was slowly killing her, not her body, but her *soul*—if there *was* such a thing. She had never honestly believed in souls or things of that nature, not until she had been assigned to this malevolent room.

Now she wasn't so sure.

Another sharp cry sounded. It hit the marble walls and dissipated instantly, for all sound was drained in this place, if not by the thick walls of the room buried deep beneath the great keep of the Citadel, then by magic spells from ancient Reavers that nullified noise.

Lying on the cold marble, upon the Star of Magha, the old man's back arched as she worked. His eyes flared wide in shock, rolling to the back of his head as he gasped in searing pain.

No more…

Meira tried not to see, tried not to feel his pain, but she couldn't help it. His straggled hair seemed to have gained white streaks of age in just days. White robes, now dirtied with blood and sweat, were stripped to his waist. Torso bared, his body was lathered in a sheen of sweat while red and black lacerations marred his arms, chest, and face.

The others continued to work. She eyed them out of the corner of her eye as she threaded, quickly assessing each. Eight Reavers in total, each chosen because of their power or their ruthlessness—including herself.

And all wore resolute, grim faces, as if preparing for death.

But not their own.

From her upraised palms, Meira watched her power join the other dark streams, like eight spokes of a wagon wheel meeting at the center where the chained prisoner lay. The old man roared as the other Reavers redoubled their efforts. His voice would go raw soon once again, but still they would continue.

It felt like an eternity that Meira had been here, assigned to this task, watching and aiding as the old man was lashed with fire, blinded, given bubbling blisters using the power of sun, and made to suffer with other bizarre tortures, all to get him to speak. He had experienced days of being shrouded in pure darkness with the threads of moon to cloud the senses and give the sensation of eternal torture, days of having sharp stones scraped slowly across his body, and days of having molding fungi fester in his wounds and grow within his lungs.

Yet nothing was as potent or as effective in torture as *flesh*. And no one was better at wielding the brutal element than her. While Meira was immensely powerful as a three-stripe Reaver, she could not bring herself to draw more than a trickle of the spark. The old man's agony ate at her, draining her as surely as the sun sucked the sweat from a man's skin.

"It is not enough. More flesh, Meira!" Guran commanded. He was the leader of the Fuse—eight wielders working as one.

Please, just give in already, she begged for the countless time.

She kept her face smooth, however, and did as Guran commanded, hiding a shiver. She could not let the others see her reluctance. Thick threads of flesh made the already thick stream of power swell like a bulging muscle, then bite into the old man, gnashing like teeth upon raw nerves. The old man's back arched until she thought it would snap. His body trembled. It was the first time she had seen that… She suppressed another shiver. How was he so strong?

Though Meira considered herself tough, she knew she would have broken during the first day of torture. But she suspected that was the difference between the man before her and all others. Even without the spark, he was a legend.

Without the spark…

The man cried out again, and she softened the threads of flesh, reflexively.

Suddenly, she felt eyes. Guran was gazing at her suspiciously. Fear flushed through Meira. Guran had a direct ear to Sithel. *No…* She had given herself up. Meira did the only thing she could think of, unsure exactly what she was doing. Twisting dozens of threads of flesh together, she made a dark spell.

Compelling—an ancient spell that would force the wielder to speak.

The prisoner gasped, words forced from his thoughts and to his lips: "He must not find me. *He must not save me. I was wrong… He must… Run…*" Ezrah began to quake violently, body railing against his chains. She thought he was done, and she prayed it was so but he spoke again, this time in single, painful words, "*Unatias … Sunthas…*"

"What is he saying?" Guran shouted angrily. "Compel him, Reaver Meira! Force him to make sense!"

She hesitated, but not for long. She twisted the threads, turning a switch in his mind from the ancient dialect he was using to the common tongue and Ezrah's rambling shifted. "*Yronia … Sithel … Voidstone … Gray… He is comin—*"

Frantically, she twisted the threads, subtly and swiftly. Ezrah's rambling halted. His eyes shut, his body limp against the marble. She saw no one was looking at her, and breathed a hidden sigh. Upon the cold, red marble, Ezrah breathed shallowly. He was not dead, merely unconscious. Whatever he was saying seemed too dire… She had started it, but she couldn't let Sithel win. Not this fight, at least.

"He's suffered the limit of pain. He's passed out," said Reaver Finn Ilunis.

"So it seems," Guran said, sounding doubtful. She looked up and found his gaze, forcing herself to meet it. She felt her body heat up and sweat pop upon her brow, but she refrained from flinching.

Suddenly, the door opened.

Reavers in scarlet robes stood in the wide entry, announcing the next shift.

Meira hid a breath of relief. *At last...*

Without waiting to receive the command, she let go of her connection with the Fuse, letting the spark fall from her. Each Reaver let go in sequence, the golden glow fading—an aura seen only by those with the spark. Meira felt her body slump, now exhausted. Sleep beckoned, but she cared not for it. A reprieve was the only blessing she was grateful for.

She made her way to the door, ignoring the others' eyes as they followed.

Outside, she attempted to feign patience, but continued to move swiftly when a voice called her name, "Meira!"

She turned to see three Reavers.

Reaver Finn Ilunis had called her name. Reaver Yuni Sinal was behind him, then Reaver Dagon Swift—a Reaver from the newest shift. The three approached her. Finn's blue eyes were red-rimmed, but his angular face looked as if he'd just seen an apparition come to life. Finn was a close childhood friend, but since the Citadel had changed, she still did not fully trust him. Oh how she dearly wanted to... But as it was, there was no on left to trust—not even herself.

She smiled serenely as they circled her. She was a paragon of poise, in full control again now that she was outside that room of horrors. "Yes?"

Finn spoke animatedly. "*How?* How did you do that? Never in my life have I seen flesh used in that way..."

"I would also like to know how you did that," said a voice behind the three. Reaver Guran suddenly pushed his way through. Tall and muscular, Guran was not only the epitome of power but of masculinity as well. Meira despised his arrogance, and even more, its effect on others. Guran grinned charmingly. "*Compelling.* I've only read about it until now in tomes of old." He sounded amused, distrustful, and hateful all at the same time.

"It was easy," she lied, having accomplished it just then for the first time.

"Then share by all means."

"Only if you insist," she said and wove the complicated threads in the air before any could reject. She pressed it forward, into Guran, taking him off-guard. He was more powerful than her in nearly every element and in raw strength, but he was too cocky, and flesh was her trademark. The layered spell hit Guran.

Guran suddenly squawked, mouth moving awkwardly, "*Stupid bitch! How'd she do it? I wish I knew!*"

The others looked at one another in amazement as Guran's face grew red with embarrassment and anger. Finn, her friend, tried simply not to laugh though a chuckle escaped.

"And now you know," she said offhandedly.

"How in the…" Reaver Yuni said.

"Meira," Finn exclaimed, amazed. "Do you realize that was nearly three-dozen threads at *once*? My eyes, woman! I never thought anyone but an Arbiter could accomplish something of that note." Meira observed Finn's enthusiasm bitterly. How could he be so full of life after what they had done? She felt wracked with shame to her core.

Guran, however, was not so amazed or pleased. "*You…!*" The man's rage mounted, his hand raising. Meira didn't flinch. It was no use. She knew she could do nothing to him before he incinerated her to a small pile of ash, but it had almost been worth it. Almost. Perhaps then her guilt, her despair, would be washed free.

"Enough!" Reaver Dagon ordered. All went silent, heads bowed. Even Guran hesitated. Dagon bore the fourth stripe upon his wide sleeves. He was nearly an Arbiter, though still chasms away. In all reality, despite being the most powerful and experienced, Dagon was pitiful compared to an Arbiter. Even Guran's raw talent with fire was but a flickering flame to an Arbiter. "You yourself asked for a demonstration, Guran. However, you know as well as any, Reaver Meira, that use of the spark against a fellow brother or sister is strictly prohibited. I shall report this to the Highmaster Venasi, and he will decide if punishment is deserved. That will be all, unless either of you wish to contest this further?"

Meira shook her head wisely. Highmaster Venasi was the head taskmaster, but all knew lately he cowed to Sithel's command. Banishment was the price of disorder as of late. *Death*, she amended fearfully. Even the hotheaded Guran growled, but said no more. He pushed his way past, shoving other scarlet robed Reavers aside and leaving a wake of fiery ire behind him.

Dagon turned to her—she saw pain behind his eyes. Could she confide in him? Was he simply worn down by exhaustion or was this dark deed sucking his soul from his body as well? She grit her teeth, wishing she knew. She could not risk it. Dagon spoke, addressing all, but eyeing Meira. "I would advise returning to your rooms for sleep as Master Sithel has instructed, my brothers and sisters, for we will be called on again soon, and you will need rest for your next shift."

The others left, though she saw Finn linger.

She ignored him, moving to leave, but Dagon grabbed her arm. "Rest well, Reaver Meira," said the four-stripe Reaver. "For I have a feeling the next shift will be the last one we will ever have, and this shall finally be over."

Meira's eyes narrowed, trying to judge Dagon's tone. Was he elated at the prospect of being done as she was? She had to know. "Finally?" she asked, her tone treading between excitement and simple curiosity.

"Spirits willing, it will be done at last," Dagon replied and sighed heavily.

Yes. I can trust him, she thought. Another sliver of relief lanced through her, thoughts brewing…

She parted ways with quick, polite words and moved through halls, venturing out of the dark, deeply restricted depths of the Citadel. More and more people moved about the higher she rose, Neophytes, Reavers, guards and servants—even a few stalking Devari strode through the white and black marble halls.

A group of Neophytes saw the three stripes on her cuff and bowed deeply, awe filling their eyes. She remembered that look, that feeling once … barely now. It seemed so long ago.

Her hands shook as she moved. She feared that servants, Neophytes, and Reavers would see it and question, but they simply continued to bow deeply in her presence, and she felt more waves of guilt with each bow of adoration. Meira clenched her eyes, trying to shove aside the darkness, to assume her normally ironclad shell of confidence, but it was not easy. Each time she did, she heard the old man's screams, and the shell shattered like the frail husk it now was. She tightened her fists to stop her hands from trembling and decided… She could not think on what she was doing or it would break her. Simple as that. It was too foul, too horrific.

But as she moved, she saw other Reavers' eyes, men she had seen Sithel commanding. Meira suddenly feared the eyes watching her from all corners. She moved faster, passing grand halls, open entry chambers, green courtyards, and more. The Citadel was alive and thriving as always, but it felt false, like a disguise. The Citadel was a graveyard of darkness wearing the guise of life, or worse, a villainous man wearing the robes of the pious. It *was* false. She entered a chamber open to the sunlit day, but the sun felt cold on her pale skin. She kept moving, towards the Eastern Wing.

She had to get to her room.

A three-stripe Reaver she knew suddenly appeared from the far hallway. Reaver Dijarik was a ruthless man in charge of torturing the old man as well. Without her shell of confidence, Meira felt suddenly vulnerable.

Show hesitancy and you may end up the same! her mind shouted. For the Citadel had changed, those who questioned the will of Sithel were never seen again. Rumors sifted that those Reavers or Neophytes had been assigned to guarding other Great Kingdoms, but Meira knew better.

They had been expunged like vermin.

Not willing to risk it, she ducked behind a large standing vase in an empty hallway adjacent to the sunlit chamber and watched as Reaver Dijarik passed.

She closed her eyes, breathing thin and fast, sweat coating her skin beneath her heavy robes. What had become of the once-great Citadel? Yet Meira knew the Patriarch would end it soon. *Once he returns from his trip to seek aid from the other Great Kingdoms, he will set it right.* She only had to wait. Though what would he do when he saw what she had done? But what could she do to resist it?

With Reaver Dijarik gone, she moved onward, gathering her calm around her one last time like a mantle. She moved towards the grand Eastern Wing of the Citadel, which housed the higher-ranking Reavers—towards her chamber and sleep.

Yet she feared slumber, for only nightmares waited there, brought upon by her dark deeds.

Gray…

The old man's words echoed again in her head, haunting her as her footsteps sounded softly on the richly woven rug that ran the marble hallway. *Who is this Gray?* Hope bloomed abruptly. Perhaps he could aid her—perhaps he could find a way to make this nightmare end... With that thought, her fists gripped her scarlet robes, and Reaver Meira pressed on faster, as if she could outrun her own darkness.

* * *

Meira scuttled through the hallways, sneaking into the kitchens.

Smells of meat and bread lingered, assaulting her senses and making her stomach growl. She had disobeyed High Master Venasi Suroth and, as punishment, the man had forbid her from breakfast, lunch, and dinner. She was starving. Meira shivered and reached out, grabbing a sweet cake from a tin near the wide double doors. Sweet cakes were her favorite.

Suddenly, something snatched her hand. "Thief!"

Fear flushed through her. "No, please!" Meira cried. "I didn't mean to! I was just hungry!"

300 *The servant woman said something she didn't understand. Her gaze was taken as a man appeared, his tall imposing frame filling her vision. Calmly, he pulled back his hood. Dark grey hair fell around a wise-looking face with stern features. He stood tall and commanding as he spoke. "Leave her be," he commanded.*

The servant woman was suddenly gone.

The man looked to her, and she tried to explain, her voice a squeak. "I'm sorry... I was just..."

"Your name?"

"Meira."

"Mine is Ezrah. And you are simply hungry, Meira. Do not apologize. No one should be hungry." Calmly, the man reached out, and the tray filled with fresh baked treats moved closer, as if held by invisible hands. The spark, she knew in awe. "Go ahead. Take as many as you want, and share with your friends."

Meira didn't question the man. Standing in the white light coming from the corridor, he looked like a spirit. Eagerly, she filled her hands with her favorites, hiding those she couldn't carry in her baggy sleeves.

"If anyone gives you any trouble, including High Master Suroth, tell him to see me. The Citadel is a place of light, not darkness. Re-

member, Meira, always do what you believe is right first, and what is told of you second."

"I promise..." she said.

Meira awoke.

Her eyes opened slowly, taking in the lacy canopy above her with its four elaborately carved posts. Her hands gripped her blankets. It had been such a sweet dream, yet sweat covered her again, making her thin shift stick to her slender frame.

Her room was shrouded in darkness—but still she could faintly make out finely made cabinets, rich rugs, velvet chairs, and several stands holding Serilian silver vases.

Outside the nearby window, it was still dark. She clenched her eyelids, hoping to drift off to sleep, but immediately opened them again. It didn't feel right. None of it did. Something inside her was stirring restlessly.

She threw off her covers, slipped on her red slippers and moved across the room, splashing cold water from her Seria porcelain washbasin before gliding across the cold stone to the huge oval window beside her bed. The night was still heavy. She'd barely been asleep for an hour, and yet the dream seemed so long—and powerful. It still clung to her like walking through a spider web. And this time, she didn't want to peel it from her. *Let it cling,* she thought. *I deserve this guilt.* It wracked her insides. Something knocked and her heart skipped a beat.

No... The summons? So soon? She hadn't even rested! How could they want her back? Despite all her strength and years of confidence, tears began to stream down her face. She couldn't do it.

She waited for another knock, but it didn't come, and she breathed a sigh and then...

It hit her.

What was this? Who was she, all of the sudden? Frightened like a little girl by imaginary knocks on her door? Terrified and intimidated into being a puppet for Sithel? Was this the price of life? Her nails scraped on the polished stone lip of her windowsill.

Ezrah's deep voice floated to her, sounding as clear as it had that day so long ago: *Always do what you believe is right first, and what is told of you second.* He had told her even then, and she had listened, always following her heart, and her curiosity. It had led her to such great heights, she knew, feeling the trappings of success around her. Yet somehow she had forgotten the words of wisdom along the way.

But no longer.

"It is time to do what is right," she said fiercely, staring out the misty window. Tears, anger, and purpose rose inside of her, and she smiled. Still in her shift, Meira moved from the window, seizing a heavy woolen cloak from her dresser and throwing it around her slender shoulders. She moved towards her door. She didn't have time to change, nor did she want to. She needed the others to see their urgency.

It was time for action, Meira thought.

It was time to save an Arbiter and a friend.

Questioning Darkness

The night was a shroud of black, the moon barely a sliver, and Karil was a shadow. A faint rain fell. It was a fine mist, but her shroud was waxed, repelling the light downfall.

Karil wrapped her cloak tight around her, moving with purpose. She had a contingent of ten Lando, her best men, including Temian, at her side. Their armor rustled as they strode briskly with hands on their weapons.

She was going to check on her prey, and she was going prepared.

Still, she hadn't told Rydel. She knew what his reaction would have been. He would have forbidden it, and she would have gone regardless, but ignoring her trusted guardian felt wrong. Instead, it was better to avoid the matter altogether. Besides, last she'd heard he was drilling her army. That was more important.

Few recognized her in the moving troop and, if they did, she moved too fast to acknowledge their bows. She could not be fazed in her current mood. The more she ruminated on Rydel's words, and on Hadrian's, the more she felt she was missing a crucial piece in a puzzle—one that may spell salvation for her people, or destruction. She would ensure it was the former.

She passed low-lying green tents, long pickets of horses, and campfires that steamed, her stomach growling from the smell of roasting stew. She saw the curious commotion among humans *and* elves. Everywhere, they were groaning or tending wounds. But most prominent of all was the sound of snoring. Man, woman, and elf lay sprawled, many half inside their tent and half out, sleeping where they fell—as if too exhausted to move another step.

She smiled. Rydel was doing his job, as she knew he would. It meant her men would be strong. The sleeping men and elves still gripped swords tightly. It was a sign that it was truly Rydel's influence.

She had a flashing memory.

Karil hit the ground hard, almost bouncing. She cracked open her eyes and realized her whole body smarted. Spots swam in her vision. When they cleared, a wooden blade dangled before her. She looked up into frozen blue eyes, to see the elf's tall, lean frame. She blew dust away from her lips, brushing aside tears when she saw a hand before her face. Karil gripped it, rising.

The elf before her was only several years older, but in that moment, despite all her training and her noble heritage, she felt like a little girl. She was young, but he made her feel small.

"What did you do wrong?" he asked calmly.

"I lost," she snapped back at him, feeling annoyed.

He shook his short-cropped black hair. Though he was the youngest Terma of all time, skill only meant so much for elves. He was still too new to grow his hair out long. "Wrong. Try again."

"Just tell me," she said, tired but mostly curious.

"You're improving, Karil, but you still care too much about my blade, and not enough about your own. You sacrificed your sword to land a hit, and it cost you much more."

She scratched her head. "Who cares? A blade is simply a tool. A person is the real weapon." A breeze passed between them, ruffling branches and leaves. Eldas was in summertime. The air was warm, but the cool breeze felt good on Karil's sweat-slicked skin.

Nearby, huge trees were in full bloom. They sat beneath their gargantuan brothers—trees that reached the heavens, a city in the rafters—and despite being fully grown oaks and Silveroots, these trees looked like tiny saplings.

"Your blade is your life, Karil."

"No, my life is my life," she replied.

"Not if it is taken from you. If you face someone stronger than you, what will you do then?"

"I have more than just the blade," she countered. "You taught me to use my hands, feet, elbows, and knees—even my head. Everything is a weapon, you said. I am the blade."

"One day you may be a blade, but not now. You've still much to learn. For now, you will treat that sword of yours like it is a part of you, and never let it go," he said, and then quoted, "'A soldier never loses his blade. Never lets go. Never surrenders.'" She sighed, but he held her gaze. "I mean it, Karil. Do you understand?"

She agreed at last, grabbing her wooden sword from the leaf-strewn ground, and Rydel attacked again.

She returned to the moment as a cart rumbled past her, carrying supplies.

Something unnerved Karil as she looked around at the starlit camp. On the surface, all was normal. Crickets chirped in the crisp air. She heard water being poured into a trough for a row of silken-haired cormacs, their coats shining in the dim night. All was tranquil. And yet… Somehow, she felt the camp wasn't safe, as if there was a deadly desrah snake in their midst—one was obvious, yet just out of sight. The Terma. And no one else knew. She felt almost guilty. Well, she would end that worry tonight.

At last, she reached the tent. On the backside of the sprawling camp, it sat alone, just as she had requested. Only a ring of guards surrounded it. Otherwise, it was a good three hundred paces to the nearest tent and closer to the nearest tree line. In the dark, the forest of Aenor looked like a black fog.

Her entourage approached, she nodded to the nearest guards in greeting, and they made way. They looked vigilant, but there was something odd about their expressions. She saw edginess in their postures and a black rim to their eyes. But she didn't ask. There was no time. She *had* been running them ragged. Perhaps they were just tired, but she didn't truly believe that.

Inside the tent was crowded. It was smaller than her command tent, but there were no tables, or chairs or beds to clutter it, simply Elvin guards and an elf in shackles.

Metal shackles were fastened around his wrists, feet, legs, and arms—each was connected to a heavy steel chain that was fixed to a thick spike driven into the ground far away. Lastly, a wide clasp around his neck led to a chain wrapped around the massive wooden post in the center of the room. He was more shackles than elf. How had she been afraid?

Despite being without sight and hearing, Hadrian looked up at her entrance.

"Remove his blindfold and earplugs. I wish him to hear what I have to say," she commanded.

A nearby elf obeyed, though he approached the elf as he would a poisonous snake. The cloth band over his eyes fell, and Karil held back a gasp, holding onto her fire and her weapon. If she expected sorrow or timidity from Hadrian, she was wrong. His eyes were all fire and, suddenly, she felt as if there were not nearly enough fetters on the elf. But then the fire was gone, as water thrown onto a flame, and sorrow returned to his sad face.

"My queen…" he said in greeting. "Have you discovered the truth yet?"

She drew a regal breath. "That is why I am here. It is time for you to tell me everything you know, Hadrian."

His faced remained impassive. "I told you all I know already. If that is the reason for your visit, then you have wasted your time in coming here." He looked back to the elf with the blindfold. "Kill me or leave me be."

"I'm afraid you will not have it so easy. I have questions."

"Then ask them and find silence my answer."

Karil strode forward. All around, the other twenty elves gripped their blades tighter, many unsheathing them. She stood several paces from Hadrian. And despite the emptiness in his eyes and the slouch to his shoulders, she felt his power and strength.

"Where is your friend?" Hadrian asked. "The one you called Rydel. The Hidden."

"On his way," she declared.

"A lie," Hadrian replied. "You did not tell him you were meeting me, did you? I suppose that is better. I doubt he would have let you come. He believes I am evil."

"And are you?"

Hadrian's eyes flashed. "What do you think?"

She waved the matter aside. "Evil or not, it does not matter to me. I simply seek the truth, and you *will* give me it. How do you not remember killing? And tell me how a Terma, one as noble as you, became so tainted?"

Hadrian's face was bluff, stone-like, once more. "Again, my queen, you travel down a path that is without sight, without end, and devoid of footing. What you seek is gone. It is simply blackness."

"I will not accept that." Karil took a steadying breath then called, "*Temian.*"

The white-haired elf came forth, a black cloth bundle in hand. He handed it to her reverently. "My queen."

Karil thanked him, and he remained at her side, hand on his hilt, which she was even more thankful for. She pulled back the cloth, unveiling a bloody sword, its blade shattered. It was Elvin-make. It should not have shattered. "Does this look familiar?"

Hadrian's eyes fell upon the blade. "What is that?"

"It is the blade of the elf you killed, or what remains of it."

Pained, Hadrian looked away.

"Do not look away!" she commanded harshly. Slowly, he looked back. "Leahwin was her name," Karil voiced, fury growing. She grabbed the broken blade and put its jagged edge to his neck. She summoned the pain, imagining what Leahwin had suffered in her final moments. She needed to feel that pain, to hold onto that anger to be strong—to never forget what was at stake. "You took her life. You will answer me how she died, or you will face a similar fate. Yet yours will be slow, and it *will* be painful."

Hadrian closed his eyes. "Put it away," he breathed.

"I will not, and you will tell me." She nodded to nearby elves, and they understood, grabbing his head and forcing his eyes open. "Look at this blade, and tell me how she died."

His eyes opened and something strange roiled across their surface—an inky blackness, like oil swimming in the whites of his eyes. *Evil*, she knew. Hadrian may not be evil, but whatever lurked within that gaze was pure evil. "I told you..." His eyes clenched again, tears welling, not from sorrow, but from an inner struggle Karil could not witness—a battle he seemed to be losing. "I saw Leahwin and Sunvai... but I did not want to kill them... I opened my mouth to speak and..." More tears leaked from his eyes, Hadrian's body began to convulse against his chains, shaking, muscles flexing. The elves struggled to keep hold of him. Karil motioned them away, stepping back herself. The chains rattled as he spoke through gritted teeth, "*Words* … I spoke … *'Lay down your weapons!'* I called," Hadrian shouted, eyes clenched shut, as if consumed in the memory. "They hesitated. I … couldn't help myself … something came over me. I remember seeing light, and then darkness. They cried out. It was too quick. I was too quick. Sunvai took my knife to his throat, gurgling blood before he could rally a warning. Leahwin was quicker, parrying my sword, but her blade shattered. She had no chance. My blade found her stomach. I cut her in two. Her gaze … it was confusion. I enjoyed it. Reveling in the difference between her pitiful strength and mine. She had tears before she died, life fading from her eyes. She spoke to me, but the words made no sense. *Terma*, she said. But she was wrong."

"Wrong? Why was she wrong?"

The chains rattled louder, and Hadrian caught Karil's gaze, head bent, "Because … I am a Hidden."

Outside, the wind was picking up. It raged against the tent, slipping through the canvas' cracks, creating an eerie howl. *It can't be,* she uttered inwardly, but kept her face strong. "You lie," she posed. "Rydel said the Hidden were nearly all dead, that there were only two left."

His body shook, and she realized he was laughing. "Lies!" he bellowed. "Your dear companion lied to you. You should ask him why."

"Then you tell me!" she demanded, "Are you the last of Rydel's kind? The second Hidden?"

"No," Hadrian laughed and his gaze flashed up, agony and amusement churning in those piercing green orbs. "I'm the third, and the weakest of the three." The chains continued to rattle in an otherwise quiet tent. Rain fell upon the roof, echoing the chorus. Hadrian's arms were coiled steel, tendons flexing. Karil's gaze flickered to the spikes in the ground. She breathed a sigh. They held.

"What did Dryan do to you?"

"*Let me go.*"

"Not before you answer me," she demanded, holding onto her own restrained fury. "Tell me, where are Dryan's forces? Their routes, their fortifications, their patrols—you will tell me everything."

"Even if I knew, and I don't, it's pointless. Dryan is too clever.

He switches his routes and changes the guards constantly. Nothing is ever the same. He trusts no one. And even if that wasn't the case, you'll never be able to get in. Not unless you can fly. The entrance is now locked."

She growled. "Locked? How did he move the Great Doors?"

"Dryan holds a strange item of power. It gives him dominion over people and certain objects. I was there the day they moved. I saw him extend the object into the air and the Great Doors shuddered and moved, closing with a thunderous boom."

Karil's brows furrowed. "What does this item of power look like?"

"A great red orb. It—" Hadrian gasped, eyes glazing. His body shook, head twitching. The other elves gripped their blades nervously, but the chains held. At last, the elf looked up. Karil froze. Death filled his eyes. Not just the lethality of power she had seen in elves like Rydel, or the high-elf Jirah, but death in the sense of the absence of life. Whoever this was, it was not Hadrian. Murky blackness filled his once green eyes.

"What are you?" she breathed.

"Death," said an elf that was not Hadrian.

Karil shivered. The way he said it. With such certainty. She knew she couldn't let him live. *I must kill him.* Her grip tightened around her sword, visualizing it piercing the hollow of his throat. Yet she remembered the sorrow in his eyes. It was still there, she knew, lurking behind this black cloud. Somehow, Dryan had corrupted Hadrian. He was still within. "There is still good in you, Hadrian," she pleaded. "I see it. Do not give into Dryan. Do not be swayed by his darkness. Return to the light while you still have a chance."

Hadrian looked to her. A light shone in his eyes, glinting amid darkness. His face contorted with pain, but then the light winked out, consumed by darkness, and Hadrian's lips twisted as he spoke. "Before your father died, Dryan said he begged for his life, that his last moments were ones with tears of fear running down his face. A pitiful but expected end to a pathetic king."

Karil felt a stab of pain to her heart, and she backhanded him across the face powerfully, hard enough that her hand stung from the force. His head, however, barely moved.

A thin trail of blood ran from the corner of his mouth. He jerked hard against his bonds, lurching forward at Karil. She leapt back.

A demonic voice emanated from Hadrian's lips. "Eldas is no longer yours, girl. Now die with that knowledge. Die, and join your father and mother in their shallow graves."

Suddenly, the Hidden's muscles flexed, sending the spikes in the ground flying forth.

Karil wasted no time, she stabbed, but Hadrian was quicker. His neck twisted slightly but with such perfect timing that the blade slipped off his skin, cutting only a shallow groove in his neck. She cut again, determined to finish the job, but it was too late. Hadrian used the back of his hand, slapping the flat of the blade. It felt as if a rock had smacked her broken sword. Her hand throbbed, numb with pain. But she didn't let go. She wouldn't. She cried out, stabbing again. Hadrian gave a primal cry, heavy muscles straining. The ground shuddered, taking Karil from her feet. Chains thundered as he climbed to his full height, dirt and root being pulled along with him.

Elves charged forward, crying out. The tent exploded in chaos as more Lando dove for her. Chains flew from the ground, every which way, lashing out. Elves leapt at the Hidden. Hadrian roared and whipped his body, and a thick chain flew, crashing and sending them flying. Karil raised her broken blade, preparing to charge, when something seized her arm.

She twisted and saw a guard protecting her. Lannor. "Rydel! He is our only answer!" Lannor said and then gasped. His eyes split wide, and blood ran from his mouth. He became limp, eyes filled with the hollowness of death. He fell, a metal spike protruding from his back.

"No!" she cried, and threw her blade with all her strength. It flew end over end, but Hadrian twisted just in time. He caught it by the handle and cut down two elves with inhumane ease. Karil swallowed… *What have I done?* Lando, her very best warriors, were no match for this elf. They were no more than wooden posts against a Hidden.

Dozens of elves surrounded Hadrian, inching forward. The Hidden suddenly bellowed, "*Enough!*" and the huge chains smashed into the ground, throwing many from their feet, others sinking to their knees. He lunged forward and grabbed a nearby elf, putting the elf's own blade to his throat. The elf struggled uselessly, and the sword pressed closer. "Drop your blades or I will kill him!"

"*Halt!*" she called, raising a hand, and the elves stopped their advance.

Hadrian looked up over the elf's shoulder. His dark blond hair was straggled across his face as sweat ran down his muscled body. The Hidden was breathing hard, but Karil didn't take that as a weakness. She couldn't take anything he did as a weakness. "I do not want to kill anymore of you," he voiced. "That is not my intent."

"You make a convincing case otherwise," Karil stated furiously.

"I simply seek to defend myself," his breathed, his voice low and burning. "You mistake me if you think I will die willingly!"

"Yet you deserve death!" she declared. "Before you wanted it, you practically *begged* me to end your life."

"No," Hadrian said, blond hair shaking. "I realize now that I did not kill those elves. It was not me!"

"Then who was it?"

Again, Hadrian looked frustrated, a murky blackness roiling across his green eyes. "I do not know—believe me, I wish I did. But I can feel it inside me still." His jaw clenched in pain. "If you approach, whether I wish it or not, you will die. Even now, it is like a demon inside that seeks only blood."

"Then if we kill you, we kill the demon."

"Unfortunately, I do not wish to die, and none of you are a match for me."

"And if we let you go?"

"This one survives," he answered. "And I will kill no more of you."

"You know too much," she said, shaking her head as her fists tightened at her side. "Besides, if I let you go, who's to say you won't just quietly hunt us, killing us one by one?"

Hadrian gave a thin breath. "You have Rydel. He is a match for me. But either way, I will not. I know you can see the truth of it in my eyes and my voice." Karil couldn't deny that she did believe him, but she couldn't risk the lives of others. Not for a gut feeling. "I swear it to you."

"A murderer's promise," she said, looking to the corpses of nearby elves.

"I kill to survive, much like you," he said, and the words hit home. "You must understand—whatever possesses me *is* not me."

"What's to keep it from taking you over?"

Hadrian laughed. "I am a Hidden, my queen. Do not underestimate me. My powers and training were not only physical but mental as well. But even as we stand, I can feel it like a poison in my veins, wanting to kill each and every one of you. I can keep it at bay, but only for so long. You must let me go. Now."

"And when we do? You will just go back to Dryan."

"I doubt you'll believe me if I tell you I had a change of heart?"

"Doubt would be a mild way of putting it. You will be lying," she said.

"*Strength is life, weakness death,*" Hadrian said, as if quoting, biting off each word. "There's an old saying, my queen, born with the elves since time immemorial: 'The heart of the Hidden is truth', but I see now the heart of the Hidden has been twisted, manipulated to fit a purpose and turned into a lie," he said mysteriously, then shook his head as if returning to the moment. "The truth is simple—I do not believe Dryan had my best interest at heart, nor any elf's, but my destination is my own. Let's just say I plan to right some wrongs ... to deal a little of my own justice. Beyond that, you will have to believe what you will."

She couldn't bring herself to do it. The answers Hadrian held could spell their victory, but looking in the elf's eyes, she felt fear. She couldn't let another die because of her. Yet if he killed more? If he killed hundreds? Fury roared through her as well. How was she to judge what he would do? She had seen Hadrian's inherent good, but she had also seen a darkness trump that light like a wind snuffing a flame.

Suddenly Hadrian cried out, limbs shaking, chains rattling. A faint, black flame surrounded his body and the Hidden roared as if trying to resist it. The elf in his grasp tried to twist, to grab his blade and attack, but Hadrian was too strong. "No!" she cried. The murky blackness in Hadrian's eyes swirled and his blade cut. The elf's throat was sliced open and he fell to the ground with a bloody gurgle.

Karil's mouth fell open, and her heart dropped. *Pitiless*...

Elves charged forward angrily, but Hadrian was too fast. He grabbed the nearest elf and Karil tensed. "Stop!" she bellowed. "Do not attack!" Hadrian held Temian, blade tight against the elf's neck. Temian's face was stone as if he knew what was coming... "Let him go, please," Karil pleaded.

"*Curse you!*" Hadrian roared. "I did not want to do that! Yet you forced my hand, and now his death is on your head!"

"No," she seethed, "you may shun the blame, but it will not save you from the truth. The darkness inside you is too strong!"

Hadrian growled. "I *can* control it. Now let me go, or see more die."

Karil felt anger and sorrow spiral inside her. He had killed too many already, and if he did return to Dryan, anything he had learned would be turned upon them. And yet… "Let him go," she ordered.

"No! Don't, my queen!" Temian shouted. "He cannot be trusted!"

Hadrian's blade tightened on Temian's throat, but the elf held Karil's gaze, shaking his head.

"Do it!" Karil commanded, louder.

Reluctantly, two Lando strode forward and unlocked Hadrian's shackles. One by one, the chains that bound him fell. She almost felt as if it had been more ceremony than necessity. She feared now with the chains gone he would be even more of a nightmare. "Go," she breathed angrily. "Go and never come back."

Hadrian's sword continued to rest on Temian's neck, blood dripping from the steel. Tension mounted and Karil feared she had made the wrong decision. Black tremors spidered across Hadrian's arms, his body shaking, muscles tense. The chains clattered, matching the howling wind outside in fearful chorus. At last, Hadrian shoved Temian forward and twisted, moving to the back of the tent. No elves followed. The Hidden slashed, cutting the heavy canvas, unveiling a windy night filled with horizontal rain.

Hadrian turned back, wind and rain tousling his hair and dirtied, battered clothes. "A final warning, my queen, for letting me go… Beware of Dryan, for his strength is not only his own."

"What's that supposed to mean?"

"He's not alone," Hadrian replied. "If you kill Dryan, it will not end his evil. It is only the beginning. You must follow the strands and kill the source."

Karil eyed him darkly, refusing to speak.

"Dryan follows a dark philosophy. Root out that, and it will lead you to the head of the snake. But beware—somehow I fear it is an ancient evil, the greatest this world has ever known." He moved towards the entry, as if to leave.

"Wait!" she called. "What dark philosophy?"

"Ask your trusted guardian, for it is the very same belief. It is the creed of the Hidden."

Karil's breath was stolen, a shiver running through her.

"I will not forget this, my queen," Hadrian said and, with that, he was gone.

Temian rose, moving to her side. "You should not have let him go, my queen. My life was not worth it."

She looked to the other Lando with their pieces of her father's crown shining proudly on their breast in the dim light. They had survived too much to die now, and so pitilessly. But what had she given up? Had she made the right choice? Time will tell. "Truth be told, I did not do it for your life alone, dear friend," she answered at last. "In the end, he would have killed us all."

And the slash in the tent continued to flap from the wind, accentuating her ominous words. Meanwhile, her mind churned.

The creed of the Hidden…

Rydel.

The Dimilioc Summit

Meira listened as Finn spoke, each in the room wearing different expressions.

Hutosh was a noble-looking man. She wondered perhaps if he wasn't of royal lineage, but now, as a three-stripe Reaver, all heritage was stripped from him. His proud features were recognizable from a field away—strong jaw, cliff-like nose, and bushy brows, though his brown hair was thinning considerably. He listened to Finn with attentiveness and worry. Tugard was a Sevian man. As such he was darker of skin and wore the characteristic short pointed beard of Sevia, thick below his bottom lip, flowing down to his chin, and ending in a sharp point. Tugard was hardened by the constant warfare of the plains, and as such, his face was blank as always, but Meira saw through the stoic exterior and saw his brow crease, listening raptly. Her dear friend, Finn himself, spoke passionately, his frame nearly shaking with the fervor that she had perhaps placed inside him.

"*We must save Ezrah,*" he said finally.

Finn's voice settled, and the room returned to its previous quiet.

On the walls, the Yunais flickered. Yunais were silver globes with hundreds of mirrored facets that would reflect light. They illuminated the small room in hoary white, making all figures appear like the already deceased returned as phantoms. It was an omen of what was to come—one of two paths.

All four were gathered at last in the Room of Dimilioc, a room with gold-veined marbled floors. On a nearby dais, a pair of white robes with gold trim was draped carefully without so much as a wrinkle. A strange, ruby-throated scepter sat on one pedestal and on another a golden ring humming with spells. Though small, Dimilioc was a place of great magic. She had chosen it purposefully, for it was the place where Reavers became Arbiters.

Finn's final word hung in the air—the cerabul in the room that no one wanted to see, or, in this case, hear.

Ezrah…

Hutosh spoke, voice panicky. "That name, you cannot say that name. It is—"

"—Enough," Meira said, interrupting the three-stripe Reaver. "You've evaded your conscience for far too long. We all have. Now it is time to do what is right." Ezrah's words echoed in her head. "While Finn is right, he is only speaking my words, words that I know each of you are thinking even at this moment, and have been since

the day we were assigned to this task, this *horror*. But now it is time. Now we must rise up. Now we must save Ezrah."

Hutosh replied, "You would willingly sacrifice yourselves? For that is what this path is…"

"Yes," she declared.

The other four looked shocked, even Finn.

"You do not mean that, do you?" Finn asked.

Please, stay at my side, a part of Meira pleaded, noticing her friend's surprise. "I mean every word," she replied, "for, as we stand, we are already among the lifeless."

"What do you mean?" Hutosh said, "We have our lives."

"That is where you are wrong," she answered. "We have bodies, and perhaps minds, but our souls and even our very wills are not our own."

Hutosh's brow crinkled, and he rubbed his jaw, striding back and forth anxiously. "Meira, do you know what you're saying?" the noble man argued. "We are rebelling against the will of the Citadel. I despise what we do as much as you, but we are an ant fighting a giant."

"It's Sithel's will, not the Citadel's," she countered.

"Still," Tugan said, speaking finally. "If we are caught, Meira…"

"Then we will die," she said. Silence reigned, and Meira felt her passion grow. "No more," she breathed in a wrathful whisper, letting down that barrier she held on to so tightly, feeling hot tears that she hadn't shed since she was a child. "No more will I let others control my life. No more will I let my own fear determine my path. No more will I torture and do what is wrong when I know what is right, even if it costs me my life, for I would rather die on my own terms than live a life like this."

All were silent, but each looked affected by her words.

"Meira…" Finn said, looking pained.

"Tell me you each do not feel it, and I will leave you be," she said angrily. "Tell me you do not feel the sorrow and the rage … the guilt…"

Tugan eyed his own hands as if they were covered in blood and replied with quiet angst, "I feel it."

"By the gods, we all do!" Hutosh said, looking equally distraught by his own deeds. "What we are doing is not right. Light, that is an Arbiter down there! He is supposed to be our leader, and more than that, he is a human being. But what are we to do?"

Suddenly the silvery Yunais flickered and stone rumbled from the heavy marble door. "They're here," Finn exclaimed, turning.

No! Meira thought in terror. *How did they find out?*

Each summoned the spark, filling with power as the door slid open and a dark figure resolved itself. Reaver Dagon stood in the entry. He was tall, with wavy black hair and tan skin. His head tilted as if curious what he had stumbled upon. Yet above all, the four black stripes on his scarlet sleeves drew Meira's eyes like a moth to a flame. She readied her power, fearfully. Behind him, however, was an empty hallway. He was alone? Silently, he entered and the door slammed shut.

"Greetings," Dagon announced.

Meira debated throwing all her power at him, but he hadn't made a move yet, and beyond that, she wasn't sure of the limits of a four-stripe Reaver. Even attacking together, they might not be enough to take Dagon, she admitted. "What are you doing, and how did you get in here?" she questioned.

"You underestimate me," Dagon said. "And a better question is what are you four doing?"

"I…" Finn stammered.

Hutosh spoke smoothly, interrupting. "We were discussing matters of the next High Rank. In fact—and uncomfortable as it is to admit—we were considering you," he lied.

A *noble man and politician indeed,* Meira thought in admiration, eyeing Hutosh. The High Rank was a title chosen by a majority of Reavers and given to the most favored brother or sister—usually the most experienced and well liked. The High Rank was the go-between to the Patriarch himself. It was a mark of prestige and honor, but none had been named for centuries.

Dagon raised a single brow.

And Meira joined in, latching onto the lie. "Indeed," she added smoothly. "However, as such we needed someplace private to discuss it. In light, perhaps it would be wise if you were not a part of this discussion. If any other found out, they may think you had swayed or even coerced us into our decision."

Dagon scratched his temple as if amused. "Clever, both of you, but I am not here to expose you, so cut the falsehoods. I am here to join you to save Ezrah."

Hutosh blinked and even Meira gawked.

"How did you…" Tugan managed.

Meira regained control. "I do not know how you found out, or why you think you are entitled to join us but…"

"Let me amend my previous statement," Dagon said with utter calm. "I will join you. You have no choice. You four are powerful and skilled, but you are lacking in one area, and it will be your downfall."

"And that would be?" Finn asked, looking skeptical but curious.

"*Authority*," Dagon replied, "someone who can make this absurd scheme become a reality."

Meira hesitated. She opened her mouth but Tugan interrupted. "He's right," said Tugan then looked to her. "Look, I know you do not trust easily, Meira, but as I see it, this makes sense."

"We need no one," she said firmly.

"Be reasonable, Meira," Hutosh said. "To have a four-stripe Reaver on our side in this fool's errand would be a great boon."

She looked to each, then to her dear friend. "Finn?"

Finn shrugged. "I don't know, Meira..."

Something felt wrong... She wanted to speak, but as she eyed their faces and saw their expressions shift, she noticed they now looked hopeful. And she realized, guiltily, that Finn had only been doing it for her. She could not have that—she needed their *wills* as well, or she would be no better than Sithel.

Hutosh chimed in again. "Besides, who would question us with Dagon at our side? He can lead us."

"I will lead," she said stubbornly, anger seeping into her voice.

Dagon answered, "And your plan?"

Meira sniffed. "You think I trust you so soon?" she asked. "What's to stop me from tying you up or burning you to a crisp right now? Who is to say you are truly on our side? Say what you will, but I find it hard to trust an entrance like that. What are you really after?" she asked Dagon.

"I came alone, did I not?"

She growled, unable to answer for that. "So? Perhaps only to root out more traitors against Sithel..."

"You want the truth?"

She met his gray gaze unwaveringly. "I do."

"Then Compel me," he said. "I saw your threads. Compel me and see the truth for yourself."

Meira began to thread the ancient spell.

"Meira! Is this really necessary?" Tugan asked, grabbing her arm, but it was too late. The spell took form in the air, a complex tapestry of glowing threads of flesh and bits of Sun, so intricate and layered that the finely meshed lines seemed to blur into one thick cord. It floated and sunk into Dagon.

Dagon gasped and fell to his knees, words flowing forth as his body trembled: "Ezrah was so kind, so thoughtful. Always watching out for me when the other Neophytes would tease me relentlessly. They were jealous, I knew. But it didn't help. I hated them. But then he came. Ezrah. An Arbiter. He, unlike lesser wielders of the spark, knew what power meant. And now I have betrayed him. I must seek justice. I must save him.... These fools... They must see reason... Perhaps... Compelling—it is the only way." The four-stripe Reaver continued to shake, but no more words came, and Meira let the threads dissolve wordlessly. Dagon controlled his breathing and slowly rose, his expression turning resolute and grim. "As I said, I have nothing to hide. I will save Ezrah. But I cannot do it alone."

It's the truth… "So be it," Meira replied, and reluctantly, she described her plan. They each nodded, though some slower than others.

"A simple but wise course to our destination, but what then?" Dagon asked.

"Bloodshed," she answered. *There was no other answer now.* Each looked uncertain and conflicted, but not wholly opposed. To kill another Reaver was akin to killing one's family, but it had to be done.

"Perhaps it may come to that," Dagon said, "but if I can suggest another route? I will not join to kill those who resist Sithel's cause. There *are* others like us, whether you believe it or not…" Meira didn't like where this was going, but she nodded for him to continue. "If you have not forgotten, I am in charge of compiling the roster for the next shifts."

"And what good will that do us?" Finn asked, shuffling closer to Meira.

Her eyes narrowed, seeing the plan churning in Dagon's gray eyes, and she spoke, "You plan to fix the roster, don't you? To make a full eight who are loyal to our cause and to Ezrah?"

Dagon nodded. "Like you, I do not trust many others, but together surely we can think of others who will aid our cause. We can do this without killing, Meira."

"No," she said adamantly. "Eight is far too many. I will not allow it."

"Eight out of nearly three hundred Reavers? Do you truly think it's gotten that bad?" he asked, almost saddened.

Meira didn't waver. "Yes."

"You must have more faith, Meira. Or have you forgotten that these are our brothers and sisters? Besides what use is saving one man if all of the Citadel is a lost cause as you seem to believe?"

"Because it is right," she said simply. "And because he is more than just one man."

"Dagon has a point, Meira, you must admit," Finn said.

Meira clenched her eyes, seeking stillness, but it would not come. "You all seem to think the Citadel is worth saving, but you must see its darkness as well. It is everywhere. Who can we ask? It was like pulling teeth to gather *three* I could trust," she said passionately. "One wrong person will spell our death."

"Then let us play this out..." Dagon posed, "What are the odds that we can even *take* those in the room? I am four-stripe, but there are several other four-stripes in Sithel's clutches. What if Guran is there? He is stronger than all of you combined. And even if we do succeed in slaughtering our brothers and sisters, what then? A clash like that will be felt by any nearby, and it will lead to our discovery and our demise. It's the same with every 'so called' traitor. One use of their spark in resistance, and no matter the size of their power they are never heard of again. Sithel finds them and quells their rebellion."

"He kills them," Meira contested. "There's no need to pretend or mince fancy words about it, Dagon, not anymore."

"We do not know that yet," Dagon said quietly. "But you are right. Even one is too many. That is why I am here, why we must do something, and why we must gather eight loyal Reavers."

"Loyal to who?" she questioned. "To Sithel? To *you?*"

"I am not the enemy, Meira!" Dagon shouted in anger. "Don't you see? You must trust again," and his voice grew soft, almost despairing, "or Sithel will have already won."

His words ran through her, shaking her certainty. Was he right? Was her distrust blinding her?

Hutosh sighed, running a hand through his thinning hair. "Sorry, Meira, but I'm with Dagon on this. I refuse to believe we are the only ones with a conscience. And I will not do this without him. Light, I will be a blasted fool to do it with him! But at least I might be a living fool."

"Enough caring about your own hide all the time," Finn said to Hutosh. He looked to Meira and clasped a hand on top of hers. "We're behind you, *savii*," he said fondly, using the nickname he hadn't used since they were Neophytes—in Yorin it meant *fierce*, "but let us try Dagon's tactic. It seems the safest path."

She released a sigh. She did not want to see others die, but she feared that the time for avoiding bloodshed had passed. "So be it," she declared. "Then we will go as a new shift, preparing to take over for the previous and free Ezrah from his bonds. Then we will make our move, and use my route of escape to escort Ezrah out of the Citadel and to a safe house I have secured."

"A wise choice," said the four-stripe Reaver, looking relieved. "But there is one last thing."

"What is it?" she asked.

"We must be quick. Time is shorter than you think. I fear if we do not succeed tonight then Sithel will either have his information or have Ezrah's death. The Arbiter is stronger than any man I've ever met, but he will break, and soon…"

"Tonight then," she agreed.

The others looked fearful, as if hoping it would be at some later date, but each nodded in turn, and Dagon spoke, "Then it is time I leave to prepare the next shift and ensure our places on the roster. Who shall I seek to fill the last spots?"

Quickly they discussed the other likely candidates for their mission and came to a unanimous decision on the final three.

Now decided, the four men looked dutiful and strong—as if their guilt had been shed and their minds cleared. It was the first time in what felt like ages that Meira looked upon the faces of true Reavers. *Power, confidence, and virtue.* It filled her with pride, and even if they were just a small ray of light in an otherwise dark abyss, at least there was hope.

She spoke powerfully, "Go now and prepare yourselves—steel your hearts and minds, for tonight may be our last, but if so, we will act as Reavers and see it through to the very end."

A Fellowship

Gray stood frozen at a four-way corridor as crowds moved around them like a river parting around rocks.

They were deep in the Citadel now, having wormed their way through hundreds of courtyards, rooms, and hallways—each more magnificent than the last, displaying the true might and grandeur of the city of fire. Twice they had passed through a grand chamber swarming with Reavers, but with Zane and Victasys at his side, he strode with the confidence of a Devari, and so far, none dared question them. As a rule, Gray avoided Devari as best he could, using the ki to sense them before they approached.

Yet now, they were stuck. Ahead were three different hallways looking exactly the same. Two odd stone pillars sat in the center of the room. If he had his power, he could search down one of the paths, but the nexus still flickered, missing a portion.

"What's wrong?" Victasys asked.

"My..." he began, then stopped and settled on a simpler explanation, "I don't think I've ever been this far." *Where are you?* He questioned of Kirin. His old self had aided him thus far, but now Kirin was strangely silent. "I'm lost. I'm sorry," he said at last.

"You've done a good job so far," Victasys said. "No one is blaming you, boy."

Yet I am blaming me, Gray thought.

So am I. You're fairly worthless without me, Kirin voiced suddenly.

Where have you been? Gray asked in frustration. *Tell me where to go.*

What do you mean? Kirin asked, amused. *You're already here… See with your mind, not your eyes.*

What is that supposed to mean? But Kirin was silent once more.

More Reavers and Neophytes swarmed around them, and Gray felt anxious standing in one place too long. *With my mind…* Kirin's words nagged. Gray reached for the nexus. The swirling ball of air sat, waiting. Again, it flickered, wanting to slip from his grip like a freshly caught sunfish from Cloudfell Lake, but he gripped it tighter and then—

A *sunfish? Cloudfell Lake?* He didn't know what either of those were… He had a vague image of a grand body of water and a strange and slimy fish that was yellow and spear-shaped, but these were not Gray's memories. Were Kirin's memories becoming his? He shook his head and focused. Faint, trembling power filled him as he surveyed the room again and nearly gasped.

In the center of the chamber sat a huge white swirling void.

"What is it?" Zane asked.

"A door," he whispered.

"Where?" Victasys asked.

"In the center of the room," he replied. "Between the two stone pillars…"

"He has gone mad," Zane said, scratching his head.

"No, it can only be seen with magic," Gray said.

Victasys grunted. "I believe it is called a *portal.* It makes sense that the Vault is restricted by use of a portal. They are often used as a means of protection, for many items of power are said to exist below the keep."

Zane started forward. "Then what are we waiting for?"

"Hold on, how do we know if we can even get in?" Gray asked. "It is magic."

"There's only one way to find out," Zane answered, walking towards it.

The air shifted, the white-door pulsing. "Wait," he said, gripping Zane's arm.

Zane's fiery copper eyes narrowed. "It's opening."

"You see it too?" he asked incredulous.

The fiery man simply nodded.

The spark... Gray had seen fire conjured in Maris' Luck, but he hadn't known it was Zane's doing. Perhaps he was another Untamed? If so, it was a boon, but something about it seemed odd. Before he could question it anymore, the white portal swirled and a gap appeared, and two Reavers in scarlet robes stepped out into the hallway.

At the same time, commotion rifled through the crowds. Men and women parted as six Reavers appeared from the eastern hall, commanding all attention. They made their way through the people as if parting grass, heads high and eyes forward with purpose.

"What's going on?" Zane asked Victasys.

The Devari shook his head. "I'm not sure..."

The group of Reavers met the first two at the swirling white door and exchanged brief looks, their faces grim, then entered. It was all over before Gray could speak.

Zane started forward and Gray followed. Zane did *something*, and the portal swirled open, widening like clouds parting to reveal what lay beyond—a hallway of white marble. Gray touched the portal and shivered unexpectedly, feeling wet, as if coated in water. He held his breath and stepped through.

On the other side, he saw Zane and Victasys looking to their clothes as if expecting them to be drenched. "This place..." Zane growled. "I will be glad to be out of it."

Their surroundings looked the same, save for a shimmering and ever present white light. The hallway ahead split into three paths.

"Where to now?" he asked.

"Well, where did they go?" Zane questioned.

Gray reached out to his nexus. The flickering ball of air came forth, barely. He reached out with it, sending tremulous threads of air down each path, not seeing but *feeling* what lay beyond. Down the middle path, something in the air lingered. He grabbed it, cupping it as if with both hands, then pulled it towards him. It was the smell of clean sweat, and freshly washed clothes, and he even smelled what he thought was a hint of fear—but he figured that was just his imagination.

Gray started down the middle path, the others following.

"You've remembered?" Zane asked.

"No, but one path is as good as another," he replied.

As they walked, Victasys spoke calmly, "You're lying."

How did he...? My ki, he realized. He winced. He couldn't lie near a Devari. He had nearly forgotten. In the future, he would have to remember that. "I can smell them," he admitted. "The other Reavers."

"Really?" Zane asked. "That's hard to believe. I have a great sense of smell, and I sense nothing."

"It's my power," he explained. "It's not easy, but I can catch their scent in the air and grapple it towards me."

"*Wind...*" the Devari breathed.

Zane looked equally stunned. "What are you?"

"A better question, what are you *both?*" Victasys said.

Zane shrugged in his dark rags. "I wish I knew. All I know is I cannot wield my power without need."

"An Untamed then," the Devari said and looked to Gray. "And you?"

"I..." Gray hesitated, feeling as if he were exposing a raw wound with his next words. "I can do small things with wind, but my power is limited now. I am not whole. We cannot rely on it."

Victasys merely nodded. Inside his hood, he knew the Devari's scarred face was expressionless. Had the man smiled once since they met? Yet he was glad to have him. The Devari was truly in his element as they moved down the airy hallways, reminding him of a stalking wolf.

Gray rounded a corner and heard sudden voices.

"*We are all here then. Are you all prepared?*" A woman voiced.

Zane reached into his jacket and pulled out a mirror, angling it to see around the corner. Gray huddled closer and took in the curious scene.

In a circular room, eight Reavers stood in a ring addressing a smaller woman. He couldn't make out her features, but she seemed powerful.

"Ready as we'll ever be," said another Reaver.

"There is a complication, Meira," said a darker, powerful voice— a tall man with raven hair and dark skin.

"What is it?" Meira asked.

"I could not stop Sithel from setting up guards at Ezrah's chambers."

Gray gripped Victasys arm, and the three exchanged looks. *Ezrah.*

The woman cursed. "How many guards?"

"Only two," the tall man said. "But I cannot be certain if they are with us or against us."

"Then we must assume they are against us. Is that all?" Meira asked.

Another Reaver spoke, "We must be careful of Jian as well. A Devari told me he is looking for you, Meira."

"*Who's Jian?*" Gray asked in a faint whisper.

"The new leader of the Devari. A man to be feared," Victasys said in an equally low breath.

Back in the circular room, the woman Reaver spoke again, "It is time," she said grandly, "Follow me." With that, she turned and left.

"What should we do now?" Zane asked.

"We follow," Gray stated and rose quietly.

With care, they moved through chambers and more hallways, watching the eight Reavers in the distance. Occasionally, he glanced out of the corner of his eye and saw his companions' grim-set faces. Wherever they were going was dangerous—the very air trembled with power, and Gray expected the walls to crack and crumble from it.

Suddenly, muted voices sounded from around the bend and Gray saw barred rooms ahead. Swallowing nervously, they continued, but he kept his grip on Morrowil. The eight Reavers disappeared ahead. With the others at his side, they neared and saw men and women huddled in the shadows of murky cells. Most didn't spare them a look, as if their wills were already broken, but several eyed Gray and his companions with strange looks. Victasys pulled down his hood, peering into the dank darkness.

A man suddenly charged the bars, and Zane's sword rung as he unsheathed it.

"Victasys!" The man said. "Brother!"

The Devari spun. "Walamros? How... What are you doing in here?"

The man's bloody fingers clenched the bars as if they were preventing him from drowning. "I questioned the divisions rising between the Sword-Forged Devari and the younglings. We are breaking, Victasys. You understand, don't you? I had to say something! Of course, once I did, that bastard Jian cast me down here like a broken sword."

"Victasys…?" another voice questioned in the dark from behind.

The scarred Devari turned, looking into the shadows. "Gremla? You're here?"

"I am… We all are," Gremla said in a grave but excited voice.

Suddenly, more faces appeared, coming forth out of the shadows and into the light of the torches. A flame appeared in Zane's hand and he lifted it. As it rose into the air, the flame grew, revealing a vast chamber, and hundreds of cells, far bigger than Gray had imagined. Gray saw the faces and counted them all. Not all were Devari. Some were Reavers, some Farbian guards judging by their gambesons—padded jackets that belonged beneath mail. There must have been a hundred men and women at least.

He looked to their dirt-smudged faces, seeing the blood upon their skin, their faces ragged, and many with sunken cheeks. Their clothes were shredded, and a foul smell emanated from their dark hovels—their own waste, he realized.

"Brother, I thought you were dead…" said a big man with arms like small trunks, a cloak of the Devari on his broad back.

In the dim light, Gray could just make out the tattered cloaks of Devari on at least two dozen. "You all have been cast down here by Jian?" he asked.

"Jian or Sithel," said a dark-skinned woman. She answered with the poise of a queen. A *Reaver.* "If you oppose the will of either of those two foul tyrants, you are silenced and forced down here, into this abysmal pit. Two of my very sisters gave me away. I was betrayed in my sleep." She cursed, looking away, as if hopeless. "Reavers, Devari, guards, even Neophytes. It does not matter. None are safe from their dark clutches."

And now Gray saw others too in the bleak shadows. Youthful faces of boys and girls. In the flashing red-orange light, he saw their round faces still held the chubbiness of adolescence, but all youth was gone from their eyes. They were craven with glassy eyes, like creatures left too long in the dark. He felt his anger rise, seeing their dirt-caked features streaked with dried tears.

"What is this hell? Who would allow this?" Zane asked, the fire he had conjured growing. His sword arm shook with bottled rage.

Gray looked down the long corridor. The Reavers were getting away. Yet he couldn't simply leave these people here… Clenching his sword, he moved to the nearest lock.

"What are you doing?" Victasys questioned.

"We have to save them," Gray said.

"What about the Arbiter?" Zane asked, conflicted.

"They have an Arbiter?" the woman Reaver questioned, looking aghast.

"My grandfather," Gray declared. "He is being tortured as we speak."

"Dear spirits… Then the Citadel truly is gone…" she breathed.

Zane growled. "What do we do?"

"What is right," Victasys stated firmly, and then spoke in a loud voice, "Brothers, sisters… We cannot see you to safety now. Not unless we dare risk a war, and we cannot win a war as we stand."

Walamros, the first Devari who had spoken, reached out, grabbing Victasys' arm. "We understand. Go, brother, but come back for us if you can," he said in a hard tone. "We will pray for your safe return. Besides, we're not going anywhere. Right, lads?"

The others gave somber smiles of encouragement, echoing Walamros' sentiment.

Victasys gripped the Devari's arm tighter. "I will return with more. We will set you free. Upon my life, I swear it."

"Good, good. Now go—you're wasting time," ushered the woman Reaver, as if chiding children. "Save the Arbiter—save your grandfather, for he is too important to lose if we wish to wage a war against this darkness."

They each nodded, and Gray swallowed, his heart wrenching as they moved away, continuing down the hall. Voices echoed in the darkness, whispering prayers of encouragement until they passed beyond, entering a different hall altogether.

Ahead sat a red marble corridor.

The walls were not straight, but seemed to waver and distort the longer Gray looked at them. It made him sick to his stomach. He avoided keeping his gaze too long in any one place. Red orbs glowed upon the wall, as if casting the already scarlet walls in shades of blood.

Suddenly, they came upon a huge, black door.

It was shattered, the cast iron slabs hanging from cracked hinges like a broken arm hanging limply at an odd angle.

Gray rushed forward, the others at his side, feeling wind propel him as he dashed past the bodies of two dead guards and into the room beyond. Inside, he froze. It was just as he had seen in his dream, only worse…

In the center of the floor, upon the inlaid Star of Magha, were broken chains and blood. Blood was everywhere. But Ezrah was nowhere. He saw bits of brown robe lying upon the ground and strands of blood-soaked white hair. "No…" Gray croaked. Emotions flooded through him, and he sank to his knees, overwhelmed by it all when he felt a hand upon his shoulder.

Zane stood over him, offering a hand. "Get up, Gray. You are not done yet."

"But the blood…"

"Trust me. Your grandfather did not die here," the fiery man replied. He said it with such confidence that Gray could only nod and rise, and they moved out of the horror-filled room.

Outside, Victasys was closing the eyes of the two dead men. Gray realized they were Devari. *Perhaps they had killed a Reaver trying to defend Ezrah?* Gray wondered, but then shook his head. None of it made sense.

Victasys stood and looked to Gray, pointing beyond. Ahead sat a dozen different corridors, each a different color, shades of blue, red, green, yellow, and even black. "Where are they?"

"I—I don't know."

"Use your power. Follow the scent of blood."

The fury in the scarred man's face almost quelled Gray's own rage, but instead he let it feed him. He reached into his mind, snatching the nexus and holding on. His mind quavered. The nexus tried to flee, but he fought it as if he were gripping a ledge by the tips of his fingers. *Listen to me!* He pleaded. Slowly, grudgingly, it obeyed. A thin stream of power sifted through the dozen halls.

He heard voices … then the pounding of feet on marble … cries and shouts of fighting, and more… It sounded like war being waged. He returned back to his body, eyes snapping wide. Gray pointed

Morrowil down the middle hall—a hallway of utter blackness, whereupon no light came forth.

Victasys simply nodded and charged forward. Zane gave a thin, wicked grin and followed. Gray, close behind, moved into the darkness. The Devari unsheathed his sword in a loud ring, and the fiery aura blazed along the curved steel, lighting the murky hall in orange flames.

Traps

"It is time," Meira said proudly, "Follow me."

They moved swiftly, gathering their powers and preparing for anything. They wove their way down, passing the sullen Chamber of Solace, cells filled with alleged traitors of the Citadel. They were filled with those who had 'legitimate' crimes brought against them by Sithel, unlike those who were simply killed and never heard of again. She saw friends in the dank cells, but did not slow. She would see them freed, but Ezrah came first.

With the others at her side, she neared the red marble hall. Fear clutched her heart as it always did here, but she let it go. Today she had no reason to fear. Today she would save, not destroy. Entering the hallway, she spotted two men standing beside the black iron doors to the Arbiter's room.

Devari.

They approached, and the Devari shifted.

"Open the doors," Dagon demanded with authority, not slowing.

The two Devari didn't move. "I'm afraid not, Reaver Dagon."

"What is this nonsense? Open the doors this instant!" Tugard roared, his always calm face growing fearsome.

"Apologies, Reaver," said the muscular Devari, the wider and taller of the two with a long komai braid. He was powerful, even for a

Devari. "Unfortunately, new orders just arrived, and they supersede your command, Reaver Dagon. Sithel has canceled the next shift. This is the final shift. You all may go back to your rooms."

The spark roared inside the eight Reavers.

Meira lifted her hand, and the roar of power abated, momentarily. *Caution*, she pleaded of her companions inwardly. *Make a scene here and we may never set Ezrah free.* "Today, I am here for salvation, not destruction," she said calmly. "As such, I will give you an option. What you do now, and what we have done, is wrong. You know it in your bones, both of you. Now, if you wish to be a part of change, a part of bringing light to the darkness that has plagued us like night without the dawn, then open those doors and announce the coming shift. If not..."

The powerful words hung in the air.

The big Devari eyed all eight of them, and a strange roiling blackness shifted across his eyes, so quick Meira wondered if it was even there.

"She is right, Dundai," said the younger Devari, gripping his blade tightly as well. "Let us stop this madness. Please—" Steel rung, and the big Devari's sword flashed, impaling the younger Devari. The boy gasped, clutching the blade in confusion.

Meira was stunned but only for a moment. The eight Reavers embraced their spark, lashing out.

But the big Devari was quicker. He turned, charging, but not at them. His blade roared with flames and he slashed at the black iron doors, and rammed his shoulder, barreling into the dark room.

"We are under attack!" he yelled. "Kill them! They are—"

Dagon lashed out with a tongue of fire, searing a hole through the big Devari's heart, and the man dropped like a sack, but a dark silence hung in the air...

All eight Reavers inside the room whirled, and the spark flared.

"No..." Meira breathed. But it was too late.

Chaos erupted.

The Reaver leading the Fusing sprung for Dagon, creating mountainous threads of stone and fire. Dagon ducked and the stone and fire blew past, consuming Reaver Isolde in a flash of blood and ash.

"No!" Dimitri screamed, watching his brother die.

"*Fuse!*" Meira roared.

As they had planned, Meira's fellowship of Reavers Fused, and fed their power into her. She gasped from the amount of power roaring through her. She felt as if she were going to explode, her skin bursting and her eyes flaring wide.

Another huge column of stone and fire soared towards her, flames howling through the air. Meira was ready. She met it with massive threads of water chilled to ice. Shards of ice and stone and fire collided—the two beams became one and rattled the ground. Strong, Meira's mind shouted. These eight were powerful. *Too strong, perhaps.* Just then, Dagon rose and lent her his spark. The column of ice exploded forth with a greater power than she could imagine, flowing over the fire and turning it all to a solid shaft of ice like a giant icicle. The ice fell, nearly crashing upon Ezrah's flayed body. Meira threaded a thousand strands of sun, and the water evaporated into steam, and then was gone.

The eight other Reavers attacked again, but this time Meira was quicker and smarter. She met their attack with the element of moon, threading a blanket of darkness to hide behind. "Get down!" she cried, and dove to the ground with the others at her side, and then

she threaded flesh. The veil of darkness fell, but it had done its job by hiding her attack. She watched the spell of flesh spiral and collide with the wielder of the other Fuse, slamming into the four-stripe, black-haired Reaver. The man gasped, clutching his heart. Feeling the beating muscle, as if she gripped it in her hand, she whispered a silent prayer of forgiveness and pulled the threads tight. Seizing his chest, the man fell over dead.

The seven other Reavers looked around in dread. Scattered, they attacked. But without the four-stripe Reaver it was no use. Meira dissolved their threads with ease, and then cast a burst of light that slammed them against the wall, knocking many unconscious. The remaining rose, and Dagon broke from the Fusing. Meira gasped, feeling the room dim, power cut in half despite the other five Reavers feeding her.

Dagon threaded strands of fire and attacked.

"*No!*" she shouted, striking the fire from the air with a burst of water. It barely snuffed the flame. How was he so powerful?

The enemy Reavers looked confused, baffled by Meira's attempt to save them.

"What are you doing, Meira?" Dagon questioned.

"What are *you* doing? Where is your pain in killing a fellow sister or brother? Your alleged compassion?" she questioned, shaking—she wasn't sure if it was from anger or from the power of the spark still thundering through her.

Dagon snorted contemptuously. "And what do you propose to do now, Meira? Ask them to join us? Or would you leave them here and have them alert Sithel to our presence and what we've done?"

Meira growled, hating the man's cold, calm logic. Without answering, she threaded bonds of light like shackles around their wrists, and a rare, intricate spell of flesh sunk into the Reavers' flesh. The spell cut a connection in their mind between them and their spark.

Again Dagon laughed, as if amused. "Impressive. I've not seen or heard of those threads since the war of the Lieon. But how long do you honestly expect to hold them like that? Hmm? For you can only stop them from holding the spark as long as you are holding those threads."

"I will hold them for as long as I can," Meira said. "I will not allow any more death than is necessary."

"Necessary…" Dagon said, repeating the word as if mockingly.

She ignored him and directed the nearest Reavers to haul their captives to their feet. "We shall take them with us. Watch over them closely, brothers." She saw hard tears in Dimitri's eyes, and she remembered they had lost one of their own as well, but he nodded, jaw set.

She turned her attention to the most important thing in the room.

There lay the symbol of the Citadel's resistance.

She dropped to her knees at Ezrah's side, surveying his condition. His gray hair was strewn across his face, and he was motionless. Panicked, she reached out and felt for the pulse of life, breathing a sigh of relief. Bruises, red marks, and scars marred his frail body. On his left side, his skin had been flayed, and a rib was exposed. Meira touched his skin. It was warm. Gathering power from the Fusing, she threaded flesh, knitting together muscle, tendon, and then finally skin. She saw smooth pale skin once more, but she was not done. She reached deeper and felt what she'd feared, broken bones.

Nearby, the Reavers made a circle around her, standing over the broken Arbiter, waiting anxiously. "He is alive," she said, "but not by much."

The others breathed sighs then Dagon spoke. "We need to move," he announced firmly, "Others surely heard—they will be coming."

"He's right. Come, Meira. It's time to go," Finn said, grabbing her shoulder.

"Not yet. I need to set his bones first," she said.

"Or?" Dagon questioned.

"Or moving him could be the cause of his death, and then all this would be for naught," she declared, silencing the four-stripe. Dagon's lips pressed tightly then he cursed, moving to watch the hallway.

But mending bone was easier said than done, setting and fusing bone was not simple or painless. With a breath, she tugged and bone shifted, grating.

Ezrah awoke, gasping loudly.

She didn't slow. Meira fused the bone as his eyes rolled to the back of his head, showing only the bloodshot whites of his eyes. She finished at last, and Ezrah slumped back against the bloody floor, unconscious once more. Retreating, Meira broke the Fusing. Power left her, and she gasped as if she had drawn a dagger from her belly.

"I will do more for him when we get to safety. This will have to suffice for now," she stated. "Let's go." Hutosh and Tugan lifted the Arbiter reverently, putting his thin arms around their shoulders, heading out of the ghastly chamber.

* * *

Meira gathered her robes about her, stepping over the dead bodies, entering the red marble hall.

"Where to?" Finn asked, eyeing the dozen multicolored hallways.

"This way," she ordered and charged ahead, the others trailed with the captive Reavers in tow as they entered the black hallway. She heard a whimper of fear. It was Chloe. She had nearly forgotten the woman. *Even the weakest of us need purpose,* she reminded herself and touched the woman's arm. "A light," she commanded.

Reaver Chloe nodded, finding a bit of backbone, and a bright red flame lit the hall a dozen paces in either direction. They continued moving swiftly when Meira heard voices and footsteps echoing in the hall.

"Faster!" Dagon bellowed, and Meira's legs pumped as they flew.

Still, the footsteps grew, louder and louder.

"They are gaining on us," Hutosh cried.

The footsteps sounded on their heels, and then from everywhere. She realized it was not behind them, but ahead.

A sudden light bloomed in the hall beyond, blue and crackling.

Meira halted, the others' ragged breaths loud in her ears.

"What is that?" Tugard questioned.

"Brighter," she ordered of Chloe.

The light bloomed, growing, shedding light down the dark corridor to reveal feet, and then dark figures in gleaming chain and plate. Farbian guards, but they had an odd look to them, something strange in their black-rimmed eyes. There were dozens, if not more. At their head, stood a man in once-white robes, their hem dirtied and frayed with obvious spots of dried blood like a butcher's apron.

Sithel.

She felt her stomach churn knowing that was the blood of her brothers, sisters, and even children. But her gaze was drawn to a bizarre glowing blue orb. It sat in the tyrant's hand, crackling. Blue lightning veined across its radiant surface. "Traitors," Sithel hissed, his tone slick. "Right beneath our noses like scurrying little rats." Reaver Hutosh began to laugh sharply, but most were too filled with rage to find mirth in the Sithel's taunting. He continued calmly, unperturbed. "That man you hold is guilty of betraying the Citadel. He is mine to do with as I will, for the sake of the Citadel's protection."

"Do you even know who he is?" Reaver Dagon questioned. "Whom you held like a beast in a cage?"

"An Arbiter," Sithel answered, sounding bored, "which is just a man." His men took another step forward, brandishing their blades. "Truly, he is no more than a relic, a dusty weapon that holds no use in our new world." The way he said new put Meira's hairs on end, goose bumps prickling along her arm.

"What new world?" she questioned.

"A world where only the strong survive," he replied, lifting the ominous blue orb. Suddenly, the men in Meira's possession, the captured Reavers, shrieked and fell to the ground. Blood ran from their eyes and ears, and an orange light was sucked from their bodies into the air until they fell, lifeless.

Meira's breath was lodged in her throat. It had all happened so fast… One man still gaped like a fish dying upon dry land. He reached out to her, desperately pleading. She released their now useless bonds and knelt at the man's side to heal him. She touched his head. Pain lanced through her as the spark fizzled and her hand grew numb. She pulled away from him, realizing that whatever malady he suffered from could not be healed by her touch. With terror in the Reaver's eyes, he gave his final breath.

"You're a demon, a monster," she said slowly, rising with anger trembling through her limbs. Hand still numb, her power grew inside of her. She felt the others summon the spark as well, preparing to level Sithel and his dark men at her command.

Sithel laughed, the sound echoing off the walls. "Demon? Hardly. I am the purification… Simply the fire that burns the dead wood, just like those captured fools. They were weak, and so they deserved death." And he smiled, his worm-like lips twisting in what was a dark mockery of compassion. "Admit it, Meira, you were just too kind or perhaps too soft to give it to them."

"You're mad," she breathed. "You've murdered Reavers and Devari in cold blood and fractured the Citadel! You have broken us!" The fire roared to life in her hand and the other Reavers summoned water, stone, metal and more. Yet confusion crawled its way into Meira's shell of confidence for Sithel merely smiled deeper.

The man shrugged, orb bobbing in the darkness. "What you see as lives that are worth saving I see as broken pieces, men and women unfit to wear the mantle of protector. Each held pitiful amounts of the spark. As for the breaking… Well, oftentimes a broken sword needs to be shattered in order to be made anew."

"And that gives you the right to kill them? Slaughter them without mercy?"

"They were not like you or me, Meira. Weakness is death, strength is life," he chanted. "This I have come to know. The Citadel was weak, like I once was, but no more." Zealous passion filled his voice, gaining strength as he spoke, "There once was a time when the world valued strength above all … but no longer. The cowards of this world, they fear power, they fear their own strength, and so they sit and do *nothing*." Then he cursed almost beneath his breath, barely audible. *"I did nothing."*

I…? Meira wondered

Sithel suddenly began to shake, his words punctuated by a voice trembling with fury and pain, his mad eyes roving in memory. "*Beaten*," he cursed, "lashed by chain and whip and made to serve on hand and foot… Treated like a useless human refuse … like metal for the forge beaten until the last glowing spark of life flees the broken body… " He growled, arm shaking.

Meira and the other Reavers at her side watched, confused and shaken. With every word, the blue veins glowed brighter along his pale face, pulsing as if ready to burst.

Until at last…

"No," Sithel said with a single, even breath. He looked back to Meira, gaze rising, fervor still roiling in his eyes, but his madness seemed under control. "Make no mistake, my dear Reaver, the Citadel *will* rise again, and strength will reign supreme."

"All your words are oiled in the mire of lies," she replied biting off every word, though her voice sounded soft after the man's ranting.

"And yet, here you stand, a living symbol that I speak the truth. That weakness is death, and strength, life."

"What are you talking about?" she seethed.

Sithel's grin grew. "What was his name again? That man … a pitiful one-stripe Reaver?" Meira choked, tensing. "Ah yes, Morgan—that was his name, was it not?"

Meira felt her blood freeze. "How?"

"Ah, but I know much more than you can imagine, dear sister," he answered with a haughty grin in the blue orb's light. "But enough talk. If you will not return the Arbiter, then I will give you what you deserve. A traitor's death." He turned to his men. "Leave none alive," he commanded and his men stalked forward.

"Kill them," she ordered her own people, and power roared to life in the halls. Balls of flame and orbs of frozen ice soared through the air, stone rumbled, lightning flashed, flesh sizzled, and men screamed and—

It ended.

As surely and as powerfully as it had begun, all forms of magic fizzled in the air, dying just as it reached Sithel's dark men. And then it hit her—

Meira cried out as the spark burned inside her, shriveling.

"What is happening?" Chloe cried.

Other Reavers shrieked too, grasping at the walls, at their hearts, as something ate at them from the inside, gnawing away their insides. Feeding on their spark.

Pain and horror filled Meira. *What is this?* She looked up and saw the orb. It glowed fiercely, as if alive. An orange essence was pulled into the air as the spark was sucked from her skin. The others reached out, trying to grab their life force as it was drawn towards the glowing blue stone. *The orb is the cause*, she realized. It was feasting upon their power. If she could only stop it! She gripped her spark, reaching for the dwindling bud of light. It was racing away, but she held on tenaciously, as if gasping for a last breath. *No! I cannot let him win!* Dredging every last bit of spark she had in her, Meira attacked. Threads formed on her fingertips. She shot them out, forming spears of fire. They reached Sithel's grinning face, and then, just like the other threads, vaporized into nothing. With that, Meira fell. Light and pain and suffering consumed her from the inside out. She realized she was screaming, as if crude daggers were carving out her heart, slowly and painstakingly. Thoughts stuttered beneath the devouring pain.

Distantly, she saw Ezrah, lying upon the cold stone. Blood ran from his head and upon the blackened stone in the fading light.

There is no hope, she thought.

All is lost…

* * *

"Think!" Meira shouted.

But it was so hard…

Visions flashed, screams from her, from all of them, still rising in the air. Gasping, Meira saw the knee-high boots of Sithel march calmly towards her. She clawed at the stone, trying to crawl away as pain racked her limbs. He grabbed her chin, forcing her eyes up as her pain began to cloud and dim her vision. Her last image would be his greasy smile. *Please, not that.* He held a dagger, running it closer to her neck. But she couldn't move, pain sapped her limbs of strength.

Because you are weak... Sithel's words echoed in her head. *No.* Sithel was wrong, again. *Strength is not everything, and it is not al-*

ways so easily seen.

She felt something grab her ankle, frail yet strong.

But it was a fleck beneath the monstrous pain.

Darkness encroached upon her vision, and she reached out with the last tendril of her power, something she hadn't known had been there. Eyeing the ceiling, she pulled with all her might.

Stone thundered and fell, crashing down upon them.

Sithel roared in anger. Something gripped Meira's arm and she was being pulled away, shards of stone exploding around her and dust clouding her vision. When, at last, the thundering stopped and the clouds of dust settled, Meira saw her act had created a barricade of stone, one she hoped Sithel had been caught in, but knew better. *Such evil does not die so easily.* She looked upon her savior.

He was a young man with gray-green eyes and brown hair, which was tousled as if he had been running nonstop. In his other hand was a brilliant and mesmerizing sword that glowed white. He wore the tattered cloak of the Devari with crossed swords, but somehow he did not seem like a Devari.

Just behind him were two men—one clearly a Devari in look and stature, with a hideously scarred face, and the other a shorter, stouter man with fiery copper-colored eyes, nearly the same age as her unexpected guardian.

"What is this?" Dagon moaned, rubbing his head and gaining his feet.

"This young man … he saved me," she said, disbelieving.

Dagon opened his mouth then cut short.

As the ringing in Meira's ears ended, she heard the thunder of armor and of footfalls.

The young man pulled her to her feet. "It is time to run," he declared. She watched in awe as he threaded *something* with his other hand. Her mouth parted as the air distorted, as if from heat, but it was not the element of fire.

And she knew.

Wind…

It sifted beneath the Arbiter, and the man rose, as if held by invisible hands. The air suddenly solidified, and Ezrah lay upon a golden glowing stretcher.

Several other Reavers had gained their footing and gasped, wide-eyed.

"Abomination..." Hutosh breathed.

"So much for not being able to use your power," the fiery Devari said.

"That was the last of what I have," her guardian declared, slumping as if exhausted. "Can you take him?" His two friends nodded, both Devari grabbed the stretcher and ran. "Can you run?" the mysterious young man questioned, grabbing her arm.

What are you? She thought, but her mouth worked soundlessly. Meira eyed the hand upon her arm as if it were a claw. *Wind*... The footsteps grew louder. Shaking herself out of a daze, Meira suppressed her fear and nodded then, together, they ran. Moving through the halls, they slowed as more fires and shouts of men sounded ahead.

"They're everywhere," Hutosh said, hand upon his bleeding forehead. "Where in the seven hells do we go?"

"This way," she ordered, turning down another series of dark halls when they hit a sudden wall of stone. A dead end. "This ... this is not supposed to be here," she voiced, panicked. Confusion and despair rose as her hands groped the solid wall.

"It's a trap," said Chloe, voice shaking with rising dread.

"Calm down," Finn instructed sharply, "Your fear does us no good here. Simply look for a door or a latch—there must be something." Despite his steady voice, his hands groped the walls frantically. Others, Chloe included, joined him.

A hand grabbed Meira, pulling her aside, and she found herself looking into the scarred Devari's face. His blue eyes shone in the dim light as he spoke, "I'm assuming you had a plan to get the Arbiter out of here. What exactly was it?"

"I have a cart waiting for us," she explained, "But we need to get to the Eastern Courtyards."

"And which way are they?"

"Straight above us."

Just then, fires appeared from behind, bobbing in the darkness—hundreds of them. It must have been an army.

"Do we stand and fight?" Reaver Dimitri asked.

"There's too many," she declared. "We must run."

"Yet there is no way out," Reaver Tugard said softly. "We're trapped."

"There is always a way out," Meira replied fervently and strode forth, joining Finn in his search. Her legs wobbled beneath her as she put a hand to the nearby wall, feeling the stone beyond. The footsteps and bobbing lights were getting closer by the second. She could almost hear their breathing and feel their heat upon her neck. Steel rang, and the Reavers pulled at their powers, but it was a dismal sight—the orb had weakened them greatly.

Meira moved closer towards the charging army, hand running along the wall.

"Meira!" Finn called fearfully.

Abruptly, she felt an emptiness. A hollow. *Here.* She summoned the spark, and felt a bit of power had strangely returned to her, but it was still like working a shriveled, atrophied muscle. Finn was suddenly at her side, grabbing her arm and feeding her his power. She smiled and stone erupted, falling and revealing a hallway beyond. At the same time, the air whistled, and something raced towards Meira. She threw up a stone fragment, just in time. Steel and wood splintered against it, and an arrow fell to her feet. More arrows streaked like hail as shouts rose. Nearby, Reavers erected pitiful shields of stone or steel, but it was not enough.

"Quickly! Into the hall!" Meira yelled to her fellowship as they leapt over the rubble and through the opening. The fires of the dark army were nearly upon them. Meira turned, but paused.

She saw Chloe lying upon the ground, eyes glazed, an arrow in her chest.

Weakness is death, Sithel's words played in her mind. Chloe's one-striped robes seemed to mock Meira as they became soaked with spreading blood.

Distantly, she thought she heard Sithel's maniacal laughter.

Hatred filling her, Meira whispered a silent prayer and ran.

Sacrifices

Just like that, the black halls ended.

Gray squinted into the blazing sun.

His eyes adjusted to the bright light, and he saw a grass field surrounded by tall black gates. *One of the dozen courtyards that surrounds the keep*, Kirin informed him. Trees dappled the grounds, with meandering stone paths flanked by unlit lampposts, benches, and even a nearby small pond. It all seemed so strange and unreal after the hours of endless dark halls, like walking out of a nightmare and into a dream. Still, relief flooded through his tired body.

"I didn't think we'd ever get out of there," Zane breathed at his side.

"Don't count your blessings yet," Victasys replied. "We're not quite out."

"Wait, where's Chloe?" a bearded Reaver asked suddenly.

The powerful woman responded. "Dead." She sounded shaken. *Meira*, they had called her. "Come. The cart and Eastern Gate are this way."

Gray took the wide, white marble stairs two at a time, then froze.

In the very center of the courtyard, a man knelt calmly, sitting upon his heels.

Had he been there before?

Gray felt Victasys tense at his side, as did the other Reavers.

As they descended the last stairs, the man's eyes snapped open.

Immediately, Gray reached for Morrowil as the man took them in, fist tightening around the blade's smooth handle. Not a hint of surprise registered on the sitting man's face made entirely of hard angles, as if he had been a piece of steel hammered by a blacksmith, but then left jagged and forgotten. Gray swallowed. Even his cold blue eyes made Victasys' seem warm.

"I guess I spoke too soon," Zane said.

Slowly, the man rose and spoke, the deep voice echoing over the courtyard. "I am here for you, Victasys. There is no more running. It is time to face your punishment."

Before the figure, a sword was stuck into the ground, pinpoints of light blazing off its shining steel. But he didn't reach for it. His cloak danced in front of him from a gust of wind, showing two crossed swords, but slightly different. The swords were larger and a brighter white. It seemed all too familiar. And he realized why. It was just like Kail's. The man bore the leader of the Devari's cloak.

Jian, Gray knew.

"And what crimes does the tainted Citadel accuse me of, brother?" Victasys replied.

"Do not call me that," Jian snapped. "You're not my brother, for you have broken the Code of the Devari. You're now a Forgotten." Gray saw Victasys stiffen, as if slapped. *Forgotten?* Gray questioned. Apparently it was a harsh accusation as the scarred man's body began to shake with anger. He did not think anything could perturb Victasys so much. Jian continued, "Though I would hear it from your own mouth before I end your sacrilege. Tell me, are you not to blame for the death of a Reaver in the Market Square?"

Zane yelled abruptly, "You're wrong! It was not his fault! Victasys killed that Reaver in self-defense and to protect me!" Calmly, Victasys gripped Zane's arm, shaking his head. And the fiery man quieted, if reluctantly.

Victasys remained silent, and Gray felt the tension build.

"Speak," Gray whispered. "Tell him it wasn't your fault, but say something!"

"I cannot," said the scarred Devari. "The man has already concluded my guilt. In the end, some men will simply not listen to reason." He sounded resigned, and yet there was a note of fear. His blues eyes wavered.

"Your silence has attested to the truth. You have betrayed us," Jian said in a deathly cold tone. "Your hands are stained with blood, but I will see them cleansed."

The tall, black haired Reaver, Dagon, spoke in a low, confident tone, "Together we can take him."

Gray nodded, gripping Morrowil tighter.

"We attack as one," Reaver Meira declared.

"No," Victasys said softly, but it cut the air like a knife. "We cannot beat him. Not even together, not as we stand." Handing Ezrah's stretcher to a nearby Reaver, he looked to Gray. "Take him and go. All of you."

Meira's eyes tightened, but she nodded, striding forward. "Come, guardian," she called.

Gray unsheathed Morrowil with a ring. "No, I'm not going anywhere."

"This is my fight, Gray," Victasys said, then nodded to Ezrah. "And you know yours. It is time we both follow our fates."

"Damn the fates!" he shouted, rage welling inside him. Yet worst of all, he knew Victasys was right. He felt his rage turn to sorrow, looking at the man as if seeing him for the last time. "I cannot leave you… We will not leave you… You are one of us now."

"Gray's right. We fight together," Zane said, his blade ringing.

"You don't understand," Victasys said. "You both are no match for Jian."

"I'm not afraid of death," Zane replied.

"You may not be, but Hannah? What will she do without her brother? And you, Gray? Do you not think Ayva and Darius will attempt to avenge you if you fall here?"

Zane cursed softly, his fiery gaze turning away.

But Gray didn't turn away. "There must be another way," he voiced.

Victasys grasped his shoulders firmly, and despite the darkness, Gray felt strangely lifted by the resolve in the man's eyes, smooth, scarred skin glistening in the sun's light. "Listen now. You two have given me hope when I had none. That is enough for me. The darkness upon my heart has been banished. But you must go now, for your grandfather is the Citadel's only hope. We still don't know what secrets the Arbiter holds. If they take him, all is lost."

Gray's body roiled in frustration and sorrow. He wanted to deny Victasys, to shout and rail against him, but he knew there was nothing he could say that would change the truth.

"Leave!" Victasys yelled, stepping back. "Now!"

"You better win," Zane growled.

The Devari's scarred skin twisted as he gave a wicked smile at last before facing Jian. Both men exchanged glares that could have melted stone. "I will not go down easily."

Zane tugged upon his arm. "*Gray*… C'mon…"

Reluctantly, Gray stepped away. Following the other Reavers, he skirted the center of the yard quickly. Heart lodged in his throat, he turned the corner, Zane at his side.

Beneath Gray's feet, the courtyard rattled as steel rung.

But Victasys was gone.

With pain in his heart, Gray continued forward, not slowing.

* * *

Victasys' grin grew.

At last, he would be able to determine if the myths around Jian were true—if the man was truly more powerful than any Devari in a thousand years, even stronger than their once-leader Ren. Perhaps in another age, when the Citadel was not broken, Jian would have made a great leader. Standing there, the sun's light bathing his imposing figure, hard sinewy muscles tense with fury and insurmountable strength, he was clearly a man of legends. *I would have followed you unto the end, had you only listened to reason...* But he did not voice the sentiment. He was not a man of many words, but now, more than ever, words were useless. All had been said that needed to be said.

Victasys unsheathed his blade, and flames roared to life all along Yuwa's surface, his named soulwed blade, weapons bestowed to a Sword-Forged Devari. He had carried Yuwa at his side for nearly six decades, as such the blade had become his closest companion. And yet he did not feel for it nearly the way he had felt for those two young men.

Across from him, in the center of the green yard, Jian grabbed his soulwed sword, and for one of the first times in his life, Victasys felt true dread. Bright red flames bellowed forth, scorching earth and burning grass in a ring around Jian.

A bead of sweat formed on Victasys' forehead, rolling down into his eye.

This man was not simply stronger. With a blade, Jian was death.

Abruptly, wind burst over him and Jian *flew*. Victasys' sword flickered, blades clashing as Yuwa met those brilliant red flames. Jian's expression didn't flicker, his arms flexing as his blade pressed down. The flames roared louder, searing Victasys' face, and he cried out, lunging and attacking with everything he had. But with every move, Jian's blade was there, meeting it almost casually. Blades clashed and steel thundered as a flood of blows sounded, echoing through the courtyard. Victasys moved faster and faster. He sacrificed sure footing and exposed vital targets all for the chance to land a blow. His battle cry grew louder and louder as he slashed at Jian's midsection and then lunged for his head. But it was not enough. *No*, Victasys thought with rage. *I will not fall here!* He used his ki, forcing all his will upon the man in an attempt to read the Devari leader's move-

ments. A barrier met him, harder than steel and thicker than any city's wall. But that was not his intent. He simply wanted to distract Jian. It worked. Victasys lunged and his sword met flesh.

Jian retreated in a rush of wind.

They stood a dozen paces away, and Victasys found himself breathing so hard he felt as if he were a youngling once more. He wanted to vomit, but he suppressed the urge. His arms were limp, tingling beneath the ringing power of Jian's blows. He wanted to let them fall to his side, but he refused, holding his sword upright, as if he was ready for more.

He looked to Jian, and tensed.

How?

Only a tiny gash marred Jian's cheek. Victasys' confidence wavered. The man casually wiped at it with a finger and flicked the blood to the ground. *But if he can bleed*, he thought, *then he can fall…* He ground his teeth, forming a plan hastily. *Confidence.* If he could feign confidence perhaps—

Suddenly his thoughts were interrupted as Jian … *transported.*

For that is only what it could be called. It was not magic, Victasys knew, not the spark, but pure strength.

He was simply too fast.

He tried to move, but it was no use.

Victasys felt cold steel pierce his gut and he gasped, pain shooting through his limbs. He felt his limbs twitch. Knowing Jian had hit his spine, he knew he was dead, that it was only a matter of seconds before Jian would cut and end it. Mercifully. He tried to speak, but only blood poured forth. He swallowed it down and tried again.

"I … would have … followed," Victasys said, unsure whether it was garbled or the words came out with any coherence. His mind started to waver, all things blurring. He fell to his knees, seeing the bright grass rustle from a subtle breeze. *Wind… Gray…* His heart warmed at the thought, despite slowing down, knowing that those two would live and see Ezrah to safety.

The last thing he saw as he felt something cut his spine and sever all life was Jian's mixed expression.

Duty… So thick it could have buried a man alive.

And beneath that: *Sorrow.*

The Trader

This way, Kirin plied.

Gray listened, anger and sorrow roiling through him with each step.

He led the others as they passed through the green courtyard and into a black tower on the eastern end of the Citadel. Several guards twisted at their sudden appearance.

The two groups reached for blades, but Gray wasted no time.

Monkfish Darts Beneath the Waves. He rolled, dipping beneath the first guard's slash, barely. At the same time, the other guard's halberd plummeted towards Zane. The fiery man sidestepped and rammed his fist into the man's gut, dropping him. Gray came to his feet, ramming the pommel of Morrowil into the side of the first guard's head. The man's armor clanked as he crumbled to the stone floor.

Gray didn't slow, but he asked… *Is he…?*

Unconscious. Don't worry, Kirin said.

A four-way split approached and, from around the bend, swords raced towards Gray. He couldn't move in time, and he prepared himself to feel steel, cringing—

The guard cried out, collapsing. Nearby, he saw Meira's hand extended, face smooth. "Careful," the three-stripe Reaver advised.

Gray nodded in thanks.

"How exactly do you know where we are going?" Meira asked as they continued.

"Call it a hunch," he lied, ducking left.

"A strong hunch or a bad liar. Why do I feel it's the latter?"

Gray grumbled but didn't slow. Three corridors. *Left*, Kirin said. Gray didn't question. He dashed down the left courtyard, the footsteps of the other Reavers echoing behind him. Though Meira had tried to wedge herself closer, Zane ran between them, near to his side. As always, he was glad for the fiery man's presence, but he felt as if there was a hollow at his other side. *Victasys*. Pained, he turned his thoughts away. He looked to Ezrah as they ran. The man's eyes were closed as the two Reavers carried him upon the golden stretcher.

An Arbiter.

His grandfather...

"If you are no Devari, then what are you?" the woman asked yet again, breaking him from his reverie.

Gray paused at a four-way intersection. "Does it matter?" *Where?* he asked Kirin, but again silence.

"If we are following you, it matters."

Gray sniffed the air and smelled dirt closer down the straight path before answering. "I am something different," he said with a small smile, then ran. He felt her emotions spike in curiosity through his ki. And he reveled in her curiosity and irritation, but her face became a mask of coolness once more. He tried to sift between her barrier. She was strong, immensely so, but he found a slim gap. All at once, her emotions rushed through him, her feelings overpowering him.

Duty and pride... Strength and reserve... Sorrow and loss...

Beneath that was a driving regret, and he knew who that was for—the man on the golden stretcher.

And at last, a wisp of love surrounded by denial, and he wondered for whom.

But most immediately, her every muscle twitched wanting to stop, to turn back. It was clear. This is the wrong way, her body shouted. Gray retreated, eyeing the woman as they ran. She was expressionless. How could she act so placid, yet be so ruffled inside? If one overlooked the sweat and blood, Meira could have been out for a simple jog. She had thick, dark brows and a slender but strong Serian nose. *Serian? Who or what is that?* Kirin, he knew. He tried to guess her age. She couldn't have been old enough to be his mother. Then again, her angled brown eyes were full of wisdom, like a woman many times her age.

Meira opened her mouth.

"And to answer your next question," he said, interrupting her, "you yourself said the Eastern Gate is blocked. This is the only way out."

Meira's lips tightened in response. "Presumptuous, are we? What makes you think that was my next question?"

Gray gave another small smile. "A strong hunch," he replied.

This time Meira's annoyance and curiosity was obvious, but she remained silent.

Gray moved through a stone hall and saw a door ahead.

The postern gate, Kirin said. The iron-strapped door was bolted shut, but they didn't slow. At his side, Zane raised his hand and a bolt of fire exploded forth. With the others at his side, Gray ran through the cloud of splinters and found himself in a dusty street of Farbs. Clay buildings surrounded them, but there were no signs of guards.

"Where are we…?" a younger Reaver whispered fearfully.

But just then, there was a sound.

With a trickle of his power, Gray felt back along the corridors from where they came, then suddenly felt the presence of hundreds of soldiers storming through the halls like a flood of barred steel, barreling closer. Their eyes, cruelly lit in the dim halls, shone with the lust for blood.

At their head, he saw a man in gruesome red-stained robes, a blue stone in one large palm, pulsating and crackling. Gray's vision snapped, racing back into his body.

Zane's hand was on his shoulder, reassuringly. "What did you see?"

"They are coming…" Gray whispered.

"Then we run?" Zane asked, gulping a breath, looking haggard. His hands were on his knees. He seemed as if he wanted to lie down and sleep. Gray felt exhaustion to his bones as well. How long had they been running? He could barely think straight let alone drive his leaden legs to move once more. A strange determination kept him standing, kept his head high and his back straight, but how much longer would it last? He felt as if he stood on borrowed time.

"We cannot run anymore!" shouted another Reaver. "Besides, where is there to go?"

Reaver Dagon stepped forward, head held high. "Then this is where we make our stand."

"But none of us can fight!" said another, "I can barely feel the spark!"

"Agreed," said a bearded Reaver. *Hutosh*, Meira had called him. He gripped the nearby wall, flexing his palm as if seeing it for the first time. "It's strange ... but I would be lucky to light a candle at this moment."

"Then what do we do?" Reaver Dimitri questioned.

"We die," Zane said, unsheathing his sword. Oddly, thin flames danced along its surface, for a mere moment, but then were gone. Gray shook his head. *Was he seeing things as well now?*

The footsteps grew louder as the hallway seemed to breathe darkness. Gray was so tired, but he held onto that inexplicable strength and lifted Morrowil, readying himself for whatever came. At the same time, the ground rattled, but it was coming from elsewhere.

Gray twisted when, from around the bend, a cart rumbled into view. The man in the driver's seat lashed the horses, voice ringing. "*Ho!*" he called, and the beasts came to an abrupt stop. The man wore a wrinkled smile and had a big nose and dark eyes that bulged from his small head. Upon his skull, a floppy cap tried and failed to contain his bushel of snowy white hair. "Need a lift?" he called.

"Liam..." Meira breathed, sounding stunned.

The scrawny man scrambled from his perch, hastening to throw open the doors of the cart. "My lady," Liam said, bobbing his head. "So sorry, but no time for any more formalities. Quickly now, quit your gawking and load him in!" And the Reavers jumped to. "Watch it now, careful with his head! He's an Arbiter for bloody sake, not a bushel of wheat!"

"Where in the seven hells did you come from?" a dark-skinned Reaver voiced.

"From the land of *It Doesn't Bloody Matter Right Now*," Liam said. "Now do you want to be rescued or not? If so, all of you get in, or I'll leave your sorry hides behind!"

Each man jumped to, leaping inside as if the ground was on fire.

Gray felt the earth tremble. He looked back towards the hallway. *They were coming…*

With Zane nearby, Gray bounded into the cart as a blue light filled the air, crackling with power, and Meira and the other Reavers gasped as if being stabbed.

* * *

Men burst from the postern door, soldiers charging towards the cart. Ignoring the pain, Meira leapt up into the side-driver's seat. Grabbing the wiry man's stick thin arm, she yelled, "Ride! Get us out of here!"

Liam winked. "Ah, but with pleasure, my lady!" he said anxiously. He clicked his tongue, and the horses burst into a gallop, racing down the dirt streets.

Meira peered over her shoulder.

Calmly, Sithel walked out of the hall, surrounded by men. His bloodied white robes brushed the ground as he watched the cart race away, a small smile upon his cruel lips. In his hand, the blue orb crackled in the dry, empty street, sucking at all life—even the golden motes in the air seemed to fizzle beneath the orb's touch. Wavering in her seat, Meira had only one thought looking upon that man and the stone in his hand: Sithel was death.

Liam shouted louder, urging the horses on, but Meira's mind was consumed in pain, watching Sithel's burning, black gaze. Her mind warped, and she clutched her head, clenching her eyes shut. Their escape became a blur, barreling down a series of narrow alleys and cluttered backstreets. At last, they turned a corner, and her mind and power returned. She breathed in sharply and noticed the other Reavers return from the darkness that was Sithel. Meira shivered, glad to be as far away from that cursed object and man as possible.

"Liam, you mind explaining what just happened?" she asked, still shaken.

"Ah, my late entrance? Added to the thrill of the moment, did it not?"

She ground her teeth, silently. She knew her eyes spoke volumes.

Liam glanced at her, and he swallowed, the man's ever present smile wilting. "I am sorry, but I had a bit of trouble with some feisty guards claiming I couldn't use that alley."

"But that wasn't even the right gate," she said.

"Ah, but it's the right package. That's all that matters!"

She shook her head. "How?" she asked. "How did you find us?"

Liam gave a thin-lipped smile. "Ah, you underestimate that man you carry, my lady."

And Meira looked through the slot behind her. Ezrah was now in the center of the wagon. Her guardian sat beside his still form, trying to wake him unsuccessfully. "But... He's not even awake. That's impossible!"

"He is an Arbiter—nothing is impossible," Liam replied, suddenly humorless. Meira felt suddenly small amidst the weight of events transpiring around her. Liam flicked the reins, and they emerged onto a wide thoroughfare and blended with the sudden crowds.

A majestic cry pierced the air.

Meira looked up as several gryphons passed overhead, swooping over the crowds and briefly eclipsing the bright sun. With the head of an eagle and the body of a lion, and eagle talons upon their fore-paws, the proud beasts stood as a symbol of the Kingdom of Fire. Just as all Great Kingdoms had a creature, gryphons were the representative animals of Farbs. The gryphons screeched again as they flew towards tall turrets in the distance called Perches—huge manmade nests used as a hub for all air travel in and out of the city.

All around Meira, the marketplace roared with life.

Liam's colorful cart became one of many.

Smells, sights, and sounds bombarded them—cooking food, blacksmiths' hammers, hawkers' cries, and much more. She'd almost forgotten how chaotic the streets of Farbs truly were. Several guards maneuvered on horseback through the throng, their eyes roving, searching.

Discreetly, Liam flipped his vest inside out, showing purple instead of white, and then swapped out his floppy cap for a conical wide-brimmed hat—the notorious garb of a Serian.

The guards neared, weapons in hand.

Liam shouted at a man moving too slow before them, "Move it, man! Make way for his Grace, or the Crown of Seria will have your head! Quickly now! His High Noble Yunta is inside this cart, and he suffers no man!" The man moved aside and the guards ahead took note. Meira was impressed. The wiry old man pulled off a Serian retainer to near perfection. And she wondered if perhaps he wasn't Serian himself. He had the bold nose for it.

Meira hid her face as well, pulling her scarlet robes over her mouth and nose, as if to shield her from an assault of dust and the smell of a nearby tannery, which admittedly was foul smelling. The last of the guards passed, moving onward, and Meira gave a shiver of relief, recalling a sudden memory as a Neophyte, flopping onto her tiny cot after a tireless day of training.

Finally safe.

"Is the safe house prepared?" she asked.

"As requested," Liam said, and then peered over his shoulder through the slot of the cart himself. "It's quite comfortably sized and luckily so, as I didn't exactly expect this many. It seems my lady makes companions quite easily."

"It wasn't intended," she replied.

"And who are these new friends of yours?"

"I'm not sure yet," she answered warily.

Liam's grip tightened on his reins. "Can they be trusted?"

"We will see," she replied, and then looked at her guardian. The young man's gray-green eyes were pools of mystery as he hovered over Ezrah. *Wind...* she thought again in equal parts amazement and dread. In all her decades, she had never seen anything like it. The element of wind. *How could it be? Who is he?*

Meira hadn't realized she'd asked the question aloud until the wiry old man squinted and squawked, "Who? Ah! Yes! That must be him!" Liam said with a loud chuckle, "That old rascal. *Fates indeed!*"

"What are you talking about?" she questioned, again doubting Liam's sanity. He had seemed trustworthy before, but now? If Ezrah had spoken to him, did he work for her or the Arbiter? She shook her head. *Does it matter? Ezrah is the only one I can trust.* Meira sighed. However true that was, she felt strangely used.

"The boy..." Liam said. "The Arbiter told me he would be coming."

"*Him?*" she questioned, eyeing Gray.

Liam nodded.

"Then he must be important."

"You could say that," the old man said mischievously.

Her eyes narrowed. "What aren't you telling me? Who is he to the Arbiter?"

Liam smiled, his wrinkles creasing, then answered, "Family."

The Tranquil House

Scrolls of amber light from the nearby window lit Ezrah's face, making him appear divine.

It was dusk now and they were on the second floor of the safe haven, which Meira and the other Reavers had begun to call the Tranquil House. Gray sat in a chair beside the man's bed, reading. Well, not really reading. That would imply that he knew the words. The language, however, was not one he could decipher.

In his hands sat the book Mura had given him so long ago—nearly a lifetime he felt—the same one that had been lost when the Vergs and Saeroks had sacked their home. He wished he could see Mura, though the book did give him comfort, as if part of Mura were still with him.

Gray's hands felt across the surface of the book, feeling its raised emblem of wind upon the cover.

Inside, he scanned the pages, wondering what the words meant. Several times he saw other symbols, all symbols he had seen before—water, stone, metal, flesh, moon, sun, leaf, and fire.

The last one stood out to him. *Farbs.* The Great Kingdom of Fire…

The door behind Gray opened, and Zane entered.

"Is he awake?"

Gray shook his head. "Not yet."

The man nodded softly. "He will be soon. Meira said he is merely unconscious now that Sithel has stolen his spark." *Stolen the spark…* The words, though mostly a mystery to Gray, still seemed like a curse, lancing through him. He eyed the sleeping Arbiter, the man's gray hair with white streaks strewn across his face—a face more weathered than when he had first seen it in his dreams. He knew the white hair and age had been a part of his torture—a dark price, but a small one in Gray's mind.

Zane moved to his side. The fiery man's presence was strangely comforting. The room was quiet with only a several-handed instrument upon the wall ticking quietly. A *clock*, Zane had called it, though he seemed more or less unfamiliar with it as well.

"What's that?" Zane asked, eyeing the book in Gray's hand.

"A present from long ago," he said, feeling the worn cover.

"No," Zane said, "this." He reached out and picked up the fragment of dark cloth with two crossed swords emblazoned in white upon the back. It still had a splotch of blood. "Kill a Devari, did you?"

As soon as he said the words, Gray felt a sting to his gut.

Victasys.

Zane realized his words, and his eyes clenched, trying to recover. With a shaky sigh he added, "I mean… Where'd you get it?"

"A friend," Gray said mysteriously.

"Why does it look different?"

"Because it is. It's the cloak of the leader of the Devari."

"How in the… This… Is this *Ren's* cloak?"

"Ren?" Gray asked, confused.

Zane ran a hand through his blond hair. In the light of the setting sun, Gray saw it had a flame-red tint. Everything about the man seemed fiery. Even his clothes had been burned in the chaos, though he had been unharmed, and he had taken to wearing a deep red vest. It suited him. Again, it seemed too familiar, too *fated*, but Gray didn't let his mind wander in that direction as Zane answered, "You don't know who Ren is?"

Gray shook his head, something stirring inside him.

"Ren was the last leader of the Devari. Some say he was one of the strongest blademasters ever to live."

Live… Kirin breathed.

You're back, Gray thought, oddly missing the voice in his head. But then Kirin was silent once more. Shrugging it off, he looked back to Zane. "You make it sound like he died. What happened to him?"

"He did die."

Kirin wailed. *What was that?* "How?" Gray asked.

Unsheathing a rusted dagger from his belt, Zane spun it on the nearby table, catching it each time before it fell, creating a small notch in the wood as he answered, "Honestly, no one knows for certain. At this point it's mostly just stories and rumors."

"Tell me," Gray pressed.

Zane arced a brow. "Curious about this, aren't you?"

"More or less," he said, trying to sound casual. "Anything better to talk about?"

"I guess not," Zane said. "Well, they say he was found with a hole in his stomach the size of a fist. The room he was found in was filled with other dead guards and Devari, full of severed limbs, blood everywhere, as if a gateway to hell had opened and unleashed all its dark fury upon those poor souls…" Zane shook his head. "Least that's what some say. To me, sounds like the work of Reavers, but the whispers said he was betrayed by his own kind, by a brother, a Devari. Though I'm not sure how any Devari could have killed a man like that. He was the strongest of them all."

"And then?" Gray wasn't even aware he spoke, his mind lost in Zane's story.

"It wasn't long before news of Ren's death spread like fire to a thatch roof. It's not often that a Reaver or Devari is found dead—or at least, it wasn't back then—least of all the *leader* of the Devari. More than that, the man was well respected, even outside the Citadel. A huge ceremonial pyre was erected for him in the center of Farbs, and thousands attended. After that, the hunt was on…" Zane said. "You should have seen the look in a Devari's eye, or lucky that you didn't. For months, thieves and others of the less than reputable sort walked on eggshells when a Devari appeared. They roamed the streets, as if searching for the one that killed their beloved leader."

Gray was riveted. He felt a distant thrumming of fear, but a burning curiosity overrode it. The whole story sounded so familiar. He heard a sound, and he realized that, oddly, his heart was hammering in his chest. He unfurled his palms and saw they were drenched in sweat. *What is going on?*

Zane spoke again, his voice snapping him out of his thoughts. The room seemed to flash back into focus, Gray's world returned. "Sometimes I forget how much, or how little you know," the fiery man said. "One day you'll have to fill me in on your past."

Gray put a hand to his head. "And you on yours…" he replied absently.

Zane swallowed, seeming suddenly pained, as if seeing demons.

"Did I say something wrong?" Gray asked.

"No," Zane said, yet his voice grew dark and resigned. "It's just … my past … I—"

Gray held up a hand, interrupting him, after seeing the man's obvious reluctance, as if he was pulling Zane's nails off with hot pincers. "It's all right. You've risked your life for me, and to save a man you barely know. You don't have to tell me anything you don't want to."

Zane's body slacked, muscles uncoiling. "Thanks," he said with a heavy breath, looking grateful.

He smiled. "Anytime." Gray knew what it was like to have someone who simply trusted you, who didn't ask questions when there was a darkness nipping at your heels—specifically a darkness that was one's past. That was Ayva and Darius for him. Thoughts of the two made his heart twist, and he prayed they were all right with Faye.

Gray looked back to Ezrah.

"We did it, Gray," Zane stated. "You should be proud."

Gray nodded. *Proud*... He wasn't sure if he was proud, but he was glad, happy even. The man was alive and in the flesh before him. It was hard to believe.

Even in sleep Ezrah seemed powerful, yet oddly vulnerable at the same time. It was somehow endearing, as if Gray was the only thing protecting one of the most powerful men in the entire world.

Ezrah suddenly stirred.

Gray's fingers froze upon the page.

"I'll leave you," the fiery man whispered. "Good luck."

Good luck? Gray thought, gulping. But then again, perhaps he would need it.

The Arbiter's eyes opened, revealing gray-green irises.

Just like mine...

Gray tried to swallow down the lump in his throat as the man's ancient gaze took in the serene surroundings—a small, cozy room made of earthen brick with simple wood furniture, white sheets, a stone fireplace, several chairs, and a long window that overlooked the busy streets below—and then finally his gaze settled on Gray. A thousand different emotions flashed across Ezrah's face, all utterly unreadable. Before he realized what he was doing, Gray reached out with the ki in an attempt to read his grandfather.

He touched the man's mind and gasped.

He was met with a wall unlike anything he had ever felt before. It glowed golden and bright, like the living wind he could thread, but brighter still—blinding even. He looked away, but it did nothing. The light beamed forth, radiating power and strength. Hesitantly, he touched it and—

"The ki, is it?"

Gray snapped out of the moment, opening his eyes.

Ezrah's voice rang deep and powerful, "Quite a powerful one too."

The man was now sitting upright in his bed, his simple, white sheets falling around his torso, which was wrapped in thick bandages that hid his wounds. The Arbiter eyed him, and a long moment passed. Gray's heart thundered in his chest. At last, Ezrah's face softened. "Gray," the man said. That simple name. As if he was saying a thousand things in a single word.

"Grandfather..."

Ezrah smiled. "Welcome home, my boy."

Gray found tears in his eyes that he didn't know were there. He blinked them away, and before he knew what he was doing, he embraced the Arbiter in a deep hug. The man gripped back, surprisingly strong.

After a long moment, both released. Ezrah's face turned suddenly stern once more. It was like staring into the gray-green gaze of a storm. "However, we'll have to have a little talk about that ki business. I'm awake for only moments and you seek to infiltrate my mind?"

"I ... I didn't mean to," he said. "I just—"

Ezrah held up a weathered hand. "I am only teasing. But you do not need to use the ki—not with me. However, I am curious... Is the ki familiar to you once more? And your memories, have they returned?"

Gray waited for Kirin to burst into his mind, but there was a strange silence. He shook his head at last, "Not yet... Just bits and pieces. But the ki, on the other hand, feels oddly familiar. It comes easily now. Just then I wanted to know what you were thinking, and it kind of happened before I realized it."

The Arbiter rubbed his chin with a thoughtful sound. "Be wary, my boy. My knowledge of a Devari's powers is relatively sparse... But what I *have* learned over my many years is that any power, the ki included, can be dangerous. Until there is someone who can guide you in the ki's proper usage, I'd caution temperance. Use it sparingly."

Gray nodded in understanding.

A moment passed, and Gray had a thousand questions flood through him in a rush, thoughts racing like a whirlwind in his mind. Before he could speak, though, Ezrah reached out and touched Gray's arm. His hand was warm, and the skin soft.

"I see..." the man declared mysteriously. "You've learned your power, then."

"I have, but it is fractured, like..." he began and fell short.

Ezrah lifted a brow streaked with white, reminding Gray of a bolt of lightning. "Like mine?"

"Meira told me about what they did to you. It sounds ... horrible." The voidstone. The woman had briefly mentioned its powers. The power to steal the spark, draining one of all their power... *And to drain an Arbiter.* Meira made the act sound worse than death. As if they had already killed Ezrah. He didn't truly understand but knew nonetheless that, whatever Ezrah was feeling, he couldn't begin to fathom. Still, he was just glad the man was alive.

"It is horrible," Ezrah said. "But I will survive."

"And your power...?"

Ezrah's eyes crinkled, as if knowing a secret. "Hand me that candle."

Gray faltered, noticing a thick wax candle on the bedside stand. Meira said she had tried to remove anything in the room that would make the Arbiter "thread" unconsciously, triggering the dark reminder that he was without his power. Yet there sat a candle. Gray handed it over.

The Arbiter took a deep breath, turning the candle in his hand. "Many believe to be drained of the spark is a fate much like death. And in a way, they are right. The spark is life. It feeds the land, the rivers, the forests, and all creatures. It is in the very air we breathe." Ezrah looked out the window, over the streets of Farbs, eyes glazing, his gaze growing distant. "Yet as we sit here, my boy, the spark is dying in the world. The creatures of Farhaven depend on it, and magical beings like Sprites and Dryads are fading from this realm. Even mortals grow weaker as it fades. Soon we will be much like Daerval in every way."

"What are you saying?" Gray asked, reading between the lines. "Farhaven has magic, but what is the difference between a man from Daerval or one from Farhaven?"

"You have noticed it, have you not? In Farhaven you can run longer, fight harder, jump higher, and sleep less, among other things. This world is different. It gives you strength. Without magic, humans will be simply humans—or what you have come to know in

Daerval as human. And elves? Well, many believe those with a strong connection to the spark and to this world simply cannot live without the essence of magic."

"Then elves and other magical beings … they will die when the spark dies?"

Ezrah sighed, holding the candle up to the light of the window. "I wish I knew, but even the wise cannot know all things. However, as for your question, the spark is life, but true power resides deeper, my boy. True power lives within." *Within?* he thought, confused. Just then, Ezrah's fingers snapped and the candle's long wick sparked to life—a small flame, but deep and red and burning brightly.

Gray gasped. "You still have your power! But how?"

Ezrah eyed the flame, watching it burn fervently, as if seeing through the flame. "Daerval is without the spark, correct? But while living in Daerval may diminish your strength and your abilities, your power is still there, is it not? In the end, it is choice, as are all things. All our power resides within, and just because you can't see something, doesn't mean it's not there. Your strength is inside you, Gray, and you cannot—you *must not*—let anyone take it from you," he said and shrugged. "Also, I am an Arbiter." And the red flame suddenly burned blue, yellow, green, white, black, tan, and then finally settled on a deep red, once again. "I am not without my ways."

Gray had trouble choosing whether to laugh or gawk. He realized his mouth was open, and he snapped it shut then shook his head. "But still, my power… I know it's inside me. I haven't let it be taken, but I can't seem to fix it."

"Then you must search deeper." Ezrah handed the candle to him. "Snuff the flame with your power."

Gray faltered, fingers tightening around the smooth wax. He wanted his power, and he wanted to prove to his grandfather he wasn't weak. He focused on the burning candle then delved inward. The nexus came, a ball of white as usual, but the missing patch seemed to be growing. Fear flashed, but he put it down and reached out. Yet as he touched the white ball it slipped through his hand, vanishing. He grasped for his power again, but the nexus was nowhere to be seen. "I cannot," he said, frustration growing. "Without need, I cannot touch my power. Wait, you can teach me, can't you?" he pleaded, looking up.

Ezrah glowered at him beneath thick eyebrows. "You wield the flow. It is a power only the Ronin can wield—it is the very essence of the spark, where all magic in the world derives from. As such, it is by nature far greater in power, but also wholly different. Now none but the Ronin know its vast limits, or how to summon it at will."

"Then how am I to learn it? The Ronin are dead," Gray said. As he said the words, they sounded like a lie, even to him. Ezrah's eyes were a mystery, again unreadable. He almost reached out with the ki by instinct, but refrained.

The Arbiter spoke. "You will have to learn by trial and error, as is the way of most things. Though I can help a little. What I do know is that the spark yields to force, but I believe the flow is like a blade. It will need the cool, quenching waters to temper the steel, or it will shatter beneath the first blow. In essence, seek your power in the moment between anger *and* stillness."

Holding the candle to the light streaming from the window, Gray pulled, but this time he *listened* as well. His eyes tightened on the burning flame. He felt the wind begin to form on the tips of his fingers, little white threads reaching for the orange fire. He wanted to pull more, to hold the power tighter, but instead he relaxed his mind. A slight breeze ruffled the sheets, and the flame wavered, but then settled, still burning brightly. Gray sighed, letting the nexus fall. Ezrah placed a solemn hand upon his shoulder. "With time, my boy, with time… There is also power in patience."

Just then, there was a knock.

"Come in," Ezrah called in the voice of an Arbiter.

Meira entered with a group of Reavers behind her. She took in the scene with her usual smooth face. He saw she was wearing a fresh set of scarlet robes, and the dark stripes upon her cuff seemed to pull in the light of the tranquil room. She spoke. "I'm sorry to delay your reunion, my—" she seemed to struggle for an honorific "—*Arbiter*," she settled on, it sounded powerful enough.

"What is it?" Ezrah asked. Again, his voice was soft, but it demanded authority like a general upon the battlefield, despite sitting in a bed on the recovery from the brink of death.

"We've only just begun, and there's much to be done. Sithel's darkness is spreading. We need you."

"His wounds have barely closed," Gray said, his jaw tightening.

"Can you not wait until his strength has recovered at least a little?" Through the ki, he felt compassion coming from Meira, but her stern expression didn't alter.

"It's all right, my boy," Ezrah said, and Gray turned to see his grandfather wearing a strong but kind smile. "I must see to this. I must heed my own words and find the strength within."

Gray nodded but paused, not moving from his seat.

His grandfather lifted a brow, "My boy?"

Gray couldn't leave. "I…"

Ezrah, seeing his consternation, looked to the other Reavers. "Leave us," he commanded powerfully. Meira opened her mouth as if to object. "*Now.*" The word boomed, and some three-stripe Reavers made flustered bows, while others just hurried for the door, but all obeyed, even Meira.

"We'll give you another moment or two, but no more," she said, shutting the door.

The room returned to silence, and he felt the weight of his grandfather's eyes.

"What is it, Gray? Speak your mind."

Gray's fist tightened around the candle. "The Ronin."

Ezrah's expression darkened. "You want to know who you are?"

"I know," he said. "I am Kail's progeny."

"You are much more than that, Gray."

"What do you mean?"

"You are a Ronin, a Devari, and the blood of an Arbiter flows through your veins." Gray swallowed at the weight of those words. "There is much that stands upon your shoulders, my boy, though you've a long path ahead of you and much to learn… You hold a greater power inside you than anything the world has ever known."

Gray shivered. "What am I to do with it?"

"That is your call," Ezrah said simply then smiled and touched Gray's hand that held the book and something seemed to sift *into* him. There was a *click* in his mind as a chill coursed through his limbs, despite the warm air in the lighted room. *What was that?* "Know this, my boy," the man said in a deep voice. "Whatever your power, you are still *you*. Your choices are yours alone. Only you can shape who you will become."

There was a rushed knock, and Meira's faced peeked back in.

"My Arbiter," she voiced calmly, but the vein of urgency was clear. "We've waited long enough. Too much is at stake. The boy is not going anywhere. We must discuss our plans."

Gray sighed and rose, but Ezrah's hand stopped him. "I've waited two years to see my grandson. I do not intend to lose him again so soon. You may stay, my boy, if you'd like."

"It's all right," he said, warmed by his grandfather's words. "I'm not needed here, I'll only get in the way. But don't worry, as far as I'm concerned, this conversation is far from finished."

Ezrah gave a mischievous wink. "Until then." Gray turned, and Ezrah called out, "My boy. Are you forgetting something?" he said, holding the worn tome in his hand. *I thought that was just in my hand?* Confused, he thanked his grandfather and grabbed the book. The chill coursed through him again. Feeling strangely drained, Gray moved to the door as the others rushed in.

A Book of Truth

As Gray left Ezrah, he moved into the adobe hall, book under his arm, making his way towards the stairs when he felt something tug upon his mind. Ezrah's words played over again. *Until then...*

He shook it off and continued. He passed a room with men and women talking around a low table and sitting on small cushions—newcomers to the Tranquil House. They had been coming in small droves. Farbian guards, Reavers, servants, and even Devari, any and all with sense enough to see the Citadel was breaking. As such, their cause was growing rapidly.

Meira had refrained from pulling out the Neophytes. Not yet at least, she said. Several had already 'disappeared' in their attempts to flee. It was too dangerous, she had decided. But Gray felt the tension building. How long could this continue? It was only a matter of time until the Citadel discovered their whereabouts. Real conflict, like a teakettle close to boiling, was bound to happen.

Sithel was building his forces, preparing for something, and Gray feared it. Whispers spoke of it throughout the Tranquil House, in every hall, sifting in and out of all corners of the large building.

"How many are left?" a woman's voice asked with authority. A Reaver.

Gray ducked back, listening to the conversation in the room.

"We've recovered only a small portion of our brothers and sisters. Too many Reavers have swayed to the darkness, or worse, are too afraid to speak up or act. Sithel has cast a fear over the Citadel that is all but tangible. More are coming to our cause, but it is dangerous to do so, almost too dangerous. As it stands, we are outnumbered ten to one. We must sway others to our rebellion or we will never stand a chance."

"What do you intend, Reaver Unuri?" a stern voice asked of the woman—it sounded like a Devari. "Do you plan to start a war all on your own?"

"War is already upon us, Devari. Ignoring it only leaves us blind. If we remain blind, then we will fall."

"Perhaps, Unuri," said the first female Reaver, placidly. "But we must be careful as well. What if Sithel simply shuts the doors to the Citadel? What then? Or openly begins the manhunt of all non-dark Reavers? As it stands, he has been tactical enough to do his dark deeds behind closed doors. How many will die if he purges the Citadel of those remaining who are loyal to our cause? We must not force his hand in this. There are too many factors to consider. One wrong action could spell our demise, and before we even have a chance to act."

"Wise words for any other time, Reaver Ethelwin, but how long is caution the correct course of action? With each passing second we grow, but Sithel grows even stronger. How long must we wait?"

"We wait until the Arbiter decides it is time, and no sooner."

There was a silence, as if this seemed the right course of action for all.

"Let us hope he decides soon then…" said Reaver Unuri.

Reaver Ethelwin spoke again, her soft voice sing-songy as if trying to lighten the mood. "How about the Devari? How fare our numbers with your ilk?"

"We are still split as well," said a deep-voiced man, sounding troubled. "The younglings side with our rebellion, but they are not Sword-Forged. The true might of the Devari still lies in Jian's hands. And he will never lead them against the Citadel. He is a man of duty above all else. Nothing will sway him but the Patriarch's hand, and he is still away on foreign matters."

"And the servants?" asked another.

"Good, *m'lady*. Sithel has not cast his foul eyes to us yet. We have garnered over two dozen to our cause. And a good thing too with our rising numbers! Or we'd never have the ovens working in such force, or beds made—"

"*Beds?*" scoffed a younger voice. "This is ridiculous!"

"Reaver Suntha, watch your words…"

"No. I'll not be silent! I watched two of my brothers die to Sithel and his dark Reavers. Yet here we sit, gossiping about bedpans and cooking when we *need* an army!"

"Enough!" Reaver Ethelwin snapped in return. "It is not Sula's fault. She is doing her best like every one of us. We can only follow the path before us until another is revealed. It is our way. Now, if you are quite finished, we have other matters—"

Feeling guilty, Gray decided not to eavesdrop anymore, and continued forward.

Those in the room saw him, and their conversation halted abruptly.

Several Devari cast salutes while the servants bowed low. Even the male and female Reavers rose and made awkward bows.

Gray swallowed and moved on. None knew how to deal with him upon discovering Ezrah was his grandfather. An Arbiter. Most seemed to flash him looks of fear, respect, but above all, curiosity. He had no spark, and they seemed to be able to read it in him. But he didn't care. Their looks were just a buzzing fly, something he carried beneath a much greater mantle.

But their words troubled him.

War.

He passed a Reaver on the stairs that was gazing out of the two-storied balcony. He paused. Despite Ezrah's warning, Gray reached out with the ki, entering the man's body. He expected a wall. The man was three-striped, but he found nothing. Literally, *nothing*. His mind was not a door left open, there was no door. He seeped into the man's body. He felt the cold metal railing beneath his forearms. As he saw through the Reaver's eyes, people moved below, but the man's gaze was distant. He saw none of it. As if he was no longer alive.

Gray retreated from the man's body with a deep shiver.

With the book under his arm, Gray left, moving outside. It was a lush, green glade split by a running brook and several trees. The neighborhood was upscale by any standards Gray knew. Over the backyard's walls, he glimpsed other large houses, and the street was wide and filled with people adorned in silks and jewels. He hardly felt it was a suitable hideout, but Reaver Meira had assured him that the large house was *normal*, at least by the standards of Farbs. As a whole, he supposed she was right. The tan brickwork of the house, though covered in vines, was relatively plain. The stables on the backside, opposite the dirt street, were no larger than those at the average inn, perhaps even smaller—making the rebel army rather cramped.

Again, his attention turned to the lush backyard.

The dry heat already sucked all moisture from his mouth, yet the glade reminded him vaguely of the Nodes. *Perhaps magic sustains this place?* He sat down on a low stonewall that encircled the glade, needing to think about what was coming.

His hand touched the book in his lap, and he felt strength radiate across his palm. Curious, Gray looked down and saw the book was *glowing* as if alive. Cautiously, he peeled back the thick cover and the warm yellow glow washed across his skin.

"What in the..." he breathed.

Suddenly the words upon the page, once strange and unreadable, were now shifted before his eyes, their lines making sense bit by bit until... He understood it. All of it. And he read.

189 D.L.

Upon these pages are the events succeeding what many have deemed the Final Age—an age that has been shattered by The Betrayal, that of the stolen blade. The ill-famed deed that caused the end of the Everlasting Peace and ushered in our age, nearly leaving the world a ruined heath, an age known by one name only now.

The Lieon.

In the following pages are the accounts of the great war of the Lieon, and of the shattered peace between the nine Great Kingdoms, but mostly here are the stories of the righteous that fought against an unfathomable darkness.

In these pages held by magic, herein lies the true tales of the Ronin...

Yet as the words formed, mouthed upon Gray's lips, the golden glowing letters upon the page took shape, forming a picture that filled his mind, stealing his sight.

He saw a world beautiful and resplendent. Brief flashes of nine grand cities. Scarlet and silver flower petals rained from the air upon cities filled with wealth and prosperity—men, women, and children joyously filling the streets. The Great Kingdom of Water, its grand falls feeding a tiered city of splendor. Moon, a buried gem of a city with thousands of arched tunnels and waterways cast in ever-present sea foam light. Leaf, the Elvin sanctuary full of life and green light, a city suspended in the towering trees. Stone, its walls thicker than buildings and hidden away in a towering field of boulders. Metal, a heaping mass of steel with walls backed against the Mountains of Soot and forges that burn endlessly, the Deep Mines burrowing to the core of the world. Flesh, a sprawling city swarming with life, man, woman, and beast worked to the bone. Wind, a magnificent bastion of spiraling towers, walkways and parapets situated on the windy, impossibly high cliffs of Ren Nar that overlooked the world. Then he saw a glimpse of a familiar city. *Farbs*. The Great Kingdom of Fire. The desert city was twice the size—and each building was not clay, but gilded in gold and greenery. Trees littered all the land, each flowing with pure silver veins. He saw creatures, thousands of them, things he couldn't put a name to, living in the lands, in the bountiful forests, in the rushing rivers that glimmered translucent blue. *The Final Age*.

Flash.

He saw a city of light. The Great Kingdom of Sun. Suddenly he was inside, and he saw a magnificent sword mounted upon a wall in the center of a grand hall. It was guarded by rows upon rows of ironclad warriors, their faces grim as death. Gray saw hidden traps as well, hundreds of them—poison-tipped arrows and countless wards of magic. But his gaze was only for the blade of light. The sword glowed golden—like a sun had been set within the folds of its brilliant metal. It was slender, tip curved, blade straight, and handle arched. Gray marveled at it. It was more a graceful work of art than a blade, but he could sense it was equally deadly. He felt a stab of pain. Suddenly, it was gone. *Stolen*, he knew. The kingdom was in an uproar, the world on edge, looking for the one to blame. War was coming... *The Betrayal.*

Flash.

Next he saw war and bloodshed, corpses stacked upon corpses, so much that he shut his eyes, waiting for it all to stop, but still it came. At last, it ended. *The Lieon.*

Flash.

Then finally, an image came to him.

Nine figures standing upon a rolling green hill.

Cloaks wavering in the winds, each showed the varying symbols of the Great Kingdoms. Gray saw Kail, his red eyes flashing. Each looked the very definition of a legend. Their swords were unsheathed, the color of the blades mimicking their powers, blazing in the morning light as they stood before an army of darkness.

And—

"Mind if I join you?"

The images shattered, and Gray returned back to the world. He turned and saw Zane and snapped the book shut, severing the connection completely. In the dusky light, the fiery man held a bowl filled with a variety of odd-looking fruits. He held the bowl out, and Gray took a few berries, hiding his uncertainty at the weird green dots upon the vivid red skin.

"Gladly," he said, glad for Zane's presence and a distraction from his thoughts.

Zane plopped down at Gray's side and looked ahead, copper eyes squinting at the purple and red striated clouds, as if seeing it all for the first time. "How was your conversation?"

"Good, and yet..."

Zane looked over, curious. Gray didn't know how to explain it. He looked up at the window above, knowing Meira and Ezrah and the others were discussing dark plans about Sithel and the Citadel, and preparing for war.

Ezrah. His grandfather.

"I have family finally. I'm not sure how to even react."

"Happy?" Zane asked. "That'd be a start."

Gray laughed. "You're right. There's still so much I want to know. The man knew who I once was..." As he said the words, he paused. *Wasn't it just recently that I didn't care about that? Who I am now is what matters.*

But who am I now? he wondered. Was such a thing so simple?

The book felt warm beneath his palm still.

A *Ronin*.

Excitement and fear swirled inside him. It was a name that many dreaded, but to Gray, for as long as he could remember, *Ronin* was a name of burning intrigue. And now he was one of them, and not just one, but Kail's progeny—the strongest Ronin. A shiver traced his spine at the thought of such power and responsibility. He lifted his hand, but the nexus flickered in his mind—its flaw glaring. He set it aside.

No, Gray knew his potential, but he was not there. Aside from feeling broken, he feared Kail's legacy. To go insane, to become the dark traitor. He had seen the man. In the end, Kail's motives had been true and good, yet how much did he really know of Kail? All the Ronin had feared him. But what had they feared? How many had known the truth? In the end, Kail had saved the world, but Gray had seen the man's red eyes. They had been filled with power *and* darkness. He knew Morrowil was part of the cause, spawning some of Kail's evil. The blade had nearly conquered Gray as well before he realized that the sword merely manifested the darkness inside him. He could not fall victim to Kail's same dark fears and desires lest Morrowil take control and feed upon it, just as it fed upon his light. But was there more? What had Kail done? Gray's hand gripped the book tighter, fingers cutling around its thick, worn spine realizing that perhaps the answers were closer than he ever imagined. In the end, he was the most powerful Ronin, or at least had that potential inside him. But was that a grand gift or a terrible curse? Or *both?*

In the rare stories that told of Kail's heroism, painting him in an uncommon, favored light, they had blamed his darkness upon the death of those he loved. How much had been laid upon the legend? And worse yet, how much would be burdened upon him? Could he stand the weight of what was to come? He took a deep breath, stopping his trailing questions.

"We can only follow the path before us, until another is revealed."

It was Reaver Ethelwin's words from earlier.

Mura would say much the same. *"Find answers first, think about the questions later."* Gray focused his thoughts, knowing what he had to do. He needed to know what being a Ronin meant, and the book would tell him.

"Well, you're still alive," Zane declared, pulling Gray from his reflections. The fiery man popped a plump berry into his mouth. Then he laughed. "So it seems Arbiters aren't the feared legends the stories say they are. Truth be told, I'm almost a little disappointed." He laughed again with a shake of his head as Gray grabbed another berry. "After all I heard, they almost sounded like the dreaded Ronin."

Gray choked on the berry.

"You all right?" Zane asked, slapping him on the back.

He coughed, clearing his throat. Nearby, two one-stripe male Reavers passed by, talking in hushed tones, moving through the enclosed yard with several servants trailing them. It reminded Gray. "Did you see the Reaver on the stairs?"

Zane grabbed his rusted dagger and began shaving a gnarled root, the black shavings falling to the grass, revealing bright pink pulp. *Is everything in Farhaven so strange looking?* Gray wondered. "The one that looked like the walking dead? I saw him," Zane said offhandedly. "He doesn't talk. Reaver Dimitri. Another told me he lost his brother saving Ezrah."

Gray looked ahead as the boughs swished from a breeze. "We paid a steep price to save Ezrah."

"Great things are not done without sacrifice," Zane said.

"Wise words," he replied, lifting a brow.

"Not mine," the man said. "Another I once considered as close as blood. Father."

Gray nodded, and vowed to remember the sacrifices. Again, his throat clenched thinking of Victasys.

Zane spoke. "I can understand his pain. If I ever lost Hannah…" Rage wormed its way into his voice. He stabbed his dagger into a fuzzy, bulbous piece of fruit.

Hannah. That made Gray think of Ayva and Darius. How long had it been? They were all right, weren't they? Faye would see them safe. But they should have saved Hannah by now, shouldn't they? He saw Zane's concerned features, the angst growing on his tanned face. He gripped the man's tense arm. Zane looked to him, and Gray had trouble not flinching.

"Hannah is alive," Gray said firmly.

The man's expression didn't shift. "How do you know?"

"Because I believe in them," he said with equal fervor, "Darius and Ayva will not fail."

Slowly, Zane's gruff visage broke, and he nodded.

Gray breathed a hidden sigh. He was glad to see the man finally relax, if only a little. "We will just have to wait until they show up. But it won't be long," he added. "Meira has sent out others to search for them, and she positioned sentries nearby Faye's house. There's nothing to be done for it now but trust them and wait. They will return."

"You're right," he said. "But waiting? I've never been known as the patient type."

Gray suddenly rose and turned to Zane who was biting into a fruit, juice spilling around his mouth. The man looked up as Gray unsheathed Morrowil and pointed it at him.

"What's this?" Zane asked, unfazed.

Gray smirked. "Care for a duel?"

"What's a duel?"

"You know, *a duel*. It's like practice fighting."

Zane scratched his head. "What's the pointing of fighting if it's not for life or death?"

"My mind finds reprieve from troubled thoughts when I'm working the forms. A reprieve I think we both could use." Zane's mouth twisted, listening attentively. "Not to mention, it seems inevitable that a war is coming. If so, there are men like Jian that we will have to fight. I think it's time we practice our skills so we are not dwarfed in power."

"Speak for yourself," Zane snapped.

"Do not deny the truth. You saw Jian's strength as well as me."

"The bigger they are, the harder they fall," the fiery man retorted sharply.

Gray lifted a brow. "Then you think you can take him?"

Zane looked uncertain. "Perhaps training is not entirely unwise."

"Then it's a deal. I'll teach you everything I know," Gray said excitedly, "and you teach me all you know. Let's train to be ready for whatever comes." He stuck out his hand, and Zane looked at it hesitantly. "Then again, you can just mope about and grow fat until the others show up. It's your choice."

After a long moment, Zane gruffly wiped his mouth with the back of his arm. Tossing the bowl of fruit on the ground, he rose, showing his intimidating stature. He was not exactly tall, but he was far more muscled than Gray. He rolled his heavy shoulders in a stretch and his thin lips curved, a fire in his eyes. "Everything you know? Sounds fun. That should take a good few minutes. But I suppose training is better than doing nothing, and I could use a small stretch, which is what this sounds like."

Gray smiled and gripped Morrowil tighter. As he opened his mouth to reply, Zane unsheathed his blade, roaring and attacking him more fiercely than a flame roared to life.

Seeking Stillness

Sifting through the streets like a shadow had been Gray's first test. He had only failed once, when he was spotted by guards in a restricted district of Farbs but had escaped with Zane's help. The key, the fiery man had taught him, was believing you didn't exist, which seemed like a sad, strange notion, yet as Gray sat, breathing in the darkness, becoming one with it, he realized Zane was right. Wary Farbian guards passed him a breath away, as if he were no more than a wisp of wind. Zane taught him other tools of stealth as well: how to skulk from toe-to-heel in order to move in utter silence, which shadows were darkest, and how reflections gave one away. The act of hiding was one that Gray thought he would have grown tired of, but learning from Zane was thrilling. The man made it practical, to the point that, when they finished, Gray felt as if he could hide in plain sight. When they were nearly caught by a pair of guards who seemed to be searching for something—*for them,* Gray knew—they had decided to confine their training to the safety of The Tranquil House.

Once there, the man had taught him how to withstand pain, using a boiling cauldron as a test. Attempted, that is. Gray had failed that. The wind had created a thin buffer between him and the molten metal handles every try. But as always, his power had only come out of need.

After that, Gray taught Zane how to work the forms. He had taken to them quickly, almost inhumanely so. It was late in the day now on the second day of their training. The last precious minutes of dusk dwindled fast, and the sky was overtaken by deeper night as Gray faced off with Zane in the courtyard of The Tranquil House.

"Is that all you've got?" Zane called again, standing with his head cocked to one side, as if curious. His blade rested casually in the verdant grass. The pose seemed somehow familiar, as if he'd seen it before, long ago.

Shaking it off, Gray set his stance. That brazen attitude was beginning to wear on him. Worst of all, he knew it wasn't arrogance. Zane was simply confident and as blunt as a hammer—it was all the more infuriating. And he had every right to be confident. The man was a weapon. *Then I will be a weapon as well.* Setting his jaw, Gray attacked again. Morrowil whistled through the dry air. Devari forms seemed to sift back, slowly but surely.

Fisher in the Shallows meets—

"Fisher in the shallows, eh?" the man called as he easily parried the sweeping strikes and slashed at Gray's flank. Gray snarled and sidestepped. *Dancing Crane.* He leapt back. Zane took the opening, lunging forward but Gray had baited it, and his sword cut upwards. Still, Zane was too quick. He smacked Morrowil aside with the flat of his hand and landed his sword a breath away from Gray's throat.

"That's amazing. Your hand… Simply slapping the blade hurt my grip. How did you do that?" Gray said, rubbing his tingling palms.

"Simple. I'll show you," Zane said flatly, and he instructed him, building up speed. Finally, Gray smacked Zane's blade. The man grimaced and breathed through his teeth, massaging his hand. "You're a quick learner."

"But not as quick as you," he answered, truly impressed.

Zane had taken to wearing black pants and a red vest, exposing his arms to the reddish setting sun. Had it really only been one day? Gray felt as if he'd grown stronger in one day than in years of training.

Sounds of the night drifted into Gray's awareness—a babbling brook, insects chirping in the bushes that clung to the walls, and birds singing in the trees. Gray knew many of the birds from Mura's tutelage back in the Lost Woods; the warbles of thrushes, the trill of a nightingale. But there was another. Gray listened, finding peace in the ethereal flute-like call of a red-throated Brenhorn—a bird of Farhaven. It was becoming more like that; names, places, forms, it was all coming back, even quicker now.

He took in The Tranquil House too.

It was a three-storied building with many rooms and shuttered windows with vines that grew along the clay walls. The whole of it sat just off the way from the main thoroughfare. Aside from that, it was altogether common looking—a perfect hideout. It looked like any number of the dozens of buildings placed along the ordinary street.

He looked up to the room where Ezrah was resting. He knew it had only been this morning he'd talked to the man, but it felt like an age ago. The Arbiter was standing by the window, looking out on Zane and Gray, his eye watchful, yet his face seemed grim, as if he was looking beyond them. Gray smiled and his grandfather returned the gesture, looking away once more.

Despite the yard's stillness, preparations seemed to be growing, reaching their peak. Men and women moved about constantly now, Reavers and Devari filling the house until it flowed over like a broken dam. Whispers hung in the air, swords at every hip…

Whatever his grandfather was planning, it was big, and it was coming.

"What's this?" Zane asked abruptly.

Looking back, he saw Zane was holding the book in his hand. The man had opened it, fingers grazing its pages as he bit into a juicy black fruit with his other. A flush of fear shot through Gray, but then he remembered Zane wouldn't be able to read the book.

"The Ronin, huh? Seth sounds kind of impressive."

Gray gawked. "*What?!*"

Zane scratched his jaw with his fruit-filled hand. "'*Seth summons the fire within to conquer the soul of his sword.*'"

"You … can read that?"

"Sure," Zane said, distracted. His eyes narrowed. "This line, it seems different. '*Fire's strength is in its fury. Feed the fury and find your source.*'" Zane seemed to concentrate. Anger swirled in his visage, growing. Suddenly, the fruit in the man's hand burst into flames. He threw it to the ground, now a burnt black husk.

"What'd you just do?"

Zane shrugged. “I don’t know. I just saw a flame in my mind and then that happened… ” He eyed his hand, then shook his head, looking up. “Gray? What’s the look for? Looks like you’ve seen a ghost come to life.”

Gray’s mind stuttered. *A flame in his mind… Just like Darius, a leaf in his mind.* “You…” he began, his mind churned, and then he shook his head at last, “It’s nothing. Give it here. You’re going to get it all dirty.”

Zane snorted, handing the book over. “Whatever you say.”

A bell rung, announcing dinner, and several boys and girls—children of the servants of the House who had come to watch them—turned and ran towards the building, squealing as they played a game Zane had called *ice tag*. Kirin remembered the game distantly.

Zane sheathed his blade sharply, heading to The Tranquil House.

“Where are you going?” Gray asked.

“I’m hungry,” he said, looking back. “We’ve been training for hours on end. Some food and rest will do us good.”

“I cannot eat, not yet. There is a war coming, Zane, and we need to be ready.”

“And we *will* be, but for now, I’m tired and hungry. You can keep training, Gray, but for today, I’m done.” His voice was fire. Not a raging inferno, just a slow burning heat that Gray couldn’t argue with. With that, Zane left him standing alone in the quiet courtyard.

With a sigh, Gray moved to the stone wall and sat. The book lay nearby. Rain began to fall, softly, and he sheltered the book with his threadbare cloak, and saw the symbol of wind once again. It reminded him of his broken nexus. At the same time, in the distance he saw glimpses of the Citadel’s black spires, waiting.

Where was his power? With it, he knew he might be able to save the Citadel, but without it, though he had grown *stronger*, he was still even weaker than Zane. And he wanted to be strong. Yet there was no answer, just the quiet stillness of the night and the pattering of rain on the nearby stones, leaves, roof tiles, and the swish of a night breeze. The moon above hung sullenly, watching him like a pale, glowing eye.

The book felt oddly warm in his hands. And the words Zane had read resonated through his mind. He spoke aloud: “Fire’s strength is in its fury. Feed the fury and find your source.”

The book.

It was an instruction manual.

Hastily and eagerly, Gray peeled back the book's cover. It seemed to open to the proper page as if by magic. On the top of the page was a picture of the symbol of wind and a rough sketch of a creature that looked to be made of flowing wind save for a pair of luminous white horns. He read the words beneath:

Wind.

It is the strongest known element in our world. We do not think of it, but always we are immersed in it. It is everywhere, and it is nowhere. It is the fierce gales of a wrathful hurricane, or a subtle, cooling breeze. It is a contradiction, inexplicable and hard to define, but undeniable in its sheer potency. To wield wind, Kail once spoke to me words that I have never forgotten:

'I must be everything and nothing. Like the wind upon the heights, I find my power in anger and serenity.'

Gray closed the book, snapping the connection. He had seen Kail's face as he read the words—his long, loose, graying hair framing that hard face and those burning scarlet eyes. Suddenly it made sense what the man held in that gaze.

Anger and serenity.

Flash.

Something pulsed inside Gray's head.

Anger and serenity… Peace and rage… Like the wind upon the heights.

The words throbbed through his core, beating like a drum inside his chest.

And in the center, he found stillness.

Gray saw a golden door waiting in his mind. His heart thrummed in anticipation. He reached out, hastily, serenity slipping. The door wavered. Releasing a breath, holding tranquility and burning anger hand in hand, Gray pushed forward.

The door opened, radiant golden light spilling forth.

He saw the nexus, brighter than ever.

It rotated, whole and flawless once more.

Suddenly, Gray realized the rain no longer fell on him, but he still heard its sound, though faintly, as if from behind a windowpane. He felt warmth on his skin and he opened his eyes. All around him, shielding him from the rain and wind, was a sphere of flowing gold.

And Gray knew—his power had returned.

* * *

Gray burst into Zane's room. Despite the dim light, his eyes adjusted, picking out the room's features: a white cot, a bedside table, and an unlit lantern upon the wall. There on the small white cot lay Zane—though now he was simply a mass of flailed limbs, as if he had wrestled with his blanket and lost.

He lit a nearby lantern, and Zane leapt up, sword ringing. Its tip trembled before Gray's neck—not in fear, but in anger. The man's expression was all fire, and in that moment, Gray saw the thief in the man's eyes, the one clinging to life in a world surrounded by darkness. *Such hardness*.

His mood unfettered, Gray ignored the sword. With one hand, he tossed Zane a globular black fruit, shaved to its pink center—it was called Yundar Melon he had discovered, Zane's favorite but far too bitter for his tastes. "Wake up," Gray said, unable to contain his grin.

"What is it? Is Hannah back?" he asked, rubbing his eyes.

Gray shook his head softly. "Not yet. Now, are you ready?"

Zane groaned, flopping back into the bed and tugging his sheets around him into a tight cocoon. "What are you doing? It's still night," he moaned. "Go away. We'll train tomorrow."

Gray said nothing but merely waited, feeling anticipation rise.

Zane feigned sleeping for another few moments than grumbled into his pillow. "I can feel your smug smile on my back, Gray." He rolled back over, eyeing him with his unnerving copper-colored eyes. "What's with that look? So eager for another beating?"

Letting the smile linger, Gray closed his eyes. He reached inside, finding the line between rage and serenity. The balance of *stillness*. The nexus flickered, not as strong as he'd wished, but he did not force it. A thread of wind wormed its way into the cot, gripping the man's covers. Gray yanked. The sheets flew into the air, pulling their load. Zane cried out as he fell onto the floor with a hard thump.

"We've only just begun," Gray announced, and left behind his speechless friend. Hiding the growing smirk, he moved into the dark hall and towards their training area.

* * *

Outside, Gray sat in darkness.

He breathed it in, enjoying the quiet. But still his anger beat a low hum, waiting to be used. And between that line, he knew his nexus waited. He had lit a dozen torches and stuck them into the ground in a circle, creating a small bubble of light. Morrowil sat in his hand, its smooth handle surprisingly tacky to the touch as usual. Above, a waxy yellow moon hung amid a starry sky.

He couldn't see the dark spires of the Citadel in the night, but he felt them. It should have been scary, knowing a war was coming, but Gray instead felt his heart beat in anticipation. *And fear*, he admitted, remembering Victasys, and his heart knotted in memory.

A figure appeared from the darkness, menacing as he strode into the fire's light. "A clever move. You can use your power at will again?" Zane asked, walking out of the dark and into Gray's circle.

Zane stood bare-chested, his red vest cast aside, his hair stuck up in a crazy array, reminding Gray of Darius, only blond. "We'll have to see," he replied. "I've brought you out here to answer that very question." Gray let the nexus fill him, and golden threads filled his hand, bright in the dark night. With it he grabbed the torches that burned in the ground, carefully twirling them in the air, as if they were lanterns held by invisible hands. He dropped them back to the ground. "I can't lift anything very heavy. Not yet at least."

"Well, if you brought me out here, I suppose it's to show me more than a few dancing flames," Zane said.

"It's time for one final fight," Gray answered.

Zane grinned in the light of the fires. "Then let's get it over with."

With that, they charged at one another. Wherever his blade slashed, Zane's sword was there. *Under the Bridge*—it was an upward slash that ducked beneath his opponent's cut. Zane met it with *Guardian's Garrote*—parrying and slashing, trying to take Gray's back. Their blades flickered as they moved about the courtyard. Quickly, Gray's exhaustion caught up with him, sweat beaded and dripped into his eyes.

Zane called out the moves Gray had taught him. *"Down the Hill! Falling Sky! Clean the Blade meets The Dragon's Fang! Two Hands*

Clasp!" His sword hammered down, and Gray backpedaled under the man's attacks, each one feeling like a mountain crashing down. But still he waited. He needed to know if he could summon it when it truly mattered. "You are stronger than this!" Zane called. "Show me your true strength!" The words were just like Faye's upon the desert, teaching him the sword and si'tu'ah.

Anger and stillness.

Zane's sword pounded down at last, nearly reaching Gray's neck.

The nexus pulsed.

He embraced it, not out of need, but willingly, calmly. Warmth and light flowed through him, and he felt his limbs suddenly coated—a thin, white wind flowed over his body. Zane's blows became less heavy, and Gray's arms, less leaden. Abruptly, Gray stopped his retreat. Shock showed in the fiery man's features as he held Zane's parry with ease, swords gnashing, sparks flying. A thin smile crossed Gray's face ... and he attacked. Zane barely had time to block as Gray's sword whipped. He cut at the man's arms, legs, head, and torso, almost all at once. His limbs moved, almost too fast for him to handle.

Suddenly a burst of fire flew forth.

Gray ducked, stunned. His vision returned, and he saw Zane.

Small flames still dancing from his fingertips, Zane looked confused, almost apologetic. He opened his mouth, but Gray didn't give him a chance, lunging with his sword and crying out. The wind powered his strike—*Boar Charges down the Hill.* Zane parried in the nick of time, and flames roared to life across the fiery man's sword. The two blades clashed, flame and wind dancing. But it was Gray who was stronger now, his blade inching closer to Zane's face.

Gray smiled. Anger and serenity thundered inside him. "Admit defeat!"

Zane snarled, fury dancing in his eyes, but beneath that was a smile. "Never." And he cried out, flinging his hands. Gray cursed, leaping back as a fountain of fireballs hurtled forth, flying out of the dark night. Fear flushed through him when a memory struck him. *Dragons descending from all sides upon a golden walkway. Shields of golden wind, hovering in the air between the rushing villagers and the horrible clawed beasts. The shields…!* his mind shouted. He conjured those threads again, and the fiery orbs clashed with the shields of wind. *One, two, and three…* Each ball of fire exploded, weakening the wind until… The shield shattered. Yet another ball of fire raced through the air. Gray shot out his other hand. A bolt of wind imploded the fire and sped towards Zane's head. The man growled and threw himself flat then he slapped his hand upon the ground and a line of flames roared, scorching grass and racing towards Gray. He began to thread a shield but—*It's too much to stop with a shield!* his nexus shouted.

It can speak? Gray felt fear and confusion.

The nexus flickered as his serenity wavered but he held on. Rage welling, he envisioned a spear, one made of wind. He threw his arm forward and a strange, giant lance of wind rushed forth. It doused the flames but didn't stop. The gust barreled into Zane, who had just gotten back up, and threw the man from his feet. Gray closed his eyes. He felt threads form around him, thick and complicated. He knew the threads, but they were not easy to wield. His anger and stillness trembled. He held the two tight, refusing to let go and…

The nexus pulsed.

Suddenly, he stood over Zane. He'd *shifted*—moving from one place to another in the blink of an eye. His sword hovered above the man's throat. "Do you concede?"

Zane's eyes were uncommonly wide. "How… How did you do that?"

"It's a skill of the Devari," he lied.

Then, slowly, Zane grinned and Gray extended his hand. Zane took it, rising to his feet. "Either way, *that* is what I call training," the man said, looking invigorated.

At his words, Gray's legs trembled. Zane caught him before he fell, and then helped him to sit upon a nearby stone bench.

"You all right?" he asked gruffly.

Gray nodded. He was. He was elated even. He'd never felt more right. Though *shifting* took a lot out of him. It was not an ability he could use often, not until he got stronger. Still, his power… It *was* back! He had summoned things he had conjured before, upon the Gates and in the desert, even new things. *What was that spear?* He had envisioned a lance, and it had come. Could he create anything he saw in his mind? If so, wind seemed limitless. Inside his mind, the nexus floated, golden and whole once more. There were no blemishes or cracks, but a swirling ball of pure wind.

Anger and stillness.

He held out his hand and the wind that flowed across his arms channeled itself into a single dense ball of white air, churning upon his upturned palm like a globe of living wind, brilliant and white in the dim night.

He looked up and saw Zane's face turn suddenly pale in the flickering flames.

"What is it?" Gray asked.

"Your eyes…" Zane breathed.

"What about them?"

"See for yourself."

Gray held up Morrowil. Despite the darkness, he saw his eyes in the blade's reflection. There was no pupil, just spheres of swirling white, like the wind within his hand. He nearly gasped, dropping the blade. Instead, his concentration slipped. Serenity and anger left him in a rush. The white wind coating his body vanished, leaving a chill through him as it dissipated in the air. Gray watched as his eyes returned to their normal gray-green.

"What are you?" Zane asked. He wore a look of burning curiosity.

Can I tell him? Is it safe? Or does the man fear Ronin like all others? He answered at last, honestly, "I'm still trying to figure it out myself. I'll tell you when I find out." But as he said the words, Gray didn't fear the uncertainty and mystery that was his future. He was Kail's progeny, but he knew he would never be Kail.

They sat on the nearby bench, exchanging a skin of water. How long had they battled for? It was still a deep night, but he felt the chill in the air soften—was that also a skill of the Ronin or Devari? He wondered if it would be difficult to decipher the two. He figured wind was Ronin and Devari was anything with ki, but perhaps the two would overlap.

Regardless, a slow fog rolled in.

Dawn was coming.

And with that, war.

"Gray… Do you think we're strong enough to take Jian?" Zane asked into the night, unexpectedly.

"I'm not sure," he answered honestly. "I hope so."

"With the way the Devari look at us now, and especially now that you've got your power back, I doubt an average brother or even low ranking Reaver will be a problem. But Jian… Thieves have told fearful tales of his prowess. They say even Darkeye is afraid of the man."

It was true. Gray felt different. With each passing moment they each had grown faster and stronger. *But Jian seems special,* Gray thought. *He seems* more *than a man.* "We will just have to see," he said at last.

"I will see Jian's blood upon my hands before this is done. He will pay, just as Darkeye will pay for laying a hand upon my sister."

Gray felt the same anger, and he swore, "Victasys' sacrifice will not be in vain." He looked over and saw Zane's eyes were swirling with thoughts. He knew he was thinking about his sister. He couldn't blame the man. His own thoughts kept drifting to Ayva and Darius. But he wouldn't allow himself to think anything negative. He knew.

They were alive.

They had to be…

The Pit of Despair

"We're almost there," Faye announced.

Darius breathed a thin sigh. He watched Faye's back as she moved like a predator through the cavernous tunnels. As they moved, red glimmered eerily off the woman's armor from the strange red rocks embedded in the dark, stone walls.

"What are those?" Darius asked as they moved.

"*Bloodstones*," Faye said from ahead.

"I've never seen anything like them," Ayva said. "Are they valuable?" Her white shirt and gold vest looked out of place in their grim surroundings, but she moved at Darius' side with confidence. Her hair was pulled back from her face, exposing her delicate features. A light burned in her eyes as she watched their surroundings.

"They are more valuable than gold. It is what Darkeye uses to fuel his small war against Farbs and the Citadel. They are only found deep beneath the earth."

"More than gold…" Darius breathed, and reached out, wanting to touch them.

Faye was suddenly gripping his wrist. He gasped in pain. How was she so strong? "Don't," she snapped. "Bloodstones are incredibly dangerous."

"Why?" Darius asked. "They don't look so dangerous."

"On their own, the stones hold no magic, but to one with the spark, someone like you… Put simply, they can accomplish great and terrible things. If you are an Untamed, there's no telling what your magic might do to it. Simply touching one could ignite these Bloodstones and cause an explosion that would kill us all. Or they could simply fizzle into dust. If you wish to live, I would advise against using your power down here."

Darius shivered, yanking his hand back as if seared. "Why does everything in this forsaken land have to be so damned dangerous? Let's save Hannah and get out of this cursed pit already," he ordered, moving forward. He watched as Ayva put her hands to her side as if that would prevent her from causing any trouble as they continued.

Ahead, the tunnels seemed to breathe darkness, and Darius felt a cold wind hit him. He reached out to his leaf, but then hesitated, remembering what Faye had said. The bloodstones could ignite and kill them all. Something in the ground felt *wrong*.

They moved onward, snaking their way deeper into the tunnels. Bloodstones now littered the walls, ceiling and even the ground, shining iridescently, their glassy surface casting them all in shades of red. Still, deeper they wound themselves, the tunnels narrowing.

As they moved, Darius heard the trickle of water and, beneath that, a faint scraping noise. It echoed off the jagged walls. "What is that?"

"We're beneath the entrance of Farbs, the Southern Gate. Water pipes run throughout these tunnels, leading up to the surface," she explained. They continued, turning a corner, and Darius froze.

Ahead was a grand, circular chamber. In the murky half-light, Darius made out a domed ceiling high above, reaching for the surface—but it was unlike any roof he had ever seen. It *glistened*. In the dim light, it appeared as though made of water, as if a dark lake was suspended above them. The walls, though also far away, were engraved with huge, strange runes the size of buildings. The floor was empty save for more unfamiliar carvings, white unpolished marble, and the occasional glittering bloodstone sprouted from its surface reminded him of little red eggs. Dim, glistening light hung in the air, touching everything faintly. Darius squinted. In the center of the grand white floor, was a curious black pit.

"Dice…" Ayva whispered, neck craning to take it all in.

Dice, indeed, he thought.

"I never thought to see something like this in such a dark hole," Ayva said, eyeing the floor. "These are words, aren't they?"

Faye nodded. "Of an ancient language said to exist during the time of the Ronin."

Each scrawled letter was thick enough for a stream to run through. *If they are words,* Darius thought, *they must've been written by a giant's chisel, for they are enormous.* "What exactly is this place?" he asked.

"No one knows exactly," Faye replied. "Both the chamber and the pit have stood since the origin of Farbs, perhaps even before, built during the first age. I often wonder at the purpose of this place for the people of old, but whatever it was, it is now lost. Darkeye has twisted it—just like all things he touches. Come. The prison is at the far end of the chamber."

Swiftly, they moved across the grand, white floor, passing by the pit. Darius slowed. The others continued on swiftly, but he felt strangely *pulled. What is this feeling?* Cursing his curiosity, he edged closer. The scraping sound came from within, and it grew louder with every

step. His heart rapped against his ribcage as he stared into the black abyss while red bloodstones glittered in the depths.

He felt a hand on his shoulder and nearly leapt out of his skin, and then he saw Ayva's face, blue eyes pinched with worry. "We can't stop, Darius, we have to save Hannah."

"Come," Faye ordered, "we must not linger here."

Darius heard the words, feeling their urgency, but he felt inexplicably drawn to the pit, like a gambler's hand to dice. *Why is this here and what is this feeling?* Ayva hesitated too, drawing closer, and she reached out.

Faye snatched Ayva's wrist, shaking her head. "I wouldn't. There is a reason this is called the Pit of Despair. Darkeye uses this hellish hole for any who disobey him."

From within the pit, something shifted in the darkness. It rasped. *Breathing.*

"*What* ... what's down there?" he asked fearfully.

Faye's grip tightened on her sword. "Remember the Darkwalkers?"

"You mean those black creatures back in the desert?" Ayva asked.

"*Those* demonic spawn?!" Darius cursed. "They nearly killed us!"

The scratching and rasping continued, the red lights shadowing as the creature roiled in the darkness, moving as if restless ... as if hungry. "And they would have succeeded too if it weren't for Gray. Now come," Faye insisted, "This place is not safe. We must not stay here long."

They continued onward.

Darius followed, forcefully pulling himself away from the pit.

Why would Darkeye keep such a beast? And he remembered his father's words, *'Evil begets evil, lad. Never trust.'* He shook his head. No, his father had been wrong before. Perhaps the creature was simply misunderstood. Being kept down there endlessly... A dark life indeed. All beasts need to feed, don't they? He scoffed. *Wishful thinking, Darius,* he thought with a shiver. He remembered those dark, flailing limbs from back then. That thing *was* evil. *Then why did I feel drawn towards that pit?*

"Darkwalkers, what are they exactly?" Ayva asked as they walked beneath the grand domed chamber, heading towards the far wall.

"An odd time to ask questions, girl," Faye said, but she answered regardless. "Darkwalkers are creatures of terrible magic. They kill by sapping the spark from anything they touch. Nothing can cut through their black skin save for *phoxes*, beings of light created to balance the Darkwalkers."

"Phoxes? You mean those things we saw before?" Ayva asked. "Those white creatures in the cages?"

Faye nodded.

Darius shivered, remembering the main cavern with its swarm of thieves and cages full of outlandish beasts—gryphons and the like. "Wait, I don't get it," he said. "If Darkeye has so many phoxes, why not simply use them to kill all Darkwalkers and then be rid of the whole lot of 'em?"

"Impossible," Faye said. "As Primordial Beings, neither can be controlled so easily. As I told you before, phoxes follow a Matriarch. She is their queen. Only the one who can bond the Matriarch can control the phoxes. A *destined* one," she scoffed, "or so the stories say. Otherwise, phoxes are nearly as dangerous and unpredictable."

Ayva shook her head. "Why would the world spawn such evil?"

Faye sniffed. "This world is full of magical creatures, some dark, and some light. Is it your place to judge what is good and what is evil?" Ayva opened her mouth, just as Faye cut her off, announcing, *"We're here."*

* * *

The prison was not much more than a black stone hollow at the far edge of the huge vaulted chamber—the open space made Darius' stomach queasy, knowing they could both see who was coming and be seen with equal ease. Rusty metal bars were embedded into the cavity and inside the jail cell he saw only darkness.

"This is it?" Darius questioned fearfully. "I don't see her."

"Hannah?" Ayva called.

Shadows twisted, and a small voice sounded. "Who's there?"

Ayva strode forward. Dappled light shone down upon them from a gap in the chamber's ceiling high above, making her appear divine. Something about the image of Ayva in the light felt familiar to Darius. "Hannah? Is that you? You can come out now. It's all right."

"Who are you? What in the blighted hell do you want with me?" the small voice called from the darkness.

Darius sighed. "That's Zane's sister all right."

Ayva cuffed his arm, and he grumbled, then the voice spoke. "Did you say … Zane?" The girl stepped into the half-light but not huddled and afraid like Darius was expecting. Though caged, she stood straight and fierce like lightning placed inside a bottle. She had flaxen hair and a soft round face, but there was a fire in her. "My brother… Is he alive?"

"He's alive," Darius said. Then grumbled inwardly. *I don't think he can die. That angry fool took on a whole inn full of thieves.*

Hannah breathed a sigh of relief.

Faye moved forward, extracting a key from a series upon her belt and unlocked the heavy bolt. Ayva rushed inside. "Hannah, we're friends of your brother—we've come to rescue you, but there is not much time..."

Darius entered the prison when he felt the ground shudder beneath him. *What was that?* Unshackling his manacles, he knelt, touching the cold stone floor. Footsteps thundered, approaching. Fear gripped his heart. He touched Ayva's arm. "We have to leave *now*. Hannah"— he turned to the young girl— "are you ready?"

She bobbed her head, snatching a tattered jacket from the ground.

Metal clanged.

They twisted to see Faye.

Instinctively, Darius lunged for the bars. Faye quickly twisted her key with a terrifying *click*. Confusion and anger flooded through him. He reached for her, but she nimbly leapt back. Standing on the outside of the hollow, Faye's expression was unreadable—only the white of her eyes gleamed from within the shadows of her hood.

"Faye?" Ayva questioned. "What on earth are you doing?"

The two women joined him at his side.

"What's going on?" Hannah asked. "Who is this woman?"

"Faye … unlock this door," Darius said slowly, as he calmly gripped the bars.

"I'm afraid I can't do that, dear rogue," Faye said.

Darius felt Ayva tense at his side.

He swallowed. "And why exactly not?"

"You see, I wasn't always at your side. When I told you I had tried to abandon my past, that wasn't the whole truth," Faye said.

"No," Ayva breathed.

"Open this door!" Darius shouted.

Faye ignored them. "It's a funny thing, trust, isn't it?" As she spoke, she unsheathed one of her many daggers, tossed it into the air and caught it by the blade repeatedly. "Life is a dance with fate. We think ourselves smarter or faster than her, but always … in the end…" She tossed the dagger high. It twirled. She caught it by the blade, but, due to the angle, the dagger's edge cut into her palm. "She wins." Faye's expression didn't shift as she eyed the blood upon her hand, as if resigned.

Darius twisted as the sound of clapping echoed through the chambers. A figure appeared, dozens of dark thieves at his back, and there was no doubt in Darius' mind as to who it was. Wearing shreds of black cloth about his slender frame, and a black mask from which blond tufts of hair stuck out, the demon thief approached.

"Darkeye…" Darius cursed.

"Name recognition," Darkeye said in a grating voice like a blade slowly unsheathed from a tight scabbard. "My, my. I feel important." The thief leader stopped before the cage. "Well done, my dear. I am proud of you." With the back of his fingers, he stroked

Faye's cheek compassionately.

Faye shirked his touch like poison, but replied in a low hiss, "I live to serve."

"Yes, well, perhaps unwillingly for now. But the glory days of old will return, and you will realize that I have only your best interests at heart," he declared. But Faye didn't answer. Darkeye looked back to the cage, hand resting casually upon the blade at his hip. "These are the two you mentioned?"

"As promised," Faye replied.

Darius' blood boiled, but he tried to conceal his rage. He held his leaf-blade close, hiding it behind his back, preparing himself.

"Greetings," said Darkeye in an infuriatingly calm voice, eyeing them in the shadows like a hungry beast. He waved to his thugs. "I'd like to see our guests of honor in the light of the cavern. Bring them out, and don't forget to take the young man's sword that he's attempting to hide, and so poorly."

The hulking thugs barreled in, grabbing Darius before he could swing his blade. They yanked his arm behind his back, and he cried out in pain as he was thrown to the ground, sword points aimed at his neck. When his blind fury died, he saw Ayva was nearby, and his blade sat a dozen paces away.

A thug moved to grab it. The huge man with a curly head of hair and barrel-like arms snatched the handle and immediately cried out in agony, falling to his knees. He continued to shudder, trying to let go of the leaf-shaped blade, his scarred muscles roiling like snakes moving beneath his skin. At last, he keeled over, silent.

Another of Darkeye's men touched the man's throat and backed away, shaking his head. *Dead*, Darius realized. The other minions looked to Darius with snarls of anger and confusion, and he felt hope rise inside of him. "What … what kind of trickery is this?" said a big thug, eyeing the dead thief and the quiet green blade.

"Go ahead," Darius taunted, looking to Darkeye. "Take it."

Calmly, Darkeye pulled off his mask. Darius fought to not look away. Darkeye's face was that of an almost ordinary man, with blond hair and a white scar that ran across his nose, cheek and over his eye. But there was no mistaking the aberrant strain of darkness within him … a murderous hunger that shone in the man's auburn eyes. "Leave the blade," he instructed then looked back to Darius. "If you think that a blade of magic is something to fear, then you are in for quite the treat, boy. I shall give you your first lesson on true terror."

Darius felt a smirk rise, but he bit off a retort as he saw Faye's expression. For a moment he thought he saw her features shift, mouth twitching in fear. But then it was gone, and her expression was almost bored once again. "If I'm done here..." she began, moving away.

"Stay," Darkeye ordered harshly. "I wish for you to watch this."

Darkeye led the way, and Faye and his guards followed, escorting Darius and Ayva back to the center of the chamber where the pit sat, leaving Hannah behind in her prison.

Darkeye pulled a glimmering bloodstone from the chamber's white floor and held it in his hand. He stalked nearer to the dark pit as he spoke, "Bloodstone is truly fascinating. Did you know in every Devari's blade a fragment of bloodstone is kept? It's what gives their swords that brilliant blaze when they embrace their ki and allows their blades to slice through weaker steel and even magic." With a sharp ring, the man unsheathed his blade. It blazed brilliantly in the light streaming from above. The blade looked familiar, and Darius realized it was just like Victasys. Just then, Darkeye twisted slightly and he stiffened. *His cloak...* It was made of bloodied, patchwork scraps of nearly a dozen crossed-swords sewn together, emblems of the Devari cloaks.

Darius gagged, as he saw bits of flesh still caught in the cloak's fabric. "You're a monster," he voiced.

Darkeye looked back, lifting his sword to Darius' throat. "A monster? No, I'm an animal, as we all are, but I am simply the strongest of them. There is no crime in strength, Darius, only weakness."

"Weakness is not a crime," Ayva whispered softly.

"What did you say?"

"You lie," she hissed.

All gazed at her, a silence setting over the black cavern. The other Darkeye officers sent cruel stares toward Ayva's small, huddled form. Her head was bent, brown hair falling around her face.

Darkeye sniffed. "Nature does not lie, girl. The truth is, we are simply beasts, and I am the strongest of those beasts. *Pity. Sympathy.* These are words that breed weakness into an already pathetic world, a world that— "

"—Enough!" Ayva interrupted angrily, looking up. "Your words are sickening, like a poison that festers, taking the guise of truth. '*Weakness is death, strength life…*'" Ayva spit at Darkeye's black boots, and Darius hid a surprised grin. Ayva's one-eyed guard snarled and raised his hand to slap her, but Darkeye gripped the man's wrist like lightning, stopping him. Ayva's voice gained strength with every word. "That rhetoric may work for those with darkness and a lust for power *already* in their heart. But the truth is you are wrong."

"Tell me then, girl," Darkeye said quietly, "how am I wrong?"

"'Weakness is death, strength is life.' That's wrong. Your clan spews those words, but they are too mindless to see that there is strength in sacrifice, and power in compassion. Your limited definition of the word 'strength' is what blinds you to the ultimate truth."

Darkeye half-smiled dangerously. "What truth is that?"

"Ayva," Darius said, warily. "Don't…"

But Ayva's voice rang with clarity and the light of veracity as she spoke. "The truth that your creed is a lie, and fodder for only the truly weak, the truly pathetic."

"That's quite a speech," Darkeye said calmly, but Darius saw rage welling behind his eyes, like a furnace of hatred.

"It's only the truth," Ayva replied.

"Is it now? *Sacrifice… Compassion…*" Darkeye spit the words out like venom, all the while circling the pit, his sickening Devari cloak fluttering behind him. "This bickering is growing tiresome. You say you speak the truth? Then I wish to be enlightened."

"What are you talking about?" Darius questioned.

"Let's play a game and test *your* truth… your beliefs against mine to determine who is right once and for all. Fitting words in the end, don't you think? *Sacrifice and compassion.*" With that, he nodded to his guards who grabbed Ayva and pushed her before the black abyss.

"No!" Darius cried. "*Don't!*"

"Show me the power of your weakness," he said and waved his hand.

Her eyes flashed wide, and the guards shoved her forward. Ayva fell, tumbling into the black pit, and a crash echoed in the darkness—the sound of bones snapping.

Horror flooded Darius.

He stared over the dark lip, frozen in shock.

Darkeye smiled at him, calmly. "Well? What are you going to do now?"

Darius snarled. He was an arm's length away from Darkeye's throat, close enough that he could grab the man.

He twisted. *His sword.* It lay paces away—*too far.* Just then, the shadows in the pit flickered.

The beast was stirring. Darius stared into the pit, terror growing.

Darkeye smirked. "What are you waiting for?"

Darius cursed. With a cry, he leapt. Air whistled around him as he hurtled into the darkness—in a flash, he remembered a dark night, leaping from Lakewood's tall roofs to escape a game of dice gone wrong. He'd tensed upon impact and had broken his leg.

Don't tense.

He relaxed and hit the ground. And the floor *cracked.*

Darius looked around. In the dim, glittering red light from the bloodstones, he saw what he had landed upon. Bones. Thousands of them. They had dulled the blow of his fall. In the murky light, Ayva knelt nearby, looking dazed. He rushed to her side and pulled her up.

"You all right?" he asked.

She gripped his arm as the darkness *shifted.* "I'm guessing you didn't have a plan?"

He shook his head. "This was as far as I got..."

And the darkness hissed, dark red gleaming off the angular blackness. He glimpsed the sheen of long, black claws. Swiftly, Darius reached for his blade but his hand felt air.

He cursed and spoke, "When I say, dive..." he began.

The beast screeched and leapt.

"Dive!" he yelled.

He crashed into more bones as the beast skittered, hurtling into the wall in a dark explosion. Quickly, Darius leapt to his feet. The beast turned. It stood near a patch of glistening red bloodstone, their dim light hinting at the creature's full form. It was monstrously huge, that much was clear—nearly brushing the walls and twice again as tall as Darius. Its skin looked like undulating black metal, but instead of reflecting the dim light, it *absorbed* it. Upon its back and arms were huge black protrusions like bladed fins. It watched him, its dozen pairs of eyes shining an even more ominous red.

"Ayva…" he breathed, seeing the creature had cornered her and was stalking nearer for the kill. Ayva pressed herself against the bloodstones, as if looking for a way out. Then, he realized … the bloodstones. Ayva realized it too. She pried a nugget of red from the wall and hurled it at the beast. The red glowed brighter, as if feeding off her power, and then collided with the beast in an explosion of fire. The Darkwalker shrieked.

"*More!*" Ayva yelled.

And Darius pried a huge stone from the wall, felt it grow warm in his hands and hurled it at the beast's back with all his strength. It burst, lighting the pit in fiery embers, searing the creature's black flesh. The Darkwalker snarled in rage and pain, and twisted to him. Yet if it was wounded, it didn't show it. It stalked forward, eyes glinting with the hunger for blood.

"Dice," he cursed, stumbling back, "bad idea..."

"Darius!" Ayva shouted, throwing more bloodstones. The red gems burst upon the creature's back. A burning smell, like putrid meat, hung in the air. He saw holes form in the creature's flesh, but then vanish, its black skin turning smooth once more. He gulped as the creature neared, ever closer.

And he shouted, "Ayva! It's not working!"

Darkeye cackled above them, "Fools! Darkwalkers cannot be killed by anything from this world. Bloodstones are useless!"

The Darkwalker hissed, and the stench of a grave filled the pit. The creature reared up onto its many legs and lunged, slicing at his neck. Darius ducked out of instinct and the claw scraped over his head.

"I will not die this way!" he roared and reached up his hand.

Something pulsed in his head.

The Leaf.

But Faye said the spark couldn't be used down here. Yet there it was. And something else as well…

His sword.

The Darkwalker reared up, ready to finish what it started, and its mass of limbs and gleaming claws flashed, cutting from all angles. Darius cried out, pulling upon the Leaf. He lifted up his hand, *feeling* the sword, as if it was an arm, waiting to be used.

Come to me, he whispered.

And it came.

He felt it whirl through the air, end over end, faster and faster—a cry shouted from above as the sword flew through Darkeye's guards and descended into the pit, racing through the darkness and finally slamming into the heel of his hand. The Darkwalker lunged, pincers plunging for him, a breath away. Darius sliced and bellowed in fear. The leaf-blade gleamed its emerald sheen as it sluiced through the darkness.

Contact.

The creature's beady red eyes flashed in confusion as its black flesh parted, his sword cleaving it in two. The dark beast let out a sickening gurgle, and the two halves fell, crashing against the bones in the reddish light, and then vanishing into nothing. *Just like the Nameless…* he remembered from long ago, the fearsome nightmare that Kail had killed.

Quickly, he rushed to Ayva's side. Reaching out a hand he helped her up, bones rattling beneath them. "Are you all right?"

She nodded. "A few bruises but no more," she said and shivered. "You?"

He checked himself in the dim light then remembered Faye's words: *a Darkwalker's touch is death.* He held back a shiver of his own. "Guess we'd know, right?"

"*Impressive,*" a voice called from above.

Both turned to see the outline of Darkeye standing upon the pit's precipice.

Darius called angrily, "Is that proof enough for you?"

Darkeye's voice echoed back, "Ah, but you broke the rules."

"What are you talking about?" he shouted.

"The sword. It was clearly cheating. The strength was supposed to be your own, and not the magic of a sword."

Darius' fist clenched at his side, "You dicing scum!" he yelled furiously. "The sword was mine. I summoned it with my own strength! You—" And he felt Ayva's fingers on his arm tighten. "*What?*" he said angrily, turning toward her. Despite the darkness, he thought he saw her eyes shining, a faint golden hue.

"He's trying to bait you to talk about the sword," she whispered, and then called, "We passed your test and more. Now let us go!"

"Sadly, I cannot do that. Sithel's gold does not entice me, but you two do, and so does your sword. Lucky for you, I've a heart of *gold*," he said, and Darius could almost *feel* his sly sneer. "As such, I shall give you two choices: a life with the clan, or a noble death, your last hours spent hungry, alone and mired in darkness. Choose wisely. The pit will give you time to contemplate your choices. Alas and woefully, this is where we part for now. There's a war coming, and I must make preparations. Come, *Diaon*, say your goodbyes."

War? Darius wondered. *What the dice is he talking about?*

Faye approached the edge of the pit. In the faint light, Darius thought he saw her face—*sorrow?* Could it be? Smoothly, the woman sheathed her blade with a hard click and spoke. "Farewell, my friends."

"Wait!" Ayva called. The woman froze. "You have a choice."

"Sometimes we simply can't outrun the wrongs we've done. Sometimes we don't have a choice."

"*Sunha*... You can't leave us here!"

"Leave you?" she echoed, amused. "A curious choice of words, wouldn't you agree? Fate truly has a cruel sense of humor," she said and turned away. "A piece of advice for the road," speaking over her shoulder, her voice echoed into the darkness around them. "Treasure family, for it is all you will ever really have, for good or worse. Safe travels, my dear companions, in this realm or the next."

With that she was gone.

* * *

As Darkeye's men followed with their torches, Darius watched the light upon the cavern's ceiling dwindle and then vanish altogether. And darkness, deeper than ever before, pressed in on them, the bloodstones flickering. The leaf-blade's green glow winked out of existence. He shivered and hugged his rags tighter.

He felt Ayva huddle nearer, her warmth giving him comfort.

"Well, what now?" he asked. "Got any bright ideas?"

Bright ideas? You're a genius, Darius.

"Why thank you," he answered, speaking to the darkness. "My intellect is often undervalued and, frankly, deserves a bit more respect."

"What are you talking about?" Ayva asked. "I didn't say anything."

"Sure you did, you said—" Darius froze, realizing she was right. She hadn't spoken. He tensed, and her hand felt it. "It can't be..."

"Darius? What is it?" Ayva asked, sounding nervous.

"I ... think I just heard your thoughts."

In the dim, red light, he thought he saw her raise a brow. "Darius, that's impossible..."

"I swear I heard something," he said. "Watch, try it again."

"Fine," she said. And there was a gap of silence. The darkness seemed to hum, and he thought he heard another scratch as if from another Darkwalker, but he knew it was just his imagination. His fear. At last, Ayva spoke, "Well? Did you hear any of that?"

He shook his head.

"Darius?"

He realized she couldn't see him. Clearing his throat, he replied, "No, I couldn't." *Odd... I could have sworn...*

"Perhaps the darkness is simply getting to you," she said.

"Maybe," he answered uncertainly.

"C'mon, we can figure it out later," Ayva said, gripping his arm reassuringly. "For now, we better find a way out of this pit or we'll be another one of these bones when Darkeye returns. If only we had more light..." Just then, a tiny spark bloomed in the darkness, like a pinpoint of gold in an otherwise black sky. It grew, slowly, illuminating Ayva's delicate features and dappled freckles. Darius saw her grin of triumph, and then her face went slack.

"Ayva? What is it?" he asked.

Ayva lifted her arm, pointing at something across the pit. Darius turned and his jaw dropped.

Upon the wall, in flowing, huge letters, words glowed. A script carved into a huge bloodstone set into the wall. Where Ayva's golden light touched, the letters burned brightly as if yellow flames were contained within the deep red stone. "What is this?" Darius breathed.

The script was foreign and strange to Darius, but the longer he looked, the more it began to make sense to him. He squinted, mouthing it out, but Ayva was quicker, and she read:

"THE RIDDLE OF FIRE

The three will become four:

Four for the warrior of fire

Whose strength is fueled by ire.
But all will fall upon the sands,
If *nature* does not find the balance.
For only the fated bonder of Light
Can slay the undying Dark."

"What does it mean?" he asked, scratching his itchy stubble.

"I … I'm not sure," she said, hands playing over the runes. "But it's prophecy for sure, and it's definitely ancient."

"Faye said this place was created before Farbs was even here," he said. "Not that we can exactly trust that traitor."

"Something tells me this time she's not far off."

Darius whistled through his teeth. "If that's true, then these words have been around since like … *the beginning of time*." He realized Ayva had grown silent. She stood a breath away from the wall, the orb pulsing within her hand. Her eyes were transfixed upon the words. It was a brilliant sight, he admitted. He felt his heart race inside his chest, as if those burning letters were calling to him. But something about the prophecy seemed to pull at her even stronger.

"C'mon, Ayva," he voiced, breaking her trance. "We gotta get out of here."

"Your power?" she asked.

He nodded and closed his eyes, reaching into his mind, but the Leaf was nowhere to be seen. "I … I don't think I can conjure it unless in need," he admitted, embarrassed.

"Well, did you try concentrating?" Ayva said.

He grit his teeth in annoyance. "What did you think I was doing? Closing my eyes to take a nap? I *tried* concentrating. Besides, something tells me even if I could there's no vines or roots anywhere near to aid us this time."

"Then we're trapped…"

"Not yet," he replied in a growl. "Besides, it wouldn't be fun if it was easy." Strapping his sword to his back once more, he leapt, trying to grab onto the gleaming red bloodstones. His fingers slipped free, absent of purchase. The rocks were too small and smooth for a handhold. Stubbornly, he leapt again.

"It's useless, Darius..." Ayva said. "Save your energy. We might need it."

Darius ground his teeth and continued until he was sweating and his arms and legs grew limp, and he knew his fingers were bleeding. *I just need to jump higher... maybe some bloodstones are thicker up there...* He grit his teeth and leapt off a bone, but it snapped beneath his weight. He tripped, cutting his hand on sharp bloodstone and falling hard onto the damp earth.

"Darius..."

"What am I supposed to do, Ayva?" he breathed. "Just wait until Darkeye comes back to finish us off? I—" he panted, throwing the splintered bone into the darkness, hearing it clatter "—I can't, Ayva. We've come so far... now we're just supposed to rot in this damned pit?"

Ayva grabbed his arm and pulled him next to her, silently.

Darius didn't resist. Holding back his tears of frustration, he moved to her side. His heart still hammered in anger and exertion, and Ayva rested her head on his shoulder. Feeling Ayva's warmth, the seconds seemed to pass like hours. But slowly his anger abated as he stared into the darkness. The pain of trying and exerting faded. His exhaustion caught up with him, and his worries melted as sleep took Darius at last.

Dreams sifted in and out, restless and almost forgotten.

He dreamt of Sophi's inn, its long bannister always smooth to the touch save for the scrawled 'D' and 'A' where he'd tried to carve his name before his beloved caretaker and godmother caught him. He dreamt of Lakewood's placid lake, trolling fishing boats skimming the glassy water ... of sweet apple pies and burnt fingers and *more* scolding. Of Sophi cramming him into his Sunday best, forced to mingle with townsfolk in the center green. The faces were all a blur, as if lost in time. *Why can't I see them?* his mind wondered as he itched, wanting to be back in his comfortable black rags and dark green cloak... What dark green cloak? He didn't wear a cloak, and he *hated* green.

Memories started to blur and bleed together.

Of the long trek to the Shining City and the stinging wind and snow while playing Cyn against the hermit Mura… He felt the darkness of those days again settling like a suffocating blanket… Running and never knowing what terror was around the corner or biting at his heels… Next he saw the Elvin camp behind Death's Gates, but instead of Karil inside her tent he saw Sophi. She turned, wearing that knowing smile. Could it be? She'd survived the chaos of Lakewood? He ran to her, heart pounding. But just as he reached her, she faded and became the face of the Ronin, Maris, with his flame-like white hair and his mischievous eyes, watching him without word.

When Darius awoke it was still dark as pitch. Confusion took hold, expecting to see his tiny cot and the once-familiar furnishings of Sophi's inn. But then he remembered where he was… His head fell back with a sigh. He wanted to sleep again, to escape the darkness, and retreat back to a simpler time, but he knew that time was long past. He let Lakewood's tranquil memories fade, as if he was saying goodbye to a close friend and took in his surroundings once more.

Ayva was still asleep with her head nestled into his now numb arm. He freed his tingling limb to gently rest her head against the pit's dirt wall. In the bloodstone's light, her freckled skin seemed paler, her features more gaunt, but he knew it was just his imagination.

Darius turned his attention to the pit.

Right, now to escape… he thought, scratching his stubble. *Think like Gray, he'd have some foolproof plan involving magic and bravery and…* He growled. *Dicing, Gray. Where are you and your white-knight antics when I need you most?* But beneath his cursing and frustration, he missed the fool hero. He hoped by now Gray was safe with his grandfather. He sighed, brushing the dirt off his hands and rising.

Bone-weary, Darius approached the wall. He gripped the bloodstone but his fingers slipped free once more. Sucking in a thin breath of pain he felt his palms—*dried blood, from my failed previous attempts.* With a sigh, he tried to think. Reaching into his pocket Darius felt something prickly and metallic. He pulled it out and in the dull red light saw the glimmer of gold—the shard of the Elvin

King's crown, the gift from Karil. *That's not much use here.* In his other pocket he felt a piece of string. *Well, that's helpful,* he thought sarcastically. Lastly, in his cloak's pocket, he found a dried piece of cheese he'd stolen from one of the many inns and wrapped in wax paper. He was hungry but not starving yet and knew he'd need to save it.

Behind him, there was a rustle.

"You awake?" Ayva called.

"No," he said. "I think I'm stuck in a nightmare."

"I think we're in the same nightmare then," Ayva replied. "Mind pinching me?"

He gave a soft chuckle, but then he felt his anger rise. "Only too gladly. Maybe then I'll realize only in a dream would we follow a raving mad woman—a woman who tried to kill me, *sell* me, then ultimately shackled us as prisoners and betrayed us."

"Don't…" Ayva seethed.

He turned and in the dim red light he saw she was gripping one of the bones, the brittle bone cracking from her anger. And he realized for Ayva that subject was still too sore.

Darius nodded to himself. The betrayal pained him too, sharp
and sickening like bile on his tongue. He sat in the dirt cross-legged, facing Ayva. "Perhaps when the dream shatters then this silly notion of being a Ronin will shatter with it…"

"Do you…" Ayva began. "Do you really believe that?"

"I don't know what to believe," he answered truthfully.

Ayva shivered and he neared, sitting at her side once more.

"Do you fear it?" Ayva voiced into the darkness.

"Yes," he answered without hesitation.

She gave a breath, as if in relief. He was glad to share the burden as well. "I'm afraid of it, but as with most things I can't help but be curious," she whispered. "Why me? Why *us*? And why now?"

Why us? The answer rung inside Darius' head. "Ayva, do you remember when we followed Gray to Tir Re' Dol?" *Or where it once stood,* his mind amended. They had traveled through the Shining City's secret tunnels to the capital city of Tir Re' Dol to find Gray … only to discover their friend amid a ruined heap of stone and sorrow, a testament to the Kage's true evil.

In the dim light, she nodded, confused. "Yes, why?"

"Well, your question—why us? Did you ever wonder why we followed him back then?"

"That's obvious. Because he was our friend."

"Is it that simple?"

"What else?" she asked.

"Doesn't it seem strange that we knew Gray for all of *one* day and the next thing we know were at each other's sides, riding with legends away from everything we've ever known?"

"We had no choice," she said, irritated. "Lakewood was set on fire ... our home was burning before our very eyes, Darius."

"And yet ... why us? You asked it. Why us instead of any other villager? Timing? Coincidence? Why two youths nearly Gray's age?"

In the murky red, Ayva's eyes narrowed, catching his implication. "What are you saying?"

"Isn't it just a tad too coincidental? Why did we all feel so close? You know me, or at least knew *of* me, I haven't had a friend since..." he hesitated, swallowing his words. "I never had a lot of friends, and yet, with us it was different, the opposite."

"A crisis can do that ... people stick together and—"

Darius shook his head "No, not like this, Ayva. Be honest with yourself. Do you really remember that trip to Tir Re' Dol?" She hesitated, looking into herself. "Because *I don't*. I barely remember asking Mistress Hitomi where Gray went. Why would she tell us?"

"I don't know," Ayva said.

"It was the *way* you asked her. There was power in your voice, a strange conviction I've never heard before except from one other person..." He didn't need to say who. "And that's not the half of it. The Sodden Tunnels, do you remember traversing those to get to Gray? Again, I *don't*," he said with emphasis. "So you might want to ask yourself, did we truly travel to Tir Re' Dol to save Gray of our own will? Or were we pulled?"

There was a long silence and he wondered if what he said was just nonsense, partly wishing he could take it back, when Ayva whispered, "You're right. I'm not sure how I didn't see it until now, but you're right." She breathed a sigh as if a weight from her shoulders was sloughed free. "I knew something felt odd about that night and it's been nagging me ever since, but until you voiced it..."

"It's a tad frightening, isn't it?" he chuckled.

"A bit. But then what's pulling us?"

"Fate," he answered. The single word bounded off the walls, reminding them and emphasizing the words that were emblazoned on the walls, but now were dark and silent, watching them. To soften the moment, Darius added, "And perhaps dumb luck in my case."

Ayva laughed. "You know, you're far smarter than you ever let anyone know."

Part of him blushed, glad for the darkness hearing how sincere her voice was, but he couldn't resist, "And a lot cuter?"

"Don't push it," she grumbled, but then smiled. "But I'm glad you're still your normal self. Now," she said, throwing the bone at the wall and hearing it clatter hollowly. "Have any infinite wisdom on how to get out of here?"

Darius eyed his hands, feeling their sting. "Running low," he answered. "What do you have in your pockets?"

Ayva rifled around and came up with her translucent dagger. "I almost forgot I had this. I guess it's not much help. How about you?"

He shook his head. "Not much."

They talked out ideas, from trying to use their blades as stepping stones, to creating a makeshift ladder out of the bones, piling them as high as possible, and more… In the end, their efforts netted Darius only a few more scratches and a lot more frustration.

"It's no use," Ayva said at last, sitting in an exasperated heap.

He couldn't agree more. Rage and frustration and exhaustion welled together but he forced himself to take a breath and replied, "It's no use wearing ourselves out any longer. Get some more sleep, perhaps then we can approach it with a fresh mind and a few less bruises."

As he turned around, he saw Ayva was already asleep. He smiled to himself and knelt at her side, unpinning his cloak and draping it over her body. As he did, she whispered softly, talking in her sleep.

"*Papa…*"

In the light of the bloodstones he watched a tear roll down her round cheek. He felt her pain, debated waking her, but instead moved to wipe the tear away. Before he could, Ayva's body rolled towards him and she snuggled into the crook of his arm. Darius sat frozen. "Uh…" he whispered. She nestled deeper, making a soft sound.

With a breath he smiled and gripped her tighter, then let exhaustion take him, falling back into the darkness of the pit and the abyss of sleep. Hours passed, Darius passing in and out of sleep. Day and night all became one long blur in the darkness. It could have been one day or one week, Darius had no clue, when he awoke for what he thought was the second time. Or was it the third?

Ayva was playing with her power, gently tossing a sputtering orb of light from one hand back to the other.

"You're getting good at that," he remarked, still tired. It was impossible to get real sleep without ever seeing light.

The ball sputtered and died as Ayva startled in surprise. "I…" she began and then shrugged. "It's nothing really."

Confusion marked Ayva's features as Darius gently unfurled her palm. Slowly, the orb of light grew once more, lighting their features. "That's not nothing."

She smiled as well, but the ball flickered. "I can only hold it for so long. I can feel it slowly draining me. But it's worth it—worth fighting this awful darkness even for a second, for a glimmer of light…"

Darius felt the panic in her words. Looking closer in the light, he realized he wasn't wrong about before. Ayva *did* look gaunter, paler, as if she was slowly being drained of life. "Ayva…"

"I know," she said and groaned. "I must look awful."

"What is happening?" he asked.

"I'm not sure," she answered. "Maybe I'm sick; you should probably stay away from me."

"I'm not going anywhere," he said, shuffling nearer. "Besides, what could you have caught? I've been at your side all this time. I think it's just the darkness, playing with our minds. It's easy to feel out of sorts in this wretched perpetual night."

She nodded. "Maybe."

His stomach grumbled again. "Dice, I'm starving."

Ayva laughed, stomach growling in unison. "Me too…" she whispered, and her voiced turned from forlorn to hopeful. "You know what sounds good? I could really go for one of Mistress Hitomi's hrofi dishes right now... Maybe some buttered bread still warm from the oven…"

"Or some of that duck in that strange brown sauce simmered in herbs…?"

"How about those roasted vegetables?"

"Exactly!" Darius exclaimed. "Carrots glazed in brown sugar, roasted yams…"

Ayva laughed softly. "You do have a good memory."

Darius tapped his noggin and made a hollow sound with his mouth. "Like a steel trap."

He got a small chuckle out of Ayva and felt a shred of hope, but then her sigh followed, long and tired. "I'd settle for anything at this point..."

Suddenly, Darius remembered the cheese in his pocket.

Excitedly he grabbed it.

He broke the piece in two, and felt the two sizes. One was clearly bigger. His stomach growled again, eating away at itself like a ravenous creature. It was painful. He'd never felt so much pain from hunger, and a large part of him had trouble not wolfing down the whole meager slice of food.

Ayva's stomach growled again.

He handed her the bigger of the two slices.

"Where did you get this?" she said in amazement.

"I've still got a few tricks up my sleeve."

Ayva wasted no time, putting out her light and eating the cheese hungrily. He followed suit. Suddenly Ayva launched into a fit of coughs, doubling over in pain.

Darius dropped the cheese, grabbing her. "Ayva!" He didn't know what to do. At last the coughing ceased. "What is happening to you?"

"I … I think it's the darkness."

"The darkness?"

She nodded in the dim red light. "I can feel it pressing in around me, like fingers around my heart… I…" she coughed into her palm, it sounded frail and rattled. As she lifted her fingers to the bloodstone's light, Darius saw blood. Ayva's eyes widened in fear. "I'm afraid, Darius. I can't stay here much longer…"

He heard her words but for once in his life he didn't have an answer.

She was speaking again, but his mind was elsewhere.

There was a clatter as a rock skittered into the pit. In his delirious state Darius wasn't sure if it was real or a dream or if he'd already passed into another realm. A scuffle sounded above, feet against dirt, and his rattled mind finally put the pieces together.

Darkeye had returned.

* * *

Lucky grabbed Dared and closed his eyes, holding him to the unlit torch.

Please work, he thought again. *Nothing.* Dared was silent, just like his name. But Lucky knew he was there somewhere. Maybe he was just sleeping? The statue did make funny noises sometimes like snoring. He squeezed his eyes harder. *Work!*

Vfoof!

The torch roared to life, flames burning and banishing the darkness. He smiled in success, and pocketed the magical statue that he'd begun to call Dared. He thought the statue enjoyed having a name, and it seemed the right name too—Dared, the Ronin of moon, was always quiet but deadly like a shadow … or so the stories said. Naming the little figure of a man who gripped a too-big sword

was the least he could do. After all, the statue had saved his life almost a dozen times already. Again, he thanked Zane, though still he felt guilty for thieving it. *I'll give it back soon, I promise,* he thought again, but a part of him didn't want to let Dared go.

Lucky squinted into the scary darkness, but saw nothing. He was sure he had heard someone! Hadn't he? Dared promised they were down here! Just then, there was a scraping sound. Yes, someone was down there. But what if they were bad, like the others of Darkeye's foul clan? His heart thumped inside his chest. Again, his legs itched to flee. He could take Dared and hide, find a small nook to call home and live in peace.

But Dared pulsed, urging him forward.

He took a big breath and leaned forward, "Anyone alive down there?"

A light from within bloomed to life, brightening the pit, revealing a young man, and girl, and a pile of bones. "Yes," the young woman said. "Who are you?"

"Lucky," he said with a smile.

"What are you doing down here, Lucky? It isn't safe," she said worriedly.

She sounds nice, Lucky thought, smiling.

But could he trust them?

Inside his pocket, the statue grew warm, as if speaking to him again. *Yes. Trust these two*, it resonated, not in words but in feelings. Lucky sighed again. Well, the statue *had* led him this far. *Fine, but you better know what you're talking about, Dared.*

The young woman was speaking again. "I don't know how you got here, but you have to leave! There are bad men down here, and if they find you, they'll kill you."

And Lucky smirked. "I know, and that's why I'm here to save you."

"You … what?"

Lucky wasted no time. He hopped to his feet and moved to grab the rope Dared had told him to bring, when he heard a voice in the distance. He stumbled towards it fearfully, only to see a familiar face in the darkness of a cell. Sandy brown hair, sun darkened skin and sharp, hard eyes. Just like Shade's. It couldn't be. *Hannah.* He rushed to the prison. "Hannah! Are you all right? Dared was right, you are here!"

"Lucky?" she voiced, baffled. "How in the…"

"Um, it's a long story," he said, scratching his head. "I promise I'll tell you it all later. For now, I'm sure Shade is really worried about you, and I don't want him mad at me for getting us caught."

"Zane?" she questioned, gripping the jail's bars suddenly.

"Yep! Now stand back, okay? I'm gonna free you, but I don't want Dared to hurt you."

Hannah scoffed, sounding like her brother. "Dared, *the Ronin?* And how exactly are you going to free me? Don't get me wrong, this is the bravest thing anyone's ever done for me, but that lock is bigger than your head."

And Lucky simply grinned. Fishing Dared out, he held him against the lock. Pressing his eyes shut, he growled, *Work!* The fat little man with his sword began to glow red and another tiny burst of flame flew forth, exploding the lock.

Hannah threw open the door, rushed forward, and scooped him up. "Lucky, I've no idea what you just did, but I could kiss you!" His cheeks bloomed red and he squawked in protest, and thankfully, she set him down. "C'mon, let's save the others!"

They rushed back to the edge of the pit.

The girl's light shone still, beating back the darkness.

"Need a little help?" Hannah called.

"Thank Lokei…" the young man breathed.

"Hurry!" the girl called. "We don't know how much time we have until Darkeye returns!"

Finding the nearby rope, they tossed it down and hauled them up.

They stood at the edge of the pit.

Lucky eyed the two and shivered. They had the look of heroes. The young woman was kind and pretty—with brown hair, bright blue eyes and freckles, but her eyes held a faint golden sheen. Her fist opened and another orb of light burst forth. It reminded him of the scary blue stone, but he knew she was good. The young man at her side didn't seem as nice. He scratched his wild brown hair, looking confused. But sizing him up, he could tell he was strong, and … his jaw dropped. *That sword!* The young man held a sword that made Lucky's hands sweat—a green blade that looked made for a king!

Hannah let out a breath of relief. "Thank the spirits you're alive! I was so afraid."

"Alive, sure," Darius scoffed. "Yet for how long? We're out of the pit, but how exactly are we getting out of here? If we leave the way we came, we're surely doomed. We got through that mess barely with Faye's help and, save for Adorry's death, I think that whole thing was a lie—a grand, staged rehearsal to bring us into Darkeye's clutches." And he sneered in anger.

Hannah turned to Lucky, kneeling. "Wait a second, how exactly did you get in here, Lucky?"

"Oh right, that's the best part!" he said, and pointed straight above them to the sound of trickling water that echoed through the grand caverns. Just then the sound of footsteps sounded faintly in the distance. In his palm, Dared grew warm again. "There's no time to explain, this way!"

* * *

Lucky reached the surface first, clambering out of the drainage pipe to stand in the cold shade of a back alley. On his heels, Darius and the others scrambled out of the hole, eyeing the sun as if seeing it for the first time as they absorbed their new surroundings.

"Sunlight," Ayva said, breathing in the warm desert air while wiping damp sand from the knees of her tan breeches. "How long were we down there?"

"*Too* long," Darius replied.

"I'd say two days in full," said Ayva. "Aside from those hours in that cursed pit, Faye seemed to be stalling us, but for what reason, I know not… The others must be worried sick."

Nearby, there was a pipe leaking rainwater runoff and Lucky cleaned himself beneath the dirty water, shaking like a dog.

"I can't believe we did it!" Hannah exclaimed. "I was so afraid when I heard Darkeye throw you into the pit, Ayva. But you were so brave. In all my life, I've never heard anyone speak like that. You stood up to Darkeye and spat in his face! And then…" She shivered as if remembering something terrible. "When I heard you fall, I feared the very worst. I thought you'd been killed."

Ayva's eyes looked haunted too, but she shook her head and eyed Darius. "And I would have been if it wasn't for Darius."

Darius smirked. "Why, you're welcome."

"I didn't thank you," she said. He grumbled, opening his mouth to retort when she hugged him deeply. "But that was truly brave."

"It was nothing," he said, waving it off, but Lucky thought he saw his cheeks redden, "still, I wasn't the one who got us out of the cursed pit."

Ayva nodded, turning to Lucky. "Right. Who is this brave young man?"

"A Lost One, like me and Zane," Hannah explained.

"A Lost One and a hero," Ayva countered.

Lucky puffed out his chest, feeling pride to the pit of his stomach. He felt as if he was about to float from the ground any second. *I can get use to this hero business. Better than the nasty streets, anyway.*

"Well, where to now?" said Hannah.

Lucky cleared his throat, opening his mouth.

"We need to find Gray," said the roguish one, interrupting, looking over Lucky's head into the busy desert streets beyond, gripping his leaf-blade tighter. "By now, they've surely saved Ezrah with Victasys' help."

"But they could be anywhere," said Ayva, pulling her brown hair behind her ear, biting her lip.

"Then where do we start?"

"*Ahem!*" Lucky coughed loudly, and they turned to him at last. "That's what I've been trying to tell you!"

"What do you mean?" Hannah asked.

He sighed, his hands balling into fists. "Dared knows where to go! He can find your friends."

"*Dared?*" Ayva questioned, raising a thin brow.

Lucky smiled and whipped out the pudgy little statue of a man with a flourish. "Dared! He's my best friend in the whole world."

Hannah's eyes narrowed in scrutiny. *Uh oh…* he thought. *Bad idea!* "That's Zane's! Lucky… How on earth did you get it?" His eyes darted, looking for a way out. *No, I can't get away. I'll have to lie.* Lies flew into his head, but Dared spoke.

The truth, Lucky, the statue ordered.

He sighed again. "All right, I stole it, okay? But I swear I was going to give it back! When I heard Darkeye was keeping you prisoner, Hannah, I knew I had to be brave like Shade and save you… It was Dared that led me to you. Thanks to him, I learned about the water pipes that wormed deep into the Lair of the Beast, and into that strange cavern. But there's no time for the whole story, I'll explain the rest later, okay?"

"Why later?" Darius asked.

"Because Dared says we're running out of time. We have to get to your friends. Shade needs us!" he said in a hurry and turned, heading down the dusty alley. He looked back.

They all watched him, looking to one another, confused.

"I swear I'm not lying! Well, *this time* at least."

"He did save us," Darius said, shrugging.

"Hm. And that statue *is* magic," Hannah said.

Ayva bent down and touched his shoulder. "Okay, Lucky. Lead the way."

"Right then!" He said proudly. "Follow me and keep up!" With that, he barreled down the dirt road, moving into Farbs—its familiar sights and smells, the others on his heels—listening to Dared's orders as they twisted and turned, moving deeper into the Nobles' District.

At last, they reached an adobe house with vines crawling up the outside walls.

There was a strange amount of activity outside, men and women coming and going on foot and on horses. A cart with a wiry-haired man in its driver's seat sat outside. The foolish man was arguing with a scarlet robed *Reaver* of all things. *Doesn't the old man know that's how you get turned into a newt or something worse?* Just then a few Devari, disguised as merchants, broke from the busy street, entering the house's big double gates. Lucky watched, taking in the courtyard beyond. The green grounds were abuzz—servants, Reavers, and Devari storming about, as if preparing. Tension hung in the air. And even Lucky knew that feeling… It was just like the night the Lost Ones' home had been attacked.

It felt like *danger.*

It felt like war.

In Lucky's palm, his fingers grew sweaty, tightening nervously around the little man. Dared grew hot—as if in welcome. And he announced with a gulp, "We're here…"

Inside the Mind of Madness

Sithel shuffled forward, dragging his bad leg like a wooden stump. He hated that thing. He'd asked his dark master to fix it but had only received the sinister reply that it would serve as a reminder of his weakness.

Weakness, Sithel cursed as he moved though the grand halls of the Citadel, ignoring the dozens of Devari and dark Reavers who moved at his side. *It is a curse upon mankind borne by fear … the fear to do what is necessary, to sacrifice anything to become something more… I will not be weak anymore.* The words sounded familiar to that day so long ago, and his vision was pulled away, ignoring the green courtyard and his lavish surroundings, lost in a world of dust, chaos, and brutality.

"Diaon," the fat man barked, "Grab me the tongs." Those words and the hissing steam of the bellows pulled Sithel out of his reverie, bringing him back to the dismal real world. He fell back into the sounds of toil all around him—strange beasts and men slogging through the ever-crowded streets beyond the small tent, sweating in the high sun. The smell of sweat, dirt, and blood was thick in the air.

Again, the bellows hissed.

This was the tenth apprenticeship he'd had in less than a year. As an orphan of Covai, he had no choice but to move on each time, accepting his allotted place. He could barely remember each horrible memory as they blurred together: the stench of dead animal from the tannery with those noxious dyes that stained his body for months, or the tailor who made his hands numb with tireless needlework, his words harsh and belittling for every mistake, but this, Sithel knew, was the worst.

The fat man's small blacksmith tent was cramped and messy, just like any one of the thousands of shops in the largest trading hub in all of Farhaven. A district of a much greater whole—it was the city of Covai, a Great Kingdom, and home to the element of Flesh, a brutal city of life and death, where one toiled and worked their fingers to the bone to get by; or one didn't, and died. Sithel had known that for all of his dozen summers that he'd been alive, but he never wanted to believe it.

He wanted to believe in something more.

Beyond, through a gap in the tent, Sithel glimpsed the vision of the merchant's terrace—a segment of Covai that was high above them, like gods watching down upon their creations. It was a place full of wealth and power, with buildings of gleaming gold, silver, and bronze, and terraced balconies, each a castle in its own right. Beyond that, in the greater distance, he saw the infamous Ren Nar Cliffs of the now-forgotten Morrow—the lost Great Kingdom of Wind, shattered during the war.

Suddenly, something smacked him in the back of the head, pain exploding as his vision flashed as he fell to the ground. When his vision returned, he realized he was coughing dust through his mouth and felt something wet—his blood, trickling from his nose. He looked up into the brutish, sweating face of his Sunha—his master. The man was furious, his eyes bulging and jowls jiggling with red-faced fury.

"You!" his Sunha bellowed. "This is the last time you daydream before me! I've had enough of it!"

Sithel looked up slowly, spitting blood. He wasn't willing to give the man a name. He was just one of hundreds of cruel, pitiless men caught up in this pathetic race, clambering to survive. Sithel was more than that. He knew it, but others didn't yet. He sneered inwardly, gripping the dirt, trying to assume a servile face. They would know, but not yet… Eyes to the ground, Sithel tried to murmur a false apology. "I'm sorry, Master," he groveled, trying to rise to his knees.

"My patience has reached its limit with you, Diaon," the man sneered.

"Forgive me, please. It won't happen again, I swear—"

"—Enough of your lies!" Sunha shouted, ramming his foot into the small of Sithel's back, creating a shooting pain like he'd never felt before. He'd felt pain, surely, but nothing like this. He tried to catch a breath but couldn't. His eyes watered, tears flowing down his face and mixing with the sweat and dirt. He waited for it to abate, but it wouldn't, and he heard himself continue to cry. This only made his Sunha angrier. "You little, sniveling coward!" the man shouted, grabbing a red-hot prong from the nearby glowing furnace. Crowds beyond paid no mind, moving past the tent as if seeing nothing—a Sunha could do this to his Diaon. It was the law of the land. The law of Covai. His Sunha pressed the hot prong into his back.

And Sithel screamed. Hot tears burst anew as he writhed in anguish. If only he could catch a breath… He was suffocating, his vision blurring, lights flashing. Distantly, the smell of burnt flesh filled his nostrils. Let it end… his mind begged distantly.

Let it all end….

But a part of Sithel, as his body thrashed uncontrollably, dying quickly, was still gazing above, at the merchant's terrace, towards power and wealth. His Sunha jabbed, over and over, until he felt his limbs stop moving and his breathing slow. At last, he realized the man had stopped, and he took a ragged breath. "I…" he tried to breathe. "Can't take anymore."

"Nor can I," said his Sunha. Sithel looked up, craning his neck painfully to see the fat man's dark, angry eyes. "It's forbidden to kill your Diaon, but an accident isn't unheard of… The governor will give me a new rat, but it will surely be better than you. Your incompetence and daydreaming has reached its end, my Diaon," the brutish, filthy man sneered with a dark grin, raising a half-finished blade from the glowing fire. Sithel swallowed in fear, eyeing the rough-hewn edge that gleamed a bloody red in the dark tent. Sithel crawled away, trying to back up, but the man advanced, slowly but surely.

"Please," he entreated, sniveling and continuing to crawl. His back hit the stone bellow. Fear shot through him. "I swear I'll do better! Give me a chance! Don't do this! I don't want to die!" It was true—that above all things he feared. He opened his mouth to beg more, to plead for his life, but knew it would be of no use. His Sunha would kill him and no one would be the wiser. Everything he'd hoped and

dreamed for, gone. Another pile of flesh thrown to the wayside.

“Enough begging,” his Sunha said, “Face your death, you miserable worm.”

“An apt reflection,” said another dark voice, filling the tent. The words chilled Sithel to the core—it was a dark rasp like he'd never heard before. A sudden gloom filled the already shadowy tent. The bellows suddenly snuffed, darkness consuming all.

“What is this?” His Sunha sneered, twisting and turning, trying to find the origin of the voice. “Come out, you coward!” It had become strangely quiet outside the tent, and he realized…

The crowds had stopped moving, as if the world stood still, and time had frozen. What's happening? Sithel wondered in terrible fear and awe.

His Sunha noticed as well. The man's thick lips trembled, “What is this? Who are you?!”

“‘What am I would be a better question,” came the dreadful voice.

His Sunha slashed at the air with his red blade, crying out. Suddenly, he was pierced through the stomach by a thick black feeler the size of the man's fat head. The living darkness wiggled in the air, peering through the man's chest, as if curious. Sunha gurgled in his blood, then fell to the ground, dead. Sithel felt nothing for it, except fear at the shadows that materialized into a tall, human figure, wearing only the living darkness as clothes.

“Rise,” the dark figure ordered.

And Sithel moved without hesitation. He tried to move his legs, despite his searing pain, but his left leg wouldn't budge… Fear spiraled through him, eyes widening. “It won't work!” he shouted fearfully. “I can't move it!”

“A lesson then,” the dark figure said—the only bright parts of its features were the burning red eyes like bloody coals. “You were too weak to fight for yourself, but beneath me, you will be strong, Sithel. Join me and face an end to your fear and an end to death.”

An end to death? Who was this figure? Terror deeper than his own Sunha's threats filled him. Who knew what this person could do to him? But a greedy thrill rose inside him as well, greater than he'd ever felt. Hope. But not the typical pathetic hope of the masses. Hope for power and strength. You'll just be Diaon, once more, Sithel's mind thought. No, he realized. The dark figure was strong, not a regular

Sunha. He would listen, and he would become something more.

He would become everything he ever wanted.

The dark figure reached out its black hand with a claw-like grip. Sithel's gaze held the merchant's terrace, unable to look away from those glittering buildings. At last he nodded, taking the figure's hand.

Sithel returned to the moment.

He realized he was sweating, and he had stopped. The others, Devari and Reavers at his side, waited, curiously. They had never seen him like this, and he tried to quickly hide the painful memories from his face. A Devari grabbed his arm in concern. "Master?"

He harshly threw it aside. "Let go!" he cursed, then he sneered quietly, "I'm fine. Come. Let us see to these Neophytes who do not wish to turn to the side of the righteous, to the side of strength." *For only the strong survive.*

* * *

Sithel found the courtyard quickly. Several dozen Neophytes sat on the dewy grass, surrounded by his dark Reavers and Devari. The little boys and girls knelt in their small gray robes, shivering in fear. A nearby fountain spouted a calming babble of water, grating his nerves, and he sent out a tremor of the voidstone's power—the water cut short in a deafening silence. Well, *aside* from the whimpers and soft sobs.

He approached with a wicked smile, assuming his mantle once more. He was powerful and he was strong. *I will never be used again, will never be weak.* A nearby Reaver bowed upon his approach as he moved through the wide, stone archway into the yard that was open to the sky. "Are they broken yet?"

"No, my lord," the two-stripe said. "Not yet … they are a stubborn bunch."

Dragging his clumsy leg, Sithel knelt before the smallest of the bunch, a little girl with big blue eyes and curly brown hair. She clenched her eyes, afraid to look upon him. "It's all right, my child," he confessed, and slowly, Sithel reached out, grazing his hand across the little girl's face. "You don't need to fear me. I've come with the message of truth."

Another spoke, an older boy. "Leave her alone!"

Sithel cocked his head, like a creature examining its prey. The boy had long brown hair, tan skin, and blue eyes, a youthful face that couldn't have been much more then twelve summers in age, but the young magic wielder's furious glare didn't falter. Amused, Sithel rose, spine cracking as he assumed his full height, a position he wasn't familiar with. The boy swallowed, sitting straighter upon his knees as he approached. "A hero, is it?" He smiled. "This will be more fun than I anticipated."

The boy in his Neophyte gray robes stared up at him with fiery pride. "The Patriarch will come and save us—he and the other Reavers will find out what you've done and they will kill you! You are nothing!"

"It that so?" Sithel questioned.

The long line of Neophytes still trembled. Yet now, with the older boy's outburst, they looked different, their young minds seeing a glimmer of hope. Nearby, other Reavers watched along the walls. Some were his own, and others were what he'd begun calling *examples*, men and women who he'd already desiccated, robbing them of the spark. At first he'd just kept them out of pity, but it'd been a stroke of genius to keep them alive, like prized but gelded stallions—the more powerful they once were, the better. They kept the rest in line and dozens already had turned themselves to his cause due to his little act of *compassion*. Yet even those hollow men and women curiously looked up at the boy's passionate words.

"You have quite the spark inside you boy," Sithel said, "Let us see just how much, shall we? This will hurt," he declared and pressed the voidstone closer. It crackled loudly, pulsing with blue energy, and … nothing happened. Fear and confusion lanced through Sithel's body as he stared down, eyeing the boy like a monster.

The boy simply smiled. "I'm not afraid of you," he retorted.

"So it seems," Sithel replied, trying to hide his fear, lip twitching involuntarily.

"Someone is going to find you and stop you," the boy jeered. "Someone with real power will put an end to you and show you…"

"Show me what?" Sithel inquired, regaining control. "*Hm?*"

"Show you … show you that you're just a weak worm!"

Rage tremored through Sithel's body. The words bit deeper than any dagger, but he quickly suppressed it. Meanwhile, the voidstone continued to crackle, draining all those nearby, but not *this* boy.

Whatever he was, he was somehow immune. How could it be? The boy was weak! He had the spark, surely, but it was nothing great. Then how could he resist? *Because*… Sithel thought in sudden realization. *He* is a *monster*. Sithel sighed and knelt closer. Embracing the boy close, he sighed, "A shame, really, that fire inside you is… remarkable," he said, his tone silken.

Confused, the boy writhed in his embrace. "Let me go!"

Sithel continued, "Even with such little spark, you would have made an excellent Reaver." The boy struggled, realizing his fate, even crying out, but it was too late. With practiced ease, he unsheathed his dagger and rammed it into the child's gut. The boy gasped. A cry went out from all nearby as the boy keeled over, dead. The others now trembled in fear, in *weakness*. Sithel hated killing children, or those with strength, but it was necessary to keep the rest in line. There was always a variant strain, a voice that rose above the others, but once one squashed that? Well, the rest followed like a leashed animal.

"Why?" cried an older girl, lying over the boy's lifeless body.

"Don't you see?" he asked, befuddled, and she looked at him as

if he were mad. He laughed, knowing how wrong she was. "Misguided girl, I shall explain to you. To you all," Sithel said louder, his voice echoing through the courtyard. "The Citadel is ours, but why stop there? To go back to what we were, *that* would be the true crime. With only the strong left, and those willing to do what is necessary, nothing can stop us! Worthless rules and pitiful hierarchies plague this world. Without them, it is ours for the taking, and we *can* take what we want, for we are the *strongest*." He laughed and it resounded into the sky. "Together, the rest of the Great Kingdoms will tremble beneath us, groveling for the salvation of the Citadel!"

The older girl looked to him over the dead boy's body, eyes brimming as if seeing something she couldn't fathom. Something *beyond* her.

Yes, he thought and continued, his voice softer, silken, "…and once they do, once they are swayed to the side of the mighty and their misguided notions of saving the weak are gone? Well, then we shall simply remake this broken land. For only the strong can banish the suffering and pain of this world," he declared, his words now shaking with power. His limbs quivered as well, and he thrust the azure voidstone high into the air, letting it crackle in raw dominance, filling the courtyard. "Let me hear your conviction!" At his command, the others began to chant his master's promise alongside him, voices rising into the chill night air.

"THE AGE OF THE STRONG IS NOW."

"THE AGE OF THE STRONG IS NOW."

As the voices thundered in beautiful symphony, Sithel's grin spread, and in his mind, he saw merchant's terrace—its glittering buildings rising above Covai's dusty streets, and he had one single thought. He would have more than he'd ever dreamed. *Soon, all the world will be mine…*

A New Beginning

Meira moved through the Tranquil House, feeling a fire growing inside her. She snorted and wondered, *Do men lack wits, or do they simply choose not to use them?* Finn was the cause of her anger this time. The man was incorrigible.

The messenger's words flashed through her mind again.

"Finn has requested your presence," said the woman.

"What for?" she asked.

"He said only that he wished to see you before the battle began."

Battle? She wondered. *What is the man talking about?* War was brewing, but they were far from deciding on any conclusive plans. To siege the Citadel was no simple thing, even with their growing numbers. It was an impregnable bastion that had not been scathed since its creation, not even in the war of the Lieon. Moreover, Sithel had surely locked down the gates and was preparing for their invasion. One wrong move could spell disaster. On top of that, too many powerful voices had created a sort of division. She sighed. She was partly to blame for that. Ezrah's voice overrode all others, but the Arbiter seemed to be … waiting for something. It set her teeth on edge.

Again she sighed, moving faster towards Finn's room.

Men… she cursed. *Stubborn as an old oak is to cut, and as strange as—*

A few Devari at her side raised their brows. *Did I speak aloud again?* She shrugged inwardly. It was no surprise. Her concerns only seemed to grow, unable to contain themselves in her head. Granted, the Devari would never quarrel with her, a three-stripe Reaver, no matter the insult. Her group, a swath of men and women, Reavers and Devari moved at her side.

With the influx of newcomers to their rebellion, the groups had begun to divide themselves in three parts beneath Ezrah's authority. Dagon led a faction, Ethelwin, another four-stripe led another, and Meira, with Finn's aid, led the third to gather supplies and intelligence, while searching for a way to retake the Citadel.

They reached the door of Finn's room.

Meira held up her hand. "Stay here." She entered and closed the door.

Immediately, she sighed at the surroundings—a simple table, chair, dark cot, and a balcony that looked out upon the courtyards where men and women trained. Despite being a leader of this little rebellion of theirs, the man had requested, no he'd *insisted*, that he have the least luxurious of all the rooms. He'd succeeded. And her eyes panned back to the man in the center of the room, and she felt her pulse flutter upon seeing him.

What … was that? She thought, taking a calming breath.

She shoved the feeling aside, watching him. Finn was working his forms—Devari stances and postures for fighting. He moved deliberately, precisely. He balanced upon one leg, slowly twisting, his sword cutting the cool air. It was a beautiful thing, she admitted, but pointless.

After completing a form, he turned to her with a smile, rising to his full height, with his shirt off and sweat glistening off his body. "Ah, Meira," he said in greeting, "Welcome to my humble abode."

"Humble indeed," she answered.

"I see that look you're giving me," he remarked, turning away and sheathing his sword.

"What look?" she asked. "You can't even see me."

"I can *feel* it."

"So now you truly are becoming a Devari," she said, hiding a smile.

He sighed and threw his shirt back on, which had lain on the lone chair. She felt a wince of … regret? She sighed. Why was she acting like a Neophyte with a crush? Finn spoke, "There may come a time when our powers cannot be used. The voidstone has proven that. Reavers are not infallible as *some of us* believe we are."

She could sense his distaste. Meira knew he was referring to Dagon. The man was exerting his power more and more of late. "I suppose," she said, waving off the matter—but the man did speak with infuriating wisdom. She didn't argue that she still thought there were more useful things to be doing than playing with a sword like a little boy. "Why did you summon me here?"

Offering her the chair, Finn lounged back in his cot. She took it, grudgingly. "Why else?" he asked. "Because I missed you, of course."

She raised a brow. "Yet the messenger said that you wanted to see me before the battle? What battle?"

"What battle, indeed," he said.

"You mean you just wanted to say you missed me?"

He nodded.

"Then why not simply say that?" she asked.

He shrugged and smiled disarmingly. "Would you have come if I had only said I missed you?"

"Likely not," she admitted, picking at lint in the dirty green chair.

"See?" he said with a wink.

She sighed.

"Well?"

"Well what?" she asked.

His grin grew. "You haven't said that you missed me too."

Despite herself, she laughed and rose, moving to the nearby balcony. "You are incorrigible," she replied, gripping the railings entwined with dark red and green vines. Below, she watched men and women training, preparing for whatever was coming.

She felt Finn approach. He touched her arm. "What are you worrying about this time?"

"Everything that you should be fearing," she said softly.

"Precisely," he answered. "You worry enough for the both of us."

Again she smiled, shaking her head. She felt heat emanating from his body in the chill night. "Do you know what is coming?" she asked, not willing to look at him.

"I know what you fear is coming," he answered.

She narrowed her eyes, fingernails scraping the steel beneath her as a breeze ruffled her hair. "I can hardly believe what we are planning," she voiced. "Since I was a little girl I dreamed of becoming a Reaver, moving through the grand halls, seeing the courtyards, wearing the red robes, and learning it all while I was sheltered behind its black walls. The Citadel is not just a keep. It is our *home*. We are planning to siege our very home."

"It is not our home, Meira," Finn said with conviction. "Not as it stands. It is Sithel's lair of darkness. We are planning to rescue it from that fate."

"Still," she said. "It's the *Citadel*, Finn. A bastion of light in a world of darkness."

"Farhaven is not so hopeless as you think. The other Great Kingdoms—"

"—Are divided," she interjected. "I fear a malevolence is rising, my friend. The Citadel has always been that barrier against evil. We Reavers are guardians, feared but respected throughout the land. But how will the world view us now? We were meant to stand against the darkness, but if we can be corrupted, what chance of salvation is there?"

He gripped her shoulders, turning her, his soft brown eyes taking her in. "We will reclaim the Citadel. I swear it." He smiled again, and it banished some of her fear and concern. "Do you see those two?" he asked, pointing. She followed his finger and saw two men. She recognized the peculiar youths; Gray, her guardian, and Zane, the fake, fiery Devari. "They have been training without rest. They owe the Citadel nothing, us nothing. It is not their home, nor is it filled with their friends and family. But still they train. For us, for something more... They are the light against the darkness that you fear so much. It is a light not reserved for Devari, Reaver or even Arbiter. It is the light of humanity, of perseverance against all odds. It is the light of compassion. So what you fear, Meira, is an end. Yet the truth is this is just the beginning."

She shivered, trying to swallow and find her words, tension and fears fleeing her body. At last she spoke in a faint voice. "I have missed you, my friend. Somehow, you always know what to say." Their gaze lingered and she felt her heart begin to beat harder and faster. She took a breath, gathering herself and looking away.

Finn spoke softly. “Meira… I asked you here for more than just telling you that I missed you. There is something else…”

Despite the chill air, her face flushed, knowing, fearing, and hoping.

“… something you’ve known for years, but I’ve never had the heart or courage to say until the other day. Seeing Ezrah and his compassion for his grandson made me think … and then these days of preparing, of battle and war brewing like a storm of swords on the edge of the horizon…”

She gave a soft snort. “Poetry, Finn? Are you trying to woo me?” Meira looked away to avoid his gaze, sighing. “Really, don’t we have better things to discuss?”

Lightly, he touched her chin, turning her to look up into his eyes. “No more. Those tongue-in-cheek words won’t work on me, Meira. *I know you.* All of that, it is just a guise that I’ve played along with, and I refuse to buy it any longer.”

“I…”

Finger upon her chin, he pulled her gently but firmly closer. His breath was sweet but hot, his lips lingering closer. Her heart was loud enough she feared it would pound its way free of her body. “The truth I’ve never been able to say is not that I love you, Meira, but that I’ve always loved you.”

She swallowed. “Finn… I…”

But he silenced her with a kiss. And Meira lost herself in his touch. Distantly, she felt him wrap his arm around her waist, pulling her tight to his body, and she moaned against his lips from the strength of his touch. In that moment, worries, fears, and even hopes seemed to disappear, pressed against his hard body and soft lips.

For once, she forgot about it all.

For once, since Morgan’s death, Meira felt peace.

Reunion

That same night, Gray still couldn't sleep. He wandered the Tranquil House restlessly. A group of Devari and Reavers approached from the opposite end of the hall, and he did not need the ki to feel their tension. Again, many cast him quick, simple bows, and though he'd grown more accustomed to it, still his skin crawled. *Who is he?* Their eyes seemed to demand.

A tall, powerful man led them, a Reaver he recognized—Dagon.

He opened himself to the ki, wanting to sense the powerful man's intentions, but was interrupted. Deep in thought, the black haired, four-stripe Reaver's course clashed with Gray, and they bumped shoulders. He shuddered. The group passed. He breathed a sigh.

A feeling of malevolence filled him. Like the danger of death—the purpose of blood.

Gray felt goose bumps prickle along his arm, the feeling following him like a clinging fog. He strode through the halls lit by flickering torches. He cast his mind from it, continuing, taking in his surroundings. The bright orange torches banished a night that pressed in from all angles, as if seeping through the windows. But that only seemed to remind him of the darkness in the tunnels and of the sword upon his back.

Morrowil is mine now, he vowed, *not the other way round.*

He found himself in the quainter side of the Tranquil House, near Zane's rooms once more. He saw the brass handled doorknobs and memories returned.

A room…

Darkness…

A bloodcurdling cry…

Suddenly, the cry seemed to echo again, not as shrill and painful, but still…

No, he thought. That was real.

"You deserve death!!" A voice boomed angrily.

He twisted and saw it was Zane's room at the far end of the hall.

Gray gripped his power and kicked the door with threads of wind powering his foot. Splinters exploded in the air. He felt the nexus roaring with life inside him. Through his anger and stillness—a haze of red and white—Gray took in the scene.

The small room was in tatters, furniture flung to one side. The plain rug was singed with flames, and the simple walls with landscape paintings held black scorch marks. In the center of it all, Zane held his sword to Faye's neck, and flames were beginning to crawl up the steel, inching closer to her face. Her expression was a strange mix of fear and acceptance.

"Zane!" he bellowed, "What in the seven hells is going on?!"

The man turned, pain and wrath flowing in his eyes so strong it nearly took Gray to his knees. They burned *red*. Not like Kail's, more copper, but still it was a gaze he'd seen before—in Seth. "She killed them, Gray," the man seethed, tears in his eyes. "She killed Hannah and the others..."

Dread, fury, and confusion flooded Gray. "What… What are you talking about?"

"She just told me everything. She led them into the pit and betrayed them, giving them to Darkeye to die. They're dead, Gray. Ayva, Darius, and Hannah… They're dead, and this lying witch is to blame…"

Zane's attention split, Faye suddenly twisted, ducking beneath his sword. She pressed against the wall, kicking him with both feet, and the fiery man grunted as he was sent flying back.

As if standing in the center of a tempest, Gray's rage and serenity *pulsed*.

He shifted.

Wind flashed around him, and he suddenly stood before Faye, Morrowil to her throat.

Faye's eyes were wide in shock. "That move..."

"Why?" he breathed, ignoring her. "Why did you do it?"

The woman before him didn't flinch, but her eyes held a hollowness Gray could barely fathom. "You'd never understand."

"Speak or I will end you right now!" he cried.

Faye looked away and spoke, "I live with blood on my hands, but there is one life I was not willing to let go," she answered coarsely. "One life I cannot see spilled, no matter the sacrifice. I never wanted to betray you—despite what you did to me. You are unlike anyone I have ever met, Gray, and you have this strange and, at times, almost infuriating effect on me. But I never wanted this."

"Then why?!" he bellowed, pressing his sword tighter, cutting deeper.

"For my sister," Faye said in fury and sorrow. "Darkeye has my sister..."

"Sister?" he questioned. "You sacrificed my friends for your sister?"

"I could not let her die, or worse, become me."

Become you? But he didn't care. "You saw them die?" he asked.

"No," she replied shaking her head. And hope bloomed inside Gray. Suddenly, he felt a voice in his head, and anger. A presence. *What is that?* Then it clicked. Zane. He was threading.

The room flared with heat, searing Gray's back as a flame roared for Faye. Releasing an even breath, feeding off his anger and serenity, the nexus spiked. With a casual flick of his hand, a gust of wind rushed through the air and dissolved the angry molten fire to nothing, blowing Zane back, slamming him into the far wall and dropping him to the ground.

He looked down. Morrowil was shaking in his hand. *The sword is giving me power.* He remembered. *Stealing too much from Morrowil will consume me just as it did Kail,* he reminded himself. Yet for now, his nexus had control. He twisted to Faye. "I thought I knew you. I trusted you..."

Faye leaned in, lips brushing his ear. "Trust is a misguided notion, my dear Gray. It will only be your death."

"I don't believe you. You have good inside you, Faye. I've seen it!"

"You saw what you wished to see," she answered, looking away, her pale red lips made a tight line.

With the wind, he lifted her from the ground, feet dangling as he held her in the air. He read her eyes as she flinched. "What are you hiding? Tell me!"

"Death is not what I fear for you friends," she admitted, wincing beneath Morrowil's edge as faint eddies of wind flowed along the blade. "It's a life of servitude."

"Then you know nothing," he snapped. "Ayva and Darius would never fall to shadow!"

"Perhaps, but Darkeye has a talent for breaking even the most righteous. No matter their strength of heart," she replied, eyes flashing as if in memory. "He finds a way." She made the words sound personal and painful all in one.

"Then why did you return? Just to die?" he asked, gripping a veil of serenity. For if he gave into his anger, his power would shatter. He knew the nexus was the only thing saving Faye from certain death.

Faye's amber eyes watered. "Because … I had to…" Abruptly, she gripped Morrowil's handle and gasped in pain, and Gray knew the agony Morrowil was giving her, having seen it before. Still, she held on, pressing the blade closer to her throat still, more blood flowing forth. "Finish it!" she seethed. "I care nothing for my life, but know in so doing that you are risking thousands of others…" Her eyes held his, swirling with pain. *How could I trust those eyes?* "I have information on what Darkeye is planning. I came to inform you all, to tell you and your grandfather, the Arbiter."

"Lies," he breathed. "I can never trust you." He thought about Ayva and Darius, and sorrow rushed through him until he thought he would collapse from the weight of it. He raised his hand, forming threads of furious wind, anger growing. The nexus began to shudder as his serenity faltered.

A voice sounded.

"*Gray?*"

That voice… It was so familiar, soft and yet strong.

He twisted.

Ayva and Darius stood in the dimly lit doorway, firelight flickering behind them, silhouetting their frames. A young girl who was obviously Zane's sister, Hannah, and a small dirty boy were at their side. Each looked ragged, their clothes soiled, oddly wet and in tatters, but they were alive…

The nexus faltered, anger wavering.

He dropped Faye to the ground and stepped towards them. "Am I dreaming?" he breathed.

Ayva rushed forward, and he met her, embracing her deeply, and then Darius—the rogue lifting him from the ground, laughing and smiling. "Dice, Gray, you're alive! I knew it! That Devari would never have let you out of his sight…"

Victasys… Gray's heart winced but Ayva's smile pulled him back to the moment.

"Zane!" Hannah cried, hurrying to the fiery man who lay slumped beside his cot, unmoving. "What's wrong with him?" Gray cringed, feeling guilty. *Perhaps I used too much force.* Hannah pressed her fingers to his head.

Zane suddenly grumbled, he rose and rubbed the bump on his skull. *The girl can use the spark?* Zane saw Hannah and his face twisted, his visage of fury becoming one of joy. Wordlessly, he gripped her, pulling her close, and she hugged him back just as fiercely. "I thought you were dead…" he breathed.

"I was so frightened," she said. "Never leave me again, deal?"

He laughed, scrubbing her hair. "Never," he voiced, eyes blazing in mirth.

Darius and Ayva's eyes suddenly noticed the woman behind Gray, and fury filled their expression.

"What in the seven hells is she doing here?" Darius seethed and unsheathed his leaf-shaped blade in a ring that filled the small room. He strode forward.

Gray stepped in between him and Faye.

"What is this? Move aside, Gray."

"No."

"Gray," Ayva said quickly, gripping his arm, "Faye is not who you think she is. She—"

"—I know," he said.

"No—you don't," she said, her eyes flared. "She betrayed us! Without Lucky, we would be dead."

Lucky? Gray wondered, eyeing the small boy in rags that barely fit his skinny frame. That must have been whom they meant. "Faye admitted her betrayal already."

Ayva shook her head, baffled, eyeing Faye. "What are you planning?"

Faye remained silent.

"Wait, Lucky saved you?" Zane asked.

"I'm a hero!" Lucky exclaimed, "Thanks to this!" and the boy thrust a hand-sized statue into the air of a stout little man bearing a sword.

"My statue…" Zane whispered. "How in the…"

And Lucky blushed red. "I swear I was going to give Dared back, Shade!"

Dared? Shade? Gray questioned.

"Yes, yes, the statue," Darius said. "That's terrific, but why is no one addressing the fact that we've a traitor and a murderer in our presence?"

"I'll deal with it," Zane replied, gripping his sword and rising, his blade wreathed in sudden flames.

"Not if I finish her first," Darius answered, hands wringing his leaf-blade and stalking forward, and even Ayva's hands glowed with a strange golden-white light, anger in her eyes. Faye simply gave a dark, empty smirk as if beckoning it. And Zane bellowed, raising his blade. With thick threads of wind, Gray reached out and gripped every person in the room. He raised his palms, lifting them into the air. He felt energy flee his body, sapped as if he'd just run for days. His left knee buckled to the ground, and he winced. It felt as if he carried all of their weight upon his shoulders, but still he held on.

"Enough," he retorted in fury and stillness. "No more!"

Zane sneered, hanging in the air. "Let me down! The foul woman deserves death!"

"I will not have it!" he answered, and he fell to his other knee, arms trembling beneath the strain. "Faye *does* deserve a dark fate, but this is neither the time nor the place. No… more…" And he dropped them to the ground with a breath.

When he looked up, Ayva was at his side, Darius as well, preventing him from falling over. With their aid, he rose to his feet. "She *betrayed* us, Gray," Ayva said. "She tried to kill us. I cannot let that go so easily."

"Nor I," he said, "but she has news Ayva—information about Darkeye and his plans that surely has to deal with Sithel and the Citadel. If I can prevent hundreds from dying in the battle to come, then I will gladly spare her life for now. She *will* meet her fate, but not now. For the time being, she is too useful."

Ayva sighed. "So be it."

Zane grit his teeth, "As long as you keep her away from me."

"And me as well," Darius said, staring daggers at the woman. But he seemed to brush the matter aside with his next breath. His fingers flit eagerly at his side, a trait just like Maris. "So what's comes next? And what's this business about a war?"

He opened his mouth when Lucky yelped throwing the statue into the middle of the wood floor. "Ouch! It's hot! Dared just burned me!" The statue glowed gold, sucking in the light.

Zane spoke, "I think we're being summoned."

"What do you mean?" Ayva asked.

"That statue, it's Ezrah's," the fiery man replied.

Gray stared up, as if he could see his grandfather up through the floors of wood and walls of clay, and he spoke. "Then it's time to return it to its owner."

A Traitor's Truth

Words of prophecy danced in Ezrah's head.

They lingered one moment, and vanished the next as his eyes scanned the page. It was a torn piece of parchment cradled in an old book for safekeeping. Candlelight shined off the parchment's ancient ink stains and long dried water spots—each as familiar to him as freckles or scars upon his weathered hand.

Suddenly, a scream sounded, jarring his reading. He ignored it and kept reading, when it came again … a bloodcurdling cry echoed through him, one that would make men shudder, women weep, and children tremble. With a long breath, he shut the book and looked up.

Aside from the ticking clock, the room was utterly silent. Outside the window, the courtyard stirred with life, but inside, shadows flickered across the wide four-post bed, wide table, and several chairs. Even the grand fireplace sat cold and black.

He knew the screams weren't real.

They were memories—the darkness enveloping him reminded Ezrah too much of that cursed torture chamber.

Flashing images came to life.

Stones scraping.

Fire searing.

Dark mold clogging his lungs.

All of it stealing his life, bit by bit, in an attempt to break him, to *turn* him. Ezrah's gaze narrowed on his hand. It trembled. Reluctantly, he threaded a spell of flesh into his own mind and breathed a sigh. It barred the images, or at least threw them to the recesses of his thoughts. It was dangerous. Threads of flesh cast upon oneself were forbidden, even for an Arbiter, but Ezrah had more important things to do than fear.

Still…

He waved a hand. A fire roared to life in the nearby hearth, crackling and eating away the darkness and, before him, the candle burned brighter. He focused his attention back on the worn parchment, its bottom edge ragged. It was only half of the prophecy. For the thousandth time, he wished for the other half, wondering who had it. He had his guesses but, whoever it was, they were doing well to counter him at every turn.

A knock sounded and he turned calmly. "Yes?"

"It's me," a voice answered.

With a subtle smile, Ezrah instructed, "Come in."

Gray entered, the others close behind. Silently, Ezrah surveyed his guests with a watchful eye. At Gray's side was a young woman, perhaps a summer younger than his grandson. She was a pretty girl. Despite her outward softness, he admired the strength in her bright blue eyes—*a light.* Yes, I see the resemblance now. *The light of truth*, Ezrah thought with a smile. "Your name, my dear."

"Ayva," she replied, swallowing beneath the weight of his gaze. "Ayva Yuni."

Gray looked to her curiously. "Yuni?"

Ayva nodded. "My last name, after my father."

"How come you never told us that?" said a young man at Gray's side with wild brown hair.

She shrugged. "Well… You never asked."

"A pretty name," Ezrah voiced, drawing their attention. *And much different than your predecessor.*

He turned to the next, raising a brow. The wild haired young man stood at Gray's other side. He wore a bright green shirt and dark trousers, and had the look of a scoundrel reformed. Beneath his scrutiny, the young man shrugged uncomfortably, scanning the room as if looking for an exit. And yet, there was a mystery to him. Then Ezrah saw it. The sword on his back... A leaf-shaped blade that pulsed faint green despite its sheath, and a handle engraved with runes of old. *The blade*. It resonated with power—a power Ezrah couldn't see, but could *feel. The flow.* He's retrieved his weapon already? What did that mean for his power? It was clear that the boy, despite his nature, was powerful.

"The name is Darius," the young lad said firmly. "Gray's grandfather, I presume?"

"A worthy guess," Ezrah answered.

"Then you ... you're an Arbiter?" Ayva asked.

He smiled. "In title only for the moment, I'm afraid."

Still, the girl's eyes widened as if he'd just proclaimed himself a living god. "*An Arbiter ... in the flesh ... my spirits...*" she mumbled, as if to herself, then looked around and realized she had spoken aloud and blushed.

"Hannah," said a girl at Zane's side.

"Welcome, Hannah. I'm glad you're safe at last. Zane once told me there were only two people in this world he trusts. I can see now in your eyes that he placed his trust wisely."

Hannah, though fierce in spirit like her brother, also looked embarrassed by his kind words, her cheeks coloring, and Zane spoke in her stead. "Thank you for rescuing my sister, Arbiter. It seems I owe you again."

The young man was clever. Perhaps he had to be to survive so long in the harsh Underbelly of Farbs and keep his sister's innocence intact. "Ah, so you figured that out, did you?" he asked.

"Who else would send a lone little boy into a den of evil?" Zane questioned brazenly. "While I don't necessarily approve of how you did it, I do approve of the results."

"Is that so? Well, your approval is appreciated," he said, then saw that Zane stood close to Gray's side. He had seen the two training over the last two days, and now he felt the bond between the young men. A bond forged by fate. Yet he could see it was genuine and real as any friendship. Ezrah felt his eyes crinkle, happy for that, and spoke. "I see you learned a valuable lesson since last I saw you."

Zane noticed his gaze and his implication. "Even a closed heart can find a sliver of space I suppose," he answered, clearing his throat gruffly.

Gray raised a curious brow and Zane grumbled.

Ezrah turned to a young boy at Zane's side, hiding behind Ayva. Something pulsed. He sensed it in the little boy's pocket. "You must be the one who discovered my statue, and the champion of this group." The little boy glowed beneath his praise, a grin splitting his face. "What is your name?"

"Lucky," he breathed.

"Might I see my statue, Lucky?"

Lucky nodded, handed the statue of the little man over, and found his voice. "I took care of him, I swear. I made sure Dared never got hurt, not even once."

"Dared, is it?" he asked warmly.

The boy nodded, but then looked nervous. "I know he's yours, but it just seemed wrong not to name him after all he did for me…"

"Dared is a fine name," Ezrah declared. "And quite accurate too. He's not much of a talker, is he?" Lucky chuckled and, calmly, Ezrah's hand played over the statue, feeling an intricate web set over the little man. As he'd suspected, someone had laid a spell of magic upon it. Whoever it was, they were powerful. *Too powerful…* Again, his suspicions flared. He knew that the culprit who laid the spell was likely the very same one who held the second half of the prophecy, the rest of his torn page.

With threads of metal, leaf, flesh, sun, and moon, he wove a complex tapestry, slowly unraveling the spell until it dissipated into the air at last. He pretended to wipe it free of dust on his robes then handed it back to Lucky. "There we are. Just needed a bit of cleaning, that's all."

"Dared—I mean the statue… *I can keep it?*" Lucky asked, eyes widening to the size of Farbian coins.

Ezrah rubbed his jaw. "Well, seeing as it did you more good than it ever did me, I see no reason why not. Consider it a reward for the brave young hero. But treat Dared well, promise? He may be a Ronin, but even heroes need someone to watch out for them."

Lucky beamed, nodding vehemently, and stepped back, fondling his treasure as if it were pure gold.

At last, Ezrah's eyes settled on the mysterious dark figure in the room, standing out like a black spider in a white web. She bore herself like a weapon—while she'd obviously been stripped of sword and bow by the Devari guards at his door, she was still a weapon like an unsheathed blade or a coiled desrah snake. Her armor was dark plate, with one tall spiked pauldron, the whole of it clearly forged by a master. Aside from the fierce armor, the woman's eyes were rimmed in charcoal, giving them a deathly glower from within her dark cowl. She stood with hands upon her hips, eyeing him mysteriously.

"My name is Faye," the woman said before he could speak. "And forgive my rudeness, grandfather of Gray, but if we're done with introductions, there's a war that's about to crash down upon your pretty little heads, and I've come to warn you about it."

Ezrah ignored her, looking to Gray. It seemed only to spur the fire in the woman who was used to commanding. He raised a brow.

"It's true," Gray said. "Or at least I think it is."

"And who is she to you?"

Faye's gaze narrowed dangerously.

"No one," Gray said at last, "but she is important to Darkeye. She believes the battle is about to happen."

"*Battle?*" Faye scoffed. "It will be a massacre. The army is coming."

"What army?" Ayva asked disdainfully but with a note of fear, the others in the room tensing.

"The army that has been brewing beneath your very noses," Faye answered. "An army of dark Reavers, a legion of Darkeye's minions, creatures included, and lastly and most importantly ... *Darkwalkers*, Sithel at its head with his blue stone of magic in his grip. It is an army ready to siege this world and throw it back into the dark abyss of the Lieon."

Though already set in night, the candles in the room fluttered, as if unable to hold back the darkness of the woman's words. Each member of the room seemed fearful. Ezrah's gaze panned to each in turn. All eyes settled on him.

Suddenly a knock sounded, as planned.

"Who is that?" Darius asked.

Gray's gaze didn't leave him though.

Twisting threads of steel and leaf, Ezrah opened the door.

A flood of Reavers, Devari, and guards entered, filling the room and spilling out into the hallway and down the stairs—their presence felt all the way into the courtyard outside. Reaver Ethelwin and Reaver Dagon filed in at their head. Meira was not far behind with Finn at her side, the two so close they were practically holding hands. He smirked, heartened by the sight. Perhaps it was the threat of looming death that showed those two the path to their true feelings. *With death comes life*… he thought. Reaver Dimitri stood amid the crowds with hard eyes, the one who'd lost his brother—he was the one Ezrah had sent to inform all others, for all men needed a purpose. Yet there were many who'd lost friends, brothers, sisters, wives, husbands, and more at the hand of Sithel thus far. As such, vengeance was undoubtedly at the forefront of many minds. But in that moment, all stood quiet and waiting, the air of The Tranquil House filled with growing anticipation.

The others in the room gawked—Gray and his friends crowded closer to him in awe.

"So many…" Ayva breathed.

Zane's eyes merely boiled with determination. "It's time."

Closest to him, Gray spoke in a low whisper. "You knew the whole time…" he said, shaking his head. "You knew about the coming army, about Faye, Lucky, all of it, didn't you? How?"

"Fate is a funny thing, my boy," he answered. "It's never true until it happens."

Reaver Meira spoke loud and clear for all to hear. "What are your orders, my Arbiter?" She looked for the first time at peace, yet equally eager. She clasped Finn's hand tightly. "We are ready."

Ezrah spoke, threading flesh into his voice, his words echoing off the walls and into every ear. "It's time to make the Citadel whole."

Fate and Will

Gray listened to Ezrah's words.

It's time…

He hid a shiver, feeling the weight in the room. It was as if he were standing in the Hall of Winds, within the city of Morrow, just like the stories … in the moment before the final battle, during the famous last meeting of the great generals of the Lieon. The meeting that decided the fate of the lands.

The moment of Kail's betrayal.

He shivered again.

All moved to leave, and Darius nudged him. "C'mon, Gray, let's get out of here. I could use a drink before the action goes down, and I saw a pint in the kitchen with our name on it. If I remember correctly, you still owe me one from the Shining City." *The Shining City?* The rogue *did* have a memory like a steel trap. An *incorrect* steel trap in this case, but it was still a distant recollection.

"Gray," Ezrah called as he reached the door with Darius, the man's voice deep and firm as iron.

Gray paused in his tracks, turning.

"Linger for a moment if you would, my boy."

Darius squeezed his arm with a look of sympathy. "*Good luck*," he whispered.

Smiling in thanks, Gray watched as the last of the Reavers and Devari glided past him, leaving the shadowed room. The door shut with finality, and he found himself under the gaze of his grandfather. The man's stance was full of power, wearing his rank like a stole upon his shoulders. An Arbiter—one of the most powerful men in all the world. With his fall of gray hair, now streaked with white, he looked ancient yet somehow ageless. His wise face was lit by the flickering firelight. Against his pristine, white robes, his gray-green eyes shone with clarity. Gray found it hard to believe that only days ago the man had been on the cusp of death. Now his grandfather looked as if he'd never been hurt, nor ever *could* be.

Ezrah spoke, "Last we talked, you were missing something, but it has returned I see..."

With a smile Gray raised a hand, embracing the nexus. He pulled at threads in the air, fingers of wind gripping a nearby pitcher. Narrowing his eyes, he lifted the steel vessel. Water sloshed into two empty glasses and he floated one to Ezrah who took it with a raised brow, looking impressed and amused. The soft threads of wind pulled back into his hand, tickling as they formed a churning white ball that hovered just above his palm. Abruptly, he made a fist and the air vanished. "But it's still hard to hold without the power of need..."

"That is a thing of time and practice, Gray," Ezrah replied. Suddenly, the room chilled as water was sucked from the pitcher in a thick stream. The man split the stream into a dozen, then a hundred different strands of water. In a delicate balancing act, he wove those into a knotted sphere the size of Gray's head—his finger twirling softly. Then the water crystalized inch by inch, turning to ice. Dropping his hand, the ice fell. Before it shattered upon the floor, Ezrah's eyes flashed, and there was a blaze of fire. The ice dissolved to vapor, then it was gone, as if never there. "If my power was an ocean, that was but a drop of my true strength," he confessed. "And yet I started just as you did, my boy, if slower and less talented."

"*Less* talented?" he said, still astounded, rubbing his chilled arms.

Ezrah's eyes glazed in memory. "Indeed," he said, amused. "Highmaster Suroth once said I was the least powerful Reaver in all history."

Gray scrubbed the back of his head. "Was the man blind?"

"Actually, he was right," he admitted. "At the time, at least."

"Then how…?"

"As I said before, my boy, strength comes from within," he replied. "Besides, a thousand years to perfect one's skills does surprising wonders. With patience and belief, Gray, your power will grow."

A *thousand years…* Gray's mind boggled at the notion. Sometimes he forgot people lived so long in Farhaven. *Life is based off the strength of one's spark, Faye had said once while traveling. Then if Ezrah is one of the most powerful wielders of the spark, how old is he really?*

"Gray," Ezrah intoned, breaking his thoughts. The man beckoned him closer. "There was a reason I asked you to stay. I see there's still a darkness that lingers behind your eyes… What bothers you?"

"What is going to happen?" he asked.

"You suspect I know the future?" Ezrah voiced with a small laugh. "My boy, I would be a very unlucky man if I knew all ends."

"But…" he began, shaking his head then looking out the window to see Reavers and Devari gathering in the center of the courtyard that was submerged in darkness. An orange glow from the torches and a full moon illuminated the men and women. Gray knew dawn was coming. "What if…"

"If?" Ezrah asked, joining him at his side to look at the preparations. Faye stood in the moon's glimmering light, looking like a mercenary of death, a separate shadow from the rest. "Life is not about ifs, my boy. *If* is only the past and future. What we have is now."

As always, he felt the wisdom in his grandfather's words but still… "It's just, I haven't even had the chance to tell you about everything. So much has happened since last I saw you."

"Is that so?" Ezrah touched his temple with a finger and a flood of memories flashed through him—everything. At last his vision raced to this moment, to where he stood. Gray gasped, pulling away. "I see," said the man, his words bearing the weight of sudden understanding and empathy for all that had happened. "You've had a long journey indeed, my boy."

It was true. So much had happened…

First came the memories of Daerval.

Living his quiet life beside Mura, then the attack of the Vergs, followed shortly by his desperate flee through the Lost Woods… His encounter with Vera, then Ayva and Darius within Lakewood… Then the Ronin ... seeing the legends taking form, alive and not dead after thousands of years, and not the true evil. Shortly after, fleeing from the Kage... The sanctuary of the Shining City and its people, convincing the king to aid them, and then fleeing on his own... Ayva and Darius joining him... Then, at last, the battle at Death's Gate.

Next came Farhaven.

The long desert journey full of magical Nodes, where they had met Faye ... si'tu'ah and training with the woman... the Darkwalkers... the Algasi... seeing Farbs upon the hilltop, a gleaming gem... The taverns and Maris' Luck... Zane's arrival. The battle within the keep ... and finally Victasys... It all lingered, like a candle's flame after one closed their eyes. *So much...* he thought again. As if he'd lived a lifetime since he'd entered Farhaven. He felt like a different man, especially after his training with Zane. He felt stronger, more secure in what he wanted. The flow was coming more naturally to him now, and Kirin... His former self was quiet now, but he knew that was one thread left dangling that would need to be cut or find its place before the end.

"That magic, I've felt that before haven't I?" he asked.

Ezrah smiled. "A long time ago."

"You look worried," he said reading the concern on the man's wizened face.

"I've seen your journey. I fear the things you've seen."

"Darkwalkers," he voiced aloud. "What are they?"

"Darkwalkers have been around since the beginning of time, though few have ever seen them," Ezrah said. "Only recently have they shown themselves and in such numbers. They appear like a dark swarm upon the land and devour all they touch. Some believe they are the reflection of a dying world of magic. Others that something is ... stirring them, awakening them from their dark slumber."

Gray read what Ezrah wasn't saying... *Something? Or someone?*

Ezrah continued, "Darkwalkers hold no definite form, appearing in all shapes and sizes. Sometimes on two legs like a man, four like a dog or horse, or eight or more legs like a giant insect. Fire, stone, metal, flesh, leaf, ice, moon, and sun are all useless against them. But Darkwalkers and Algasi?" Ezrah voiced, his gaze distant, as if seeing a game of Elements but not knowing the next move. "The prophecy mentions both of them, but I do not know how it unfolds.

It is dark to me. But somehow I know your friends have a role to play."

Gray felt their presence, just beyond the wall, waiting for him.

Ezrah nodded. "Just as you have a role to play in this coming fight, they also have a purpose." His grandfather's eyes softened. "Your life is one of great dualities, simply because you have greatness in you. Moreover, your power, while truly yours now as I sense, will never be so simply held."

"Like Kail," Gray said, "just as he fell victim to the power and his darkness. Was that his fate?"

"Perhaps," Ezrah said. "The Wanderer faced great adversity time and again, and in the end, perhaps he did fail, or perhaps he was meant to fail."

"Meant to fail?"

"Perhaps in failing the wanderer actually succeeded, aligning events as they were always meant to be."

"How so?" he asked.

"You arrived, did you not?"

Gray shook his head. "Fate," he cursed. *Ayva, Darius, and now Zane*, he thought. He cared for them dearly, but was it his own choice to befriend them, or was it simply destined? "Is that all I am, a product of fate? A simple cog in the wheel of time?" he questioned angrily.

Ezrah smiled and it banished the darkness in Gray's heart, the stubborn fear rising. "Have you learned nothing of prophecy, dear boy? Fate or prophecy may be written, but we always have a choice, just as you had a choice at the Gates. What you do will define you *and* strengthen you, giving you the ability to fight greater odds and meet tougher choices ... but never believe that our troubles or challenges will fall off once we simply 'know who we are' or 'make one right choice'." Ezrah paused, throwing on a long, elegant coat over his white robes. "When I look at you, I will not lie, I see the potential for the terrible darkness you fear—it is the mantle all those with power must bear—but I see a brilliant light too, just as powerful if not more. Which one you choose is up to you."

"Will I ever be rid of the darkness?" Gray asked.

Ezrah looked out the window. "Darkness will always exist," he said, "but just as night needs day, all things have balance, and for that very reason a terrible darkness must always be met with a brilliant light such as yours."

Ezrah opened the door, and Darius leapt back having obviously been eavesdropping. He grumbled and then moved off, standing beside Ayva. Along the walls were a dozen Reavers and an equal number of Devari. At their head, Meira waited, her ever-present friend, Finn, never far from her side. His grandfather turned back to Gray and spoke with a wise smile, "In the end, my boy, life is always a knife's edge, whether it is written in prophecy or not."

A Game of Elements

Gray moved close to his grandfather's side, watching the man's white robes whisk along the desert streets. Not far behind, the others trailed, moving beneath the moon's dappled light. An army of Devari and Reavers.

Despite the time of night, citizens of the great desert city still moved about as well—though many secluded themselves in their homes, for the tension in the air was all but palpable.

It was clear this was a night for blood.

Ezrah, however, with the aid of a dozen Reavers, had used the element of moon and cloaked them all in shadows. It felt strange upon Gray's skin, as if a dark cloud clung to him. Ayva and Darius rubbed at their arms as well. Only Zane seemed at home in the strange shroud of gloom. And Faye, of course.

They entered a simple alley. Gray breathed a sigh. Immediately, he recognized where they were. It was cold and dark like any other. High above, clotheslines held drying garments of green, blue, and red, with a yellow moon in contrast. A memory of a day long ago sifted back to him.

He looked around. The alley was empty save for the tall, tan brick walls, and hanging clotheslines high above. On his left, in the damp sand lay the pendant. He grabbed it and rose to his feet, moving to leave when he felt something. Gray looked back. There, in the shade of the alley, lay the sword. He sheathed it and with a deep breath he stepped forward into the desert street…

Gray's vision snapped back to the moment before him.

He looked around to see if the others had noticed his reverie, but Ayva and Darius were just entering, looking confused, by the strange narrow alley. He felt a hand on his shoulder and saw Zane's copper eyes.

"You all right?" the man asked, looking genuinely concerned.

Gray nodded. "This place … it's familiar."

"It should be," Ezrah announced, ahead of him, coming to a stop. "It was your last memory as Kirin."

The words were like a slap. A strange terror welled inside his breast, a voice and memory trying to bubble forth, but he pushed it down. *Was that Kirin's dread?* But before he could ask anymore, the Arbiter lifted a hand. A block suddenly slid inward, as if someone had punched the seamless clay wall with a square hammer.

A *transporter*, Gray realized.

Abruptly, a sphere of purple appeared in the air and hung, suspended and weightless.

"A transporter?" Meira questioned, stepping forth, shaking her head of dark hair. Her scarlet robes were freshly cleaned, her three-striped cuffs in stark contrast to the bright red cloth. "Why here? I thought all of them were contained to the Citadel."

At her side, Finn scratched his head as well. "You never cease to amaze, even for a man of your rank."

"But more importantly, where does it lead?" Reaver Ethelwin asked, her head held high, stately as ever, looking down her sharp nose. Her eyes glinted with intelligence. Gray had grown accustomed to that expression, passing her in the halls of the Tranquil House. It was neither cruel nor kind, simply unyielding. Reaver Dagon was at her side, only a hair behind—as if both four-stripes had argued where they would stand in position to Ezrah and had resolved this particular arrangement. The four-stripe Reavers bickered like cats, despite their power and rank.

"A valid question," Dagon echoed. "This transporter looks as if it hasn't been used in decades. It could be faulty—if so, it could land us on the top of an ice-capped mountain, or place only *half* of a person in one location, and the other half somewhere else entirely."

At Gray's side, Darius shivered and mumbled, "In that case, I vote to go last."

"It works," Ezrah declared firmly.

"*But*—" Dagon began.

Arms folded inside his billowing white sleeves, the Arbiter cut Dagon and Ethelwin's objections short with a mere glare.

"How *do* you know?" Ayva asked softly.

Ezrah looked to Gray. "It's been used before. Two years ago to be exact, and by my own grandson." All in the alley eyed Gray. He felt the weight of their stares—powerful Reavers, menacing Devari, and his friends, each questioning. He held his stance, unwaveringly, but still he had no answer. "If I can trust his life to it, I can trust yours."

"Enough delaying," Faye stated, striding forth smoothly, "Who's first?"

"I'll go," Gray said. He felt their eyes on him as he stepped into the waiting sphere. As if suffocated in stone, the purple haze vanished around Gray, leaving behind the cold, wet alley, replacing it with a warm room and stone walls. The walls were lined with books, an elegant white desk sat in the corner, and against a large window that showed a keep cast in shadows was a table. Upon the table sat a board game, pieces laid upon the checkered surface as if the game were in progress.

"This place…" he whispered. It was beyond familiar.

He heard a *vwoom* sound, and he leapt back as another purple sphere appeared, filling the room. The sphere dwindled and in its place stood Ayva, Darius, Zane, and Hannah.

Darius gripped his stomach. "That … was unpleasant…"

Ayva simply looked around, mystified. "That was incredible… I've read stories about transporters, but my spirits, I never thought it would be like that!" She suddenly took in the room, eyes wide. "What is this place? It has the look of a library."

With one hand, Darius gripped his leaf-blade sword as if there were hidden enemies behind the ornate bookshelves. "I don't like it… It feels like magic."

Ayva smacked his hand. "Can you stop that? The desk isn't going to attack you."

Darius grumbled but let go.

"It's Ezrah's room," Gray declared, scanning the chamber.

The four turned to him curious. "How do you know that?" Zane questioned.

"Your memory has returned?" Ayva asked, touching his arm warmly.

"Not yet, not all of it at least…" he admitted, but what he didn't say was that it felt as if his memories were a deluge of water held behind a dam. And that dam was on the verge of bursting.

Kirin was about to return…

Fondling a glass figurine upon the board shaped like a small, orange flame, he knew he'd played it before. It was a game of hidden tactics. A game of war—it felt like a fitting metaphor for what they were here to do.

"What is that?" Darius asked, nodding to the small flame.

Gray opened his mouth to answer when a deep voice intoned, "Elements."

All turned to see Ezrah. A group of Reavers stood behind the Arbiter: Reaver Ethelwin and Reaver Dagon included, Reaver Meira and Finn not far either. Among others, Faye was there as well, watching him with her mysterious black-rimmed eyes.

"Quaint," Faye snorted, eyeing her surroundings.

Soon enough, all of their forces were amassed in the dark halls with long windows that overlooked the grand Citadel, and Ezrah spoke. "We shall form two groups—one to search the grounds for resistance while gathering those not yet swayed by Sithel to our side, and the other faction will head directly to the prisons to release our shackled brothers and sisters. I shall lead the second company, while Gray shall lead the first."

Gray froze. *Me?* He eyed his grandfather. He opened his mouth to object, but before he could, Ayva, Darius, and Zane joined his side, Hannah included. A group of Devari joined them as well, and a smattering of lower-rank Reavers. They stood behind him, their expressions hard.

Dagon spoke. "Surely, I, or Reaver Ethelwin, or even another should go with the boy—he is your grandson, my Arbiter, but still he is just a boy."

"He's right," Gray said. "Another would be more suited to the task than I."

Meira stepped forward, Finn close behind. "I will go with the boy."

Gray gave a breath of relief as she joined his side.

Ezrah nodded and the two groups exchanged looks. "Once it is done, we shall meet at the northern entrance of the Citadel. May the winds be at your sides," his grandfather declared.

With that, they split, heading down opposite halls.

"Come," Meira voiced. "This way."

Gray wasted no time, moving quickly with the others at his side.

"Where are we?" Ayva asked as they ran.

"The restricted halls," Finn replied. "None but the most powerful are allowed here."

Ayva swallowed, not in fear but in awe. Darius shivered and Zane merely looked purposeful, his hand upon his blade's hilt. Gray took in their surroundings as they moved. The halls were sparse, aside from dark stone that seemed to pulse with magic, as if thousands of Reavers had left their mark upon the stones. Twice, he saw rooms that were huge libraries with limitless ceilings and endless rows of books. As he passed, the musty scent of ancient tomes wafted forth. Windows to either side showed more glimpses of darkened courtyards or stone ramparts, familiar and yet not. They continued on and a strange feeling filled Gray, growing with every step. It was in the very air—it felt lifeless, absent of laughter, chatter, or the warmth of another.

A *feeling of absence.*

He saw Meira and Finn react too, as if their scarlet robes itched.

They breached the dark halls suddenly, appearing in a white courtyard with grass and alabaster stone statues. In the center sat a pool with a huge statue of a flame—sigil of the Great Kingdom of fire—spouting water, and the Citadel's Star of Magha, drawn in red tiles in the water's shallow depths.

Finn looked around, puzzled.

"This doesn't seem so dark and dangerous," Zane declared, scratching his stubbled jaw. Hannah was close at his side. The two hadn't parted more than an arm's length since their reunion.

"Because we aren't in the upper halls anymore. In fact, this is the Neophytes' Chambers," Meira explained. "Or it *was*, for whatever is going on here is not normal. We were preparing for an attack, but this is much worse."

"This ... this isn't right," Finn agreed.

The others, Devari and Reavers, seemed equally unnerved—a few of each running off to scout.

"I don't get what's going on," Darius said. "What's all the fuss?"

"The room is empty..." Gray said, lifting a hand to the air, feeling its coldness. It felt strange, as if he was reading both the ki and the flows of wind at the same time. "Whatever used to be here is gone."

"How long?" Finn asked.

Gray breathed in the scent, using his ki and his nexus. He almost thought he could feel the emotions on the air, stale and faint, but there. *Fear. Sadness. Chaos.* There was no sensing how long it had been. At last, he shook his head, frustrated. "I'm sorry, I can't tell."

Darius growled. "Would someone mind telling me what in the seven hells you're talking about?"

Reaver Meira answered darkly, "This room is empty, and it's not supposed to be. Women, men, and children normally fill this room with life..."

A chill ran through Gray, and he saw the others give equal reactions.

Ayva eyed the surroundings, sidling closer to him. She wrung her silvery dagger in her hands and spoke, hopefully, "Perhaps Sithel simply took them elsewhere?"

Two Devari returned, breathless.

"What did you find?" Gray asked

"Nothing," the Devari answered. "A few dead, but that's it. They're all gone."

"Gone..." a few others whispered, Reavers and Devari.

Gray gripped his nexus with anger and stillness, searching. The wind flowed along the halls, running through hollow courtyards and vacant halls. Sheets ruffled from the wind's presence upon tousled but empty beds in a hundred different rooms. The ramparts were clear as well. No guards. Nothing. He retreated back into his body with a gasp, opening his eyes. The others were looking at him curiously. "It's empty—all of it," he announced. "Not a single sign of life."

The others shook their heads, baffled.

"How is that possible?" questioned a short, brown-haired Reaver with two-stripes upon her cuff. "There must be some life—something!"

"I speak the truth," Gray answered.

"Then what now?" Zane asked at Hannah's side.

"We must do what we set out to do," he pronounced. "We will join the others at the Citadel's entrance once they have rescued the prisoners. Until then, we will search for any that I might have missed. Whatever the case, they had to have gone somewhere."

"He's right," Meira said. "Besides, we've dawdled here long enough. Come," she ordered, leading the way.

As they moved, Finn joined his side. "It seems you have a knack for sensing what's ahead," the Reaver said insinuatingly.

"Is that a question?" Gray asked.

Finn lowered his voice. "Is it truly wind?"

Eyeing the Reaver, judging if he could trust him but knowing Meira had—and for some reason he trusted Meira—he at last nodded. He was no longer afraid of the wind and its power, but he realized that in this world it was a banished element. As such, others seemed wary of him, as if debating whether to treat him as a demon or a spirit. Glancing over his shoulder, the other Reavers and Devari gave him strange, almost brooding looks. "It seems it's not as common as I expected."

"Wind is a banished element as you know," Finn explained. "Many fear what they don't understand, but do not blame them. Their hearts are in the right place. But a word of advice if I might?"

Gray nodded for the man to continue.

"I would be cautious with that power of yours if I were you," he said. "The world may be less forgiving of a man who threads wind… A man who reminds them of The Wanderer."

Gray felt sweat flash across his brow, but he remained silent.

As he moved through the Citadel, he realized the truth of what he'd seen. *Absence*. The quiet was thundering. Ayva and the others stayed close as they moved, as if hoping to banish the silent night with the sound of their breaths. Moonlight lit the eerie courtyards, shining like a gravesite without headstones.

They passed a dark hall, and he slowed.

The others stopped.

"What is it, Gray?" Ayva asked.

Gray looked down the hall, gaze narrowing and his vision racing towards a wooden door at the end of the hall. Something pulsed inside him, like fingers gripping a string within his heart, pulling him towards the door. He listened. Distantly, he felt the others following.

Zane fell in at his side as he reached the door. "Do you sense someone inside?"

He shook his head. "Not someone, but something. What is this place?"

"This is the Neophytes' Quarters," Reaver Finn stated.

Gray gripped the door knob, and his arm began to tremble. His heart hammered in his chest, but he wasn't scared. It was Kirin. He twisted the handle but it was locked. He felt a hand on his shoulder as Zane pulled him aside. "Allow me," the fiery man said, raising a hand and a bolt of fire blew open the door, wood shards flying through the air.

"*Agh!*" Darius exclaimed, coughing from the cloud of dust. "*Real* subtle. My favorite characteristic in you, Zane."

Zane snorted, uncaring.

The other Devari and Reavers stood behind them. "Gray," Meira said. "We have no time for this. We have to meet the others and search for survivors. There is nothing in here." Gray ignored her, leaping through the debris into the room, then with a thread of his power he used a gust of wind to wash away the cloud of dust, revealing a room set in pitch-black. A colored-mosaic window took up the back wall, though shattered. Boards were set over its gaping holes, letting in a faint, eerie wind that cut through his clothes and chilled him to the bone.

"Little cold and dark in here, isn't it?" Darius voiced, rubbing his arms.

"Allow *me*," Ayva proclaimed, eyeing Zane with a playful smile. Then raising her hand, a globe of light formed, golden and brilliant, bursting the shadows around them and revealing the room.

The others gasped.

The stone was stained a deep red, almost black.

Blood, Gray knew, *and lots of it*, as if a war had been fought. Someone had obviously attempted to scrub it away, but to no avail. On the sides of the walls, furniture lay shattered. Otherwise the room was barren.

A Devari cursed, "This room, it is forsaken… We must leave it at once!"

"What are you talking about?" Zane asked.

"So this is it then," Finn said in realization, eyes tightening. "The room in which the last Leader of the Devari, Ren, met his end."

"What happened?" Ayva asked.

"Ren was betrayed," the tall Devari answered spitefully, hand on his blade.

Finn shook his head. "The truth is no one knows exactly, all we know are rumors."

"What rumors?" Darius questioned.

Gray remained silent as they conversed. His arm shook at his side. *What is this feeling?* he thought in rising dread. Morrowil grew hot upon his back, rattling in its sheath.

Meira answered, "Rumors that a boy, a young Devari, killed his master and his brothers. But it is impossible—no single Devari, let alone a non-Sword-Forged one, could kill the Leader of the Devari."

Gray closed his eyes and had flashing visions and searing emotions.

Scarlet robes. *Flash.* A beautiful face—Vera's. *Flash.* A sword in her stomach, blood covering his hands. *Flash.* Dark tentacles. *Flash.* Blood-curdling screams, rending the cold air.

With each vision, his heart raced faster and, distantly, he felt his nails scraping stone.

Flash.

This one came sharper and harder.

A vision of a man, a familiar face, a long graying braid, fighting to save him. He watched as horror and confusion filled the man's eyes as he fell—dying, blood and gore everywhere.

Terror and sorrow rent his heart.

It was his doing, all of it.

Gray's eyes snapped open, and he saw others were looking at him. Slowly he rose to his feet, catching his breath. But the memories still lingered, and his mind felt full and pained, as if the dam was on the verge of collapse, his memories bursting at the very seams. Frustration, fear, and anger rose inside him, and he cursed Kirin.

You're taunting me, aren't you? He asked the voice within his head.

Silence.

Speak! He ordered. *I need to know. Are you … am I … evil?*

More silence, but Gray thought he heard distant sobs or perhaps laughter.

He clenched his eyes, ignoring the looks of others. *I know you're there, Kirin. Show me the truth. I beg of you. I need to know once and for all—let me remember what happened or be gone forever.*

Soon… came the soft reply.

With a shaky breath, Gray embraced his nexus—finding anger easily but stillness with difficulty. The line between all things. It afforded him a veil of serenity and he opened his eyes, seeing the others still staring at him, and spoke. "Let's continue then, shall we?" With that he pressed forward, leaving behind the dark room and the puzzled looks of the others.

Yet Gray knew the shadows of his mind were about to be revealed.

* * *

Jian sat in the cold, mist swirling about his form.

The red sun was just beginning to crown over the dark walls beyond. Red. An omen he knew all too well. His hand played over his scabbard, touching its handle, once leather, now worn to the nub. He pondered what was to come. His men stood behind him—dozens of Sword-Forged Devari, simply waiting for his command. He directed his attention back to his sword. Every little bump upon his hilt was familiar to him, and it gave him comfort now, not knowing what he had to do.

Behind him sat the Citadel, empty.

"What are we doing here?" he whispered.

His second in command, Orrick, spoke. "*Sometimes, when you know not what to protect; when even the direction of your blade is unknown, you have to trust what is familiar.*" It was a saying of Renald Trinaden, the first Leader of the Devari, the man who took the oath and bound himself and all Devari to the Patriarch and, in turn, the Citadel.

"Wise words," said another, older Devari.

"The Citadel is our home," Orrick declared. The scar over his eyes knotted as his brow furrowed in anger. "We must defend it at all costs, my lord. That is what we must do."

Others nodded, but Jian remained silent.

He knew those quoted words. They all did. Renald Trinaden was considered the father of their kind, his words passed down from Devari to Devari. Trinaden was the only man more revered than Ren, the last leader who was named after the father of Devari. But did those words mean what he thought they meant? Times were changing, the Citadel crumbling beneath him with Sithel and his charge corrupting the very fabric of what they stood for. The flame of the Citadel beneath Jian's feet felt a mockery of justice. Then what could a man do? *Trust,* his thoughts echoed. *Trust what is familiar.* What was familiar was his duty and his honor, like every scratch upon his sword.

He looked up into the red sun and spoke with a heavy breath, "Prepare yourselves. It's time to move."

A Moment of Fate

Gray froze in his tracks, eyeing the chamber ahead.

"Well, this is familiar," Zane announced.

"What is this?" Hannah breathed.

They stood in a huge room with walls of shimmering gems and a ceiling simulating the sky above, a more vivid blue than Gray had ever seen, the billowing clouds all too real. But this time, however, the transporters were silent, and the room as barren as all the others. Gray moved across the grand floor, the others at his side, the silence unnerving as he recalled the life that had once filled this grand chamber.

At his side, Ayva spoke, short of breath. "This … this is…"

"Wayfayer's Hall," Gray stated.

"I was going to say *amazing*, but that too," she replied.

Zane snorted and said bluntly, "If this is impressive, you should see it when the transporters are working."

"It's true," Meira admitted proudly. "It's a place unlike any other, a hub of life and magic. Over the centuries, nearly all of Farhaven has passed through here at one time or another."

Ayva's mouth was open in wonder.

Darius nudged her, and she clamped her mouth shut, but when the rogue looked away, his eyes rolled in his head like loose marbles.

They continued. Gray's neck craned as he took in the giant statue in the center of the floor. The statue was the height of several buildings stacked one atop another. Its sandaled foot alone reached above his head. In the vast room, the robed figure's gaze felt heavy, as if accusing their company of the odd absence of life, and consequently standing in judgment with its scepter and living flame. Gray suppressed a shiver. Then he saw Seth in marbled form, once again. At his side, he felt Zane stir, fingers playing along his sword. The carved likeness of the fire Ronin knelt at the robed statue's side. Seth's face was hard as always, gaze fixed ahead as if still seeing a danger or hope beyond sight.

"The northern entrance is just beyond," Meira announced. "Let us not linger."

Quickly, they passed out of Wayfayer's Hall, the sound of the giant flame dwindling. Gray moved into the courtyard seeing stone benches and fading yellow lampposts. A dawning crimson light peered over the bailey of the Citadel, as if announcing a bloody dawn.

Suddenly, from around the keep's bend, a fleet of men appeared. Their steel-colored cloaks wavered, and Gray saw the familiar insignia of crossed-swords. Devari. They fanned out in a long line, blocking their passage. Gray noticed their faces were grizzled with age and experience. He tensed. *Sword-Forged, all of them.*

Suddenly, their ranks parted and Jian stepped through.

Eyes fogging with rage, Gray took in the leader of the Devari with his sweep of blond hair, sharp blue eyes, and strong features. He wore a long coat that brushed the ground, faded black pants, and dark brown boots folded at their tops. At his waist, hooked to a thick and metal-tooled leather belt, was his blade. Though the man couldn't have looked ten summers Gray's elder, the hilt of the blade looked worn to the bone.

"Jian..." Finn breathed angrily. "Is this your doing? What has happened to the Citadel?"

"I know not, but if you seek Sithel, he is gone," Jian said.

"Then what are you doing here?" Meira snapped.

"What am *I* doing here?" the leader of the Devari replied calmly, stalking forward with deadly grace. His coat barely shifted as the man moved, as if by way of magic. "Restoring order, of course."

"Order?" Meira scoffed. "The keep is empty, you fool! There is nothing left here to save!"

Jian's eyes blazed. "Nothing? While there is honor and truth in this world, there is always something left to save," he replied darkly. His gaze passed over the Devari of their group, and scorn riddled his hard, handsome features. "I see not all of you believe the same. Duty is a hard mantle to bear. Many are not strong enough for it. Duty is a thing as old as time. The Ronin Kail bears the title of traitor for failing in his duty and abandoning his brothers. There will always be those who uphold their duty to the last breath and those who are twisted or run from it, like each of you..."

Finn shook his head, baffled. "Enough of your twisted logic. Sithel is the one we've come for. Tell us where he is and then step aside."

"I know not where that worm went," Jian answered casually. There was a sharp ring as the ground trembled, a wave of heat rushing over him. When Gray opened his eyes, Jian gripped his blade that was coated in dark red flames. Jian wore the gaze of an executioner. "As for the rest, I shall step aside when I finish you just like I finished Victasys."

A rage-filled cry cut the air.

Gray twisted to see Zane charge.

Dozens of Devari unsheathed their blades as one, fire blazing along their curved steel.

"Zane, no!" he cried. With a hand, tapping into the nexus like lightning, Gray reached out. He extended thick threads of wind. They were suddenly seared, but he sent more, thicker and faster, but again they were burned to a crisp, falling short. The other Devari shifted to aid their leader, but the man held up a hand. Zane reached Jian, his cry pitching. In the last moment, Jian coolly ducked Zane's slice, ramming his fist hard into the fiery man's gut.

Zane collapsed to the ground, motionless.

"Zane..." Ayva breathed.

Darius gripped his leaf-blade tighter.

One blow... Gray thought, stunned. He reached out with the wind, and felt the air before Zane's mouth. *He was still alive.* Gray shivered. He remembered their training. The fiery man could take far more punishment than him. How hard had Jian hit him that he wasn't moving?

This man was no mere mortal.

Worse still, the Devari leader hadn't even glanced at the worn handle of his blade. That confidence was unnerving. Yet he feared it was justified. Reaching out with the ki to Jian, Gray felt … *something.* It was like touching a mountain of fire cloaked in stone and steel. *How did I ever think I could face this man?*

Jian's gazed panned up with a sigh. "Proud but foolish."

"Are you mad?" Finn questioned. "He's just a boy! We are not your enemy, Jian!"

Hannah suddenly cried out, pulling a blade from a guard's sheath and racing forward. This time, Gray was quicker. He grabbed her in bonds of wind, holding her in place. She screamed, limbs thrashing to reach her brother, but he held on. At his side, he felt Ayva, Darius, and the others ready themselves—threads taking form in the air. Meira and the other Reavers' hands swirled with molten fire.

Just then, a brown-haired Devari with a knotted scar across his left eye interjected, "My eye, it can't be… I know that boy!" he said in disbelief, sword aimed at Gray. Kirin shrieked something, as if trying to flee. "It's him! The rumored one, the boy who slayed Ren and the other brothers!" Silence fell upon the crowds—Devari, Reavers, and all others.

He felt the pressure of their gaze bore into him like hot awls.

"Are you certain, Orrick?" Jian asked, "That boy, if he ever did exist, was rumored to have died or crossed Death's Gate."

"I swear it," the Devari, Orrick, answered, grinding his teeth, and that gnarled eye squinted in distaste. "I'd know that smug face anywhere. Ren and he were as thick as thieves all those years ago. I always found it odd the liking the man took to him, a non-Sword-Forged. It was … unnatural. *Kirin,* yes, that's his name. I'm sure of it now—it's him."

Inside Gray, Kirin suddenly tensed, flooding him with caution.

"Orrick's right," said another Devari, baffled. "He's aged, and there's a different look to his eyes, but I remember him. He's a Devari, a youngling."

"Kirin?" voiced another Sword-Forged, looking crestfallen standing beside Jian. "It can't be... How could you? Ren loved you as a son. You … you betrayed us all…"

Gray's heart panged, at a loss for words.

Orrick's sword blazed brighter as he spoke, voice dripping with venom, "You don't remember me, do you, Kirin? This—" he pointed to his missing eye, striding closer, "is a present from you when Ren wanted to demonstrate to all that *strength* is more than title. You wounded me in more than flesh that day, *boy*, but I will have it out of you and more." He was now only a pace away. "I wonder do you even know how to wield that hunk of metal any longer?"

Beware! Kirin sent. *Orrick holds a grudge that only blood can slake.*

Gray lifted Morrowil to the man's throat. "Another step and you will find your answer and your end."

Orrick sneered, tension thundering. "A man's pride is more than his life." And he struck. His hand moved fast but, gripping Morrowil, he writhed in pain and agony, his palm spurting blood. But still he stabbed, lunging for Gray's throat. By a hairsbreadth, Gray ducked the man's sword but its flames singed his hair. Growling, he pulled hard, but Orrick was faster. As if sensing his action before it happened, the one-eyed man released Morrowil and roared. His boot slammed against Gray's chest, launching him across the yard. As he fell, Gray caught himself with a cushion of air. Just then, the air parted as Orrick's blade plummeted, racing for his head—the man's single eye bloodshot with rage.

Roots shot out, gripping the blade.

Darius, he knew.

Suddenly, the courtyard exploded in action.

Devari scattered like a swarm of ants, racing forward. Fire ruptured the ground, launching dirt into the air. Devari moved amid the chaos with liquid ease. Vines raced, but the men cut them down. Meira cried out, and several Devari fell, oddly, spasming uncontrollably as if grappling with invisible arms. Fire, stone, metal, leaf, and more roared across the impasse between the two groups. Gray's eyes burned with the images, but a seething voice drew his attention back.

"Do … not … ignore me!" Orrick bellowed. The man flexed, snapping the thick roots with his brute strength, and charged forward. Gray realized he couldn't contend with his sword—he needed to end this with his power. He summoned the nexus and reached out with thick threads of wind, attempting to grab Orrick. The wind raced and Orrick sneered. Gray reeled as the man cut, his threads sliced down as if his arm was lopped clean. Fear flashed. He barely ducked an overhead swipe. Out of instinct, from his training with Zane, he stabbed. *Parting The Needle*—a quick thrust aimed for the gut. But it was too slow as Orrick, despite his girth, danced back.

"Wind?" Orrick cursed. "I knew you were demon spawn. Luckily you've forgotten the power of a Sword-Forged Devari. Bloodstone pays no heed to magic, and I can sense your every move." That was it. *The man's sword.* Orrick's ki could sense his reactions and somehow that blazing sword could dissolve even the flow. *I can't beat this man, not without my power.* Orrick was simply too fast and strong. How in the seven hells did he think he could ever face Jian?

Fortunately, in the corner of his vision, the Devari leader simply watched the chaos, his gaze riveted to Gray, as if waiting his turn. Then dread filled him as he realized that even if he beat Orrick, his next opponent would be his last.

Orrick leapt high into the air—higher than any man should be able to.

He crashed down upon Gray, and his knees buckled beneath the man's strength. "Give in!" Orrick ordered, "You have lost."

Summoning his will, muscles shaking, Gray rose to his feet. "Never."

"Then die!" Orrick roared, and suddenly, his eyes rolled to the back of his head, legs buckling as he fell to the ground.

"Your pride was always your downfall, Orrick," he uttered, eyeing the man on the ground.

The words were his, and yet not.

Kirin.

He looked up to see Darius, who stood in Orrick's place, breathing hard. His leaf-blade was in hand, pommel raised. "I just tapped him on the head. It wasn't that hard, was it?"

"Thanks for the help," Gray replied with a sigh of relief.

"Oh, it looked like you had it under control, but he was just really annoying."

Gray smirked when he remembered Kirin's words. *How had he spoken without my will?* Confusion gripped him, but he shoved it down. The battle still raged, but it was a blur—through a clear path, he saw Jian. The man's face was expressionless, watching him.

Darius cleared his throat. "I suppose it'd be too much to ask you to take this one on your own?"

He snorted and asked, "Are you with me?"

Darius grinned, gripping his leaf-blade. A faint emerald aura radiated from its glassy, green surface. The rogue opened his mouth when another answered—

"Of course we are." Gray twisted to his left to see Ayva, her white dagger in hand. Her white shirt was singed, but otherwise she looked ready for battle—blue eyes blazing.

Gray nodded and, with the others at his side, he strode forward towards the waiting Jian, fear pounding in his chest. They neared and Jian waved a hand, indifferently. Devari leapt from either side, and Darius and Ayva reacted, roots sprouting from the ground and bursts of light flashing, blinding those nearest.

"Gray, go!" Ayva shouted.

Darius laughed beneath a Devari's parry. "We'll hold these thugs off! You just take him down and end this nonsense!"

Torn between aiding his friends and fighting Jian, Gray at last turned, striding toward the waiting leader of the Devari. As he approached, flames danced upon Jian's sword, eating at the chill air, and the man spoke, "You are no match for me."

Gray gestured angrily to those nearest. "Look around you, Jian, we are not your enemies! You must sense it!" The battle raged, but Gray could feel the hesitation in the air. Even those who fought knew this was wrong.

"We can only do what we must—upholding the law of the Citadel is my duty."

"Laws are nothing without reason!" Gray shouted.

The Devari leader sighed, beckoning him forward. "I've said all that needs to be said. Now come. Show me the strength of Ren's murderer."

Gray felt rage build, and he breathed in the magic around him, letting it fill him. He attacked with a cry. Jian coolly raised his blade, parrying. Morrowil collided, and Gray's arms shuddered as if he'd run into a wall of steel. He didn't relent, however, slashing in a series of advanced Devari forms. But wherever he moved, Jian was there, his roaring blade flicking Morrowil aside like a gnat. The man had barely taken more than two steps, and Gray realized Jian's blade was not simply a blade. It was him.

Every limb in Gray's body began to burn. His battle with Orrick had sapped him, and he was reaching the limit of his control with the nexus. With a hand, he threw out a bolt of wind, and Jian cut it from the air disdainfully.

"Wind…?" the man spat. "What are you?"

Gray didn't answer, throwing a dozen more bolts of wind, hardened like lumps of steel.

Jian slashed them from the air, retreating.

He'd bought himself room, but Gray sagged from the effort, feeling leaden, as if his simple black pants and green tunic were made of steel, dragging him to the ground. He feigned confidence, standing straight.

The battle raged around them, fire exploding, swords ringing, dirt erupting as the Devari whirled, spells cut from the air fizzling beneath the Sword-Forged Devari. Gray realized his group was on the verge of being surrounded and overtaken.

"Impressive," Jian called loudly, ducking impassively beneath a bolt of whizzing fire, "for a man without honor, but I hardly believe this is what defeated the last leader of the Devari. Show me your true strength!"

With that, the man *disappeared*.

Shifting?

No, but still—

Immediately, Jian reappeared in front of him, scarlet blade lashing. Gray barely ducked and dodged the man's lightning-fast attacks. Each blow grew heavier, rattling Gray's arms as he dodged a cut that would have taken his arm. *He's too strong!* Kirin raged.

It was true.

He was going to lose.

Jian knew it too. He moved faster as if confident of his win, whipping his blade and making crimson flames ripple, devouring and scraping closer to Gray with every strike. With a grunt, Gray threw himself forward, clashing against Jian's blade in a desperate parry. "You don't have to do this," he breathed through gritted teeth. Their swords ground, their steel sparking.

"It is time to finish this," Jian declared. "In the end, it seems Ren wasn't nearly as strong as the stories claim." The crimson flames roared, searing Gray, singing his clothes and flesh.

He cried out when he heard a presence murmur: *Use me.*

Morrowil.

Let go, the blade uttered—in *feelings*, not in words. He listened to the sword, uttering a strange breath from his center. Morrowil listened, something unlocking within. The blade vanished, hard steel becoming white eddies of wind. However, Gray had simply used the move to get closer. Jian's sword still continued, heading for Gray's neck. He let it. And he reached out—not with his sword, but his hand, touching the man's arm.

Suddenly, images collided.

Kirin's memories.

He remembered it all.

It flooded through Jian as well. The dark room, the death and chaos, and even Ren's death. He saw the darkness consuming Kirin's mind back then, controlling him against his will as the oozing black tendrils murdered the guards, Devari, and finally his friend… But it was not Kirin. It was not *him*. "It's not my fault," he whispered aloud in sudden realization. The epiphany of his words rumbled through him, shaking him to the core, and he gasped as if emerging from a frozen lake. The memories were so clear, so strong.

More memories came.

Sithel, his darkness, and the voidstone. Lastly, a vision of Ezrah's torture. He saw the dream he'd had in the desert of Farbs—his grandfather screaming in agony beneath the cruel hands of eight Reavers as flames, stones, water, and more assailed his starved, half-naked body.

When he opened his eyes, Jian's sword was held against his throat. The flames were gone, but the blade had begun to cut, blood trickled down the cold steel. The man had seen everything. Gray breathed a thin sigh, backing away. Both were on their knees, gusts of golden wind pulsating over all. A silence hung in the air in the wake of the powerful visions. Slowly, Jian lowered his blade.

The other Devari froze. Darius, back to back with Ayva, watched Gray and Jian in confusion. The vines dropped, and Ayva's light withered. A dozen Devari fighting with Meira and Finn simply lowered their blades—the two Reavers' brows pinched curiously.

Gray spoke, "You know what happened now. I killed Ren, but it was not my fault. And there is a darkness here, Jian, that is greater than you or I—greater even than the Citadel. I fear Sithel is only the beginning. But if you have eyes to see, then you know the last thing we must do is fight amongst ourselves."

"My ... duty..." Jian said, eyes watering as if something were breaking inside of him.

"A wise man once told me a Devari's duty is to protect life," Gray replied. He felt pain, remembering Victasys' words, but he let it go and continued, "and *Farhaven*, not just the Citadel is in danger. The world needs us. It's time to accept your fate."

And Jian rose, standing tall and imposing once more. He waved a hand and his Devari took up a line, standing behind him in a perfect file as if nothing had happened.

"You have shown me a harsh truth this day, Gray," the Devari leader uttered. "But I will tell you one as well. I see the look in your eyes. I know there is more to you, that sword, and your powers. We, however, have suffered enough betrayal to last all time. Kail's treachery shattered us for a thousand years, and Ren's death nearly broke us again. Know now, our allegiance is to ourselves. We will fight, to save the Citadel and combat Sithel's darkness, but that is all."

Gray squinted. His words sounded almost like a threat.
 "That is all I ask."

Darius and Ayva, as well as the others, approached.

"Blood and flesh..." the rogue breathed. "What just happened?"

Looking around, Gray saw the courtyard looked as if a war had been fought, benches shattered, trees splintered, lampposts cracked, and dirt upheaved, but miraculously no one looked more injured than scratches or bruises—flesh wounds easily healed.

He looked down. In his hand, he felt the smooth marbled handle of Morrowil. He remembered, even all those days ago when he had scrubbed the blade clean of blood and brought it to Mura. He had feared long ago where the blood had come from and if it was his doing. Now he knew it wasn't his fault at long last. It felt like a weight being lifted from his shoulders. He felt lighter, breathing easier.

Whoever Kirin was, he wasn't evil. And while Kirin might not have been who Gray was now, the two were no longer halves—the memories would return he knew, and when they did, he would be whole.

Ayva scanned him. "Are you all right?" she asked.

"I am," he answered.

Suddenly, a breeze tousled cloaks, flowing towards Gray like a tempest. As it ruffled the hairs on his arms, every muscle in his body stiffened. He gagged upon its smell. *Darkness.* An evil so heavy it nearly took him to his knees. *What is this?* He looked up at the ramparts, as the red-orange glow of dawn bathed the walls.

He knew he'd sensed that smell before, and the memory came back as clear as day. It was just before he'd nearly died upon the sands. The smell was mixed with the odor of man and beast, but the ancient evil overrode all others.

Darkwalkers.

He eyed the red dawn—the direction where the breeze had come from. There was a noise, distracting the others, and he slipped away. In a trance, Gray moved towards the ramparts, following the scent of death.

The True Threat

There was a loud crash as the double doors of the Citadel opened and a flood of dirty men, women, and children flowed into the courtyard. Joy filled the air as Reavers, Devari, and gray-robed Neophytes reunited, battered and bruised, embracing in tears and laughter. Ezrah stood on the steps, watching the scene, and Ayva breathed a sigh. *We did it.*

And yet…

Something wasn't right still. *What is this feeling?* Absence, she realized, like a page missing from her books, or the moment before a coming storm. She knew they weren't done yet.

Ayva looked over and saw Darius sitting upon a rock. The dawning light spilled over him, making him look oddly heroic in his fine, green tunic. Over that, he wore a black coat with a high flaring collar that he'd picked up somewhere along the way. He stared at a leaf between his fingers while his strange blade lay in his lap, close as always. She remembered it slicing through the Darkwalker as if the beast was made of clay. He was nothing like the rogue she'd always known.

Speaking of changes… She stood in the center of the courtyard, feeling the curious stares of both Reavers and Devari. But it didn't make her nervous. Perhaps the old Ayva would have shirked beneath their gaze, but not now—not after everything she'd been through. She was stronger, and she felt it to her bones. They all were, not just Darius, but Gray too. Suddenly, she realized that's who was missing.

"Where'd Gray go?" Ayva asked. "He was just here."

Darius looked up from the leaf he twiddled. "He's on the ramp above."

"Why?" she asked, "And how do you know that?"

"You can't sense it?"

But as she dug into her mind, there was a strange knot—a presence. She shook her head, and the presence faded. No, the rogue was just making her imagination run wild again. But still… "C'mon," she said, pulling Darius up.

"Wait," he protested as they wove between men and women, "Where are we going?"

"To find out what's coming," she answered, dragging him along.

* * *

Finn lowered his hands, letting the roots slither back into the ground, deep beneath the earth's crust as the Devari moved away, gathering around Jian in a large cluster. He shivered, he didn't like fighting Devari, but luckily it seemed Devari didn't like fighting Reavers. It was obvious that was the only reason none had died.

At his side, Meira raised a brow, "Not so trustworthy, are we?"

He laughed, brushing flakes of dirt from his once-clean, scarlet robes. "Not all of us are so talented with flesh—a more easily concealed weapon." She raised a brow, as if unsure what he was insinuating. Finn sighed. "I can still sense you're holding your spark, Meira. In case you've forgotten, dear friend, we're both three-stripes."

She sighed and at last released it. "So I was, suppose I barely noticed it."

He nodded, "Oh, surely."

Meira grumbled something, which sounded like 'fool'. "And did you say *friend*?" she asked, as if amused. "Is that what we are?"

"Well, I meant…" Finn began then cleared his throat, feeling a heat rise in his cheeks. He knew a dangerously loaded question when he heard one. Suddenly his head spun, and he felt woozy upon his feet. Light flickered. When his eyes opened, he realized he had fallen and Meira had caught him. Her face wore a look between concern and annoyance, but beneath it was true caring.

"You're hurt," she said, dabbing a finger upon his forehead, and he winced in pain as she showed him his own blood.

"Is that what that looks like?" he asked, summoning a woozy grin. "Been a while since I've seen that, being the tough guy I am and all."

"Being the fool is what you are," she muttered. "That smile… You know, despite being nearly two hundred years old, sometimes you act *and* look just like the Neophyte I remember so well, that reckless 12-year-old who just couldn't stop himself from getting into trouble."

"I'll take that as a compliment," he remarked as he stood.

Meira sighed and reached out to heal him.

He gripped her wrist, stopping her. "No. Others need it more than I." He felt Meira retract, looking hurt. "I'm all right, I promise. It's only skin deep. You need to conserve your strength."

She relented, but before he could stop her, she ripped off a strip of her robes and tied it around his forehead, stopping the flow of blood. "Always the valiant fool," she said.

"When this is done, remind me to thank you properly," he said mischievously.

Meira sighed, but he could see a hint of amusement in her beautiful, dark eyes. "How you can think of something like that at a time like this is beyond me. But…" she said and looked up into his gaze. "I do look forward to being in your arms."

He smiled, holding her eyes.

Meira shook her head, as if clearing those thoughts, and looked around at the wounded Reavers and Devari. "This was just a taste, Finn."

"But a taste of *what* is the real question. Let's find out," he declared, moving to meet the others. Meira nodded and they moved forward, towards Ezrah who stood on the top of the white, marble steps. The orange light from the dawn washed over the Arbiter, making Gray's grandfather look like the legend he was. "For the record," he added, "I only got in trouble because I was half as good as you at my studies. You and Morgan had the intellectual side covered, I figured we needed a rogue to round out our group."

"Sounds familiar," Meira said, looking over her shoulder.

And Finn knew where her gaze settled without looking.

How had Gray ended that fight? Even before seeing his power of wind, he'd known the boy was different. *Now?* He shivered. Gray was more than extraordinary but he did not envy the boy—for he knew that, with a destiny like that, great and terrible things were on the horizon. Finn looked over his shoulder and saw the crimson dawn. *For that matter, he thought, great and terrible things are on the horizon for us all.*

* * *

Zane winced, squinting from the bright sun.

"Ah, welcome back," Hannah announced.

"How am I alive?" he asked.

They sat in the yard, commotion rumbled around them, but he paid them no heed, finding Hannah's soft brown eyes instead, which were watching him warmly. "I healed you again. I think I'm getting stronger. See? No spark fever," she said, pointing to her face. "Course, some other Reavers tried to shove their noses into the matter, saying I'm just a puny *Untamed*." She huffed, and then beamed smugly. "You should have seen their looks when I proved them wrong. It wasn't that hard really."

He sighed. "Really, Hannah, challenging Reavers?"

She punched his arm, hard. "Look who's talking! This coming from someone who just tried to take on the leader of the Devari! Besides, I just saved your life, all right? Show me some respect!"

He grunted from the blow and growled, "I'm sorry, all right? It's just you're an Untamed and I... I worry about you, that's all."

Luckily, he didn't need to expound anymore as she nodded. "I understand. I'm sorry too. I'll be careful."

"Good," he grumbled and rubbed his sore arm. "You're getting stronger, you know? That didn't used to hurt so much." She smirked, looking glad. "But I suppose that answers whether or not I'm still dreaming." Though, as Zane looked around, he questioned his last statement. The courtyard teemed with life—thousands filled the grassy grounds. He sat in a pocket amid the commotion. "What is this? Where did all these people come from?"

"The prisoners," Hannah explained, looking equally staggered by the milling throng. It was an army. "Turns out Sithel had banished all those who had resisted him to the prisons. *Thousands* were down there. Neophytes, Reavers, Devari, and guards—practically the whole Citadel."

Zane nodded. That explained the absence.

Hannah's nails slowly clawed at her pant legs, and she shook her head in anger. "Zane, how can a man do such a thing? He caged little boys and girls in those dark cells." She shivered, and he knew she was speaking from experience. He still felt a dark rage at what Darkeye had done to her, but he kept the rage in the back of his mind lest it consume him.

Darkeye will pay in blood, he swore. He'd refrained from asking more about her experience, knowing any detail of it would only stoke his ire. Looking around, Zane realized the truth of her words, seeing the children huddled together by a group of Reavers, their small bodies barely filling their gray robes. His anger for Sithel spiked, but between all that, he glimpsed another group. Meira and Finn stood beside Ezrah alongside Reaver Ethelwin, Dagon, and other high and mighty threaders of the spark. Meanwhile, more Reavers tended to Devari who bore bruises and cuts, but nothing more. "Was there a fight?"

Hannah laughed. "You could say that."

He growled, wishing he had been a part of it. "How did we survive?"

"Gray," she answered. "He saved us."

Zane grumbled, frustrated and angry, but glad Gray had shown his true strength. He knew the man was strong—he'd seen it, felt it. But part of him was truly relieved. "Then Jian is dead and Victasys' is avenged. That is good. I only wish I had been the one to see his face—" Hannah winced, and he halted as she pointed.

A group of Devari parted, revealing Jian.

Wrath shook through Zane.

Hannah gripped his face, turning him to face her. "Zane..." she pleaded, holding his gaze. He tried to push her away, but she held on. "*Please*, don't. I know that look in your eyes, but please, let it go. He's on our side. Sithel, he's the real enemy, remember?"

Grudgingly, Zane took an even breath, letting the pulsing fire inside him subside, somewhat. "So be it," he admitted at last then rose, picking up his blade from the shriveled grass. He hadn't realized, but he'd seared away a patch of earth from his presence alone. Luckily, Hannah hadn't noticed—admitting his power to her was something he wasn't ready for. "I think it's time to find Gray. This is far from over." He extended a hand. "You coming?"

She laughed, grabbing his hand. "And miss out on all the fun so far? Not likely."

Zane nodded, pulling Hannah to her feet. "Of course, you know I only asked you because I knew you would come anyway."

"Of course," she agreed, and together they moved through the crowded yard in search of Gray.

* * *

Ayva walked up the wide, stone rampart, reaching the top of the bailey when she saw him.

Gray stood, looking out over the Citadel's walls. She couldn't see his face, but she *felt* his tension. It sat heavy in the air. Beyond the black stone crenulations lay Farbs—a sprawling city of colorful tents and tan buildings—and beyond that, the rolling Rehlias desert.

Darius found her side.

Suddenly Zane appeared from behind them, Hannah in tow. "What's going on?" the fiery man asked, "What's with him?"

She shook her head and approached.

Finn and Meira emerged from the adjacent rampart, a dozen paces away. They came with a trailing entourage—she even saw Faye and Ezrah among them, as well as a group of Devari and powerful Reavers in their scarlet robes. They neared, but she ignored them, intent on Gray's back, his cloak wavering from a slight breeze. With each step, she felt her heart thump. As she neared, she saw that his arm shook. She touched it—his coiled muscles were tense as rock. He twisted slowly, and she repressed a gasp.

His eyes were white.

"Gray?" she breathed, forcing herself to hold his gaze. "What's wrong?"

The others were at her side.

"They're coming..." he answered and pointed with Morrowil. "There."

Ayva looked up and beyond, into the desert and—*what is that?* she wondered, seeing a thin black line on the horizon like a dark forest. And then she realized it was moving, like an undulating wave of gloom, and dread flowed through her. Distantly, she felt the others have similar reactions of terror.

"What is that?" Zane questioned.

"Death," a voice announced.

Faye's auburn eyes still glowed from within a bed of smoke. Her plated armor was bloodied from the fighting in the dungeons below the Citadel, but as her gaze held the dark moving mass, for the first time Ayva saw fear in the coldhearted woman. A wave of something washed over Ayva, and she turned to see Ezrah. He stood tall and imposing in his white robes, as if banishing or contrasting the darkness of Faye, the sun to her night. Reavers formed around him, powerful in their own right but looking like children at the Arbiter's side. All save for Meira and Finn.

"Darkwalkers," Darius cursed with a shiver, gripping his leaf-blade tighter.

"That and much more," Faye answered.

"Sithel is out there then," Meira stated, face gleaming with hatred. Finn held her shoulder. "If Sithel is out there, then so is the voidstone."

"Don't forget Darkeye," Faye said, hand resting upon her crossbow.

"Why is Darkeye at Sithel's side?" Ayva asked.

"The leader of the Underbelly sees this as a chance to seize an even greater hold of Farbs and the Citadel—whether at Sithel's side, or in the wake of the chaos, like a scavenger bird picking at the flesh of the dead after it's all said and done."

Ayva felt the chill morning air heat, and she saw Zane had unsheathed his blade, the flames along its surface blazing. "Darkeye's head is mine," the man declared quietly.

A voice spoke from behind them, calm and powerful. "We must meet them."

Jian. Ayva had trouble judging the man. *Whose side is he really on?* Most of her felt hatred towards him for what he had put them through, not to mention for nearly killing Gray, but there was a side she knew he hid—the side that had proven good. He was a mystery. It didn't help that he was the most handsome man she'd ever seen. *Man*, she thought with emphasis, distinguishing him from Darius and Gray who seemed like boys beside him. He was tall and brooding, with dark features, a sharp jaw and startling green eyes—rugged growth on his face only added to his rough nature.

"What did you say?" Faye questioned.

"We must march out as one and meet them upon the desert of Farbs," Jian said again, calmly, as if he were ordering a fence to be built. "Our army against theirs."

Faye cackled, drawing all eyes. "Our army? Have you seen *our army?*" she pressed, pointing to the ragged throng in the courtyard below. "Men, women, and *children* all starved half to death from the Citadel's charming dungeons. I'd be surprised if they can fight to stay awake, let alone wage a war."

"There are Devari and Reavers among us, many of them," Jian answered. "By my estimates, we number nearly five-thousand strong—including my Sword-Forged, of which the enemy has none."

"Devari," Faye scoffed, but Ayva had seen the admiration she gave Jian who stood like a statue, the perfect warrior.

"...and we have an Arbiter," Jian asserted.

Ezrah had said nothing until now. The man seemed immortal. The Arbiter gave a deep sigh. "It is a strange thing to admit, but I'm afraid you overestimate my powers, for now. As I stand, my power is far from what it used to be. I will only be of so much use in this fight. Moreover, I fear I am not the only Arbiter to partake in this fight."

"Arbiter Fera?" Reaver Meira breathed.

"I do not know," he answered. "There is a darker presence of magic overseeing all this. But I have not seen Arbiter Fera in some time while the Patriarch has been abroad seeking help within Vaster."

"The Patriarch will save us," said another Reaver—a tall woman with short-cropped. white hair. "He will be here! We are his children." And she muttered beneath her breath, barely audible to Ayva's ears, "*Blessed is his name, as we are sheltered and protected beneath his eternal light.*" *The Patriarch,* Ayva thought in awe—the most powerful Arbiter of all time.

"No," Reaver Finn interjected, shaking his head. He kept one hand to the hilt of his blade. His hair was spiked in a dark fray from a bandage across his forehead—a strip of red cloth. Reaver Meira stood at his side. Finn continued, "For a week now, we've attempted to slip messengers past Sithel to alert the Patriarch, who has been abroad seeking unity with the other Great Kingdoms. Every messenger has been found and killed. I'm afraid Ezrah is right, we must rely on ourselves."

Fear pounded as Ayva looked at the dark army advancing relentlessly forward. "And how exactly do you plan to kill a legion of Darkwalkers?" Faye asked. "For that is what is at their side."

"Darkwalkers would never follow the rule of mankind," another Reaver said. "The stories say—"

Faye sniffed contemptuously. "The stories are wrong. The two are lifeless nightmares, Darkwalkers and that pale worm. Darkeye informed me that Sithel, with his voidstone, can command the spark deprived beings. It's clear he left the Citadel to gather his nightmare army and take this city. So unless you, Devari Leader, have a way of killing a thousand Darkwalkers, we will be fodder for that horde. Perhaps you have a full tribe of phoxes with a Matriarch at its head?"

Jian's eyes were cold and steely, silently watching.

"No?" Faye asked, looking amused. "As I suspected. There's no way. We are doomed." Ayva felt something, a coldness, like an absence or the wind withering. She turned, looking around for Darius.

"If they breach the walls of Farbs, there will be no hope of stopping them," Jian said.

"Then we fight from behind our walls," said another Reaver.

"Darkwalkers pay no heed to such edifices," said Faye. "They will climb your walls like ants to an anthill."

Silence settled, and Ayva's palms sweated, watching the roiling darkness. It looked leagues closer, but she knew it was her imagination.

"We will meet them," Gray announced. "It is time to face Sithel. If we can shatter the voidstone before he reaches Farbs, then perhaps we can break the command he has over the Darkwalkers."

Ezrah took to Gray's side, as if backing his grandson's word.

"So be it," Meira affirmed and looked to the others. "Give the command. Gather all who are able. We make for the gates to end Sithel's reign once and for all." The other Reavers and Devari gave solemn nods and turned away.

Ayva watched Jian stride towards Gray.

She felt her hand reach for the blade, but then it fell short as the man gripped Gray's forearm. "Rekdala Forhas," the man uttered, eyes gleaming with a fierce intensity. His hard features looked ready for blood, and yet there was a crease at the corners of his gaze like the beginning of a smile. The two might not have been friends, but it was clear a bond of sorts had been forged between them.

"Till honor and death," Gray replied.

The Devari leader gave a thin smile.

Jian moved past her, his men at his side, and she shivered—the air was frozen around the man, as if he and his Devari carried a shroud of death. She felt a hand on her shoulder. Gray regarded her, calm and confident. Ezrah was at his side. Gray's eyes had reverted back to their normal hue. The two looked related in that moment, both with their resolute gray-green gazes.

"Where's Darius?" Gray asked.

"I don't know," she answered, worriedly, "He was just here."

Ezrah replied calmly, looking up. "He's gone to do what must be done."

"And what is that?" Ayva asked.

"His fate," Ezrah replied.

Puzzled, she opened her mouth to ask more when she felt the darkness wash over her. She turned to see the massing darkness only miles from their walls. She imagined she could hear the nightmare's dark, inhumane sounds, claws and feet racing across the sandy stretch. "So close..." she breathed. "Do you really believe we can take them?"

"No," a female voice announced firmly, and Gray's eyes narrowed, looking over his shoulder as Faye approached, joining their circle. "They will crush us like an ant beneath their boot. Madness doesn't begin to describe this path you all have carved for yourselves."

"Then run," Ayva snapped, "bury yourself in a hole or some dark hovel and leave us once and for all."

"There is no place safe now," Faye answered, shrugging. "Besides, I won't see Darkeye taint the clan further."

Ayva laughed. "You're truly insane, aren't you?"

"Ayva..." Gray began, but she waved him off.

"No, not this time, Gray," she said, anger growing. "This woman deserves death. Can't you see? She tried to sacrifice us to Darkeye, and now she claims to want to see him dead? She's using us again—that's who she is: a manipulator, a liar, and a *murderer*."

"And yet you wish to see me killed right here?" Faye questioned.

"Don't even try to switch this around," Ayva replied, amused.

"You left us to be killed by Darkeye. If anything, I simply have more guts than you to see the job done."

Faye sighed, shrugging dismissively, "If you say so."

"Tell us, why should we trust you?" Gray asked.

"It doesn't matter if you trust me or not anymore, dear Gray," Faye answered. "I am coming. Darkeye has tainted the clan, turning men and women into a mindless mob that simply regurgitate his ideals of strength and weakness—a sudden change I've yet to understand." Then she sniffed. "But I've no need to explain my motives to any of you, especially not my *Diaon*. To put it simply, I will see him dead or upon a spit for doing this to the clan. I *am* coming. If you wish to stop me, you will have to kill me here and now."

Ayva felt her anger reach a peak. "Gladly," she answered and gripped her dagger, warmth blossoming inside her.

She felt a hand upon her own and saw Ezrah's face, warm but firm.

"We need every sword possible," said the man softly. "When it is over, I will ensure her punishment. I know what I ask is not easy, but I swear she will not avoid her fate." *Her fate?* The way the man said it… At last Ayva breathed a thin, shaky sigh, letting go of her anger and her dagger.

"Never call me Diaon again," Ayva spat at Faye.

Gray coughed, clearing the tension. "Well, if that's settled…" He stood beside a block of stone that protruded from the rampart, a purple sphere expanding into the air. A transporter. "This should help us catch up with Jian and the others."

"How'd you know that was there?" Ayva questioned.

"Memories," he answered with a smirk.

Suddenly a loud screech split the air. No, Ayva realized. It wasn't the sound of one cry, but thousands, intertwined in a cacophony of shrieks. They echoed in the morning light, shuddering through the city.

It was the sound of death.

And the Arbiter intoned powerfully, "Come. We make for the gates to finish this once and for all."

A Rogue's Task

Darius itched in his fancy clothes as he maneuvered out of the courtyard, passing through those giant, jaw-dropping gates of black stone and into the city of Farbs. Here, it felt as if nothing had happened. He could scarcely believe it as he watched men and women in the bright early morning with smiling faces and purposeful strides, going about their day, unaware of the dark army at their doorstep.

He shivered, trying not to think about it, for he had another mission at hand.

He itched again, but it wasn't his clothes that felt uncomfortable. Besides, he was growing used to the color green, even if it was so bright it hurt his eyes—he rather liked it.

A woman—pretty, if a tad matronly—caught his eye as if sensing his nerves. He smiled disarmingly. She merely lifted a brow, looking back and handing a thick coin over for a basket of bread. Darius shrugged it off, catching snippets of their bland conversation about the weather.

He had somewhere to go…

What in the dice am I doing? he thought and shook his head, throwing his hood up as guards in glimmering plate rushed by him towards the Citadel, obviously joining the army. He laughed to himself. *Better not to question. Think on it too long and you'll come to your senses, Darius. Better just to keep moving,* he decided. *But why didn't I tell anyone?* Well, it didn't seem right. They had their mission—to face that foul army.

His was elsewhere.

Suddenly, a gust of wind made him jump, and white wings flashed overhead. When he looked up, his gaze caught as the giant beast—a gryphon—flapped its way to the zenith of a distant tower. With a deep breath, he made his way, running as fast as he could, glad that he'd strapped his sword to his back for ease of movement. As he moved, he fingered something idly in his pocket, something sharp yet metallically smooth.

He reached the top quicker than he'd expected—as if his feet were guided by purpose, by *fate*. Darius scoffed, and absently felt for the object in his pocket, but it was gone. He crested the wide stone rampart, reaching the top short of breath. He saw a man dismount from the giant beast.

The tower's summit was a stone platform, barely larger than Mistress Sophi's common room. Beyond the crenulations was an empty expanse of blue sky, and he knew Farbs lay far below. But before even *that*, he saw a flock of the creatures, all in giant hay-filled baskets like oversized hens. He refrained from gasping. The rider who had just left the creature was speaking with another, a scrawny man in strange white-gold livery, obviously a trainer of the beasts. As the rider turned, he saw it was no man.

An elf.

Darius tried to duck back around the stone bend, but it was too late. Instead, he strode forward, owning his hair-brained idea. The trainer turned too, the man's thin lips peeling to show mismatched teeth. "Greetings!" Darius bid, "I'll be needing one of those … gryphons there, if you don't mind. I've a long journey ahead of me, and very little time."

The trainer eyed him, blue eyes gauging Darius. The elf, however, could have taught a stone emotion. He was *tall*—Darius wasn't exactly tall, he admitted, but this man was huge. Taller than Gray or Ezrah and even broader than Zane, but his waist was narrow, his torso cut like a 'V'. Blond hair fell all the way to his brown, leather belt. Otherwise, he wore a plain green tunic and white pants, both torn and dirty. But that face… It was filled with such strange impassivity, like most elves Darius had seen but even more so. Darius knew that look. It was the face of a man with a dark secret. When the elf's eyes fell upon him, he felt sweat break out along his skin—the man was powerful, like a Devari, but *different.*

"Your badge!" the trainer demanded, shattering Darius' trance. The man extended his bony hand. His other held the reins of the giant white and brown creature. It flapped its wings as if restless.

He hesitated, trying to construct a lie. "You see, funny story 'bout that, I…"

"Quickly," the man barked, "Show me your badge or be on your way! No one leaves Farbs without proper consent, by order of the Citadel."

Darius sighed. *Enough of this.* He grabbed his leaf-blade, unsheathing it in a ring. He raised it to the man's scrawny throat. The green hue shone off the trainer's pale skin. "I don't like you, but I'm still sorry to do this. Move aside."

"No," the trainer retorted.

Darius gawked and thrust the sword closer, and the man gulped beneath the blade's tip. "*Really?* I've a blade to your…" He waved the matter off with a hand. "*Look*, there's a war coming, and well—*ah*, dicing hell, there's no time to explain, man! Just give me the beast and we'll call it even, all right?" He reached for his coin purse and threw it on the ground. "Take this too, just hand over those reins."

Until now, the elf hadn't flinched. Darius saw he held a blade as well. The elf's gaze seemed strange… There was something unsettling about him. He eyed Darius' blade hungrily. Was the elf mad? Shaking his head as if waking, the elf questioned abruptly, "The war has reached your borders?"

"Reached our borders?" Darius scoffed and pointed with his leaf-blade in frustration. "See for yourself." The elf looked to the horizon and saw the dark, roiling horde, eyes widening slightly.

"May the Eternal Spirit save us," the elf whispered.

The trainer laughed mockingly, drawing Darius' gaze. "So you've seen Sithel's ultimate plan then, have you? Well, no matter. It's too late for you and for Farbs. *He* is coming to lay waste to it all and reward his servants. You're all doomed." He grabbed a strange red instrument that dangled around his neck and blew. A shrill whistle split the air, stinging Darius' ears. He raised his sword, but abruptly the skinny man crumpled to the ground. When Darius looked over, he saw the elf held his own blade in hand. Calmly, the elf sheathed his sword and proffered the reins of his beast.

"There's no time to waste," said the elf. "You best be quick, if I'm not mistaken, more like this one will be coming soon."

"Why help me?"

"Do you truly think you have time to question my motives? Or do you want to save Farbs?"

Darius hesitated but only for a moment. The elf had a way of getting to the point. With a breath, he snatched the reins. Stuffing down his hesitancy, he threw a leg over the beast, settling into the worn leather saddle. The gryphon shuffled beneath him, sensing his urgency or perhaps the fear that pounded through Darius as his hands shook upon the reins—but his heart felt like steel, calm even. Distantly, that strange leaf pulsed. Darius ushered the beast forward, and like the cormacs, it understood. Moving to the edge of the stone, it flapped its elegant, snowy wings ready to take off.

He paused, looking back to the elf whose expression was a mystery. "I have to know," Darius said. "Who are you?"

"A friend to those who aid the queen, the rightful ruler of Eldas," said the elf, and he nodded to the small trinket upon Darius' breast that he had almost forgotten was there—the small, golden lacework remnant of a crown. It was Karil's parting gift to Darius what felt like ages ago. But it had been in his pocket, how did it…? He realized he must have placed it there without thinking as he had been walking.

Fate, Darius cursed.

"Is Karil all right?" he asked.

"She is, but you won't be if you don't go, my friend."

"*Darius*," he offered, extending his hand as the gryphon teetered on the edge of the long drop.

The elf eyed it oddly, as if confused, and then took it at last. "Hadrian is my birth name." The big elf swiveled calmly as the sounds of plate on stone echoed, and a dozen guards appeared on the small turret all bearing swords. The elf looked back, unperturbed. "Now it's time you go, friend."

"There's too many," Darius said, grabbing his leaf-blade. "You need help!"

The elf simply smiled. *As if mad*… "Good luck, Darius," Hadrian intoned and, with that, he slapped the gryphon with the flat of his blade upon its rump, *hard*. With a screech from its bird maw, its talons pounded free from the stone tower, leaping into the air with astonishing grace. Gripping the reins in terror, Darius' heart leapt into his throat, and he plummeted. Wind lashed at him, eyes watering as he dropped like a rock towards the roiling masses below, towards the clay buildings and colorful tents.

He screamed in the moment before the gryphon's huge, white wings fanned wide, catching the wind. "*DIIIIIICE!!!!*" Darius bellowed at the crowds, and his body jerked as if caught by a rope, then swooped upwards, settling into a glide over the masses' heads. He gripped the beast's fur and white feathers, pulling himself closer. "*Never … do that … again…!*" he shouted at his mount, yet, as the wind coursed over him, the crowds rushing by in a blur beneath, he found himself beaming, laughing into the wind. He flew like a tempest—knocking off hats and ruffling coats and cloaks.

But then a grim realization settled over him as he rose above, seeing the dark mass nearing, closer still, their approach inevitable. It was a sea of evil. He heard a rush of screams from the crowds below—men, women, and children, thousands of cries of terror. It was clear they had seen or heard the darkness as well and many were fleeing towards the gates.

It reminded Darius too much of Lakewood.

Never again, he vowed inwardly, eyes watering from the rushing wind. He squeezed his legs, pressing his mount faster with his will. It was time to find a different kind of creature altogether.

In the distance, he saw a green patch amid the endless tan desert.

A Node.

"C'mon," Darius called to the creature beneath him as they soared over the land at dizzying heights. "Let's find us a Matriarch to bond with."

Facing the Enemy

Riding tall upon his cormac, Gray approached the colossal tan-colored gates. His pulse raced, memories coming back to him of that day long ago. He remembered it all—running through the streets, the fear of guards chasing him, and above all, the terror of Kirin losing his memories. *His* memories, that's how he thought of it now. The memories of running and his fear were still fresh like a raw scab, but he put them aside, focusing on the gates ahead.

Gray knew this time it was different. This time, Morrowil was his, and most importantly, he wasn't alone.

Ezrah, Ayva, Zane, and the others were at his side riding upon mounts—not to mention an army of Reavers and Devari, Jian at their lead. Not for the first time, he wished Darius were with him as well. Wherever the rogue was, he hadn't taken his cormac, and they had left his elfin mount in the stables. He missed the rogue's presence. But there was nothing to be done about it now. He trusted Ezrah was right and Darius was safe, whatever he was doing.

Around him, the city was alive with the shouts and chaos of fearful men and women. Citizens of Farbs swarmed the tan streets. The word of what raced to their doors, the terror beyond the walls, was now well spread. Many tried to escape but, ahead, the monolithic doors were shut. *Tighter than a Landarian seal*—he thought lightheartedly, thinking of Balder, the foolish stonemason. Ahead, the last of the Farbian guards had congregated to form a wall of flesh and steel in order to keep any from leaving.

The guards in red cloth and chainmail spotted them and lifted their tall pikes and halberds before spreading to either side, making way for the army of Reavers and Devari. Ezrah, at their head, commanded all eyes. Stillness followed his grandfather, but as he passed, whispers rippled through the crowds in his wake.

Murmurs of awe, most uttering a single word: "*Arbiter…*"

Ezrah didn't slow. He lifted a finger and the gates split wide, revealing the desert beyond. They moved through, slowing at last. Through the mist of morning, Gray gazed upon that dark column as it hurtled closer, nearly upon them.

Darkwalkers.

He remembered Faye's words: *a Darkwalker's touch is death.* He shivered. *And so many…* Worse yet, he knew they had little to fend them off, and he looked back at the host of men and women, each battered and bruised—whether from the dungeons of the Citadel or the fight against Jian. They were a sorry lot, but instead of filling him with fear, it gave him hope. Despite all that they had faced, they still rose to fight again. *Heart,* he realized, *that is what wins battles.* With a breath, Gray ushered his cormac forward, and the others followed. He kept his head high, trying to show his strength of heart.

Ayva edged her cormac closer, joining his side, with Zane and Hannah close by.

"I wish Darius were here," Ayva whispered.

"He won't miss this," Gray answered.

"Something's wrong," Ezrah announced ahead, drawing short. "This fog … it's not right."

Gray felt it too, as did the others. Mist swirled around his cormac's feet rising from the desert sand, seeping around them. Gray breathed in the wet air, swiped at it and felt it cling to his skin. At his side, a miniature sun blossomed in Ayva's hand making the white vapor hiss as it burned. But then her brow knit, the sun sputtered. The mist rushed in, swallowing it whole. "*What is this?*" she whispered, panicked.

"Enough," Reaver Dagon said and lifted a hand blasting it with a bolt of fire. The fire sizzled the fog, but again it returned as if unharmed. Dagon's noble features went slack. "What is this madness?"

"It's regenerating," Ethelwin answered.

"Clearly," said another Reaver, "but why?"

More mist rose from the ground, thickening, and the Devari slashed at it, but where they struck it formed again. It was everywhere, rising from the sand like a living entity, turning the desert into a fog-filled graveyard.

But Gray knew.

"We cannot fight what we cannot see," he whispered.

* * *

The gryphon's powerful wings beat as it settled to the ground. Darius leapt off without waiting. The beast cawed, and he looked back to the giant creature. "Wait here," he ordered, ushering with a hand. He heard clawing upon the dark mulch and looked back to see the beast's birdlike head tilted, blinking in confusion. He growled, realizing the beast had taken a sudden liking to him. "I'm flattered, really, but I can't have you scaring off ... *whatever* this thing is, all right?"

Darius reached out, feeling the Leaf pulse in his mind. Vines from a nearby tree lifted, curling around the gryphon's feathered white neck like a collar. *That'll do,* he thought smugly. "I'll be back soon, I promise."

With that, he took off running.

The air hummed with enchanting music, and gold motes of the spark still danced before his eyes, but something felt off. He eyed the trees, bushes and ground. Dark vines with feathered moss clung to old trees—strange, black-barked things. They stooped, their branches stewing in puddles of fetid water, like hunched, old men reaching for a drink. He smelled mildew as the air grew clammy. Of course, life still flourished, simply a different kind of life. A huge, black beetle the size of his hand strolled across his path, and he grimaced in disgust. Before he could sidestep it, a snake that had looked like a vine snapped out, encircling the black-shelled insect in its coil.

"Why couldn't it be one of the other bright and shiny Nodes?" he grumbled aloud but pressed on. He unsheathed his leaf-blade. As he did, he noticed the green seemed to shine brighter, the air smelled cleaner.

Suddenly, there was a screech—loud and fierce, though followed by a child-like wail. Darius' pulse raced, grip tightening on his sword. *It's here*, he thought, remembering the call. But why the human cry? Deep down, he knew. *It's baiting me*.

Darius pressed forward, moving into the clearing beyond. "Well, this is what you wanted, isn't it?" he called, turning in a full circle, arms outstretched. But there was no answer. Only an eerie silence. "If you truly are a matriarch of these creatures, come and get me!" he beckoned. As he looked around, he noticed the sudden stillness. No insects or birdcalls, and even the gold motes were absent. He swallowed. His arms trembled as the ground pulsed.

Slowly, Darius twisted.

As he did, he looked down to see his legs trapped in a strange white film. Ayva had warned him about it in the desert, but only *now* it appeared. A thump sounded from behind, louder, rattling his bones.

The footstep of something huge.

He pulled at his leg, hard, nearly feeling the knee pop, but nothing changed. Instead, he sank deeper. *No*, he cursed. He pulled harder and faster, trying to claw his way free, but the sticky sand stuck to his hand and trapped his arm. Anger, frustration and terror grew as he attempted to free himself, now frantic.

Again, it thumped, louder still, nearly upon him.

He gripped his blade tighter, palms sweaty and trembling.

Closing his eyes, he felt a hot, rancid breath tickle the hairs upon his neck. Slowly, twisting his head, he uttered a silent prayer and opened his eyes. It was the face of a colossal white beast. Large, swirling white eyes blinked at him, and its large maw opened, saliva dripping from long fangs.

Still, he clenched his blade painfully tight.

Just then, there was another screech. A white figure descended from above, crashing down in a flurry of feathers and dirt. His gryphon landed between him and the huge Matriarch. He grinned. "You!" Just then, the matriarch cried out, thundering forward, but the gryphon cried and flapped its wings, blowing wind and dust at the monstrosity that was many times its size. Immediately, Darius knew the gryphon was no match for the Matriarch, but it was buying him time to escape. He felt the Leaf pulse in his mind again.

With the Leaf in his mind, he reached out and grabbed huge feathery vines, lashing them to his wrists. He pulled with all his might, grunting as he painstakingly pried himself free from the sticky white film.

The gryphon slashed in a terrible flurry of claws and feathers. At the same time, the matriarch raised a huge limb. Talons the size of great swords glinted, ready to strike. Vines shot forth, hundreds of them, embracing the Matriarch, but it roared, snapping free of their bonds.

"No!" Darius bellowed, reaching out a hand.

Then something happened he never expected.

The Matriarch stopped.

The gryphon's chest heaved in exhaustion, ready still to defend itself to the death, but the Matriarch's blow wavered. Cautiously, Darius stepped forward. He placed a hand upon his mount's lion-like haunch. "Thank you," he uttered, and the gryphon snorted, bucking its head. And it strode forward, taking its place to stand before the matriarch.

The terrifying beast snarled. Its swirling white eyes looked like clouds in motion. But Darius saw confusion in them, even curiosity. "I need your help," he said, unsure what he was doing, but it felt right. "Many are going to die and soon… With your aid, we can save them." The beast cocked its head. "You may not be able to speak, but I know you can understand me."

The Matriarch's broad chest puffed in and out with huge breaths, enough to power a ship's sails. It raised its huge talon once more. This time, Darius didn't fight. He bowed his head and uttered solemnly:

Four for the warrior of fire
Whose strength is fueled by ire.
But all will fall upon the sands,
If nature does not find the balance.
For only the fated bonder of light,
Can slay the undying Dark.

The Matriarch roared in response, a terrifying bellow. "Please," Darius whispered clenching his eyes, waiting for it all to end.

Mist and Madness

Finn staggered through the madness.

His whole body ached, the spark draining him as surely as a day spent working the Devari forms. Though what gave him hope and confidence was Meira. She moved at his side, using threads of flesh to disable thieves, or sand to blind them as Devari clashed with dark Reavers, their soulwed blades cutting spells from the air with ease. He had witnessed the talent and dexterity of those men, and was glad they were on his side this time.

Abruptly, a dark Reaver—Ingard—leapt from the mist, throwing a bolt of fire at the two, and Finn wiped the man's fire away dismissively while Meira cast threads of flesh, buckling his legs.

"Where is he?" Meira questioned the man in a dark tone, violence in her eyes.

Ingard laughed. "He will end you and your pathetic flock, Meira."

Meira sighed and waved a hand sending threads of searing flesh through the man, cutting at his nerves. Ingard cried out, quivering in pain. "I'll ask again, where is Sithel?"

Ingard trembled but shook his head. Upon his scarlet robes, a mockery of his station, were two-stripes. He was no match for two three-stripe Reavers. "You won't get anything out of him," Finn said again with a sigh. "The pawns never know where the king is held."

She scowled at him of all things, and then flicked a hand. Ingard's eyes rolled to the back of his head and he collapsed, unconscious.

"You shouldn't scowl," he remarked. "It doesn't suit your pretty face."

She scowled deeper if anything. *She really is beautiful*, he thought, *even in this madness.* Her dark hair framed her thin, furrowed brow and sharp features, but her eyes held intelligence and integrity deeper than he had ever seen.

"We'll find him," he told her, with a reassuring touch. "I swear it."

* * *

Gray moved like a tempest.

As much as possible, he avoided Darkeye's men, leaving them to Jian and the other Devari, but wherever he found Darkwalkers he stopped, attacking with abandon. He heard screams through the white fog of men and women. Suddenly, searing claws lanced out of the mist, reaching for him. Gray sucked in his gut and the claw burned his clothes, barely missing his own evisceration. Gray cut blindly. Morrowil sliced the fog and a Darkwalker screeched. With a casual wave of his hand, Gray blew away the nearby mist to reveal the bleeding creature—a strange, insect-shaped head with a dozen eyes gleamed lifelessly. The creature's many limbs, like large black knives the length of his arm, twitched in the throes of death.

A *dozen*, he counted, adding up his kill toll of the foul creatures.

"Ayva!" he called, but there was no answer, only mist and the muted cries of war. "Zane!" he shouted louder, but still nothing. Abruptly, he saw a horse bolt through the mist. He prayed the others were all right, and when he glimpsed flashes of fire and sunlight, he hoped it was them.

With that, he gripped Morrowil tighter, cleaving his way through the fog, searching for both his friends and for the foul blood of more Darkwalkers. *If I can kill them all, then maybe this madness will end.* The desperate thoughts sounded too much like something Kail would have said.

Suddenly, Reavers appeared at his side, and he raised his sword as if to cut.

"It's me!" the voice sounded, female and strong. Gray let his rage subside as he recognized Meira.

Gray lowered Morrowil but did not apologize.

Meira released a worried breath. "By the Star of Magha, I'm glad to see it's you, Gray. I saw you slay that Darkwalker and thought you were a demon of neither side," she confessed. "But I'm glad to find that you are on ours. An Arbiter's grandson indeed."

The way she said the words made Gray shiver. "I barely know which side I'm on in this chaos. I can't see a thing."

Finn appeared at her side, sword in hand. He thought it strange the Reaver bore a sword, having seen his prowess with the spark. But the man appeared a capable swordsman, his fighting side told him. "Are you all right?" the three-stripe Reaver asked.

He nodded. "I am, but where's Ezrah?"

"Fighting beside Jian and his Devari against a legion of Darkwalkers that I would not dare to face if there were a hundred of me," the man answered, pushing his red-scarlet headband up to pull the hair out of his eyes.

"Your friends?" Meira asked, concern in her dark eyes.

Gray shook his head. He'd lost Ayva in the beginning of the fight, and Zane had seen Darkeye and chased after him like a cerabul—he envisioned in his mind a large, black animal with a temper like an unquenchable fire. *His* memories.

Abruptly, a group of thieves wearing the bloodshot eye appeared from the mist and leapt at them. Finn reached out his arm. A wave of fire rushed towards the men. But Gray tapped into the nexus, waved his hand, and a gust of wind snuffed the fire. In the same gesture, he pulled deeper and wrapped the men in flows of wind, holding them in place. Paces away, the thieves' eyes were wide, swords still raised like statues. "There is no need to kill them," he proclaimed firmly. But his body sagged from the effort, and part of him, the *Kirin* side, wished Finn had just killed the men. It would have been easier, at least.

"Ever the savior," Meira said softly.

Oddly enough, Finn shivered, hand upon his sword. "I don't think I'll ever get comfortable with you using the banished element, but I do approve of your methods," the three-stripe Reaver answered. "It's a horrible thing to kill a man."

With a flick of her fingers, the dozen men sagged in his bonds. He let them go and the thieves crumpled to the ground. He looked at

Meira, angry, and she answered, "Not dead. With the right threads, *flesh* can convince the simple of mind to slumber. Not that sleeping amid this insanity is the safest of paths."

A sudden cry of men and women sounded.

"Meira," Finn ushered. "The other Reavers need us."

"Good luck, my guardian," Meira advised sincerely, and with that, the two vanished into the mist once more.

* * *

Finn led the way when there was a break of fog, and he saw Guran, the vile three-stripe that had led their Fusing when they were torturing Ezrah. Guran fought other Reavers and Devari with bouts of flame and earth, and Finn tensed, watching the horror.

"He's there," Meira announced. "Sithel." She marched forward.

"Wait," Finn said, sensing the man's level of the spark. It was almost more powerful than his and Meira's combined, but she was right. Where Guran was, surely Sithel was as well. "We have to gather help, for Guran and the others are too strong. We cannot fight them alone."

Suddenly the ground rumbled, erupting in a cloud of dust and flames. Finn cried out, reaching for Meira. "No!" he bellowed. The world spun, stomach churning as the ground lurched. Finn gripped the spark, trying to balance himself, when it flickered… The dust settled, and he saw Sithel marching through the fog, Guran at his side. Finn saw Meira too, closer still. She rose to her feet, bracing herself with all her power, and he choked, staggered by the sheer amount of spark she held, brimming in her hand. Finn rose, racing for her when pain lanced through his limbs. He gasped and saw Guran curling his fingers in spite. "Stay!" the man shouted, as if speaking to a disobedient dog. Meanwhile, Sithel continued to stalk forward, hobbling with his feeble leg, wearing a slick smile, face pinched like that of a rat. Meira waited. She raised her hand, trembling from the voidstone, and unleashed all the power she had in a torrent of fire that raced for Sithel. In the last second, the man raised the blue crackling orb and the fire sizzled.

Finn tried to thread bits of his own, but every time he did, his mind burst with new pain, shattering all thought with searing agony. *Guran*… he seethed through his jumbled torment. The man was just too strong.

Sithel stood, looming over Meira, and more dark Reavers appeared from the fog like phantoms, Darkwalkers at their side, ambling like misshapen nightmares. Skin burning as if on the point of rupture, Finn tried to catch a desperate breath. Blackness crept across his blurred vision, distantly aware of his mind breaking. He reached out for Meira, watching her surrounded from all sides. Then, before it all faded, in a rare break in the mist, he glimpsed a vision of white high above.

* * *

Gray spun, looking for more Darkwalkers, his temper growing.

He had a feeling they were losing. He heard thousands of cries of anger and pain and very few screeches from the inhuman beasts. He knew the Darkwalkers were too many. Twice more he found Darkwalkers, one scuttled across the sand on eight limbs like a spider, and another walked upon two spindly legs. He moved away from its horrible body quickly. However, as a whole, they were avoiding him now, as if growing smarter.

Reavers, Devari, and Darkeye's thieves misted in and out of the heavy, white fog like apparitions in a nightmare. Gray spun with each new muffled cry. Bloodcurdling screams sounded from everywhere until he thought his mind would implode. Suddenly—I'm coming… a voice said inside Gray's head.

"Darius…"

Where are you? The rogue's call was distant, the sound of rushing wind tied to the panicked thoughts, although Gray sensed elation and triumph in Darius.

Parrying a dirty thief's rutted blade and slamming his foot into the man's chest, Gray twisted to the east and looked up. He cursed. Through the heavy mist, he couldn't see a thing.

But he *knew.*

Drawing deeply upon his nexus, his vision flashed, blackening, and he fell to the ground. In his mind, the nexus flickered as well. "*No…*" He gripped the sand beneath him. It was draining the last of his energy, pushing him too far again. His weakness frustrated him, but worse was the fear of losing his power.

Strength is within, my boy, Ezrah's voice echoed in his head.

Just a little while longer, Gray pleaded of his nexus and stumbled to his feet. Tying threads of wind to his blade, he slashed. Morrowil cut the air and a gale of wind followed it, kicking up a tempest of sand, and blowing away a swatch of mist to reveal hundreds of Reavers and Devari fighting. He saw Ezrah and Jian battling, but above that, he saw a patch of sky. Ayva suddenly was at his side, dagger in hand. "Is that...?" She questioned.

"Darius," he answered.

Through patches of the fog, Gray saw a gryphon flying through the brightness, a rider on its back. *Darius.* On the rogue's tail was a huge, strange and white beast but with giant black wings. With curling horns the size of a man's leg, Gray knew what the creature was. *A phox.*

I can't see through this mess! came Darius' voice, fearful. *Where are you?*

"He's brought help, but he can't land," Gray explained hurriedly.

"I heard," Ayva answered. "We need to clear a path for him."

Zane was suddenly at his side, Hannah close behind. His red tunic was riddled with gashes, but the blood in his blond hair didn't

look like his own. In his hand, his sword blazed a brilliant red to rival Jian's who fought a score of Darkeye's thieves a dozen paces away. "I heard something," Zane announced. "Is that Darius?"

Gray tensed. *How had he...* He shook his head. There was no time. "We need to clear away this mist," he ordered.

Fire leapt to Zane's hand, searing the clinging vapor. "Then stand back."

A burst of light blinded both Gray and Zane. They turned to see Ayva holding a golden sphere of light in her palm, much larger than before, banishing the nearby mist with an even greater force. "How about together?" she posed.

"Together," Gray agreed, and as one, they poured their powers forth. Wind rushed along his arm, gushing outward and blowing away mist. Fire seared, and the sun took chunks out of the living vapor. "*More!*" he bellowed. He felt the nexus pulse, and he asked for more. *Stillness and anger,* he reminded himself and another gust of wind issued forth. But where he struck, more mist took its place.

"What is this?" Zane bellowed. "It's not working!"

More screams echoed through the mist—without sight he knew

they would all be slaughtered. Time was running short. Darkwalkers flashed about them, killing Reavers and Devari. They were growing bolder despite Morrowil.

It was only a matter of time…

"Look!" Ayva shouted suddenly.

Nearby, he saw a group of Reavers—none that he recognized, their hands raised to the sky, a white haze pouring from their palms, filling in the gaps they created, allowing the misty killing-fields to continue. Gray growled, using more of his power. His knees grew weak, legs trembling again and he collapsed, but still he held up a hand, issuing wind for Darius to see. But it was not enough.

They were going to lose.

* * *

Faye stalked towards the line of dark Reavers. They were the backbone of their army, the men and women who issued the nightmarish mist, creating this chaos. Eight huge thieves moved at her side. They wore leather vests that exposed the knotted scars of the bloodshot eye on their upper arm. She knew how fearsome they looked, stalking forward like death. Just then, a ratty looking thief with Darkeye's badge, who'd been overlooking the carnage and obviously in charge of protecting the summoning Reavers, caught her advance. Nervously, he elbowed the others and a fan of bows rippled through the ranks of Darkeye thugs. They looked relieved to see her.

Two dozen, she counted distantly.

"Officer Faye Silverus," the ratty-man sniveled, "thank the blasted heavens you are here! The battle is turning and you are a sight for sore eyes in this fetid hell-hole. But with you at our side…" And he grinned as if already victorious as she broached the last few paces. Without flinching, Faye stabbed the man in the stomach with a long hidden dagger that had been pressed to the inside of her forearm. She didn't break stride, moving towards the Reavers.

Confused, he fell to the ground.

The rest weren't so easily confused and chaos erupted.

Her men leapt to defend her, and the fighting became a blur. Faye's only thought, only vision, was of those dark Reavers casting that perpetual mist. She cut down the first one-stripe Reaver and ducked a fireball, slitting the next man's throat. "Enough!" A tall, dark thief bellowed, blocking her killing spree. She sliced but he was surprisingly nimble and parried her blade, throwing her back. "Stop this madness! You're a part of the clan—what do you think you're doing? Don't you know Darkeye will have your head on a pike for this?"

She cocked her head, as if confused. "Precisely."

Her crossbow had been drawn, and she fired three thick darts into the man's neck. The tall thief choked, gripping the arrow's shafts, then garbled something and fell over lifeless, his handsome face and bright brown eyes now vacant.

"Let him come…" she seethed, knowing the price of her betrayal.

Shouts sounded as more Darkeye brutes leapt at her. Many cried out words and questions of anger and protest, but Faye didn't care or answer as she cut ruthlessly into their ranks. Their blades sliced at her, but she was fluid and one with the mist and shadows. Where they struck, blades clanged off her impregnable armor. She scored cuts along her arm, and two skimmed past her face cutting shallow grooves, but it only fueled her thirst for blood.

At last, and finally, it was done. The mist from the dark Reavers
500 dissipated. With it, the cries still continued, and the vapor still clung, but at least they would have a chance now. A slim chance, but a chance. Besides, her only real concern was whether she would be able to find Darkeye in all this madness. Three huge men moved out of the mist, wandering over the dead thieves, their *brothers* only moments ago. With faces like hewn stone, each sporting scars from a thousand fights, they were far from pretty, but they were hers and loyal to the bone. She smiled at them. They were the ones she'd encountered in the dark pit of The Lair of the Beast. They knuckled their foreheads in respect then smiled back. She counted them. Five out of the eight officers sworn to her had died, but three was better than none.

Finally, it was done.

Finally, she would see Darkeye dead.

* * *

Just like that, the regenerating mist ended, but still it lay over everything. The cries continued. Gray felt Ayva and Zane huddle closer to his side as the sounds and flashes of Darkwalkers narrowed in closer and closer.

They were surrounded.

He looked at them, exhausted to his bones and beyond. They exchanged a knowing final glance, having given it everything they had when…

A burst of fire so bright that it seared his eyes shot over Gray's shoulder and burned a clean path through the mist. A dozen, then two dozen, then a hundred more streams of fire burst behind it, scorching the thickening mist like a burning sun. Gray looked over his left shoulder and saw his grandfather.

"We're here, my boy," he said. Gray felt a wave of relief quickly overtaken by awe as, behind Ezrah, a hundred Reavers in scarlet robes stood—Dagon and Ethelwin with hands extended, rivers of red fire flowing forth from each to match their rank.

Ayva and Zane pulled Gray to his feet and watched as the mist broke. And in their place, Gray saw *real* clouds. No… he shook his head, realizing the clouds were moving too fast. *White creatures.* Gray found his feet. The white beasts soared through the air, growing closer, their shapes resolving. He recognized their forms. *More phoxes.* At their head, Darius rode upon his gryphon with the Matriarch right behind. The rogue hooted and hollered, whipping his leaf-blade above his head in triumph.

As the mist parted, the Darkwalkers were revealed.

The phoxes shrieked in unity. A thousand cries of ravenous hunger filled the air as they descended like hail upon the Darkwalkers, ravishing the evil beasts in a flurry of white feathers and translucent talons. Suddenly, a huge Darkwalker leapt from the mist. Fire rained upon the beast from nearby Reavers. But the flames bounced off its gleaming obsidian skin, useless. The huge nightmarish creature tore through their ranks, killing with its dozens of taloned limbs. Devari bounded towards the beast boldly, but their blades pinged off its skin. They leapt back, but the creature was too quick. It sliced two across the waist, dropping them to the ground, and another two it impaled upon its black, spear-like arms, holding them high in the air. Abruptly, the creature's dozen eyes looked down, having cleared a bloodied swath around it.

Hannah stood beneath the writhing evil, rooted in horror.

"*No!*" Zane bellowed.

Gray reached inside, summoning the flow.

Listen, Morrowil beckoned again.

He released that strange breath again, giving into the sword. The steel vanished and Gray cut. Three slashes in the air—just like he had upon the Gates, but this time he *knew* what he was doing. Three golden arcs of wind flew from his blade. The Darkwalker's featureless face parted to reveal a maw with dripping black fangs. It reached for Hannah. But the wind raced as well. It cut, slicing limbs from the creature's body. The two dead and suspended Devari fell to the ground and the reaching arm was severed.

The creature roared in fury, turning and lunging at Gray.

Too fast, he thought in sheer panic.

Ezrah cried out. A flood of water filled the air, crashing against the beast then freezing into a pillar of ice. The beast was only slowed as it shattered the ice and lunged the last pace. Before Gray could raise Morrowil, a white blur plummeted from the sky crashing into the beast and smashing it into the ground with an ear-piercing cry. When sand and fog cleared, Gray saw the massive Darkwalker was pinned beneath the Matriarch's huge weight. The equally colossal Darkwalker flailed its dozens of sharp limbs and shrieked—but its talons were useless. They ripped at the Matriarch, but the giant phox didn't seem to care. Gray saw the Matriarch's form blur where the Darkwalker's claws struck, as if turning to wind and then flesh once more. The Matriarch's pure white eyes widened with primal hatred as she gave a single loud screech and plowed her razor-sharp horns into the Darkwalker's gut, thrashing it to pieces. Dark blood splayed onto the desert sand, and the beast let out a dying groan—then vanished altogether, as if never there.

Through the disappearing mist, and the shrieks of Darkwalkers, Gray saw a figure.

Faye.

Her armor was even more bloodied than before. In one hand, she gripped her long, curved sword, and in her other fist she held a severed head. Casually, she threw it to the ground and looked up, finding his gaze. Pulling back her cowl, she eyed him. A lingering smile traced her pretty face, her dark-rimmed eyes amused and a bit remorseful. Abruptly, a horde of phoxes descended, colliding with a swarm of screeching Darkwalkers and obscuring his view. When they tumbled away, Faye was gone. He felt a strange absence, sensing that she was truly gone.

Another loud thud rattled the earth.

Zane held a ball of fire in his fist, red and angry, Ayva a sphere of brilliant gold, and Gray forced his heavy arms to lift Morrowil—even Hannah summoned a shred of her power. But each power fizzled as Gray turned to see the rogue, riding upon the back of a huge gryphon, its white feathered wings flapping as its lion body clawed at the sand beneath it.

"Darius..." Ayva breathed.

Laughing, the rogue dismounted smoothly and rushed forward. Gray found himself smiling as he embraced Darius. Pulling back, he shook his head. "*How?*"

"With luck, pure terror, and a bit of charm," the rogue answered.

The tide has been turned, Gray realized. The last of the army of Darkwalkers cried out, clashing with the white phoxes, their translucent claws and horns brutally killing the black beasts. As they fought, the phoxes *blurred* with each strike. It was too fast to make out, but Gray's gaze crinkled, embracing his power, and he saw the truth just as a dozen paces away a big Darkwalker leapt upon a smaller, white phox. Just like the Matriarch, the phox *blurred* disappearing into a gust of wind. Sifting through the black nightmare's claws, it reappeared on the Darkwalker's back as flesh and bone once more, slashing. A dozen more phoxes rained down, biting and tearing into the Darkwalkers in a frenzied blur of white wind, shrieks cascading through the air.

"The way they move..." Ayva said in awe. "As if made of wind."

Gray remembered the creature on the top of the book—a creature of wind. *Phoxes*, they were of *his* element, his creatures. It explained why he felt a strange affinity towards them, even now. And he realized, as they evaded the creature's blows, they were *shifting. Of course,* he thought, *how else would an army of wind creatures fight?*

Gray saw the Matriarch, the leader of the phoxes. Like children, the other phoxes all fell in behind her, landing silently. As the last of the phoxes alighted upon the desert sands, silence settled over all. Reavers, Devari, and guards eyed the hordes of white creatures with respect and trepidation for there were thousands of them. They watched the humans with curious, uncertain, silver gazes that reflected the morning light. Their deer-shaped heads bore small thorns where ears should be, and twisted side to side, like inquisitive birds. Most were on four legs, but some rose up on to their heavier hind legs, which made them appear more human-like. He saw Hannah scuffle closer to him and Zane, unnerved. Ayva held her ground, as did Darius.

The Matriarch's footsteps rattled the ground, stepping forward.

She was almost a different creature entirely—though still white, her huge wings were black, like huge furry feelers, and her eyes were swirling white orbs the size of Gray's head. Horns the girth of a man extended from her forehead. Though translucent, they glowed, filled with magic of the spark. *No*, he remembered, not the spark, but the flow. That was the reason they could not be killed by a Darkwalker's touch alone.

Without warning, the Matriarch roared, a cry that was reedy yet deep, making even the hardened Devari flinch. Abruptly, Darius broke from them, moving forward.

Ayva snagged his arm. "What are you doing?!"

"We're old friends," he replied with a smile.

Gray watched dumbfounded as the rogue ambled forward to stand like a child beneath the Matriarch, and he reached out a hand. The beast eyed him with her swirling white eyes, blinking. She looked ready to take off his head in one simple snap from her elongated snout with its rows of glistening sharp teeth. Then, astonishingly, she leaned forward and nuzzled Darius' outstretched hand. A throaty gurgle emanated from deep within her throat.

"It's purring..." Zane remarked in disbelief.

Darius stroked her huge deer-like head, rubbing the long snout.

Just as abruptly, the Matriarch cawed, and its giant black wings beat gusts of wind, kicking up flurries of sand as it rose into the sky, towards the burning sun. Its brood of phoxes flapped their small wings, trailing after. Moments later, they were specks on the horizon. Darius returned back at their side, wiping his hands upon his jacket cavalierly. "Well then, that was fun."

Ayva strode forward. Darius lifted his chin as if expecting a compliment when she punched his arm.

"What was that for?"

"Why else do you think?" she huffed. "You could have gotten

yourself killed! What in the seven hells of remwar were you thinking?"

Darius' grimace became a smile. "You were worried about me, weren't you?"

Ayva snorted, looking away.

"Aw', c'mon," he said. "She really was more bark than bite, kind of like you, *or so I thought*," he added rubbing his arm.

Gray didn't quite believe that. He had seen the way she had torn into the large Darkwalker, ripping it to shreds like a ragdoll. "How?" he asked. "How did you know it—I mean she—was going to listen to you?"

"I didn't," he answered, shrugging. "I simply hoped. After I heard that the Darkwalkers couldn't be defeated by anything but the phoxes, I knew what I had to do. I remembered that when we first found Faye, she was searching for the Matriarch in a Node—*that's where magical beings reside*, she said. So naturally, I just had to find a Node and hope the Matriarch was there. After that, I just had to bond with the beast. She took a strange liking to me."

"I'm not sure why," Zane said.

Darius grumbled.

"I'm just so glad you're all right. Even if that was utterly foolish, it was also incredibly brave," Ayva said.

Gray took in the scene. With the fog gone, the world was suddenly bright, but then he saw the aftermath. Many lay wounded, Reavers tending to them, but some lay unmoving—Reavers and Devari, but not nearly as many as he'd expected. Gray said a silent prayer for them, knowing their lives could never be replaced.

"Speaking of which, where is Faye?" Darius asked, fondling the broken piece of a crown that Karil had given him in his idle hand. "Without her endless hints, I would never have remembered the counter to Darkwalkers."

Gone, Gray knew.

But before he could answer, there was a moan of agony, splitting the air and drawing all eyes. He looked over the battlefield to see Finn and several bloodied Reavers staggering forth. Finn's red robes were in tatters. He fell to his knees before the crowd of Reavers and Devari. In his arms, he cradled a body, bloodied and limp. He unfurled her, and Gray recognized the fall of brown hair and sharp features, even lifeless as they appeared.

"Meira…" Gray whispered.

Reavers rushed towards Finn's side.

"Heal her!" Finn pleaded of Ezrah, "You cannot let her die!" His grandfather said nothing, closing his eyes and putting his hand to her bloodied head.

Zane grabbed a nearby Reaver. "What happened to her?"

"Sithel," the woman cursed, clutching her bloody arm as another Reaver healed her. "Meira conquered the voidstone, ending the vile Guran and the others. But just when I thought we had won, Sithel tricked her somehow. There was an explosion, and the next thing I knew there were dozens dead…" She shook her head, eyes clenched. "When I looked around, Sithel was gone, and Meira was..."

"I'm so sorry, Finn," Ezrah said, eyes filled with sorrow. "There is nothing I can do… She's gone."

And Finn buried his head into Meira's body and sobbed, cries wracking his body.

Several Devari sunk to their knees and stabbed bloodied swords into the wet sand in anguish. All the remaining nearby Reavers bowed their heads, sorrow plastered to their tired faces.

"She was the best of us," said a Reaver with a thick moustache and deep accent. "She—" his voice cracked "—Meira deserved more."

At Gray's side, even Ayva and Darius looked heartbroken. Zane's anger was palpable, heat emanated from the fiery man. Only Ezrah seemed distant, face heavily lined in mystery, but there was a deeper sadness in his grandfather's eyes, as if he was holding a profound secret.

Gray gazed up to the bright sky. Sadness filled him to his core. Meira had helped him and saved Ezrah at the risk of her own life, much like Victasys. Now she was dead too. It all seemed so pointless.

He knelt beside Finn, putting a hand upon the man's shoulder. Finn looked to him, eyes brimming with tears, still holding Meira's body. *Her corpse*, his mind corrected cruelly.

"And Sithel?" Jian asked, joining them suddenly. "What of the betrayer of the Citadel, and the cause of all this madness?" His men fanned out behind him—hundreds of Sword-Forged Devari, bloodied and battered, with expressions as grim as death, and Gray noticed their numbers were thinner than he remembered.

"Gone," Finn whispered without looking up.

"Then the voidstone is gone as well," Dagon proclaimed, striding forth. He, surprisingly, looked unharmed but drained. A company of Reavers flanked the four-stripe Reaver.

Ethelwin was not far, but she had blood upon her face and a long gash down one cheek. Those two seemed to have made an uneasy truce. "No voidstone, Sithel lives, and Darkeye is missing, and in all likelihood still alive as well. It seems we have lost."

"No," Ezrah said, the word rising like a bird on a current of hot air. Men and women stood taller, leaning against blades or gripping others to stand straight as the Arbiter spoke. "Sithel is beaten, and, as for the voidstone, it is not the same threat it once was. We've proven its powers can be overturned." A flame sparked to life in his hand before he clenched his fist, winking it out. "True, it is a shame to lose such a powerful relic, but we have succeeded. The Citadel is once again ours, its darkness banished, and Farbs is safe at last. It has not been without cost or sacrifice, but we have won."

Gray felt hope return to all those nearby.

Quietly, he rose and moved away, into the sand beyond. A frost-bug buzzed in the air before him despite the strange time of day, humming enchantingly. He felt a presence and knew who it was. The man stood at his side, a boon of comfort. "Do you really believe it's over?" he asked his grandfather softly.

"For now," Ezrah answered.

Looking over his shoulder, he saw Ezrah's lined face staring into the distant dunes—seeing what could not be seen. Gray shook his head. "It seems so strange, fighting so hard but nothing turning out the way I ever imagined," he said. Behind him, Jian moved carefully through the field of battle with his legion of Devari not far away. He picked his way through dead thieves and strange beasts, clearly looking for wounded men.

"Sometimes life's bounty is in the unexpected," Ezrah answered. Suddenly, the frost-bug landed upon the Arbiter's robed sleeve, glowing its beautiful cerulean hue.

Gray remembered first seeing them when he traversed the desert to reach Farbs with Ayva and Darius. It seemed like so long ago, their journey to discover who he once was and how he'd lost his memories.

Now he knew.

"As for Jian, he is an honorable man, but be careful of him," Ezrah advised. "Even those with righteous intentions can lead us astray. I believe he and his Devari will be a point of contention since the Ronin were the once-generals of his kind."

"But the Ronin are dead," Zane said abruptly.

Gray turned to see Ayva and Darius at the fiery man's side.

Darius held his leaf-blade in hand, his eyes swirling with power and duty, far unlike the scoundrel he remembered. Those eyes seemed different but familiar. The sword in his hand too.

Ayva, on the other hand, wore her faded white shirt and fitted breeches, but with all the chaos upon the sands, it had turned the shirt a dusty gold just like her vest. Otherwise, her eyes shone harder and wiser. No surprise, he thought, with all that they'd been through. She wore a shrewd expression now. Her brows pinched and she spoke hesitantly. "I've been thinking about that … a lot, actually…" She looked to Ezrah and asked, "The Ronin aren't dead, are they?"

Silence held all four, even Zane looked to each of them in understanding when a sudden breeze picked up a flurry of sand, assaulting them, and Ayva pulled up her black shawl, covering her face—all but her eyes. Her bright blue gaze shone fiercely, the only thing visible just like Omni, and Ezrah replied with a mischievous smile, "I believe you just answered that yourself, my dear."

Gray felt a chill run through him.

It all made sense.

Hannah approached. "What's going on here?"

"Ah, perfect timing," Ezrah announced. "We were just discussing your journey."

"Our journey?" Gray asked, confused.

"Of course," his grandfather answered.

"What are you talking about?" Zane questioned, twisting his blade in hand. "My place is here, in Farbs."

"Is it?" the Arbiter folded his arms into his billowing sleeves and spoke, "Magic is fading from this world, slowly but surely. The Great Kingdoms are in danger and far from united. Order has not yet been restored to Farhaven. Not to mention I fear there is a greater evil here, something that stirred Reavers to darkness and even pulled the strings of Sithel."

Darius scratched his jaw and spoke up curiously. "For argument's sake, where exactly would one begin to fix all that?"

"Follow the Algasi, of course," said the Arbiter.

"Vaster," Ayva whispered.

"The Kingdom of Sun," Ezrah said. "Besides, my boy, it's just begun. You know who you are, so it only stands to reason that the others would like to discover their fates, don't you think?"

"Others?" Gray asked.

"You mean us, don't you?" Ayva questioned.

The Arbiter looked to each in turn. "You all, and the rest."

Darius cleared his throat. "The rest?"

"The other Ronin," Ezrah replied.

Hannah swallowed, fearfully. "What is he talking about, Zane?"

"I..." The fiery man shook his head.

"Where are they?" Gray asked, heart pounding.

Ezrah gave an amused laugh and turned, walking away. But over his shoulder he spoke, the words barely reaching them. "Waiting," he answered, "for you." A strange excitement brewed inside Gray as he watched the lone frost-bug fly, dancing in the warm air, then flit off, as if to find its brothers.

The Face of True Evil

Sithel stood in a gloom-filled room without furnishings or windows. The stone walls *crawled* with the darkness, as if a black river flowed upwards to a dark void above, the shadows ending as wispy, lacy fingers, alive and moving. He dared not look down and find the same. Huddling closer in his white robes, now soaked red from the bloodshed, he took an even breath.

He waited impatiently for the dark figure to arrive. Despite his fear, anger and frustration raged like a storm inside him, barely contained.

They had failed, miserably. He cursed.

His legions crushed, and Darkeye missing. *Where was that miserable thief?* he thought again. He'd vanished in the middle of the chaos to fight some fool woman. In the end, Sithel had barely escaped with his own life. He was not prone to delusions. They had failed, but he knew the cause beyond those foul, white beasts.

That boy and his companions.

Somehow they had rallied against the misguided Jian.

But Sithel smirked inwardly, for he had taken his share of lives, those pathetic Reavers who believed themselves infallible with their precious spark. *Meira*, he thought with a dark hunger, remembering her last breaths and the fear in her eyes. Besides, it was not over.

Sithel waited now because he *would* get what he was promised. The Citadel was his, and he would not let it go so easily. For he still had what the shadowed figure wanted.

In one hand, he cradled the voidstone. The azure, crackling light was a comfort against the strange shadows, stone cold and yet warm in his curled palm as always. But this time, he kept it hidden. It was time for a new lord to reign supreme in this world.

It was Sithel's time.

Abruptly, a gap in the huge black wall opened and a shadowed figure stepped forth. A strange, brilliant light surrounded his frame, as if a sun was hidden behind his back. At the shadow figure's side, in the darkness, was a strange, black creature. *A Darkwalker?* Sithel questioned. *Strange*… Yet despite the gloom, he saw the hint of translucent horns, and white fur upon its breast. Part phox and part Darkwalker, the creature was an abomination. *It couldn't be*… he thought. *Her?* No. She was evil, but not like this. Upon seeing the figure, as always, Sithel began to sweat in dread. But he rose higher out of his ever-stooped posture and addressed the figure. "Master," he said in greeting.

"Greetings, Sithel," the figure uttered in that loud, unearthly rumble that made his bones ache.

Sithel hesitated, but his master did not seem upset. Though he couldn't see his face in that dark cowl, he seemed *pleased* of all things. He had expected his master to reign down his anger, only to fall short with the aid of the voidstone. Whatever his master was, he had to at least be human, and all humans who wielded magic used the pitiful spark. And in that, his master would fail. He reached for the voidstone, but hesitated. "Master," he posed, licking his lips, "You … are not mad?"

"Mad? Why would I be?"

Anger surged again inside Sithel, limbs shaking with wrath, but he hid it well. "Your—" he corrected himself, "*Our* plans have failed, master. My armies are all laid to waste. Only a handful of Dark Reavers even survived. It's clear, is it not? We have lost." *But I haven't lost. Not yet.* The voidstone grew warmer and colder behind his back, ready to be used.

"Lost?" the figure questioned, perplexed. "No, dear Sithel. We've done exactly as planned. You, my pet, served me perfectly."

Confusion spiraled inside of Sithel. "What are you talking about?"

The dark figure took a step forward, growing in size and girth, filling the room with every deliberate stride. "You have shown me amazing truths at little cost. I know now that the boy has companions. I have seen them. I know their faces and even their names. I've seen what will rally these people together. Sacrifice, compassion," the figure said and laughed. "Now I know what I must use to break them. Most importantly, you have proven to all that there is a darkness, but it is not me."

Sithel shook his head, his plan momentarily forgotten in light of his confusion. "But at what cost? Thousands of our men have died and…"

"Useless pawns," the figure rasped. "True strength is far beyond their reach, or even your imagination, my pet. The final prophesized war is rising, and this time, there will only be one victor. Sadly, you will not live to see it."

Suddenly, dark feelers reached from the ground, circling around Sithel's limbs and lifting him into the air. Fear rooted him, but not for long. A limb shot for his arm, but he sneered and grabbed the voidstone, lunging it forward. The black limb was seared by the blue aura. "You underestimated me," Sithel seethed. "You forget, never give the object of power to one who you intend to kill."

"Power?" the figure asked, amused. "I gave you an object of power, but you were always weak."

The darkness continued to writhe in pain, shadows hissing beneath the voidstone's blue glow. Sithel's dark sneer slowly wilted. He could always see the orange aura around his victims in the moment before it fled and their terror filled them.

Their spark.

But as the voidstone glowed, Sithel didn't see an orange glow around the figure. Instead it was gold, like a bursting sun, pervading the room with divine light. It nearly blinded him. *It couldn't be…* This man, he wasn't just powerful. He was a god. Shards of pain ran through him as he stared into the light, but he couldn't turn away. He cried out, blood running from his eyes, limbs shaking uncontrollably, and tears streaming down his face in terror. "You…" he sputtered. "What in the seven hells are you?"

The figure raised his glowing gold hand slowly. Sithel felt the dark tentacles raise him higher in the air, curling painfully tighter around his wrists, legs, and one strangling his neck. "When I found you in Covai, Sithel, you were just another pile of useless flesh, lost like so many. I offered you something beyond your wretched life. I offered you more. That is what I prey upon, all those who wish for more out of their pathetic lives. I gave you that, but in the end you have proven there is nothing great inside you after all. You have served your usefulness, my pawn. It is time for you to die as the insect you were all along."

No... Sithel thought. *I am strong*... His childhood terror filled him, the only thing he feared more than death. "You're wrong. I am strong!" he bellowed. "You cannot kill me!" He thrust the voidstone further forward, and the blue light flared, then sputtered and the black limbs continued to crawl and writhe forward inevitably.

"No," the dark figure hissed. "You are *nothing*."

Sithel screamed as the tendrils flashed. They plunged through his body, and he felt his insides twist, innards tugged brutally, and he sprouted new tears of agony. He shrieked, begging for it to stop, but the twisting pain continued, as if his limbs and body were being stretched and picked apart, piece-by-piece.

At last, it ended.

When he opened his eyes—lids sore from the pain of holding them clenched so tightly—he expected to see himself in the realm of the dead, but instead, he saw a vision of terror: the obsidian walls glimmered, showing the reflection of a demon. But it was not his master—it was *himself*.

His master spoke in a deadly cold tone. "I've decided to reform you, sparing you for now. Yet raise your hand against me again, my pet, and I swear to deliver unto you pain so horrifying that it will make death seem the lightest of breezes."

And the light hit his dark lord's face, showing features that he both knew and feared. "I shall obey, *mistress*," Sithel answered, voice rumbling and dark, strange in his own throat. But he reveled in it—terror and delight filled him, his grin spreading as he eyed his clawed hand.

He was powerful, at last.

Life Restored

The nearby fire warmed Gray's back as his quill scratched against the parchment, writing his letter to Karil. In the corner of his

eye, he saw his strange book that Mura had given him resting upon the desk. Occasionally, he thumbed through it to aid his burgeoning poem. Beside it sat his dinner, a spicy vegetable soup from the kitchens of the Citadel. It was tasty, but it was growing cold as he worked to find the words to describe what was coming, for them and for the world as a whole.

It had been two days since the battle upon the Reliahs desert, the disappearance of Sithel, and the death of Meira. They now were in Ezrah's room, in the upper restricted halls of the Citadel. With the influx of Lost Ones, the keep was packed tighter than a school of Inago fish, for nearly every room was filled. Zane, with Gray's help, had convinced Ezrah and the Reavers to house the Lost Ones until they got back on their feet. It only made sense with the loss of all those foul dark Reavers.

But it wasn't so bad. Ezrah's room was quite comfortable—stuffed chairs, gold stands, vases of priceless Saerien porcelain, and a warm fire glowed in the marble hearth. Despite its opulence, the room felt as familiar and comforting as Mura's hut, reminding him of his slowly returning memories.

Still, Gray was growing restless.

They all were, for this was their last night in Farbs.

Nearby, Darius and Zane lounged on a rich, purple and gold-scrolled rug in the center of the room. The rogue puffed on a new pipe, while he and the fiery man played a game of Elements. The rogue hummed a quiet tune, scrutinizing his next move,

> *"I've seen the darkness come and go*
> *I've seen the light sway and fro,*
> *But all I've really hoped to see,*
> *Was your sweet beauty,*
> *Gazing—gazing, up-on me."*

Gray had taught both of them the basics of Elements from his memories. Zane was on a winning streak. He had backed Darius into a corner now with two orange flame-shaped figurines. "You swear you've never played this?" Darius asked, breaking his tune, making his move with a disgruntled sound.

"Not once," Zane said. He plopped a glass flame closer to Darius' side of the board then returned to idly spinning his dagger on a patch of bare stone.

The rogue grumbled. "How are you so good at this?"

"You forget, fire is my *element*," Zane said with a sly smirk.

"*Oh*, so clever," Darius said sarcastically, a bitter tinge to his voice.

"It was clever," Gray remarked without looking up. "Don't be bitter."

"Bah, this game is over anyway," Darius exclaimed. "It's your turn, Ayva."

Ayva sat across from Gray. Cradling her head with one hand, her elbows rested upon the only table—a polished desk made of a strange white wood—while she gazed wistfully out the nearby window. Outside, the sun was setting, but Gray could see men walking the ramparts, guards and Devari, others strolling through the green yards far below. But he knew that's not what Ayva was thinking about. Her mind instead fixated upon the woman who had called her *Diaon*. "Let Hannah take my turn," she said distantly.

Hannah sat close beside Zane as always, cross-legged, wearing a blue dress. "I'm busy," she said with a stone figure gripped tightly in her hand, beads of sweat growing on her forehead in concentration. Zane's sister was everything the fiery man wasn't—innocent and quiet. He knew that was something Zane had fought for, but Gray had seen fire in her too, much like her brother's.

"What are you daydreaming about anyway?" Darius asked Ayva.

Absently fingering a notch in the smooth, white desk, she answered quietly, "She's still out there."

"Don't get me started on that woman," Darius cursed, pulling his leaf-blade closer. "I still don't get why she had to steal Mirkal. Why not your steed, Gray? You said it was your *deal* after all. First my pipe, *now* my cormac. The woman truly is evil," he said with a snort. Despite the fact that she'd tried to kill him and Ayva, Gray thought the rogue seemed more upset at the loss of a pipe and his mount. Though he knew that wasn't the truth. The woman had left her mark on the rogue, and Ayva. On them all for that matter.

Gray recalled Faye holding a head in her hand before she had tossed it to the ground, and he asked suddenly, "I never asked by the way, but what did Darkeye look like?"

Zane stirred. He was scratching his stubbled cheek with his dagger and his hand froze. Gray knew he still held a bitter hatred towards Darkeye for kidnapping his sister. A hate that only seemed to burn deeper at his disappearance in the battle.

"Darkeye?" Ayva asked. "Well, like a thief. He had dark auburn eyes, unkempt blond hair, and a black mask, oh and a white scar that ran across his face."

The quill snapped in Gray's hand. "Are you sure…?"

Darius snorted. "I was face to face with that murderer. That's him all right. What's gotten into you?"

Gray looked down to his hand and saw he'd cut himself from the quill. It was only a tiny laceration, but blood was beginning to ooze. It reminded him of Faye and his blood pact within the Node, and her words echoed in his head. *Farhaven will hold you to it…* "Darkeye is dead," Gray announced quietly. "Faye killed him."

"What?" Zane questioned, eyes burning.

And Gray explained quickly what he saw. "That's the strangest news I've ever heard," Darius remarked. "Good news, but *strange*. That woman continues to boggle my mind."

"I'll believe it when I see it," Zane countered. "But in either case, it's still clear Sithel got away."

"Was he really the one behind it all?" Darius asked.

"I fear he wasn't," Zane answered. "Before Lucky left, the little champion told me something. He said that Sithel was stealing boys and draining their spark under Arbiter Fera's command. Worse yet, she had asked to see me..."

Those in the room grew even more darkly silent. "Then Arbiter Fera is the cause of all this madness?" Darius whispered. "She is the puppet master pulling Sithel's strings?"

"Perhaps..." Zane said hesitantly. "As dark as this may sound, she didn't kill any of the boys. In fact, Lucky said she even stayed Sithel's bloodthirsty hand. Instead, she seems to be searching for something."

"For what?" Gray asked, curious.

The fiery man shook his head. "I wish I knew..."

"Where is she now?" Darius questioned.

Zane's dagger rasped at the stubble on his jaw and he sighed. "I asked around and no one has seen Arbiter Fera since the battle on the sands. It seems she's gone as well ... for now." Suddenly, the stone figurine in Hannah's hand burst with a tiny flame. Hanna gave a surprised squawk, and then smiled in success. "You did it," her brother said approvingly.

"Well, we can't all be as talented as you with fire," she said. "A talent I can't believe you hid from me all this time. But mind you, I'll get there, and then watch out."

Gray was having trouble focusing on the letter, his mind a churning cauldron.

"Well if Ayva's not playing, care to join us, my poetic chum?" Darius asked.

Gray looked up, realizing he was being spoken to. "Soon, I promise," he said, then scratched his temple, trying to think of another word for 'belittled.' *Disparaged*, his memories said.

"Almost done with that letter?" Zane questioned.

"Almost," he answered.

"You didn't forget to add what I told you, did you?" the fiery man replied, humorless. "She owes me."

Gray chuckled without looking up. "How could I possibly forget?"

In the corner of his eye, Zane nodded, satisfied. "As long as the Lost Ones are safe, the rest is hers."

Hannah spoke, "Wait, there's still one more thing I don't get... With Darkeye dead, does that mean the Darkeye clan is no more?" Again distracted, Gray looked up from his letter, half-listening.

"At the least now it seems they're leaderless," Darius said, puffing smoke rings from his pipe. "Good riddance, I say, for it should be a long time until Farbs is troubled by their ilk."

Gray hesitated as he remembered Faye and the look in her eyes. He wasn't so sure, but he kept his silence, glad for the look of hope and peace in his friends. A fire crackled in the nearby hearth, banishing the chill in the room, promising security. And all seemed to settle into its right place.

Ayva rose and moved outside.

"What's with her?" Darius asked. "I said something wrong, didn't I?"

Shrugging, Gray set down his pen and followed. He found her on a large stone balcony that overlooked the Citadel's grounds. Again, he saw they flowed with servants, Neophytes, Devari, red-robed Reavers, and its flock of Lost Ones—men, women and children. *Life*. It had returned to the Citadel. Beyond that was Farbs. The desert city glowed in the light of the fading sun, which sat on the horizon like a golden flame. A breeze flowed over them, tousling Gray's cloak and playing with Ayva's short-cropped hair. The wind fell down the steep black walls and sifted into the crowded streets full of life, nighttime settling over Farbs.

The people are safe, he thought again, content.

Ayva held the twisted black metal railing as he approached. He debated using the ki, but refrained. Instead, he touched her arm. "Are you all right?" he asked. "I was worried..."

"No," she said and twisted, wearing an unexpected smile. "I'm not all right. I'm terrified, and yet... I've never felt more alive." She looked away, north—over the clay buildings and colorful tents, into the desert and beyond.

Vaster, he thought.

"Vaster," she uttered, voicing his thoughts aloud. "The Great Kingdom of Sun. I can feel it, Gray. I swear I can almost see its gleaming walls shining like a jewel, those turrets of shimmering glass." She turned to him, grabbing his hand in her soft palms. "Can you?"

He only nodded, slightly. Again, his heart thumped against his ribcage. "It's waiting for you."

"For us all," she replied.

"What's waiting for us?" Darius' voice echoed from behind.

Quickly, Ayva let Gray's hand drop as the others came from the wide doorway onto the large balcony. "Adventure," Zane said, hand upon his blade, his wide and muscular frame nearly twice that of Darius.

Hannah spoke, wiping her hands from the stone dust. "You can't be thinking of joining them, can you, Zane? How can we leave the Lost Ones?"

"There's nothing for us here anymore," Zane said. "The Lost Ones are safe now. I wish I could have found that traitorous little cur who nearly sent me to my death, but his little tip ensured that the Lost Ones will never be left cold and hungry again."

She nodded and huddled closer to her brother. "Well, it doesn't matter where I am as long as I'm at your side."

"You're both coming," Darius stated firmly.

"Who says I care about you?" Zane asked.

Darius scoffed. "And here I thought we were becoming fast friends over Elements. Is it because I beat you too many times?"

"You beat me?" Zane asked, amused. "You have twigs between your ears."

Darius interrupted him. "Psh, who are you talking to, fire for brains?"

Zane growled. Suddenly Darius yelped, grabbing his rear in pain. "What were you saying?" the fiery man asked.

"I changed my mind. Feel free to stay," Darius said.

"Try and stop me from coming," Zane replied.

"Only too gladly," Darius retorted stepping towards him, but Ayva interjected, calming the two.

Gray watched them all, as if from a distance—Ayva the light of reason, Zane the fire of passion, Darius with his ever-changing nature. *Sun, Fire, and Leaf.* Each balancing the other. It was like watching Omni, Seth, and Maris all over again. And in that moment, he knew the Ronin really had never died.

"We're going," Gray declared suddenly, heart thumping in his chest in anticipation. "All of us." They turned to him, and he twisted looking to Vaster—past the golden flame of the setting sun, towards the Golden City. "It's time to find our brothers."

EPILOGUE

“Mistress Hitomi!” a girl called, racing down the half-constructed steps that were still missing their railing. Hitomi grimaced inwardly. How she still missed The Dipping Tsugi’s railing that was polished to a ruby glow by thousands of hands. A testament of a well-loved inn.

It’s strange what things one misses, and coincidently doesn’t, Hitomi thought. Her first thought was for that strange, affable hermit… Karil said he was safe, but she knew he was deep in enemy territory. From what she could tell, or at least had heard, Eldas was the last place to be in this magical world. But that gruff old hermit had surprises up his sleeve. She knew Mura wouldn’t die so easily.

“Hitomi!” the young girl called again, leaping the last stairs into the mostly empty common room, save for the hearth made from large polished river stones—the only thing finished in the large chamber. A *hearth is the heart of an inn.* “He’s coming back soon! Just like he said he’d be!”

Hitomi had been watching from the corner of her eye. At last, she looked up from her ledger and saw the men surrounding her—elves, she corrected. Strong and dutiful they were, and not so surprisingly handy when it came to woodworking. “Slow down, girl,” she instructed, putting a hand to Piper’s arm. The girl was one of the villagers who'd survived the chaos, a refugee of Daerval. "What are you talking about? Aren't you supposed to be in charge of the Aviary? And who's coming back now? With all this ruckus, it better be the devil himself."

"*Gray!*" the girl exclaimed.

Hitomi raised a dubious eyebrow. "Piper, has Balder been putting tales into your ear again?" She knew she should put the man to work on her inn, for he was incredibly talented, *for a drunk*, but he'd taken more to being the resident mischief-maker and storyteller of the camp. "I told you not to talk with that fool, anymore."

Stuffing her hands on her narrow hips, Piper shook an admonishing finger. "Hitomi, you really ought to be nicer to Balder," the girl chided. "It's not very polite, you know. Besides, he only says nice things about you."

"I doubt that," Hitomi snorted, holding back a scowl. But it was the girl's attitude and appearance that made her frown. Piper had taken on a whole new look recently. Not two days prior, the girl had chopped her pigtails off trying to look older. Her raven black hair was now strewn in a short, edgy mess. She wore *white* pants and a *white* shirt. If that wasn't enough, she even wore a makeshift gray haori. A haori was a cloth vest—what the Ronin were said to wear in the stories. On the breast and back of the vest she'd painted a symbol of wind she'd copied from one of Hitomi's books. It was safe to say that Piper had developed a bit of a crush on Gray since the aftermath. Not to mention, her tall-tales were growing quite infamous around the camp. Stories concerning the Ronin. "Piper, if this is another one of your stories, I'll make sure you're scrubbing pans until those pretty little hands are more wrinkled than my own."

"It's not, I swear!" the girl protested, and handed over a crisp letter with a red wax seal that was broken. Piper winced guiltily, wringing her hands. "This came in from the Aviary… I *might* have opened it."

Hitomi grumbled, but then saw the marking on the red wax.

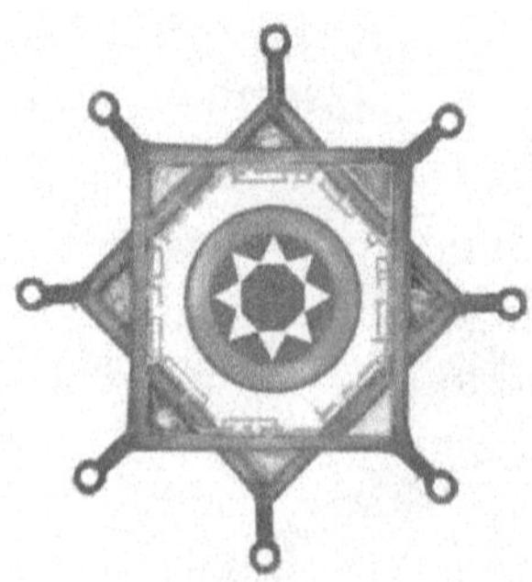

It was the Citadel's sigil with all eight elements, the red flame brightest for Farbs, the Great Kingdom of Fire.

Quickly, she read it and stiffened.

"Turn it over," Piper said, eyes wide as she teetered on her toes.

On the front was an etched symbol, not stamped but drawn meticulously by hand.

"See?!" Piper exclaimed, breathless, "It's him!"

"Spirits take me," she cursed softly.

Piper tugged on her arm. "*So?* Can we go already?"

Hitomi looked up, in a half-daze. The girl looked ready to leap out of her skin. Despite being on the short side of fourteen summers in age and as skinny as a well-picked bone, Hitomi doubted she could stop the girl. "Yes, yes, let's see what this is about. I suppose the inn can wait."

Piper giggled in glee and darted for the gaping entry where the doors were still missing.

"See to the Aviary," Hitomi informed the elves. "If the queen is having me run letters for her then I will see it properly constructed as a center for communication. If she wants an army ready for war, then intelligence, which is all too underrated, comes first."

"Wisely stated, innkeeper," said the lead elf, Yuna. He hadn't liked giving his *birth name*, but she couldn't go on calling him "*big elf*" forever. Oddly, he hadn't seemed to mind that name. "However, if this is the Eminas indeed, we shall join you as well."

She waved a hand. "Fine, fine. Come on then. The whole family it is."

With that, Hitomi lifted her heavy skirts, gathering the others behind her, following after the fool girl into the wooded camp.

* * *

Flanking Karil were a dozen of her elite guards who bore the fragments of her father's crown upon their breasts. She was glad to have them at her side as they moved proudly in their broken, dark green plate. Rydel moved at her side with his gaze set ahead, his presence giving her comfort as always. But she could sense his curiosity too. Hitomi hadn't said much, save for impressing urgency. Perhaps it was unwise she'd elected a woman of few words as her intelligence gatherer. But the woman did seem talented, even suited for it.

Gray… she thought, again. *Is he really here?*

Karil had dropped everything to see if it was true.

As she moved through her camp, she eyed the commotion again. The air seemed alive with activity. Amid the tall, heavy green trees, blacksmiths from the illustrious Maldon hammered anvils in canvas tents, steam rising into the canopy above. Men and women, villagers mostly, moved about aiding in one errand or another. Karil passed long picketed lines of horses and silken-haired cormacs. Beyond them, everywhere, were elves in moss-green leather armor.

Not a camp, she amended. *A city*.

The once-small camp was growing day by day. She knew it needed to be, too, if they were to contend with the might of Eldas, a Great Kingdom. However, beneath it all, she saw the deeper, darker truth.

The little signs were everywhere, from empty quivers, to the smell of sweat from the lack of soap, or even the frustration on her blacksmiths' faces. The last was almost the worst. *For what is an army without swords?* Without money they were reduced to little more than a rabble with a cause. Iron was becoming a scarcity all too quickly, and what little they had was riddled with impurities. As they stood, only half of their men could be fitted with real blades, and the other half had holes or chinks in their armor. No, the worst was the men, women, and even elves that went to bed with empty stomachs, hungrier every night. Her already hollow stomach soured at the thought, seeing gaunt faces at every turn.

Rations had been thinned. Elves ate roots or tubers and the refugees of Daerval dined on soup so thin it was nearly water. As of yet, no Great Kingdom would come to their aid. In less than a week, they would all be starving. She shoved all her growing worries aside and continued. Perhaps this news would be a boon, she thought hopefully. *The spirits know I need it.*

At last, Karil reached the clearing that Hitomi had indicated.

A ring of tall, wooden poles surrounded her camp, and at the entrance was a host of elves, including Hitomi and the young girl, Piper, whom the innkeeper had warmed to.

They approached and the elves gave her deep bows.

"Is he here?" Karil inquired.

The elves looked to Hitomi. "We've not been told, but *this* arrived with those two."

Karil looked over to see a simple cart and a chest upon the ground next to it. The wood of the chest was aged, ashen Silveroot. A faint silver sheen of the magical tree still coated the well-polished chest, but otherwise it was plain, held together by rusted metal rivets.

In the driver's seat of the rickety cart, sat a tall man with dark, haunted eyes. He bore the red robes of a Reaver, and she immediately felt a note of caution. Once, Reavers were respected throughout Farhaven, now they were darker and much less trusted. But that hollow expression... The man seemed more dead than alive. At his side, was a young boy, perhaps no more than ten summers in age. He had wild yellow hair, reminding Karil of Darius, and the look of a scoundrel. *Again*, reminding Karil of Darius. But his ragtag clothes seemed clean, and he wore a beaming smile.

"Greetings," she said in introduction.

The Reaver simply nodded, dully, looking away.

At her side, she felt Rydel stiffen and whisper beneath his breath, "I don't like that man."

"Whom do you like?" she asked.

The young boy jumped off the cart. "Hello!" he said in a reedy, jubilant voice. "We come from Farbs with a message, but I was told you should read the letter first." He motioned to the innkeeper who held a white envelope.

"So be it," Karil said and approached. "Hitomi." She nodded in greeting.

"My queen," Hitomi bowed, low but not very, as if she were a noble herself.

"How's the inn coming?" Karil inquired.

"Well, unexpected delays of course, but what can you expect in wartime?" she answered, "I'd say we're a month from completion once we find the funds, but I thank you deeply for the generous aid of your elves and the other villagers."

She knew Hitomi hid the fact that she'd spent half her fortune on the inn, and the other half towards Karil's cause and *still* she was running low on supplies. But Karil smiled, sincerely. "Then Piper has been helpful?"

"Quite," said Hitomi with a wry twist to her mouth. "That is, when she isn't mooning over someone in particular."

Piper blushed fiercely but didn't look ashamed.

"You should really get Balder on it. I thought the man had a knack for masonry?"

Mistress Hitomi grumbled. "Yes, I suppose. One matter at a time," the innkeeper said and indicated to a chest sitting on the moss-matted forest floor.

"What's in it?" she questioned.

"I'd advise you read this first. This is what our messenger was referring to—they arrived together," Hitomi said with a curious smile, handing over a letter. Karil noticed the wax seal had been broken and lifted a brow in question, and the woman nodded to Piper. "Curious, young minds. A crush is a powerful thing."

"Indeed," she answered and read the scrawled lettering with Rydel at her side.

> *Dear Karil,*
>
> *I wish I could begin with pleasantries, but the hour is late. I leave early in the morning for Vaster with Ayva, Darius, and two new companions. Let Mura and the others know we are all right … but Farhaven is not.*
>
> *The war is just beginning.*
>
> *Eldas was the first victim, and now Farbs. Though the cost was great, we have fended off the rising darkness. Sadly, the shadow of evil does not end there. I promised you I would return, and I will. But it is not time yet. I have somewhere else I need to be first. Others need me. It feels strange writing this, almost hard to believe for myself, but somehow I know it's true. This feels right. If anyone will understand, I figured it would be you. It is time to take up a mantle of duty far beyond me, to repair what*

once was broken.
It is time for the Ronin to ride again.

Karil stopped reading for a moment, her heart skipping a beat.
"My queen?" Rydel asked. "Are you all right?" He gripped her shoulder in concern. She read on without answer.

I send this to you in my stead, for I believe you will have more need of it than I. But be forewarned, a fiery individual told me to inform you that you 'owe him.' If you find the chest a little lighter, it is because there are lost souls in need within Farbs, men and women who have been disparaged and are in need of a new home.
I only hope this will suffice until I see you next.
Tell Mura … I miss him. We miss you all.

"What is it?" Rydel asked gruffly, growing impatient at last.
She looked up, wiping a tear, and answered, "A gift." Bending to the lock, Karil noticed it was tied with a simple string. Casually, she broke it and lifted the wooden lid and found her breath stolen.

Hitomi cursed. "Dear spirits…"
Inside, thick gold coins glittered, nearly three-quarters full.
"That's enough gold to build a kingdom!" an elf remarked.
"Or fuel a war," Karil answered and looked to the young boy. "And what is your role in all this?" she asked.
"Well, I'm your protector," he said proudly, puffing out his chest.
Mistress Hitomi raised a brow. "Well then, it seems I've no need to hire a bard for my new inn as we've a hero in our midst."
"Exactly!" Lucky declared, and then blushed, as if remembering heroes had to be more modest. "I mean… I'm here because my home was destroyed. It's being rebuilt, but I wanted adventure like the stories. When Ezrah asked me to deliver this with Reaver Finn, well, I knew what I had to do. Also, I've always wanted to see the elves, cormacs, and the magical forests," he said, eyes the size of the fat coins before her, panning around to the sights about him—the towering trees and her elves clad in green plate.
"Wait a moment," Rydel said, "Who's Ezrah?"
"Ezrah's my friend," Lucky answered. "He's an Arbiter!"

"An Arbiter?" Karil scoffed in disbelief. While the boy had the look of a scoundrel, he seemed to have a good heart. Could she believe him? Could he really have meant an Arbiter? "Surely, you're mistaken, my child."

"Nope," he said, "Ezrah is an Arbiter, and Gray's grandfather!"

At that, there was a unanimous sound of incredulity from all nearby. Even Rydel looked doubtful. "Really now?" Karil asked. And yet somehow, the idea of one of the most powerful threaders of the spark being Gray's grandfather wasn't as surprising as it should have been. If her prophecies were true, then the boy was destined for great and horrible things... She shivered in memory, pushing it to the back of her mind.

"That's why I'm here too!" Lucky exclaimed, "Ezrah said he wants to talk to you."

"And how exactly would he do that?"

"Through my friend Dared," the boy said and held up a small strange statue that pulsed with a soft orange glow—obviously containing the spark.

"My, my," Hitomi said. "I think I've seen the like of that before

in my books. It's a Simulacrum used to communicate messages over long distances."

"Yes, but Ezrah said only I can use it," the boy countered quickly, pulling the object close. *Dared*, Karil thought. The silent Ronin was one of the most mysterious, beyond Kail. She had seen him in person, and thought that the legends and their infamy would fade, but the stories seemed ingrained to her bone.

She smiled, touching the boy's arm. "Well, I'm so glad you're here, Lucky." She looked up to see the Reaver's troubled eyes. "Welcome, both of you," she said, letting the words linger, hoping they had some effect on the troubled-looking Reaver. Her smile brightened. "Come now, let's find something to eat shall we? A good rest and a full stomach is what every hero needs."

The Reaver alighted from the cart with a bare nod of thanks. It's a start, Karil thought as an elf grabbed his horses' reins, and Hitomi and Piper guided the two off. Karil lingered, however, as did Rydel, listening to the wind whisper through the woods. It rustled the emerald leaves, as if speaking, and her eyes settled one more time on the glittering gold before her—knowing that, at last, she would retake

Eldas and the throne that was rightfully hers.

Wherever you are, Gray, Karil thought, *thank you*.

Bastion of Light

Book Three of The Ronin Saga

The Black Hive

Odaren's stout legs chafed as he hurried with news certain to see his own death. Turning, he entered an intersection swarming with thieves, opening up to hundreds of archways and canals—all of it coated in the famous turquoise glow of Narim. It was a hub of sneers, dirty bodies, and tangible threats—where one cross look meant a swift dagger in the back. He tasted the tang of sweat on his upper lip and covered his nose from the stench of death that clung to the nefarious men and women who walked the pathways of Narim, the Great Kingdom of Moon.

Death...

Odaren gulped a sweaty, fearful breath.

He stopped amid the watery halls. *What if I run?* Hope like a sharp lance made his pulse race. Dark thieves continued to flow around him. He looked up. A dirt ceiling loomed hundreds of feet above—a barrier between the dark underworld and the subterranean land above. A land of air, of light, of *life*. Yes... *I can head for the hills, hide in the crevasses of the Narim Foothills*... Smiling, Odaren grew emboldened by the idea. *I can feed myself on the farms of the surface—those dim-witted peasants would never be the wiser. But most importantly, I would live*... Abruptly, his smile wilted.

All around him the people moved en masse, heading towards one place. A coliseum-like structure, rising from Narim's grand, turquoise lake like a shattered black blade.

The Black Hive.

No. There was no running, not from him.

For the Shadow King's orders were always obeyed. Besides, if Odaren was anything, he was servile to his core. If he had a shred of pride, it was in that. In a life full of depravity and sin—a life clinging to life, like his threadbare clothes upon his heavyset frame—Odaren was at least loyal.

With a heavy breath, he made his way up the long rise. Sweaty and tired, he maneuvered through the maze of arches and ramps, reaching the last barrier of guards—thieves really—between him and the Shadow King. They lounged beneath a wide archway in their black rags. Festooned upon their breasts was a poorly stitched half-gold half-black crown of their master. Odaren approached. They made no move to stop him, but beneath their breath he thought he heard the words, "King's rat."

Odaren ignored it and entered the Shadow King's hall.

Perhaps at one time long ago, the hall was a place of grandeur, filled with rich rugs, tapestries, bloodstone murals, and other symbols of the Moon Kingdom's wealth. Yet after the last rightful king of Narim was killed, all of that was pilfered and wasted, those relics now scattered across the lands. Now it was little more than a round hemisphere of worn stone. Broken chandeliers hung like paralyzed giant spiders far above his head. A fissure in the ceiling like a broken egg showed the much nearer earthen roof of Narim.

Darkness was prevalent. It lingered in the air like cobwebs Odaren couldn't brush aside. Luckily, on the far walls, turquoise light peeked through the slates of boarded-up grand windows. The light of Narim fought back against the dark aura of the Shadow King's throne room. It gave Odaren a strange sense of comfort to know that, despite the corruption from a dozen years of defiling at the Shadow King's hands, the Great Kingdom still had a pulse.

Gaze fixed in deference to the stone, he made his way across the long, cold expanse of floor to stand before the Shadow King's throne. His heart thudded, the weight of hundreds of eyes bearing down made him twitch inside his skin. In the corner of his gaze, he glimpsed the crowded walls packed with an assortment of characters:

sycophants mostly, and dirty little youths the oh-so-magnanimous king kept as errand boys to filch—Odaren thought this compassion odd, and often questioned the true reason for their presence.

His attention snapped back as Halvos, the Shadow King, spoke:

"*What news?*" the man asked from above, words echoing in his skull.

"The news is…" he muttered, lip quivering, trying to find the right word. The silence stretched and he licked his lips finally croaking out. "*Unsavory*, master."

"My patience runs thin, Odaren," Halvos said. "Tell me of the rumors from the south of Farbs and Darkeye's Clan. Tell me, or you will find your end equally *unsavory*." Odaren glanced up finally, taking in the Shadow King. The man sat upon his throne, one leg draped over the stone arm. He wore a black coat with a high flaring collar. Upon his fall of ghost-white hair, a crown, one-side black, the other gold, teetered, a symbol of his reign which he had stolen from the previous monarch of Narim after killing the man in his sleep some dozen years ago. His skin was the sickly white of an underdweller, or what Odaren had heard called an albino. But worst of all were his eyes… They were a cloudy white. The Shadow King was blind, but somehow his eyes pierced Odaren to the core.

At the man's side, a woman knelt on the stone, her head bent. Odaren had never felt a woman's touch before, but this one was pretty. She had been a present from Darkeye for the Shadow King. With long, curling, red hair, a sylvan face—narrow chin, light eyes, and high, if a tad gaunt cheekbones—she was out of place in this dark hollow made for only the greedy and the damned. Upon closer inspection, Odaren saw her hair seemed to be hiding a livid white scar near her temple. Abruptly she glanced up and Odaren shivered. Her gaze was vacant, dead. The woman may have been flesh and bone, but he would be surprised if her skin still held the warmth of the living.

"Well?" Halvos pressured in that eerily calm voice of his.

Where did he begin? "The Lair of the Beast has fallen," he stated bluntly.

"Fallen?" Halvos repeated.

"Crushed, master," he answered. It was true, hundreds of accounts retelling an epic battle and thousands of thieves dead upon the blowing sands.

"Then the rumors are true," said the Shadow King. "What of Darkeye? Does he still live?"

Odaren shook his head. "The rumors pile higher than a midden heap, master. Some say he fled for his life, others that he was killed amid the fighting. I only know that there are whispers of a new ruler of the Darkeye Clan taking over The Lair of the Beast."

Halvos mused on this, tapping his lip in thought. He made a casual flip of his hand and a lanky, greasy-haired man shuffled forward out of the shadows of the raised throne. "Send word," the Shadow King ordered, "I wish to see this new ruler, tell him—"

"*Her,*" Odaren corrected.

Halvos' head twisted.

Immediately he regretted the outburst, shrinking in his rags, trying to disappear into a ball of nothing. But Halvos' calm voice held a note of anger—that was when you didn't have to worry; it was only when it was absent of all emotion that men died at his whim—as he spoke again, "*Her?*"

Odaren bobbed his head, jowls shaking. "Indeed, master. They are calling her Mistress of Shadows."

Halvos snorted and a smile creased his thin, black lips. "A woman... I was almost worried for a moment there. But yes... I see this is all working out for the greater good. *Strength is life, weakness death.*" His tongue licked at the familiar, comforting words well known to all thieves, especially of late. Halvos continued, looking up from his reverie. "After all, it only stands to reason that the Mistress of Shadows should meet the King of Shadows, should she not?"

"Yes, master."

"Strength is life, weakness is death," the man purred again beneath his breath. "Yes... Fortuitous indeed. With Darkeye gone, there is nothing stopping me from ruling all of the Clan of Shadow." He looked up, hand stroking the woman at his side once more. "This Mistress of Shadows... Do the rumors grace us with her human name?"

"Faye, master."

His hand paused on his precious prey.

The girl beneath his hand still looked like a doll, more dead than alive, but she stirred now. Her vacant eyes held a glimmering spark.

"That name…" the Shadow King began. "I know that name… But how? *Who is she?*" The girl beneath his hand trembled and Odaren saw the king's mighty grip was squeezing the girl's neck like wringing a calvas vine for its juices, his anger flowing through him. The girl's neck would be crushed in a matter of seconds. Odaren didn't mind witnessing death, but watching her choke silently made something in his heart pang. Maybe it was her beauty or his lonesomeness, or perhaps he was simply warmer of heart in that moment.

Either way, he found his voice, and spoke quickly. "She's no one, master. No one compared to you. But if you wish it, I will find her for you directly and bring her to you … under the pretense of *reestablishing* allegiances." He was never silver-tongued, but somehow he found his words.

Slowly, the Shadow King's rage came back under his control and that tempered voice, the one that sent terror into Odaren's marrow, came in a bare whisper. "Perhaps you're right." He blindly waved the servant at his side away. "I shall give you the honor of this duty. Go now, and see it done, my fat little rat," he said, using the title all of Narim whispered behind his back. It rankled Odaren, but he kept his head bowed, hiding his anger.

Wordlessly, he flourished an ungainly bow.

When his eyes glanced up, he turned, leaving as quickly as he could—feeling sweat slowly dripping down his back as if he'd escaped the headman's axe once more. But as he reached the exit, he could almost swear the vacant shell of a girl at the Shadow King's side spoke, lips forming a silent word: "*Sister…*"

* * *

Odaren stepped out of the hall of the Shadow King and onto a balcony with no railing, one of hundreds that rimmed the Black Hive. The balcony watched over the dark halls of Narim, the Great Kingdom of Moon. Beyond the lip was a steep fall—a sharp drop that ended in the churning walkways hundreds of feet below filled with thieves. One might live if they landed on a person, that is if they missed the sharp black poles that decorated the Hive, like barbs upon the back of a great nightmare beast. Sweat dappled Odaren's forehead and he swiftly mopped at it with a dirty handkerchief, giving a shaky breath, eyeing the city that lay beneath it all—for Narim sat hundreds of feet below the surface of Farhaven, the only Great Kingdom once-called 'the subterranean gem' of the world.

The air was warm here. One might even call Narim serene, with its hundreds of slow-moving canals, babble of water—though now drowned beneath Odaren's husky breaths—and the ever-present turquoise glow that clung where shadows should be, but beneath it all was a darkness.

Men and women moved among the canal's narrow pathways in droves, most with the sly gate and shifty eye of thieves. They were the Shadow King's Army; really just a ragtag group of lost mercenaries, and once-bandits—those who sought shelter from the cruel world while adding to that cruelty in turn, their job to pilfer from the rich *and* the poor all in order to line the Shadow King's pockets. But now their numbers were growing, their training intensifying...

A chill breeze cut through the air. The breeze of change. Odaren knew what was coming. *Something grand*... Something that would shake the very pillars of Farhaven. His stubby fingers stuffed his kerchief away in his snug jacket as he looked up. Above, a dirt ceiling extended for miles, the odd murky half-light of the canals barely reaching the roof of the ancient Great Kingdom.

His thoughts turned inward.

The Shadow King had charged him with finding this woman, the Mistress of Shadows, but was it a death sentence? From the few rumors he'd heard, the woman was nearly as fearsome as the Shadow King himself. Well, no one was as frightening as the Shadow King, but the rumors of her *had* grown to legendary status practically overnight. Stories claimed she was taller than most men, with dragon scales for armor, mowing down legions with fire-breath, and a sword of lightning and wind.

Wind! Odaren scoffed. That was preposterous enough, almost more so than the foolish notions of a woman breathing fire like a dragon of old, those draconian beings now extinct from the world by all accounts. But the thought of the banished element made him feel sick and coated in oil. Only one person had ever been able to wield that element—Kail, a Ronin, and worse still, their *leader*. Odaren knew that stories always told a deeper truth. Just like this Faye, this Mistress of Shadows...

He wasn't daft enough to believe half the things he'd heard, but what he did believe and made him fear for his life was the *other* accounts—dozens of witnesses told of the woman killing men and women, both the enemy *and* her own. They said she slaughtered them while they called out her name, turning the tide of battle against the Darkeye Clan.

Well, perhaps she was simply out for power. What better way to supersede Darkeye? He shook his head. Something about all the tales didn't add up, however.

This woman would be his death a deep fear told him.

Again Odaren thought about running, hiding in the hills.

"Yes… It can work…" he whispered, fumbling with the kerchief in his stubby fingers.

A rat squealed.

Odaren startled, nearly tumbling over the sharp abyss, but caught himself. A young man sat on the lip of the balcony, cast in shadows. The turquoise light somehow didn't shed light upon his swarthy features. His feet dangled over the side as he stared out into nothing, something in his hands glinted brightly. A *dagger?* It moved methodically, as if cutting.

"You…" Odaren said, gaining control. "How long have you been there?"

The boy turned, looking up to him with eerie, alien blue eyes.

Silent and unmoving, Odaren suppressed a shiver when he recognized the boy. "You… You're the king's new pet aren't you? The little rat that all the others are afraid of." Odaren felt the irony at him calling another *a little rat* and he still felt the wrath and sting from the Shadow King's *little* jab. Yet the boy before him didn't flinch. He just kept shaving something that Odaren couldn't see. Odaren decided to vent his anger. "Yes, that's right, his new favorite toy. The silent one… Modric, that's what they call you—yes Modric, after the fabled stories."

The boy said nothing.

Odaren's curiosity spiked and he licked his lips. "They say you murdered your own parents, is it true?"

Still, the boy continued to shave, silent.

Odaren sniffed sharply, giving an uncomfortable shrug. "You're just a mute little rat. Scurry off and leave me in peace." He turned his shoulder, but the boy rose. He was tall, far taller than Odaren imagined now outside the gloom of shadows. Odaren suppressed his surprise, clutching the kerchief in his sweaty hands. With wide shoulders and lithe build, the young man looked almost elvish in stature, but there was no threat to his stance. Still silent as the grave, the boy bit into the object in his hands, red juice spilling around his mouth. At last, with a faint smile, he let the object roll from his fist to the ground and moved off into the darkness.

Odaren released another shaky, pent-up breath, sagging in his skin.

Rumors of the silent boy had seeped into every corner of Narim—a boy who had slain his own parents, who had killed and raped his sister, who had done a hundred other untold things each more devious and dark than the last. The boy unnerved Odaren to the core. What the Shadow King wanted made him curious, and what the boy's role was in all this was still beyond his sight…

Odaren hobbled forward and saw what the boy had eaten.

A skinned dead rat lay upon the cold stone, veiny and red, a chunk missing; for a flickering moment he imagined himself just like the rat. Water dripped off the cavernous walls, matching his beating heart. He kicked the rat over the side of the cliff, watching it tumble to the masses below.

The world was changing, Odaren knew, watching the swarm of thieves like a pot ready to boil… and he would have to change with it or be cast to the wayside. Currying favor with the Shadow King was one option, and the other was running. But what use was running when you were weak? Yet strength was not always in sharpness of wit or sword, he knew well, but also in the play of power, following those who rise and fall. And Odaren knew how to ride that rising tide—he could grovel and lick the Shadow King's boots, if only to live another day.

He looked up, deciding.

There is no running.

He had to go to Farbs, to The Lair of the Beast, and convince this Faye to see the Shadow King—to see her death, and ultimately, secure his life.

Glossary

The terms within are not equal with regards to the timeline of the Saga. Lastly, what you see below are terms mostly pertaining to the Ronin and their legacy, for a detailed background on the history of the Ronin and the war of the Lieon see www.roninsaga.com.

Algasi (ALL-gah-si) – Nomadic warriors who are believed to hail from the lands of Vaster long ago. They are dark-skinned with light, curly hair and are often short but they are considered "as hard as stone," with every moment spent training their bodies to be weapons. They value light, truth, and courage.

Arbiter – A supreme wielder of magic, born of the Citadel. There are only three and some say ever were. Their power is equivalent to their rank.

Arbiter Fera – The third most powerful wielder of the spark, Arbiter Fera is a force to be reckoned with. Enigmatic and playing behind the scenes her nature and ultimate plans are hidden to almost all. She is also one of the few spark users who attempts to understand the flow, and researches and experiments with magical creatures. Her half Darkwalker half phox pet is always at her side.

Aurelious (Oh-RAIL-ee-US) – A Ronin, also known as the Confessor. His element is that of flesh and his home the Great Kingdom of Covai. He is brother to Aundevoriä and known for having a small temper, but a fierce love for his brother, and loyalty for his Ronin brothers.

Aundevoriä (ON-de-voria) – A Ronin, also known as the Protector. He wields Durendil, the stone blade and his home is the Great

Kingdom of Lander, a fortress of stone, its walls thicker than most cities. He is known for his willingness to sacrifice all for the sake of humanity.

Ayva (AY-va) – Ayva is the tomboyish, intelligent friend of Gray and Darius. She and her father ran The Golden Horn in Lakewood. Ayva is an avid reader of the world that lies outside Lakewood.

Balder [Jiro] – A man who claims to be the leader of the Stone-mason Guild (a well reputed guild), who lives in the Shining City.

Baro (bah-ro) – A Ronin, also called the Bull and Slayer of Giants. His element is that of Metal, and his home is the Great Kingdom of Yronia—a city that is a mass of steel and steam. Its forges were once lit with undying fires but now it is one of the "forgotten kingdoms". Baro wields the blade Iridal, a giant sword made of unbreakable steel. In all the stories, he is larger than any man known, described as having a waist like an oak trunk, and shoulders as broad as an ox, often known as the one who led the vanguard of the Ronin into battle.

Burai Mountains (boo-rai) – Endlessly tall mountains that reach towards the heavens, and are often called the spine, or back of the world. Death's Gate is nestled between these impassible peaks.

Calad (Kah-lahd) – One of Hiron's famous twin swords.

Citadel – A great keep of black stone within the Kingdom of Fire, and home to both Devari and Reavers.

Cloudfell Lake – Lake beside Cloudfell, turquoise waters and low-lying mist make the lake look like it hovers just beneath the clouds.

Shining City – The great city in the mountains. It is a part of a massive kingdom, and the last remnant of the Kingdom of Ice.

Cormacs – Cormacs are elvin steeds. They have long legs and broad, powerful chests which makes them formidable sprinters.

They have shorter muzzles than a horse, long silken tails, and slopping backs. Karil also mentions they are attuned to the spark.

Covai – Kingdom of Flesh, the city of men, women and beast, land of the Mortal Being, one the largest spiritual sects of all the lands.

Covai Riders – A vast horse tribe from the Kingdom of Flesh that controls much of the plains of Farhaven.

Curtana – Dared's twin daggers, thin with broken tips.

Cyn (KIN) – A game played with small, carved figurines, consisting of followers and a mark.

Daerval (dare-vahl)– A land without magic, on the other side of Death's Gate.

Dalic – The leader of the Algasi tribe—a two-stripe Mundasi warrior.

Dared (DARE-ED) – A Ronin, also known as the Shadow. His element is that of moon and his home is the Great Kingdom of Narim—a vast subterranean gem located in the dark hills, half above the land, half below. The least is known about Dared. He is said to never have spoken. Rumors of his powers include the ability to turn completely invisible in the night even under the brightest moon.

Dared [the statue] – Dared the silent Ronin in statue form.

Darius (dare-ee-us)– Darius is a wiry young man of seventeen who is from Lakewood, and we learn very little of his parentage; he appears to be an orphan. Darius is perhaps most well-known for his love of gambling, a skill he holds no modesty about.

Darkeye – Leader of the Darkeye clan whose hold is called Lair of the Beast. He is famed for his brutality and malevolent deeds.

He wears a cloak that flaunts these skills, showing the patches of slain Devari.

Darkwalkers – Creatures that are neither living nor dead. They are immune to the spark and most weapons save for a Devari's blade. They are described as black beasts with many forms, like a "hundred-limbed spider" or even walking on two legs. Most, however, are faceless with black prism-like bodies that shine like obsidian and knife-sharp limbs and beady dark eyes.

Death's Gate – The infamous gates that divide the two lands. The origin of the name is said to come from all those that died during the Great War, specifically during the final battle that stained the White Plains red.

Desiccating – To remove one forever from their innate spark. It is a dreaded occurrence that is often worse than death to any wielder of the spark.

Devari (duh-var-ii) – An elite group of warriors who live within the Citadel, and they are masters of the blade. Using "Ki" they hold certain powers, including inhabiting another's body and feeling their sensations. They have two ranks, apprentices and "Sword-Forged", Devari who wield powerful soulwed blades.

Diaon (die-on) – Translates to "knows nothing". It is title given to apprentices and slaves of Farhaven.

Dipping Tsugi –Mistress Hitomi's inn in the Shining City.

Dryads – Fabled magical creatures of the forest of Drymaus, a great mythical forest to the north of Eldas.

Dryan – High Councilor and elf who assumes the throne when Karil's father, the old king, is murdered.

Drymaus – Home of the mythical dryads.

Dun Varis – An offshoot and fragment of Lander, the Great Kingdom of Stone, rumored to exist again within Daerval, and Aundevoriä's homeland.

Durendil – Aundevoriä's famed sword. It has a wire-wrapped handle, and turns to stone.

Eldas – Home of the Elves, one of the nine Great Kingdoms, also the Kingdom of Forest.

Elders of Eldas – Also known as the sages or High Council of the Kingdom of Eldas. They are the ruling council of the Great Kingdom of Forest.

Elementals – Magical beings of Farhaven.

Elements – A game of Farhaven that Ezrah and Kirin play.

Eminas – The name for Gray used by the elves, and literally means eminent one, but its variant meaning is harbinger.

Ester – A city once bound together with Menalas in what was called a "false kingdom".

Ethelwin – A powerful Reaver and lecturer who is only a few below in rank and prestige of the female Arbiter.

Ezrah – Arbiter of the second rank who lives in the Citadel, and Gray's grandfather.

Farbs – The sprawling desert city wherein the Citadel resides.

Farhaven – A land full of magic, on the opposite side of Death's Gate.

Faye – Enthralling and unpredictable, Faye is a woman of many talents. A skilled fighter and a Farhaven-versed individual, she aids Gray, Ayva, and Darius on their journey to Farbs. Though with strange ties to Darkeye and his clan, she finds a way to be both a curse and a blessing in disguise.

Fendary – Also called the Stormbreaker, or the Sentinel. He is Fendary Aquius, a high general during the Lieon who supposedly fought the Ronin.

Fisher in the Shallows – An advanced technique where one flows through Low Moon stances, and makes several sweeping horizontal slashes directed at the attacker's legs.

Fisher in the Shallows to Dipping Moon – A snaking thrust to an upward strike, from which its power is derived from the bending and swift upward lift of the legs

Flow – What is often called the source of all magic, or the "essence." It is what the Ronin wield.

Frizzian Coast – Located in Farhaven, full of peaceful towns and villages along the coast and in the Northern provinces.

Full Moon – A defensive stance where one's blade is above the head and their knees are heavily bent in order to absorb and redirect coming blows. It mimics the pattern of the arcing moon in the sky or a sphere, where water flows off the perfectly round surface, unable to find solid contact.

Fusing – A bond between magic users that wields even greater power. It is said hundreds of Reavers were used in ancient times to forge epic creations, including the transporters.

Heartgard – The name for Seth's famed sword; meaning brave, enclosed.

Great Tree – The tree that is at the center of Eldas, and bears the spire; the great buildings where all nobility reside.

Gryphons – Mounts of Farbs that are half eagle and half lion.

Hall of Wind – Within the legendary Morrow, Great Kingdom of Wind. Mura claims Kail stashed his most precious of weapons in the "Hall of Wind."

Hando Cloak – A black and forest green cloak Rydel wears. It signifies that he is one of the Hidden.

Haori (Ha-o-ri) – Colored vests, each matches the powers the Ronin hold, and the color of the Kingdom they represent.

Heartwood – Harder than most human metals, most of Eldas is constructed out of it.

Heron in the Reeds – A powerful and agile strike from above—most often where one baits with the front leg, then pulls it into a "Heron" (a stance upon one leg), and strikes down at the now lunging and exposed attacker.

Herbwort – An herb that aids with shivers and insomnia.

High Council – The council of elves in Eldas that oversee affairs; see also Elders of Eldas.

High Moon – A Devari stance where the back leg is heavily bent, and holding the majority of the weight, while the other foot rests lightly upon the ground. The fighter's shoulders are angled, just enough to minimize a target, but enough to engage their upper-body, turning for powerful strikes if need be. It is a stance few ever master.

Hitomi – Often called "Mistress" Hitomi. Hitomi is the proprietor of the Dipping Tsugi in the Shining City. When the others stumble upon several rare books in her packed library, they discover her obsession for books.

Hiron (He-row-nn) – A Ronin, also known as the Kingslayer. His element is that of water, and the Great Kingdom of Seria. He is known as the peacekeeper, and the Ronin of wisdom and serenity.

Iridal – Baro's famed sword, rumored to be impossible to shatter.

Jiryn – A high elf healer from Eldas.

Kage (KAH-gey) – The nine nameless evils who pose as the Ronin and hold equal powers.

Kagehass – The saeroks and verg's name for what others refer to as the Nameless (the Shadow's Hand).

Kail – The once leader of the fabled Ronin. He is known by many names, from many eras including the blight seeker, betrayer of men, and the wanderer. He is rumored to have survived the Lieon, and still exists, told in fearful tales for the past two thousand years.

Karil – Karil is the queen of Eldas, home and kingdom of the Elves. She is half-human and half-elf. Karil is tall and beautiful, with silver eyes, and white-blonde hair. Her beauty is only equaled by her intelligence.

Ki – The source and power of a Devari.

Kin – Dark men and women who are agents of the "shadow", specifically the Kage. Gray runs into one in Lakewood when trying to retrieve the sword.

King Gias – Karil's father and the King of Eldas.

King Katsu – King of the Shining City.

King Owen Garian – King of Median, the rebuilt Great Kingdom of water—said to be a righteous man of conviction with a blue-tinted beard.

Koru Village – The town Gray and the others run across. It is just north of Lakewood.

Laidir – The second of Hiron's famous twin swords.

Lair of the Beast – The home of the Darkeye clan within the Underbelly.

Lakewood – A peaceful town, but resides close to the ill-famed Lost Woods. It is the home of Ayva and Darius.

Lander – One of the "forgotten kingdoms". Lander was the Great Kingdom of Stone. It was a city that had walls purported to be thicker than small cities.

Lando – Translates as "redeemers" or "liberators" in the common tongue. They are the group that saves Karil in the woods of Eldas.

Lieon –The Great War during the Final Age that lasted over a thousand years.

Lokai/Lokei – The god Darius evokes; the god of "luck".

Lopping the Branch – A slashing strike, twisting the torso and attacking the opponent's head.

Lord Nolan – Steward of Vaster, Great Kingdom of Sun.

Lost Woods – The infamous dark forest where Gray and Mura live, and said to be full of direbears and other nefarious beasts. Villagers say the woods come alive at night, and travelers who venture in are rarely ever seen again.

Low Moon – A Devari stance where one leg is heavily slanted for a low center of gravity for balance and stability, and the other is heavily bent and holds the majority of the swordsman's weight.

Malik – Leader of the Kage. He has a spiked pauldron and is bigger than his brethren. He speaks to Vera and is the voice of the dark army.

Maris (mare-is) – A Ronin, also called the Trickster, a Ronin of many names and faces. He wields Masamune, the leaf blade—its powers unknown. His element is that of leaf, and his homeland is the Great Kingdom of Eldas.

Maris' Luck – the most dangerous inn in Farbs and perhaps all Farhaven.

Masamune – Maris' famed sword.

Mashiro – Guard captain of the Shining City.

Matriarch – leader of the phoxes.

Menalas – A southern city of Farhaven that was once part of Ester, together they were deemed a false kingdom denied the position of power as one of the nine Great Kingdoms. They were forced to split and divide up their power. Many of their inhabitants, however, still lust for a throne that no longer exists. Moreover, they share an iron mine with Ester that was too difficult to upend in the Lieon.

Mirkal – Darius' cormac.

Mistress Sophi – She owns an inn in Lakewood, and taught Darius how to dance.

Morrow – A city upon the windy high cliffs of Ren Nar that oversaw the world. It is the Great Kingdom of Wind. It is the last of the three lost Great Kingdoms and the most famous. It is Kail's homeland. It contains the Hall of Wind, the famous meeting place for the great kings, queens, and generals who fought for the armies of Sanctity and against the Alliance of Righteous in the Great War of the Lieon.

Morrowil – The infamous sword that Gray inherits from Kail.

Mortal Being – A religion of Covai that often encourages self-

inflicted bodily harm to achieve a higher spiritual state.

Motri (moh-tree) – Gray's hawk and companion, who also seems to have a mysterious alliance with Karil.

Mundasi – The elite warriors of the Algasi tribe.

Mura – Mura is a charming, but irascible hermit of unknown age. He lives in a cabin in the middle of Lost Woods where Gray stumbles upon him. Mura is wiry with thick gray brows and an often stern, heavily-lined face, and black and gray peppered hair. He is Karil's uncle.

Nameless – Created from Reavers, a horrible evil that mists from thin air, and is rumored to be invincible to "mortal blades." Their armor is made from overlapping dark plates. Gray and Darius fight them in the back alleys of Lakewood, behind the Golden Horn.

Narim – The Kingdom of Moon in the dark hills, half above, half beneath the land, and is a vast subterranean gem.

Neophyte – A threader of the spark, a rank below a Reaver. They reside in the Neophyte Palace and wear gray robes.

Nexus – The source of Gray's power. It is a swirling ball of air that he focuses on to tap into his power.

Niux – A unit of twelve, that consists of vergs and saeroks.

Nodes – a magical oasis and a safe haven for all living creatures of Farbs especially in times of dire need.

Omni – A Ronin, also known as the Deceiver. Omni's element is that of Sun, and from the Great Kingdom of Vaster. Omni leads the Ronin in Kail's absence.

Oval Hall – Where the Seven Trials takes place in the Citadel. It is beautiful and ancient.

Phoxes – angelic white creatures with long snow-white fur, sharp elongated teeth, and huge silver eyes. They move in a way familiar to Gray and to the element of wind. They are led by the Matriarch.

Patriarch – the well-known benevolent ruler of Farbs, Great Kingdom of fire. The most powerful wielder of the spark and first rank Arbiter.

Quenching the Fire – A Devari stance.

Reaver – A powerful wielder of magic born of the Citadel.

Rekdala Forhas – "Honor and duty" in the Yorin tongue.

Reliahs Desert – The desert surrounding Farbs, sometimes called the Farbian desert.

Relnas Forest – The forest of Eldas, home of the elves.

Ren – Close friend of Kirin's and leader of the Devari. He wears a graying Komai tail, a long braid, and is described as ageless. Most characteristically, he is a man hardened from years of training and battle, both mentally and physically.

Renald Trinaden – Warden and Keeper of the Silver, and author of The Lost Covenant.

Rimdel – Trader's paradise or jewel of the Eastern Kingdoms – capital with no central rule, inhabited by only thieves, ruffians and traders as hard as stone, destroyed by the Kage.

Ronin – The legends of the Lieon, nine warriors who each holds a supreme power. According to the stories, they are dreaded and the bane of mankind.

Rydel – An elf of the rank of Hidden, the most elite of guards that protect the royal family of Eldas, the Great Kingdom and home of the elves. He is Karil's ever-present companion and guard. He has shoulder-length dark hair and piercing eyes.

Sa Hira – "I see", in Yorin.

Saeroks – Creatures in the Kage's dark army. They are tall beasts with thin, patchy fur, sinewy muscled frames, and long gangly arms and legs with long claws. They walk on two legs, but can run on all fours for greater speed.

Salamander – A powerful lackey of Darkeye who can wield the spark.

Sanctuary – The home of the Lost Ones within the Underbelly.

Seth – A Ronin, also called the Firebrand. Seth's element is fire, and his home is the Great Kingdom of the Citadel, a dark keep whose fires light the night sky. He wields the sword Heartgard. Seth is known for his fiery temper, and proud spirit.

Sevia – Green lands known for their wine, silk, and, unfortunately, bandits.

Shifting – Kail's rumored ability to transport great lengths of space in a short amount of time.

Si'tu'ah – 'Way of the sword' literally translated from the Sand tongue; but more generally, it is a vast philosophy attributed to tribes dating as far back as the First Age, before even the Lieon. Its principles include both fighting and everyday life. Its core tenants revolve around using all facets of yourself (mind, body, spirit) and your enemy in order to succeed.

Silveroot – A tree of both Farhaven and Daerval. Within Farhaven it is described as having veins of glowing silver that flow visibly beneath its bark, and bark that shimmers like a fish's scaled belly. Within Daerval, where there is no magic, it is simply a large evergreen, producing nut-sized fruits.

Silvias River – A magnificent river that flows south and divides much of Daerval.

Simulacrum – A statue that holds the spark and can be used to convey messages over long distances.

Sithel – The madman who takes over the Citadel. Possessed by a fear of his own weakness Sithel strives to be powerful. Though deprived of the spark, he uses others and finds power through servitude to a higher, darker cause and individual. He is described as oily in every manner, possessing a white robe that looks like a butcher's apron.

Spark – The magic that all but the Ronin wield, including Reavers, Neophytes and Arbiters, and the majority of Farhaven's magical beings. It is said to be derived from the Flow.

Spark fever – A potentially deadly fever induced by using too much of the spark.

Spire – The highest building of Eldas where the council, king, queen and their family reside.

Sprites – Magical beings that have no form.

Star of Magha - The famous insignia that symbolizes the eight recognized kingdoms.

Stice – Aurelious' famed sword.

Sunha – translates to "the learned".

Taer – A land within Farhaven.

Tales of the Great Schism – Stories about the end of the Lieon and the Devari's split from old alliances to new ones, including their origin in the Citadel.

Tales of the Ronin – One of most famous books about the deeds of the Ronin.

Temian – An elf with long golden hair, and strange golden eyes. Gray befriends the elf in the encampment beyond the Gates at the border of the woods.

Terus – A game of Farbs where one flips a dagger in the air and attempts to catch it by the handle or blade.

The Great Kingdoms –The legendary cities. There were nine. Stone, Ice, Leaf, Fire, Flesh, Moon, Sun, Metal, and Wind. Each kingdom was the home of one of the Ronin, and coincides with their powers.

The Red Moon – A mythical event that is said to coincide with "The Return" of the Ronin.

The Return – The fated return of the Ronin; an event the world fears. It is said they will finish the destruction of the lands they were rumored to nearly destroy during the Lieon.

The Rift – A rumored chasm where the world split thousands of years ago, before the Lieon and the Ronin even existed.

The Seven Trials – The trials that a Neophyte must pass to become a Reaver.

The Sodden Tunnels – The tunnels that lead out of the Shining City; a dark and dismal place with no light, full of thousands of misleading paths. At one point, Mura says darkness called his name within the Tunnels. Karil also refers to them as the "Endless Tunnels".

The Terma – Elite elvin warriors, the second highest in rank and skill in the armies of Eldas.

The Wasteland – A vile land where vergs and saeroks are rumored to be born. It is east of the Lost Woods.

Tir Re' Dol (teer-reh-dol) – Often called The First City. Appropriately named as it was the first city to rise from the ashes of the Lieon, and soon became the capital of Daerval for millennia.

Transporter – A device that transports its wielder to a specific place by use of magic. They are hidden around the Citadel. Ren says they were created by a hundred Reavers working as one through the use of a "link."

Trimming the Stalks – A move that uses the rotation of the upper body and shoulders to lash at lower extremities, arms and sword moving in a figure-eight fashion.

Underbelly – The halls and tunnels beneath the Citadel and Farbs, including The Lair of the Beast, and Sanctuary. Some parts are said to have existed since the beginning of all the lands, created by unknown creatures.

Untamed – A threader of the spark who is untrained by the Citadel (neither Neophyte, Reaver, or Arbiter.) They are often considered dangerous to themselves and others.

Yorin – The old human tongue for all of Farhaven.

Yronia (YOR-own-ee-uh) – Great Kingdom of Metal once known for their gleaming steel and mountainous walls of iron, and home to the Ronin Baro. Also home of the Great Forge and the Deep Mines. However, its "unbreakable" walls were shattered during the Lieon and it now lies as one of the forgotten kingdoms.

Vaster – The Great Kingdom of the rising Sun, named for the shining keeps that gleam like alabaster jewels, always in the dawn's light. Omni's homeland.

Vera – A woman, originally from the Citadel and connected to

Kirin. She is beautiful, but equally dark and would gladly use her looks as a tool to gain even more power.

Vergs – Brutish, behemoth like creatures born from the taint that are said to be intelligent.

Victasys (vic-tay-sis) – A powerful scarred Devari who Gray and Zane befriend.

Zane (ZAY-nn) – An orphan from the Underbelly, the refuge for all misfits and reformed thieves of Farbs. Zane is a hard-bitten young man. However, his rough, fiery exterior softens (somewhat) as he befriends the Devari Victasys and Gray. His beloved sister is Hannah.

Author Biography

Matthew Wolf was born on March 14, 1986 in San Diego, California. He graduated from UC Santa Barbara as a literature major with a specialization in medieval studies and Japanese. Throughout college, he studied Old English and Japanese extensively, both of which are strongly tied to the languages of the book. He has also traveled considerably, from Switzerland and Scotland to Bonaire, and these sights inspire much of the land of Daerval.

Aside from the book (which is his main passion), he is also a Kung Fu instructor. His hobbies include woodcraft, archery, and of course, writing. Matt Wolf is currently building the brand of the Ronin Saga, giving rousing speeches, and encouraging others on the exciting path of writing.

FARHAVEN
Frizzian Coast
Ester
Kalvas Ocean
The Dragons Tooth
Mountains of Soot
Kalvas Ocean
The Abyss

VASTER
Tacrian
LANDER
Cloudfell Town
Cloudfell Lake
Aster Plains
FARUS
Helians Desert
Drymaus Forest
Helnas Forest
ELDAS

CPSIA information can be obtained
at www.ICGtesting.com
Printed in the USA
BVHW090008290722
643205BV00006B/9/J